CH00841927

The Authors

GENE WAS born in the exotic town of Bedford. He rapidly escaped – though only as far as Suffolk, where he was condemned to attend a rural comprehensive school. In spite of this, he managed to get into Bristol University, where he was sectioned into the psychology department. There he gained the only first of his year after the lecturers got confused and mistook him for a student rather than a case study. He has remained in academia ever since, and now lives with his partner and daughter somewhere in The Mysterious East.

Andrew came into this world fully formed; a bit like Venus except for the beautiful bits. He too survived the state school system, shining in the subjects of skiving games, acne and chemistry. His ability at science sent him to Bristol University to study the dark arts of the test tube, crucible and distillation apparatus (*particularly* the distillation apparatus). He still lives in the British university system where he survives in The Cold North as a plaything of physicists.

The two authors met at university whilst standing outside a geology lecture wondering why they were here when they'd each signed up for something completely different. After much beer-drinking, curry-eating and world-travelling in search of the perfect night out, they decided to write a book about such a quest. This is that mighty tome.

At this point, Gene would just like to make it very clear that the rudest jokes in the book come from the depraved mind of Andrew. This is funny really, because Andrew is keen to take credit for all of the rudest jokes, but would like to disassociate himself from all the 'psuedo-literary nonsense', for which he blames Gene.

THE QUEST FOR THE HOLY ALE

or
Three Sheets To The Wind

By

GENE ROWE
and
ANDREW SCHOFIELD

Published by

**MELROSE
BOOKS**

An Imprint of Melrose Press Limited
St Thomas Place, Ely
Cambridgeshire
CB7 4GG, UK
www.melrosebooks.com

FIRST EDITION

Cover designed by Bryan Carpenter

ISBN 978 1 906050 96 2

Printed and bound in Great Britain by:
CPI Antony Rowe, Chippenham, Wiltshire

CONTENTS

We would like to dedicate this book to real ale lovers
everywhere, especially to the worthies of CAMRA
(your cause is just!) and The Fat Cat in Norwich
("probably the best pub in the world").

The Prologue

THIS TALE begins in a temple in the land of Frembolia. Well, we say *temple*, but we might just as well say *museum*, or even *brewery*, for this particular building used to be a brewery until the brewers died and the recipe for their beer was lost. So now it is mainly a temple: a place to worship ideals and to pray for the return of better things and better times.

In this place, in the shadow of a pillar, there is a man. *Sneaking.* And he's good at this – he's even got a diploma for it. He's actually quite good at many things, although you might not suspect this on first seeing him. There he goes … slinking across the lamp-lit floor from one shadow to the next. Amazing! Just like a cat in STEALTH mode!

The little, wizened, yellow-skinned man was a monk by training, and a seeker of knowledge by inclination. Unlike his brethren, however, he believed that life's great mysteries *could not* be solved by such common strategies as spending years alone upon a mountain, or perching silently atop a tall pole, or bruising your cheeks upon a hard floor as, for hours on end, you twisted your legs into improbable positions and chanted the word "om". He was instead a believer in the principle of direct action, in whatever form – or indeed, state of legality – this might take.

The monk (for that was how he thought of himself) skittered along a wall covered with horse brasses and headed for an annexe. There, he knew, he would find a fragment of parchment on which was drawn a particularly *interesting* map …

———•••••———

The scene swirls and changes, as it is wont to do in stories like this.

Two weeks have passed since a particular individual half-inched a bit of parchment from a druidical temple-cum-museum. Frembolia is but a memory: the present is a clearing in the wilderness beside a crossroads …

At this crossroads, four figures huddle around a small fire. A cauldron hangs from an improvised wooden support above crackling twigs and orange-red flames; a small barrel of ale lies empty and discarded beside it. Two of the figures smoke contentedly, and all stare into the mesmerically dancing fire.

These four chance acquaintances had been talking for some time about the great mysteries of the universe, and had just reached an important conclusion about one of its very greatest conundrums. There was a moment's silence as they pondered their decision. And then the ranger, called Angred, cleared his throat. "So, we are agreed then," he said, with great solemnity. "The answer to the question is: *big breasts are best.*"

The others nodded slowly with great satisfaction. As if to toast their success, the four men simultaneously took up their mugs and tilted the ale within to their lips. Four arms were then lowered in unison. Each of the men stared into the bottom of his mug and thought about *big ones.*

Tugon the barbarian sighed and drained his mug. As the last dregs of ale slipped down his throat the bearskin-clad adventurer coughed. "This Monegrin brew is foul!" he complained, eyeing the bottom of his tankard with suspicion.

"Monegrin ale is truly piss!" concurred Gerontas, a merchant.

Angred and the fourth member of their impromptu party – whose face was hidden by the hood of his cowl – both nodded their assent.

From this position, it took little effort for the conversation to be turned to the next of mankind's great debates.

"Here," said the ranger, after a second's thought, "what about ale? Now that *is* a big question. What is the best ale in the world?"

"I know this," declared the barbarian. "Listen to me, and I will tell all."

When a barbarian declares himself ready to speak, others tear up their queue tickets and accept the inevitable. The men prepared themselves for the tale, adjusting their postures for greater comfort. Angred shifted his weight to allow blood to flow back into his other buttock; Gerontas re-lit his gnarled pipe and puffed it to life; and the hooded man kicked his boots aside, crossed his legs, and folded his arms, burying them in sleeves so voluminous they could have hidden a hundred decks of cards.

As the barbarian began his tale, the hooded man showed particular interest. He had heard many such tales before – and indeed, he had tracked down many of those ales that had been declared by half-cut fireside companions (with slurred voices) to be The One. Some of the nominees had been good and others very good, but none had been as exquisite as the one he now sought. And so now the hooded man watched and listened as his companions took it in turns to voice their own opinions.

He heard the barbarian boast of the Blood Ale, and the ranger counter with Impo's Bitter. The sneering merchant had then dismissed both claims, going on to relate his own tale about how the angel Cirrhosis had brought the Celestial Light Ale to the priests of the temple of Worth-in-Ton. According to Gerontas, Cirrhosis had paid dearly for this charity, for the gods had chained him to a rock, where a voracious beagle feasted upon his continuously regenerating liver.

After the merchant had finished his tale, the party sat around the fire in silence, thinking about the stories they had heard. But the hooded man simply shook his head, for he had learnt nothing new.

At last, the barbarian broke the silence and turned to the hooded man – who had until then kept his own counsel. "You have been silent throughout, but I see from your garb that you are a monk … and monks are renowned throughout the world as great brewers of ale, aye, and great consumers too. With all your experience of ale and your access to the gods, surely *you* must be able to shed some light on the question: what is the best ale in the world?"

The monk wriggled upright and slowly lowered his hood, revealing a heavily weathered oriental face assembled beneath a bald pate. The lines and creases around his mouth, and by his eyes, and across his brow, exaggerated every facial expression so that he appeared to be perpetually gurning. The monk cleared his throat and gave a frown that made him look like a frog with indigestion.

"Your tales … maybe true, maybe not." In the monk's native tongue, pronouns and articles were largely superfluous. As such, he didn't believe in them, and only used them under duress. "Maybe explain how certain ales reached certain parts of world. *Maybe.*" The monk slowly raised one clawed hand and made a curious gesture in front of his mouth, as though trying to pinch an invisible fly using just thumb and forefinger. "But what none can say is which ale is *best*, for none have tried others." Suddenly, the monk's hand darted out and his fist clenched. There was a faint *crunch*, and the monk brought his hand back to himself. Opening his fist, he revealed the crushed remains of an insect. "Ah, grasshopper!"

He flicked the bug away, then continued. "So ... barbarian – have tried Impo's Ale?" He gave Tugon no chance to reply. "No! And merchant, have tried Blood Ale? Have not! Why then say it *not* best?" The monk sneered and made a dismissive gesture.

Gerontas frowned. "And I suppose you have tried all of these ales?"

"*Yes!*" cried the monk, suddenly animated. "Have tried all! Have made this mission in life: to find perfect ale. Have talked to master brewers; have scoured ancient parchments; have humbled self before gods. And now ... now *know* answer!" The monk began to tremble with excitement. His eyes widened. The others in the band leant forward to catch the words of this man who claimed to know the best ale in the world and, more importantly, was about to tell them for free.

"What is it?" asked the barbarian.

"Tell us!" demanded the ranger.

"Go on," cried the merchant.

"Yes, *will* tell," said the monk, "but first must tell story." He sniggered to himself as though at some private joke. "It said that alcohol discovered by wood spirits when noting strange effects caused by rotting fruit on creatures of forests, like, ah, bees and wasps that fly around and crash into trees ..." the monk had a spasm of laughter as his hands imitated an inebriated bee swooping this way and that "... ha, and wild boars that stagger about and fall into bushes, and – ha-ha-ha – like squirrels that fall out of trees ..."

"I think we get the picture," grumbled Gerontas. "Get on with the story."

The monk's face adopted the exaggerated expression of an affronted gargoyle. "Ai-la, you rude bugger!" He stood up suddenly as if to leave. He was torn between punishing the foolish one and relating his story – a story that had to be told. After a moment's hesitation he nodded to himself and squatted back down again. "Will tell, but you shut face, okay!"

"Yeah yeah," muttered the merchant, aware of the intent looks being directed at him by the other men around the fire. "Sure. Go on."

"Humph. So, wood spirits tried rotten fruit too and liked very much. Then was great party with singing and games and dancing. But pretty soon some bugger offered cup of new drink to gods as gift – and this number one mistake!" A serious expression crossed the monk's rubber face. "La, for gods liked drink and demanded wood spirits make more and more for them, until all rotting fruit in forest gone. But still gods wanted more, so spirits forced to experiment. They collected fresh fruit and put in vats to moulder, and so invented brewing." The monk paused to collect his thoughts. "At first, spirits used apples and pears, but soon ran out and forced to try other fruits and flavours. Then one day spirit called Boozer used small fruit of climbing plant called *hop*, and made first true ale."

The monk smiled ecstatically now and a tear formed in the corner of one eye. "La, Boozer invented ale, and all tasting drink agreed it divine. Then other spirits tried to make miracle ale, and many types were made, for Boozer would not reveal mix of ingredients added to hops. Tcha! Then other spirits tried to trick recipe from Boozer, who fled, and after much wandering hid recipe where no god or spirit would think of looking … in secret place in realm of man! And this place guarded by great warrior priests and protected by traps, and location … ah, that been mystery. *Until now.*" The monk scrunched his face into a mischievous expression and stared into the flames of the fire. The other men held their breath, waiting for the story to continue …

But it did not.

"Go on," urged the ranger. "Where is this 'secret place'?"

"Aye," snarled the barbarian, "you've whetted our appetites. Tell us more!"

The monk cackled dementedly. "Want to know more, eh? Good!" He rocked back and forth on his haunches. "Learnt of secret place from dying man, who told where to start search for place of recipe." Again he paused.

After several moments more, the merchant threw up his hands in frustration. "This is like pulling teeth!" He glowered at the monk. "How do you know this ale is the best anyway … from the lips of a dying man with a tall tale? You haven't even tasted it!"

"Ai-la," cried the monk triumphantly, making a perverse shaking gesture with one hand. "*Have* drunk ale! Man had some in water bottle and for small service gave sip. Is best! Even now, thought of ale makes me shake with lust!"

"A little service?" wondered Gerontas, with a smirk. "I don't suppose that involved a quantity of ointment, your tongue, a large wooden truncheon and—"

"*Shhhh!*" hushed Angred. "Enough! Monk – this hidden place: do you know its location? Its name?"

The monk gave a wry smile. "No, do not … but there instructions … this what man had learnt. Boozer made map of route took when wandering realms of man, and when returning to forest in Frembolia tore up map and left parts here and there on way back. Each part shows way to next, but all must be viewed before full path can be known."

"And the first step … the first part of the map … do you have it?"

Again the grin. "This is so, but not second. But know where is."

"Where?" exploded the barbarian. "By Grom, you must tell us!"

The monk cackled and rocked backwards and forwards with even greater vigour. "Tell you, eh? Barbarian is enthusiastic? This good! Need men of vision, strength and cunning to help find secret place. And maybe *you* will do!" The monk giggled like the demented owner of a Chinese restaurant who had seen one order for sweet and sour pork too many. Around the fire, the other men looked at each other with uncertainty in their eyes. Surreptitiously, the merchant made a rotating gesture with one finger at the side of his head.

The monk at last regained a degree of self-control. "So … are interested? Barbarian, think of slaughter and glory … and ranger, think of challenge to skills … and merchant, think of profits to be had!"

"Let me get this straight," said Tugon suspiciously. "You know the location of the recipe for the greatest ale in the world, and you want us to go with you to get it? Why us? You'd never met us before tonight."

"Fate!" cackled the monk. "Fate brought together. This major crossroads … *in lives*. You are Men of Action – cannot resist challenge any more than dog can resist sniffing bum of other dog. And now moon losing height in sky and new day soon be here. Suggest sleep."

"Yes, good idea," responded the ranger carefully. "After all, we'll need all our strength for the long quest ahead, won't we?"

A grunt of assent emanated from the barbarian, and the men settled down to sleep. As they prepared their sleeping mats they thought about the potential bloodshed, the challenge, the riches that they might gain, and the inevitable death that they would suffer. And anyway, who was to say that the monk spoke the truth? What a loon! Yes, surely his tale was the result of delirium …

When the morning broke, the monk awoke to find himself alone: the other men had gone. Next to the ranger's empty sleeping hollow, scratched into the earth, was the message: *Grandmother lost in woods – gone home.* By the barbarian's pitch was scratched the excuse: *Grandmutha kild in battle – gon home.* And by the merchant's, written on a piece of parchment: *Had a good offer for my grandmother – gone home.* The monk shrugged his shoulders in resignation. This had happened to him before during his journey. No matter what crafty lures or ruses he used he was unable to persuade the travellers he met on the road to join him on his mission.

"Men of Action – pah!" he muttered to himself. "What really need is men who desperate for a good drink!"

CHAPTER 1

THE BEAR ESSENTIALS

AT THE meeting of the Great East and North Roads, at the intersection of two perpendicular valleys forming a geologically improbable 'X', lay the small town of Cross-My-Way. This town – to whose peculiarities we will return shortly – was surrounded on all sides by steep, forested hills and sullen mountains. The sprightly River Rockbelow tumbled past the settlement in a series of rapids, chasing one of the Great Roads through the east-west valley like a wild, frothing horse desperately seeking a warm barn, a bale of hay, and a nice sugar cube from the hand of a buck-toothed girl. The river gambolled along the valley until, further east, it disappeared over a steep cliff face and so became the Sunbirth Falls.

As a consequence of its watery assistant, the so-called Valley of Latitude was a pleasant, verdant place of trees and flowers and bumbling bees; of greens and blues, yellows and reds; of life and noise, youth and energy: like a whole chorus line of frantically whirling Carmen Mirandas on speed. In contrast to this, the water-deprived north-south valley – the Valley of Longitude – was an empty, dry, and barren place, littered with cracked rock and scrubby trees. The nearest that *this* valley had ever got to the stage, metaphorically speaking, was after the audience had gone home, when – armed with a bucket and mop, and dressed in a pair of wrinkled tights – it scrubbed the boards. And as for colour … well, the Valley of Longitude held no terrors for the colour-blind there, for it was brown: *only* brown; *very* brown. The naked trees, the rocks, even the creatures that lived there: *all* were brown. For its inhabitants, this brownness was both boon and curse. Nature, with its wicked sense of humour, had demanded that every creature wanting an even chance at life beyond a couple of minutes adopt this colour scheme. While the anonymity of

The Brown was all very well for those creatures wanting to avoid becoming the starter to something else's meal, or for those creatures that believed in letting the steak tartare deliver itself, it also proved something of challenge for those *wanting* to be noticed. In terms of finding a mate, for example, the valley had the success rate of a dating agency. If it moved it was about to eat you, if it didn't, it was probably still going to eat you *and* give you a bloody big shock into the bargain. The Longitudinal wildlife lived in constant uncertainty about when it would next taste of the Forbidden Fruit, and indeed, whether the next piece of Forbidden Fruit might not instead turn out to be the Forbidden Amusingly Shaped Piece of Wood. Still, what were a few splinters when the alternative was becoming the source of something else's indigestion?

Even the top predators had difficulty in affairs d'amour. The ferocious brown bears, for example, were frequent victims of the deceitful scenery. Indeed, it was not uncommon to see one unleashing its full and oblivious passion upon a comely boulder, only to disengage with that *Oh No, What Have I Done* morning-after feeling. As such, the bears were too often seen hurriedly retreating in embarrassment from some particularly unfulfilling liaison to cause the odd traveller *too* much trouble. Which was not to say that the valley was safe – it was just the case that, since it was the amorous rather than the dietary appetites of its inhabitants that tended to be in greater need of sating, the passing convoys of traders had other things to fear than the loss of their lives. The golden rule – learned by generations of travellers – was thus: never, ever, *ever*, rest against any boulders …

The strange geography of the environs of Cross-My-Way was subject to all kinds of bizarre rumour, blind speculation, and dogmatic assertion. Sages claimed that the Rockbelow had once flowed in a different direction, carving out the Valley of Longitude before perversely changing course. Why it should do so, however, even they dared not speculate. But what did they know? Could sages throw axes to split the pegged-out tresses of comely blonde maidens? (Indeed, could they even lift the axe?) No! Could they match Old Blunster, Cross-My-Way's awesome ale-drinking champion, in a contest to find the bottom of a barrel of Olde Gutrot? They could not! And if they were so smart – the townspeople joked – then how come they were so poor even beggars gave them alms?

A second explanation for the geographical peculiarities of the region was provided by the devout worshippers of the god Clovory, who claimed that the unusual valley formation had come about from a heavenly game of Noughts and Crosses, when Clovory – excited at the prospect of victory – had placed the winning cross squarely upon his own enormous big toe. Indeed, the townsfolk were more than willing to embrace and propagate the Clovorite belief – at least, in the presence of any brown-robed figure – for the constant pilgrimage to the small Clovorite shrine brought the town (and the Relic Marketeers in particular) plenty of income. And if the odd acolyte searched too deeply into the Valley of Longitude for fragments of Lucky Toenail … well, at least the bears had something to smile about, and the occasional buttock-clenching holy man could always pick up a soothing balm from the market place.

It was a third perspective on the valleys' strange geography, however, that was generally embraced by the town's inhabitants. In the manner of people who have been brought up in the shadow of wonder, the source of others' fascination seemed to them merely mundane and not at all mysterious. And hence, the cross-shaped valley was simply *So*, while the average river-cut valley was, to them, an object of amazement and clearly the product of faulty theistic craftsmanship. Occum the barber summed up the townsfolk's views eloquently. "Where's the mystery in crossing valleys, eh?" he would say. "You want mystery, you look into the beards of some of my customers. Astonishing what you find in there – lamb kebabs, small hunting knives, Ye No Parking Tickets … Amazing. Now do you want a short back and sides or what?" Hence Occum's Razor: don't go worrying about complicated things when a nice cut and shave will set you up for the day. The sages hated Occum's homely wisdom which, in part, explained their hirsute untidiness.

The epicentre of the crossed valleys also formed the epicentre of the town: the large cobbled expanse of the Old Town Square was where the two Great Roads that followed the valleys met, mingled in confusion, and then parted. And, in many ways, the Square was the town: it was the life, soul and reason for the place. The houses and shops behind the Square's frontage were merely bunting, simply places for people to go when they'd had enough of living and wanted somewhere quiet to pass out, be alone, or indulge in solitary pleasures. These zones of relative calm and sanity were known as the Four Quarters: Nostrum, Kelloon, Sarsus, and, of course, the Latin Quarter.

The better-off and more fortunate denizens worked in the shops, hostelries and inns that formed the perimeter of the Square, while many of the rest of the townsfolk set up their stalls in the scrummage that was the daily market. Here could be found all variety of goods: trinkets, jewels, exotic foods, spices, rude carvings, *very* rude carvings, ancient scrolls, clothing … anything bought, traded or pillaged to North, South, East and West, was sure to pass through the ubiquitous colourful stalls at some stage. While gay and festive during the warm sunshine, the market became a sodden mêlée during rain, or with the simultaneous arrival of a number of large caravans. Then, squawking, frantic traders in muddy attire and ridiculous hats would clash in the Square, eager to gain the best price for their merchandise, or to bargain down the price of some curiosity or relic. The crush would swell to and fro across the Square like a huge game of rugby, with dozens of teams scrapping for dozens of balls on a single pitch with a multitude of goal posts. Occasionally, whole stalls would disappear, trampled underfoot or swept away (sometimes with their stallholders), never to be seen again, or to mysteriously re-appear one day presided over by a bandaged owner with improbable tales of the Far East, or the Great West Forest, or Yegoran, the White City of the North.

On days such as these – when the market resembled a cross between open warfare and 'It's a Knockout' – the only place for the sensible traders, or those with enough time or money to say "I'll come back tomorrow" were the shops and inns along the Square's perimeter. It was here, too, that the townsfolk would gather to spend their earnings on choice meats doused in fiery, exotic sauces, or to quench their thirsts with the huge selection of ales that were always on offer. Indeed, the favourite civic pastime was to slowly drink away the afternoon while ensconced at a red-and-white-parasol-sheltered oaken table outside a well-stocked inn, and to watch with humour and amazement the furore of the marketplace.

Although well-served in the drinking department, Cross-My-Way had two establishments in particular that were famed the world over, and known for the quality and diversity of their ales, the warmth of their welcome, and the biceps of their barmen. To the north of the Square lay The Compromised Pilgrim, and to the south, The Merry Bear. Each boasted that it was 'Ye Best Inne In Ye Worlde'. Each claimed to have the largest cellar, and each claimed to have the very best of ales. Travellers and traders from miles around came to Cross-My-Way to test out these competing claims. They came with great expectations – and greater thirsts – and usually left with the sort of headache that made them ask *why*?

Though opinion on the matter of which inn was 'best' varied as greatly as the list of brews that each offered, there were champions aplenty for each contender. The townsfolk, too, tended to have their favourites. Occum the barber, for example, preferred The Bear. "More

4

of an ambience," he would tell his victims, as he strapped them down into the barber's chair, "you can sense the ale as you enter. I once got drunk by breathing too deeply." It was funny how rarely Occum's customers disagreed with him, although cynics would often note (though not while in 'the chair' itself) the astonishing correlation between the *depiliates'* agreement and the proximity of their barber's particularly sharp cut-throat razor (cold steel possessing a certain *persuasiveness*).

On the other hand, the members of the local chapter of 'Ye Hull's Angels' preferred The Pilgrim. Among the latter's attractions, they claimed, was the spacious stabling for their long-horned yaks and the presence of draught Rear Thruster. Rumours that their choice was the result of being on the losing side of a 'who-can-knock-who-cold' encounter with Terry Testosterone, The Bear's chief troubleshooter, were vigorously denied.

In a sane world, the two inns would have rejoiced at their successes and contentedly accepted their slice of the ample custom, perhaps sharing out the various niches in Machiavellian collusion over a pint of Best Bitter. "Right," sane proprietor number one might have said, "we'll stock Clovory's Golden Shower and Bishop's Todger for the religious set – you take the Brown ales for the Southerners, and we'll hold promotions on alternative nights." Idealistic, maybe, but it *could* have worked. *Surely?*

Instead, like competing television stations on Christmas Day, the inns and their proprietors (Hops at The Bear and Manis at The Pilgrim) were determined to have it all. Over the years, the rivalry between them had developed into the sort of competition that could only be called *friendly* by someone who lacked any grasp of semantics. It was as friendly as a game of 'It' between lions and Christians, as good-natured as a game of chess between grand masters, and as gentle as an ice hockey grudge-match. The lengths to which the innkeepers and their staff would go to undermine and discredit the opposition knew no bounds. Indeed, the animosity between the two inns did not stop with their proprietors. Each had a hard core of devotees who eagerly expounded the virtues of their home inn to the town's transitory population *without even being paid*. These patriots would happily bash anyone they encountered from the other pub – provided they caught them *alone, off-guard* and *from behind*. To protect their pubs from such unruly, over-enthusiastic customers, each landlord had hired troubleshooters.

In the case of The Pilgrim, the doorman was a hulking brute with more muscles than a shellfish merchant. Since nobody knew his real name, the regulars – who had frequently observed his *modus operandi* – had christened him The Berserker. His sole job was to enforce The Pilgrim's motto of 'Damage the company's property and we damage you'. To judge the mood of a fighting man, the experts say, you should look into his eyes, as these never lie and will tell you whether he is about to fight or flee. The regulars of The Pilgrim had learned over the years, however, that there was nothing to be gained from looking into The Berserker's eyes: in the first place he *never* fled, and in the second place you ought to be *slightly* more concerned about what his hands were doing. On one occasion, for example, the Demonic Brotherhood (of the Broken Altar of the Possessed Nanny of the Mother of the Second Cousin of St Johool the Mad) had descended into town from their mountain stronghold for their annual summer beano and got into a fracas over a game of dominoes with the Barabary brothers (the meanest trio to ever drop from one woman's womb). As tables had begun to fly, the Berserker had not even paused for thought: within seconds, he had waded into the middle of the mêlée of flailing hair, black robes and knuckle dusters, and Sorted It Out. As far as The Berserker was concerned, when it came to brawls, the size and number of his opponents *only* mattered if they were too few or too small to put up a decent fight. Indeed, when that man was in a state of rage, it usually took a large bucket of cold water to bring him back under control, and generally that bucket had to be thrown base-first.

The Bear, on the other hand, employed a far more serene trouble-shooter – although initial appearances tended to deceive. Terry Testosterone was a barbarian-and-a-half. He stood about seven feet tall in his bearskin boots and possessed the sort of body that made girls go weak at the knees (and men at the bladder). His sole contribution to the clothing debate was a bearskin loincloth that hung down to his knees, leaving his immensely muscled torso bare for all the world to see. Visually, he was the quintessential savage, and yet much of the appearance told a lie. In fact, Terry liked cats, enjoyed wine (but never in public), and had a secret desire to spend his life cutting hedges into those funny animal shapes that the more-educated refer to as 'topiary'. He would have ditched the mangy bearskin if he could (probably for some fine silks), but wore it to please Hops, who thought it gave him a suitably menacing appearance (although Terry had managed to draw the line at having his muscles oiled). Indeed, Terry was courteous, if not a complete gentleman. He was the sort of man who would apologise to an unruly customer *before* ejecting him from the inn, and *then* go out and bandage his wounds before calling him a yakxi.

To Terry's father – who'd had the sort of career that barbarians called "bloody stonking", and the rest of mankind just "bloody" – all this *civility* was more than a little disappointing. It was not that Terry did not know how to handle himself – in fact, in his youth, he had quickly mastered the Nine Ways of the Sword and the Eighty Ways to cripple an Opponent without touching his Balls – it was just that he never seemed to enjoy applying this knowledge. With Terry around fights tended *not* to happen, and he had never, ever been known to start a single one! The Elder Testosterone had at last sent him off into the wider world in the hope that something, somehow, would provoke him into the life of carnage and Putting It About that was his cultural inheritance. Terry, for his part, knew of his parents' disappointment, but could not find the rage in him. Instead, he spent his spare time concocting outrageous letters home in the hope that he might provide some cheer to his long-suffering parents. Indeed, at this very moment he was sitting in the back yard of The Bear, by the stables, chewing on a piece of straw and furrowing his brows in concentration as he considered the text on the parchment before him.

Hi mum, hi dad, the letter began. *This morning I crushed my enemies, drove them before me, and listened to the lamentations of their women. It's definitely the best thing in life. I only wish there had been more of them. Er, the enemies that is, not the women. Well, it would have been okay if there were more women, I guess, but the wailing gets on your nerves a bit. Not that I don't mind a bit of wailing you understand – I know us barbarians like that sort of thing – but it does tend to put me off my breakfast ...*

Terry chewed on the tip of his quill. He was finding it increasingly difficult to invent new, believable scenarios. In his last letter, for example, he had described how he had slaughtered a whole army with a small gardening trowel, ravished *all* of their women, and then lost his new-found kingdom in a game of cards. Had there been any truth to his letters, Terry mused, he would by now have been ruler of the entire world, and have sired enough illegitimate children to turn the globe into one vast, squabbling nursery.

Terry lowered the page before him and sighed. "Having trouble with the letters again?"

The huge barbarian looked up and saw his friend Roffo, leaning on a broom beside a neatly swept pile of hay.

"Oh, hi Roff, yes, I'm afraid so. I just can't get the hang of this embo ... embel ... embulabising ..."

"Embellishing?"

"Er, yeah, that too."

"Let's have a look."

Roffo came to look over the barbarian's shoulder, but an undulating deltoid – like a giant wave – kept obscuring his sight. "Keep still!"

"Sorry!"

To the casual observer, the sight of the slim young man with a long nose peeking over one gigantic shoulder must have looked something like a Chad (perhaps declaring: "wot, no shirt!"). Even seated, Terry dwarfed his friend.

"You haven't got very far ... how long has it taken you to write this?"

"Um, well, er, all morning."

"I see. You definitely need a hand. Now ..." Roffo disappeared briefly, then reappeared with a second battered stool. He carefully laid down his broom. "What about rescuing a princess? Have you done that yet?"

"Er, I'm not sure we *do* that. I mean, rescue people."

"What about captured friends?"

Terry grimaced. "I think we're meant to let them escape themselves. Or commit suicide. Then we destroy the enemy's village and ..."

"See them driven before you, hear their lamentations ... I get the picture. But surely princesses are different?"

"Nope. My dad says that we can break into fortresses, slaughter guards, and ravish prisoners – but we *don't* help them to escape."

"Hmm, I can see this is going to be a problem. What about a quest of some sort? I know! A holy quest! Do something for your god."

Terry slowly shook his head, his grizzled mane swishing about his unshaven face (another of Hops's little suggestions). "Our god is Grom, Lord of the Battle Mound, Sharp Pointy Steel, and Really Long Hair. He gives us life and the will to fight, but Cares Not A Toss. My dad says he'd rather sit on a cactus than do anything for Him."*

"Ah, I see," said Roffo, scratching his unruly shock of hair. "No holy quests, and no rescues. What is it you *are* allowed to do then?"

"Um, *slay*. We can do lots of that. *Slaughter. Pillage*. We definitely

---

* Which, coincidentally, just went to show how out of touch Terry was with his culture, since he had failed to link the following facts: a) the frequency with which his dad came home with cactus spines embedded in his cheeks, b) the look of sublime pleasure that crossed his father's face as each spine was ripped out by his wife, and c) the fact that his dad kept all of the spines and was in the process of creating a rather interesting chair that would not have gone amiss at a sado-masochists' convention.

like *ravishing*, though only if the ravished sort of agree. My mum would kill my dad if he didn't get permission first. *Plunder* is good too. Oh, and there have got to be lots of *lamentations*. That's a must."

"So, basically, what you're saying is that you've got to, ah, *inconvenience* people?"

Terry thought about this for a moment, a slight frown on his face. "Er, yes, you've got it there."

"And do they always have to get hurt?"

The barbarian held up his hands. "Oh no. Not at all. Not *really*." He lowered his hands and thought a moment more. "Er, only slightly. Not fatally, you understand." His brain continued its methodical progress. "Okay, yes," he admitted at last, "they do. Have to get hurt, that is. Quite a bit, actually."

"Barbarous!"

Terry's face suddenly lit up. "Yep – that's us!"

———•••••———

Within the inn, Hops was frowning. He often frowned – it was something he liked doing. Years of experience had taught Hops that frowning tended to get things done. At the very hint of one of Hops's frowns, oversights would suddenly be rectified and wrongs would be righted: barrels that should have been changed ages ago instantly became top-priority; mighty pyramids of empty glasses teetering on rickety tables began to draw staff like flies to a corpse; and the money-box would rapidly fill with the coin owed for surreptitiously poured beverages. Sometimes, when he was in the right mood, Hops would frown *all day* as a pre-emptive strike against mischief.

This day, however, Hops's frown was a genuine one. It was the sort of pure, concentrated frown that, had it come in a bottle, would have been marked 'dilute to taste'. A brawl could have erupted beneath Hops's very nose and he would not have noticed it. Resting on the bar before him was the source of all his troubles: a sheet of parchment on which were scrawled a dozen names. Beside these he had made various marks and annotations, most of which had been scribbled out, re-drawn, and scribbled out again. The entire effect was like the shopping list of a drunken, stoned, demented surrealist. Among the comments that zig-zagged across the sheet were: *he playeth like a nancy, but bools like the demon-possessed … 8; fingers of butter and scores like a decrepit maide, 5*; and *this one they dare not smite, else next visit their ears will be taken home in ye bagge* (an arrow linked this comment to the name 'Occum'). But, bold, at the top of the list, was one name about which no doubt was expressed or comment needed: 'Ye Barbarian'.

It was a day away from the most important event in Cross-My-Way's calendar – an event so important that even the eternal market would close for it. More important than Founder's Day, more anticipated than Zmas, more critical than any World Cup Final, the morrow was the day of the annual Bear-Pilgrim cricket match. Not only would victory in the contest bring great kudos, it would also ensure a healthy increase in bar sales for weeks to come. For such an important event, however, the immediate reward was incongruously nondescript, being a tiny trophy known as 'Ye Ashes'. This contained the burnt remains of a walking stick that had belonged to one of the umpires in the very first match – this having been ceremonially incinerated by The Pilgrim team after their defeat. The walking stick had, in many ways, been an innocent bystander in the affair, having been caught *between* the pyre and the umpire – but only for a very brief, very *hot* moment. The other umpire, not being perambulatorily challenged, had made it over a hedge and into a wood – a posse of screaming, firebrand-waving Pilgrims in his wake – never to be heard from again. As Occum often said: "you just can't beat Natural Deselection."

Hops considered the list anew, and sighed. The responsibilities of the selector! For a fleeting moment he was tempted to ink his own name at the bottom of the parchment. The very thought caused one corner of his mouth to twitch upwards into a half-smile of remembrance. In his youth, Hops had been a doughty stroke-maker and a terror to The Pilgrim's bowlers. Part of his success had, paradoxically, come from his very lack of fitness. Hops had always eyed with uncertainty and suspicion the twenty-two-yard distance to the opposite wicket and, deciding that 'running' was not his kind of thing, he had settled on a 'hold your ground and smite the blighters to all boundaries' approach. He had been a legend! Alas, the years had seen his barman's belly inflate to the point where it actually interfered with the free swing of his bat. The humiliation of being given out Belly Before Wicket had at last driven him to hang up his bat for good. Now his duties had diminished to team manager and motivator (as in "drop that catch, my lad, and ye'll be sweeping the stables for the next week *without a broom*").

A thought suddenly struck Hops. He crossed out one name and, in a still-pristine corner of the parchment, scrawled another: *Grimwade*. Also known as Ye Devil's Scholar, the head teacher of one of the town's three teaching-houses was a regular at the inn and a man reputed (by the town's terrorised children) to have a good arm and a true aim, particularly when he had a plank of wood in one hand and a nearby target of the soft, white, moon-shaped variety. Hops dipped his quill in ink and quickly wrote: *this one will spanke their balls – 3.*

A scent of cheap perfume stole up the barman's nose and gave his nasal reins a tug.

"Hopsie, what are you doing? Is that the team?"

Hops made a grunting noise, something like a bear with indigestion, and tried to shield the sheet from view.

"It is, isn't it! Oh, let's have a look – please?" Soft breath fell onto Hops's ear and feminine anatomy pressed into his arm. Hops began to sweat. A bead of salty water slid from his forehead and dropped onto his hand.

"Hrumm, urhuhuhm. Haven't … " Hops's voice dried up like a British reservoir after the first hot day of summer. "Maddy," he squeaked, "haven't you got work to do?"

The voluptuous young barmaid with matted blonde hair and provocatively tight attire put on a little pout. "Oh, Hopsie, I just want a look. You can trust me!"

Hops tried to *frown*, but his lips just quivered. "No. You can't look. Go away. *Please.*"

The girl turned away, but only to call out to Heddy and Eddie, the other barmaids (Hops having a liking for girls with a double-d). "He's got the teamsheet and he won't show me!"

"Oooh, is my Ned playing – is he?"

"Come on, Hopsie, let's have a look!"

The barman was suddenly surrounded by three young women who weren't just dressed to kill, they were dressed to annihilate! He found himself in a scrum of clawing arms, murmured encouragements, cajoling, prying, pressing, squeezing, hot breath, and the smell of rank perfume …

Hops's sensory systems reached the point of overload. At about this time in a cheap sci-fi B movie, a red light would start to wink and klaxons wail. And Hops did the only thing a repressed, red-blooded male could possibly do in these circumstances.

He fled.

CHAPTER 2

MARKET FORCES

SUNLIGHT SPRAYED down onto the damp, early morning streets of Cross-My-Way, prying into half-drawn shutters, searching out secrets, dissolving shadows. On the crumbling tiles of a rooftop, a mangy grey cat blinked its eyes and looked accusingly at the yellow face peering over the roof horizon. The small ball of fluff that lay nearby – lightly wedged between two russet tiles to thwart the unjust demands of gravity – suggested that there would be one more reason this day for Jer-Ey, God of Mice, to remonstrate with To-Mas, the Nemesis, the Mewing Destroyer.

Several houses further down, a furtive figure with a blackened face and a demeanour that suggested Up-To-No-Good, was startled as he emerged from a second-floor window. He quickly recovered his composure, however, and – still clutching gains that were definitely ill-gotten – he grasped a sturdy drainpipe and swung himself expertly onto the roof. He bounded away across the rooftops as though they were afire, leaping over alleyway chasms with the dexterity of, well, *a thief.*

Nearby, upon the top of a still-warm chimney, a small flock of pigeons indulged in their favourite pastimes, cooing like a feathered choir and whitewashing the flues. If humans could have understood their speech it would surely have hastened the advent of Pigeon Armageddon.

"Watch this, watch this … aaaaah! Classic!" cooed a large fat pigeon with an unusually full complement of toes.

"Waste! Wot a waste!" jeered his nearest companion, who also had all his toes but had only one eye. "Bet you can't do that again!"

"Bollocks! Bet I can!"

"No way …" twittered another – this one with hardly any toes at all.

"Hah, that's nothing," declared a pigeon with two toes on each foot. "Cop this!"

A squelchy eruption followed that caused a couple of the more nervous birds to flutter away a short distance, fearful that their companion was about to explode.

"God, what *have* you been eating?" cooed the fat one, unable to keep admiration from his voice.

"Heh heh heh! Never you mind! But I'll tell you this, I've got plenty more for the humans!"

"On the head, on the head!" cheered an enthusiastic youngster.

"A head shot – *maybe*. But I likes to get it in their beer. Some of it is so shite the punters don't even know when they've been *done*!"

"Ho-ho, ho-ho!"

"Stupid humans, cooo, cooo."

"Let's go, let's go right now! Let's *do* it!"

The rest of their conversation, following a similar vein, needs no reporting.

———•••••———

Meanwhile, in the street below, the thought processes of the man ambling along under the new sun were far more serene. Hops enjoyed his regular early morning stroll from his home – in the Kelloon quarter – to The Bear. As he walked along the slick cobblestones on this day, munching an apple, his mind filled with thoughts of bar rotas, possible drinks promotions, the price of ale, and the conniving of the big brewers. It pleased him to think that, just about now, Cook would be preparing his substantial breakfast, Terry would be weeding out the last of the night's malingerers, and Heddy and Roffo would be giving the bar a quick clean – slopping out the worst of the drinking man's excesses and hiding what couldn't be shifted (the *stains and remains* as Hops called it) under handy beer mats, ash trays and bar towels. Hops did, after all, pride himself on being proprietor of the cleanest inn in town!

Hops continued past a number of narrow wooden houses, a small convenience shop, and a Travel Agent advertising sensational excursions to Foreign Parts. He paused for a moment to peruse the offers on display, just as he did every day. To travel! The hectic life of a publican offered little time and few opportunities to leave the world of the inn for more exotic parts. But Hops had always dreamed, and the tales from the passing traders had only served to whet his appetite further. Tales of adventure, of lust, of weird and grotesque architecture, of spicy foods, of lust, of fabulous landscapes, and of lust … Hops bit hard into his apple, mopped his brow with an unwashed sleeve, and tried to think of other things. In spite of this intent, his mind filled with visions of comely maidens attired in the fabled sex-clothes of Nudia …

With an effort, the barman turned his attention to the bargain of the week: a long weekend in famed Colloidia, land of hot springs and hotter nights! Alas, thought Hops, wistfully, for the nine weeks it actually took to travel there …

The rotund man continued along the road, scurrying past the premises – two doors down – of Awful Puns's Bakery. He gave an involuntary shudder and moved swiftly on. No-one knew what exactly went into Puns's pastries – and perhaps it was better that way – but the smell alone was enough to make a strong man retch. Puns! One of Hops's least favourite people! Indeed, there were only two things in life that Hops detested more. One was that Manis at The Pilgrim, and the other – which his suddenly attuned hearing brought instantly to mind – was pigeons!

The sound of cooing from the rooftops caused the hairs on the back of his neck to stand up. *Aha! Sitting on that chimney pot! I see you!*

Hops took a final bite from his apple and calculated the angles. Trajectory *just so*, arm back *so far*, and … let it fly!

The apple core made a splendid arc through the air, a perfect parabola, a dead-eye shot. The core dive-bombed through the cluster of conspirators and struck a particularly fat pigeon full on the head. As Hops clenched his fist at this little triumph, the remains of the small flock took to the air like a scrambling squadron of Spitfires. There was a great fluttering of wings, and momentary confusion. The birds rose – and dispersed! Unfortunately for a creeping, black-clad man – who had strayed into territory the pigeons usually claimed as their own – they dispersed right into his path. The man swatted at the blur of black-and-white feathers, lost his balance, and careened towards the sloping edge of the roof. A grey cat, which had been anticipating a main course of pigeon to follow its mouse starter, suddenly found its prey scattered and a huge shape blundering towards it at speed.

Below – his view somewhat impeded – Hops heard a feline wail, a dreadful curse, and the thunderous sound of a dozen extremely agitated pigeons venting themselves in fright. And then there was a brief, oh-so-brief, split-second of silence. From out of the sun came a dark, eclipsing figure, filling the air. But this figure could not fly, and gravity – earlier denied the embrace of a dead mouse – now snatched at this instead.

The thief plummeted to the ground in front of Hops, right into the very middle of a puddle whose origins were, to say the least, *dubious*. As the suddenly sodden man attempted to absorb the full fall through the powerful shock-absorbers of his thighs, a meteorite of flailing grey fur descended in his wake – and clocked him firmly on the bonce. Both thief and cat were pitched into the odorous mire. Hops watched with curiosity as the stunned pair regained their feet and, drenched, staggered off down the street in opposite directions.

Somewhere, in the bowels of the earth, a huge rodent with immense ears and a slowly fading golden sceptre squeaked in glee. As it shovelled a piece of cheese the size of a family saloon into its spacious cheeks, one thought pervaded its mind and was transmitted, ineffably, to small squeaky things everywhere. Mice capered, voles got down and grooved, rats turned somersaults in the air, and a high-pitched chant rippled down the sewers and through the fields and along the skirting boards of the world: "*one-aaaaaall, one-er-un aaaaaall, one aaaaaall, one aaaaaall!*"

Unaware of the furore, Hops – the castaway instrument of a god that had a bigger stock of cheese than a whole *arrondissement* – gingerly brushed the splashes of brown 'water' off his tunic, shook his head slightly, and continued on his way.

The streets of Kelloon wove about drunkenly, never keeping to a straight line, never allowing the pedestrian to become bored, and forever throwing surprises in the way. Hops passed beneath a little oak bridge that linked two second-floor rooms above a pair of antique shops. Further on, he swerved through a chicane, emerging to find a heavily laden camel attempting to do a three-point turn in the narrow street, chided by a wailing, yellow-robed merchant. The innkeeper stepped into Rusty's Ironmongery, passed a row of barrels containing nails and horseshoes, and emerged through a second door on the far side of the traffic jam.

Hops heard the market before he saw it. Even at this early hour of the morning, the babble of business 'being done' was considerable. As he got nearer, the noise rose from a faint hum – a background to more immediate sounds: someone coughing, a bell jangling, the splosh of a night-bucket being emptied onto the street, the howl of someone on whom a night-bucket had just been emptied – to a noise not unlike that of a vast continental lake flush with flamingos. By the time Hops shimmied around the last kink in the road and emerged onto the fringes of the Old Square, the din was such that it sounded as though the flamingos had gone to war with an army of howler monkeys while urged on by cheer-leaders of the demented-cockerel persuasion.

On this morning, however, the cacophony was even greater than usual. As Hops stepped into the Square proper, the tension in the air slapped him around the face like a manhandled maiden. The merchants and stall holders – unstable individuals at the best of times – were burning high octane in their attempt to make up for the loss of trade that would result from the enforced closure caused by the afternoon's cricket match. With a large caravan due in from the East on the morrow (and hence the need to clear out old stock and build up the coffers), and the almost-unanimous extension of the businesses into the field of bookmaking, the combination of events had sent adrenaline levels surging. In these circumstances, the slightest provocation or affront tended to lead to quarrels and bloodshed. A low offer from a customer on this day was as liable to bring forth a flurry of blows as the usual sneer of derision, while the snaffling of a customer from a neighbouring stall was likely to lead to arson or assault. Regulars from the two inns rushed back and forth throughout the market, comparing quoted odds, placing some bets, trading on others – and stopping to rage at opposition supporters. On the outskirts of the Square, teams of stretcher-bearers stood at the ready, looking anxiously for custom, while the Market Police – in their swanky white uniforms – milled around at the fringes, looking scared.

Hops stopped dead in his tracks. He would normally pass through the market on his way to the inn, placing orders for food to be delivered later in the day. But looking at the heaving, shouting mass, his mouth suddenly went dry. If the balloon went up, he didn't fancy his chances. Already, nearby marketmen and their customers were beginning to turn Hops's way. *Eyeing* him. *Wondering.* He could almost sense their thoughts: *What if he doesn't make it to the match … How will the odds be affected if … Just a little accident, nothing serious, a broken leg or two …* Hops shuddered, tried to turn up the collar of his tunic, and turned away. As he scurried along the southern perimeter of the Square, with burning eyes boring into his back, he rapidly came to a plan of action. The food had to be got in, there was no doubt about that. After all, he couldn't let his customers starve. Right. Fine. So, he would just have to send someone else out to get the provisions. And if a few menials got, er, *hurt* in the process … well, it would be worth it, wouldn't it? A slight smile played across Hops's lips as the thought passed through his mind: *today, about 100 gold coins worth it.*

Still thinking happy thoughts of profit, Hops sidled his way around the edge of the market towards his beloved pub. Upon reaching the front door he yelled inside. "Terry! Roffo! Where are you? I have a job for you."

Roffo slunk through the propped-open front door to stand before the publican. The manfully-striding Terry came up close behind him. "I have a bad feeling about this," whispered Roffo, over his shoulder. "Look at the sheen on his face. He gets like that when he's excited … or scared."

"Right, lads," declared Hops, "I need you to get the grub in." He ticked off the list on his fingers as he spoke. "I need thirty steaks, some spicy sausages, three big bags of potatoes, some salad vegetables, and a couple of packets of extra-hot curry powder for today's special – the good stuff mind you, not that weak Lingulian rubbish. Aye, if our customers can sit down before the week is out, they'll know they've been short-changed! I think we've already got the other ingredients." Hops gave a knavish grin. "I would go myself, of course, but I've got to stay in and wash my hair. Aye, cleanliness is very important in the hostelry trade: the punters wouldn't want to find a *dirty* hair in their food, now, would they?"*

"Into the market to buy salad – *today!*" whined Roffo. "I don't want to die for a lettuce!"

"Tush tush," chided Hops. "A much under-rated thing, the lettuce. A very important commodity it is. Add a couple of slices of cucumber, a quarter of tomato, and a bit of cress, and it sets the meal off a treat. Let's the customers know that you *care* about their meal. So, it's not just lettuce you'll be dying f— … er, *getting*. It's a token of goodwill."

Hops dug deep into one of his pockets and started searching amongst its contents. With a satisfied grin, he pulled out a small, leather bag. He coaxed some coins from this and handed these to a disgruntled-looking Roffo. Before any further excuses could be made by the 'volunteers', the innkeeper turned on his heels and headed through the open door.

"Off you go, then," said Hops's back, as it disappeared into the pub. "I'll see you later …" The final, unspoken word "possibly" was left drifting in the doorway.

The two stood for a moment at the front of the inn, looking out over the market. A cold wind suddenly arose from nowhere, causing the chilled men to wonder whether it was the icy hand of fear they felt, or simply the flatulence of God. Even Terry, to whom the concept of fear was as alien as a creature from Alpha Centauri, experienced an instant of doubt, causing his heart to beat a little faster. In subconscious response,

---

* Whereas a clean hair, of course, would be perfectly all right.

he clenched his fists and sent two bicep tidal waves sweeping up his arms to crash against the rocks of his shoulders.

"It's quiet out there," said Roffo, who was a dead hand at spotting cliché opportunities, "*too* quiet."

Terry looked askance at his quivering friend. "Er, no it's not. It's, er, quite noisy actually ..."

Roffo waved the comment aside with a brief flick of a hand. "It's the coming caravan – like a coming storm. It's got them all on edge. And The Match. You can taste the tension in the air, feel its clammy hands on your skin, smell its putrid breath ..."

"Um, well, not really ..." interrupted Terry.

"Smell its putrid breath," continued Roffo, insistently. "Is it a mark of doom? What does this portend? Will we *end* today? So much still to see and do, so much ..."

Terry gently placed an over-sized hand atop his friend's head and gave him a shake. The effect on the slim young man was something like that of an earthquake on a skyscraper.

"Er, *when* you've finished scaring yourself ..."

"Oh, er, sorry Terry. Got a bit carried away. I didn't get to 'oh, woe is me' did I?"

The barbarian grinned. "Not quite." He then added reassuringly: "There's really nothing to, um, *worry* about, just because I'm reckoned to be The Bear's best batsman and half of the town has bet on the opposition." He turned away and started off. "The butcher's first, I think."

A pale and shaking Roffo trailed closely in his wake.

In a back room of The Pilgrim, a squat middle-aged man with slick black hair and a lumpy nose held court over his minions. Manis looked around the table at the seven men who were taking liberties with his Rear Thruster and digging holes in the furniture with a variety of sharp objects – and what he saw did not inspire him. These were men who had risen to the top of life's rich soup (i.e. the *scum*). They were bullies. They were thugs. They were the sort of men who never washed their hands after going to the toilet. Indeed, the best that could be said about these men was that, when it came down to it, they weren't even that *good* at being *bad*. Manis scowled. And he was meant to ensure victory over The Bear *with this*?

"We are getting nowhere," sighed Manis, "except to the bottom of a barrel of one of my finest. I am not a charity! The problem remains:

how are we going to ensure victory over the Hearth-Rugs? What are we going to do to tip the balance our way?"

The other men exchanged worried looks, fearful of speaking, fearful of invoking the kind of scornful reproach at which Manis (like a French teacher) was adept. Five of these villains were members of the local chapter of the Hull's Angels: black-clad (entirely), large (mostly), and bearded (also mostly). The other two members of the party comprised the man-mountain known as the Berserker, and a slim, balding individual called Picket who, perhaps unsurprisingly, was a fence.

Trespass – the black-bearded leader of the yak riders – appreciated that more was expected of him. He cleared his throat uncertainly. "Well, er, maybe we could *kidnap* Occum? I mean, that damned barber is a demon with the bat – cutting and slicing and whatnot."

"Yeah, I like that," growled Grunt, a huge, round, brown-bearded moron. "I know," he continued, "maybe we could get 'old of 'im and sort of, well, tie 'is limbs to our yaks and then, like, leave town by different gates!"

"You mean, just for a bit of 'armless fun?" noted Burble, with a smirk. Burble was both the shortest and the least hirsute of the Angels – a man who suffered from that terrible affliction of only being able to grow one of those ridiculous wispy beards, in the face of which (as it were) he had opted for the whole-head clean-shaven approach. Because he was somewhat shorter than his brother, Frunge, Burble had been nicknamed *The Shadow*. This was an appellation he had accepted with relish and given an interpretation all of his own …

Manis scowled. He had been taking suggestions of this ilk for the last hour or so. "Ripping one of your opponents in quarters, though having merit in certain situations, is perhaps a bit *drastic* in these circumstances."

"Dat's wot you said about my suggestion," pouted the Berserker. "I still don't see wot's wrong with my idea of just 'ittin their best player on the 'ead with my club."

"Actually," sneered Manis, "your suggestion was to hit *all* of their team with your club, and *then* anyone who might take their place, and *then* anyone who looked like anyone who might take their place …" Manis was beginning to lose it "… and *then* the family of anyone who looked like anyone who might take their place. Don't you think this sudden act of genocide might make the survivors just a *little* bit suspicious? *Damned fool!*"

The Berserker thrust out his bottom lip still further. He had never learnt how to respond to a telling-off when violence was out of the question. For a moment it looked as though he might blub.

Picket stepped in quickly to save a lot of embarrassment. "I suggest," he ventured, "we focus our efforts on taking out their key player and forget about the others. And that's not Occum. It's got to be the barbarian. He may be strong in body but, well, is he as strong in mind? A devious plan might lure him into our clutches."

"You're right," said Manis, with exaggerated calm, "we need a devious plan. I'm glad that's established. Well done. Splendid. It's good to know that after all this time we have managed to come to the conclusion that we need a plan. But," and now Manis rose to his feet and pointed at the fence, "*what in the name of Bulabothel* do you think we've been trying to decide here*? Give me a plan ... *give me a plan!*" Manis collapsed back into his seat.

"Er, right boss. I do have an idea as it happens." Picket hunched forwards conspiratorially. "Right. We need to lure the barbarian into a trap, agreed? So, what can no man can resist?"

"That's easy," exclaimed Grunt. "A Harleck Dravidian with gold-tip chopper-'orns, a black pelt, go-faster stripes, and ..."

Picket shook his head. "No ..."

"Och, I ken," declared Bruce, a red-bearded hooligan from the Highlands. "A hundred barrels o' Fullney's Black Death, a dozen crates o' pork scratchings, an' ..."

"No! *Interesting*, but ... no. A—"

"A palace of jools and ivory and gold," cried Frunge, a man who had twice the girth and half the brains of his younger brother, "and a thousand slaves to do everything for you, like wipe your butt and stuff ..."

"No, no, NO!" shouted Picket. His hands clenched into fists and his eyes whirled about in their sockets. He took a deep breath to calm himself. "No."

"Interesting," mused Manis, as he rasped at the stubble on his chin. "I do believe you're thinking of a *honey* trap."

"Er," exclaimed Frunge, in confusion, "you mean brain him with a beehive?"

"No, you dolt," said Trespass. "He means we smear him with honey and tie him to the nearest anthill. That's a great ..." Trespass ground to a halt as Manis *looked* at him.

Picket nodded enthusiastically. "That's right. We get some floozy to lure him off somewhere and detain him using her feminine wiles. And I think I know just the woman we need."

"Go on."

---

*   An evil god, reputed to live in Hull.

"Well, what about that girl in the bar? The looker with the tattoos and the flame-red hair. Rumour has it she'll do anything for a silver sovereign."

The assembled men nodded in unison. A smirk started out on Bruce's lips and – like a bad disease – rapidly spread to the rest of the company. As the infection took hold, secondary symptoms were manifest: sniggers, chortles, and giggles broke out. There was even a touch of foaming at the mouth.

Grunt held up a hand like a child in desperate need of relief. "Oy, boss," he cried, "can I go *on the job* with 'er!"

"Och nae," cried Bruce, "if she needs a hand I can *gie her one*!"

"Hur hur hur," laughed Frunge, "let's give her an *audition* and see if she's any good!"

Trespass laughed along with the innuendo merchants, but at the back of his mind he knew that something wasn't quite right. The description of the temptress was somehow *familiar*. At last he changed mental gear and Mr Realisation tapped on the dashboard to signal an emergency stop. "Here!" cried the leader of the pack, "that's Sonia! That's *my* bird!"

The laughter choked off ... but not for long. A gasp of breath escaped here, a snort there. Hands appeared in front of mouths to tactically cover strangled coughs. Grinning faces sought desperately to avoid the eyes of the head yak rider. Shoulders heaved up and down. And Trespass began to hyperventilate. As he struggled for indignant breath his face started to turn white, and then blue. "You ... her ... on the ... job ... give her ... one ... ahhhh ... ahhh ... ahhh!"

"Enough of this," snarled Manis. He leant across the table and belted Trespass on the back, making the bearded one exhale like a rabbit-punched whale. "Calm yourself! We're not suggesting she drag him back to her boudoir and shag him senseless – eh, Picket? And take that grin off your face! Okay. Call the wench in and I'll proposition her."

Trespass's eyes bulged. "You'll *what*?"

Making progress through the market was akin to wading through quicksand with an elephant on your back and hidden obstacles in your path – while blindfolded. Normally, people parted before the barbarian like the Red Sea before Moses, but this day there was just nowhere to 'part' to. What was worse, the natural inclination of people to get out of the giant's way had, like self-preservation, goodwill, and humour, gone right out of the proverbial window. This was Market Rage, where normally sane people – frustrated beyond all endurance, pushed, shoved, trampled, ignored, short-changed, and anonymous within the crowd – lost all sense of proportion and did things which, in many cases, they would regret for quite some time (particularly when the source of some surreptitious blow or kick was traced – correctly or otherwise – to *them*).

Terry trudged along, a human steamroller, calmly picking people up and putting them aside or, when there was no place to put them, draping them over his shoulder until there was. At one brief eye in the chaotic storm the barbarian unloaded a Yegoran trader, a Clovorite priest, and two evil old ladies – one of whom turned and booted him on the shin for his 'cheek'. As she hopped about clasping her now-crumpled foot in one hand and her tartan pumaskin-lined 'shopper' in the other, Terry made apologetic noises.

"Layorf you big oaf! Assaulting me poor tootsies with yer great shin. You should be ashamed of yourself! When I was a lass we knew how to deal with hooligans like you *aaaark* …" and a sudden surge in the crowd trapped her shopper and dragged the old woman off into the midst of the mêlée.

"Thank Clovory for that," panted Roffo, as he leant against his friend. "Wicked old harridan – I hope she drowns in her own drool."

"Oh, I thought she was sweet."

"Terry, sometimes I wonder about you."

Nearby, a stall gave way under the weight of demand. A sudden cheer went up, and a swell of people – sensing free plunder – surged in that direction. From Terry's exalted height above the crowd he recognised the stall holder as Long Jon Con Dom, Purveyor of Devices of Sexual Education and Gratification. He watched as that man clambered onto his ruined stall and began fending off groping, grasping hands with a large, suspiciously shaped knobbly object. Various bits of merchandise flew through the air, some bouncing about on the heads of the members of the crowd: Eroto-balls, cages of hamsters, weird devices that looked like improbable drills. Bottles began to break, essences and scents were released, and Jolobo Fly was sprayed over a part of the crowd. At last, Long Jon's resistance ended and he was pulled down into the maul. A great scrap broke out on one side of the destroyed stall, while on the other, people started ripping off their clothes and … Terry turned away.

"This is madness," cried Roffo, ducking as an iron contraption – a bit like a bikini bottom with a lock – whistled over his head. "We've got to get out of here."

"I'm all for that," shouted Terry, "but I'm lost. Which way now?"

"East – head east," yelled Roffo. "And if you can't tell where that is, just follow the flies!"

The majority of the meat vendors set up around the eastern end of the Square, near to the exit of the Great East Road, close to the town's slaughterhouse in the Sarsus Quarter. This juxtaposition was very much a consequence of refrigeration – or rather, the lack of it – which meant that stalls selling meat had to be as close to their source of raw material as possible. And let's face it: death is Nature's way of saying that something has passed its sell-by date: for the purchaser of bits of defunct animal it was then just a question of *by how long*. Of course, there were also plenty of independent butchers scattered throughout the town – and these had their own shops and did their own meat processing (i.e. turning live animals into dead animals) – but their premium rates only tended to appeal to those who planned to feed themselves rather than others.

Terry and Roffo breasted through the tangle of humanity and came to a little clearing before one of the meat vendors' stalls. This stall was laid out in a methodical manner: a section was allocated to each individual animal (comprising the various cuts and joints that it furnished) and was fronted by a sad-looking head that wordlessly, eloquently declared that 'this was me.' The heads – and their state of decay – also served as barometers of the number of days that the meat had been feeding the local fly population. Sausages hung from the top of the stall and, from between two extremely green, furry strings of these, there peered Mr Baker, the butcher. On spotting the approaching pair the man let out a squeal of joy and rushed around to the front of the stall to greet them.

"Gentlemen, gentlemen, I'm so pleased to see you," fawned the butcher. "All ready for the big match, I hope? If there is any way I can be of assistance please don't hesitate to ask. I'm always ready to help those at The Bear – praise you! Up The Bear, I say, and down with the cursed Pilgrim!"

"Hmmm," mused Roffo, "then why do I note The Pilgrim's mark on your order board beside the comment 'ten beef steaks'?"

"Oh – that," laughed the butcher, "a trifling order. I had ten manky bits of meat, not fit for dogs. I hope it poisons them. But for you, sirs, only the very best!"

The owner of the neighbouring stall – which a large banner proclaimed to be 'Noble Candles' – spotted the star player of The Bear and called out to him. "Oi, Terry, over here!" He gave the barbarian a thumbs-up. "Give 'em Hull for us, eh? I've money on you, son, so don't let us down!"

This show of support was instantly countered from the stall directly opposite with the blowing of an extremely loud raspberry, courtesy of Rene Heap (also known as 'The Reek'). Rene was a regular at The Pilgrim, where he collected dung from the stables, which he then dried and sold as firelighters, giving a whole new meaning to the concept of 'throwing a log onto the fire'.

"You've no chance," sneered Rene, in a menacing manner. "You're gonna lose and lose baaaaaaad!" The firelighter salesman started to make a number of offensive gestures.

"Er, haha, that Rene – what a card!" said the butcher. "Always jesting and japing, though he never means no harm by it. Ignore him! Now, what can I get you?"

"We need ..." Roffo stepped to one side as an embryonic firelighter pitched onto the cobbles beside him "... thirty steaks. Of top quality, mind you!"

"Naturally," cried Mr Baker, "you'll have the freshest cuts!" He cupped one hand to his ear as though listening to some far-off sound. "In fact, can you hear that?"

All the intrepid duo could hear were imprecations from around them as the argument between the nearby stall holders threatened to get out of hand. Terry also cupped a hand to his ear. "'You ... *damned whoreson'*?" he queried. "'You ... foul canker on the anal hairs of ... *Bulabothel*?'"

"No no ... not that. *That*! Mmmmm ...." went the butcher, looking at Terry encouragingly. "Mmmmmoooo. Mmmmmmooooooooo. Moo?"

Terry shook his head. "Sorry."

"Well, ha ha," the butcher slapped the severed cow's head. "Anyway, 'tis almost as fresh as a live 'un, so it is."

Roffo frowned. "Yes, well, we also need some spicy sausages – Mrs Hops likes a bit of spicy sausage."

"So I've heard!" sniggered the butcher.

"Please, no more!" moaned the barman.

Out of the corner of his eye Roffo suddenly caught sight of Rene advancing across the cobbles towards the candle-maker, armed with a particularly large clod of pre-firelighter. His aim, this time, was much better. The missile flew high over the intervening (and now ducking) crowd, to land with a sickening splat on the candle seller's head. The crust on the partially dried lump of dung broke, releasing the rather less solid internal contents. Momentarily, the candle seller stood stock still, his face a mask of tranquillity, the liquid sludge oozing down his cheeks. Then, slowly, ever so slowly, he bent down – dislodging the brown beret –

to reach for a box containing a number of his brother Alfred's *special* red candles. He extracted one, lit a match, and applied it to its wick ...

The butcher had also spotted this exchange. *That Rene,* he thought, *sometimes he goes too far!* "Excuse me, gents," he said to his customers, "duty calls ..." and with that he grabbed a hock of meat from his stall and danced across the road. With the cry of "Have a free sample of tenderloin!" he swung the meat straight up between the firelighter salesman's legs, lifting the man a good foot off the ground. His now cross-eyed adversary groaned once before slowly sinking to the ground. A split-second later, brother Alfred's Special landed on Rene's stall right in the middle of a large pile of raw materials. Mr Baker lowered the tenderloin and looked at the pretty candle, quizzically. *My,* he thought, *that's a fast burning wi*—

The huge explosion blew the large pile of dung fifty feet into the air, showering pieces of turd over a wide area of the market. When the smoke cleared — and after the last splatter of dung had descended from the heavens — Terry and Roffo slowly picked themselves up from the cobbles. All they could see of the unfortunate butcher was a pair of smoking boots. It looked like there was going to be a sale today.

"This is insane!" yelled Roffo, above the moans and wails of the fallout victims who lay around them. "We're never going to get everything by lunch-time. Maybe we should split up?"

Terry looked down at the slim young man. "Er, are you sure that's a good idea?"

"Listen, anything that gets me out of this mayhem sooner is a good idea. I'll get the veg, you get the curry powder, okay?"

Terry nodded absently, with half his attention drawn to the wrecked stall. A barbecued lump of meat dropped from the sky and landed on the prostrate Rene. The barbarian hoped it was the tenderloin.

———————

Roffo was covered in bruises. It could, however, have been worse. Although widely known to work at The Bear, it was also generally recognised that the barman's chances of playing for its team in the forthcoming match were about the same as those of a penniless beggar — wearing an embroidered "Manis *Likes* Squirrels" vest — getting a freebie in that proprietor's inn. Consequently, the worst that Roffo had so far encountered had been a couple of attempts to bribe him into poisoning Terry's tea, an odious inquisition by a syndicate of rat exterminators about the form of the team, and a bit of a near miss when Bestial Bob —

The Pilgrim's chief fast bowler – had decided to get in some early practice throwing hard things at opponents' soft parts. Roffo had escaped with his bails intact, but a considerable lump on his head.

At present, Roffo's main concern was how to transport his various purchases (three large bags of potatoes and various salad accompaniments) across the market and back to The Bear ... on *this* of all days. In retrospect, he thought, it might have been a better idea to have gone for the spices himself and left Terry to deal with the heavier provisions. Roffo eyed the pile of veg with distaste. It was clear that his own physical condition – or rather, the lack thereof – militated against a prolonged battle across the square while burdened with an exhausting weight of vegetables. What he needed, he told himself, was a plan.

Roffo looked around to appraise possibilities. What he saw did not encourage him: wall-to-wall people – struggling, shouting, sweating. To his right, a man travelling head-high above the throng cracked a whip at his truculent camel, urging it forward. If anything, the moody creature seemed to be moving in the *opposite* direction as it was caught and driven by the predominant swell of the human tide.

Then, out of the corner of his eye, Roffo noticed the sudden appearance of a gap in the crowd – a gap that was quickly filled by the large, shaggy head of a long-horned yak. As this huge beast made its ponderous way between the stalls, people either got out of its way or got bulldozed. Various bits of cloth and haberdashery hung from the yak's horns – a testament to the fate of stalls that had not left enough room for the passing of such a creature. The yak's fat, bearded rider appeared completely oblivious to the carnage he and his steed were wreaking in the crowded environment. In the wake of this hairy monster, there followed a second, no-less substantial beast, on which two passengers rode: a black-bearded rogue and a stunningly beautiful red-haired woman. The yaks disappeared behind a large grocery and florist stall. A few moments later, the trio of dismounted humans re-appeared by the side of the stall.

A Yakzi? thought Roffo. He grabbed his load and struggled off in the direction of the threesome, hoping to hire a ride back to The Bear. As he approached the stall, however, recognition smote him like a hammer: recognition of the two yak riders *and* of the cowled symbol on the pennant fluttering over the grocery stall. His heart skipped a beat and he turned his back on the scene – so close that he could almost feel the rank breath of the Hull's Angels on the back of his neck. Now, not only was he weighed down with an excessive amount of produce, but he was also in enemy territory! If caught, there was a not-insignificant chance that he would end up being boiled along with the potatoes and served up to Manis with a nice salad garnish. The thought of being the *Special of the Day* in The Pilgrim kicked Roffo's slumbering mind awake. There was no time now for fancy plans or niceties. Direct action was the order of the day. Roffo knew what he must do: he must steal one of the yaks.

As a youth, Roffo had done a bit of joyriding – nothing serious, mind you, just mules and donkeys – and so he knew all about hot-wiring. Roffo patted his pockets, and frowned. Damn! He had no heat source! Not that *that* was much of a problem, really, as he had no wire either. He would just have to kick-start the beast. From the corner of his eye (as he edged around the stall) Roffo watched the smaller of the two bearded riders pluck a flower from a display and proffer it to the girl. He couldn't help following their conversation.

"Are you going *soft*?" snorted the redhead. "*Can I smell the beautiful flower*? All I can smell is that yak … don't you ever wash the bluddy thing? *Either* of you? And as for *you*," she turned to Grunt and prodded him with an iron finger, "what *have* you been feeding yours? You should try riding downwind of it sometime. I don't know why I put up with you lot … and don't you 'my sweet' me, Trespass, or it'll be the worse for you! Now, which way to the spice stalls?"

"Um, this way, Sonia," said a timid Trespass, jerking his thumb over his shoulder.

As the leader of the pack passed in front of Grunt, the large yak rider tapped him on the shoulder and whispered into his ear: "Wash me yak? Why'd I want to do that? I don't even wash meself."

Roffo watched the trio disappear into the market, then made his move. He hauled part of his load onto his right shoulder to hide his visage, and then nonchalantly made his way to the side of the stall. As soon as a customer drew the unsuspecting proprietor away, Roffo nipped around the back, where he came upon one of the yaks. The lack of any horns, however, in addition to a sudden gust of acrid wind, gave the young barman a hefty clue that he was not actually at the right end. Roffo put a hand to his nose, then staggered, semi-conscious, towards what he hoped was the sweeter-smelling front of the animal. Pausing only briefly to clear his lungs, he slipped the noose tethering the beast to the stall and climbed aboard, lugging his shopping with him.

The slim young man nervously scanned the crowd. The stall holder was still engaged in business, while no-one else in view appeared to suspect (or care) that a crime was in progress. Roffo frantically felt about for the starter. Behind the ribcage … here? He gave an experimental kick. Nothing. He gave another, harder kick. The yak stood still, obliviously chewing a cud. Where were the damned thing's kidneys? Maybe he wasn't kicking hard enough? He stood up and, with a peculiar leap, sent his legs out laterally. When he dropped he brought his heels in together forcefully. As his feet met flesh they bounced off as though they had struck rubber. But the creature still ignored him. Clearly, it had yet to notice Roffo's diminutive presence.

The beast swallowed its cud and turned to help itself to some of the grocer's stock. As Roffo noticed this, he nodded to himself. Plan Two! Perhaps if he offered it some food he might gain its trust? He stood up on the yak's back and slipped his hand into one of the boxes of groceries that was precariously balanced on a stand at the back of the stall. He grabbed a large handful of something that felt like soft nuts, and threw these down in front of the yak. The beast's wide mouth greedily vacuumed them up, and it moved one pace forward. Roffo's hand went back for a second grab. This time he took a look at his ill-gotten gains to see what type of nuts they were …

There are times in life when sudden terrible realisation descends upon a person with a massive hot-faced, tingly-stomached horror. It comes to the person who, having just had an immensely satisfying bout of diarrhoea in a public convenience, turns to find that there is, in fact, not a single piece of toilet paper left in the dispenser. It comes to the mischievous pair who, having sniggered at the hairstyles of the gang of punks sitting in front of them, suddenly realise – with the slow-turning of a head – that their *voces* were not quite so *sotto* after all. This feeling now descended upon Roffo with the crushing weight of a battalion of elephants. The world seemed to fade at the edges as tunnel vision put the object in Roffo's hand in clear, sharply focused view. For there, in his hand, he held a small, fresh, exceedingly red fire-chilli. Indeed, at precisely the same moment that The Bear's junior barman recognised the enormity of his error, so did the yak … The sudden and extreme burning sensation in its mouth told the beast's brain that it needed water, and it needed it NOW.*

---

* The heat from a chilli generally comes from the seeds which, when crushed (say, between the teeth), release the fire as an oil. As the heat comes from an oil, drinking water only brings more of it to the surface. The best antidote to such a burning sensation is to consume something containing fat – such as a dairy product of some description. Even the yak knew this. What it really desperately wanted was a yoghurt … but without money? Who would serve him? Sometimes it's a bummer being a yak.

With a huge bellow, the yak took off in the general direction of the river: one ton of maddened destruction, like a bovine god with a whirlwind up its arse. A still-standing Roffo desperately fought to keep his balance as the beast, regardless of all obstacles, took the straightest route towards the river. People, stalls, and other animals flew past – some of the more unfortunate ones at head height.

Whether by fate, luck, or some contrived narrative design, Roffo noticed (through the shrieking carnage before him) that they were actually heading straight for The Bear. At that instant, mental processes began to regain control over a body wracked by visceral terror. Roffo groaned as the image flashed through his mind of the resultant devastation should the yak charge through the main bar. The prospects of promotion suddenly seemed slim. He closed his eyes. He could not bear to watch the imminent dénouement of his quest for garden produce. In particular, he dreaded the thought of watching the lower half of his body going through the main bay window of the pub, while his upper half remained on the outside, spread over the exterior brickwork above it.

Just as the end of The Bear seemed as inevitable as another Cliff Richard Christmas single, the yak took a sharp turn right to pass along the frontage of the Square's inns and shops, heading for the main road towards Kelloon and the river. This sudden change in direction finally caused Roffo to lose his balance, and he was thrown over the small fence surrounding The Bear onto one of its wooden benches. Splinters gathered in his chest as he slid across the table, pitching head-first into one of the small flower beds that nestled against the wall of the inn. Potatoes rained down around him like a hailstorm. And then, with more than a little relief, Roffo passed out.

The barman was brought round a few moments later by Hops, who shook him vigorously by the shoulder.

"… bruised!" said Hops, finishing a sentence that Roffo had only partially registered.

"Bruised?" replied Roffo. "I'm black and blue, boss, black and blue!"

"Not you, you dolt," wailed Hops, "the spuds!" The innkeeper examined a manky-looking potato. "If any of these are bruised I'm going to dock your pay, lad. I can't serve second-rate vegetables to my customers!"

Roffo groaned, closed his eyes, and toppled back into the flower bed.

Terry could have found the area of the market that dealt exclusively with spices and herbs with his eyes shut. Most people could. Indeed, all you needed to do was raise your nose to the air and sniff, and then head in the direction of increased aromatic bouquet.

Having survived a barbecuing at the butcher's, Terry hoped for a quieter encounter with Janus, Hops's preferred spice seller. Janus – a wizened, white-haired man in an ill-fitting green tunic – was presently engaged in conversation with a slight oriental man in a monk's habit. Their discussion revolved around the price of a bag of green, withered herbs. Terry lingered, passing a knowing eye over the baskets of wares. Presently, money changed hands between the spice seller and the monk.

"Terry, my friend," effused Janus, greeting his next customer. "What will it be today? Some Burbur powder for a Chadoori dish? Or perhaps a sprig or two of Green Vermenelle if you're thinking along the fish theme?"

"Er, no thanks. Hops is doing curry for the team, so he wants some hot stuff to, er, fire us up for the match."

"Ah," sighed the still-present monk, "perhaps he want to ensure you in the runs?"

Terry frowned, looking at the monk askance. "Er, yeah. Um, anyway, Hops says that if we can sit down before this time next week he'll go somewhere else for his spices."

"A demanding man is Master Hops!" sighed Janus. "Oh well – if it's hot curry powder he wants, then it's hot curry powder he gets!" He dived under his stall, reappearing a few seconds later holding a small bag in one hand. The hand had acquired a gauntlet for protection.

"This is the hottest stuff this side of the Black Mountains. I can't tell you what's in it, of course. Trade secret thingy. Recipe passed down from father to son for generations and all that." Janus lowered his head in a conspiratorial manner and scanned the crowd with flickering eyes. "However, I can tell you that there are spices in here so intense, and so piquant, that your tastebuds will think they've died and gone to heaven. And as for the colour, ah, fiercest red it is, hinting at the inferno that burns within. Aye, and you know why? For these spices were grown in *Bulabothel's own allotment!*"

The monk spluttered. As the spice seller turned to glare at him, he developed an inscrutable look. "Yes, Terry my friend," continued Janus, turning his attention back to the nodding barbarian. "It's true: Bulabothel's own allotment I say! I picked them up from a fallen angel who just happened to be passing through. And what's more, he gave me the cloven-hoofed one's favourite recipe for a real scorcher of a curry!" Janus tapped the side of his nose. "Very hush-hush this. Got to keep it secret, y'know. After all, we don't want Mr Pointy Horns sending his Hullish legions against us, eh? But seeing as this is for good Master Hops an' all, I'll let you have a copy of the recipe too for, er, a *small* remuneration only."

"Char-latan!" cried the monk, in sudden anger. "Deceiver! Do not listen, barbarian! His tongue wags like serpent disco dancer! Spice seller, tell how powder can be product of recipe handed down through generations *and at same time* come from devil's garden, eh? Cannot be both!"

Janus laughed nervously. "Did I say that? Silly me! Slip of the tongue, take no notice of the mad monk, heh heh. Believe me, Terry, I got it from a genuine 'oops, there I go again, tripping over me own robes' angel. And with the recipe too ... well, just think about it: how many inns can claim their food was prepared to a god's own instructions? Of course, it might not be wise to tell them *which* god, heh heh, but that's up to you."

"Ai-la!" exclaimed the monk in distaste. "Why not also claim got barrel of god's ale too? Could do offer on pair: Bifold Blasphemy Special!" The monk made a disgusted gesture and, still muttering, turned on his heels and stalked off.

"Pay no attention to him," said Janus, jerking his thumb in the direction of the departing monk. "He's a bit *uptight* at the moment, if you know what I mean. Those herbs I sold him ... for constipation. I expect all that seeking wisdom and enlightenment plays havoc with the digestive system." He rubbed his hands expectantly. "Anyway, that's five copper bits for the spices, and another five for the recipe."

"Um, I'll just take the spices please," said Terry apologetically. "If I went back to the inn with a recipe there'd be Hull to pay. Mrs Hops would spend the rest of her life persecuting me for implying her recipes weren't good enough. Um, sorry."

Janus sighed. "Ah, Terry my friend, you drive a hard bargain! Okay. Let's say four bits for the ..."

"Excuse me!" A sultry female voice interrupted the flow of BS. "Excuse me! Could someone help me?"

"Of course, miss. You're obviously looking for some henna and rose water to wash that astonishing red hair of yours for 'that shine to drive men crazy'?" Janus rubbed his hands. He had herbs and spices for every imaginable purpose from flavouring food, to pasting on skin, to snorting through a straw. "Or perhaps some perfume or cosmetic?

I've got a special stock in this here sack, all made from natural ingredients of course!" Janus's eyes wandered. Occasionally, they *bulged*.

The flame-haired lovely, in the way of many a sensitive, paranoid beauty who knows that her looks are everything and appreciates the shallowness of 'skin-deep', homed right in on innocent implication. "You what?" said Sonia, her sultry tones slipping from the heights of Lauren Bacall to the depths of Wendy Richard. "Are you suggesting I need to wash my hair? What's wrong with it? Are you saying it's dull and lifeless?" She grabbed Janus by the lapels of his tunic and, with surprising strength, pulled his face to within an inch of her own.

"Calm yourself, madam," pleaded Janus, attempting to extricate himself from Sonia's iron grip. "I was simply explaining some of the items I have in stock. I should also note that I have a free sample of perfume here for my thousandth customer and, would you believe it, that happens to be you! Now, if you would just release me, *please*, I will get your, um, prize."

As Sonia loosened her grip, Janus dived under his stall and started frantically searching through a large, tatty sack.

"Oh woe," moaned Sonia, dramatically, "what a place this is – full of rogues and brigands. What is a poor girl to do?"

"Er, miss?" ventured Terry, who had been having the sort of barbaric thoughts that would have warmed his parents' hearts. "Is there anything I can do to help?"

"That's so kind of you," said Sonia, pretending to dab away a tear, "but I couldn't possibly impose on you. No-no. At least, well, maybe … maybe you *can* help. Would you really? Oh what a darling!" Sonia fluttered her eyelashes and pressed herself against the barbarian. With acting of such atrocious quality she could have been a major soap opera star. "Oh, I'm just a weak, defenceless woman who wants to visit her poor, ill mother on the other side of the square … but it's *so* crowded and rough out there. Would you help me? I'd be ever so grateful." The coquettish Sonia stroked the biceps of the barbarian, who stood rooted to the spot, gritting his teeth with determination and trying to avert his eyes from the barely covered *embonpoint* which seemed to be swelling to fill all available space. The temptress gave a satisfied smirk – she knew she had him. Then, with a less-than-feminine finesse, she began to drag Terry across the market.

"Got it!" shouted Janus, from under the table. "It's good perfume this. If you like it I can let you have a job lot for … *Damn!*"

A short distance away, two very large, very hairy gents conspired together. One of them was not at all happy.

"Grunt, I want you to get that big bastard!" growled Trespass, pointing. "I want you to sit on his head and suffocate him between your buttocks, and I don't care what Manis says. No-one goes walking off arm-in-arm with *my* woman but me, especially not to *her mother's!*"

"'Er mother's? Oh yeah. Don't she run that brothel?"

"*Guest-house*, Grunt, guest-house!"

"Er, yeah, whatever you say ..."

"By all the boils and buboes on the balls of Bulabothel – where is that blasted barbarian?" alliterated Hops, to no-one in particular, as he stared anxiously out of the bay window. The lunch-time punters had come and gone, and now The Bear's team milled about outside, waiting to head off to the cricket ground. But of Terry there was no sign. The innkeeper dragged himself away from the window and shuffled forlornly over to Heddy, who was stacking glasses behind the bar.

"I should have known they'd get him," moaned the innkeeper. "Aye, I should have kept the lad safe in the inn ... locked in the cellar perhaps? But no, I just had to send him out into the market to get some grub so I could make a few extra coins on the day. Oh, how the gods do punish poor Hops for his greed: no star batsman, and no meat for the team's tea!"

"Poor Hopsie!" Heddy smiled at her employer. "But don't you worry your head about it. Terry will make it. He always does. He's a barbarian: he lives his life like a story in a book, with dramatic escapes, turning up in the nick of time to save the day, and all that sort of stuff." She ruffled Hops's drastically thinning hair and pinched his crest-fallen cheek. "Don't worry. He'll be there."

CHAPTER 3

THE PILGRIM'S PROGRESS

THE EARLY afternoon sun shone through a light-blue cirrus-wisp sky, thirstily ogling the world below. Not content with supping the early morning dew from the cobblestone streets, it now drained puddles, water barrels, and neglected drinks, and slyly slurped the sweat from everything that lived and moved. And there were plenty of victims for the vampiric orb, too, as the town's population converged on the Great Road that led to the west and the venue of The Match.

As the human tide passed by, shopkeepers flipped their signs from 'open' to 'closed', guardsmen hung up their helmets, artisans put down their tools on unfinished jobs, thieves turned away from silver-laden mantlepieces, and (as the throng reached the edge of town) farmers and shepherds abandoned their flocks – all rushing out to add to the swelling entity. But this horde was no ill-disciplined rabble. Indeed, it possessed a pattern that had re-imposed itself year after year from a time well before the patronage of Hops and Manis.

At the very front marched Cross-My-Way's Supporters' Clubs: two bantering factions bedecked in the colours and signs of their favoured inn. The Bear was represented by fellows dressed in brown, many of whom wore the pelts of ursine creatures that had succumbed to that unfortunate condition known as old age. A passing bear might have easily mistaken the occasion as a march of militant OAPs, though a closer inspection of the pictures on the marchers' banners might have caused it to doubt the sanity of its elders' demands. Index-linked berry entitlement? No thanks. These bolshie ancients appeared to want the provision of cowled humans for the purpose of non-consenting sexual gratification. And as for their chants … well, let's just say that whatever it was that the marchers wanted, it *wasn't* for the Pilgrimites to be *victimised by thieves, supplied with 100-percent whole-beef fast food*, or *serenaded by military chaps with small stubby brass instruments*. Let us leave it at that. In contrast, the Pilgrim supporters wore grey robes that were fastened at the waist by chains from which depended (from behind) protective iron plates, on which were written a variety of messages, the gist of which was that ursine creatures were not welcome *within*. The bears depicted on *these* supporters' banners tended to be about as Merry as one could get, when skinned and tied to a roasting spit.

Behind the mangy furs and the tatty grey robes, in the middle of the procession, came the bulk of the townsfolk, loaded down with casks of ale and baskets of food. Children rushed ahead of the adults, forming a milling zone of mischief behind the vanguard of bantering supporters – giggling at suggestive choruses and using stuffed bears' heads and anal plates as targets for volleys of apple cores and rotten fruit. The parents strolled along in the sun, occasionally berating their offspring, but more often than not calling out encouragement and hailing particularly well-aimed shots.

Next, following the main force, came the barrow boys and stall holders, pushing their wares before them, jostling for position and panting with exertion. The age-old ploy was to leave the market late, snatching the custom of lingerers and bemused foreigners, and then pushing and shoving to the front of the merchants' rabble in the hope of securing a prime pitch by the ground … although tactics *did* vary. Some traders set out with the steady pace of long-distance runners, hoping to pass spent adversaries on the final stretch. Others felt compelled by fear to lead the field from the off, energetically guiding their carts and worriedly checking that the nearest runners were not detested opponents selling similar wares. Still others used trickery or malice to take out their bitterest foes, ramming carts or surreptitiously slicing the straps holding goods onto transport, and laughing evilly as mounds of apples cascaded onto the cobbles or elegant fabrics caught the breeze and wafted into the air. Forget Ben Hur – these guys meant business!

And finally, bringing up the rear, came the Miscellaneous: the passing visitors in strange garb who realised that something was up and were bloody well determined to find out what it was; the insane, who didn't like cricket, and only followed in the hope that rain might fall and stop the match so that they could say I Told Ye So; the late-sleeping drunks, who despairingly shambled after the town's landlords; and the protesters, who waved placards and shouted their condemnation of the match (but not *too* loudly, just in case anyone should hear). Indeed, it was for the reason of self-preservation that the protesters lagged at the very rear of the throng, to ensure their unhindered escape from wrathful supporters. And chief among these protesters were the white-robed Clovorites.

"Booo! Booo! No to the match! No to the abuse of balls!"

"Shhhhhhhh you moron! Ohgodohgodohgod I think someone *heard* you!"

"Good! Let them hear my voice – Yea, for did not Great Clovory say that, on this day, His day of rest from The Creation, that all should rest?"

"Er, yes, of course He did, but He probably said it a *bit* more quietly …"

"And did He not also say that, on this day, His Holy Orbs of Creation being Well-And-Truly Wrung Dry, that no balls should be played with? Nor fondled, nor nibbled, nor licked, nor smitten?"

"Someone shut him up …"

"I'm trying …"

"Well try harder!"

"And did He not further say, Yea, I Shall Not Even Play Ye Noughts And Crosses Today, And By 'Eck My Toe Hurts? *Oooooooooomph!*"

"Brother Veritas – was that necessary?"

"Sorry High Brother Frostus."

"Hmm, yes, well! Do ten *ave Clovoris*. And Brother Veritas … *well done!*"

———•◦•◦•———

Terry was growing concerned. He knew the market was big, but this was getting ridiculous: they had been walking for over an hour now and had still not managed to break free. Either they had wandered into a part of the universe where matter (in the form of market stalls) was being constantly created, or they were wandering around in circles. The latter case seemed slightly more likely, but the girl had acted as though she knew where she was going and Terry had been loath to question her navigational skills. After all, it was *her* home for which they were heading.

With the crowds beginning to thin and merchants closing up and stowing their goods, Terry's thoughts turned to his employer. Hops would be wondering where he was and what had happened to his lunch (much of which was currently resting across Terry's broad shoulders). Then something familiar caught the barbarian's eye and *this* time he did decide to say something.

"Um, miss?" he ventured. "I'm sure we walked past that stall earlier."

"Nonsense," replied the girl, curtly, "you must be imagining things. Anyway, it's only a little bit further to mummy's."

"Ah, er, yes, still, it's funny that there should be *two* hunchbacks in the market, *both* wearing black eye patches, *both* with hooks for left hands, and *both* selling custom-made sundials." Terry frowned in puzzlement. "I wouldn't have thought there'd be *that* much demand."

Sonia shrugged. "They're probably twins." She was glad Terry had at last shown signs of noticing something was amiss. She was running out of different routes to take him around the market and her feet were beginning to ache. *Surely mum must have got the drugs by now*, she thought. "Anyway, it's just down here." She pointed at a narrow, dark, and forbiding alley.

Terry frowned at this sight. It was the sort of alley that even muggers might fear to tread. No wonder the girl had wanted an escort! Terry stiffened his back.

Sonia watched the barbarian from the corner of an eye. "Yeah," she said, "most men gird their loins for action before walking down *this* alley. Come on then." She led the way to a set of iron gates that were hidden in shadows three-quarters of the way down. She twice tugged on a dangling bell rope, paused, and then tugged thrice more. While awaiting a reply, Terry attempted to decipher the small, grimy wooden sign nailed to one of the gateposts. He could make out the first letter, a 'W', but then there was a smudge, which was followed by the letters 'rehouse'.

Terry's mind churned through the alternatives, his lips mouthing possible solutions. Suddenly, his face lit up and he beamed like a man who had just worked out his first ever *Times* crossword clue. Almost immediately his expression turned downcast. He turned to the red-haired girl with a look of sympathy on his broad face. "I'm sorry miss, I didn't realise – poor woman! Your mother, she lives in a *warehouse*?"

"Er, yeah, that's right. Just above it actually. She looks after it for the ... mayor? He doesn't keep much in here now, just ... *some beds*? Well, quite a lot of beds actually. They're from before the time he was mayor, you know, when he ..."

"Sold beds?"

"Yeah, that's right." And at that, the gate creaked ajar as though it had a mind of its own. With a touch of relief Sonia pushed it fully open and beckoned the barbarian inside. "Come on in," she purred. "You must stop for a *coffee*?"

"Er, I'd love to, really, but I've got to get back." Terry suddenly felt as uneasy as a fly that had just received an invite to a *Bring a Bluebottle* party at Number 1, The Web, Top Left Hand Corner, The Bay Window. "I should have been back at least an hour ago. I've got to get these sausages back to Hops, you see, and ..."

Sonia giggled. "Don't worry, your sausage will be in good hands here!" The redhead coughed, but managed to maintain her composure. "Surely you can spare a few more minutes? Mummy would be *so* disappointed if you didn't stop by and say hello. She doesn't get many visitors, you see, the poor dear, and you wouldn't want to disappoint an old lady, would you?" She smiled again – a dangerous smile; a smile that had no right to be let out by itself; a smile that belonged in secure accommodation under twenty-four-hour guard. It was the sort of smile that led to twenty year wars or, at the very least, to paternity suits.

Terry began to sweat. His mouth attempted to form the word "no". He took a deep breath. What would a real barbarian do? Terry's cheeks began to flush at the thought. He would just turn and go. That's it. That's what he would do. He would just ... *follow meekly after the beckoning woman.* Before he could fully comprehend his actions he was through the gate, into the building, and standing in a large foyer at the foot of a spiral staircase. An attractive, semi-clad girl was sitting on the lowest step.

"Um," said Terry, "I thought you said your mum didn't get many visitors?"

"Oh – her! Take no notice. She's just a scrubber ... er, *cleaner.*" Sonia led the barbarian past the girl and up the stairs.

At the top of the stairs they came to a large wooden door. Here, as at the gate, Sonia gave a deliberate response: she rapped twice, waited a moment, then knocked three more times. A slit appeared in the door, revealing a pair of eyes. From somewhere beneath these a grunt emanated. The door opened. Terry stepped through – behind the redhead – and found himself in a large, drab reception room. A wizened, grey-haired old woman stepped from behind the door; Sonia kissed her affectionately on the cheek.

"Terry, this is my mum. She's called Sonia too. Mummy, this is Terry." The younger Sonia grinned at the barbarian, slyly. "Terry was kind enough to escort me through the market to protect me from all the hooligans who have come to town to watch the match. He should be opening the batting for The Bear, you know."

"Arrrr, so, he's the one," said the crone, "and such a fine specimen too!" She gripped Terry's proffered hand and salaciously ran one wrinkled finger up and down his palm. The barbarian felt an urge to wipe his hand on his bearskin, but instead he gritted his teeth and endured the ordeal. At last, the old one released Terry's hand – reluctantly – and continued: "I'll have to prepare an extra strong batch of, err, *coffee*, to keep you quiet, my pretty lad. Take him up to the *special* room, young lady, and I'll come up presently. Then we'll all have a nice little nap – I mean *chat* – before your friend goes." Cackling in a manner that would have gained her instant admission into any coven in the land, the woman – popularly known as Grey Sonia – disappeared behind a curtain.

Terry took this opportunity to look around the room. A number of interesting paintings gave colour to the mottled walls. One in particular caught his eye. In this, two people appeared to be engaged in a strange wrestling match. Somewhere along the way, both contestants' clothes had fallen off.

"Isn't that the Nudian left-legged back-breaker?" enquired Terry. "I did a bit of wrestling when I was younger. Um, I mastered *that* move when I was seven."

"Seven!" gasped Sonia, turning to look at the barbarian in astonishment. "Seven? I, er, I couldn't tell from personal experience." Her wicked grin returned. "But maybe you'd like to show me later? Anyway, Mummy's special room is down here. Come on." She led the way along a corridor. Doors to other rooms led off from this. Each door had a heart painted on it. A name was inscribed within each heart.

"Tricksie?" queried Terry, who was not a complete fool. "Don't you spell that with an X?"

At the end of the corridor they came to a thick iron door. Sonia opened this and gestured Terry inside. Only a little light filtered into the room through one heavily barred window, but it was sufficient for Terry to make out the large number of metal rings and chains that were bolted into the walls, the ceiling and the floor. In between these strange fittings was an interesting selection of metal cages and boxes. An assortment of multi-studded leather garments was strewn around the floor.

"Mummy won't be long. It'll only take her a minute or two to knock up the drinks." Sonia turned to face Terry, suddenly stern. She pointed at a large metal chair and barked: "*Take A Seat!*"

Terry shucked the sack of sausages from his shoulder and did as ordered. The chair in which he sat seemed to be only half-built, with various strands missing from the intertwining slats of metal that formed the seat and backrest. His contemplation of this peculiar piece of furniture was shortly interrupted by the door swinging open. The old woman entered, carrying a tray holding three steaming cups.

"That was fast," noted Sonia. "Are you sure you mixed it properly?"

"Of course, me dear. I had the pot on the boil, ready for your return. Now, drink it while it's hot, young man. It works better that way."

Terry hesitated. "Um, I don't know if I should be drinking coffee before the game. Occum once told me there's something in it that can send you a bit, well, *manic*. I wouldn't want to fail a drugs test or anything."

"I assure you, laddie, there's nothing in *this* that'll make you hyperactive, heh heh. Quite the opposite in fact. Here you go then, take a cup."

As the tray was extended towards the barbarian, the two women looked on expectantly. Terry observed the cups, and noted that the one under his nose held more than the others. Being a polite guest, and not wanting to appear greedy, he selected one of the further cups instead. *After all*, he thought, *better safe than sorry when it comes to stimulants.*

"Not that one!" screeched Sonia. "That's, er, *mummy's* cup. It has something in it ... a *woman's* thing. Take this one!" She grabbed the mug from Terry's hand and exchanged it for the one he had originally been offered.

"Come on then," cackled Grey Sonia, "drink up! After all, you don't want to be late for the game."

Terry took a sip from his coffee. "It's a bit sweeter than I'm used to," he commented.

"I use special beans grown only in one particular spot of the White Mountains," explained the crone. "You finish your drink off now, Mr Testosterone, and I'll go and get some biscuits. Back in two shakes of a lamb's tail!" Sonia senior left the room.

Terry drained his cup, while wondering how Sonia's mother had known his surname given that neither he nor the girl had told her. He gave a mental shrug and turned his attention back to the room's interesting furniture.

Sonia sauntered over until she stood directly before her guest. She bent down until her face was level with his and her hot breath fell upon his cheeks. A slight sound, like a cross between a growl and a purr, escaped from between her lips.

"You've been a bad boy, you know," she said, in an impish-yet-predatory way, " ...a *very* bad boy."

"Er?"

"Yeah, a *very* bad boy. And you know what happens to bad boys, don't you?"

Terry gulped. Barbarian youths had a hard upbringing to prepare them for a less-than hospitable world … one that was *especially* inhospitable towards barbarians.

"Er, they're forced to climb vulture-inhabited Mount Gringlerod wearing a bearskin infested with fleas while carrying twenty stone of festering mammoth carcass, and they're not allowed down until they've slain fifteen razor-clawed scavengers with their bare hands and made a war-kilt out of their feathers?"

The girl was momentarily taken aback, but quickly recovered. "Er, no, *this*!" With a deft movement forward, she flicked two iron braces from the arms of the chair over the barbarian's wrists. She stood back and smiled. A kick from each foot performed a similar operation on his ankles.

Terry felt an instant of relief as the thought *Is that all?* percolated through his mind. But after relief came puzzlement.

"Er, what's going on, Madam? I haven't been, er, *bad*. I think you ought to release me."

"Oh no!" laughed Sonia. "Actually, it's mummy who's the Madam, and this is the room where bad boys come to be punished. And you're a very bad boy, aren't you, because you've not done something you should have."

"Yes I have! Um, well, maybe not … um, what then?"

And, with a smirk of ultimate triumph, Sonia cackled: "You've not joined your team for the match."

"Oh, that!" A thought occurred to the barbarian. "Er … is this a trap?" He groaned to himself. "Not again! This happens every year, you know. You're in with The Pilgrim aren't you?" Terry sighed, then groaned, then sighed again for good measure. "Last year it was the laxative beer, but Roffo drank it instead of me and spent the entire game fielding behind that tree that grows just inside the boundary. And the year before I was drenched in camel urine of the female-on-heat variety. That's what Roffo said afterwards. He could tell, you know, because of the way every male camel I walked past got *excited* and *went* for me. One good thump tended to see them off though. A cousin of mine taught me how to do that. He has his own kingdom now, you know, but I don't think he's happy."

"I'm not particularly interested in your family," interrupted Sonia. "And this time you have a more knotty problem to sort out if you want to get to the game. First, you have to get loose from this chair, and second you have to find an antidote to the sleeping draught you've just drunk."

"Sleeping draught – what sleeping draught? In the coffee? The sweet taste?" Terry shook his head in wonderment at the things people got up to. "Oh. I'm sorry. They never seem to work on me. From an early age we barbarians are given small draughts of poisons with our dinner to build up an immunity to them." He looked at Sonia, sheepishly, and shrugged his broad shoulders. "So you see, it probably won't *worzzzzzz* ..."

"But then again," said Sonia, "it just might. Especially if it's only a sleeping drug that's not worth building up an immunity to."

The door of the room swung open again and the old Madam peered inside.

"Has it worked?"

"Yeah, he's out. Those special beans will knock out an elephant for a week."

"Good, good!" cackled the crone. But then she frowned. "Oh, and there's some people here to see you. Some of those nasty, hairy yak riders you hang around with. I don't know why you can't get a nice boyfriend – someone like nice Mr Testosterone here."

"I'm sure drugging him will really endear me to him, eh? Anyway, if you want to make your living on the wrong side of the tracks you've got to take what you can get. Are they down in the lobby?"

"No, we're here," said a gruff voice. Trespass entered the room. "Take what you can get, is that it? I suppose you'd prefer Sleeping Beauty there. The way you walked around the market with him – arm-in-arm – you'd've thought so."

"Can I sit on 'im now?" enquired Grunt, hopefully.

"Listen you two – go and report to Manis immediately. Tell him our mission is successful. He'll probably want to give you a reward or something." Red Sonia's impish grin returned. "Meanwhile, I'll stay here and make sure nobody comes to rescue the barbarian."

Trespass looked from his girlfriend to the sleeping barbarian, and then back again. His voice softened. "You will behave, won't you, my sw—"

"Of course," she said, abruptly. "Now go!"

With a backward look, and doubt in his eyes, Trespass turned and left the room.

———◆•◆•◆———

The ground was idyllically set. Mountains clustered along the length of the Valley of Latitude like an anorak* of train-spotters around a rail

* The collective noun.

timetable. These white-topped bastions looked down onto a valley floor infested with trees so leafy they could have kept Adam and Eve in clothing until the tolling of The Last Orders (an event predicted to follow The Last Trump and The Last Belch, when the waters of life would flow no more). In one particular area of the valley, however, an ancient flood plain spread between two parts of sundered forest, forming a perfect oval of flat grassland that had been adopted as the main venue for the town's sporting occasions. To the north, this plain was bounded by the Great Road, and to the south by the Rockbelow. The playing area of the ground roughly followed the lines of the flood plain, the northern limit being the furthest edge of the Road, and the southern limit being the furthest bank of the River, while the eastern and western boundaries were marked by two stretches of rope that linked Road and River. An anomaly existed just within the southern boundary of the ground in the form of an ancient oak tree known as The Twelfth Man. In the very centre of the playing arena was a carefully tended strip – approximately 22 yards long and an unmemorable length wide – that formed the cricket pitch itself. This pitch was presently guarded by half a dozen extremely nervous young men in the green uniform of the Town Guard.

The horde from town rampaged along the Road and then began to disperse at the eastern edge of The Oval. Spectators lined the furthest edges of the Road and River, often amongst the trees or perched in the strongest branches, while the merchants set up their trades beyond the two rope boundaries, the leaders nearer town, the also-rans – often pushing crippled, war-scarred barrows – to the furthest western extremities. As all available space was gradually filled, pre-match anticipation began to rise.

At the entrance to The Bear's tented pavilion, on the town-side of the ground, a rotund man with flushed cheeks sat on an upturned barrel and cast a worried eye over the crowds. Behind him, desperate mutterings emanated from the inn's gathered team. At present this numbered just nine for, in addition to the absent barbarian, Rude Lubblers – carpenter par excellence and quite the most foul-mouthed villain in town – was also missing.

Hops started chewing his fingernails. Normally this was one of his joys, as Mrs Hops didn't allow it anywhere within her sight or hearing (which were surprisingly acute), but at present his chewing was of the nature of a desperate man.

"What are we gonna do? What are we gonna do?"

"We're doomed, I tell you, doomed!"

"Where *is* he? Just when we need him …"

"Oh, the humiliation … my family will disown me for this …"

"Um, boss … *boss*?"

Hops felt a hand gently shaking his shoulder. The innkeeper looked around to see the flushed countenance of the diminutive Roffo. He gave a sigh. "Not now, lad, I've got things on my mind."

"Um, yes, well it's about these things really." Roffo paused and scratched at his unruly mop of hair, searching for appropriate words. "Now, I know what you're going to say but … but … well, you're two men short and …"

Hops shook his head. "After last year? Roffo, lad, you spent the entire game hiding behind The Twelfth Man *having* runs when you should have been *saving* them. I swear that damned tree has grown a dozen feet since then."

"But boss, that wasn't my fault! It was something in the ale. It was! And anyway, who else can you get now?" Roffo looked over the top of the innkeeper's shining pate – and what he saw caused his lips to twitch into a smile that hinted at sudden hope. "By the way," he said, "here come the umpires!"

Hops turned around so quickly the momentum nearly carried him off the barrel. It was too soon! He wasn't ready! With a degree of dread he watched the ominous approach of officialdom from the direction of the pitch. This came in the guise of two white-clad individuals who had earnest intent in their eyes, an aura of power about them, and – in the case of one of the pair – a rather large bandage about the head.

Umpires! Now there is a problem the world over and no mistaking – a problem that has afflicted humanity since the beginning of time and will continue do so until The Final Whistle (that signal for cataclysmic violence, destruction and pitch invasions, predicted in the mythology of The Officious Sect of Referees to take place at the end of the 90th Millennium *or* several millennia into Extra Time provided someone bungs The Divine One a few quid). Indeed, the people of Cross-My-Way had tried various and numerous refereeing alternatives over the years in their search for the perfect solution.

They had, naturally enough, started by employing qualified members of The Sect of Referees. Although results were not entirely satisfactory – largely because the referees were, to be blunt, completely crap – this experiment had endured for some years. The end of the experiment had come rather suddenly after an enterprising supporter of an aggrieved losing team had temporarily *borrowed* the certificate of one of the refs. Until this time, no-one had truly appreciated what was taught at the Rakor Shana University of Referees, but the details noted on the certificate had proved rather informative. While the population were willing to forgive the fact that the referee had barely scraped a pass in the module 'Ye Rules of Cricket', they were less forgiving about the distinctions he had gained in the modules 'Knowinge when to take ye Bribe', and 'Ye Seventy Wayes of unfairly penalising teames with Fistes as Tight as a Constipated Baboon's Bottom'. The referees had been run out of town and never invited back.

Next, the good people of Way had tried using court judges on the not-unreasonable assumption that such venerable old codgers would be beyond temptation. Unfortunately, cricket being what it is, and judges being what they are, the experiment had failed badly. The umpires had had the tendency to fall asleep between each delivery, only to be roused by the cry of "Objection, M'Lud!" The experiment had come to an end after the abandonment of a game in which one batsman had been sentenced to banishment and forfeiture of all chattels. It had taken five hours and plenty of lubrication with linseed oil to extract the enraged batsman's willow from the judge's estimable seat.

Voting for umpiring candidates had also come a cropper. Invariably, each candidate was found by one inn or the other to have some dubious link to the opposition that might affect their impartiality – such as once having been seen patting the innkeeper's chief barman's grandmother's dog in an affectionate sort of way. The initial tenet of the Umpiring Selection Committee had thus rapidly contracted from 'All candidates are corrupt unless proven otherwise' to the more pithy (and accurate) 'All candidates are corrupt'. Pretty soon, however, even the Selection Committee had been accused of dubious practices and disbanded.

A flirtation with town-wide democracy had also been only brief. The most popular inn always seemed to get favourable individuals elected as umpires and – quite coincidentally of course, in a 'Did we win again? My word, aren't we lucky' kind of way – retained Ye Ashes for the duration of the experiment.

Finally, a rather unique solution was settled upon. No-one was entirely happy, of course, but there was a final acceptance that it was this or nothing, and nothing was not an option. The inns were agreed. The only people who could possibly be relied upon to be utterly impartial and unbiased were *thieves*. Of course, a more disreputable band of villains was hard to find, but the thieves had a peculiar brand of honour, plus an utter disregard for whoever (wittingly or otherwise) paid their wages. Indeed, they had no need of remuneration *per se* because what they didn't have – but wanted – they soon acquired. Bribe them, and they would take your money with a look of distaste, and then later go burgle your house.

The two umpires crossed the boundary rope at a point midway between the two pavilions – these being a mere forty yards apart, with The Pilgrim's black and white striped tent being the nearer to the Rockbelow. Here, the umpires stopped and beckoned over the team managers.

"It's time to go, boss," said Roffo, wetting his dry lips. "I think they're ready for the team lists now ..."

Hops groaned. He withdrew a creased parchment from within the folds of his tunic and looked at it. Two down! Without the barbarian their chances were slim enough but ... No. They simply couldn't do without him. There was nothing for it. They would have to start the match with ten men and hope that Terry arrived later. Hops reached for the quill and inkpot that were resting on the ground by his feet and, with a shaky hand, he drew the quill. The innkeeper scratched out the name of Lubblers and, with an air of resignation – and quite aware of the heavy breathing at his shoulder – he inked in the name 'Roffo'. Behind him, Hops heard a squeak of joy.

With team captain Occum in tow, Hops wearily shuffled up to the umpires, studiously ignoring the converging deputation from the pavilion to his left.

"Ready for the off, eh?" sneered Manis, as they came together. "No barbarian, I see? Still, it wouldn't make much difference – just delay the inevitable." He laughed and then gestured at the near-cloudless sky. "And not even the weather can save you today!"

"That's enough of that, Master Manis," declared Occum, in the stead of the dumbstruck, weakly grinning Hops. "*Antagonism* is a nasty word – but I know some too. And some pretty nasty phrases." He looked at the opposition innkeeper in a meaningful way. "Like, *whoops*, and *sorry about your ear mister*, and *did you really want this close a shave, sir?*"

"You know, Occum, one day this town will get another decent barber and then your time will be up."

"That's as may be, Master Manis, but until then you'll show some respect in my hearing or you'll just have to find some other amateur butcher to slash your hair and lacerate your skin. Or you could just go *au naturelle* like those darned Angels you keep about you!"

Manis shuddered at the thought.

The two parties reached the umpires.

The taller of the white-coated fellows – who had a bandage about his head and a number of parallel scratch marks across his nose (which just *might* have been made by a cat) – opened his arms in welcome. At this sudden gesture, Hops instinctively stepped back, while Manis, Occum, and Sly Herrold (The Pilgrim's captain) protectively reached for their hidden wallets. The bandaged umpire gave a knowing *gotcha* grin.

"No need to be nervous, gentlemen!" said the umpire. "I only want your team lists … *for now.*"

Two pieces of parchment were hesitantly proffered to the umpire and two hands were rapidly jerked back out of range. As an afterthought Manis checked the rings on his fingers …

"Ah, whoops," said the umpire, with an unrepentant smirk, "your fine gold ring appears to have fallen off into my hand. Here you go. Have it back."

The Pilgrim's innkeeper reached out to reclaim his missing property. His fingers snaked to within a couple of inches of the umpire's outstretched hand … and then paused and withdrew. Manis looked wistfully at the ring, and then looked down at the three others on the fingers of his questing hand. He made a slight whimpering sound of indecision. Then he gasped: "That's okay, I don't want it any more. You can keep it."

"Very kind of you, Master Manis. Mind you, it won't sway my decisions on the pitch in any way."

"Of course not," blustered Manis, "your integrity is legendary! But let us not delay. Time for the toss, I think, before I lose any more jewellery. Er, I mean …"

"I know what you mean, sir!" The bandaged umpire turned to his companion. As he did so he swatted at one of the smaller man's hands which had been gliding towards his pockets. The second umpire shrugged and turned to address the delegations.

"Right then, the toss, yes indeedy!" He delved a hand into one of his own pockets – and then paused. A look of consternation invaded his face. His hand began to rummage about more vigorously. At last he gave in. With a frosty look askance at the bandaged official – who had suddenly found something of intense interest on the far horizon – he said, "Ah, I seem to have mislaid it. I don't suppose anyone has a coin we can use?"

Hops started to reach for his purse, and then stopped. "Ah, yes, Occum: a coin if you please?"

"Do I look stupid?"

"Never mind," said Manis. "Sly – supply the man."

With a grumble, Sly fished out a gold piece and flicked it to the short umpire.

"Right then right then. The Pilgrim to call. In the air please …" He tossed up the coin.

"Heads!" cried Manis.

The coin went up, up, up, reaching its apex, and then began to descend. Down it came, glinting in the sunlight, down, down …

"Hey!" cried Manis. "Where's it gone?"

"Ahem!" went the umpire. "Well I never! Vanished in thin air! An inauspicious omen if ever I saw one!"

"Hmm, yes," snarled Sly, "inauspicious for a certain bloke in a white coat if this next one goes missing!" He found another coin – this time of much smaller denomination – and chucked it to the umpire.

The short man frowned at the coin. "Oh well. Here goes. Heads to The Pilgrim."

This time the coin managed to complete its journey to the ground, with four pairs of eyes concentrating on it with an intensity rarely seen in men outside of a strip joint. The coin pitched into the turf, rolled briefly on its rim in a decreasing circle, and flopped onto its back.

"Heads it is!"

"We'll field," cried Sly. A foot leapt out and made contact with his shin. "Ow! I mean, bat!"

Manis turned to smile at Hops and Occum – but there was no warmth in that smile. "See how you like fielding with ten men!" he laughed. Then, clapping Herrold on the shoulder, the pair turned to head back to their pavilion. After a brief moment, and more slowly, so did their opponents.

———◆•◆•◆———

Sitting on an exposed wooden platform, thirty feet up and just behind the Rockbelow-marked boundary, Blewers and Jombers surveyed the ground and fiddled with their sound amplification equipment. This comprised a pair of bucket-shaped bowls attached to a couple of long metal wires. These wires – imbued with superb sound-conducting properties – led down from the platform and around the entire ground. Every five yards or so wooden poles supported the wire, and these also held bucket-shaped instruments from which the original sound was reproduced and transmitted to the eagerly awaiting crowd. Knots of supporters clustered around the speakers to get the best of the commentary, particularly at those parts of the boundary where the view of the match proceedings was less than optimal.

"My word, what a splendid day for it, Blewers!" began Jombers, in a voice full of enthusiasm and *joie de vivre*. "Oh, and I see that the teams are leaving their pavilions and making their way onto the field. And, oh ho, my word, look at umpire Mitchkin – sporting a rather large bandage around his head. Just like a turban, poor chap. What do you think, Blewers?"

"Fancy dress party I should think. No ... no. Definitely a bandage, poor fellow. Perhaps he's fallen out of somewhere he oughtn't to have been? Oh, I say, look at this!" A rustling sound transmitted to the assembled thousands. "Jombers, what do you think of that!"

"Splendid, absolutely splendid! What a remarkable cake! Our first of the day and the match hasn't even started."

"Yes, it's quite superb. A sort of chocolatey icing. Wonderful. I look forward to tucking into it as soon as we get a break – not now Jombers, hands off for now! It's from a Mrs T. Waddling. Our heartiest thanks Mrs Waddling."

"By Jove yes! I think we can guarantee it a good home here ..."

On the ground, the members of The Bear's team took up their positions as directed by their gesticulating captain – ambling about dejectedly like a troop of pathetic puppets with half of their strings cut. Occum stood at square leg and glowered. "First one to drop a catch gets a free haircut first thing Saturday after I've been on the piss the night before! Understand?"

A number of half-hearted voices were raised in response.

At the wicket, Herrold leant on his bat and waited for the fielding team to sort itself out. The Berserker stood beside him, gnawing on his bat in a restless way. Herrold slapped the bat away. "Idiot! How many times do I have to tell you ... the less bat you have, the harder it is to hit the ball!"

"But I'm hungry!" The Berserker looked sullen. "Anyway, I could beat dis lot with a toothpick."

"It seems you're going to get your chance – they're ready at last. Let's go!" Herrold turned and stalked up to the receiving end. He had only gone a couple of steps when he noticed a second shadow keeping pace with his own. He turned and pointed. "The other end, you buffoon!"

The first over was bowled by Horus the farrier – a man with forearms like a pair of cantaloupes (the result of years of wrestling yaks into their new shoes), and a beard so thick it protected him from the kick of reluctant horses. He lumbered up to the stumps, like a fat bear running from a hunter, and hurled the bright red ball down towards the waiting batsman. It whooshed past Herrold's nose a foot outside off-stump and thudded into the gloves of Ancient Willy – the wicket keeper. Willy shrieked at the impact and tossed the ball to the man at first slip as though it was a hot chestnut. The next two deliveries followed the same pattern ... lumber lumber lumber, whoosh, *aieeeee*!

The fourth ball passed Herrold just a little bit wider and sailed beyond the outstretched arm of Willy – who had kept wicket honourably for twenty years but now found it a bit difficult, owing to his arthritic joints – and rocketed to the river, skimming across the surface of the Rockbelow and crossing the far bank boundary. The umpire signalled "four byes", and a part of the crowd groaned. Horus glared at the wicket keeper.

"I don't know what you're looking at, young man!" declared Willy truculently. "Can't you see where I'm a standing? Eh? *Eh?* Need glasses I think! Look! Here I am!"

"Silly old codger! That was a good ball that! See if you can catch this next one, old fool!"

"Old fool indeed!"

The next ball sailed past Willy only a foot away and went down to the boundary. The wicket keeper smirked at the bowler. "Sorry – guess I'm a just too *old* to fetch that 'un, heh heh heh! Too *slow*, yes. Just a bit of a *codger*. Pity I wasn't a *great wicket keeper*, eh, *eh?* Then I might just stop a few. But no, I'm a just an *old fool* ..."

Standing at mid-on, Occum slapped a hand to his forehead, and groaned.

The opening partnership piled up runs, scoring as quickly and as frequently as a field of randy rabbits downwind from a pheromone factory. The Berserker blazed away, smiting the ball to all parts of the boundary, while Herrold was content to nudge the ball away for quick singles or cheekily run twos. And the extras mounted.

"Whoops, there it goes again. *Elderly pillock*, eh? *Eh?*"

"I'll kill him, I'll kill him ..."

"You're doing that already, my laddo, with your shite bowling. A man could seize up waiting for you to get one on target, eh!"

"That does it!"

They eventually wrestled Horus to the ground. Occum stooped to talk to the man, who was now foaming at the mouth. "Listen," he whispered, urgently. "Just humour him ... remember what I always says – truth is as helpful in getting a quick shag as a face full of pox. *Flatter* him!"

"But I don't want to shag him ..."

"Shhhh you moron! I don't mean it literally!"

"Oh, ah, I see." Horus stopped struggling and Occum gestured for Jepho and Grimwade to let him up. The farrier looked towards the smirking wicket keeper and, somehow, he forced a smile.

The wicket keeper somehow conspired to miss the next ball too, though an appropriately placed fielder stopped it from entering the river. For five seconds Horus fumed and fought with himself. And then he did it. "You ... you ... you ... ah ... er ... you ... unlucky ... *thing*. Yes! *Unlucky*. Bad luck there Willy! Er. No-one else would have even touched that!" As Horus headed back to his mark, past his captain, he noticed Occum's upraised thumb.

Two balls later, Herrold edged the ball and the ancient one made an impressive catch falling to his right, aided by gravity and a still-competent pair of hands ...

———•••••———

"My word, Blewers, The Bear appear to be fighting back. Good show! What do you think?"

"Splendid! The texture, the taste, marvellous ..."

"Er, no, old chap, I meant the match not the cake ..."

"Oh – yes. Well, one would expect that. Horus has a good bowling average ... where is that parchment? Yes, here we go. He takes a wicket on average every *raisin*. Ah, no, I see, just a crumb. Mmmm ... very nice indeed ... and I think we should also thank Miss Drumble for a rather spiffing fruit cake."

"Yes, it's jolly nice too ... oh, and there's some commotion on the pitch – it's a new over by-the-way – and I do rather think that young Roffo has just put down a catch!"

———•••••———

"Roffo, you dolt!" cried Nev Tweeky, bar fly and, at present, the operating bowler.

"He should never have been picked," moaned Jepho, a barman

51

colleague of the offender.

"I couldn't help it … I didn't see it … it was those bloody pigeons … you saw them. I swear they flew right at me!"

"Excuses excuses! We would of dun better with a scarecrow!"

"Okay lads," cried Occum, "back to it." He looked over at Mr Butterfingers, smiled grimly, and made a cutting motion with his fingers. "Morning-after haircut to Roffo. And I'll even do it for free."

———————

The pigeons settled back to the ground ten yards from the downcast barman, clustering in a cackling conspiracy.

"Heh heh heh!" laughed Fat Sixtoes, leader of the last action. "Did you see that? Coooo! Coooo! What a classic!"

"Stupid humans … they're no match for us!"

"Pigeon Power! Heh heh heh …"

"Yes, not bad," declared a pigeon with one toe on each foot and repulsively matted feathers, who went by the name of Filthy Twotoes. "A good one for starters, lads, I'll give you that, but next time let's *bomb* him too!"

"Coooo – yes, good one, yes!"

"Bagsie I take point …"

"No, me me me, coooo!"

"My turn, my turn …"

"Hold up lads, hold," cooed Filthy, seeing things getting away from him. "I thinks the one with the biggest bombs should go first …"

"And that," declared Fats, sourly, "I suppose is you!"

Filthy ruffled out his feathers in pride, causing various bits of unspeakable detritus to cascade to the ground. He wriggled his tail feathers in an ominous, look-out-here-it-comes manner. "Well," he said, "do you know anyone else who can do *this* …"

The pigeon exploded.

Rank feathers fluttered slowly to the ground.

"Bloody Hull!"

"What happened?"

"Spontaneous Pigeon Combustion?"

"No, no," cackled Fats, nodding his head towards a point in the distance, "there he is … over there!"

"Cor – was that the ball? I didn't see it, did you see it?"

"It's that Berserker bloke … hits it faster and harder than anyone I've ever seen bar the barbarian."

"Crumbs, that could of been me … whoops, just guanoed meself!"

"Cooo, is he all right? Let's go and look …"

"No! Wait! Who's that coming onto the ground to see him?"

"No …"

"It can't be …"

"*Poor Filthy* …"

"I can't watch …"

The pigeons groaned together in a desolate chorus: "*PUNS!*"

"I say, Blewers, is that a spectator on the pitch? Does he think it's all over?"

"Hmmm," mused the addressed commentator, "I'd say it was that, er, *interesting* fellow Mr Puns. It looks as though he's chasing something. Ah, I see, it appears to be the pigeon stunned by that last shot … he's made quite a remarkable recovery!"

"Not surprised, Blewers old chap, I think you would too if you had *him* after you!"

"Good point … anyway, back to the action. Which cake next, old chum?"

The Bear's team made slow progress in whittling away the batting order, but The Berserker's presence was steadily taking the game away from it. The ball thundered around the ground as he smote it with relish. *And dis one*, he thought, *dis one is dat drunk I roughed up last night … kapow! And next is dat man who sold me dat horrible pie … blam! And now, now, er, it's the pieman again … wham!*

The Berserker was a simple man who thought simple things, but he did so with such passion. To him, life was a never-ending comic book story in which he blatted various things. He even ate violently. Roast chickens were known to suddenly come to life and start inching off the spit rather than be ravaged by him. But whatever one said about the man (quietly, of course, and well out of earshot), it could not be denied that he was an athlete-and-a-half. He brought up The Pilgrim's hundred with a huge six, and the hundred and fifty in the same way. His century came from a relatively tame single. But his innings could not last …

Young Festers, who was now at the opposite end to The Berserker, had watched the star batsman with some concern over the last fifteen minutes. Festers had somehow managed to hog the strike and, with nothing else to be legitimately violent against, The Berserker had resumed gnawing at his bat. Indeed, that piece of willow was now beginning to look distinctly frayed at the edges. At the end of the over Festers went to talk to his partner.

"Um, Mr Berserker, sir, don't you think you should, um, wait until tea?"

"Ugh? Wotsat? Wot you mean?"

"Your bat. It's, um, looking a bit chewed ..."

"You got a problem with dat? It's as good as yours ..."

Festers backed off and raised a hand. "No no ... I didn't mean it's not as good as mine, I just, well ... don't you think you should save it for your actual, sort of, batting?"

The Berserker scowled menacingly. "Are you trying to tell me how to bat? Rrrrrr!"

Festers retreated to the non-striking end with alacrity and hid behind the umpire.

The Berserker scowled up the pitch for a moment longer, took a challenging bite out of the shoulder of his bat, and returned to his crease.

He shouldn't have done that.

The next delivery from Tweeky was ripe to be hit, and The Berserker duly hit it. But he knew as soon as he struck that something was wrong. For a start, one object flew at him but two flew away. He looked down at his hands. He was holding a handle, but the rest of the blade was nowhere to be seen.

"Catch!" cried half a dozen players.

Fat Grevis stood looking at the ferocious missile that was heading straight for him. He tentatively put out his hands. *That's a funny shaped ball*, he thought, in the split-second before the wooden javelin passed narrowly over his head. Unfortunately for the smith, his hands were already in an upward motion: there was a sound something like a buzzsaw in action. Grevis pulled down his hands and stared. *It's funny*, he thought, in the brief moment before he collapsed onto his back, *I never knew fingernails could catch fire.*

As Grevis landed with a *thud* he heard a huge roar go up from the crowd, and then the sound of drumming on the ground – something like a herd of wildebeest at a tap-dancing class. Looking into the sky Grevis noticed his team mates charge past him to either side; a couple even leapt over him. They were heading for The Twelfth Man.

"Come on, Grevis," cried an unidentifiable voice, "don't just lay there ..."

Grevis watched the sky for a moment more, then hauled himself up, shook out the last of the flames, blew on his fingers, and trudged towards the tree.

"It's there … see it … there! Get a move on, Roffo, they're still running!"

Roffo muttered something unprintable and tried to increase the pace of his climb. But he could now see the ball where the branches thinned, lodged in the topmost fork, a fingertip away. *If it weren't for me,* he thought, *this damned tree wouldn't have been tall enough to catch the ball. And will I get thanked for it? Bollocks will I!*

"Don't you dare drop it!" howled Tweeky.

"Carefully does it, lad!" cried Occum.

Grevis stood beneath the tree, holding his palms out and examining the scorch marks. "Yes, I'm fine, thanks for asking," he grumbled to himself. "The burns? Oh, don't worry, superficial I'm sure. A soothing balm you say? Why, thanks, that's just what I need … bah!"

Above, there was a crack. An *ominous* crack. Roffo knew what was coming. The branches were just too thin to hold even his insubstantial weight. But he could see the ball. If he could just … The branch gave way. With a last, desperate flail he launched himself, grasped the ball lightly, slipping, moving …

Roffo dropped through the branches like a ball in a pachinko machine. And so did the cricket ball. Unfortunately, the two did not fall as one.

"Roffo, you …"

"Catch it …"

"Where the …"

Something dropped into Grevis's hands. He looked at it in puzzlement for a moment, and then slowly raised his head to see a ring of faces. Staring at him. Everyone appeared frozen, as if afraid to move. There were so many gaping mouths it was like being at the entrance to a grotto. Behind the ring of mannequins, in the background, there was a dull *thud* and an "*ooof!*"

Grevis suddenly realised what was happening. He looked down at the ball nestling in his burned hands. He looked up again. And grinned. Holding up the ball he queried: "Howzat?"

And a mighty roar erupted from around the ground.

With the loss of The Berserker, The Pilgrim's scoring rate lessened to a dribble. But the damage had already been done. Instead of an immense score, the batting side had to settle for a huge one. In the final over of the innings, Bestial Bob – the Pilgrim's tearaway fast bowler – bludgeoned the tired Bear attack for a dozen more runs. Jepho bowled the last ball and watched Bob belt it over his head and across the Road for four. A cheer resounded around the ground from The Pilgrim's supporters. Grey-robed individuals pranced about, their anal plates clanking up and down, their banners waving furiously. Two-hundred and forty, they knew, would be a difficult target to get – and without the barbarian, a nigh-on impossible one.

The batsmen skipped from the pitch, their arms raised as though victory was already assured. The fielders trudged off disconsolately. Jepho handed the ball to umpire Mitchkin, who sympathetically patted him on the back. It wasn't until Jepho reached the pavilion, however, that he realised he had somehow been divested of his gold necklace, his purse, and, amazingly, his finely woven wool vest.

Hops greeted his returning warriors with a weak smile. He looked as though he was about to be sick.

Occum peered at him from under bushy eyebrows. "You okay? You look as though someone's just told you that all of Mrs Hops's relatives have decided to come and live with you. It's not that bad. We can still do it, *if* that blasted barbarian turns up."

"Ahem, yes," said Hops, quietly. "It's not that – well, it is, but … well, it's your *tea*."

"What do you mean, our tea?" piped in Fat Grevis suspiciously.

"Well … you know how I sent out the barbarian and young Roffo there to get in the lunch-time grub …"

Nine angry faces suddenly switched their gaze to the much-bruised Roffo.

"Go on," growled Grevis, his stomach gurgling in misery.

"Well, yes, because I didn't get the provisions I requested, ahem, I, er, had to feed the lunch-time punters with the food I'd made up for your tea." Hops shrugged his rounded shoulders and raised his hands. "Sorry!"

Slowly, very slowly, Roffo began to back away …

"Well, Blewers, an entertaining first innings and a magnificent knock from that brutish chap."

"Yes, marvellous, wasn't it? The Bear are going to have a job overhauling that total. Perhaps we should just go through the scorecard once more for those who have only recently joined us."

"Certainly, old fruit. The scorecard. I make it three chocolate cakes, one strawberry gateau, five fruit pies …"

In the Pilgrim's pavilion, tea was a jovial affair. There was much congratulatory back-slapping and hand shaking, and many glasses were raised in a toast to the magnificence of the innings. Everyone was certain of victory ... or *almost* everyone. Manis sidled out of the tent and summoned Trespass to follow.

"Don't you *dare* call me paranoid or anything, but I want you to go and check on the state of the barbarian. I can't believe he's not going to show. And take fatboy with you." He waved a digit at the loudest and biggest shadow visible through the flimsy fabric of the pavilion.

"Boss you're para—"

"Don't you dare!"

"You're, er ... a *paragon* of caution is what I was going to say. You go and give your half-time speech, and me and Grunt will go and have a look."

Manis watched Trespass drag Grunt from the tent – away from the barrel of Rear Thruster that he had been trying to empty – then hammered on a large silver serving tray and called for order.

"Gentlemen! You have performed exceptionally well so far, and for that I congratulate you. However, I expect a similar performance in the field this afternoon. We may have an edge here. As you *may* have noticed, their star batsman has not turned up." Manis gave a wicked smile. "I hear he's a bit tied up."

"And I hear he's a *lot* tied up!" shouted a wag from the back.

"Gentlemen, *please*! We don't want to start any unnecessary rumours of foul play, do we? Anyway, when you go out onto the field in a few minutes remember that you're playing for the honour of The Pilgrim. And remember, also, that honour doesn't come cheap." And now he grinned even more broadly. "So, that'll be a silver coin from each of you for your tea. Leave the money on this tray as you leave the pavilion. Thank you."

In The Bear's empty pavilion, Hops sat on a barrel and sighed. He had taken plenty of profit from the lunchers at The Bear (he could feel the satisfying weight of his purse resting inside his tunic), but even he would give it all to see the barbarian striding through the tented doorway now. He gave another sad sigh, bit into an apple, and pondered the injustice of existence.

On the road back to town, Grunt was still complaining. "We're gonna miss all the celebrations! Look, Tres, why don't we just sneak back? The boss won't notice, will 'e?"

Trespass grinned at his companion. "Oh, I have a much better idea than that. We'll do as Manis says all right. But he didn't say anything about *not* taking a detour!"

Grunt looked puzzled. "Why'd we want to do that ... ah, I *see*!"

In his hand, Trespass held a key. It was a very special key, a key to earthly delights: it was a key to The Pilgrim's now-undefended beer cellar.

CHAPTER 4

BOUNDERS AND BOUNDARIES

THE ANNUAL Bear-Pilgrim cricket match was *the* highlight of Cross-My-Way's social calendar. For the men it was an opportunity to drink prodigious amounts of ale, chant repetitively, and wear silly costumes, and for the women it was a chance to flirt, gossip, meet old friends, and, of course, wear ridiculously over-sized hats decorated with lots of feathers and ribbons and fruit, and maybe a veil, and perhaps a stuffed animal …

And that was where the two Sonias *should* have been. Instead, they were confined to *The Warehouse*, acting as nursemaids to the unconscious barbarian… and they were *truly* bored.★ After all, there is only so much pleasure to be had from drinking tea and playing cards, and now – in the middle of their umpteenth game of Domina-Tricks – frustration was adding an edge to their play.

Grey Sonia cackled and laid a number of cards onto the red felt top of the table. "A set of *Willies* – *Elephant Todger* high! My game, I think!" She started to reach for the small pool of coins in the centre of the table, but Red Sonia touched the back of her hand and smiled.

"Not so fast, mum!" The younger woman selected a number of cards from the fan in her hand. "Three *Rubbers* cancels your set …"

"Not the *'Phant!* It's still my game …"

"Ah ah ah," demurred Sonia. She threw down another card. "And my *Jumbo Shears* takes out your big todger!"

"Bah – you're stalling! I can count cards y'know! Let me see …" The old woman peered at her hand while rasping the fine grey stubble covering her chin. A wicked smile crossed her face. A liver-spotted hand

---

★ As occupants of a bordello, you would have thought they'd have been used to this.

flicked three more cards onto the table. "Beat that, young madam: a set of *Tarts With Whips* …"

"Got it, got it!" cried Sonia, flourishing a pair of *Chastity Belt* cards. "I *constrain* your *Tarts* …"

"Only two of them, and anyway …" the grey-haired one laid down her trump card, "I have a *Key!*" The old Madam threw back her head and cawed. "You can't beat me, young lady! Now shovel over them there pennies!"

"How do you do it?" wondered Sonia, in disgust. "And look," she revealed the remaining cards in her hand: "A *Whale Schlong*, two *Iron Maidens*, and a *Jar Of Lubrication* …"

The old Madam smirked. "It's no good if you don't have the sets. I only had a pair of *Bound Skinny Men* left, but I had me sets!"

"Oh well," sighed Red Sonia, pushing back her chair and standing up. "I suppose someone should go and check on our guest."

"Hold on there, young lady! You checked last time!"

"Don't worry about it, mum. You just put your feet up and rest your little old legs. I'll save you the walk."

"Me legs are fine, thank you," squawked the crone. "I know your game all too well, my dear! Let's just say I just hope you fix his bearskin properly this time!"

The red-haired beauty hissed in displeasure. "What are you saying, you harridan! Think I'd take advantage of a drugged man?"

"It's been known to happen!" laughed the wrinkled one.

"How dare you, you bag of bones! I can get any man in town just like that," Red Sonia snapped her fingers. "Besides, I know you've been at him with your scabby claws. Last time I checked there was a damp patch on his chest, like some brazen hussy'd been drooling on him!"

The two women faced up to each other. For several seconds it looked as though there was about to be the mother of all cat fights. But then Red Sonia lowered her head and did something she would not have done with anyone else in town: she backed down. "Okay mum," she said meekly, "you go check. I'll put the kettle on."

The crone squawked in victory and headed for the stairs.

The Bear's openers marched to the wicket with glum expressions on their faces and hunger in their bellies. The frowns, however, told little about the two men's particular moods for these were regular residents on the two men's faces: a consequence of world-weary scepticism in the case of Occum, and of intense disapproval in the case of Grimwade. The hunger, though, was genuine enough and had little to do with a desire for victory. Indeed, the good wishes that had been heaped upon the pair as they left the pavilion had had less to do with a hope that they should plunder runs and notch up a famous victory, than a hope that they should last long enough for their team-mates to scavenge up some food for themselves.

With such a large total to chase it was imperative for The Bear's batsmen to get off to a good start, and in the person of Occum they had a supreme batsman whose skill was scarcely less than that of the barbarian. The batting talent at the other end, however, left something to be desired, and wickets soon began to tumble like an insatiable country girl in a hayloft.

Grimwade proved to be less proficient at striking a moving target than a stationary, bending-over one, and was bowled. Horus the farrier was caught behind. Jepho the part-time barman was run out when he stopped to pick up a gold piece that had mysteriously appeared mid-pitch. And Fat Grevis pulled a muscle while going for a run and had to be carried from the pitch by a dozen volunteers and a brace of oxen. But while all this was going on the redoubtable Occum stood firm, wielding his bat like a well-honed cut-throat, slicing and carving and cutting his way towards the victory target.

———•·•·•———

With each new wicket to fall, Hops's heart sank a little further until it was in serious danger of holing his boots. After a while he ceased watching the match altogether and directed his attention to the road leading to town instead. "Where *is* he?" he asked the world at large. "Oh, I should never have let him out into the market, not on a day like this. What have I done?"

"There there," simpered Maddy, gently taking the innkeeper's balding head and resting it upon her ample chest, thereby proving that, yes, three does make a crowd. "Let Auntie Maddy make it better."

"Mumfumphferumph ..."

"What was that, dear one?"

"I think you ought to let him breathe," said Heddy. "Look! The top of his head is turning purple!"

Maddy released the pressure and the innkeeper emerged from between the comfort pillows of doom. He gasped for breath and held his throat.

"Quick, somebody, give him something to drink!"

"Here," said Eddie, "take a belt of this. It'll make you feel better … *probably*."

Hops instinctively grabbed for the proffered glass flask and quaffed deeply of the yellow liquid within. He lowered the flask and wiped his lips with a free hand, then looked at the concoction in the flask. The arched eyebrows of suspicion made a bridge over his eyes. A moment later, dawning realisation caused his face to transform into a mask of terror. "Ahh-hwooooooo!" howled the innkeeper. "Etch etch etch etch etch …"

"Ere, what did you just give him?" asked Heddy, in concern.

"Um, that flask out of your bag," said Eddie, guiltily. "Looked like finest ale …"

"You mean," said Heddy, aghast, "that *you've* just given our dearest Hopsie my sample for Doctor Feare's Pregnancie Test?" Heddy began to go white with rage. "It took me all bluddy week to fill that flask!"

"Never mind that," cried Maddy, "what are we going to do about *him*!"

Hops was crawling around in circles on the ground, howling and retching.

"Water! Get him some water!"

"Ain't got none … will ale do?"

"You drank the last of that you witch, why do you think I was rummaging through your bag!"

"You harlot …"

"Food – what about something to eat … clear away the taste, like!"

"Good idea!" said Heddy. She reached into a pocket in her dress and, rather appropriately, plucked out a tart. "Get him to eat this. Hold him down, girls!"

Hops suddenly found himself pinned to the ground, with the large smiling face of Heddy looming over him and a red-topped pastry heading his way. As he opened his mouth to suck in some more air the tart was thrust into it. A hand was then clamped over his mouth to prevent him from spitting the thing out.

"Go on, Hopsie, chew for mummy."

Hops's eyes bulged. His face went a peculiar colour.

"He don't seem to be enjoying that much," said Maddy. "What was in that tart?"

"Eh? Oh, that nice Mr Puns told me it was a jam tart. I says, 'looks like fresh gizzards to me', but he says, 'no, it's definitely jam'."

"*Puns!* Heddy – you fool!"

"*Aaaaaaaaaaaaaaarghh!*" The strength of desperation allowed Hops to break through the cloying bonds of flesh. He sat upright. As a roar erupted from around the ground with the fall of another Bear wicket, the innkeeper ejected the tart in a huge and colourful geyser.

Hops staggered to his feet. Still queasy, he swayed about, trying to evade the grasps of his female tormentors while simultaneously trying to see through the crowd to the events on the pitch. He pulled at the scant remains of his hair and wailed to the heavens. What more could go wrong?

And then, suddenly, he sensed a change in the atmosphere. All around him went ominously calm – in the same way (divers say) that the sea becomes calm when something large and nasty with lots of teeth, an appetite, and a bad attitude, swims into the locale. Hops dropped his arms. The girls had vanished. But there was something, or someone, behind him …

"Innkeeper!" cried a voice. "Yes, you there! Defiler!"

Hops groaned. *Oh, please*, he thought, *not them!* Knowing what he would find, and dreading it, the innkeeper slowly looked around.

The plackard-waving Clovorites moved to surround him.

Hops held up his hands and cowered back. "Ah, er … I suppose you'd like me to stop the match?"

The Advance of the Incensed Religious Nutcases came to a halt. The senior monk, Brother Frostus, gaped in astonishment. His intended harangue about the sacrilege of having fun on Clovery's special day had been brought to an abrupt halt somewhere between cortex and voice box.

"Stop the match?" whispered one of the Clovorites.

"That's what it sounded like," said another.

"Bloody Hull! Er, pardon me …"

As the Brothers turned to face each other, gabbling excitedly, a plan leapt into the mind of the much-put-upon innkeeper. This plan – like all things new-born – required careful handling and appeared repulsive to all but he who had conceived it. A wicked smile stole across Hops's face. It was the sort of smile that ought to send any sane person running in the opposite direction exceedingly quickly. But the smile had slipped away by the time Brother Frostus returned his attention to the rotund innkeeper.

"Okay," said Hops, sweetly. "The match is off. Aye, I hereby call it off. Let's all go home."

"Do you mean it?" asked an astonished Frostus. This would really be striking a blow for the Toenail-less One!

"Of course I mean it. I've suddenly seen the light and suchlike. Hallelujah and all that! The match is over. Let's go." Hops turned towards the road, then paused and turned back. "Except that ... Ah, well, no matter ..."

"What, *what?*"

"Well, someone's got to tell the players. I'll signal mine, but who's going to tell the opposition?" Hops adopted the look of a musing man. "Now, if I went on the pitch I'd be lynched, and I'm not about to risk that for anyone, lad. So, ah, I guess that's that."

"No, wait!" A sheen of sweat sprung upon the High Brother's brow. He felt the weight of his Brothers' eyes – and expectations – upon him. "Okay. You call in your fellows, and we'll do the rest!"

"Hallelujah!" cried a noviciate. "Let us go and break the great news!"

"Oh Great Clovory!" pleaded another, with hands clasped in thankful prayer. "This we do for you! Yea, on this day – Your Day – no further balls will be smitten! Your balls, which are in everything, shall be rested; no seed shall be wrung from them; no injury shall be perpetrated unto them!"

"Yea yea!"

"Let's do it, Brothers!"

Hops nodded and grinned and raised his hands in encouraging mimicry of the Clovorites' own gestures. With the cowled contingent in tow, Hops strode to the boundary's edge, where he began a frantic and mystical signalling with his hands.

———•◦•••◦•———

At the crease, about to take strike, Occum suddenly pulled away and raised a hand towards the bowler. He walked to the middle of the pitch to meet up with his partner, Phlip, The Bear's outie cleaner.

"What is that damned fool Hops doing now?"

"Looks like 'ees trying tuh fly."

"If man were meant to fly," declared the wise one, "he would be born sitting on a very, *very* large pigeon. Let's see what he wants."

———•◦•••◦•———

"See – I've done it!" shouted Hops nervously as the batsmen appeared to abandon the wicket. He vigorously pointed to the middle. "Behold: they come!"

And so, with much rejoicing and songs of praise, the hooded horde joyously bounded onto the pitch. They capered about and waved their banners. Frostus led a small party up to Sly Herrold, opening his arms to embrace The Pilgrim's captain.

Hops turned away. For all his foibles he was, basically, a decent man. Besides, he had an aversion to the sight of blood. He therefore didn't see the first blow land, although he *did* hear it. And soon there was an awful lot of shrieking.

"What's the score, our leader?" said Occum, suddenly coming up behind the innkeeper.

"Eh, what's that? Oh, er, nothing. Just yawning." Hops shrugged his shoulders sheepishly. The Bear's star opener about-faced and, muttering, started back towards the middle. By the time he took his guard again, most of the battered holy men and their abused placards had been carried from the pitch. In many instances, *inseparably*.

Around the boundary, the living trees shook their leaves in utter horror at the sight. In tree language there is a curse. It is a potent curse. It is the sort of curse that makes even strong oaks weep like willows. It goes like this: rustle rustle rustle *rustlerustlerustle* rustle. To you and I this translates as follows: 'May you be chopped down, stripped of your bark, turned into a signpost, smeared with burning paint, and then shoved up the back passage of the sort of human who eats a lot of bran.' The events on the pitch had shown the trees that their worst nightmare could, indeed, come true.

———◆·◆·◆———

It was Red Sonia's turn to check on the captive.

As she entered the room, the sight of the trapped barbarian caused a small shiver to run down her spine. For a moment she stood and admired his physique. Terry seemed like an heroic statue of some warrior god. But this god was not stone, he was alive. His huge chest rose and fell gently in his sleep, and his eyelids flickered slightly …

Flickered?

Sonia went over for a closer inspection. She peered closely. There was no more movement. To get a better look, she sat down on the arm of the chair. Being this close to the barbarian made her heart beat a little quicker. Temptation smote her. She reached out a hand, paused for a brief moment, and then ran it gently over the man's muscular chest.

The barbarian's eyes shot open.

"What the …!" cried the startled girl, jumping back off the chair.

"You scared the life out of me!"

"Er, sorry," said Terry, who had been a bit startled himself. "Anyway, what was I saying? Oh, yeah, the potion. It probably won't work. I don't feel tired at all."

"Actually," grinned Sonia, her heart still beating as furiously as a heavy metal drummer, "you've been asleep for five hours. Mummy reckoned the drug would knock you out for a week. But then again, you're not an elephant, are you?"

"Five hours? An elephant? Um, I've not been asleep... have I?"

"Yeah. Sleeping like a baby!" Sonia oozed forward, a gleam entering her eye, her breasts heaving up and down like a pair of mating pillows. She reached out again and stroked Terry's cheek. "And speaking of babies – did you really learn the Nudian left-legged back-breaker at seven? *Very* impressive. But I've learnt a few things in my time too. Let me show you some." She ran her tongue about her lips in anticipation and began to hitch up her dress. "This one's called *bare-back riding.*" And with that she moved to straddle the *unfortunate* barbarian.

At that instant the door slammed open. Two grizzled, bearded men stood silhouetted in the doorway. Alcohol fermented out of their exhaled breath.

"So, this is how you look after prisoners," observed Trespass. "I wish you'd look after *me* that well!"

"What are you doing here?" screeched the compromised woman. "Checking up on me, eh? Following me around? Think I'm going to get up to something, do you?"

Trespass considered the scenario before him and began to clench and unclench his fists. He laughed, but there was no humour in his voice. "Get up to something? You? Of course not!" He pointed at the woman. "And there you are, sitting astride that barbarian like you're about to ride him to paradise and back ... totally innocent. Yeah. Happens all the time." The leader of the pack had a sarcastic streak in him that he had picked up in prep school, sometime during his embarrassingly un-macho (and well-hidden) past. Such subtlety, however, tended to be over the heads of his men (save for Burble, who had a bit of nous about him). "I wouldn't call what you're doing *getting up to something.* No. Not me. Others might, but not me. And what about you, Grunt, what do you think? Would you consider *that* to be getting up to something?"

The brow of the other yak rider furrowed visibly. You could virtually track the thoughts as they slowly waded their way across the morass of his mind. "Er ... actually I would. The way she was licking 'is face was a big 'int, but the real clincher was the way she was caressing 'is—"

"Thank you, Grunt," interrupted his companion. The green-eyed monster of jealousy started to waltz across his bruised pride. "You don't need to go into detail."

Sonia climbed off Terry's lap in as dignified a manner as she was able. She put her hands on her hips and glared at the bearded men. "I was just making sure he was securely locked in place, wasn't I! You know what his lot are like. You chain them up in the deepest dungeon in town and by the time you've climbed the stairs out of the pit, they've escaped, ravished your grandmother, stolen your valuables, and are getting drunk down the pub." She pouted aggressively, using womankind's age-old skill of turning the blame back onto the victim. "How could you even *think* I could fancy a bloke who comes from a race whose idea of foreplay is to give you a ten-minute head start?"

While Trespass and Sonia stared at each other in a kind of Mexican stand-off, Grunt wandered up to the restrained barbarian. "Hey – what's this!" He squatted down to look at the chair more closely. "What're all these spikes under the seat for? I bet if we give this little wheel 'ere …" he reached for a small wheel on the back of the chair "… a turn or two, these spikes will rise penetratingly into 'is flesh, skewering 'im slowly and agonisingly!"

At this, Trespass smiled. "Good idea, Grunt! Let me at it!" Glad for an excuse to evade Sonia's microwave gaze, he joined his second-in-command by the chair.

"Er …" exclaimed Terry, as his brow furrowed, "before you start turning that wheel I should warn you I have a low pain threshold."

"Ha!" chortled Grunt. "So the barbarian can't take it! I knew 'e was soft really!"

"No, I don't mean I can't *take* pain," said Terry, matter-of-factly. "It's just that pain makes me angry, and then, well, things start to *happen*."

Trespass rubbed his hands in glee. "We'll see about that!" Vengeance would be sweet indeed! He grasped the wheel and gave it a hefty turn.

As the spikes perforated the back of his loincloth, Terry groaned.

While Sonia covered her eyes, Grunt pointed at their prisoner and laughed. "Look at 'im writhing in agony. And… crikey, look at the way 'is muscles are bulging … and the way the veins are standing out on 'is forehead. What was that crack?"

"… Arm's broken," cried the occupant of the chair.

"Wot do you mean, your arm's broken?" said Grunt, stooping to peer at the barbarian. "The spikes are in your bum, not your arm."

"No, not *my* arm. The arm of the chair. *Look* ..." and with that Terry smashed his free arm into the face of the startled Grunt, sending him staggering backwards into Trespass. The head yak rider tripped over a metal chain and crashed to the floor, the bulk of Grunt falling on top of him.

"Look!" cried the barbarian. "Now you've made me break the other one!"

"Holy Bulabothel, he's got his arms free!" screamed Sonia. "Get up, you two – get him before he releases his leg shackles! Oh *shit*," she added.

With a roar, Terry ripped the rusted metal rings from the chair legs, holding them above his fallen tormentors like battle trophies.

Spotting the detached expression of victory in Terry's eyes, Grunt took his chance. He rolled across the floor, grabbing a large knobbly object of dubious phallic representation on the way. Trespass, however, remained on the floor, his tongue lolling from the side of his mouth, his eyes glazed over, his consciousness squashed from him.

"You celebrate too soon, barbarian!" yelled Grunt, righting himself with an agility not to be expected in a man of his dimensions. "And now," he added, as he waved his improvised weapon in the direction of the barbarian, "I'm gonna 'ave you."

Grunt charged across the floor, swinging his impromptu tool at the head of his adversary. Terry blocked the blow with his left forearm, causing the icon of manhood to shatter on the metal chair arm still tied to that limb. Quick as a flash, Terry returned the blow in the form of an upper-cut into Grunt's midriff. His arm sank up to the elbow in the layers of fat around his opponent's waist. The flab dissipated the force of the blow, only partially winding Grunt, but causing the yakker to stagger backwards, blowing and snorting like a wounded bull.

Grunt took a deep breath, lowered his head, and charged.

Terry stood his ground and braced himself.

The irresistible force was about to meet the immovable object ...

The power of the charge forced Terry to take a couple of steps backwards, but then his gigantic leg muscles locked, and the charge was halted. Terry slipped his arms around Grunt's chest and, with a mighty roar, straightened up, lifting Grunt off the ground and spinning him at the same time so that his head ended up earthwards while his feet pointed to the ceiling. With the skill of an all-star wrestler, Terry kicked his legs behind him and allowed mass and gravity to combine to produce the most forceful pile-driver ever seen in a ring of combat. The floorboards shattered under the impact of the two combatants, and Grunt's head disappeared below floor level. Only the broadness of the bearded-one's frame stopped the rest of him from following.

Terry stood up and glared at the frantically waving legs in front of him. Through them, he could see Sonia desperately trying to bring the prone Trespass around by slapping his face as hard as she could.

"Are you trying to wake him up or keep him unconscious?" enquired the barbarian.

"Oh no! Please don't hurt me! It was just a joke. They made me do it. Said they'd throw my poor, defenceless mother onto the street if I didn't help them!"

"Your mother – queen of the Mickey Finns? The Cross-My-Way Poisoner? Poor and defenceless? I don't think so!"

"They gave her the potion. Made her give it to you. Said they'd kill her little dog – her only friend in the world – if she didn't help them stop you getting to the match."

"They said a lot ... the match!" Terry slapped his forehead. "Grom's goolies – the match!"

"Er ... yeah, the match. If you run you might still be able to make it ... Oh! Where's he gone?"

Sudden recollection of the match spurred Terry's legs into action. He dived through the door, sprinted down the corridor, and leapt down the stairs. As he passed the upside-down head of Grunt he paused to give him a two fingered wave, then powered out of the front door and away down the street ...

———•◦•◦•———

Out in the middle, The Bear's already weak hopes were fading like the colour from a new shirt in a bleach wash. While Occum scored freely from one end, his partners succumbed timidly at the other, mainly as a result of some hostile bowling. With the latest departure, Cross-My-Way's premier barber was joined at the wicket by Ancient Willy. The only good thing about this – in the eyes of the nail-biting bearskin-clad supporters – was that Willy *was not* Roffo. The bad thing about Willy's arrival, however, was that it meant that there was *only* Roffo to come. Barring the unlikely arrival of the barbarian, this partnership was – in the eyes of many – effectively the last of the innings.

On his laboured arrival at the wicket, Willy stooped over to regain his breath. After five minutes of wheezing and hawking (with fielders scattering this way and that to avoid the vigorously ejected phlegm), The Bear's new batsman began to scratch out his mark in the crease. As this slow gardening process continued, the fielders began to get restless. After a further five minutes, and the digging of a trench that properly belonged in the fields of Flanders, Willy looked up.

"Are you ready now?" asked Frunge, the bowler, through grinding teeth. He stood beside the umpire, but not *too* close.

"What's the hurry, young ruffian, eh, *eh*?" Willy hawked again, and this time the fielder at short square leg was slow to react. Young Festers squealed as though he had been scalded. "I'll tell ee when I'm a ready! Now, let's see where you've hidden away these fielders of yours, eh?"

As Willy stood back and slowly – very slowly – scanned the ground to check the field placings, Frunge groaned. Several of the fielders began to bite on their hands or punch their arms in frustration. Willy's ability to wind people up was famous. A couple of minutes in his presence would be enough to turn Mother Teresa into a screaming hellcat, or the Dalai Lama into a homicidal maniac ("Om mani *bloody* padme om … Om mani … *right*, that's it, I've had enough! Where's that axe? Sod it, I'll do you with me prayer beads! *Aieeeeeee!*"). Sane people had been known to take desperate measures to avoid Willy: mothers would sweep up toddlers and run screaming into their houses; ashen-faced pedestrians would ditch their groceries and race for cover; invalids would throw themselves into piles of refuse and dig their way into hiding; and animals would break into desperate stampedes. Willy was the biggest single cause of RTAs in town.

At last, after a bout of coughing, a slow amble down the wicket to pat Occum on the shoulder in encouragement, and a further bout of gardening, Willy stood ready to face his first ball. By now, Frunge's mouth was flecked with foam and his nails were dug deep into the ball. He began to babble. Rivers of drool started to course down his rank beard. Herrold went up to his bowler, walking stiffly in an attempt to keep himself under control. Blood trickled down the captain's bitten lip. He reached the Angel and turned to point him towards the smirking wicket keeper. "Kill!" he muttered.

"Come on come on," cackled Willy. "You gonna throw that thing or what! I ain't got all day y'know! Got some verrucas to lance afterwards. And these incontinence pants don't empty themselves y'know!"

At this final provocation, Frunge howled, turned, and threw the ball at the gibing batsman. His aim, however, wasn't that good – quite possibly because of the tears in his eyes. Festers ducked. Fingers – the wicket keeper – made a despairing dive down legside. But he missed the ball by about ten yards. It sailed to the boundary.

"No-ball!" called the umpire, who then signalled a "four".

Frunge rested his head on Herrold's shoulder and began to sob.

"Pies, get yur pies here!" yelled the black-cowled man. "Lurvely pies … only the very best ingredients. Get yur pies here!"

The Yegoran merchant was new in town. How was he supposed to know? "Ven-dor! Over here! Yah, pies! Goot, goot!"

Awful Puns slimed up to the bulky man in white fur apparel. He rubbed at the nest of blackheads that beaded the side of his hooked nose, leaving a smear of blood behind. "Ah, yes, noble sir! What sort of pie would you like? I have here prime beef, choice lamb, and here," he lifted up a slightly burnt offering, "fresh fish pie, brought in from the sea this very morning!"

The merchant sniffed at the pie. It certainly smelled of fish … but the sea was hundreds of miles away. Was the vendor a magician? He looked over the stooped man's shoulder and noticed a number of people looking his way. They appeared to have what the merchant translated as joyful, blissful looks upon their faces. Indeed, one was making frantic motions, pulling a finger across his throat: the Yegoran sign for good health! He hadn't realised Yegoran customs were known this far south. And the man's partner had tears in her eyes and appeared to be praying. These pies must be heavenly indeed!

He returned his attention to the pie. "Yah yah! Ze fish pie zounds most goot! I weel take eet! How much?"

A mischievous look stole over the vendor's face. "Ah, well, good sir, this is my very last fish pie, and I was going to have it for meself." Puns sighed. "But for you, sir, I will let it go for … a *gold* piece?"

Behind the pie vendor a look of utter horror crossed the face of the religious woman. *Ah*, thought the Yegoran, *the face-gesture of victory!*

"Yah – ein gold piece – a bar-gain! Here …"

The money disappeared and so, almost instantly, did the vendor. The miming woman – the Yegoran saw – had collapsed, and was being brought around by her bearskin-wearing partner.

The first thing the man noticed about the pie was the oozing slime – white and purulent – escaping through a breach in the pastry. *Fish sauce?* He shrugged his shoulders and bit into it. *Funny tasting fish*, he thought, as he began to chew. Something caught in his teeth. He picked it out. A dirty white feather? He looked at the opened-up pie. And there, staring out at him, from the midst of various internal avian organs and their partly-digested lavatorial contents, was the head of a pigeon.

It did not look best pleased.

<hr />

The problem with Willy – or, at least, *one* of the problems with Willy – was that he didn't just wind up his opponents; he wound up *everyone*. And Occum was not exactly the most patient or considerate of men. Now, after nearly half an hour of Willy's antics, The Bear's captain was nearing breaking point …

And the partnership had started out so well. The bowlers had been so uptight that they had sprayed the ball all over the place. The sages manning the scoreboard had been hard pressed to keep count of all the no-balls, wides, and byes. And when Occum had got a chance to face the ragged bowlers his elegant shot-play had been rattling up the score. But The Pilgrim's bowlers had started to tire from emotional exhaustion, and as they did so their bowling began to improve. In itself, this need not have been fatal, and Willy could not be blamed for it. The problem was that Occum had become stuck at one end and Willy at the other, chiefly because The Cantankerous One refused to take even the easiest of singles. "Run you say, eh, *eh*? That might be all right for you young 'uns, but these legs aren't made for running! Heh heh, they're barely made to keep me stood up! No sireee, I ain't a budgin'!"

After a while, Sly Herrold had realised the way the wind was blowing and called his bowlers over for a huddled discussion. Thereafter, the bowlers – their ears now filled with rolled-up leaves – peacefully and gently bowled at the old codger and collected the ball as it was rolled back to them. With each scoreless over, Occum fumed. In the end – during the alternate overs when he faced the bowling – he was forced to play in a risky manner that was not at all to his liking. For a short while, Occum prospered. But it could not last …

Herrold himself bowled the fateful ball. The looping off-spinner was really too good to try to heave out of the ground. But red mist now obscured the barber's sight and, with a roar that would have put the wind up Godzilla, he flailed at the ball … and missed. Occum stood as though dazed. Momentarily his hearing left him, so that when he closed his eyes he was in a sightless, soundless world. A quiet voice inside his head squeaked "whoops!"

When Occum opened his eyes he was aware of a great dancing around Herrold, who was being patted on the back by jubilant team-mates. Occum didn't need to turn around to know that his wicket was shattered. He closed his eyes for a moment longer.

"Ahem," went a voice. "Ahem, mon capitane." Occum opened his eyes and looked down. It was Willy. "That was a damned stupid thing to do, eh, *eh*?"

"Well, Blewers old fruit, I do believe The Bear are in a jolly difficult position now. Here comes young Roffo to the wicket – a sight to warm the heart of any bowler."

Blewers wiped some crumbs away from his mouth. "Yes, old chap, I very much fear that we may be in for an early finish. Such a pity!"

"A pity indeed," echoed Jombers, "all these cakes still to eat! Let us hope he lasts long enough for us to consume Mrs Frettal's splendid cream cake with the cherry on top!"

"Amen to that, old friend!"

Terry pelted through the deserted market place, down the Kelloon road, and out of the town gate. The empty road now allowed him to reach speeds that Olympic sprinters could only dream of. As he thundered towards the ground a large cloud of dust rose in his wake. The people at the match with a good view of the road saw this first. A number remarked to their friends, rather prophetically, that a storm appeared to be coming.

They were right.

Roffo met Ancient Willy in the middle of the wicket.

"Well, er … only a hundred more to get off ten overs. How do you want to play this?"

"Eh? Whatsat? Who're you? Oh, yes, I remember. How's your bowels?"

"Uh, no," said Roffo, "that was *last* year, Willy. Remember?"

"Oh, er, I dare say. I think the sun is getting to me." The ancient one wiped a white sleeve across his brow. By the time it reached his side again it was brown. "Well, can't stand here chatting. Let's get to it. But no running about mind you! I won't be having with such tomfoolery, eh?"

Roffo managed a weak grin. He felt sick. The hopes of The Bear rested on him – and he had only managed a single run before in his entire career, and that had really been a leg bye. Where on earth was Terry? He looked

73

at the road that led to town. He stared for a moment, wishing, hoping. And then he sadly shook his head. He was just turning away, however, when he caught sight of something out of the corner of his eye. His head snapped back. What was that? A mirage? His misbehaving subconscious? A trick of the light? There seemed to be something kicking up dust on the road. Something that was either very big or moving very fast.

"Come on, boy, quit stalling!" cried Herrold, from the opposite end, as he spun the ball from hand to hand.

"Uh, er, sorry!" Roffo paused a moment longer. There was definitely something coming along the road towards the ground – but what? What had seemed like a puff of dust had already grown into a mini whirlwind. It would have been easy to dismiss the vision as a delusion, or as something real but mundane. But Roffo didn't. He *knew* Terry. Hope rose in his heart like a spout of water up the backside of a pervert on a bidet. It *had* to be Terry!

With renewed hope, Roffo turned to face Herrold. The fielders around him were chatting away without concern. They didn't think he'd even be able to hit the ball. Well, he'd show them! He didn't have to score a century; all he had to do was stay in and wait. With an uncharacteristic snarl, he set himself to receive the ball. And for the remaining three deliveries of the over he defended his wicket with tenacity. *They shall not pass!* he thought.

And they didn't.

Terry stepped up another gear. He could see the ground laid out before him, and the first of the stalls of the hard-working vendors hove into view. He lengthened his stride and ate up the intervening ground. With dust swirling behind him like a mighty contrail he thundered past the first stalls on the road. Astonished bargain hunters and stall holders stared at him agog. A part-time bookmaker rapidly recomputed probabilities and turned to his board. With a piece of chalk he struck a couple of zeros off the odds of a Bear victory.

Terry's pace did not falter. He wove through some stalls, leapt over others, and left a babbling commotion in his wake. Some burst into encouraging cheers, others tugged at their hair and wailed to the heavens. Soon – from east to west – a reverberating roar coursed through the spectators. At his pavilion, Hops suddenly looked up, taking his head from his hands. A grin as broad as his belly swept across the innkeeper's face. Nearby fans threw placards into the air and began a rendition of a song that was not at all complimentary about Pilgrims, casting doubt upon both their parentage *and* the size of their manhoods.

By The Pilgrim's pavilion, Manis fumed. He looked out to the middle to where Frunge was about to start a new over, and then back to the rapidly approaching barbarian, and then back to the middle once more. He wiped his sweat-stained palms onto his trousers and made some rapid mental calculations. A part of his mind comforted him: *It's too late!* it said. *Not even the barbarian can save them now!* But the pessimist within the innkeeper groaned and gnashed its teeth and derided him.

Terry skidded to a halt in front of Hops, smoke steaming from his fur boots. A cloud of debris swirled up around them, and a throng of supporters closed in to encircle them. A hubbub of noise swept over the scene from the excited crowd.

Terry stood before the innkeeper, his huge chest heaving with every breath. Dust and masonry powdered his untamed mane of hair, streaks of blood trailed down his forearms and right fist, and a metal chain trailed from one ankle. The barbarian took several deep breaths, then smiled meekly at his team manager. "Er, sorry I'm late, boss, but I got a bit tied up."

"Never mind that," squeaked Hops, as he picked up a nearby bat and thrust it at the barbarian. "We've got to get you out there RIGHT NOW!" He took Terry by one of his huge arms and tugged him towards the boundary. By this time, the entire population of the ground was looking towards them. Sly Herrold was on his hands and knees thumping the ground in frustration. Other fielders simply stood about, staring towards The Bear's pavilion in disbelief, or cursing under their breath (or indeed, out loud).

Roffo knew what was needed. Even before Hops's bizarre signalling began, he had reached Willy's end and was trying to explain the situation to the ancient one.

"Eh? Get out? Me?" Willy hawked and spat. A small patch of grass sizzled and died. "I think you've misunderstood the game, young man. *We've* got to try to stay *in* – *they've* got to try to get us *out!*"

"Yes, Willy," sighed Roffo. "Usually you're right, but Terry's just arrived and our only chance to win is to get him to the wicket NOW. He's the only one who can score quickly enough. So, you've got to get yourself out."

"Me, eh? Why not you? You youngsters are a selfish lot. No respect for your elders, eh?"

Roffo groaned. "Look, I can't get out because I'm not facing the bowling, am I? But *you* are. But if we change ends, then I *can* get out, can't I?"

"Change ends ..."

"Of course," noted Roffo, "it means you'll have to go for a run ... Ah, no, but you can't run, can you? So that's that then."

"Whassat? Run? Of course I can run. What are you talking about? That's what the game's all about. Are you stupid, or what? You just get back to your end, laddie, and be ready to run when I say so. Okay? And no dawdling, you young whippersnapper, eh, *eh*?"

As a still-grumbling Willy took up his position, Herrold got to his feet. He looked at Willy, then at Roffo, and then back towards the pavilion to where the barbarian was now warming up, swirling his bat around his head like a war club. Herrold scratched at his ear. He looked at Willy again. Then Roffo. And then he smiled.

The Pilgrim's captain walked up to Frunge and whispered into his ear. Soon, the yakker was smiling too. Next, Herrold called out to his troops. "Okay, lads, we all know what to do now, don't we? We all know who *we don't want to come in to bat*, right?"

It's difficult to say whose fault it was. Perhaps Herrold should have been more explicit. Perhaps he should have checked that everyone understood what was going on – particularly given the nature of his team. As it was, he didn't notice that the Berserker was standing about with a puzzled expression on his face. And, after all, maybe it was just fate that the next ball that Frunge bowled (wide of the stumps so that he couldn't possibly hit the wicket) was struck by Willy straight to that fielder.

"Run!" cried Roffo, who made no effort to leave his ground. Willy, on the other hand, put his head down and surged out of his crease like a turbo-charged hare, his old joints moving as swiftly as greased pistons. Indeed, the ancient one was mid-way down the pitch before he bothered to look up ... and the sight that greeted him then was a confusing one. Roffo had not moved. In fact, the barman was grinning at him in an embarrassed manner. Willy slowed. *Eh?* he thought. *Eh?*

The Berserker swept onto the ball like a demon. He picked it up one-handed, took aim, and then, with the astonished cries of his team-mates ringing in his ears, threw down the stumps. The throw was so hard that one of the stumps disintegrated into matchsticks.

It seemed to the horde of spectators that Terry was at the wicket before the last splinter had drifted to the earth.

Now *this*, this was the sort of plundering that Terry did enjoy. He struck the ball so hard that men everywhere winced and crossed their legs in sympathy. The ball fizzed away from nearly every delivery, skipping across the road or river boundaries for fours and sixes. Catching the thing was not an option unless your hands were protected by war gauntlets with enough padding to fill a king-sized duvet.

Terry bludgeoned twenty runs off the first four balls he faced, and then took a single to keep the strike. No matter what The Pilgrim's team attempted the barbarian was equal to the task. Different bowlers came and went. Runs were piled on. And the victory target grew nearer and nearer …

Victory would have been certain had there been two or three more overs to bat. It probably would have been assured, in any case, had Terry's batting partner had slightly more skill in wielding his bat than a blind nun with a stick of celery. But Roffo was just pleased to keep his wicket intact, and the added task of looking for runs, or trying to give the strike to Terry, was beyond him. And, despite Terry's best efforts, he couldn't keep the strike all of the time. Some of the balls he gently pushed away in the hope of taking a single, roared to the boundary as though jet-propelled. In its own way, however, Roffo's feat was as heroic as that of the barbarian: not a single run did he score, but by not getting out he gave The Bear the chance to get as close to the target as it actually did.

But all, ultimately, appeared to be in vain.

With only two balls to go, The Bear's batsmen still needed eight runs to win – seven would level the scores, but victory would go to The Pilgrim for losing fewer wickets. Roffo looked sadly at his bat as this calculation ran through his mind. He then looked up to see Terry standing before him, a kindly smile on his face. Behind him, Roffo noticed a desperate scrum forming around Bestial Bob.

"I can't do it, Terry. Eight runs! It's not possible!"

Terry patted him on the shoulder, making Roffo's legs buckle, so that he bobbed up and down like a jack-in-the-box. "Sure you can. Two sixes would do it."

"Er, I think you mean two fours."

Terry scratched his head. "Really? Uh, well, it's easier than I thought."

Behind the barbarian's bulk Roffo noticed The Pilgrim's captain slapping Bob about the face. Strains of the conversation carried to him …

"No, no, no, you dolt! It's still legal to underarm it – so do it! If you no-ball it, Manis will skin you alive – and probably the rest of us too."

"Er, why dat den? I can bowl dis geek and den it's all over in one ball."

"Aaargh! For the last time …"

Roffo returned his attention to his friend. "You could do it, Terry, but I'm useless. Can't you hear the crowd jeering? It's all over. I'll have to leave town – *if* I manage to escape the lynch mob. I wish I hadn't asked to play!"

"Don't worry – no-one will harm you while I'm around!" Terry tried his best to look menacing. "Just give me one hit and I'll do the rest. Get a single."

Roffo sighed. "Even if I could, you still wouldn't be able to do it. Seven off one ball? It's not possi—" And then a thought occurred to him. Roffo looked to the southern boundary, to where the crowd behind the Rockbelow were chanting, singing and wailing. In anticipation of the result a couple of fights had already broken out. He noticed a cowled man using his anal plate to beat at something that looked like a were-bear as the creature simultaneously attempted to throttle him. He saw Awful Puns race before this scene in full flight, with half a dozen people chasing after him – all wearing peculiarly bright, multi-coloured tunics that were clearly the result of Stomach-Rejecting-Pie Syndrome. Roffo's hands started to sweat. He dared not speak his mind for fear of tempting fate. But he now knew what he had to do.

Roffo noticed the sudden calm. Even the mob on top of Puns had ceased from forcing the contents of the vendor's tray down the man's throat, and were now looking up, mid-action, motionless in anticipation. Roffo turned to look at Terry. The barbarian gave a rueful smile, about-faced, and – in half a dozen giant strides – reached the opposite wicket. The umpire behind the stumps looked on impatiently, fidgeting with the bandage about his head. Bestial Bob was there, too, standing next to the umpire, tossing the ball from one hand to the other, red marks on his cheeks and a scowl from Hull on his face.

The diminutive young barman took several deep breaths and looked around the field. The fielders were all set deep, saving boundaries and twos, but leaving space for a single. They had understood the scoring situation too. And Roffo suddenly grinned. All he had to do was get bat on ball and then run.

"Play!" cried the umpire. Bestial Bob looked at his captain and growled, but did as demanded. Well back from the crease he under-armed the ball at Roffo. Even without a run-up the strength of Bob's 'bowl' might have taken the batsman's head off. But Roffo held his ground. He tried to get his bat near the ball, but wasn't quick enough. He watched it speed through the air, past the inside edge of his bat ... and hit him in the ribs. "*Run*," he gasped, as he tottered down the wicket. Terry was past him in an instant. The crowd roared. From the outfield, the captain himself raced in, picked up the ball, and – rather than throwing it in and risking overthrows – chased in to the wicket.

Roffo made his ground with a yard to spare, but there was no time to turn for a second run, with Sly hovering to administer the *coup de grâce* should any such attempt be made.

A great cheer came from the direction of the Pilgrim's Supporters' Club and from the various people who had bet on the vanquishing of The Bear. The air was suddenly full of objects, celebratorily thrown: half-eaten chicken legs, hats, placards, rotten fruit, opposing supporters, betting slips, articles of clothing. Manis punched the air in triumph while Hops buried his face in his hands. People yodelled and cursed. Part of the crowd invaded the pitch, capering onto the outfield, shaking fielders' hands, or kissing them, or rifling their pockets (the thieves and pickpockets invariably being the first onto the pitch).

Slowly – very slowly – the crowd began to settle from their rehearsal. The fielders regained their places, many now bereft of items of value or pieces of clothing, while Young Festers had been completely mobbed and now stood in the nude, his hands protecting his last remaining assets. Manis hushed those around him, wanting to savour the ultimate triumph – The Bear's humiliation.

Roffo walked down the pitch towards Terry, rubbing his ribs and summoning the barbarian urgently. They met mid-pitch.

"How are you?" asked Terry, in concern.

"I'll live. But that's not important right now. You've got to listen to me ..."

"Sure, Roff, but I don't see what we can do now ..."

"There is a way!" hissed Roffo, urgently. "Terry, you've got to tell me ... tell me if you can hit ... the river!"

"Eh?"

"The river, *the river*! Can you land the ball in the river?"

"Sure – I can try ..."

"The middle, mind you. The *fastest flowing* part."

"Er, okay. And then what?"

"And then run like you've never run before ..."

Manis was one of life's pessimists. To him, the pint was always half-empty. Too often he had seen silver spoons turn to wood, and defeat snatched from the jaws of victory. And now, as he watched the urgent conference in the centre of the wicket, doubt surfaced like a turd in the waves at a Blue Flag beach. *That damned stable boy*, he thought, *he's too clever for his own good. What is he planning?* The innkeeper walked to the edge of the prancing Rockbelow and tried to catch Sly's attention. "Herrold you oaf – Herrold …"

But Sly's mind was elsewhere. He clutched at the pouch hanging around his neck, and smiled. Madame LooLou's Lust Potion would come in handy tonight! Victory would mean a constant procession of wanton lovelies wanting their own souvenir from the occasion – and he was never a man to disappoint the ladies. "Nice and steady, Bob," he cried. "Just make sure it's in the lines!"

Bestial Bob growled. He then grunted. He then roared.

"Bet you no-ball it," said Roffo, leaning on his bat.

"Eh?"

"I said, you jerk, I bet you no-ball it. Then Terry will hit a six and we'll win. I wouldn't like to be in your shoes, oh no."

"Shut up you midget, or I'll rip your head off!"

"Probably illegal that. In fact," said Roffo, looking thoughtful, "I believe Rule 5B says, and I quote, 'Any acts of dismemberment on the pitch shall result in instant disqualification of the offending side'."

"Rrrrrr … I'll get you afterwards …"

"Not if you're hung up by the testicles outside The Pilgrim for no-balling you won't!"

The umpire cleared his throat and gave Roffo an intense look.

"Sorry!" said Roffo. "Just trying to save Bob's life."

"No need," sneered the bowler. "I ent going to no-ball, no way!" And with that he turned to face Terry. He hefted the ball in his right hand, took careful aim at the middle stump, and dollied the ball to the batsman. The bruised red ball travelled so slowly that the barbarian could have won himself a kingdom, ravished loads of princesses and slaughtered whole herds of dragons in the time it took to reach him. Instead of the above, Terry took careful aim and then, with a flourish of confidence, he took one hand off the bat and placed it imperiously on his hip. With the bat in just one hand, *he struck.*

The ball sailed into the sky, higher and higher and … "Don't just stand there," screamed Roffo, "RUN!"

The batsmen had completed two runs before the ball even touched the ground, or rather, the water, for Terry's aim had been true. As the ball had gone up, the crowd had halted in mid-victory sprint. A sense of *oh oh, what's going on here then* descended onto the watching population, snuffing out joy and despair with the duvet of puzzlement. Manis watched the ball climbing higher and higher. He looked around, wonderingly. *That's a six*, he thought. *We've won!* He thought some more. *We've won?*

Half of the fielders were already dancing about in celebration – but not all. Sly, for one, was watching the cherry projectile. He was suddenly concerned, although he didn't know why. He started into a walk, stepped up to a trot, and then broke into a run. As he passed Frunge and Rudy Brassrubbers he grabbed at their triumphantly raised arms and pulled them along. "Go and get the ball now ..." he said to them. "There's a couple of fine fellows." As the three of them broke into a run, it became clear from the trajectory of the ball that it wasn't, in fact, going to clear the river ...

Manis realised before anyone else what was going on. He watched the ball pitch into the Rockbelow. *Into* the river. *Not over ... not across ...* he thought, *not four, not six, not ... not ... dead!* "The ball's still in play – it's still in play!" he screamed. "Get it! Get it NOW!"

And then the crowd knew it too, the knowledge rippling out from the Manis-focus in an ever-expanding circle. Realisation burst forth like an atomic explosion. Screams and cheers broke out. On the commentary platform, Jombers started to choke on a piece of cake. A thunder of voices rocked the ground. But many of the fielders were the last to know, being separated from the crowd by their own private joy. One by one they cottoned on.

By the time Sly had reached the point where the ball had entered the river, Terry and Roffo were on their fourth run – with Terry loping along at a painfully slow pace so as not to overtake his out-of-breath partner. Unfortunately for The Pilgrim's captain, however, the ball was no longer where it had landed. The Rockbelow had caught it up, and was mischievously rolling it out of reach. Frunge stood on the bank looking confused. "Er, wot noooooooowwwwww ...."

"Now you swim!" cried Sly, from the bank where Frunge *had* been a split-second earlier. "Go go go – oh, bugger!" Accepting the inevitable, the captain jumped in too. He twisted at the last moment to drag Rudy into the icy water with him. From the opposite bank Manis was running along, keeping pace with the ball, tearing at his hair and foaming at the mouth. As he passed by, along the front of the cheering and wailing crowd, one little old lady with a puma-skinned shopper thrust a stick between his legs and tripped him up. The ranting innkeeper plunged into the water with an almighty splash.

"What the Hull," cackled the ancient crone, who raised up her voice to shout: "Go on you hooligan! You call that a run? In my day ..."

On the pitch-side of the knee-deep river, the remainder of the team (bar the wicket keeper) were now frantically charging along after the ball. They converged from various parts of the field, reaching the bank together. The very last to arrive on the scene was the Berserker, who was, in a number of ways, the slowest of the lot. Unfortunately for his colleagues, however, he was also the most single-minded. When Manis cried "get ball", this was exactly what he did: everything else in the universe became simply a collection of obstacles in his path to this goal. And on this particular occasion, the obstacles numbered seven.

"Got you," cried Sly, in triumph, as he scooped the ball up from the water. A split-second later he appended the comment "Aaaargh!" as six of his team-mates piled on top of him, followed by the rather irate Berserker.

As Frunge and Brassrubbers also arrived on the scene, and Manis floundered up to the mêlée too, Terry and Roffo turned for their sixth run.

"I've got it I've got it!"

"Aieeeee, that's *my* ball!"

"Where is it – look there, aaaargh!"

"Getoffofmyhead ..."

"Blurbleurghll ..."

A foaming, thrashing pandemonium ensued, reminiscent of the feeding frenzy of a contact group of deprived chocaholics in the presence of an eclair. Amongst flailing fists and groping hands the ball skittered about in the wash, eluding this grasp, being knocked from that. At last, the Berserker gained his feet and started heaving people bodily from the water. Sly flew head-first into a muddy bank; Young Festers flew through the air, but was saved from falling to the hard ground when his exposed tackle got caught in the branches of a tree; Hughie Puke was tossed into the gathering crowd. Suddenly, the Berserker saw the ball. He picked it up, turned, and – with an amazing throw – hurtled it directly at the wicket keeper, who was standing by the stumps.

The crowd took in a great draw of breath. The batsmen were on their seventh and final run ... and it was Roffo who was running to the danger end! The diminutive batsman and the mightily thrown ball simultaneously reached the crease and wicket keeper, respectively. Unfortunately for The Pilgrim, such was the strength of the throw that the ball didn't stop. As

Fingers tried to push the ball onto the stumps, the red missile ploughed into his hands and continued on obliviously. Fingers – still holding the ball – was carried half-way to the opposite boundary.

"IN!" cried the umpire, and – to steal a cliché – the crowd went wild!

———◆•▪•◆———

Outside The Bear's pavilion, Hops beamed expansively at the ongoing celebrations. Terry was bobbing above the proceedings on the shoulders of his team-mates; people were singing and dancing and embracing; and the barmaids were kissing everyone in sight (even Roffo, who stood about with a slightly peeved expression on his face). Hops took a deep pull from his glass of ale and mentally turned his thoughts to the evening's entertainments. It was going to be a splendid occasion, no doubt about it! He'd make enough money during the coming night to keep him in his favourite vices for a whole year. If only he could somehow give Mrs Hops the slip, he thought, he might even be able to afford a holiday. Perhaps he could persuade her to visit her relatives? Hops smiled even more broadly and tried to remember where he had hidden the travel agent's brochure for Nudia.

As Hops supped once more from his glass, a shadow passed before the late afternoon sun. The innkeeper glowered and turned to see what it was. A weak smile spread across his face. "Ah, er, Manis. It's you. Um, has it been raining?"

The sodden proprietor of The Pilgrim scowled at his bitterest foe. "You may mock me now, fatso, but the boot will soon be on the other foot, oh yes!" Suddenly, Manis pointed a finger at Hops, causing his saturated sleeve to slap against his arm and little droplets to splash onto the target of his venom. "By this time tomorrow … by this time … arg! What's the use? You'll see. Enjoy your time in the sun … *while you still can*!" And with that, the river-soaked innkeeper about-faced and stalked back to his pavilion, occasionally stopping to kick a celebrant who had gotten too close.

Occum sidled up to Hops, a glass of ale in each hand and lipstick wounds across his face. "Not exactly a good loser, that one. But I wonder what he meant?"

Hops shrugged his shoulders and stared at Manis's retreating back. All he knew was that his enemy rarely made threats in vain. With a now-glum face he turned away and went off to have a word with Terry.

Chapter 5

Shit Happens!

M ELANCHOLY AND despair were making their annual visit to the losing inn, their presence sapping it of its usual convivial atmosphere. Those customers who were present sat slouched in their seats, staring mournfully into their drinks. The only sound to disturb the miserable contemplations of The Pilgrim's clientele came from Young Festers, who stood in one corner facing the wall, blubbing softly.

Manis raised a hand and attempted to swat a hole in the blue haze of depression that hung in the air. "Well, we're a sorry lot aren't we," he said, leaning over the bar and addressing his customers in the manner of a priest delivering a sermon from his pulpit. A few sad faces turned towards him. "Do you think it's all over? Do you think we are finished?" He glared at his pathetic followers. "No! We have merely lost the battle, not the war! Let us learn from our defeat and grow stronger as a result. Already, as I speak, our forces have taken to the field of combat, and soon, oh, so very soon, new weapons will be arriving from the East! And then, my people, my friends, my followers, we will rise again – rise to claim out rightful place as the number one inn *in the entire world*!" As he finished his speech with a screeching crescendo, Manis thrust one hand into his shirt, flung a beer towel over his head, and stood to erect attention, his head tilted upwards, assuming the classic pose of a great leader. To a man, his customers let out a long, sad sigh and went back to staring into their ales. "Tossers," muttered Manis, sullenly.

In the background a blues minstrel started to sing.

"I woke up this morning, oh yeah,
I got them cricketing blues …

Our physio is a doctor … treats people with the pox;
There's a gigantic family of pubic lice … living in my
box.

Ooooh, I can't get my hand round my balls … can't get
my googlies to spin;
There's a large barbarian on their team and … we've no
chance to win, uh-huh.

Yeah, I got myself a short leg and captain – he's made
a silly point;
Took a bouncer in the face and … got my nose knocked
out of joint.

Oh yeah, I … got them blues, uh-huh, them … cricketing
blues …
I got them blues until I die …"

Manis stormed over to the warbler before he could get stuck into the
next verse. "If you don't shut up," he bellowed, "or sing something a
bit more cheerful – and I don't mean 'Down in The Pilgrim' either –
I will personally cure you of the Blues once and for all!"

The blues minstrel grinned to himself. Threats – yeah! That was the
ticket! Now, if he could just get beaten up, and have his lute broken,
and maybe have his nose bitten off, that would be really inspirational!
Believing whole-heartedly in suffering for his art, the minstrel waited
until Manis had regained his place behind the bar before launching into
a maudlin song about a puppy dog, a cliff, some lightning, crocodiles,
lots of rain, a mis-directed arrow, a little lost girl, and a savage pervert
with serious mental problems. When the Berserker began to feed the
lute down the ministrel's throat the inn's clientele actually showed a
modicum of interest. But the entertainment was brief, and all were soon
sighing and staring into their pints once more.

In The Bear, Hops beamed broadly. The inn was full to bursting point
and a comradely good-naturedness pervaded the place. Better still, Hops
had been forced to empty the cash box twice already with no more than
a couple of broken glasses on the debit side. He had not even had to call

Terry into action. And – best of all – he had been able to observe his reluctant employees earning their pay for a change.

"Heddy, my lass," he chortled, "there's a gent at the other end of the bar who either wants your address desperately, or else desires a pint of our finest. Jepho, you rogue, it's about time we had some clean glasses. Jump to it! Roffo, lad, go and sweep the room for empties ..."

"Aw, boss!" groaned Roffo, "it's bedlam out there! A man could die in that crush! And I'm knackered ... all that *running about*, you know, *helping to save the day ... valiantly fending off the enemy ...*"

Hops laughed. "Aye, and I remember a dropped catch or two along the way! Just see to it that my glasses don't suffer the same fate!"

Roffo developed a glum expression. "*Well played Roffo, my lad!*" he muttered to himself. "*I know, why don't you take the evening off? Yes, and have a drink on the house, too, why don't you? After all, nothing is too good for the hero of the hour ...*" But Hops had already turned away and missed the bitter mimicry. The young barman sighed to himself. He had not received a single freebie – not one! Occum, propped against the bar, had not had to dip into his purse once, while Terry had consumed the best part of a barrel of gratuities – without any apparent effect! Roffo felt a moment of pique at his friend: there he was, with his mighty constitution, able to out-drink the combined efforts of a whole division of rugby players, while Roffo could happily get out of his skull on a couple of pints. The ale almost seemed wasted on the barbarian. Of course, Terry would have cheerily passed some of his drinks Roffo's way, but that wasn't the point. *Even Horus* had been the victim of liquid generosity – and he had been out for a duck!

Roffo made a face at Hops's back, then girded his loins to enter the chaos of the lounge bar.

The Gebrullian Islander hopped about nervously as he waited for the proprietor of the inn. He was very much on edge and wished himself back at the caravan where the Potoon's authority – and more importantly, his scimitar-wielding guards – could protect him from the dangers of the outside world.

This was Yershah's first time away from the island of Gebrull – a half-drowned brown hillock that squatted in the Perdan Sea off the Samark coast (from whence his master came). The wispy-bearded young man had already experienced enough excitement to last a lifetime; enough, indeed, to make him yearn for the boring, olive-tree-scattered, goat-strewn slopes of home. And this place, this town … it was madness incarnate! Great Basmati protect him! The evening had started poorly and then gone downhill. To start, he had been chased by a lamenting group of grey-cowled individuals, who had responded to his polite request for directions with a shower of rotten fruit. He had managed to escape from that horde only to blunder into a party of singing bears! Well, how was he been supposed to know that they were merely men in disguise, performing some strange rite? It had scared *more* than the willies out of him, and made him glad of the *room to move* afforded him by his baggy red pantaloons … but the washer women were going to hate him tomorrow! And since then, every request he had made for directions to The Pilgrim had either been met with wails of grief, or with unkind suggestions as to what he could do: to himself, with what, with whom, and in what way. He had only stumbled upon the inn by chance after following the Great Road into the Square itself.

And now Yershah had been left waiting outside of this gloomy place – reminiscent of a funeral parlour – alone, untended, and with none of the basic courtesies or amenities that (in his land) were the due of the guest. Where was the warm water, fresh towels and perfume for him to refresh himself after his journey? Where were the delicacies to assuage his hunger from the road? Where was the customary glass of wine? True, he was not due to stop for the night, but even the sight of a winsome bed-maiden would have warmed his chilled heart! But what he really, *really* yearned for, right now, was a temporary change of clothes, a stout brush, some soap, and a toilet. He shifted on his feet uneasily and something solid rubbed stickily against his leg. Yershah winced. He turned his attention to the inn across the Square. He was sure he would have got a warm welcome there! The place was well-lit and jovial, with sounds of merriment and song providing a constant background noise. And it was busy, too, with more and more people joining its complement even as he watched (though many of these wore the frightening bearskins). Indeed, the inn was so full that its clientele had been forced to spill outside onto the cobbles of the Square, forming a great, joyous semi-circle about the portal.

The messenger heard a sharper noise, near to, and turned in time to see the front door of the dimly lit inn creak open. A stout, black-haired man bustled out, followed closely by an immense man with a naked, well-muscled chest.

"Is it here?" asked Manis, urgently. A shiver of anticipation coursed through the innkeeper, causing him to feel light-headed. He wiped his

slick palms upon his greasy tunic and looked about. "Do you have it …
I don't see it … no! *No!*" A sudden wave of fear and concern swept across
the innkeeper. "Don't tell me – it's gone! Lost! Stolen!" Manis began to
gibber. "Bandits in the valley? An attack of giant slugs? Swallowed by
an earthquake? Please, tell me, where is it?"

The Gebrullian tried to shake off the tightened fists that had suddenly
attached themselves to the floppy lapels of his scarlet tunic. "Calm yourself,
oh munificent one! The cargo is here. It is safe. It is a meagre three miles
from town, bivouacking for the night with the rest of the caravan."

Manis was momentarily dumbstruck. "Three miles? What good
is it to me three miles away? I need it here, now!" He paused to slick
back his hair with one hand, giving him time to regain his composure.
He looked the messenger up and down, realising for the first time how
young he was. An imperious look crossed the innkeeper's face. He dug
into a pouch on his waist belt and fished out an insultingly small coin.
"Quick, boy," he said, flicking the coin to the Gebrullian, "return to
your master and urge him to leave the caravan at once. Tell him to come
on into town. Tell him I will make it worth his while."

Yershah stared at the coin in misery. All those frights he had suffered,
and the revolting discomfort too, and now he had to return to the caravan
on the instant – unrefreshed and unrested – with nothing to show for it
but *this*! His shoulders drooped. He about-faced and slowly set off back
up the road to the east. He had only gone ten yards, however, when the
ungracious innkeeper bellowed after him: "And hurry!" Cursing under
his breath, Yershah started into a trot. As he jogged away, his every stride
was accompanied by a rhythmic sound …

Splat-splat, splat-splat, splat-splat.

"You really think this is going to work?" asked Burble, the shortest of
the yakkers. His tone indicated that he, at least, did not.

"Our orders are to sabotage The Bear," said Trespass, with some
exasperation. "Just how do you think we're going to do that from the
outside? And if you want to walk in there *without* a disguise so that
everyone can recognise you, well that's your choice. But I won't be
going to the funeral."

"Yeah yeah, okay," said Burble mournfully. He stared down at the
flimsy, ankle-length gown and shook his head. "But why do we have
to be disguised as *women*?"

"Aye," said Bruce, "this is daft. We'll nivver get awa' wi' it."

"'Sright," said Frunge. "*And* my yak-mask thingy won't stay up. *Look!*" In the dimly lit outer reaches of The Merry Bear's lamplight, the burly yakker attempted to fix the thin, blue fabric of a veil onto the side of his head covering. After several unsuccessful attempts he found that the only way to make it stay in place was to tilt his head backwards, letting gravity aid the frictional force between fabric and facial hair. "Anyway," continued Frunge, with his neck angled at forty-five degrees to the vertical, "with our beards it makes us look like we've all got swollen waffles!"

"*Wattles*," corrected Picket, with a sigh, "I think you mean wattles. And that veil thing is called a *yashmak*." Picket stood at least a foot shorter than the shortest of the five lovelies clustered around him. He suffered from the same problem as the hirsute ones, but in his case his slippery pate provided so little friction for his headscarf that he had been forced to smear a sticky black unguent onto his head to act as a glue. Aside from the fact that the unguent was beginning to melt, giving off an odour like a sweaty bear's crotch, *and* the fact that he had been hustled by Manis from a salacious assignation in order to chaperone the yakkers on this mission (to ensure that they *definitely did* get into trouble), *and* the fact that his gown was several sizes too big and hideously uncomfortable, *and* the fact that he was consequently as hot as the contents of a cannibal's pot ... everything was just fine. Oh yes indeedy. "Bollocks," said Picket, quietly.

"Yeah, that's wot I think!" said Grunt, overhearing the fence's *sotto voce*. "And wot if we're caught? I can't even get in a proper punch, wot with all this lace and stuff ..." The giant attempted to demonstrate his point by swishing his arm about ineffectually.

"Shut up!" growled Trespass. He liked the plan no better than the others, but it was Manis's scheme and he wasn't about to gainsay Mr Tetchy. Besides, the leader of the pack had his own score to settle with The Bear, and with Terry in particular. "First, we'll never get noticed in this crowd, and second ..."

"Second," interceded Picket, "even if we are, no-one will be able to catch us because they'll be too busy laughing their balls off."

"Right, er, *no!*" Trespass glared over the top of his veil at the joint head of the mission. "Second, we're not to get into any fights ourselves ..."

"Aw, Tres ..."

"Come on ..."

"Please ... just a little scrap ..."

"No, no, NO! No fights! And remember, we've got to stay in character too." Trespass scowled at his men. The time for talking was over: *now* was the time for action. He started to usher his men forward. "So," he continued, "remember that you're Eastern ladies who've recently arrived in town with a caravan. You're here to sell your, er, *wares*. You act ladylike. You *do not* act like animals. You sip your pints gracefully. You *do not* drink them down in one go and then belch loudly. You talk playfully with men." By now they were outside the portal. "And *do not* ogle the women. And, most importantly of all," he brought his party to a halt, "you *do not go* to the *Gents*. You go to the *Ladies* instead. Got that? And you can take those smirks off your faces. I know they're there, yak-masks or no yak-masks. Right. And when you're there, in the *Ladies*, what do you *not* do?"

"Ogle the women again?" suggested one.

"Steal the soap?" posited another.

"No!" cried Trespass. "*You do not pee standing up.*"

"Wot!" cried Frunge, in shock. This was all over his head. "You mean, we've got to *sit* in the urinals?"

———•••——

Jombers and Blewers were enthroned at a corner table upon a raised step of floor that gave an excellent view of the interior of The Bear. This was their table – a fact that was known, and respectfully acknowledged, by all of the inn's regulars. Occasionally, the odd foreign johnny unknowingly occupied the fellows' pitch, but this never led to ill-feeling. Indeed, being the gentlemen that they were, Jombers and Blewers ensured that even inadvertent trespassers received no less than splendid courtesy, a pint of ale, and perhaps, at the very end (should the message not otherwise get through) a light-hearted chivvying to another table.

"I say, Blewers old chap," said Jombers, out loud, as though he were still in the commentary box, "a jolly roisterous occasion this is turning out to be!"

"Er, roisterous, yes, yeees," pondered Blewers, thoughtfully, "though I *rather* think that a few of the fellows could do with some singing lessons. I also think they could learn a few more notes."

"My word yes – a bit monotonous is it not? Still, I rather like that song they're singing ..."

"Is that the rather *risqué* one about the things that pilgrims seek, or the Here We Go one. There are," Blewers explained, "only two songs."

"Only two – is that so? Well spotted old man! My word, they're singing them rather a lot then, aren't they! The travelling song is nice though … a bit repetitive, but jolly good fun!"

"You mean," said Blewers, "the one that goes something like: Here we go Here we go Here we go, Here we go Here we go Here we go-oh-oh …"

"I say – well done Blewers! A masterful rendition that! Do you know any more?"

"I'm afraid that's all there is to it. It continues that way *ad nauseam.*"

"Oh, that's rather ungenerous, old chum. Don't you mean *ad infinitum?*"

"In this case, Jombers old fruit, I am afraid I *do* mean *ad nauseam.*" He gave a wry smile and explained: "You see, they keep on singing until they're *sick*, and *then* they stop!"

"Oh Blewers," gasped Jombers, in the early stage of a fit of giggles, "you're such a wag!"

———————

Having successfully infiltrated The Bear, the fifth columnists forced their way through the shouting, singing, giggling horde towards the bar, a compact wedge of determined (and somewhat butch) femininity. They reached the bar and then spread, like a glob of spittle hitting a wall.

Trespass found himself next to Occum. The Angel looked down at his arch-enemy and, beneath his gown, he slowly clenched his fists. He took a number of deep breaths. What he was about to do next was the hardest thing he had ever done – but duty called, and Manis was not the most forgiving of masters. He cleared his throat and, in a staccato voice said: "Buy … a … nice … girl … a … drink?"

Occum looked around – then stared at the monstrous vision beside him. He raised his ale to eye level, frowned, and slowly shook his head. But when he lowered the glass he discovered that the horror was still there. It took him a moment to regain his usual sharp-tongued poise. "Sure," he replied, uncertainly, "know where I can find one?"

"You bastard!" Trespass began to raise his fist, but the clinging fabric impeded its progress, giving the cross-dresser time to compose himself. He settled for: "Oh, you nasty man!" in a strained falsetto. He then added sniffily, for good measure: "Well sod you then!"

"Cor, that's fine language for a lady I must say," noted the barber to Grevis, his erstwhile drinking companion. "They breed these foreign girls rough you know. Look – this one's got the hairiest arms I've ever seen on a woman. Ever seen on an ape come to that."

"Phaw, yesh," slurred Grevis, in the sort of overloud voice characteristic of the well-and-truly 'faced. "An' look at the size of her mate! I like big women and that is def'nitely a big woman! Oy! You! Come here! Want a drink?" He gesticulated wildly in the direction of Grunt. The huge Angel looked around in confusion, wondering why anyone here would want to buy him a drink. He pointed to himself and mouthed the words "Who, me?", forgetting the obscuring presence of his veil.

Grevis leaned heavily into Occum, spilling the remainder of his drink down the barber's finest green felt tunic. "A playful tease of a thing ain't she, eh?"

A free drink was, as far as Grunt was concerned, a free drink. He shrugged his huge shoulders and stepped around his worried-looking leader to stand beside Grevis. As soon as he was in range, however, the first thing he received was a hard slap on the rump and a lecherous wink from his would-be benefactor.

"All right my darling, what do you fancy?" leered Grevis. "Something with a lot of *body*, eh?"

"Sod off you git!" yelled an indignant Grunt, using a most unladylike turn of phrase. With one fist he grabbed Grevis by the collar, while he drew back his other for a knock-out punch. But Trespass reappeared and draped himself heavily about Grevis's neck.

"Heh heh heh," giggled Trespass, in his best girlie voice. "She's just teasing you. Maybe if you bought us both a drink she'd be more, er, wotsit, *easy*. Isn't that right Grun ... er, Greta?"

"Er ... Ahh ... Yeah – heh heh heh heh."

Grevis turned sullen and started to massage his vice-clamped throat. "Erm, yesh ... cor, you foreign fillies are strong!" He leant over the bar and called out to the nearest barman. "Jepho! Oy, Jepho! Another pint of Old P. here." He gestured inaccurately at his new companions. "And I'll have a couple of halves for the ladies."

"Halves!" yelled Trespass and Grunt, in unison. Looks of *utmost* horror settled upon their partly shrouded faces.

The queue to the *Gents* outie – which lay beside the stables in The Bear's back courtyard – was long and slow-moving. The customer-contact part of the outie was raised on stilts and reached by stairs. Normally, such waste collection pits were dug into the ground, but most of the earth beneath the inn's courtyard was hard and rocky, and so the pits had been constructed above ground level. For this, and a number of other reasons, the scrawny, ginger-haired youth called Phlip looked over the scene with growing concern. It may only have been an outie, true, but it was his responsibility and his alone – and he was proud of it!

Philip had come from a family whose highest previous social standing had been as scarecrows. In his childhood days they had moved from hedgerow to copse, from one temporary home to the next, always seeking enough work to get by and to enable them to afford the odd luxury or two – like a bar of soap, or a second pair of underpants. But now ... now Phlip had a roof over his head, a responsible job and, the greatest of all possible honours, he had played for The Team! The thought of the day's victory still left a warm glow inside him and he periodically paused in his shovelling to bask in the memory. Okay, he had scored a duck, and dropped a catch, and nearly run out Occum during his short stay at the crease, but he had been there! He was a winner! Life was looking up!

An intestinal rumbling, followed by a series of low explosions, brought the ginger-haired lad back to himself. He eyed the queue again and started to chew upon his lip. The punters were going through the moss like nobody's business, while the waste level in the pit was starting to rise precariously near to the High Tide Mark. A tiny germ of guilt began to grow in the youth. Phlip had been so excited by the match preparations that he had forgotten all about the consequence of victory. He put his shovel down and walked over to his hut, which was situated at ground level beside the much smaller *Ladies*. Inside, he discovered just how desperate the situation had become. One box! Was there only one box of moss left? A hot, sticky feeling passed through him. He broke out in a cold sweat. He rummaged about through old wooden crates, under the rickety table, through the discarded sacking at the back. From next door came a sound like that of a mortar, and the hut trembled slightly.

A squeaking sound caught Phlip's attention. He turned to examine a cage on the table, within which were half a dozen lemmings. These had been part of a new Waste Disposal System that he had learned about at an Out-keepers' Convention, but which he had never managed to put into operation. *Re-usable arse-towels* they were called, but you needed a good supply of the critters plus plenty of soap and water to clean them up after use. *And* you had to take their teeth out. If the truth were told, Phlip had never had the heart to prepare the little things properly. Indeed, he would not have wished *that* fate on his worst enemy (although his Uncle Lombo, the old pervert, would probably have paid for the privilege).

Phlip bustled outside again and started to push his way through the queue to the *Gents*. When he reached the front, however, a brawny arm barred his way.

"'Ere, wait your turn, you!"

Phlip eyed the man at the door – a hulking brute with a goatee beard and a yellow kilt who was obviously from out of town. The man looked as though he could go through a whole box of moss in his own right.

Phlip was not a particularly courageous man, but this was *his* patch and no-one was going to mess with him here! He puffed out his chest. "Do ye know who I be?"

"I dunno, and I dun care. Back in line, squirt!"

"*Squirt!*" squeaked the indignant Phlip. "I'll have 'ee know this be *my* outie. *I'm* in charge here! Now let me pass!"

"A likely story – *not!* On your way, boy."

"Now look 'ee here …"

Phlip never completed his sentence. The kilted man – a warrior from Brigoon – picked him up with one hand and, with a flick of the wrist, sent him hurtling across the courtyard into a freshly swept pile of ordure. Phlip slipped into unconsciousness.

And in the collection pits, the level of waste continued to rise …

<hr />

A bead of sweat trickled down Hops's nose and, like a high diver from a travelling circus, threw itself from a great height into a small tub of liquid. Unfortunately for the bead (and for the recipient of the container) no-one noticed its death-defying leap, and its heroic actions went unapplauded. Hops passed the pint over to the monk who had ordered it.

"Barman," said the monk, "I search for men to aid me. Men who big in stature and heart – like angry mother water buffalo defending young. Men who need adventure – like lotus blossom addict need lotus. You have seen such men?"

The barman eyed the monk suspiciously. He opened his mouth to suggest that they did not really approve of *that sort of thing* in his inn, when his gaze alighted upon the shiny coin that had magically appeared in the brown-robed individual's hand. He wet his lips.

"Adventurous blokes, here?" Hops's gaze never left the coin. "We've got merchants – no? Traders? Tinkers? There are some Smiths in here: they're quite hearty blokes?" With each suggestion, the monk gave a short, curt shake of the head. "Ah, well, I'm sure if you stay around long enough you'll find some men who are, er, suitable for whatever you want, ha ha. The whole world is in The Bear tonight!"

"Ai-la!" exclaimed the monk. "This coin … is too much?"

Hops chortled to himself, but greed clawed desperately at his soul. "Er, no, not at all. Now, yes, ah, let me think… of course!" The innkeeper snapped his fingers. "Adventurous types … yes! I remember! Saw a couple a few moments ago … big blokes, *walked with a swagger*." He winked at the monk. "Went out back they did, to the outie I expect. You could go out and have a look, but I'm sure they'll come inside shortly."

"At last! Thank you!" The coin was released and the monk took his drink and turned away. He returned to his table to wait.

Hops scooped up the gold piece with an expression of triumph.

The mini-caravan moved along the deserted cobblestone street that divided Sarsus from the Latin Quarter, heading towards the Old Square. It moved through the night like a ghostly procession, the only noise of its passing coming from the occasional snuffle of a camel, or jingle of harness, or muttered curse from one of the green-turbaned drivers as he goaded a recalcitrant charge. Every now and then the troop would pass a band of staggering drunks, or a well-lit inn from which sounds of merriment could be heard, but by and large the houses and shops they left in their wake were dark and empty and silent, their denizens either asleep or out celebrating/bemoaning the day's events.

With the Square in sight, a figure stepped out from an alleyway and softly hailed the guard at the head of the procession. As the troop came to a halt, a brief conversation ensued between the two figures. After a bout of hand-waving and head-nodding the troop continued on its way, now following the new arrival. The caravan was led up a side street, and thus diverted from the Square and the possibility of being observed by unwanted eyes.

Manis waited by a gateway that served as the back entrance to the courtyard that lay behind his inn. As the first of the glum beasts of the caravan hove into view – trailing behind Spotty Wembers (The Pilgrim's junior barman) and a huge red-turbaned man who appeared to have lost his vest – Manis's heart skipped a beat. It was the sight of the lead camel's cargo, however, that really roused the innkeeper's excitement: a cluster of heavy, darkwood barrels on which – in the dim light cast by the smoky street torches – he could just make out the picture of a monk with an impish expression on his face and a startling bulge in the lower part of his habit. Manis rubbed his hands in anticipation and beckoned the plodding beast into the courtyard. As each animal passed by the innkeeper tallied up the complement of barrels: six per beast, fourteen camels (plus a few assorted carts and one palanquin, all disappointingly empty of barrels), giving eighty-four in all. Eighty-four! Would it be enough? As the score of heavily muscled caravan guards – with their red turbans, curly red slippers, and naked torsos – started to unload the cargo into a neat pile, Manis gnawed on his lip and tried to calculate how long his investment would last. His musings were interrupted by the nearby sound of someone clearing his throat. Manis looked around and found himself staring at a pair of nipples poking out of an immense brown chest. He slowly looked up.

"Effendi!" declared the man who had led the troop through the gates. "His magnificence, the Potoon, commands your presence to speak on matters of business."

Manis grinned at the man sheepishly and wondered where the Berserker had got to. "Ah, yes, of course. Lead on."

The guard led the innkeeper to one side of the courtyard, where eight more men stood about in various states of exhausted distress. A reinforced palanquin with yellow silk curtains rested beside them. As the pair approached, one of the burly bearers collapsed in a fatigued heap. The head guard once more cleared his throat. "Oh Magnificent One, the vile infidel who runs this unworthy hovel begs your attention."

Manis squawked at the insult, but before he could remonstrate with the guard the curtains twitched aside and a spectacular bejewelled slipper appeared. This was shortly followed by an attached leg that was like a great ham wrapped in silver foil. This was followed by a bit of a body, and then a bit more body, and then even more body. And then even more. The huge torso appeared to be wrapped in a silver and red tent. And then, finally, there emerged a small fat face beneath an absurdly large golden turban. The fat man held one chubby, beringed hand out to the head guard, who bowed low and took the hand. With a grunt of effort, the guard hauled the Potoon to his feet. Each of the ten fingers on the merchant prince's hands, Manis noted, held enough gold rings to ransom a kingdom. Not that Manis was *impressed* by wealth – oh no. He was *awed* by it.

The innkeeper somehow found – in his limited facial repertoire – an obsequious grin. He bowed. "Welcome to my inn! I hope your journey was a good one."

The Potoon wrinkled his face in displeasure. "It was okay," he said, in a squeaky voice. "But it was quite wough foah the bandits who twied to wob me … as you can see." The Potoon snapped his fingers. A man appeared from behind the palanquin, bearing a large chest. As the fat merchant snapped his fingers again, the red-turbaned man opened the chest. Not knowing what to expect, Manis leant forward to peer inside. What he saw were several dozen severed hands. He gulped hard.

"You see," continued the Potoon, "I took gweat care of yoah goods. I now expect you will take gweat care of me!"

"Uh, yes, wight on, I mean, right on." Manis mopped his brow. This was big time! This bloke had style, and money, and lots and *lots* of guards. The innkeeper straightened his back. Well, he could be big too! He was not just any old dumb hick – maybe not yet a prince, but who knew what the future might bring? Manis knew all about the Samarks' obsession with decorum and form: he would show the fat git that he also had sophistication and style, aye, and a modicum of power too! Manis turned and snapped his fingers at Spotty Wembers – who was standing a dozen yards away, supervising the unloading of the barrels and directing the burdened guards to the cellar. The youth looked at him in puzzlement. The innkeeper snapped his fingers again, but Wembers did not move: he simply cocked his head to one side, uncertainly. The innkeeper sighed. "Spotty, you moron," he bellowed, "get over here, and get here quick!"

As the blonde youth with the acne-infested face started to trudge sullenly over to his boss, he was brought to an abrupt halt by a rush of people suddenly passing in front of him. A young man with a wispy beard was being chased by a howling pack of beefy viragos wielding an assortment of scrubbing brushes. The women did not seem amused. Spotty let them pass and shook his head: *foreigners*! He ambled up to Manis. "Yeah boss?"

"Spotty," said Manis, severely, "we have an important guest tonight!" The innkeeper looked at the Potoon and effected a small bow. "We must show him the meaning of the word 'hospitality'."

Wembers scratched at his chin, causing several spots to erupt in white-and-yellow fountains. "Oh-kay. Spare bedroom?"

"Is it vermin free?"

"I think there's just a few rats left. Nothing serious."

Manis nodded. "Good! See that the bed sheets aren't too soiled, and then go to Sonia's and get her to send one of her girls over as a companion for our guest."

Wembers continued to scratch at his face, causing carnage amongst the zit population. "Anyone in particular?" He looked at the Potoon askance. "Perhaps Lame Blind Sally ... at least she wouldn't be able to run away."

"Good choice. And get Varicose Val as well. After all, no expense is too great for our esteemed visitor, eh?" The youth made to turn away, but Manis touched his arm. "Oh, and Spotty – you'd better rustle up some grub too." He turned to the astonished Potoon. "Will eggs, beans and chips do? Speechless, eh? I'll take that as a 'yes'."

The Potoon simply stared.

———————

Trespass was becoming desperate. They had been in The Bear for two whole hours now and their only successful act of sabotage had come when Bruce had emptied a small pot of vinegar into someone's pint. In fact, they had spent most of their time fighting off the amorous advances of the more drunken members of the clientele. Subtlety, Trespass mused to himself, was just not his forte. If only Manis had said "Kick the door in, beat up anyone you find inside, and then burn the place down" – he could have handled that. But this – skulking around in a dress and trying to use *subterfuge* – no, this was not him at all. He racked his brains for an idea. Maybe he could knock one of the lanterns off the wall and set light to the straw on the floor? No: the straw was probably too damp from spilt ale to burn. Maybe he could play two suitors off against each other? No, that wouldn't work either: he was only too aware of the imposing presence of the barbarian behind the bar: he'd quash any trouble in an instant. They had not even been able to drink very much, having rapidly discovered the impeding nature of the veil. Lifting this briefly for a quick gulp was risky in the extreme. Trespass had finally come upon the solution of using his veil as a sponge and then sucking the ale from it.

While Trespass's sluggardly mind churned through a variety of mischievous alternatives, an oriental fellow in a brown cowl walked up to him.

"Excuse, miss, but ..."

"I'm taken," said Trespass, hoping to deter further unwelcome advances.

The monk bowed. "Am happy for you. No. What want is directions to toilet, la? Do you know?"

"Sure, they're ..." A wooden door by the bar caught Trespass's eye. He knew the conveniences were out back, but what would happen if he sent the guy through that door? There was a *slim* chance some mischief might come of it. Oh well – at least it was something. "They're over there, mate," he said, pointing at the door.

The monk thanked him and headed for the door, with Trespass's amused eyes glued to his back. The monk made it to the door and reached for the handle. There was a scream from the bar. *Yes!* thought Trespass triumphantly.

"Oy, what are you doing in my cellar!" cried Hops. "Terry! Terry! Stop that man … he's after my ale."

Terry appeared as if by magic and gently grasped the monk by the scruff of the neck. "Mister Hops doesn't like anyone going too near his cellar. Um, *sorry*."

"Ah – apologies," said the monk, turning to face the barbarian. "Thought it was *Gents*. Obviously not."

"No," said Terry, with a jovial smile. "They're out back." With one hand he carefully turned the monk to face the correct direction.

"Ai-la! Your grip – it is like *hai-lo* of vixen after intercourse, when dog fox cannot escape her clutches!" The monk wheezed in laughter, his little face gurning in delight.

"Er, thanks."

"That okay!" The monk now eyed Terry up and down, taking in his huge stature. "Ah, yes, have met before … in market this morning by spice seller, that char-latan!"

Terry's face lit up. "Yeah, I remember. How're you doing?"

"Am fine now." The monk started to nod to himself thoughtfully. "Hmmm. See from attire that you barbarian from Northern Wastes. Obviously taken menial job while waiting for next adventure to come along, la?"

"Er … yeah, I guess so. Well, um, you *can* get a bit bored with ravaging kingdoms and, er, a nice quiet job can help, um, re-invigorate you."

"And been in quiet, boring job how long?" The barbarian held up a number of fingers. "Three months!" exclaimed the monk. "That long time indeed for barbarian!"

"Er, no," corrected Terry, somewhat uncomfortably. "I've been here three years. It's not bad you know. The pay's okay, and I've got a nice little room upstairs, and …"

"Three years!" exclaimed the monk again. "Three …"

"Shhhh!" hushed Terry, with vestigial racial embarrassment. "Don't tell everybody!"

"Three years! We must talk. Ai-la! It must be so. Will go and re-cycle some of this magnificent ale, then come back to speak more." He started off, then turned around and called back: "By the way, do you know story about origin of ale?"

Trespass, who had been watching these proceedings with some interest, had by now acquired a smile as broad as a yak's shoulders. By some anomaly, the door to the cellar lay beside, and yet actually *beyond* the confining wooden bastion of the bar. Perhaps the bar had once been longer, extending further to protect the door. Whatever the reason for this peculiarity, it now gave Trespass an idea. He had a plan. He rescued his men from their admirers and gathered them together in one corner.

"Right then you lot," he began, "this is what we're going to do ..."

On his return from the outie, the strange monk sought out the barbarian, then trailed after him like a loyal dog. Every which way Terry turned he found the monk already present, trying to monopolise his attention, trying to recount his tale. Due to the high background noise and the constant interruptions – as people bought him drinks and as he went about his bar duties – Terry only caught half of the story. As far as he could make out, there had once been a woodland geezer who had invented a really good ale which everyone had been trying to concoct ever since. The monk knew of a map that would lead him to a place where the recipe was guarded. Unfortunately, the map had been ripped into pieces to help hide the secret, and the pieces were distributed around the land. Also, there was something about great warrior priests who were a bit wary of strangers.

The monk brought his tale to an end and looked at Terry expectantly.

"Er ... nice story," said Terry, as he pulled another pint for a desperate customer. "And these warrior priests ... are they mates of yours?"

The monk gurned in displeasure, his face warping into a guise something like that of a lemon-sucking John Merrick. "You not been listening to word I say!"

"Of course I've been listening," replied Terry. "I've just not been *hearing*. It's a bit noisy in here."

"Pardon?" said the monk.

Terry frowned. "I said it's too noisy!"

"Ah, yes. This is so. Come. Must talk in private, in quieter environment, la? Let us go outside."

"I can't desert my post," said the barbarian, suddenly feeling rather uneasy. "I may be needed at any moment."

The monk gestured at the sudden calm that surrounded them. "Look – all empty glasses collected, all customer served …" and remarkably, it *was* true. This was one of those freakish moments in pub life when, with bedlam occurring all around, the bar itself seemed to be a zone of utter calm, like the eye of a storm. Terry turned to look to his left and found that Jepho, too, was suddenly leaning back against the counter, bereft of duties. "Let us go outside back door," continued the monk, "then can get back to duty pronto. Promise to be brief."

"Okay then … but for five minutes, max. I can't spare any longer. It's amazing how quickly mounds of dead glasses build up whenever I turn my back."

Yes, thought the monk to himself, nodding sagely, *mounds of dead things always build up whenever barbarians around!* He led the way outside.

The wealth of The Bear lay in its cellar: destroy the contents of the cellar and you destroyed The Bear. This Trespass knew, and this was his plan. All he needed now was a little distraction to give him and his crew time to get through the cellar door without being seen by Hops or his staff. The villains sidled near to the door – at the edge of the bar – and formed a dense hemi-circle of fluttering blue-black fabric, obscuring the doorway to all except those behind the bar. They waited. Trespass watched as the barbarian was led away by the curious little monk: soon after, Jepho disappeared too. Then the temporary calm around the bar came to a sudden end, and the barmaids were once more busied with frantic serving and fetching, while the diminutive Roffo was hidden within the heaving mass of the interior. And so that left just Hops, who never strayed far from his cellar. Trespass's nerves began to fray. Any longer and one of the missing bar staff might return. And then Trespass smiled, for he had seen the ultimate distraction. He signalled his colleagues to be ready.

Ancient Willy approached Hops. "There ain't no moss in your outie," complained the indignant one, "just a jug of cold water. What do you expect me to do, eh, *eh*? After I launched me brick boat I found there was nothing to swab me decks with. And I can't use cold water, not at my age. I'll catch me death! Besides, it brings me piles down. If there hadn't been some young whippersnapper in the next cubicle with a particularly long cloak I don't know what I'd have done!"

"Sorry," cringed Hops. "It must be the large crowd we've got in tonight and, er, the fact that moss is scarce at this time of year. I'll talk to Phlip about it later." A fly passed between the two men and made the biggest mistake of its short life: it buzzed into a cloud of Willy's foul breath. Even for a creature whose idea of a gourmet meal was a nice pile of runny shite, *that* atmosphere was toxic beyond endurance. It spluttered, falling lifelessly into an ashtray. Hops himself turned away, but was further disquieted by the appearance of one of the large, veiled women who had been mooching about and drinking very little. *This* one seemed to be on the verge of coming around the bar to talk to him. Hops's gorge rose as she waved playfully at him. He turned back from the devil to the deep blue sea. He hoped not to catch her eye again.

"That's as may be, young Master Hops," continued Willy, "but it's no excuse! This place has gone to the dogs since you took over, sonny. I remember when they used to have soft, scented moss all the time. Everyone used to say that this was *the* place to come to ease the strains of the day. And if they ever ran out so's you had to use leaves, they'd give you a free pint!"

Hops suddenly stiffened. "Nice try," he said, through gritted teeth. "Aye, I think that's the most original attempt to get a freebie all evening. You can have a pint of your usual … at the usual price of course."

"Bah, maybe I should take my custom to The Pilgrim, eh, *eh*?"

"If you want," replied Hops, with the unconcerned shrug of a man who knew that Willy would not get within ten yards of any other inn in town. Indeed, he was only suffered at The Bear because Hops believed it was his sacred duty to save all those poor little coins from the pits of horror otherwise known as Willy's Pockets. "However," he continued, "I do hear that the only thing they have in the outie at The Pilgrim is a clump of nettles. Blast! This barrel's run out. Do you want to wait while I change it or do you want something else?"

Willy gave Hops a wrinkled scowl and pointed to the next pump. The innkeeper shouted into the chaos of the lounge at Roffo – who was collecting glasses. "Oy, Roffo my lad! Go and change the barrel of Old P." For some reason Hops could not work out, the bilious woman at the end of the bar started dancing a little jig on the floor.

They were in! The five man wrecking crew bundled through the door, leaving Grunt outside as lookout. They quietly descended the stairs to The Bear's lower sanctum. At the bottom they stopped and stared, in reverential silence, at the scene that stretched before them. Nearby, housed in hive-like alcoves, were barrel upon barrel of life's great elixir: the mature ales, each bedded down perfectly, each carefully maintained at the correct temperature. Some were connected to verdigris-copper pipes, which sucked their contents upwards to the thirsty horde above, others were stacked close by, ready to be connected when required. Chalked symbols identified The Bear's own brews, while painted pictures and neatly lettered words, mainly in reds and yellows, identified the guest beers. A bit farther down, there were rows of other barrels whose contents were still maturing and developing their distinctive *Hoppy* flavour. Farther still were the bubbling vats where the landlord produced his own multitudinous brews. The panorama presented the invaders with the perfect picture of how to organise and run a small-scale brewing operation, and was a far cry from the disorganised scene of leaky patched barrels, dirty straw, and general filth, that Trespass and Grunt had found in Manis's cellar earlier that afternoon. Could they really wreck something so beautiful?

"*Yes*," hissed Trespass, rubbing his hands together in manic glee. "Let's do it! Don't touch the barrels connected to the pumps, we don't want them coming down to investigate. Concentrate on the others."

Suddenly there was a frenetic tapping on the ceiling. "We are discovered," wailed Picket, clasping at his headdress, "so close and yet—"

"Shut up!" hissed Trespass. "Quick – hide yourselves! It might just be someone changing a barrel!"

Picket spotted a large empty barrel and jumped into it, pulling the lid over his head. Trespass grabbed Frunge and dragged him behind several large bags of hops. Burble crawled into the only free alcove in the wall, pulling straw over the entrance in a desperate attempt to conceal himself. Meanwhile, Bruce looked around this way and that, only to discover that there was nowhere else left to hide. There was a commotion on the stairs and he panicked. Running pell-mell to the end of the cellar he dived head first into the nearest of the vats, hoping he could hold his breath until the danger had passed. If they caught him, he thought fatalistically in mid-dive, at least he would get a free bath.

———•••••———

At the top of the stairs the source of the commotion tried to extract himself from an extremely large woman who had taken a sudden liking to him.

"Unhand me, madam," demanded Roffo, "I'm not the sort of man who goes for any old floozy you know!"

"Really? Why not?" asked Grunt, surprised that there were men in the world who had standards when it came to choosing a partner. "I am."

At that, something clicked in Roffo's mind. Maybe it had something to do with the sheer size of the woman, or the gruffness of her voice, or perhaps it had to do with the yakky nature of her perfume, or maybe, just possibly, it was due to the fact that half of a very bushy beard was now showing out of the side of the woman's badly adjusted veil. Roffo reached up and snatched the veil away to reveal, rather than the face of an exotic maiden of secret charms, the lumpy visage of a man with a huge dirty beard like an inverted Christmas tree. The surreal nature of the situation temporarily befuddled Roffo's normally lucid mind. "You're a man!" he stated, unnecessarily. He made a grab for a passing customer. "Oy, she's a ma—"

Grunt gave Roffo a shove through the cellar door and rapidly followed, shutting the portal behind him with a sinister thud. He paused to listen at the door for a moment longer, but heard no more than general sounds of revelry. Nodding in satisfaction, he focused his malevolent intent on the barman, slowly moving toward him.

Roffo cautiously backed away down the stairs, keeping a worried eye on the scowling, 280-pound transvestite. His situation looked bleak indeed. And then it got even worse …

The creaking of a barrel lid distracted Roffo's attention; he looked around. A pair of evil eyes stared out at him from the gap between lid and barrel. A sack of hops rustled, and another shadowy figure stood up. "What are you doing here?" it asked the transvestite.

"This runt rumbled me," replied Grunt. "But don't worry. Nobody saw us come in." He grinned at Roffo and added, "We're all alone in the night."

To Roffo's horror, a second figure appeared at the shoulder of the one behind the sacks, and then, like a maggot wriggling from a rotten carcass, a third crawled out from one of the alcoves. Out of the barrel with the evil eyes rose yet another. All were wearing dresses. They stared at Roffo menacingly.

"Grab him, Grunt," ordered Trespass. "We'll stick him in a barrel and have some fun later."

"Stay away from me, you perverts!" screamed Roffo, who had heard tales about sailors being locked in barrels. "I warn you – I'm an expert at the ancient art of judont!" He made various chopping motions with his hands to back up this claim and then, as he attempted a high kick, proceeded to lose his balance and topple to the stone-flagged floor. The bearded face of Trespass loomed over him.

"Judont? Would that be the ancient art of making up stories?" A pair of large hands grabbed Roffo by his collar, lifted him to his feet, and then tipped him head first into the barrel recently vacated by the evil eyes. The lid was replaced, leaving Roffo in the dark. Shortly, the sound of hammering rang in the junior barman's ears.

Trespass called his men together. "Right, let's get organised. Grunt, you and Burble deal with the barrels in the wall. Picket, you and Frunge do the fermenting barrels. And Bruce and me will take care of the vats. Bruce? Now where's he got to?"

"Here I am," sang a somewhat slurred voice from one of the vats. "Jus' comin'."

A sodden Bruce pulled himself upright using the lip of the vat for support. After grinning broadly and idiotically at the rest of the party, he attempted to cock his leg over the side of the vat to scrabble out, but with little success. He overbalanced and fell back into the ale. The noise of the *splash* was shortly followed by a moronic giggle.

"I think he's as drunk as the proverbial smelly beastie," noted Burble, somewhat unnecessarily. "It must be good stuff: he's only been in there a couple of minutes."

"Leave him to me," said Trespass. "Now get moving!"

Grunt and Burble grabbed mashing mallets and set about the barrels in the wall, hammering out the taps with a whirl of arms. Frunge decided that he didn't need a mallet and attacked the stoppers in the fermenting barrels with his teeth. Once he had extracted a cork, Picket stepped in to tip the barrel over. The floor was soon awash with beer.

Trespass meandered around the vats, opening their taps and letting their contents flow away. When he finally reached the one in which Bruce was still imprisoned, he took a certain pleasure in twisting the tap and watching his inebriated comrade swirl around and around with the draining ale. While it emptied he turned back to see how the others were faring, finding that Burble and Grunt had finished de-tapping the barrels in the wall and were now taking a shower in the cascade of ale that flowed from them. Each stood facing a barrel, head up, mouth agape, drinking in the brew that rained down upon him. A floundering noise in the vessel behind brought the leader's attention back to his own task and indicated that Bruce had reached the bottom of the vat. Trespass leant over and proffered a hand.

"Help! I'm drownin'," moaned Bruce, as he lay on the bottom of his wooden prison, trying to do a doggy paddle.

"No you're not," replied Trespass, matter-of-factly. "Give me your hand."

Employing a swimming motion, Bruce crawled up the side of the vat and grabbed hold of Trespass's hand, allowing himself to be pulled from the receptacle.

"Trespass, ye've shaved my life," slurred the grateful Bruce. "Ye're my beshtist pal ivver an' I love ye!"

"Geroff, you pissed git – somebody get him off me!" As Trespass struggled to escape the clutches of his new amour, Picket came to stand nearby. His dress was plastered onto him and his yashmak had been washed away in the deluge, as had his head covering, although the black unguent still adhered to his pate and made him look like the victim of a particularly malevolent seagull with dysentery. He was rubbing at his jaw in a thoughtful way. "Er, when you've finished *mein leader* ... may I *enquire* how you plan to get us out of here? I mean, isn't it a *tad* risky to go through the bar door in our present state?"

"Och, Picket, ye wee baldie – I love ye tae! I want tae have yer bairns!"

"Shut up Bruce *and get your hands out of my pants!*" There was a brief scuffle and a flurry of blows. Trespass brushed his hands in a satisfied way, then turned back to Picket and affected an insulted voice. "Do you really think I'd come in here with only half a plan? That I would lead you into the lions' den and not know how to get out? Er, isn't it obvious how we escape?" The shaking of Picket's head told him that it was not, but this was something Trespass knew already. He looked skywards in a gesture that said "Why me, god?" – and that was when he saw the trap-door above his head. A smirk spread across the yakker's face. He looked down at Picket and sneered. "I'm not as dumb as you think, matey! And just remember, when we see Manis later, this was *my* plan and not yours. Okay?"

Picket nodded meekly.

"Right then. How do you think they get all these big barrels ..." he pointed at the empty carcasses that now littered the cellar "... and all these big bags of ingredients in here? They don't carry them down that small, windy staircase, that's for sure. No, they lower them in from the outside through a trap-door. In fact, through the trap-door that's above my head."

Frunge, who had waded up to join them, looked up. "Brilliant! I don't know how you come up with them, Tres."

"Natural talent! You roll a barrel underneath the door so we've got something to stand on. I'll collect the others."

With a considerable amount of effort, and no small protest, Trespass managed to drag the others away from the free ale that they were desperately consuming. The fountains had declined to a trickle, so Burble and Grunt had dropped to their hands and knees and were slurping the escaped ale up from the floor before it could seep through the cracks between the flags. Pushing the pair ahead of him, Trespass watched as Frunge tried to shoulder the door open. But the door pushed back, obstinately refusing to move. Frunge tried several more times.

"It's either rusted up or there's something resting on the other side."

Trespass groaned. "Grunt – you're strongest. Give it a go."

Grunt climbed onto the barrel and gave the door an experimental shove. There was definitely something on the other side, but from the slight give in the door he thought he might be able to move it. He shifted his position and stood directly under the door with arms and legs bent. He screwed up his face into an expression akin to that of the chronically constipated, and heaved. Slowly but surely his arms and legs straightened. A gleam of moonlight lit his reddening face and the dancing veins that stood out on his temples. When he was almost vertical he tipped the door back. His face became a picture of ecstasy as the strain was released and the load dumped. The accompanying crashing and braying told the story of a mule that had chosen to stand on the wrong corner of the street that night.

Grunt gave an almighty roar and pulled himself through the trap-door. Trespass and Picket quickly followed while Burble and Frunge tried, firstly to get Bruce onto the barrel and then, secondly, to keep him there. After two false starts and one painful accident they got him up, then Grunt pulled him through the door. The two remaining yakkers scrambled through the opening and into the side-street. The gang crept around the corner onto the Square. They silently stole past the throng of people clustered outside The Bear's front entrance and made their escape across the empty market.

Manis, who was standing in the darkness of a nearby shop doorway, watched them go, wondering what they had been up to. He gestured to the Berserker and headed off towards The Bear. After a moment's thought, the Berserker picked up his drum and followed.

———◆·◆·◆———

Hops pulled at the pump. *Nothing*. What was the lad up to? He should have changed that barrel of Old P. by now. It was one of his most popular brews, and the customers were crying out for it. The innkeeper stared out of the window, thinking of all the nasty jobs he would give

Roffo in revenge for denying his customers the chance to give him their money. And then he saw a strange sight. There, outside, was a donkey, apparently *growing* before his very eyes! Up it went, getting taller and taller until… it toppled over and collapsed out of sight. Hops looked around the room, but no-one else appeared to have seen it. Maybe he had been working too hard? Maybe he had just imagined it all? Yes – that was it. Funny thing, the imagination. He would just take a quick break to clear his head.

"Maddy," he cried. "Maddy … ah, there you are, lass! I'm just off to see what's keeping Roffo. I'll be back in a minute." And, before any voice of objection could be raised by the remaining overworked barstaff, he made a quick escape through the cellar door.

Hops mopped his perspiring brow and staggered down the stairs. He didn't usually hallucinate … in fact, the last time he could recall was when he had accidentally eaten one of the ghastly Mr Puns's pies (when the blighter, aware of his reputation, had hired an innocent lad to purvey his evil wares). Maybe it was just a mirage thrown up by the combination of the intense heat in the bar and the vast clouds of cigarette smoke that hung over the tables like miniature mushroom clouds? When Hops reached the cellar, however, he stopped short in shock – and this time he sincerely hoped that the sight before his eyes *was* an hallucination …

While Hops stood in his cellar, in shock, Manis entered the inn. *Enemy territory!* He looked around the crowded bar and thought about how soon this might all be his. He grabbed a chair that an unsuspecting member of the public was about to sit on, and laughed evilly as the man collapsed backwards onto the floor. He then placed the chair in front of the door, climbed on top, and cleared his throat.

"My friends, hear me! I would just like to …" his voice trailed off as he realised that no-one was taking any notice of him. He gestured to the Berserker and pointed to the drum that he was holding. The Berserker handed up the instrument.

"Thanks," said Manis absently. He looked down at the thing in his hands. "Wait a minute … I don't need to bang my own drum. That's your job!" He thrust the drum back into the Berserker's midriff and made a drum-playing motion with his hands. The Berserker drew a stick from the back of his trousers and proceeded to give the drum the beating of its life, only stopping when its taught brown skin ruptured. The noise in the bar reduced to a low hum, as the punters fearfully looked towards the hooligan and his doomed drum.

"If you will excuse this brief interruption to your celebrations," began the chief of the intruders, "I would like to show you that we in The Pilgrim have no hard feelings, and I would like to congratulate you all on your fine performance this afternoon." A loud raspberry greeted his overture of friendship. Unperturbed, Manis continued. "I know that in the past we've had our differences, but I think it is now time for change. I think we should bury the hatchet."

"In whose head?" shouted a wag from the floor – to enthusiastic laughter.

Manis made soothing motions with his hands to try to quell the whooping crowd. A sour look fleetingly passed across his face. "Ah, yes, the old ones are still the best! Anyway, to show my commitment to our friendship I would like to invite you all over to my inn to try out some of our fine ales, which are on special offer this week." This proposal was greeted by various puking noises and obscene gestures. "This week, we have on tap our usual Rear Thruster, Lethe Ale, Jock Strap, and the rare BR Porter. Our guest ale is the renowned Fullney's Black Death." And now Manis paused. This was it, his big moment. A tingle of excitement traversed his spine. "Oh, and one more thing," he said casually, as though it were no more than an afterthought, "we also have, as of half an hour ago, from the famed temple of Worth-In-Ton, their marvellous, much-praised, and much sought-after ... *Mardon's Pedigree ale!*"

The crowd went silent.

A pin made a huge racket as it hit the floor.

"Not *Mardon's Pedigree?*" said an astounded voice from somewhere in the midst of the bewitched crowd.

Manis smiled and nodded.

"Did he say Mardon's Pedigree?" asked another, scarcely believing his ears. "Mardon's Pedigree!"

"Yeah," said a reverential voice near to the speaker, "they say it tastes like nectar ... alcoholic nectar, of course!"

"Sod that," said another, "isn't it also supposed to, er, wotsit, make your, um, *manhood* grow in size? I mean *really* grow!" The man, who was near to the door and standing, turned to face the eager punters and drew his hands apart to designate a dimension that would have embarrassed a compulsively lying fisherman.

"No ... *really?*"

"*Mardon's Pedigree!*"

Manis cleared his throat to regain the crowd's attention. "Er, as to the claims of Pedigree's *enhancing* properties, well, there *are* rumours. How can I put this? Earlier, our dear friend Rudy Brassrubbers purchased a small sample of the brew. When he got up to go to the outie he, how can I put this, knocked the table over *without using his hands*!"

The silent crowd thought about this for a moment. The famed Mardon's Pedigree! And the rumour ... apparently it was true! A short grey-haired man by the bar put down his glass and addressed his friends.

"I've, er, just remembered, er, I've not put the, er ... cat out. I'd better go. See you tomorrow," and he shot out the door to the cry of "See ya Stumpy!"

The awed silence allowed Stumpy's pathetic excuse to be broadcast across the entire inn. People looked at one another askance. Waiting. Deciding. Weighing up options. Some looked around for the barbarian, and others for Hops, but neither man was to be seen. The men began to get restless, while the women hid their smiles (and anticipations) behind handkerchiefs or raised hands. *Who next?* they all thought. And then, suddenly, as though some unconscious collective decision had been reached, every man in the room slammed down his tankard, rose up, and headed for the door.

Manis screamed.

As they headed towards The Pilgrim, the tide of desperate men swept the innkeeper from his chair and trampled him underfoot. As the stream of people bottlenecked in the doorway, many a man was inadvertently pulled to safety by the Berserker, who desperately fought to find his employer. Occum was carried away in the rush (as he later claimed to all who would listen – which was quite a few, given his propensity to wield sharp implements). Jepho deserted in the face of the enemy (vaulting over the bar), and was one of the first to pass over the new Manis Welcome Mat. Fat Grevis was bounced about like a gigantic beachball. Heddy leapt onto the bar in a desperate effort to avoid the stampede. And Ancient Willy, unable to make headway against the crush, grabbed hold of Eddie as she passed him by.

"What do *you* want a big dick for, eh, *eh?*" he enquired, above the hubbub. A raised eyebrow, a wistful look, and a licentious smile told Willy all he needed to know.

In the space of a single, solitary minute the inn was cleared. A track cut across the market from one of Cross-My-Way's favourite watering holes straight to the other. Fragments of clothing, dropped hats and broken glass littered the path. The last of the exodus to leave was Manis, now much-flattened, who was carried out on the muscular shoulders of the Berserker. The Pilgrimites left a scene of carnage in their wake.

———•••••———

After the passing of a long minute of silence, a head appeared above the bar. Maddy surveyed the destruction before her: crushed tankards, shattered glass, overturned tables, chairs that had been splintered and strewn about the stone flags like big pieces of straw. Many of the horse brasses had been jostled from the wall, while the portrait of Hops's dear old daddy now hung askew. Around the room, three small fires from upset candles burned away cheerily.

"Shit!" said Maddy.

Heddy, the only other soul in the room, climbed off the bar. Her feet crunched as they touched the floor. "If Hopsie thinks I'm going to stay on late to clean this mess up," she began, "he's got another think coming!"

"Too bluddy right!" said the other barmaid. "And where is he anyway? Skiving off while we've been working our butts off *and* nearly been stampeded to death! It's not right!"

"And where's Terry? He should of stopped this … that's wot he's paid …" a low rumbling sound cut Heddy off, mid-moan. "Whassat noise?"

———•••••———

Outside the back door, Terry had listened patiently to the monk as he had run through his tale for the umpteenth time. Even before the monk had come to The Point, Terry could guess where all of this was leading: a request for help; the offer of untold riches, fame, excitement, *adventure*. The barbarian shifted about uneasily on his feet. It sounded as though he was about to be made the sort of offer that no red-blooded barbarian could refuse.

As Terry pondered how to refuse the unrefusable, he suddenly noticed two very striking things. The first was that the noise from the lounge had, incredibly, abated. He thrust a muscular finger into one ear and twirled. No difference. But it couldn't be his hearing, for he could still hear the excitable voice of the curious little oriental. He was about to go and investigate when he noticed, out of the corner of his eye, the second unusual thing. It was a pair of feet. The strange thing about *these* was that they protruded from under a huge pile of ordure.

"Hold up," said Terry, deciding that this definitely needed investigating, "what's that?"

He stalked over to the heap of dung with the silky intent of a panther on the track of game. The monk threw up his hands. "Barbarians!" he muttered. "Why I bother?"

Terry reached the scene and surveyed it for a moment, working out how to extricate the poor buried individual without dirtying his hands. He found an angle of attack, bent down to grasp the mysterious ankles, and gave a yank. A body slid out from under the pile. Who it belonged to, however, was not initially obvious. It looked like the perverse result of a genetic experiment to cross a man with the contents of a sceptic tank. Terry grimaced, brought out a glass-cleaning rag, and smeared some of the excrement away from the body's face.

"Phlip!"

The turd-man groaned.

"Phlip ... are you all right? It's me, Terry."

The outie cleaner groaned some more and then started to thrash about. "No ... NO ... not the straw hat again dadda ... *please*, don't make me do it ... ah, the birds, *the birds*!"

"Tsk tsk!" muttered the monk. "Him not right in head. Shit in brains."

Terry frowned, then looked around. He noticed a bucket of water against one wall and went to retrieve it.

"Nice Mr Lemming," raved Phlip, flopping about like an incontinent beached whale. "Nice lemmies, yes, nice nice. Ye know I wouldn't of dun it ... no I wouldn't ... no. No lemmies ... what are ye doing? Let me go! Not him, no, don't give me to him ... please sir, no, not the bum, no ... *aaaaaagh*!"

The water from the bucket slapped into Phlip's face. The outie cleaner suddenly quietened. Then he opened his eyes and sat up.

"Are you okay?" asked Terry once more, concern etched onto his unshaven face.

Phlip looked down at himself. His face contorted in horror. "Oh, no! I thought it wuz just a dream... the lemmings ..." Realisation brained him like the well-thrown saucepan of an angry wife. He shook his head, causing gobbets of poo to fly off at various angles. Terry and the monk beat a hasty retreat. "Now I remember!" continued Phlip. "The hooligan in the dress! Bastard! Alls I wanted to do wuz check the moss situation." He smiled sheepishly at Terry. "Then I wuz going to drain the pits. Urm, how long have I been out?"

Incomprehension settled onto the barbarian's face. "I don't know. Why?"

A low rumble from the direction of the *Gents* outie came back in reply.

"Ahem. Good sires!" said Phlip, getting rapidly to his feet. "I does suggest we find high ground ... and does it *quick*!" He broke into a sudden sprint and headed into the stables, where ladders led up to a loft. Acting on pure instinct, Terry swept up the monk and sprinted after him.

In the outie, the evening's last customer sensed that he might, in more ways than one, have just done a boo-boo. Without even stopping to hitch up his slacks, he waddled desperately towards the door. Beneath him, the straining dam of the outie walls began to protest and buckle ...

The man would never make it.

———•◦•◦•———

In the cellar, Hops still stood and stared. Occasionally, his eyes bulged and his mouth puckered like a gobstopper-sucking goldfish. His brain had reached a curious state, caught between switching off, denial, and horrified acceptance. As it swung between the options, various further activities animated the mannequin: his knees would start to go, and then recover; a wide-eyed smile would begin to spread across his face, and then recede; and tears would start to squeeze from his eyes, and then run dry. At last, the stand-off was broken by the heavy sound of the last escaping drop of ale from a once-splendid barrel ...

Hops's hands gripped at the two tuffs of hair that still fended off the wave of bald-patch from the shores of his ears. He would have howled, but his throat was suddenly as tight as an aerobic teacher's leotard. Instead, overwhelmed by the destruction of all that he held dear, he whispered desperately to himself: "The horror ... *the horror* ..."

In the dim light through the open cellar door he shambled forward. He reached out to stroke a broken casket, to collect up a drop of nectar. Surely this was Hull. *Nothing* could be worse than this ...

And then, suddenly, it *was*.

From the room above he heard a womanly shriek, a crash, and a curious slurping sound. He turned around just in time to see a monstrous brown waterfall start to cascade down the stairs, sweeping into the cellar, spattering the broken debris and the walls, lifting up bits of wood and other flotsam and jetsam, splashing against his boots, rising up his legs, pushing him back into the depths of the cellar. In a moment of self-preservation, Hops scrambled on top of a still-whole fermenting barrel.

The shriek that came from beneath him nearly made the innkeeper jump from his skin.

"Help!" wailed Roffo. "Get me out of here ... I'm gonna drown ..."

"Roffo, my lad, is that you?"

"Get me out ..."

Hops rolled his eyes at this utmost perversity of justice. He dropped into the waist-deep slurry. Eventually, he managed to lever off the lid of the barrel and rescue the youth.

By the time the flow had eased enough to allow Hops and Roffo to ascend the stairs, the trio from the stables had joined the two barmaids in what was left of the lounge. The group looked at each other disconsolately. Even the monk appeared upset. Then Hops smiled broadly and stupidly at everyone. And fainted.

CHAPTER 6

A RECIPE FOR DISASTER?

CROSS-MY-WAY WAS like a gigantic student pad the morning after the mother of all parties …

--------◆◆◆◆◆--------

Just off the Old Square, a bleary-eyed Occum fumbled with the key to the front door of his shop. Once inside, he flipped the sign on the back of the door to 'Open' and staggered across to the shelves on which his implements of barberdom were arranged. He carefully placed a hand on one shelf, far away from any of the cut-throat razors, and – like an arthritic spider – crawled his fingers towards the blades. They touched metal. "Aha!" he cried, sweeping up a razor. "No problem!"

A tinkling at the door announced the first customer of the day. Occum turned around to greet the man, cut-throat in hand, squinting to identify his victim. "Morning Sid," he said. "You're up early. A funeral to conduct, eh? What'll it be? The usual short back and sides?"

A look of complete and utter terror settled upon the face of Horus the farrier. His eyes momentarily alighted on the weaving razor, and a hand involuntarily jerked to his throat. He turned and fled back through the door …

--------◆◆◆◆◆--------

On a rooftop in Sarsus, a thief dressed in russet-tile camouflage gear staggered about like a victim of Mad Cow Disease. Mitchkin frequently had to pause to lean against a chimney stack to steady himself. He looked down and giggled: he actually had to crane his neck to left or right just to see his feet! That ale was amazing stuff! And as for his silhouette … Mitchkin's incredible anatomy was exaggerated still further by the long shadows cast by the early morning sun. The thief giggled once more and rotated his pelvis to point, in turn, at each one of a row of houses. "Eenie, meenie, minie moe … *you're* the lad, so in I *go!*"

Like a half-cut orang-utan, the thief swung down off the roof-top. His feet alighted on a narrow window sill. He slapped a treacle-covered piece of parchment against the pane. Mitchkin adjusted the bandage about his head and grinned dementedly. He'd not even need his cosh for this one! He swivelled his hips and brought his unnaturally reinforced tool against the window. The glass broke *almost* noiselessly, and Mitchkin pushed the parchment inwards.

Mitchkin's pleasure was to be short-lived. Inside the second-floor room, Satan the dog was half-asleep and dreaming about shredding cats, which, unfortunately for the thief, *also* meant that he was half-awake. The muffled sound of the parchment and glass shards dropping onto the floor brought him further from his reverie. Now, Satan was not a clever dog by any stretch of the imagination: whereas some dogs plot ways of getting their masters to take them for walkies, or devise plans for ambushing cats, or worry about the attractiveness of their testicle-scented breath to saucy little poodles, no such thoughts ever entered Satan's skull. In fact, Satan's mind did no thinking at all. Why should it, when his stomach could do the job just as well? For Satan, life was simply a succession of eating opportunities. Indeed, he was famous throughout the town as the only living creature able to keep down one of Awful Puns's pies. And now, here he was, barely able to believe his eyes. It was like a dream come true! For there, approaching him through the window, like a gift from the gods, was the biggest salami he had ever seen. Satan licked his slobbery lips and advanced …

Stumpy couldn't understand why it was light. He had set off for home *hours* ago, but still hadn't made it. He looked around in confusion. This was still Plum Street. He shook his head to try to clear it. He *did* remember walking along, thinking about the surprise he was going to give his plump little Katy… but then, for some unaccountable reason, he had found himself staring up into the sky, flat on his back. Weird!

He walked on a bit farther. With each step the confusion ebbed away and his thoughts returned to Katy. The little she-devil! Cor, she was going to be in for a bit of a surprise! Stumpy looked down, and as he did so, a further pint of blood rushed into the admired object and away from those parts of his body where it properly belonged. He managed to get out half of the thought: *What a whopp …*

Stumpy couldn't understand it. Why was he on his back? The sun shone down onto his face. Mid-morning? Was this still Plum Street?

"Cor, this is great!" enthused Junior, a young pigeon with a dash of purple on each wing and a total of five toes. "I ain't never seen so much food in all me life!"

"Yeah, Filthy would of loved it!" said another. "Puke: his favourite!"

"Who knows," said Fat Sixtoes, malevolently, hopping over to a piece of diced carrot, "maybe we're actually *eating him* at this very moment!"

"Cooo, that's sick!"

"Did you have to, cooo cooo, you've put me right off!"

"Heh heh," said Fats, "shove over then and let me at that piece of bile."

For a couple of minutes the pigeons fluttered about, hoovering through the multicoloured puddle. Junior paused for breath. "Do you know wot my favourite food is?" he asked. "Favourite food" was the flock's most popular topic of conversation, somewhat akin to the human debate about what one would do with a lottery win.

"Stale bread crusts?" suggested a one-eyed pigeon called Nelson.

"Nope."

"Rotting dog carcass?" suggested another.

"No."

"Fresh sewage?"

"Not even close. Give up? Goat waste, that's wot. I dunno wot they eat, but it comes out all spicy and stuff. Puts a real fire in the hold."

"I always said you were full of shit!" cackled Fats.

Nelson raised his good eye to look at Junior. He nodded his head in disagreement. "Coooo, you can keep your filthy foreign muck. Give me good old local fare any day. Mrs Balook's medicinal phlegm cakes for a start …"

"Cooo, yeah!"

"Or raw offal from behind the slaughterhouse …"

"Yeah yeah," interrupted Fats, "but this puddle's done and I'm still hungry. Come on, there's another one up in that doorway …"

"*One?*" commented a scraggly old pigeon, who had been staring at the target for some time, trying to work out whether his eyes were deceiving him. "One? That ain't a puddle, Fats, that's an inland sea! It looks like half the town gathered there for spewing practice. Either that or no-one likes whoever lives in that house."

"Yeah, whatever … last one there is cat food. Come on!"

The pigeons took to the air and fluttered over to the town's newest man-made lake. They had only just taken up residence, however, when an horrendous scream rent the air, sending the most nimble of the squadron into panicked flight. Unfortunately for Nelson, who had suffered a wing injury in the past, he was not amongst these …

A brief moment later, the air was filled with a flailing figure in russet garb. The most notable thing about this particular skydiver was his unprofessional demeanour, for he had clearly not been properly trained. Thus, instead of adopting the appropriate 'swooping eagle' pose, he had instead settled for a bizarre groin-clutching posture that was not at all aerodynamic.

Mitchkin looked in horror at the rapidly approaching sea of vomit and the rapidly-growing white speck in its midst. He passed through a confusion of wings and feathers. His speed increased as he continued to accelerate at 9.8 metres per second per second. The ground, relativistically, flew up towards him …

"Oh, *shiiiiiiiiiiit!*" cried the thief.

"*Bugg*—" went Nelson.

Splosh! went the lake.

Above the scene, Satan the dog looked down upon his escaping breakfast. For a moment he felt a terrible disappointment … but it was for a moment only. Then his eyes bulged. He couldn't believe what he was seeing. His mobile salami had fallen into the most delicious of sauces! Spattering big dollops of drool on the floor, Satan waddled to the door, nosed it open, and moved down the stairs as fast as his fat little legs could carry him.

Outside, the thief – now plastered from head to toe in the potpourri of Hull – limped away as fast as he could. A spitted pigeon, like a ship's figurehead, proudly pointed his way …

"You call *that* polished?" scolded Heddy. She stood over Jepho with hands on hips, supervising his burnishing of the bar. "I want to be able to see my face in it. Come on! Give it some elbow grease!"

Jepho stood up from his work and blew a bead of sweat off the tip of his nose. "How long are you going to keep this up? If I rub any harder I'll take the varnish off. I've already said I'm sorry …"

"Traitor!"

"Look, I was carried away in the press, okay? I struggled for my life, I did. But it was no use. Before I knew it I was across the Square, bundled through the doors into *that place*, and sandwiched against the bar. I had no choice!"

"Oh-aye," scoffed Heddy. "And I suppose various freebies were thrust into your protesting hands by the ever-generous Manis, eh? But of course not. You didn't drink a thing, did you? You spent all your time fighting to get out. *Hours* in fact."

Jepho frowned. "No comment." He bent back to his task, but then straightened almost immediately. "What if I plead temporary insanity?" The look on the barmaid's face told him all he needed to know. "Oh, ah, right, like that, is it? Okay. Best get polishing."

Heddy swivelled around to redirect her glare. "And *you* ... what are *you* scowling at?"

"Nothing," replied Eddie, testily, "nothing at all." She lowered her head and put some extra effort into cleaning a despicably soiled tankard. If last night had been as good as it had promised to be, then a few broken nails, some calluses, and a desperately soiled dress would have been a small price to pay, but as it was ...

"Good. Then get on with it!" Heddy scoured the ruined interior of the inn with searing eyes. Her expression softened as her glare alighted upon the innkeeper. She started to walk towards him. "Don't worry, Hopsie. We'll sort it."

The dejected figure – who was sitting on a stool (of the wooden variety) in the centre of the floor of the devastated inn – slowly lifted his head out of his hands. Two large plugs of ripe cheese were wedged up his nostrils to filter out the smell. The odour had initially been excruciating, although – as the rank toilet sludge had gradually solidified to form a crispy brown carpet upon the floor – it *had* declined somewhat. Now it was simply horrendous.

Hops watched as Heddy gingerly picked her way towards him. In places, the repulsive carpet had crumbled away to leave a number of filthy pathways on which it was *relatively* safe to walk. These had formed through accident rather than design, since they had decided to leave the cleaning of the floor until last. But the floor was a minor problem compared to the cellar ... Hops shivered at the thought. He didn't know whether he would *ever* be able to go down there again. Roffo had bravely volunteered for *that* task, while Heddy – with the determination of a matron in a ward full of motorway pile-up victims – had taken over the cleaning of the lounge and bar. In the meantime, the innkeeper simply sat and stared. Occasionally he groaned. And now, he thought miserably, it was about time for another …

"*Oooooooooohhhhh,*" went Hops. "*Ooooooooooooooaaaahhhhh.*" He thought a bit more and then decided to elaborate. "Oooohh … what's the point?" He briefly buried his head in his hands, before raising it again. "We're ruined. Ruined! Even if we get rid of the smell and make this place habitable again, the only ale we've got left is the stuff in the barrels that were on tap last night. And when that's gone –" he drew a finger across his throat "– we're out of business."

"Now now, Hopsie, things aren't that bad," soothed Heddy, who stood in the middle of the floor at the end of an incomplete path. She had nowhere else to go. "Something will turn up."

"Optimism is not what I want," moaned the innkeeper. "What I want is ale. What I want is money. What I want is some new furniture. But most of all, what I want is to know *why* the barbarian let Manis steal my customers, and *how* an entire horde of marauders managed to get into my cellar to destroy my beautiful ale. That," he concluded, forlornly, "is what I want!"

"I think you're being a bit hard on Terry," chided Heddy, gently. "After all, you did have him serving behind the bar for most of the night. How could he have carried out his protective duties at the same time?" The barmaid suddenly had a thought and looked around. "Er, where is he?"

Hops considered issuing another groan, but settled for a weary sigh instead. "I sent him to the cellar to help Roffo. Cleaning out a huge load of muck seemed an appropriate labour for a muscle-bound lad like him." The innkeeper smiled sadly. "And after that we can see how badly damaged the cellar is. After all, it'll affect the value of the pub …"

"Sell the pub?" gasped Heddy.

Eddie dropped the tankard she was cleaning.

"Marvellous," said Manis, rubbing his hands together in glee as he surveyed the debris-strewn interior of his pub. It had turned into quite a party last night and no doubt about it! The innkeeper would never have thought it possible to squeeze so many people into such a small space – and that was *before* the effects of the ale had even *started* to be manifest! It had been like squashing a dozen bull elephants into a telephone box and then, outside, letting loose a herd of suspender-belt-wearing cow elephants plastered with trunkstick and scented with *eau de pachyderm* pheromone. Once the ale had begun to take effect, the uncomfortable male clientele had found it very difficult to leave their seats without embarrassment, which had aided Manis's efforts at emptying their wallets ...

"Marvellous?" sneered Spotty Wembers, the acne-faced barman, interrupting his employer's musings. "What do you mean *marvellous*?" Spotty had a deep-seated aversion to work, and the ruination before him looked like Work with a capital *W*. "*You* don't have to clean up this mess, or repair the fittings." He then smiled mischievously. "But you *do* have to fork out for the damage. Have you thought about that?"

The innkeeper laughed. "Not me, Spotty, oh no, not me! I won't be paying for any of this. I'll leave that to my new customers." He rubbed his hands together some more. "And if the reports from a certain hairy cretin are true, there'll be an even bigger crowd tonight. You see, Spotty, my very own bag of pus, The Bear appears to have run out of ale."

"Run out of ale?" Spotty looked at his employer suspiciously. "How?"

"Apparently the taps fell out of Hops's barrels *all by themselves*, and the ale just leaked away." Manis grinned. "I also hear they've had a bit of *flood* damage. An Act of God, perhaps?"

"Hmph, more like an act of sabotage!"

Manis casually stretched out a hand and grabbed his underling by the collar, drawing their faces close together. "I am known throughout town as a fair and equitable employer who treats his staff with a generosity that would awe the gods – don't say a word! However, if you repeat such a scurrilous rumour to anyone else it'll be the last thing you do. Understand?"

"Sure boss," said the barman, nervously. "Just my little joke."

Manis let the youth go. "Sometimes, Wembers, you tread a fine line. Still, we must have taken a lot of cash last night: I noticed you and the boys carrying out a huge number of drunks." Manis chortled to himself. "I also noticed you dumping them in the horse troughs around the Square. Now, I would normally approve of this behaviour, but I'm presently trying to show a caring new image to the public, so I'd prefer it if you desisted in future. Okay?"

"Well, um, *actually* ..." replied Spotty, with some trepidation, like the bringer of bad news in the presence of a mad, deranged, foaming-at-the-mouth despot, "most of them weren't, well, *drunk*. Not *as such*. Mind you, it *was* the ale that made them, sort of, *pass out*."

Manis frowned. "What are you talking about? Are you saying the ale knocked them out *without* getting them drunk?"

"Er, well, I don't know if *knocked out* is exactly the right, wotchacallit, *phrase*. Not if you mean, like, *falling asleep* or *becoming unconscious*."

"What do you mean, boy? Out with it!"

"Well, in some cases ... not *all*, you understand, *just a few* ... we had to, sort of, *resuscitate* them."

Manis simply stared.

Spotty continued rapidly, holding up his hands defensively. He had hoped to toy with his employer over this one, but something about Manis's mood suggested danger. "Er, you shouldn't worry, um, *too* much. We didn't let on how bad a couple of them got, but ..."

"Explain!"

"Well, you know how this Mardon's ale makes you, um, *grow*? Well, I reckon the bigger *it* gets, the more blood it needs ... it sort of sucks out your blood like a vampiric snake. And if too much flows away from your brain you become light-headed and pass out. *At first*. Well ... we had to throw some blokes in cold water to bring them round and cool their ardour. Anyway, it was all a bit much for Old Gillie's heart and the Berserker had to, well, *kick start* it."

Manis gawped at his employee as the ramifications of this new information sank in. "So," he said, a multitude of emotions rippling across his face, "what you're saying is that if you drink too much of this brew, not only do you have to consider buying a new wardrobe of three-legged trousers, but you *also* have to consider making a will?" Manis slammed both hands down onto the bar top. "I've been done! Right, where's that bloody Potoon?"

"He's upstairs," said Wembers, with a sudden sneer. He was reprieved! "I just took him breakfast."

"*Roffo!*" bellowed Jepho. "You've got visitors!"

"Whassat?" Roffo's unkempt hair preceded the rest of his head out of the doorway to the cellar. He wore thigh-length boots (currently caked in a dubious brown substance) and a pair of soiled gloves.

"It's the filth!" sneered Jepho, gesturing towards the three white-uniformed men hopping about beside him, trying not to touch any of the contaminated furniture. "Almost camouflaged in the muck, ain't they? They want to talk to you ..."

The three men of the town constabulary, accustomed to such slights, reacted in their own particular ways. Constable Hendy, a young man with a pudding-bowl haircut, looked down at his scuffed brown boots in embarrassment; Sergeant Boomber, an ugly man with warts, looked aghast; and the grey-haired Inspector Yavlo closed his watery eyes and winced.

"That's quite enough of that, sir," said Yavlo meekly. "We are the town constabulary, here to get to the bottom of a crime ... a crime against *your* employer." He looked around the devastation and wrinkled his nose. The smell was enough to stun a herd of charging buffaloes. "Really, sir, we are on *your* side."

"Yeah yeah," said Jepho cynically. "Anyway – there he is. I've got to go. You've just reminded me: I've got to get to the market as we're running short of *bacon*."

Boomber reached for his truncheon. "Right, *that's it*! Guv, let's book him."

Jepho laughed, made an offensive gesture at the seething sergeant, and ambled unconcernedly away. He pushed the front door open with one foot, then sidled out rapidly before the foul thing could touch him on its back-swing. Yavlo reached out to pat his deputy on the arm. "Let it go, Boomber. We have got bigger fish to fry."

"But guv – that was at least Insulting An Officer Of The Law While On Official Business! We could send him down for ten years for that!"

Yavlo sighed. "Please, Sergeant, let it drop. Besides, you know the prison is full." It was full all right, thought the Inspector, mournfully, but not of the sort who really belonged there. In fact, the only people they had managed to detain over the last few years had been people who had *wanted* to be arrested. You could always tell when someone wanted in, as they usually headed towards the station with a brick in one hand. And who could blame them? Three square meals a day, bathing facilities, daily exercise in a pleasant enclosed courtyard, and a good view over the small stadium in Sarsus that served as the venue for most of the town's smaller sporting events. Indeed, the prison was more highly regarded than Cross-My-Way's three hotels. It was booked solid for months to come.

Yavlo had joined the force thirty years ago as an idealistic young man who had hoped to really Make A Difference. He had donned the white robes (representing purity and justice) with honour, and he had taken noble pledges to uphold the law and to punish the wicked. But for what? Yavlo shook his head. The constabulary was little more than a catering service for down-and-outs and holiday-makers, or else a roving task force responsible for cleaning up the town's messes. He had rounded up more stray dogs than made arrests. The problem was that the townspeople tended to look after themselves, preferring to accept the risk of thieves than to pay the taxes for a proper force (in the one case they *might* be robbed, in the other case they definitely *would* be), while public justice tended to take care of any particularly irksome troublemakers. Occasionally, however, there were real cases that challenged Yavlo's detective skills and filled him with excitement and new purpose – like The Mysterious Affair of the Missing Pantaloons, and The Bizarre Case of the Exploding Outies (of which he was much reminded by the present incident).

Remembering these successes, the Inspector was much cheered. He looked at the wiry youth who stood before him and wondered what delicious mysteries the present case might bring. "Ah, yes, and you are Roffo, junior barman and stable-sweeper at The Bear?"

Roffo nodded sullenly.

"Ah, yes, good. Now, sir, in your own words, can you tell me what happened on the night of the thirty-first of Maynot? Hendy, are you taking this down?"

"Yes, guv, just let me dip me quill."

Roffo looked from one man to the other, avoiding the glare of the much-miffed Sergeant. Hendy carefully inked his quill and laid his pad of parchment on a still-upright table. He then stuck his tongue out of the side of his mouth and looked at Roffo expectantly.

"Well," said the barman, "I was sent to the cellar to change a barrel …"

"Of what?" asked Yavlo.

"Er, Old P., I think. And then …"

"And what time was this?"

"About one in the morning. Anyway …"

"Can you be more precise?" queried the Inspector. "How do you know it was one o'clock?"

"Er, dunno really. Look, is all this detail necessary?"

"Detail!" cried the Inspector, enthusiastically. "Yes, young man, it is! Detail is the essence of detection. It is part of the artistry of police work. We gather up every detail, no matter how small and seemingly trivial, and then we sieve, extract, and collate. Trust me. This is my forte."

"Yeah, but we know who did it …"

"Do we indeed?" Yavlo smiled condescendingly and shook his head. "Such cases are rarely so simple, young man. I suggest you leave the detecting to us and simply report the facts. The pure and unadulterated facts. I assure you, this detecting is a tricky business and not quite so straightforward as you might think."

Roffo gave a sour look. "Okay. The facts. I went into the cellar and these big herberts, otherwise known as the Hull's Angels, jumped me and stuck me in a barrel and smashed up the joint."

Hendy and Boomber exchanged worried glances. Hendy frowned, and the Sergeant shook his head unhappily.

"Aha!" said Yavlo. "But how do you know it was they? Is this not speculation on your part? The fact is, the only unopposed way into the cellar is through this door here." He pointed at the door behind Roffo. "Now, we know the villains exited the cellar through the delivery trap door ... we know this by the way its interior lock was broken, and because of the exterior presence of a rather bruised donkey. Consequently, the intruders could not have entered the cellar that way. *Fact!* Now, as you can see, to get to *this* door one must pass through the lounge bar. And we know – *for a fact* – that the Angels *did not* enter the inn. No-one saw them. And let us face it, they are fairly unmistakable. Furthermore, we know *as fact* that they have been barred from this once-splendid inn, and hence they would not have been allowed inside in the first place."

"But ... but ... I saw them!"

"Interesting. That would make it your word against theirs. Circumstantial evidence? Why did no-one else see them? Were they invisible?"

Roffo sighed. "Look, they were in disguise. They were dressed up as women ..."

"Aha!" exclaimed Yavlo. "Now we are getting somewhere. Who were the, ah, *large* unsightly ladies of foreign extraction who were seen hanging around the bar? What was it that the smith said?"

Hendy leafed through his parchments. "You mean Grevis? Um, he said 'Ah, so you've had a vacancy then, I'll just go and get my things ...'"

Yavlo shook his head vigorously. "After that."

"Um, ' ...well get stuffed then you pigs'?"

"No ... let me have a look." The Inspector swiped the pages from his Constable. "Here we go: '..it was only coz I was drunk, see, and they wore them veil things too so I couldn't see how bilious they were. One even called me a git!' So, we are looking for exotic women who I would guess to be from Chadoor, given other descriptions we have of their attire."

"They were Angels I tell you!"

"They may well have seemed like angels to you, sir – there being no accounting for taste – but I suggest we stick to the hard facts. Right." Yavlo handed the pad back to Hendy. "Perhaps you could show us to the barrel in which you were incarcerated, and after that a pot of tea would be nice.

If that wouldn't be too much trouble? And then I think an eye test is in order. Now, let us proceed to the cellar."The Inspector turned to his men. "And mind the steps: they still appear to be slippery. Ha! Reminds me of The Case of the Exploding Outies, remember that one? Come on men." And with that, Yavlo turned and ushered the protesting Roffo through the door. The Sergeant and the Constable hung back a moment longer.

"Er, well, Sarg, I think we ought to concentrate on finding these exotic ladies then, don't you?"

Boomber nodded. "Clever lad. I can see you'll go far. Stick to issuing parking tickets, finding missing husbands, and chasing exotic women, and you can't go wrong. And, what's more, you'll live to see the year out. Let's go and humour the guv'nor. And don't touch that door handle: that could be mud, but I wouldn't bet my salary on it."

———•••••———

Manis stormed up the stairs to the spare room. He barged past the surprised guard standing outside, flung the door open, and stomped in. His determined progress was then brought to an abrupt halt by the bare chest of the Potoon's personal bodyguard, his nose lodging between the tight pectorals of the man's chest. One muscular hand grabbed the innkeeper by the throat and lifted him off his feet, dangling him in front of the Potoon for inspection. The merchant prince took a peeled grape from a beautiful handmaiden and considered his visitor. He clicked his fingers and a weedy, bald-headed man – who had been standing to attention beside him – took a step forward and cleared his throat.

"His Magnificence the Potoon would like to know why you have housed him in a room that smells like the love nest of two incontinent skunks." The Potoon nodded encouragement and the emaciated servant continued. "He would also like to know why you have given him a room infested with voracious vermin – vermin that have eaten his fine silks and terrified his handmaidens. And he would like to know the nature of the strange yellow rain that occasionally flows down the walls." The Potoon leaned forward and prodded the man, grimacing in a peculiar manner. The servant nodded sagely. "Ah, yes, and His Magnificence would also like to know why you have provided him with comfort maidens as hideous as the purulent behinds of a pair of ancient, dysenteric camels. He would further like to know whether you realised that they had more fungal infections than a three-week-old cheese sandwich?"

The Potoon nodded vigorously at this and looked expectantly at Manis. Realising that he was unlikely to get an answer from a man who was slowly turning purple, the Samark clicked his fingers. The red-turbaned bodyguard released his grip on Manis's throat, and the innkeeper crumpled into a heap on the floor. He lay there for several seconds recovering his breath, then for several seconds more recovering his composure. In that time he came to the calculated conclusion that *now* might not be the best moment to unleash a vitriolic harangue on the shortcomings of Mardon's Pedigree. He stood up, adjusted the collar of his tunic, and manufactured a hurt expression.

"Your supreme being-ship!" declared Manis, oozing like a lanced boil. "I am but a poor, humble man. Though it may not seem like it, I have done my best to entertain you. I have given you the best room in the inn, and the best bed, and I have provided you with the very best ladies to be had ..." (Behind his back, Manis's fingers were firmly crossed.) "If *you* were to give me a fortune in gold you would still have a fortune left to give, whereas I ... well, I have given you all that I can afford. I cannot be more generous. What else could I possibly give?"

"Maybe yoah wife," responded the Potoon, pre-empting the skinny servant. The head guard placed a hand upon the hilt of his huge scimitar and looked hopefully towards the Potoon's clicking fingers.

"Wife? *Wife?* If I were married, oh light of the East, the lady would be yours. *No?*"

The fat Samark waved his chubby, ring-laden hand in a peeved manner.

"Oh, ah, I see, *life*! But who, then, your magnificence, would buy your wonderful ale?" Inwardly Manis seethed. He cursed himself for not pausing long enough to fetch the Berserker before storming up here. Then the boot would be on the other foot! If the fat git thought he'd had a bad time *last* night, well, he'd pretty soon have to change his definition of the word *bad*. And probably *nightmare* and *horror* too. Manis had more tricks up his sleeve than a bent magician. He idly wondered, for starters, whether Gorgon Gail – the nymphomaniac transvestite and three-county arm-wrestling champion – was still on Sonia's books.

The Potoon considered Manis thoughtfully over another peeled grape. "Vewy well, I will wet you wiv *today*. Unfoahtunatewy, I must *suffah* yoah hospitawity foah anothah night. We weave tomowow."

"Your eminence is *so* generous," replied Manis sarcastically, giving a little bow. He turned to leave, but then halted as though suddenly struck by a new thought. He turned back. "Oh, yes, and before I go, I wonder if you might give me the benefit of your great experience in dealing with the Pedigree?"

The Potoon made to speak, but then remembered himself. He snapped his fingers and the bald man said, "Yes?"

"Well, it appears there is a *tiny little* side-effect that you neglected to tell me about when we arranged our original deal."

The Potoon's brow furrowed. The servant observed his demeanour and translated it into words. "What?"

"Well, now, it seems that the ale has caused a number of my customers to have *blood flow* problems, with the result that they tended to *faint* at the sight of an attractive woman. Or *worse*."

The Potoon's eyebrows leapt over his furrowed brow like a pair of mogul skiers. He placed a hand on the arm of his mouth-servant to silence him. "This cannot be twue. How much did these cwients dwink?"

"Who knows?" Manis shrugged his shoulders. "Five ... six ... ten? Could be more."

"Goodness gwacious!" gasped the Potoon. "They must not dwink it wike watah! They will end up with a huge one onee usefah foah wassoing warge wiahd animaws. Death may even occah! No, Pedigwee must onee be dwunk in wittah wations. A pint an evening ... maybe two if you have a wendezvous with a fwiend."

"What do you mean a pint or two a night?" Manis's jaw dropped. He struggled to get his mind around this concept. It was a nightmare scenario. He could just imagine his punters draining a couple of pints and then declaring, *right, that me done, good night landlord.* "That's *not* the way we do things around here, mate! You go out and drink until you drop, or at least until you're thrown out ..."

"Yes, that is okay foah most beeah but not foah the Pedigwee. If you dwink too much the wepahcussions could be wuinous. You must wimit each customah to one pint an evening. The wandwoads of my wand give away a coupon with each pint of weguwah beeah and when the customah has cowected five or six coupons they are awowed to buy one pint of Pedigwee."

"Hmmm, yes, *I see!*" Imaginary pouches of gold began to manifest themselves before the innkeeper's eyes. This put a whole new complexion on matters! "That's clever, damned clever! It'll stop people from just nipping in for a quick one *and* it'll help conserve my stocks." Manis clenched a fist in triumph. "Potoon, my old chum, you're a genius!" And with that, the innkeeper swivelled on his heels and headed cheerfully through the door. As he made his way downstairs he contemplated – for a moment, an ever-so-brief moment – easing up on his pompous guest. *Tonight,* he thought briefly, *maybe, just maybe, I won't let the punters use that leaking lavvie over the spare room …*

The monk gingerly pushed open the front door to the lounge of The Bear. "Hello? Anybody in?" He crept inside – then paused. A suspicious crunching sound assailed his hearing and he found himself sinking into the ground. As the monk looked down at his boots his expression changed into something like that of the phantom of the opera on sampling a carton of two-week-old milk. "Ai-la!" he cried, swiftly skipping from the disintegrating crust of effluent onto a patch of cleared floor.

From the centre of the otherwise-silent room came a soft groan.

The monk looked up to see Hops sitting in the midst of carnage, his face buried in his hands. "Ah, innkeeper!" the monk enquired, gently, "I look for barbarian. He is here?"

For a moment the innkeeper remained still, as though he had not heard the question, but then he slowly raised his head. A look of utmost misery drew the man's fleshy jowls downwards into an expression like that of a chronically depressed beagle. Light glinted off spots of sweat speckling his thinly thatched pate. Tear-streaked grime covered his cheeks. A faraway look filled his slightly bulbous eyes.

The monk waited for a few moments, but no answer came. He was about to address the innkeeper again when Hops spoke. "The barbarian?" he sighed, as he started to rock gently on his stool. "Ah, the well-meaning lad! Maybe I shouldn't have been so hard on him …"

"He is here?"

Hops's gaze became vacant for just a moment and his head began to nod forward, but then he recovered himself. "What? Terry? Oh, yes. He's around."

The monk examined the innkeeper with sympathetic eyes and nodded to himself. Such disaster! He began to edge towards Hops along a trail that led to the bar. "Please," he said, "do not wish to intrude on despair – ai, what a thing to happen! – but must speak to barbarian. It is important."

Hops sighed again. "Important, eh? What could be more important than cleaning out the cellar?"

The monk frowned and looked towards the doorway leading to The Pit. He shivered at the thought of what must lie within. How the barbarian must rage at such a lowly task! Surely this would unchain his wild spirit? How could he reject the offer of adventure now? The monk looked back to the innkeeper. "Yes – of greatest importance. He is to join me on quest."

Hops stiffened. Not Terry! Surely the lad wouldn't desert him now, not in his hour of greatest need? He gasped: "Quest – what quest?"

"Eh," replied the monk, distractedly, "he not say to you? Quest is to recover greatest ale in world."

A welter of thoughts and emotions swirled through the mind of the innkeeper: despair, desolation, wonder, hope, amazement, concern. He stared at the monk as he stood there, chewing on his bottom lip and peering into the cellar. He wasn't smiling, so it couldn't be a joke. A quest? Terry? The greatest ale in the world? Nonsense! And yet … it was almost as if in this, his moment of greatest despair, some divine entity had decided to balance the scales of justice and misfortune. But it couldn't be true … these things never happened except in the most ludicrous tales of scurrilous storytellers. Could Lady Luck really be smiling on him? A crazy grin began to twist the corners of his drooping mouth. And then – at the very moment that hope flickered in the innkeeper's mind – a leg of his over-burdened stool broke, and Hops was pitched face-first into a particularly malevolent pool of sludge …

The three men settled around a table in a cleared corner of the lounge. A huge piece of ripe cheese was set on a platter before them, providing a ready supply of anti-stench filters. As the oriental and the innkeeper discussed his future employment, Terry shifted about uncomfortably on his seat and occasionally frowned at the monk. Conveniently within earshot, Roffo busied himself swabbing down the walls.

"So what you're saying, then," said Hops, in a business-like delirium, something like John Harvey-Jones on E, "is that you have the first part of a map to the stash of this wood spirit, Boozer?" The innkeeper gave an uncharacteristic giggle. "But of course you have. Happens all the time. Got several myself *and* my old mum's a tooth-fairy!"

The monk looked non-plussed, rather like a toad with indigestion. "This is so. Will say it no more times. Ai-la! World full of unbelievers!"

"No, no, I believe, really, I …" Hops reached across the table suddenly and grabbed the monk by the front of his habit. "Please, I *need* to believe. I *need* proof. Have you … can't you … do you …" The innkeeper's voice trailed off, but his eyes continued to plead.

The monk disengaged Hops's hands in a gentle-yet-firm manner. "Very well!" He reached within his habit and slowly brought out a flat leather wallet. He placed this upon the table and carefully opened it up, sliding out an age-yellowed scrap of parchment. The innkeeper's eyes bulged. He leaned forward to examine the thing.

The parchment was clearly one piece of a larger map. In the top left-hand corner was inscribed – in black ink, in some forgotten language – five short lines of text. The rest of the yellow fragment was covered in a black scrawl that traced out a tiny map, with a thin red line marking out a route. This line began at a point in the top left-hand corner just below the text, then meandered diagonally towards the bottom right-hand corner. The line passed through a small X near the corner, continued a short distance further, then disappeared off the right-hand edge.

Hops looked at the monk quizzically. His breathing had quickened. "What does it all mean ... this writing ... and the line ... and the rest of the map? Where is it?"

"Language is of Wood Spirits. It say 'Here is route to Bliss, Here is route of Boozer, Find the shards of map, X marks the spot, Go to paradise.'"

"Crap poem," said Roffo, whose cleaning duties had brought him close to the conversation.

"Hmm, yes. Loses something in translation."

"But these places?" wondered Hops. "Where's *this* ...?"

The monk looked at the location indicated by Hops's pointing digit. It was the point at which the red ink line began. "Ah, that Frembolia. Temple there where ancient druids worship spirits of trees and flowers and stuff. It where Boozer died and where he laid to rest. It also place where I, ahem, *found* map."

Terry rolled his eyes. Hops ignored the implication, following the line further with his trembling finger. "And *this* ...?" He pointed at a place mid-way along the line where it suddenly did a 90 degree turn.

"Ah, this is *Here* ... Wood Spirits knew town as 'Which-Way-Now Ville'. See ... I come down Valley of Latitude to town, but must leave by Valley of Longitude."

"But there's no X here," observed Roffo, who was now standing behind the monk and not even pretending to clean.

"That right ... no piece of map here ..."

"But," said Hops feverishly, "there *is* an X on the edge of the map, *here*. I can't work out where it is though ..."

"It's Nudia!" cried Roffo. "I see it! Look, this is the South Road *here*," he pointed, "and *this* kink is the diversion around the Golag Bogs. Next stop after that is Nudia. It has to be!"

The monk turned to peer at the diminutive barman thoughtfully. "Yes – you right ... that is where next piece of map is."

"Then that," declared Roffo excitedly, pounding one fist into the palm of his other hand, "is where we have to go next!"

The three men at the table turned to him, and stared ...

———•••••———

As Hops paced about, the other men looked on with concern. "Yes, I see it now ... a holding action ... aye, that's the job! There's a big brewery in Greenwing ... Bravo Ale ... not that nice if truth be told, but they'll supply me until I get my own stuff back in production. Yes, that's the ticket! And I've still got some regulars who'll pop by, even if it is for just a swift one before they go ... *over there.*" Hops turned and paced back the other way, the eyes of his companions following him as though he were the ball in a tennis match. "Maybe some promos ... some bands ... I know! A quiz! My old dad used to do quizzes ... said they were right popular ... have to ban Occum though ... oh, and need some substitute staff ... can't really replace you, Terry my lad, but ..."

"Er, that's okay boss. Maybe I should stay then ..."

"No no, lad! You're needed by our new friend here: roughing it in the field, beating off bandits, breaking into fortresses ... just up your street! I need you to get that recipe back here. And then we'll show that Manis. Best ale in the world! That'll put me back in business for sure. We'll be the most popular inn on the continent!" Terry's face turned downcast as Hops continued his pacing. "Hmm, have to start interviewing tomorrow ... yes, you'll have to leave tomorrow ... can't delay, eh lads? Time is money and all that. I'll go to the market later and get your supplies in ... have to raid my savings, but the time for caution and prudence is past ..."

"But boss," said Terry, lifting his huge hands in a disconsolate way, "how do we know *any* of this is true? The only evidence we have for it is ... er, and no disrespect intended here, Mr monk ... from a rather *tall* story. And from a single piece of map. But that's all." It was not that Terry feared the road or the danger that might lie ahead – he was, after all, a barbarian. But over the last three years he had grown attached to the quiet life. In Way he had everything he wanted: a soft bed in a neat little room upstairs, numerous friends, and plenty of time to himself to go on forays into the market. He had also been taking lessons on the culinary art from Cook, and it seemed a shame to leave now, just as he was beginning to get the hang of making the sort of goulash that could take the skin off your tongue. He now looked around the soiled interior of the inn – his home – with a deep sense of affection. He wondered when he would see it again.

"Well *I* believe the tale," said Roffo, whose eyes kept stealing to the map. "And this parchment is old, and when I say *old* I don't just mean old, I mean, well, I reckon it's *even* older than Willy, and Willy is, well, *Ancient.*" Roffo gave a lop-sided grin. "I've heard of the ale too. It's called *Boozer's Very Peculiar.* It's legendary!"

"Aye, lad, it's a legend all right," concurred Hops, whose mood had yo-yoed back into credit. "That's the spirit! See, Terry! You should take a leaf from young Roffo here. Be positive! Thank you, Roffo, now back to them walls. I think we can take it from here."

The young barman's face sagged as though he had suddenly aged a thousand years. "But, boss, the quest … I *have* to go! I can help out, honest! You know, do the cooking and whatnot. Carry Terry's weapons and stuff. And I'm good with maps, too! In my home village I got every scout badge you could get: animal footprint recognition, starting fires with two twigs, *everything* …"

Hops affected a stern expression. "Now now, lad, this questing is dangerous work, meant for the likes of heroes and such. Trust me! One day you'll thank me for keeping you here …"

"But … but …"

"No, lad, no more arguments …"

"Wait!" The monk held up a hand and looked between the arguing pair. He saw the desperation in the young man's face and nodded to himself. "La! It said in my land that should not spurn lion cub, for one day it turn into lion and come back to eat you!" He turned to peer into Roffo's face. "But most important of all, lion-cub, tell me this …" He leaned forward slightly and, with utmost seriousness asked, "Do you know how to make decent egg fried rice?"

The market was unusually subdued. The morning had already fled and the afternoon was well in progress, yet half of the stalls were still untended, and those that *were* set up for business were presided over by shambling, grim-faced beings. Instead of the usual babble of trade and passion of bargaining, the present stall-holders stood solemnly by their wares and scowled at the few customers in evidence – the latter creeping about like ninja ghouls on rice paper. Any stumble or raised voice was met with an instant volley of dagger-looks or a chorus of *shhhhhhh*s. The whole scenario was like something from a film called *The Mid-Afternoon of the Living Dead*.

Indeed, the only stalls that were doing anything like decent trade were those dispensing medicinal products. Dr Feare – a tall, languid individual with a shock of frizzy black hair – was doing a grand trade in both hangover cures and anti-inflammatory balms.

"Have you, *uhhh*, got anything for me bollocking head?" croaked Rude Lubblers, foulest-mouthed man in town. "Nightmare fucking headache scenario!"

"Ah, yes, you'll be wanting some of my hangover cure," said Feare. He looked his customer up and down with a disapproving frown. "I'm afraid, however, that I'm running rather low …"

"Don't give me that bollocking shite, just give me the potion, you git!"

"Ah, yes, ahem, well, as you have so rightly judged, I do have some bottles set aside for my special customers."

Feare produced a little blue bottle and placed it on the counter. Lubblers looked at the potion and nodded, then wished he hadn't. He covered his eyes with a hand and swayed about for several seconds. Eventually he stopped swaying. With trembling hands he fetched out a pouch from inside his tunic. He cautiously counted out a number of coins.

"Ah," observed Feare, "you appear to be under some misapprehension about the price. Because this is my SPECIAL stock, the price is DOUBLE the usual."

"*Ah ah ah*," whined Lubblers, holding his hands to his ears. "No need to shout, you bastard …"

"Oh, did I say DOUBLE, of course I meant TREBLE."

Lubblers held up his hands – conceding defeat – and counted over the requisite coins. He grabbed the little blue bottle and instantly took a huge glug. With open bottle still in hand, he staggered off into the depths of the market, muttering quiet expletives.

Feare turned to his next sheepish-looking customer. "Ah, Mr Brassrubbers," he declared, "I see that you are discomfited. Perhaps you'd like something to ease the strain?"

———◆◆◆———

Hops strolled through the market with something like a spring in his step. It had been quite a day already and his poor mind was in a confused state of mania. Occasionally he burst into unprovoked giggles or broke into a jolly skip. Given the nature of The Bear's disaster of the previous evening, the innkeeper's behaviour might have drawn more attention than it actually did were it not for the dazed state of those in the market, added to a kind of mass shame that prevented many from looking the man in the eye. Wherever Hops passed, like a ferry through calm seas, a bow-wave of guilt spread out behind him.

At Crusty the Baker's stall, Hops was offered loaves at half price and free delivery. Janus the spice seller let him take his pick of condiments and seasonings at a special 'exhalted customer' rate. The innkeeper got a barrel of apples for the price of a crate; quality salted beef from under-the-counter at the same rate as the regular offal; and three rugged goatskin tents for a price that would have made the shades of their previous inhabitants sit up and bleat. Before long, a stream of deliveries began to head for The Bear and a ripple of interest started to spread through the market. Pretty soon, stall-holders were turning to their neighbours and whispering their opinions.

"'Ee's packing up and shipping out I reckon ..."

"NO – sorry, I mean no. He can't do that!"

"Then what's he up to?"

"Probably going on vacation – that's wot I'd do. Let the staff clear up, then come back refreshed ..."

"Then why's he buying weapons and stuff? I hear he got some knives and a shield from Rusty's lad's stall ..."

"Maybe he's goin' to declare war on ... Oh. Ah, afternoon Master Manis."

Manis glowered at the little gathering of stall-holders. "What's this? Plotting some mischief to swindle your poor customers out of more of their hard-earned cash?"

"Ah ha ha ha," went Joban Bile, fruit-seller. "Very good, sir, but if you could *just* speak a *little* less loudly, I'm sure all here would be grateful."

Manis planted his hands on his hips and smirked. "So, like that, is it? Well, if I don't get some service pretty pronto there's going to be Hull to pay. Bile – you first. I'm making my guest a pie. Got any rotten fruit? You know, things with maggots in? Just the regular crap you sell me ... *aha*! And what is this?"

Hops hove into view with Horus, Jepho and Eddie trailing in his wake, balming their guilty consciences by carrying the innkeeper's purchases. At the sight of his arch-foe, Hops came to a sudden halt. A sickly smile spread across his face.

"So," mused Manis, "what's going on here then?"

Hops looked down. "Um, it's … it's, er, none of your business."

"That's it," croaked Horus, "you tell him!"

"Master Horus," said Manis, wryly, "it is so good to hear where your loyalties lie. I guess this means you won't be stopping by The Pilgrim anymore? Is the Pedigree not to your taste?"

"Um, er," squirmed the farrier, "what I *meant* was, er, you tell him what you're doing. That's all."

"*Traitor!*" whispered Eddie.

Manis grinned and turned back to the suddenly sweating Hops. "I hadn't expected to see you up and about so soon after your *accident.*" He gestured at the provisions being carried by the party. "And I wouldn't have thought you'd have much need of grub, not having any customers to feed, eh? So then, what *are* you up to?"

"Um, sorry," replied Hops, desperately, "can't chat … much as I'd like to … got to get this food back, er, need to feed the clean-up party, er, yes, um …" his voice trailed off. He shrugged his shoulders. Then he smiled sheepishly, about-turned, and led his small party back the way they had come.

For several minutes afterwards Manis stood where he was, following the disappearing Hops with his eyes. He rasped at his chin and chewed on his lip. There was something going on here, but what? He had to know. That Hops – always something up his sleeve. Ignoring the concerned looks on the faces of the cluster of stall-holders, and forgetful of his own shopping list, Manis stalked back to his inn. He would send for Picket – that's what he'd do. If anyone could find out what was going on, then the fence was that man.

Back in The Bear, Roffo could barely contain his excitement: he was going on an adventure! Heroic deeds awaited: slaying dragons, discovering treasures, conquering foes in mighty combat, rescuing damsels in distress (damsels who would, no doubt, show their appreciation in varied and wonderful ways). Roffo had dreamt about such feats of heroism ever since he was a child, when his Grandfather had sat him on his knee and regaled him with tales of dangerous exploits in foreign lands. Of course, his Grandmother had pooh-poohed these tales, once confiding to the young Roffo that her husband had never made it beyond the next village, and even then he had suffered a panic attack and rushed home. According to his Gran, the old man had only made it back thanks to the help of a couple of kindly strangers. But the young Roffo had not believed her, and had instead set out to follow Gramps to glory! Indeed, the fact that he had made it to 'the big city', as his bucolic kin referred to Cross-My-Way, was considered no mean feat in itself, but to the young barman it had not been enough – no way enough!

As he sat on his bed contemplating those halcyon days, Roffo's mind turned back to the practicalities of the quest. Following Gramps's remembered advice he had already piled up a fair amount of stuff for the road. So far, he had stacked up a thin cotton jerkin for desert travel, a waterproof tunic for rain forests, and a sheepskin coat for the high mountains. He had put out a broad-brimmed hat for the plains, a kepi for the desert, and a balaclava – knitted by his mum – for the polar regions. He had set out several pairs of trousers in various camouflage colours so that he could blend into any surrounding. He had also included three pairs of shorts for hotter climes, plus his best matching tunic and trousers – just in case they should be invited to dine in the magnificent halls of some corrupt-but-fabulously-wealthy tyrant and his one hundred stunning and available daughters. Footwear-wise, Roffo had limited himself to three pairs of boots, two sets of sandals, and a posh pair of leather shoes. The young barman looked at the mountainous heap of clothes and nodded: he had surely remembered everything; Gramps would have been proud of him!

Next, Roffo turned to consider a second heap piled up on the floor by the bed. This comprised equipment. Here were set his junior animal footprint recognition chart, his Swizz army penknife with its twenty-six different blades, several pots of varying dimensions for cooking, a plate, a bowl, and a tankard looted from the bar. He also had a packet of extra-thick rubber balloons that his grandfather had once given him in one of his less sober moments. Roffo did not know, in truth, what they were for, but correctly guessed that they played a part in celebrating the rescue of damsels in distress. All he needed now, he thought, was a weapon. His grandfather's rusty sword or his father's notched short-handled axe? Or perhaps both? Terry would know. Roffo picked up the two pieces of ironmongery and set out for the barbarian's room.

Terry was also sitting on his bed, examining his neat little room. He passed a sad eye over his bookcase, with its tomes on gardening, cats and cooking. He contemplated the little red and brown Samark rug that lay on the wooden floor. He considered the shelves that he had made with his own hands, on which were stacked his assorted bearskins. And in the corner of the room, resting against the wall near his bed, Terry noted his axe. He reached across to touch it but, an inch or so from its haft, his hand trembled slightly as though it had come into contact with some invisible barrier. Terry frowned slightly and stretched a bit further until … a mist seemed to draw down in front of his eyes. A tingle started in his fingertips then raced up his arm to his shoulder. His heart began to beat a bit faster and his breath came in shorter bursts. A small surge of adrenaline rushed through his body. The muscles in his arm trembled and bunched. A look of serious intent etched itself onto his face …

In Terry's ears he heard the sound of battle, and with his nose he scented blood and death. Anger – unaccountable anger – began to surge and bubble in him. His eyes flickered around the room … but this time he did not see the parchments, or the neatly folded clothes, or the bird's nest outside his window, or the colourful-yet-naïve painting of a cat hanging on one wall. Instead, he saw shadows; silhouettes that might have been enemies; shapes that needed slaying; folds in space that may have held threat. Steel, the substance of Grom, the curse and boon of the barbarian hordes, had woven its spell on him …

And then the door opened.

For a split second, Terry's eyes drew wide, his grip tightened on the haft of his axe, and danger was in the air. But recognition interceded, and a startled Terry pulled back, releasing his grip on the weapon.

"Ah, you too!" said Roffo, peering enviously at the great silver axe with its stout, black ironwood haft. "Taking that, eh? Well, what do you think of this?" and the junior barman waved one of his rusty pieces of weaponry at Terry. The force of the agitation made a small sliver of metal fall off.

Terry shook his head to clear it of the last traces of barbarian rage. An amused smile spread across his face. "Death by tetanus, eh?" he chortled. "Is this a special local technique?"

Roffo gave his sword a disappointed look. He rested it gently against the wall, then brought out the axe from behind his back. "Okay. What about this then? My father claimed he killed a hundred marauders with it!"

"Wow," went Terry, "a bastard axe!"

A broad grin spread across Roffo's face. "Yeah, it's a mean-looking weapon."

"That's not what I meant," replied Terry. " In my culture the *bastard sword* has the usual hand-and-a-half grip, but it also has a serrated edge – you know, like a saw? I've seen lots of weapons in my time, but this is the first time I've ever seen an axe with an edge like that. It was made that way, was it?"

"Er … of course. But if you don't think it's suitable …?"

"Perhaps you should take something with a sharp, smooth edge – like mine. Give it a heft." Terry pointed to the tool of his trade, but almost instantly wished he had not made the suggestion. A strange feeling, something like jealousy, washed over him.

Roffo eagerly grabbed the axe by its handle. As he did so an unpleasant tingling sensation shot up his arm, causing him to hesitate for a second, but then he shrugged his slim shoulders and made to give the axe a huge swing. "Arggh!" he cried, as he nearly wrenched his arms from their sockets. "It's stuck to the floor!"

"No it's not," said Terry, through gritted teeth. He casually leant over and picked up the axe with one hand – at which the jealousy fled – and wafted it under Roffo's nose. He put the weapon down again and turned back to his friend. "Maybe something lighter would be better. There are some weapons in the spare room that I confiscated in the past. Maybe one of those will suit you? Let's go down and see."

"Okay," said Roffo. He then looked around Terry's undisturbed room. His brow furrowed. "Uh, but maybe you'd like to pack first?"

"Sure." As Terry walked past his bed he gave the end of his sleeping mat a flick sending it rolling up into a bundle. "Finished," he cried. "Let's go."

Picket strolled across the lounge of The Pilgrim, passing through the intermittent cones of late-afternoon sunlight spearing through the windows. "Ah, Spotty, where's the boss?"

Wembers scowled and pointed through a doorway leading to the courtyard out back. "He's in the kitchen, and he's in a funny mood. If you ask me he's finally flipped. Watch yourself."

"Hmm, thanks for the advice."

The kitchen was adjacent to the lounge but inaccessible from it because of an absence of doors: food and orders were exchanged between the two rooms by way of a serving hatch. Picket walked into the courtyard and then around to the kitchen's stout wooden door, where he paused. As usual, the door was propped ajar. A billow of steam wafted through it, followed by a bout of manic laughter. Picket patted the sweat from his shiny pate with a plum-coloured handkerchief, then he girded his loins and entered.

Baal the cook was standing behind Manis, wringing his hands and watching with concern as the demented innkeeper shovelled another handful of chillies into a wok. "Spicy food? I'll give the bugger spicy food!

Doesn't like our *primitive cuisine*, eh? Well, let's see how he likes *this!*"

"Urrr, maybe you should lay off them chillies," whined Baal, "I don't think my pots and pans were made for such stuff. Look! It's starting to dissolve the metal!"

Manis turned to growl at the chef. "If you don't bugger off *right now* I'll do the cooking for *everyone* this evening, and then tell them the blisters on their tongues are your doing – got it?"

Baal nodded his head and, wiping a tear from his eye with a clean corner of his apron, he trudged off into the depths of his domain.

"Ah, Picket, did you get those turnip and weasel pies from Puns? Or the rat crumble? A dessert fit for … a merchant prince, perhaps?" Manis threw back his head and gave a lupine laugh.

"No … remember … you sent me after *information*. About Hops …"

"Oh. Yeah. Right." Manis took the wok from the flames and laid it aside. He was suddenly intensely serious. "What did you find out?"

"Weeeeeell … he's been buying up lots of provisions …"

"I know that!"

"Yeah, okay, but there's also been some activity in their stables. I saw them checking out a yak team and loading up a cart. And there's this funny looking foreigner hanging about. A priest or monk or something. Looks like someone's going somewhere, and that character is somehow involved."

"I guessed as much," snarled the innkeeper. "But where? And why? And who is the stranger?"

"I dunno where they're going," said Picket, cautiously, "but I did see the barbarian sitting on the cart and adjusting the reins. Suggestive, eh?"

Manis chewed on his lip. "I smell a rat here. Hops wouldn't let Testicles out of his sight unless it was really, *really* important. I don't like this at all. Right, go and fetch the lads and tell them to get ready for a little journey, just in case. After that, go and get some travelling fare from the market, then go and keep an eye on their stables. And keep your boy with you as a runner. I've got to know what's going on."

Manis returned to his cooking. After a few moments it became apparent that his spy had not moved. He turned back to face Picket. "Well?"

"Um, just a small point really," said Picket, "but, er, won't I need some dosh for the supplies?"

Manis grinned wickedly. "Of course you will. You'd better fetch one of your secret stashes, eh? I'll reimburse you later … as long as you have the proper receipts." And with that, he turned his back on the unhappy fence to continue with his culinary sadism.

———•◦•◦•———

Within the hour, the stable behind The Pilgrim played host to the Way chapter of the Hull's Angels.

"Damn! I've got a flat!" complained Frunge, flicking ash from a freshly lit cigarette. His beast had lost a shoe. He angrily slapped the ample backside of the long-haired Noughton, raising a cloud of dust. "Anyone got a spare?"

"There's a shoe over the door," replied Grunt, as he extracted a dipstick from the backside of his own steed. This was a giant Ducrapi, a species so wide it was considered an act of gross indecency to let a woman ride one. He ran his finger along the length of the dipstick to remove the gunge, then rubbed the brown goo gently between his fingers. "Hmm, a bit oily. Think I should put less rape-seed in 'is feed?" But Frunge had turned away and was now trying to wrestle the lucky shoe from the wall. Grunt shrugged his shoulders and opted to give the a ooze a second analysis: he put his fingers into his mouth and sucked.

"Purring like a cat wot's just shat on the mat," remarked Burble to himself, as he removed an ear-horn from the side of his 1000cc (crap capacity) West Highland yak. "Running smooth and ready to go!" he announced, loudly.

Bruce, who had his ear pressed to the flanks of his own charge, complained: "Och, mine's a wee bit rough." The Black Mountain yak, whose mane was as dark as a pint of Guinness, lowed plaintively. "I think he's got a tank fair full o' gas. I'm gaein' tae have tae vent him."

"Hold it!" yelled Trespass, flinging down the cloth he'd been using to polish the horns of his Harleck Dravidian. "You're not doing that while I'm in here. Last time you nearly killed me. It was like trying to breathe in a brick."

"Aye, it's a dirty job, but someone's got tae dae it."

Trespass ushered the rest of the gang to the door, passing the knitting-needle wielding Bruce. In the courtyard, the four men waited for the rush of air that would indicate that Bruce's operation had been successful.

"Give us a fag while we wait," Burble asked his brother.

"Last one," replied Frunge, pointing to his empty mouth. "'Ere – where's me fag gone? Some bugger's nicked it. Er …"

"Unless," growled Trespass, maliciously, "you've left it inside. You clot! Go and get it before …"

The stables exploded.

Burble picked himself up from the cobblestones and looked over to Frunge, who had been blown into a nearby horse trough. The beardless one went over to give his elder brother a hand. "Maybe, bruv, it wasn't such a good idea leaving a naked flame in the same room as a yak that's being degassed?" Frunge managed a damp shrug.

A moment later, a steaming figure emerged from the stable door. The only bit of Bruce that seemed to have survived intact was his red beard, an entity so matted and dense it would have required a thermonuclear detonation to harm it. His complexion, on the other hand, had changed radically from anaemic to black, his shoulder-length hair was now flying vertically above his head, and his eyebrows had gone AWOL. In his hand he held a set of limp reins. The beast to which these had previously been attached now lurched out of the stable. It, too, had undergone a considerable transformation, now being the only hairless yak south of the Great Grebe desert.

And so the afternoon passed. Evening hurried into town and then, realising the error of its ways, hurried out again. And night sneaked in through the backdoor ...

Hops had dismissed the bar staff early from the near-deserted inn, sending his two intrepid questers off to bed so that they would be well rested for an early start tomorrow. The monk had soon followed, having been allocated the guestroom that Hops normally used when his presence wasn't otherwise commanded at home by the missus. The innkeeper himself had kept the bar open to continue serving Occum (his sole customer) as long as ale remained in the pumps.

The atmosphere in the darkened bar was hardly convivial. The two men stared into different distances, each distracted by their own particular concerns. Hops pondered a variety of strategies for staving off bankruptcy until the return of his heroic adventurers. Meanwhile, Occum mused on the worldly lack of a decent hangover cure. The barber had tried just about everything during the course of his long life – including a number of Dr Feare's dubious potions – but all to no avail. He now frowned at the little packet resting beside his pint. His latest experiment had thus far shown no greater effectiveness. Maybe he needed a stronger dose? Pulling a disgusted face, Occum reached into the packet and brought another handful of mank curly locks to his mouth. So much for the 'hair of the dog' …

Upstairs, tucked up in his warm bed, Roffo smiled to himself in his sleep. He dreamt of riding across a vast green plain, with the wind in his hair, a strong horse beneath him, a towering mountain before him and – in the distance – a castle with cruel turrets, strong battlements, and a thousand fluttering flags. The dream-Roffo threw back his head and laughed, and as he did so, the thundering army of warriors charging in his wake laughed with him. This image dissolved to be rapidly followed by a succession of others that were equally improbable: scowling bad guys fleeing before the sword of Roffo the Ruthless; dusky maidens swooning at the sight of Roffo the Ravishing; liberated people calling out the name of Roffo the Redeemer. Again, scenes swirled and changed. Now Roffo smacked his lips as spicy food was spooned into his mouth by a wanton temptress in scanty attire, while – through bow-shaped windows – the vista of a mysterious white city shimmered in a heat haze. A stupid smile affixed itself to the young dreamer's face …

In an adjacent room, Terry tossed and turned trying to find sleep – but the images that kept him awake were not half so pleasant. The barbarian pondered long, tiresome days and cold nights. He imagined himself sitting on a stinking horse collecting sores in places not normally visible to a man (unless you were Mr Bendy-Wendy the Double-Jointed Contortionist). He thought about the unpleasant prospect of arriving in a foreign city and not having change for the parking meters; of being unable to speak the lingo and accidentally ordering frog sputum sauce with his chips; and of having his luggage go missing at Baggage Reclaim. He mused about being pestered by scabby foreign women whose only interests were in lightening his purse and spreading novel sexual diseases; about encountering bandits with more cunning than the condensed cunningness of every fox that had ever lived; and about the grim certainty of Delli Belly or Brumbay Bum. And when Terry eventually dropped off to sleep, his dreams were clouded by thoughts of blood and septic wounds and all the other supposed delights of a barbarian existence that he had once hoped he had left behind forever.

The Angels had also been ordered to retire early, but in their case the gods of sleep were fighting a losing battle with the gods of revelry. It was two o'clock in the morning and the sound of carousing mingled with the warbling of a local rock band, Stevenlupine, to create an annoying racket that carried across the back courtyard and through the thin wooden walls of the stable – where the yakkers' uncomfortable straw beds were arranged. Even worse than the sleep-disrupting quality of the noise, however, was the fact that it reminded the Angels of all the fun that they were missing.

"Cor," said Burble, enviously, "sounds like it's really rocking tonight!"

"Yeah," agreed Grunt. "Bastards!"

"C'mon, let's join them. The boss won't notice, not if we, like, stay out of the light …"

Trespass turned over and propped himself up on one arm. "Shut it, Burble! No-one's going anywhere …"

"Aw, Tres …"

"No no no NO!" He scowled at his sullen gangsters until they dropped back onto their pallets. After extending the scowl for a further minute, Trespass grumpily beat at his straw pillow and lay down himself. He was just getting comfortable when, to his other side, a deep snore boomed through the air. Bruce was the only one to have found sleep, having done so by stuffing wool into his ears (this from one of the many fleeces now adorning his yak). Trespass rolled his eyes in frustration as the bass beat to his left was accompanied by a louder one to his right. He eventually rolled onto his front and heaped straw over his head. The images that teased his mind concerned the terrible things he was going to do to all the people whose loud voices he recognised from the inn. Cutting their vocal cords and beating them about the head with their own larynxes was his initial favourite, though the more-practical idea of banging a large drum outside their homes early the following morning as he left town rapidly gained ground. Deciding he needed to be more imaginative, he set about thinking up more inventive methods of revenge. Eventually, with a smile on his face, he drifted off to sleep.

CHAPTER 7

ON THE ROAD

IN THE grey light of early dawn a small flight of bedraggled pigeons roosted under the gable of a smithy, cursing the Gods of the Storm. Not only had they been deprived of a restful night's sleep by a sudden downpour, but the laughing torrents of water in the gutter were even now washing away their bounty of the last couple of days.

A short distance away, outside The Merry Bear, a pair of yaks stood dolefully in the rain. The yaks were yoked to a large, covered wagon upon which sat a cowled figure, staring at the road, apparently oblivious to the cloudburst. The figure played with the reins impatiently. It turned to address the small knot of people sheltering under the eaves of the inn.

"We leave today – yes?"

"Yes!" cried Roffo excitedly. "Let's rock and roll!" The young barman dragged the last of his bags of adventuring prerequisites through the front door of The Bear and heaved it into the back of the wagon. Scrambling up beside the monk he hurriedly declared: "Bagsie I'm up front!"

The bald oriental squinted at the young man, then meaningfully turned to look at the huge heap of bags, boxes and cases that made the covering tarpaulin bulge like the lumpy cheeks of a greedy hamster. "Any more bags," he declared sourly, "and you break axle!"

For the fourth time Terry tried to extricate himself from the three wailing barmaids – who embraced him like a human straitjacket – and for the fourth time he failed.

"Come come girls," pleaded Hops from the doorway, "let Terry go, eh? Can't you see how much he wants to be off? Ah, Terry my lad, I almost envy you: to feel the wind in your hair, to ride the open plains, to go adventuring, *to see Nudia*! What could be finer for a barbarian, eh?"

Terry looked at the innkeeper unhappily and started to speak, but then closed his mouth and frowned.

"Look at that!" continued Hops. "Overwhelmed he is! Well, we can't delay you any longer. Come on girls, we'll watch them go from inside, where it's warm and dry." The innkeeper grabbed Eddie and gave her a gentle shove through the open front door and then followed after. He reappeared a moment later behind the big bay window with the blubbering barmaid at his side.

Heddy and Maddy reluctantly released the barbarian and stood dejectedly in the doorway. With a rueful backwards glance Terry strode to the wagon. Finding Roffo already settled in beside the monk – his eager head poking out from a huge, green waterproof poncho – Terry let out a resigned sigh and trudged around the back, squeezing in amongst the baggage. Hearing the barbarian crashing about behind him the monk let out a guttural cry and gave the reins a heavy flick. As the yaks started to slowly plod off down the road they left sobbing, handkerchief-waving barmaids in their wake.

"Hope you've packed enough spare undies," yelled Heddy, unable to think of anything sensible to say.

At this, Roffo jumped up in sudden alarm, only to be restrained by the monk's strong arm. "Twenty pairs!" he exclaimed, in panic. "Do you think twenty pairs are enough?"

Terry waved half-heartedly at the girls from the backboard of the wagon. The sudden twitching of curtains within The Pilgrim caught his eye, but the significance of this eluded him. Had he been able to understand semaphore, the waving fittings would have spelt – clearly enough – the word 'trouble'.

"They're off!" yelled Manis, dropping the corner of the curtain he was holding. "To your steeds, men, and sharp about it!" Corners of curtains were thrown down as the yakkers turned to race to the stables. Manis stopped briefly to pat Picket's son on the head and absently slip a few small coins into his hand. With the other half of his attention the innkeeper urged the others on. "Go go go – you mustn't lose them!"

Manis was about to continue after the retreating pack when a thought struck him. He turned around and, to his great relief, discovered that the messenger boy had been too awed by the innkeeper's unexpected generosity to put his tip away: the lad was presently staring at the coins with wide eyes. A fatal mistake! Manis bent over and removed a couple of the coins from the boy's still outstretched hand. After a moment's pause for thought he removed a couple more, leaving the boy with just one small, lonely, bent copper disc. After a second's further reflection, Manis plucked this up too. He tousled the boy's hair. "Good lad! Go to the kitchen: Master Baal has some grub left over from last night. It's fit for a merchant prince, so it is! Tell him I said you could eat your fill. Go on then, off you go!"

With a wicked chuckle, Manis turned and stalked off towards the stable. The scene that greeted him there, however, soon wiped the smile from his face. Chaos reigned!

"What the … I thought I told you to be ready. You're not even properly packed!" He ducked as a small knapsack of supplies shot over his head and landed squarely between Burble's eyes.

"What do you expect," responded Trespass, tying a moth-eaten blanket to the back of his saddle. "You tell us to go to bed early and *then* throw a huge party *next door* so's we can't sleep. *Then* you come storming in here at an ungodly hour and *kick* us awake, *demanding* that we come to the bar to watch what's happening over the road. And *then* you try to hurry us off when we haven't even had breakfast or anything!"

"Yeah," concurred Grunt, "and I'm not paying the rip-off prices of them roadside service stations either. Wot about a sub?"

Manis ignored the request and scowled at the leader of the pack. "Do I have to do everything myself? Just get to it, you morons!" He turned around to discover that Bruce was nearest, thereby qualifying for his help. The innkeeper set about stuffing everything in reach into the two broad panniers that depended from the saddle of the highlander's fleece-covered yak. After five frantic minutes, filled with more foul language than an archive of films by Tarantino, the packing was completed and the party was ready to depart.

"Gerroff!" growled Trespass, as Manis tried to throw him physically into the saddle. "Look, boss, we've got loads of time! We don't want to be so close they shake us off the first time they wipe their arses." The yakker hauled himself onto his steed, then looked down at his employer. "Besides, with all that gear they loaded they'll leave a trail in the mud a blind man could follow!"

"If you don't leave now," explained Manis irritably, "the farmers will start turning up for market with their produce and, more importantly, their carts. Now," he added sarcastically, "won't that obscure your trail just a teensy weensy bit?"

"Er, yeah, okay. Good point. Let's go lads. Up and at 'em!"

"Which way?" asked Grunt.

"They're heading for the South Gate," answered Burble, clambering onto his yak. "If we use the back streets we can get to the gate before 'em and watch which way they head: south to Nudia, east to the barbarian lands, or west to the mountains."

"Fine suggestion," said Trespass. "I'll lead. Grunt: you're tail-end Charlie."

In single file the Angels streamed past Manis heading towards the gate, with Grunt bringing up the rear. Just as the last in line passed Manis, he gave his yak a hearty squeeze with his powerful legs. A deep, resonant, and extremely menacing sound emanated from the bowels of the yak, shortly followed by a rank wind that ruffled the innkeeper's hair and assaulted his olfactory senses.

"Watch that back-fire!" said a grinning Grunt, as he turned back to check on the gagging innkeeper. Addressing his steed, he cried: "Look wot you've dun now? Bad boy ... *bad* boy!" With a snort – that just might have been a stifled laugh – he goaded his mount onwards.

The thought that – a few seconds previously – the present contents of his lungs had been up a yak's bottom, sent a nauseous wave of bile rushing up Manis's throat. By the time he recovered from this particular bout of chemical warfare, the Angels had moved out of sight.

<hr />

"What now?" demanded The Potoon of his panting ancillary.

"Your Magnificence, the infidel has left the bar and is presently occupied in the stable with his hairy horde. They appear to be preparing for a trip." The Potoon looked out of the room's back window and caught sight of the first Hull's Angel exiting the stables.

"Wight, this is our chance. Wet us begone fwom this pwace befoah we die of some tewibble disease. To the cawavan!" The Potoon normally ran from no man, but in Manis's case he was prepared to make an exception. In his early travels, before his trading talents had brought him success and wealth, he had endured countless hardships ... but the last two days had been something else. Never had he eaten such disgusting food, slept on such festering ground, or been rained upon by such fetid waters. Even though he was 'doing a runner', however, he comforted himself with the thought that he was still going to leave by the front door. "I want absowute siwence. The fust sound I heah will be quickwee accompanied by a second – that of the pahpetwatah's sevahed head webounding off the gwound!"

The Potoon's personal guard crept over to the top of the stairwell and peered cautiously down. The coast appeared to be clear. He signalled to the Potoon who, with the rest of his band, silently stole down the stairs. Meanwhile Manis, having recovered his composure and seen off the last of his troublesome minions, headed back to the bar in search of something short and strong to take away the vile taste that presently clung to the back of his throat like a limpet with BO. A strange sight greeted him. There, coming down the stairs on tiptoe, carrying their long, curly, red slippers in their hands, were the Potoon and his men.

"Going without breakfast?" enquired Manis.

"Awgh," went the surprised Potoon, ducking just in time to avoid being decapitated by an over-eager guard. "Yes," he explained, rapidly recovering his aplomb whilst beating his almost-executioner around the head with his shoes. "Wegwetabwee we must now weave. We have many weagues to go."

"Oh well," said Manis, with a shrug, "that's a shame. I had something special planned too." And indeed he had: sausages filled with the natural product of pig intestines; black puddings made from the blood of Fungian Septic Skunks; and pickled goat eyeballs served in a sauce of sheep spittle. He'd even had Baal dye the eyeballs yellow so that the dish looked like fried eggs. It had been the innkeeper's intent to serve the Samark a breakfast so vile that he would never, *ever* want to stay at The Pilgrim *for free* again. It was a shame about the wasted food (he'd probably donate it to the town's orphans), but Manis felt confident that he had already done enough to ensure that the Potoon would remain with his caravan on his next visit. "See you in a few months," he said. "Oh, and by the way: what's with the shoes?"

"Shoes?" queried the Potoon, extracting the curly tip of one of his slippers from the nostril of a guard, then looking at it as though he had never seen such a thing before. "Oh *these*! We, ah … wemoved them so as not to wouse you and yoah guests."

"So thoughtful," said Manis, following the party into the bar. He poured himself a large one as he watched the Samarks head out the door, before breaking into a run across the market. *Pagans*, he thought to himself, shaking his head sadly. *No gratitude.*

"*Infidels*," said the Potoon, to his personal bodyguard, as they sped across the damp market square. "No idea of hospitawity!"

149

"I'm feeling sick," complained Roffo, as they bumped along the Great South Road. Brown, tree-covered foothills lay off to either side of them, while mountains rose up to east and west forming two high, parallel walls in the middle-distance. Behind them, the South Gate of Cross-My-Way still loomed large on the horizon. "I occasionally," he continued, "er, *very* occasionally you understand, suffer from travel sickness."

"Occasionally!" cried the astonished monk. "We only been travelling ten minutes!" He shook his head and gurned in displeasure. "Fortunately, have medicine that will fix sickness. Hold onto reins while I fetch from back."

Roffo grabbed hold of the relinquished reins and watched the cowled figure dive into the bowels of the wagon. Here, the monk started fishing around amongst his stores and jars. *Yes*, thought Roffo, in secret triumph, his nausea disappearing with suspicious suddenness, *in charge at last*! Casting a cunning glance back at the monk – who was now studiously examining a small brown bottle – he gave the reins a sly flick. Nothing. *Damn*, thought Roffo, *it's going to take a bit more than a whip across the back to make these buggers speed up*. His mind went back to the chilli incident earlier in the week, and the painful memory of splinters caused him to squirm in his seat. He wouldn't be using *that* approach again! It was then that the handle of a fishing spear caught his eye. A quick prod in the right place should provide appropriate encouragement! He slowly slid the barbed harpoon out of its holding, spun it in his hand to get the point facing in the right direction, and rested its tip against one of the animals' buttocks. He leant on the end to give it a little penetration into the yak's thick hide … with a result somewhat greater than planned. For, at that exact moment, the front wheel of the cart encountered a particularly deep and uneven pothole. The diminutive adventurer was pitched forward …

The yak let out an horrific bellow – scaring the wits out of its companion – and both beasts took off as though powered by rocket fuel. Roffo silently voiced the words *not again* as he desperately sought to rein in the charging yaks. The monk suddenly found himself pitched from a standing position in the front of the cart to a prone one at the back. Terry was not so lucky: one minute he was sitting glumly on the backboard of the wagon, and the next he was flying through the air, and then the next he was sitting on the road, having hit it with a force that would have broken the buttocks of an ordinary man. He dusted himself off, stood up, and turned to watch the rapidly receding cart. An obscenity formed on Terry's lips. Resignedly, he set off in pursuit of his comrades.

Outside the South Gate the yakkers waited on the summit of a small hill, watching the road below. A copse of trees sprouted from its peak, providing cover from the rain and prying eyes.

"They seem to be heading south to Nudia," said Trespass, peering out from under a hand, "and it seems they're in a hurry."

"Do you think they're gonna go all the way?" asked Frunge.

Burble laughed obscenely. He was well acquainted with the tales of Nudia and the famed sexual-hyperactivity of its denizens. "In Nudia, *everyone* goes *all the way*."

"No wonder they're in such a hurry," said Grunt, suddenly wide-eyed.

"Er, no," said Frunge, "I meant, well, you know wot I meant!"

"Sure, bruv," said Burble, "don't worry your head about it." He turned to face Trespass, who was mounted up beside him. "By my reckoning, there's nothing of any possible interest on the road between here and Nudia ..." The beardless yak rider was well aware of the concept of an *ulterior motive*, and he could feel one coming on now. He shook his head in a sage manner and pursed his lips in a contemplative fashion (while simultaneously wiping his suddenly damp hands on his black leather trousers). "Nothing at all. Just some hills, a swamp, and endless rolling plains ..."

"Aye, an' endless rollin' when ye git there," leered Bruce.

Burble ignored him. "So they *must* be going to Nudia."

Trespass mused on this fact as he watched the tableau before him.

"Do you think they're going to make Testicles run all the way?" wondered Frunge.

"If they dae," said Bruce, "he'll be fair shagged oot afore he has a chance of *bein'* shagged oot ..."

Trespass nodded. *Damn that Manis*, he thought. *If we make a logical decision and it goes wrong, so that we have to suffer days of sexual ecstasy, well, we can hardly be blamed for that, can we?* "Right," he said at last, making an executive decision. "That's it. I think they're going to Nudia. Agreed? Good. We'll go straight to Nudia and intercept them there." This decision was met with a general nodding of heads and mumbling of assent. Lecherous smiles formed on hairy faces. Grown men began to dribble like infants. And Grunt removed his helmet and placed it over his lap.

151

"Er, yeah, but what if they're laying a false trail," queried Frunge, who still hadn't quite cottoned on to the hidden agenda. "We'll look like complete dick-heads just waiting there amongst all those, um … *naked beauties*?" Light began to dawn. "Er, with their, um, pert breasts?" Frunge gulped hard. "And, er, their smooth round butts and, er, soft silky thighs." Frunge was now sitting bolt upright in his saddle.

"It's a risk," replied Trespass, stoically, "that we *have* to take!" He wiped a bead of sweat from his brow. "Okay, Burb, you claim you can read maps. Lead the way."

<hr>

Although the summer's day had remained warm, the rain had continued to fall for all of the morning and most of the afternoon. It was not until the late afternoon that the sun finally managed to pierce through the leaden skies to patchily illuminate the damp landscape. For Roffo, the day had started off on the sort of emotional high not usually achieved without the use of habit-forming substances, but the seemingly endless hours spent bumping along the soggy road had gradually begun to take its toll. Now Roffo sat glumly on the backboard, his poncho tucked beneath his chin, glowering at the slowly moving trees. "One tree … another tree … another *bloody* tree … *yet another* tree … *a* tree …"

"What's that?" asked Terry, who'd struggled into the depth of Roffo's expeditionary gear in search of a cloth to clean his axe.

"Oh, nothing. Just commentating on the landscape. Oh look: a *tree*!"

Terry came to sit beside him. "You look bored."

"What – me? Bored? What makes you think so?"

Terry looked at his friend askance. "Er, is that sarcasm?"

"I'm sorry, Terry. I didn't realise adventuring could be so dull. We must have travelled *miles* and we haven't done anything exciting yet. Where are the bandits? The wood spirits? The dragons? I haven't even seen any bears."

"I should think they're sheltering from the rain. I'm sure they'll appear soon enough." Terry grinned at the barman. "Why don't you take over the reins?"

"The monk won't let me. Called me an 'imbecile' he did! I mean, it wasn't my fault the yaks decided to have a race …" Roffo noticed Terry's grin. "Er, okay, it probably *was* my fault. I just thought we ought to, you know, speed up a bit. And, well, you enjoyed your run didn't you?"

Terry chuckled quietly. "Having spent the last few hours sitting on my butt, I now appreciate it a bit more than I did at the time!"

Roffo had the decency to look a little sheepish.

The two men stared at the passing landscape for several minutes in silence. Just outside of town the land had been largely brown: barren fields, brown earth, grey-brown boulders, the odd brown-leafed tree, and steep mountains in the background. But the mountains had fallen away from their flanks as they had passed out of the long, dry Valley of Longitude, emerging into rolling plains. Here, the colour of the land had gradually changed from brown to green: the hills, now well watered, had first supported grasses and ferns, and then trees. Now the land through which they passed might almost be considered a forest.

As a shaft of sunlight broke through the layer of purple-grey clouds, skimming the treetops, Terry shielded his eyes. "Well, I suppose we ought to make camp soon before it gets dark." He nudged Roffo in the ribs and smirked at him mischievously. "And who knows what *terrors* the night might bring!"

Roffo gulped hard. "What – terrors? You think so? That'd be something! Yeah!"

"Okay. Look out for a place to pull off the road and camp. I'll tell the monk."

As Terry clambered forward through the wagon, Roffo rubbed his hands in recaptured glee.

———•◦•———

They camped in a small clearing just off the road. Night had fallen quickly and, for Roffo, with surprising suddenness. They had barely had time to light a fire and hobble the yaks away from the wagon before the sun disappeared below the tree tops. Now, a half-full moon held dominion in the sky, casting feeble light onto the world. Occasionally, the sky's new monarch slipped from sight, playing peek-a-boo behind the few remaining clouds – stragglers from the cold front that had earlier blighted the party's day.

Roffo sat by the fire, shivering slightly in spite of the extra-thick lambswool jumper he wore. Occasionally, the young adventurer jumped at the sound of snapping twigs or fluttering wings, or at the caress of the wind, or at the buzz of an insect attracted to the flames. When a large moth decided to test out the suitability of his face as a landing pad, he gave a shriek and batted at it with his empty supper bowl.

"Bloody bugs! Piss off! Yes, and *you* ... and *you* too ... and you can have some of it too ..." Roffo leapt to his feet and flailed about with his bowl. "Aha! Got you, scumbag! Take *that* and *that* ..."

153

"Ai-la!" cried the monk, materialising from the darkness. "What going on? You make enough noise to wake the sleeping!"

Roffo came to a sudden halt in mid-swat and cocked his head to one side in a quizzical fashion. "Um, don't you mean *the dead*?"

"Hah! Foolish one! How can wake the dead when they are dead?" The monk shook his head like a teacher who'd just been given a particularly stupid answer by the classroom dunce. "Now – calm self!"

Roffo slouched down beside the fire next to the monk – who had crossed his legs in a bizarre double-jointed manner and was now rubbing his hands before the flames. Opposite the pair, Terry sat quietly in a world of his own, apparently undisturbed by Roffo's antics. With long, slow sweeps, the barbarian slid a whetstone up and down the curved edge of his huge battleaxe. The *schlick schlick* of whetstone on axe seemed to have mesmerised him.

A cracking sound from somewhere out in the forest made Roffo hunch further forward until he was virtually in the flames. He looked around warily. He imagined he saw a flicker of movement off to the left, and then to the right. He strained his eyesight, which made the shadows seem to waver and move even more. A prickling sensation ran down his neck. He closed his eyes for a moment and shook his head, trying to clear it of the imaginary demons. He looked across the fire at his friend, seeking a comforting sight, but the barbarian's trance-like state caused him to frown uncertainly.

"Hey – look at Terry," he whispered to the monk. "What's up with him?"

The monk nodded to himself. He spoke quietly. "Is *steel*. Has caught him."

"What do you mean?"

"Steel of axe is ... *magic*. Barbarian magic." The monk leaned closer to Roffo as though afraid that the sound of his voice might break a spell. "Is said by *barbarians* that *steel* is gift to them from gods. Hmm. Others say reverse ... that barbarians are gift to steel. Sometimes steel seems to *control* them. Is *through* barbarians that steel makes mark on world, and shapes it, and breaks it. Steel is fearsome thing!"

"How can steel ... wait a minute ... what's that smell?" Roffo raised his nose to the air and sniffed. "I smell burning. What's burning?" He looked down in front of him. What he saw caused his eyebrows to spasm into the sort of arches that must once have inspired a certain triumphal French dictator. "Aaaargh!" cried Roffo, leaping to his feet and prancing about like a mad jester on a bed of coals. Flames licked up from one of his shoes. Startled by the cry, Terry looked up with eyes that were fearsomely wide. *Fight. Blood. Death. Fight.* The steel urged him on, whispering promises and endearments. For a moment, the barbarian's muscles bunched and tensed, but then the mist cleared, and all that Terry could see was his young friend hopping about on one foot while waving the other in the air.

"Ah … oh … ah ah … oh …. me foot me foot!"

Terry put down the axe, and relief flooded over him. Laughing, he picked up a blanket and tossed it to the barman. "Go on then, beat it out."

"Ah … yes … ah … oh … thanks … Oh oh. Bugger!" Roffo came to a halt and peered at his now-smouldering shoe, and then he looked up at the others. "There you go," he declared. "You both laughed at all the gear I packed, but Gramps was right!" He planted his arms on his hips and elaborated: "Day one, and I've already got through a pair of shoes! Good job I packed a dozen more!" And with that, he about-turned and stalked off to the wagon to arrange his attire for the morrow.

———◆•◆•◆———

The wagon bumped along the road at the same steady pace it had set for the past week. Roffo glowered at the landscape with a look approaching enmity. The forests had withdrawn somewhat so that they could once more see – between the trees – stretches of green hills and the odd rocky outcrop. A whole week, thought Roffo, and the most exciting thing that had happened to them during all that time was when a bird had shat on the monk's head, and he had even missed *that* because he'd been sent to a stream to get some water. *And* the monk still refused to let him have the reins.

Roffo looked at the monk – who now sat beside him, reins in hands, scowling at the road ahead – and an idea began to form in his mind. Flattery, he once remembered Eddie saying, could get you anywhere. True, she had said it to Terry (in a pleading kind of way) and *not* to him, and it was also true that his own efforts at flattery with Maddy had usually resulted in a free ale-shower, but he was sure that this was just a case of lack of practice. He manufactured a jolly smile.

"Cor," he noted to the monk. "You really know how to handle a team. The way you keep them in a straight line – amazing! Must take a lot of skill that!"

The monk slowly turned towards the young man, a look of utmost incredulity etching his face. He simply stared.

"Um, I mean, they haven't bolted once, um, must be something to do with your masterful …"

"No."

"Er," stuttered Roffo, "no what?"

"No – I not give you reins." The monk's face adopted the expression of a disgruntled gargoyle. "And no, I not teach you how to use them …"

"But …"

"No!" With one last gurn, the bald-headed one turned back to his driving.

Roffo chewed on his bottom lip for several minutes, his mind toying with various mischievous options. The monk was clearly too wise to be fooled by flattery. Perhaps Roffo could somehow disable him? Pushing the obdurate one into the path of the wheels, however, did seem rather extreme. Perhaps logic was the answer?

"Er, Mr Monk, sir, have you thought about what might happen if you somehow, er, got hurt? Who would drive …?"

"Barbarian!"

"Er, yes, *but* what if we were under attack by bandits at the time? Terry would be needed to repel boarders, and then who would …"

"Me."

"Yes, but, remember, you're injured and …"

"How?"

Roffo scratched his head. "I dunno … perhaps you've got an arrow in your arm …"

"Then still able to drive."

"Ah, but, what if you had *two* arrows in *each* arm, and you were knocked out too?"

The monk gave this a moment's consideration, enough to start raising Roffo's hopes. The oriental frowned. "We in battle, yes?"

"That's right!"

"And it noisy and scary, yes?"

"Of course!"

The monk nodded curtly. "Then yaks scared and run. Best they given their heads. No need to steer. So."

Roffo stared at his companion with an open mouth. Logic had failed! Time for extreme measures. Begging!

"Oh, please, go on, please please please, let's have a go. Go on, you can trust me …"

"No!"

"I'll cook your favourite grub tonight: roast duck in black bean sauce?"

The monk hesitated for a moment. "No."

Roffo slumped back in his seat and crossed his arms. There *must* be some way to move him. Perhaps, yes, *perhaps* if he got to know the monk better then he could work out his weak points, or at least, maybe become a good enough friend to appeal to his good will and camaraderie. A sly look stole over Roffo's face.

"Okay. I don't want the reins. Subject closed ..."

"Good."

"Well, anyway, what shall we talk about? I know, why don't you tell me about yourself? Hey, yeah, I've just realised – I don't actually know your name!"

At this, the monk stiffened. His eyes widened.

"Go on," wheedled Roffo. "What's your name? It would make communication a bit easier, eh?"

"No it not! My name is ... *secret.*"

"Eh? You don't know your own name?"

"Of course know!"

"Does your mother know?"

"Yes! Too many know ... that is ..." and he trailed off into silence.

"A secret monk thing, is it?" wondered Roffo, mischievously. "Or is it just that you've got a bit of a silly name? Maybe it's something a bit girlie like, I dunno, *Leslie*?"

The monk started. A bead of sweat formed at the corner of his brow.

"Go on! It can't be! What about *Eustace*? Or maybe *Rosemary*?"

"Here," cried the monk suddenly, thrusting the reins into the barman's hands. "Feel ill – think go into back and lie down for a while!"

With a crow of victory, Roffo grasped the leather leads.

Hops considered the interviewee sitting before him. "Well, Jon," he enquired, "what experience do you have of troubleshooting in the service sector?"

The innkeeper – fearing further sabotage or, at the very least, high-spirited customers – had reached the point where he could no longer ignore the lack of muscle behind the bar. Although business over the last week had not been great, things had started to pick up as a consequence of the return of a number of The Bear's regulars. Some of these repatriated beer guzzlers had been dragged back by their guilty consciences. Others had simply returned because they could no longer afford the exorbitant prices being charged at The Pilgrim for Mardon's Pedigree, or because they could no longer stand the bowel-stressing effects of the Rear Thruster that all Pilgrim customers were now required to sup under Manis's new voucher scheme. Further custom had come from the occasional caravan trader or traveller who had heard of the inn but not of its recent disasters. Indeed, the smell from The Outie Incident had now diminished sufficiently that the barstaff *occasionally* managed to relieve the latter visitors of the price of a drink *before* the oppressive odour drove them to more fragrant pastures.

Long Jon Con Dom, ex-Purveyor of Devices of Sexual Education and Gratification, frowned at the question and wriggled in his seat nervously. He was generally a confident fellow, but attending this interview had put him in mind of his last visit to the dentist. The trick to this situation, he knew, was to lie through his teeth, but not so outrageously as to be disbelieved. "I used to own a stall in the market," he began, "which provided a very popular *service* to the *public*. As such, there was many an occasion when I had to deal with, ah, *over-excited* customers." At least that was true, thought Jon. "I believe I handled these situations with tact, diplomacy, and discretion. Oh, and with a bucket of cold water when necessary."

"A bucket of cold water?"

"Yes, it's a new sedation technique." Jon spread his large hands and grinned lop-sidedly. "I find it cools off the riff-raff and brings them to their senses without the need to resort to physical violence." With growing confidence he leaned forward and declared: "And I really think it could work quite well in the hostelry industry."

"An interesting idea," said Hops, mulling the concept over. He scribbled onto the piece of parchment before him and chewed thought-fully on the tip of his quill. Still looking at the parchment, he continued. "Okay. You say you *used to* run a stall. What happened?"

"There was a crash in the market," replied Jon, carefully.

Hops looked up at this. "I see. The value of your stock dropped and you lost your business? That's a terrible thing to happen to an honest trader!"

Jon smiled sorrowfully and shrugged his shoulders. He was not about to admit that the drop in his stock was unrelated to adverse trading conditions on the Cross-My-Way Stock Exchange, but was instead due to his loss of control over the licentious mob that had overwhelmed his stall during the market frenzy prior to The Match. His business truly *had* been lost: into the pockets, pouches, and bags of the town's amoral

158

majority. A decent troubleshooter, Jon mused, would never have allowed such a thing to happen.

"It's the up and down life we entrepreneurs lead," said Jon, watching the innkeeper intently. He was relying heavily on the sympathy vote here, but he knew he had to be wary of going overboard. "We work every hour that Clovory sends us. We invest our very souls into our work. We live for our professions. And then misfortune strikes, and all our endeavours come to naught. So much for the vicissitudes of life! Still, I can't complain. Such perils can strike down the very best of us."

Hops nodded glumly. "Aye, so they can."

"But we're survivors, eh, you and I? We will prevail in the end. What doesn't break us, makes us stronger." Jon allowed a smile to slip onto his lips. He could sense that this was going well. "Now, can we focus on details? I believe this is a temporary job, available while the present employee is away on a religious pilgrimage. This is precisely what I am looking for. This job would give me the chance to get together enough money to repair my … er, to start a new business."

Although the innkeeper felt a certain empathy with the stricken trader he would never allow emotion to overwhelm logic where business was concerned. He looked down at the parchment before him and leafed through the sheets beneath it. Long Jon was the sixteenth man he had seen for this position and was clearly the best so far. Indeed, none of the previous applicants had lasted more than a few minutes, proving to be either mischievous, deviant, dishonest, alcoholic, lazy, or, indeed, *all* of these things.

Rudy Brassrubbers (one of The Pilgrim's stalwarts if ever there was one) had only made it through the door because Hops's attention had been diverted by the list of questions he had been perusing at the time.

Mitchkin the thief – his head bandaged and his middle-thigh region wrapped so thickly in gauze that he looked like a baby wearing a nappy that hadn't been changed for a year – had lasted barely three minutes. Hops had dismissed the part-time umpire in a rage as soon as he realised that he was suddenly trying to write with a quill that had *mysteriously disappeared from his hand* onto a *now-invisible* piece of parchment. Peculiarly, the chair upon which Mitchkin had been sitting had also gone missing on his departure. Hops couldn't even bring himself to *think* about where the man might have stashed it.

Rude Lubblers had lasted even less time … about thirty seconds in fact. Generally, mused Hops, it was not considered good form to answer the first question of an interview, "And why do you want this job?" with the pithy response: "Mind your own fucking business you fat git."

And Fat Grevis had been completely incoherent as a consequence of a conditioned response that led to his mouth filling with saliva at the very sight of a beer pump. The row of unprotected, vulnerable temptresses that were ranged behind the bar had clearly been too much for him.

Hops frowned at the memory of the previous interviews. Nightmares! He looked up at Jon and cast a critical eye over the man's physique – as honesty and integrity were not the only requirements for this special post. Although Jon was imposingly tall, the middle-aged man was also somewhat on the thin side. Hops chewed on his bottom lip. Maybe he could bulk him out somehow? He nodded to himself.

"Well, I have a few more people to interview," Hops said, suddenly beaming, "but I think I may have found my man. Come back tomorrow morning and I'll let you know." The innkeeper waited until Jon had departed through the front door then cried out: "Next!"

———

They crested a damp hill and saw below them, stretching off into the distance, a carpet of tall grasses and reeds.

"There's the road," declared Trespass, indicating a faint line off to their left. This ran between two hills and then arrowed into the swamp. "And that must be the Golag Bogs. Bloody Hull, Burble, have you been this way before or are you just lucky?"

The short, barrel-shaped yakker flashed a grin. "Luck's got nothing to do with it, mate. I've got a compass in my head!"

"Aye," muttered Bruce, "sae that explains why there's nae room fo' any brains."

Burble glared at the man. "That's good, coming from the moron who set his own yak on fire!"

"Wasnae ma fault," snarled Bruce, "wasnae me who left a lighted fag layin' aboot …"

"Enough!" bellowed Trespass. He stared menacingly at his motley band, holding the stare for several seconds until he was sure he had quashed the quarrelling. "Right. We must be ahead of the others by now. Let's get back on the road."

"Bollocks," said Burble, eloquently. "Look, the road only goes part of the way into the Bogs and then it curves out and misses most of it. If we cut straight through we can gain even more time on them." He smiled. "And that means we should have *even more* free time in Nudia."

"Hmmm," mused Trespass, "a convincing argument! The more

time we have on them the, er, the longer we have to plan a trap. But are you sure you can get us across?"

Burble drew himself up to his full height in the saddle (which, admittedly, was not great). "No probs! I can navigate by the stars and everything! All we have to do is keep the sun on our left and we'll get across in half the time."

"Are you *really* sure about this?" asked Grunt, who did not like the look of the swamp at all.

"Course he is," said Frunge, lending fraternal support. "Let's go." Before anyone could raise any further objection the brothers set off down the hill. Trespass gave a shrug and gestured for the others to follow.

"Croak!" said the frog. "Croak croak ribbet *croak.*"

A newt, sunbathing on a nearby log, gave the frog a hard stare. "You've been at those mushrooms again, haven't you? You always talk funny afterwards. I don't know why you do it."

"No I haven't!" said the frog, with some indignation. "I've been off the mushrooms for *days* now. Been through *cold duck* and everything. I'm clean."

"Then what's with the frogspeak? You a *revivalist* or something? A *recidivist* who yearns for, wotsit, past times when all Golag swampthings spoke their own tongues and we couldn't understand each other, and our days were filled with, y'know, strife and stuff?"

"Nah. I'm just practising in case those humans come by again. We can't let them in on the Big Secret can we? Anyway, it's been such a long time since we got any in *this* part of the swamp that, well, I'm a tad rusty at the old tongue."

"You're telling me," replied the newt. "Croak! Croak croak ribbet *croak* – indeed!" He shook his head from side to side. "I'm assuming you're trying to say Croak! Croak croak *ribbet* croak. Which is to say, that classic rebuke: *Oy! Get off of my lily pad!*"

The frog looked non-plussed. Being corrected on his native language by a newt really took the water biscuit. "Well, what was I saying?"

The newt gave a gargling laugh. "You said: *Oy! Get off of my willy lad!* Which, as you can see, is a request of an entirely different nature!"

The frog gave his eyes a lick and considered the matter.

"You know," said the newt, with a hint of envy, "I never get over that tongue thing. I bet that really excites the girls!"

"Too right," replied the frog. "But not quite as much as *this* does

..." He unrolled his tongue like a mad Turkish carpet salesman, wrapping it around an unsuspecting fly.

"I'm speechless," said the newt, who clearly wasn't. "I wonder how ... eh-up! What's that?"

A loud splashing noise came from a point in the swamp a few yards away. The newt started to twitch his tail nervously.

"Relax," soothed his amphibian chum, while gumming methodically at his snack. "It's just those humans again. And their giant ducks."

"Oh, yeah, I see now." The newt scampered up onto a grassy mound to get a better look. "Funny looking ducks though. Why do you think they have big branches poking out of their heads?"

The frog expanded its throat to produce a vesicle that would have been the envy of any contestant at the world bubblegum championships. "Weapons I reckon. Probably War Ducks. Something like that. I expect they impale things on them."

"Cor! And look at their feathers: they're so long you can't even see their wings. That's weird that is. And why are the humans shouting and waving their fists at the smaller one in front?"

"It's a mating ritual!" declared the frog, confidently, adding a 'Croak' in the *lingua amphibia* just in case any of the passing men were listening.

"How do you know?"

"Well, when they went past this morning they were all quiet. When they went past this afternoon they were shouting loudly at the bod in front. And now they've come back a third time and they're even more excited. It's a classic scenario. Soon they will mate."

"Hmm!" wondered the newt, who was beginning to suspect that his companion had sex on the brain. "Are you sure it's related to bonking? They just look very angry to me."

"Of course I'm sure. Only a second ago I heard one of them say he was *going to have* the small one if they were still in this *bloody swamp* by midnight. Well, there's no way they're going to be out by then, so sex is looking pretty likely."

The newt flicked out its tongue and tested the air. "Well, that's definite then. But why do you think they keep going through Stinky Bottom? I mean, it's a nice area and all that – distinctly *des res* – but I always thought humans considered it to be the foulest, most rancid, most putrid part of the swamp. Is it all part of the mating ritual?"

"Dunno. Maybe they've come here to feed their ducks. After all, the flies here *are* particularly fat and plentiful. Or maybe they just like the smell? You can never tell with humans. Thick as two short clumps of marsh-grass, the whole lot of 'em."

"Hey," said the newt, suddenly enthusiastic, "that reminds me of a joke Old Warty told me yesterday. My log's got no nose ..."

"Heard it," said the frog, and he hastily leapt into the mire.

———•••••———

"Golag Bogs ahead!" shouted Roffo over his shoulder. Behind him, the monk squatted in a little hollow amongst the supplies. This was a position he'd occupied for the last couple of days, complaining of some mysterious ailment that appeared to have no symptoms whatsoever. Behind the wagon Terry was doing his daily exercise, jogging with several hundredweight of Roffo's heaviest sacks perched on his massive shoulders.

As Roffo brought the yak team to a halt beside a signpost, a bald head poked through the canvas and peered at the road ahead.

"Why stop?" asked the monk, sourly.

"Swamp," declared Roffo. "Time for a change of clothing I think. Ah, Terry, there you are – just what I need! In that sack there!"

Ten minutes later they moved off again. Roffo was now clothed in an anti-mosquito hat with a net veil, a bright yellow tunic (which his Gramps had once told him was an ideal bug deterrent because the colour made insects feel sick), and a pair of thick gloves to protect his hands from bites and stings. The monk sat beside him, attired in his usual brown habit, muttering under his breath. Behind these two, Terry stood up in the back of the wagon wearing only a bearskin loin cloth, his hands braced on the frame, looking out over the heads of his companions.

The green hills had become more lush over the last few miles, during which the road had followed a winding path between them. Now the hills drew away to either side of the travellers – forming an encircling wall – while the Great South Road continued straight ahead, dipping into a wide depression in the landscape. This depression acted as a sink for the surrounding land: numerous small streams poured into it from off the hills, and a greater movement of water secretly drained into it through permeable subterranean rocks. In this water-rich environment, tall grasses reigned, and weeds and rushes clustered around shallow pools and muddy bogs. The road surged into the Bog, initially confident, but as the ground became more and more treacherous it started to meander, as though trembling with doubt. At last, the road appeared to realise that it could go no further and, accepting defeat, it swept away to the encircling foothills, detouring around the worst that the swamp had to offer.

The travellers had no sooner started down the road on a gentle descent into the Bog when the first attack came – in the form of a wave of ferocious horse flies the size of impudently raised middle fingers.

"Zzzzz," went one, "look at ze plonker in ze loud shirt!"

"He thinkz it will deter uzzz!" said another.

"Zzzz zzz zzz," laughed the first. "Letz show him. Follow me!"

The squadron of flies darted towards Roffo and buzzed within an inch of his nose, causing the diminutive fellow to shriek.

The flight reformed a few feet away. By now it had been joined by an air armada of mossies (which had scented human blood from a mile away) plus several hundred bandit midges. Wing Commander Eeee, of the 6654th Mosquito Air Force, whined up to the chief of the horse flies.

"Greeeetings Buzz Master!"

"Zzzz! Iz that you Ee?"

"No, it's Eeee!"

"Zzzz, ah, yez, Eeee – 6654th?"

The mossie flitted up and down in acknowledgement.

"Zzzz – good! Let uz co-ordinate our attack!"

The Wing Commander whined assent. "What ees their deesposeetion!"

"There are, zzzz, three of them! A plonker in armour, a baldy, and a Big Mother!"

The mossie darted away to have a look, then returned as rapidly. "Eeeeow, I don't like theee looks of theee barbarian! Iron Man! Weeee probably cannot harm heem! You can have heem!"

"Zzzz – no way! He izz yourz!"

"What! Are you scared?"

The two winged leaders danced about nervously. In the end they came to an unspoken understanding. "Zzzz, okay, we will concentrate on ze other two. We'll annoy ze crap out of ze one with ze hair net, you take ze one with ze shiny head wearing ze sack!"

"Vvvvv," went Bandit Leader VowVow of the midges, "don't, vvvv, forget us!"

"Zzzz – good, maybe you can penetrate ze net. Come with us …" The fly buzzed up to its command. "Squadron! Zzzzz! Attack!"

Several thousand insects drew up into a great cloud, preparing to descend mightily onto their scarcely protected foe.

On the front seat of the wagon the monk calmly produced a pair of chopsticks from one voluminous sleeve. He clacked these together between three fingers, then nodded contentedly to himself.

"What are you doing?" asked Roffo. "It's not lunch-time yet?"

"For us – no. For them …" he gestured at the black cloud that was now hurtling towards them, "it is. This for defence."

"Eh? How, er, what …?"

"Watch!"

The cloud of bugs crashed into the men like a black tidal wave. Roffo screamed and thrashed about, while the monk suddenly came alive like a hyper-animated whirling dervish, clicking his chopsticks like lightning and squishing the life from bug after bug. During all this, Terry stood behind the pair – a slightly confused observer – watching as the swarm dashed itself at his two companions but refused to close with him.

"Wheee!" said Commander Eeee, as he swooped down on the monk's head. "Landing pad ahead! Mine, all mi—" the chopsticks *clicked*.

"Zzzz – what ze fucking Hull is going—" the chopsticks *clicked* again.

"Vvvvv," went the midge chief, caught up in Roffo's face net, "pull back, pull back, vvvv, the net is too fine, vvvv, I repeat, the net is—" a giant pair of fingers *tweaked*, and the bandit chief became a black smudge.

The assault was brief and nasty and, for the insects, remarkably costly. Leaderless, the various armadas retreated back to their stagnant mires to regroup, think of revenge, and tell their numerous young the legend of the demon with the chopsticks.

The yaks, protected by their thick coats, continued along the road, oblivious to the great battle that had just been fought.

"Wow," said Roffo, removing his hat. "I ain't never seen anything like that before – have you Terry?"

The barbarian shook his head and whistled. "Impressive!"

The monk smirked like an imp that had just won the Lottery, wiping his soiled chopsticks on his habit. "Old trick taught at Temple."

"They taught you how to take out flies with chopsticks?" asked Roffo, incredulously. "Boy, you must have had one Hulluva insect problem!"

"No no," laughed the monk, bouncing up and down on his seat. "It taught as part of Eating Ritual. You know? For when accidentally knock over bowl of rice?" The other two looked bemusedly at one another. "Now get driving," continued the monk. "Not want to be in swamp when night falls and little buggers come back!"

Roffo needed no further encouragement.

———•◆•———

"Here you go," said Burble, plonking a tray on the table. "Five pints of the landlord's finest." The four seated men glared at him. Grunt muttered something obscene under his breath; Bruce began to toy with his knife. Burble pondered the injustices of existence and wondered at the quickest way out of the bar. "Well, bugger you lot then!" he said. "Anyone can make a mistake!"

"You're dead right," said Trespass, affecting a philosophical tone, "anyone can make a mistake. However, it takes a *real bloody idiot* to believe it's possible to take a short cut through *that* swamp." In spite of his best intentions, an edge of steel crept into the lead yakker's voice. "Two days we spent wandering aimlessly in that stinking cesspool – *two bloody days*! Did you see the landlord? He almost fainted from the stench when you went to order! Owning an inn on the edge of *that* swamp you'd expect him to have come across the worst of it, but no," and now Trespass stood up and clasped the table top with both black-smeared hands, looming over the shortest member of the pack, "along comes Burble to discover a bit that is so disgusting it dwarfs even *his* most horrific experiences … a region so rank, so foul, and so putrid that it's probably the current holder of the title for Ye Worlde's Most Festering Hull Hole!" He sat down, seething, but instantly leapt to his feet again. "Oh, yes, and another thing: all that time we made up on the other lot … lost!"

"Yeah, and you'd better 'ave lots of shampoo with you," fumed Grunt, thumping the table with one weed-encrusted arm. "I only washed Votan to impress the girlies in Nudia, and you *know* 'ow much I 'ate washing. Now 'e wouldn't impress the foulest and most desperate crone in the universe!"

"Hah!" sneered Burble, whose temper was beginning to fray. "That sounds like an admission that you're *trying* to bait foul and desperate crones! That's moving up a league for you, isn't it! I suppose *Madam Sonia* isn't good enough for you any more? What's the problem? Too many teeth? Too few wrinkles?"

"Are you suggesting I'm dating that 'arridan?"

"Steady on …" said Trespass, worried about the slander of his potential mother-in-law.

The two men ignored him. "Got the pictures, mate, got the pictures!"

"You … you … *aaaaiiiiiieeee*!" Grunt launched himself at his pro-tagonist. The distance he had to cover to get to the man, however, and the fact that this involved going *through* the table, gave the three observers time to react. Frunge made a grab for Burble, pinning his arms to his sides and pulling him back off his chair, while Trespass shoulder-barged Grunt, deflecting his lunge for the smaller man. Bruce, seeing an opportunity to settle a score with the man who had been making sarcastic comments about his hairless yak for the past week, jumped on Grunt's back. He grabbed the fat one around the neck and tried to get his teeth into one of his ears. It was from his lofty position on Grunt's shoulders, however, that Bruce caught sight of something that drove all thoughts of revenge from his head. For there, pulling up outside the inn, was a wagon being driven by a certain very large fellow in a bearskin loincloth.

"Oy!" screamed the landlord. "We don't allow *excessive male bonding* in this inn!"

"Right!" snarled Grunt. "First I'm gonna kill 'im," he pointed at Burble, "and then," he spun around and pointed at the publican, "I'm gonna kill 'im! Nobody accuses me of *that*!"

"Och nae!" went Bruce.

"Och yes!" responded Grunt. "And wot are you doing up there?"

"Look! Through yon window! It's Testicles!"

Trespass leapt onto a chair to get a better look. "It's true. Bloody Hull! Quick – into the bogs!"

The five yakkers, their animosity suddenly forgotten, made a mad dash for the toilets. Unfortunately for Bruce, the five seconds it took to reach the *Gents* was more than long enough for Grunt to forget all about the passenger on his shoulders: Bruce was knocked unconscious on the door lintel as Grunt passed under it. As the four remaining yakkers frantically dragged the prostrate body of Bruce into the privy, Terry and his party entered through the main door.

"Wait a minute," said Burble, who had been squashed into a urinal. "Aren't we supposed to be intercepting them, *not* hiding from them in the loo?"

"Well," pondered Trespass, rubbing his bearded chin, "we *could* take them now. Sure. And then, of course, we wouldn't need to go to Nudia …"

"Ah, well then," said Burble, "maybe we shouldn't be too hasty."

"Besides," said Trespass, "we still haven't found out what they're up to. I'm sure Manis would be pissed off if we didn't find that out …"

"Och, the stars the stars," moaned Bruce.

"Right then. It's decided. We'll continue to Nudia. Quick, Grunt, pull out the window frame and let's get out of here."

Meanwhile, the landlord stood outside the *Gents* listening at the door, a stout stick in one hand and a worried expression on his face. The sight of men jumping on top of each other and then running into the toilets had ruined the reputation of many an establishment. He looked at the stick in his hand, and was suddenly struck by how *small* it appeared when compared to the size of the men who were now holed-up in his lavatory. *Oh well*, he thought, *live and let live!* He shrugged his shoulders and went to greet his new customers at the bar.

CHAPTER 8

FOREIGN CUSTOMS

THE THREE adventurers gathered outside of Ye Swamp Thynge inn. An overnight downpour had left the world glistening and green, though the rain clouds had already cleared and the mid-morning sun was shining bright and warm. A heady perfume exuded from the purple and red blooms of a dozen hanging baskets that depended intermittently along the front of the inn. Fat bumble-bees hummed in delight and blundered drunkenly from one flower to the next. The air had a crisp, clear, invigorating lightness to it.

Roffo drew in a deep breath and closed his eyes as though savouring a fine wine. "Ah, get a lungful of that! Reminds me of the mountain air from back home. It's good to get out of the big city, eh?"

The monk frowned at the barman. "Which big city? You never been to big city before."

"Well, Way is a pretty big place."

"Pah! Way is tiny town. Should see Yegoran or Kishif or Femori: they big cities. You not know what talking about!"

Roffo looked askance at Terry, grinning and raising his eyebrows.

The barbarian grinned back. He was in a fine mood too. He'd had an excellent night's sleep, followed by a breakfast fit for a very fat, very greedy king. Terry patted his stomach in appreciation. "It was good grub, wasn't it?"

Roffo nodded in agreement and loosened his belt. "I'm so full I could burst. Now that was a *real* breakfast – all you could eat for a silver piece! Mind you, I reckon our host regrets the offer now – especially after the way *you* sacked his larder."

The monk broke into a grin at this. "Innkeeper never had to feed barbarian before." He chuckled to himself. "Ha! Saw tears in eyes when had to send son to slaughter pig for more sausages and bacon!"

"And fifteen rounds of toast," continued Roffo, in awe. "Fifteen! Where the Hull do you put them, Terry? And as for all those eggs you guzzled, well, I swear I could hear the hens complaining out back!"

A broad smile fixed itself to the barbarian's face. "Maybe this adventuring isn't *so* bad after all."

"Well, this place definitely gets into my 'Good Hostelry Guide' ... ah, landlord, we were just commenting upon your fine inn."

The apron-wearing landlord smiled weakly. "Aye, well, thank you sirs. If you could pass on your opinions while you're on the road I'm sure I'd be grateful."

"Of course!" cried Roffo. "Splendid stuff! Now, I suppose we must be on our way – you know how these Quests are, eh? How far is it to Nudia then?"

The landlord gave a knowing smile. "Ah, I see! It's *that* sort of quest is it, sir! Just stick to the road and you'll be there in five or six days, tops. You'll know when you're there, believe me!"

Roffo's face reddened. "Uh, it's not what you think, um, *really*, um, I mean, we're not going to Nudia for *that* ..."

"Aye, that's what they all say. Never mind, sir, your secret is safe with me." The landlord winked at Roffo then turned to re-enter his inn.

The much-embarrassed adventurers walked to their wagon.

———●●●●———

In a nearby ditch, five extremely wet men squatted in dank grass and slimy mud and attempted to listen to the conversation emanating from the front of the inn. Trespass nodded at the mention of Nudia. "There you go. *Nudia.* It's confirmed. We'll go cross-country and meet them there."

Frunge's stomach rumbled miserably in response.

Burble stifled a violent sneeze.

Grunt wrung some water from his beard.

"Och, it'd better be bloody worth it," moaned Bruce, who squatted gingerly on his haunches. The hair on his singed yak had started to regrow, producing a stubble that had rasped terribly against his delicate sub-waist anatomy. Bruce's saddle had been lost in the dreaded Golag Bogs, along with most of the party's provisions.

"Sod that," declared Grunt, looking critically at the frizzy mess of his beard. A small black beetle crawled from some recess and dropped into a pool of water at his feet. "I'd give everything I 'ad now for a nice bath."

"You're sick, you are!" noted Frunge, aghast. He dropped onto his butt and took his head in his hands. "Food … all I want is some food," he wailed.

"Let's get in there then," said Burble. "Did you hear that? All you can eat for a silver piece!"

"We cannae," sneered Bruce. "We lost all but one pouch o' oor friggin' funds in that *Pit o' Putredness* an' spent most o' what we had left on the beer last neet. Aye, an' we *didnae e'en git a chance tae drink that* 'cos o' *ye!*"

Burble snarled back and started to strap on a pair of knuckle dusters.

As the inevitable brawl ensued, Trespass merely sighed, closed his eyes, and leant back against the sodden wall of the ditch.

———◆◆◆◆———

"Why do I have to wear this furry nappy?" asked The Bear's new troubleshooter unhappily. "It's considerate of you to provide a staff uniform, but I don't mind wearing my own clothes. It's not a problem, *honest.* Besides, it's damn cold wandering about with nothing on but the remains of a mangy cat. I'm starting to turn blue!" Long Jon gripped the waist of the garment tightly to prevent it from escaping to his ankles. "*And* it's too big!"

"You've got to wear the right gear," explained Hops. "It makes a statement, you see. This here attire tells everyone how tough you are. It declares: Here Is A Man Who Should Not Be Messed With! Don't worry about the size, lad, I'll get one of the girls to take it in a bit. Now, do you have a weapon?"

"Yep. Sure do." With the hand that was not holding up his bearskin attire, Jon waved a dubiously shaped club in the air. "A knobkerrie."

"Good!" Hops rubbed his hands together. "That should cause any would-be troublemakers to think again. Now, where's Heddy … ah, here she is. Hurry along, lass! Have you got it? Excellent!"

"What's this?" asked Jon, suspiciously, as the barmaid approached him bearing a pot between her hands. She was grinning broadly.

"Heddy is going to give your muscles a bit of an oiling." Hops appraised the new troubleshooter once more and frowned. *Muscles?* Long Jon's muscles were about as prominent as a dose of mumps.

"Why? To make me slippery in case a drunken customer grabs hold of me in a bear hug?"

As the winsome barmaid started to massage the oil into Jon's thin chest, his eyes widened. "Hmm," he ventured. "I suppose I'll have to *suffer* this *every* day?"

Heddy nodded, then frowned, her reverie broken. She took a step back to appraise her work. "Your chest is a bit flabby," she noted, before returning to her task. "Now, Terry had lovely tight pecs. Very well defined. And he was beautifully proportioned. And talk about a six-pack, well, he ..."

"Terry this, Terry that!" sneered Long Jon Con Dom, as he hitched up his loincloth. "I'm pretty well regarded in my own field, you know. In fact, I've got a famous contraceptive device named after me!"

"Oh-aye!" said Hops, whose knowledge of contraception stopped at abstinence. "What's that then?"

"*The Longman Special.* Very big in Nudia it is."

Heddy finished her ministrations. She slapped Jon on the chest. "Right, that's you done. Go get 'em!"

Jon took a deep breath, gave his frame a quick shake, then walked through the door to the lounge. There were only two people in residence at opposite ends of the lounge, and they didn't look as though they would be any trouble. Jon scanned the room and noticed, with some satisfaction, the two buckets of cold water that he had earlier put by the fireplace. He nodded to himself and walked up to the bar where Jepho was absentmindedly polishing a glass.

"Business still not picked up then?"

"Nah. There's only old Grumpy. And that stranger over there –" he nodded in the direction of a corner booth "– asked for a pint of *large,* he did, whatever *that* might be."

Just then the doors swung open and a caped newcomer walked into the tavern. He looked around, spotted the man in the booth, and waved at him. Then he strolled over to the bar. He removed his black fedora to reveal a face framed by a grey beard.

"I'll have a banana daiquiri please."

Jepho sighed. It was not going to be his day. "Do you want a pint of that, or what?"

Night was falling fast as the wagon crested the hill. Below, the road wove down into a valley thick with lush bushes and squat, lumpy trees. A gurgling stream paralleled the road. A short distance away, in a clearing between the road and the stream, a small caravan of half a dozen wagons was encamped. A score of camels were hobbled further down the stream bank.

"Companions for night?" suggested the monk.

"Sure," replied Roffo. "And they might be able to tell us a bit about Nudia, too. Someone in the caravan might have been there before."

"They look harmless enough," commented Terry, passing a professional eye over the cluster of vehicles. "See: they've not closed the wagons in a defensive formation, and they've only posted two lightly armed guards. They don't look like the type to cut our throats as soon as we fall asleep."

The monk cracked the reins and urged the yak team forward. The wagon trundled down the gentle slope towards the encampment. The two guards, noting their approach through the twilight gloom, moved slowly but purposefully on an intercept course.

"Good evening, friends," said the monk. "Night is near. Time for travellers to come together and share fire and company and defence, la? May we share camp for night?"

One of the men looked back into the camp. A short distance away, seated beside an embryonic campfire, a smartly dressed man of wide girth gave him the nod. The guard gestured the party to advance and pointed to a place for them to park on the edge of the clearing.

Terry jumped out of the back of the wagon as soon as it came to a halt. He surveyed the scene with his trained eye. A campfire and a captive audience! A primeval urge rose in him. His brows knitted. He licked his lips and felt an urge to speak. *By Grom*, an inner, ancestral voice cried out, *surely this is the place to recount tales of bloody battle and mighty feats, of wounds gained on a broken field and of great feasts in the halls of kings.* This sudden strange thought caused Terry to stop in his tracks. He felt rather *strange*. He shook his head, hefted the tingling axe over his shoulder and, almost without volition, strode towards the ring of men around the fire.

As the moon had risen high into the sky, the fireside conversation had waxed and waned. The men from Kirdost had spoken first: of their dreams of wealth, of the grand marble towers of their homeland, and of the perils that they had faced on the road; and then the monk had replied, telling his tale about the source of ale and the feats of Boozer.

Now silence prevailed as the men stared into the flames and thought about beer and legends and other such weighty matters. As Terry squatted by the fire, with his axe lying across his lap, his hands moved restlessly. In front of him, a log crackled its death throes and sent sparks flying into the air. One of these landed upon the barbarian's thigh. While half of Terry's face frowned the other half, peculiarly, appeared to smile – as though two aspects of his personality strove to interpret the event. Perhaps in town, amidst civilisation, the frown would have won. But here, in the wild, with the wind ruffling the barbarian's hair and the sounds of nature all around him – the hooting of an owl in search of prey, and the laughing of an untamed stream – the smile could not be vanquished. As he watched the spark burn itself out, revelling in the pain, something in Terry's character *changed*. An ancient spirit, as old as his race, stirred within him.

"You know, monk," said the barbarian, in a voice so deep it caused the monk to frown and the drowsing Roffo to sit up in bewilderment, "you tell an interesting tale. The best ale in the world? Hmm. *Perhaps.* But let me tell you what I think." The barbarian slowly leant towards the fire. The flames half-lit his face and gave him an eerie aspect. Roffo opened his mouth to speak, but the monk touched his leg firmly and motioned him to remain silent. Terry rumbled on. "I think this ale of yours cannot match the Blood Ale of my homeland. *That* is the best, and I will tell you why. Heed me!"

The other men around the fire sat up suddenly as though forced by some command that they could not ignore. Some looked around at their colleagues in confusion; one of the caravan guards scratched his head unhappily. As one, the company turned their attention towards the barbarian.

"There is no better death," began Terry, "than one that comes in battle – facing the enemy with an axe in each hand and a curse on your lips!" He clenched his fists in sudden passion and a half-smile – as though from fond remembrance – settled onto his lips. "The warrior who so dies is borne aloft to the Great Halls of the Gods, where old comrades wait, and where there is much feasting and drinking. And the drink … ah, it is no ordinary brew, but it is Blood Ale: the first and the finest of ales; the *due* of all who die honourably …"

Terry looked around the fire at his startled companions and almost seemed to *grow*. His brow furrowed and his half-smile turned into a snarl. "Aye, it is their *due*," he repeated, "but – once – not all of the gods were pleased that this was so, and most displeased of all was Lokran, the Housekeeper, who is guardian and dispenser of the ale. For Lokran resented having to replenish the tankards and the plates of the Fallen. And so, at a time when the fathers of Men were still young, he made a decree – which the other gods, fearing that he would keep the ale to himself if confronted, dared not dispute – that the Fallen would remain at the table only so long as they stayed conscious. Thereafter, whenever a warrior passed out from the ale, he was carried from the table and cast back into the world to be reborn."

Terry picked up a stick and stirred the embers of the fire, bringing more life to the flames. As he did so he gathered his thoughts – the memory of a childhood tale, but now seen through different eyes – then continued. "But in the past, in the time of glorious anarchy before cursed civilisation, there was no ale in any of the lands and the world was as dry as the Great Grebe Desert. For the gods – when they made man – gave him death, but kept the ale for themselves." Now the barbarian looked up at his companions and gave a wry smile that, to Roffo, seemed totally out of character … and yet so *natural.* "And because the warriors were unused to the ale, when they reached the Halls and quaffed from the horns and the tankards, the ale went straight to their heads and they became giddy like foolish youths, and before long they passed out and were expelled – and Lokran was happy!" The barbarian shook his head and howled in laughter, causing the others to start. "Ha – Lokran, you rogue, curse your name! But Grom – who gave us steel – ah, he was not happy at all! For he enjoyed the company of men with their glorious deaths and their great tales, and he loved to hear how well men had used his gift. And so Grom came down to the world of earth as a dream, and he entered the minds of two brothers called Smyth, and gave to them the secret of the Blood Ale, so that warriors could drink and harden themselves to the brew, and prepare themselves for the next life. And these brothers … they were the ancestors of my tribe, and their knowledge has passed down through countless generations to us and us alone!"

Terry now stared into the fire, resting his elbows on the haft of his axe. The other men looked around uneasily, uncertain as to whether the tale was now over. Some licked their lips nervously, others mopped sweat from their brows and looked askance at the unseeing barbarian, and others wondered whether it might now be wise to make a break for the nearest bushes. There was an unspoken recognition that it might be wise to first get permission before making any sudden move. Only the monk and the merchant who led the caravan maintained any degree of calm.

At last, the pipe-smoking merchant, fortified by drink, decided to check the temperature of the water. He cleared his throat. "Barbarian … your tale is fascinating, but I detect an anomaly …" Was "anomaly" going too far? He gulped hard. "Um, your tale doesn't explain why there is ale throughout all the lands in many forms. Why is this so?"

Without taking his gaze from the flames, Terry scowled. "When the first ale was brewed it caused much envy. Some said it was blasphemous to drink the ale that was the *due* of the Fallen, and others merely wished to steal away the secret for themselves. Great wars were fought – which further pleased Grom – and the secret was stolen and passed from one Lord to another, until it was known to the whole world. But with each passing of the recipe it was corrupted – like the steady corruption of a rumour – so that the new ales were always inferior versions of the old. And the recipe for real Blood Ale is known to one tribe alone, and that is my own."

The barbarian now blinked and turned away from the flames. He looked around the fireside at his companions. When his eyes met those of the monk they locked. With a growl of challenge he asked: "How then, monk, can your ale be better than mine? Even if your ale is not just an inferior descendant of the Blood Ale, it is still only the product of a common wood spirit, whereas the Blood Ale is the brew of gods!"

The monk let out a long sigh. "Ah, Terry, my friend, do not see that tale is parable? It says to barbarian people: look out! Beware! It says: do not get drunk or will become slow and lose control of self. Will be thrown from paradise; will be separated from comrades; ai, *will be killed!*"

"Bah," snorted the barbarian, "you have been on your quest so long that you can't accept that there may be other ales in the world superior to the one you seek. There is always someone out there trying to improve on what is already perfect."

"This true," replied the monk serenely, "and will be pleased if some bugger improve on Boozer's recipe, for that will be drink worth sampling! But now suggest get some rest, for dawn not far off. Perhaps, friend, your axe is heavy, no? Why not put it down somewhere safe, la?"

And – as he made to get up – the axe slid from Terry's knees. For a moment the barbarian stood stock still. Then he looked up at the assembled company – who stared at him with a mixture of emotions, and quite a bit of fear. He smiled sheepishly. "Er, um …" he ventured. "Ah, I'll just, um …" He stuttered to a halt. And then he shrugged his shoulders and, in embarrassment, slunk away to his pallet.

Half-awake and half-dressed, Grunt stumbled towards the smell of cooking. "Wot's for brekky then?" he enquired, rubbing his ample stomach and sending a tsunami of fat rolling across his belly. Since the loss of the bulk of their provisions in the Bogs they had been on emergency rations. "I could eat a yak."

"Beans," replied Frunge, giving the large pot in front of him a stir. He held up a ladle for his companion's inspection: it was coated in a congealed mass of pulses. The beans, in turn, inspected their prospective host. Not liking what they saw, they slowly oozed back into the cauldron.

"Wot about some bangers?"

Frunge nodded in the direction of a plume of smoke with a pair of legs protruding from it. "Bruce is cooking those."

Grunt ambled over to the column of smoke and tapped its occupant on the shoulder. "Maybe you should try using *dry* twigs next time, eh? Then you won't get so much smoke."

Bruce leant back out of the smoke to reveal a face almost completely covered in ash. Little rivers of tears flowed down his cheeks from streaming eyes. "Och, are ye tryin' tae be funny? This *is* dry wid. The smoke is comin' frae the cookin' oil Manis got us." He pulled his frying pan from the fire and shoved it under Grunt's nose. It was half full of black crude. Occasionally, a small, sad-looking sausage surfaced for a gulp of air before sinking back into the depths.

"You've put in too much oil, you moron," observed Grunt, "*and* you've burnt it!"

"I havenae! I only put in a spoonful. The black stuff *came from* the sausages. They've shrunk tae aboot a fifth their original size. I tried tae fry an egg in there a minute agae. It dissolved!"

Grunt looked unhappily at the content of the pan. "I'll go and wake Tres and tell 'im breakfast's ready," he grumbled. "And you'd better 'ave some coffee ready, cos you know wot a gripe 'e is if 'e 'asn't 'ad 'is morning cuppa."

With some trepidation, Grunt walked over to the slumbering Trespass and kicked him in the thigh.

"Not again, Sonia, no," mumbled the prostrate figure, "Mr Wimby's tired …"

Grunt gave him another kick.

"Eh, what? What's going on?"

"Brekky's up."

Trespass rubbed the sleep from his eyes with two dirt-encrusted fists. He looked about the campsite and frowned. Something malodorous assaulted his nose. "What's that smell?" The leader of the pack sniffed the air and screwed his face up. "Bloody Hull, it smells like yak shit!" He rolled over and got to his feet. In the space where he had just been sleeping was a large patty of yak excrement. "Brilliant! Just brilliant! Covered in crap. A perfect start to the day!"

"They say it's good for the roses," commented Grunt, backing away and wafting his nose.

"Yeah, and so are ladybirds, but I wouldn't want them coating various part of my body!" He peeled off his black tunic and dropped it to the ground. "Right, this breakfast had better be good."

Trespass stormed off in the direction of Bruce. "Food!" he demanded.

Bruce dropped three small, burnt sausages onto a plate, where they landed with a *dunk*.

"The last time I saw something like that was when I went skinny-dipping in the Rockbellow in winter. What have you got to go with them?"

"Beans. Frunge is daein' them."

"Yeah. Here they are. One lump or two?"

A crack shot across Trespass's plate as a wedge of beans landed on it.

"I can't eat that!" cried Trespass. "I'll break my teeth!" He threw the plate down in disgust. "Right, get me some coffee, and get it NOW!"

Bruce handed over a caffeine-stained mug. "Er ... sorry aboot the oil slick. The fryin' pan wiz a wee bit tae close tae yon water pot."

"This is the most disgusting crap I've ever seen!" cursed Trespass. "Bloody Manis! He must have bought the cheapest scrag-ends in town. We can't eat this rubbish. Let's go. To your rides!"

"Och, wait a minute," said Bruce, "where's Burb? He wiz on watch earlier."

The yakkers looked around but could see no sign of the diminutive Angel. "Bandits?" wondered Bruce.

"Bandits? Where?" said Burble, appearing from behind a rock and heading swiftly for the safety of the pack.

"Where've you been?" asked Trespass, angrily.

"Eh? Oh, just to that inn around the corner. Excellent breakfast I had, too. Bacon and beer. So, what have you lot had then?"

A fuming Trespass had to be restrained.

———————

The wagon rumbled up to a red-and-white painted swing barrier and came to a halt. Beyond this barrier, off to one side of the road, was a large stone building. A small wooden hut was situated beside the barrier itself. From within this hut there emerged two white-suited individuals. Unnecessary lengths of blue fabric depended from each man's neck and sheathed knives hung from their smart leather belts.

"*Passport* control!" cried one of the men. "May we see your passports, sirs?"

"Passport?" whispered Terry to his friend. "What's that?"

Roffo turned to give the barbarian an incredulous look. It was the sort of look, he imagined, an experienced traveller might give a novice. "You don't have a passport? Then how did you get across the border to Way in the first place?"

The monk leaned forward from his place amongst the baggage and cackled. "Barbarians don't need passports. Have big weapons instead. Passport to anywhere!"

Terry grinned sheepishly and shrugged. "I don't think we're allowed to have them. They're probably seen as a bit *sissy*, you know, like a civilisation thing …"

"Sirs … please … if you wouldn't mind stepping down?"

"Er, right, okay." Roffo leapt down from the passenger seat and, with a backwards glance at Terry, pulled his pristine parchment pamphlet from an inner pocket in his tunic. Somehow, the gloss of gaining his first ever passport stamp had been taken off the situation. Still, the diminutive barman-cum-adventurer straightened his back and thrust out his documentation. "There you go, my good man. I hope all is in order!"

The speaker, who distinguished himself from his colleague by sporting the sort of thin black moustache that would later become *de rigeur* with Fascist dictators, took the pamphlet dubiously and opened it up. He frowned at the rather flattering portrait of Roffo. "Do you realise, sir, that passport portraits are meant to be at least *vaguely* representative? The character portrayed here, sir, is so handsome he even turns *me* on, and I am not of that persuasion." Roffo began to blush as the man continued his lecture. "Furthermore, it is customary in such portraits to adopt a serious demeanour, and not a knavish, come-hither grin. And I must also say, sir, that hand gestures of this nature …" he turned the pamphlet to the beetroot-coloured barman and indicated the hand that appeared in one corner of the picture, "are liable to lead to imprisonment and expulsion." The second official nodded at this and folded his arms.

"Um, er, well, you see, I, er …"

"Enough!" The moustachioed one sighed. "If I were in a worse mood than I am, I would bar your entrance. You are very lucky, sir, that I am feeling rather affable today." He produced an ink pad and a stamp from some inner recess of his white tunic and pressed a mark onto the first blank page of Roffo's passport. "It goes against my better judgment," he continued, "but you may pass."

Roffo meekly took his passport and, with head bowed, returned to the side of the wagon. The monk passed him on his way. With a small bow, he handed his aged yellow pamphlet to the officer. The moustachioed one leafed through page after page and, after a while, gave a whistle of appreciation.

"You are certainly a well-travelled man, sir. I must admit I don't know where half of these places are. 'Chundibundinumbipundiland'? Quite a mouthful!"

The monk nodded. "Yes, this is so. Ai, because of name, coins of land are size of large platters and stamps are size of pillow cases."

"Ah, yes, ha ha, very good sir." Mr Moustache pressed his stamp into the small space that remained in the bottom corner of the last page. "You may pass. Ah, and now, sir, what about yours?" Terry had ambled up to join the pair.

"Um, sorry, I, er, haven't got a passport."

The monk nudged the barbarian and pointed to his broad belt.

"Oh, yeah, sure." Terry slowly pulled the giant war axe from his belt. Sunlight glinted off its razor-sharp edge. "Unless, of course, you count this?"

The two passport officers retreated several steps in unison. "Ah ha ha," laughed the voluble officer, nervously. "A barbarian! Your weapon? Yes, that'll do nicely!" He licked his lips, inked his stamp, and cautiously crept forward. With a rapid motion he jerked forward, pressed the stamp onto the flat of the blade, and leapt back. "You may pass!"

The three adventurers mounted their wagon and passed beneath the raised barrier. As they did so the moustachioed one called out: "And now, sirs, if you would kindly make your way to Customs. That's it – into the building on your left. Thank you very much, and welcome to the Great Empire of Yerrowe."

———•◦•———

Terry goaded the yak team through the broad entrance to the large stone building. Inside the dim, torch-lit edifice, a wooden partition divided the interior into two. A sign to the left, in green lettering, noted 'Nothynge to Declare', while to the right a red-lettered sign noted 'Thynges to Declare'.

"Which way now?" asked Terry.

"Go left," said Roffo, whose pallor had nearly returned to normal. "Quick, while no-one's looking!"

Terry nodded and flicked at the reins. With a snort, the yak team ambled forward through the green channel. They had nearly traversed the building when, from a hidden alcove in the left wall, a voice cried out "Halt!" From out of this alcove stepped a moustachioed gent in a white suit with an inverted noose about the neck and a small dagger depending from his belt. "Could you lead your team over here please, sirs."

"You again!" cried Roffo. "I thought you were Passport Control!"

"Indeed I am, young sir, but with The Empire's resources being what they are, I am also employed as an Excise and Duties Inspector … along with my colleague, Fred." The silent Fred stepped out from behind Mr Moustache and folded his arms in a stern manner. "Now, if you would kindly unload your baggage onto this desk …"

"Look," said Roffo, in exasperation, "is this really necessary? We're not staying here. We just want to pass through your land to Nudia. We're not traders or smugglers or whatnot!"

"That, sir, remains to be seen! Now, the quicker you unload your baggage and allow us to inspect it, the quicker you can be away."

The three adventurers looked at one another resignedly. Terry clambered down and started to manfully heft the supplies from the wagon onto the large counter. Immediately, the Excise officers began sifting through their belongings. Occasionally they tutted, or shook their heads, or glanced meaningfully at the three potential Duty Evaders. A small pile of goods was separated from the bulk of the equipment. This began to build up steadily. At last, Mr Moustache came around the desk to address the adventurers.

"Well well well, sirs, it seems we've been rather naughty, haven't we?"

"What do you mean?" asked Roffo.

"Well, for starters, I count here ten bottles of spirits. The limit, as you should know, is three bottles per person. So – even assuming that the spirits are evenly distributed – that means there is one extra bottle on which duty is due."

"Um, well, we're on a long trip …"

"That, sir, is no excuse for evading Duty! Furthermore, what is *this*!" The official held up a pie of the most revolting dimensions. A globule of pus-like drool formed at one broken juncture in the crust and dripped onto the floor. It hit with a disgusting *squelch*.

"Oh my god!" declared Roffo, clasping a hand to his mouth in an attempt to stop himself from retching.

"Ai-la!" cried the shaken monk.

Terry turned green.

"It's one of ... Puns's ... pies ..." stuttered Roffo. "I don't know how it got ... god! You mean we've been carrying that with us all along?"

The monk tapped him on the shoulder. "Turn away! Do not look!"

The official wrinkled his nose. "Were you aware, sir, that biological weapons are expressly forbidden in Yerrowe?"

"Sorry ..."

"And as for this ..." the moustachioed one put the pie down on the counter and swept up a bottle of ointment. "All medicinal products *must* be accompanied by a contents manifesto."

"La! That is for bowels! Put it down, char-latan!"

"Hmm, yes, well, talking about bowels, I have to say that I am not entirely convinced by your *bona fides*, and I must take my searches further. Fred!"

The silent, grim-faced official began to pull on a pair of thin, pale gloves. A filthy leer settled onto his face. "Right," he said, speaking for the first time in a bear-like growl, "who's first? You, monk? If you would kindly step this way, please, and bend over ..."

———

Half an hour later, the three adventurers sat on their wagon as their yaks plodded down the road. The three quietly stared off into different distances. Copses of trees slowly trundled past them. At last, Roffo spoke.

"That was a bit unnecessary, don't you think?"

The monk grimaced and gave a curt nod.

"I mean," continued the diminutive one, "trying to stick his hand up ..."

"Yes yes ... okay! That enough!"

Silence reigned for a few minutes more. A bird squawked overhead; a rabbit chased across the road in front of them.

"I mean," ventured Roffo, "if they'd just asked for the extra duty, we would have paid, wouldn't we?" No-one answered the young man. The embarrassed silence stretched. One of the yaks sneezed.

The barbarian was the first to break. He chuckled gently to himself. "Where *did* you learn to *kick* like that?" he asked the monk. "I couldn't of felled him better myself!"

A smile twitched at one corner of the monk's face. "Shao-Bin temple. Ancient art of Fung-Chu."

Roffo's face could not restrain the smirk any longer. "Did you see the way his eyes crossed? I've never seen that before. Surprised the Hull out of me …"

"… and him!" laughed Terry.

"Do you think," said Roffo, "that we've just caused an, um, whatsit, *Diplomatic Incident*?"

The monk sniggered like a naughty schoolboy. "Ai – assuredly so! Whole empire will be after us …"

"Until, that is, we cross the border …"

"Yeah," said Terry, "speaking of which … here it is! And another Passport Control. Smallest damned Empire in the world!"

"Do you think *they*'ll be there?" wondered Roffo.

"Shouldn't think so," said Terry. "Last time *I* hit someone *there* – um, *accidentally of course* – they weren't able to walk for a week."

The three adventurers looked at one another and burst into laughter.

———•••———

"Steel yourselves, men," commanded the grey-haired Inspector Yavlo, addressing his troops. Sergeant Boomber and Constable Hendy looked uncertainly at one another, the close proximity of The Pilgrim's grey portal – two doors down – providing a worrisome prospect. "Today, events beyond our control have forced our hand and mean that we must undertake a most dangerous mission. We must enter a foul pit of evil and, once there, we must interrogate the very devil himself."

"Why are we doing this, guv?" asked Hendy, fearfully.

"Why? Because that *bast* …" Yavlo took a deep breath and attempted to regain control of his temper. He was not a man to show extreme emotion, or even to swear, but he loathed interference from pen-pushing bureaucrats. "Er, because that *fine gentleman* Mr Hops has called in a favour from the mayor, and our esteemed civic leader has personally ordered me to go and have a word with Manis. Ha! Pen-pushers! As you are aware, gentlemen, I am frankly uncertain about this direction of enquiry. But my hands are tied."

"I agree, guv," intoned the wart-covered Boomber. "Why don't we just return to the station and let young Hendy here put the kettle on? No-one need know we didn't interview Manis. You can tell the mayor that after *extensive investigations* we concluded that Manis had nothing to do with the destruction of The Bear." Boomber laughed nervously and crossed his fingers behind his back, "which, of course, I'm sure he didn't. The mayor would never know."

"Sergeant, that is a rather dishonest suggestion and it is hardly in the fine traditions of the Constabulary!" Yavlo frowned unhappily. "Besides, I have already thought of this idea and dismissed it. The problem is that as soon as we finish with Manis, that demon will be straight round to the mayor's office complaining about police harassment. The mayor knows this, and I suspect that he knows that I know that he knows this. If he does not hear from Manis by tomorrow I predict that our pristine copybooks will be well and truly blotted. Besides which, the mayor is eager to find out about these exotic women that everyone has been talking about, and I believe that a certain Mr Hops has been directing his attention in a most unlikely direction. Exotic women at The Pilgrim? Preposterous!"

Boomber took a final drag on an imaginary cigarette, dropped it to the ground, and snuffed the life out of it with a booted foot. He reached for an imaginary blindfold and tied it around his eyes. Hendy pulled a tattered parchment from his tunic. It was entitled 'Ye Last Will and Testyment of Goodeman Hendy, Esquire'. He signed it.

Yavlo sighed. "Gentlemen, please refrain from the amateur dramatics. Come along. Let us get this pointless charade over with."

The Inspector set off for The Pilgrim. After three steps he halted. He turned about and walked three steps back. Taking hold of one hand each of his unwilling comrades, he turned once more and dragged his men towards their perceived doom.

———•◦•◦•———

"Hello *ladies*," sneered the pustulous Spotty Wembers, acknowledging the arrival of the Constabulary at the bar. "And what can I get you *dearies*? Three halves?"

Yavlo dropped the hands of his men. "Frankly, sir, I do not like the tone of your voice! Now, I wish to talk to your employer about a very serious incident that happened a couple of weeks ago at a rival establishment."

The barman pondered this request for a few just-to-be-irritating seconds. "Oy boss!" he cried, at last. "It's the pigs!"

The bar fell silent. In an inn where nobody tried to catch anybody else's eye, it was the first time that most of the clientele had noticed the presence of the enemy. The silence was broken by the soft *swishing* of knives being drawn. Spotty Wembers waved good-bye to Cross-My-Way's finest.

"Tell them to bugger off and come back when I'm not so busy," responded a voice from a dark corner. "I'm free in about two years."

Yavlo turned to address the dark corner in question. "Indeed, sir, you *will* be free in about two years ... for that is the length of sentence you can expect for refusing to answer the questions of a senior officer of the law during a criminal investigation."

To a man, the clientele inhaled sharply. They waited for a sign from Manis that would signal the violent expulsion of the three men at the bar ... but the sign never came. "Now, now, Yavlo my man! There is no need to get shirty at my little joke. Come over here and have a drink. Spotty, get his men a drink." A disappointed collective sigh emanated from the onlookers.

Yavlo walked confidently towards Manis, safe in the knowledge that he was not going to die *just* yet. Boomber and Hendy stood at the bar in a less assured manner.

"What you investigating then?" enquired Spotty, selecting the dirtiest glasses he could find. He emptied the slops into them.

"It's, um, The Case Of The Befouled Cellar," stuttered Hendy. "You know, at The Bear."

"Ah, that incident, eh?"

"Do you know anything about it?" hazarded Hendy.

"Maybe. But it'd be more than my life's worth to tell you. And more than *yours* too." Wembers laughed obscenely. "Now, that'll be two silver pieces for the beer. Cough up!"

In the meantime, Yavlo had joined Manis at his table. The Inspector found himself surrounded by some of the biggest and meanest looking men he had ever seen. Trying to ignore their stony stares, he produced his notebook. "Now Mr Manis, sir, I was hoping you would be able to help us in our investigation into the vandalisation of a nearby hostelry. The names of some of your associates came up in our preliminary enquiries and ..."

"Tut tut," tutted Manis, disrupting Yavlo's opening gambit. "How could you suggest such a thing? I've *heard* about the destruction of The Bear, of course, and my sympathies go out to poor Hops. In fact, I've hired myself some new guards to make sure this place doesn't suffer the same fate." He waved a hand dismissively at the new bunch of heavies surrounding him. One badly scarred face pressed close to Yavlo, eyeing him up as though considering which part to dice first. "I'll retain them until Trespass and his lot get back. They're visiting his sick grandmother, you know."

"Hmm, I see." The Hull's Angels were certainly not exotic, nor womanly, but Yavlo suddenly got the sense of Something Going On.

Why *had* the yakkers left town? Why *had* Manis assumed that it was *their* presence he was interested in? "I guess, then, that their absence from town has nothing at all to do with them hiding out for a few weeks until the storm blows over?"

"There you go again making ludicrous suggestions! Never before have I met such a friendly, conscientious, harmless bunch of lads in all my life. The thought that they could get up to any villainy whatsoever is simply ridiculous." A smile flickered across Manis's face. "Now, I'll tell you this once and once only. I had nothing to do with the destruction of The Bear's cellar. Everyone will tell you I was here all night selling my new ale."

"Yeah, that's right," growled the scar-faced thug. "I saw him and I wasn't even in town at the time."

"Hmm, that is interesting." And Yavlo's interest *was* roused. The innkeeper was being rather defensive to say the least. "Perhaps you could provide me with a list of witnesses? I will need to collect statements regarding the times at which these people saw you, and then I would like ..."

"*Enough!*" growled Manis. "Neither I, nor my barstaff, have got the time to waste on this. Now *sod off!*"

Yavlo found his feet suddenly dangling above the ground as two of Manis's heavies picked him up by the shoulders and frog-marched him to the front door. A boot connected with his backside and sent him hurtling through it. The heavies then turned around and looked eagerly at the two policemen standing by the bar.

Boomber dropped his drink, while Hendy chose that moment to test the dampness-retaining properties of his pants. The young Constable desperately looked around for an escape route. He caught sight of the window and went for it, or more accurately, *through* it. Boomber followed his comrade through the newly made exit.

Yavlo watch the rapidly retreating backs of his men as they ran across the market heading for the nearest town gate. *Thirty years*, he thought, *thirty years of this humiliation!* He clenched his hands into fists and for the first time in many years he lost his legendary composure. "I am not going to take this ... this poo anymore!"

He stormed back towards the station.

Roffo had been fidgeting about on the front seat for the last hour or so. He was sitting beside Terry, who currently had the reins. The young man wiped a bead of sweat from his forehead and re-crossed his legs for the umpteenth time.

"It's hot, isn't it?"

"Uh-huh."

"Probably something to do with having a continental climate and whatnot ... you know, very hot in summer, very cold in winter. We're a long way from the sea, you see."

Terry nodded, but kept his eyes on the route ahead. The road had been steadily increasing in gradient over the last few miles, making long, slow, gentle switch-backs between the curves of hills. The switch-backs were gradually becoming more pronounced, and occasionally the land to one side of the road would drop off into a little scree slope – not steep enough to threaten life and limb, but enough to wreck the wagon of a careless driver. Trees marched up the sides of the hills, further obscuring the road ahead.

Roffo reached into a pouch and produced a white bandanna, knotted from previous use. For some reason he found it difficult to untie the knot, his hands clumsily twitching and jerking at the fabric. After a brief bout of fumbling he gave up and tossed the bandanna at his feet. "Okay okay, I have to know ... I want to know ... is it *true*?"

Terry shrugged his massive shoulders. "Dunno."

"Yeah, but haven't your lot pillaged this way before? Surely you must have some uncle or cousin or someone who's swept through this land, putting people to the sword and generally throwing their weight around?"

The barbarian thought a moment. He shook his head. "Not that I know of. I don't think the Nudians have got much to plunder ..."

"Aha! Not got much *of what*, eh? *Fine clothes*; jewellery and pendants and such stuff to pin on *fine clothes*?"

Again Terry shrugged.

Roffo pondered matters for a moment, then turned to look back into the wagon. "Monk ... Mr Monk, sir? Do you know if it's true?"

There was no response. Roffo grinned mischievously. "Oh, *Rosemary*! Sorry, that's probably not it, is it? *Abigail*? Are you in there?"

A bald head appeared through the canvas flap. "Shhhh, foolish one! That not name!"

"Sure ... *if* you say so."

"Ai-la!" the monk winced as though he had been forced to suck his way through a crate of bitter lemons. "Okay, what want?"

"Is it true? You know … *thingy*. The Nudians. Their, er, *sartorial habits* …"

"You mean, do Nudians spend days clothed in manner of new-born infants?"

"Er, yeah, that's it."

The monk folded his arms, placing his hands into the depths of the voluminous sleeves of his green silk kimono. He nodded curtly. "Hear it is so."

"No! Really?"

"Nudians are logical people. Also people without inhibitions or embarrassment. Believe that clothes should be worn for warmth. In day it hot, so wear nothing, at night it cold, so dress up for bed. Makes sense."

"Cor!" Roffo crossed his legs yet again. "You hear that, Terry?" He turned back to the monk. "And you say they don't have any inhibitions?"

The monk nodded. "Want to know about nooky? Yes. Nudians do it when feel like, with whoever want."

"Bloody Hull! Terry, can't you move this crate any faster?"

"Ahem." The monk cleared his throat and suddenly looked serious. "It good you raise this point now, for must discuss something."

"Don't worry," laughed Roffo, "I'll leave the redheads for you!"

"No, foolish one! Be serious! Must be diplomatic here. I not know where map fragment will be …"

"Doesn't it say on your map?" asked Terry.

"No, just give general location. So. Must be careful. Must be on lookout. Must see everything … not in that way, ai-la! And must hear everything. Must be friendly – stop sniggering like schoolboy! – and must also fit in … ah, I give up!"

"No, no, oh ho, oh ho, sorry!" Roffo wiped the tears from his eyes. "Honest! I mean it. Go on."

The monk scowled at him. "What I try to say is this: must not offend them. Must obey Nudian customs and rules."

"Er … are you saying what I think you're saying?" wondered Terry, with a slight grimace.

The monk closed his eyes and nodded gently. "Yes. Should disrobe too."

"*What?*" Roffo turned pale. "You can't be serious!"

Look lively," said Terry, as they took another bend in the road. He pointed at a guardpost in the near distance. "I think we're there. There's a couple of guards ahead, and they're wearing the least impressive armour

I've ever seen."

Roffo gulped hard and covered his eyes.

"Cor!" exclaimed Grunt, peering through the bushes at the group of naked people going about their business in the field below. "Look at that woman's jugs!"

"Aye, they're bonnie," muttered Bruce, "but I wish she'd put them doon. They're obscuring ma view o' her breasts."

Burble's mouth moved as if to make some comment, but his dried-up throat allowed no words to be formed. He continued to stare at the throng whilst contemplating a game of pocket billiards. Frunge wiped the sweat from his brow. And Trespass simply gawped.

"Reet," declared Bruce, at last, making to part the branches of their cover. "Let's git in there!"

Trespass put his hand on the red-bearded man's shoulder to restrain him. "You can't go in there dressed like that, you moron. You'll stick out like a sore thumb!"

"Hoots mon, if I gae intae toon dressed like yon lot," he waved his hand in the direction of the citizens of Nudia, "then it willnae be ma thumb that's stickin' oot! An' since nane o' them hae got big stiffies we'll be spotted as strangers just as quickly, sae we may as well keep oor breeks on!"

A general nodding of heads revealed that the rest of the pack were of like mind. Everyone was keen to watch the show but not take part.

"But they'll never let us in," grumbled Trespass. "I haven't seen a stitch of clothing in the last hour. I bet The Bear lot won't be ashamed of going native."

"You're gonna find out in a minute," said Frunge, pointing to the small guardpost on the road. "'Cos here they come!"

"Right then," announced Trespass, "if they're starkers, we go starkers, if not, then we keep our kit on too."

The gang watched closely as the wagon came to a halt. One of the guards – who wore a plumed helmet but nothing else – ambled up to it. Several more birthday-suited guards hung back, watching the strangers suspiciously and playing with their spears. From the yakkers' vantage point on a hill overlooking the road – which wound towards The Buff, the exposed capitol of Nudia – they watched an animated conversation ensue between the chief guard and Terry. After several minutes, the barbarian climbed down and a pair of guards clambered up into the wagon to inspect its contents. The Angels craned their necks in the desperate hope of catching a glimpse of the famed loincloth.

"Damn! You can't see a thing," complained Burble. "He's using his axe to hide his chopper. Wait a minute. They're chucking the wimpy one out the back to get a better look inside." Necks stretched further.

"He's got his shirt aff," commented Bruce, "but I cannae see a'thing doon below 'cos his bonnet's in the way." On the road below, Roffo turned around. "Och, he moves quicker than a fan dancer!"

The monk jumped out of the wagon and started remonstrating with the guards.

"Well, there you go," said Trespass, pointing towards the wiry form of the religious man. "Naked as the day he was born!" A collective groan reverberated around the group. "Right then you lot – clothes off!"

"Sod that!" grumbled Grunt.

"Look," said Burble, "we can hide our bits with some twigs. If we're stopped by anyone we can say we're collecting firewood."

Trespass nodded. "Yeah, good plan. Let's do it." He turned to smirk at his companions. "And if you still can't control yourselves just think of that sight over there," he pointed in the direction of the monk who, having seen off the guards, was bending over to examine one of the wagon's wheels.

"Cor – that's a scene to put you off *It* for life!" moaned Burble, while unbuttoning his jerkin. The rest of the troop slowly undressed and started stripping the branches from the bushes. Being more reluctant than the others, Grunt soon found himself lagging behind. By the time the fat man stepped out of his smalls, their bushy cover had been totally denuded. He gingerly loped across to another patch of shrubs.

"What are you doing?" enquired a soft female voice.

"Er, wot?" stammered Grunt, as he turned to confront the beautiful girl who had caught him unaware. He attempted to hide his privies in the privet. "I'm, er, just admiring your bush."

"Ooo, you cheeky boy," tittered the girl, nibbling one of the berries she had collected. "Would you like to walk with me into town?"

The girl took hold of Grunt's hand and led him like a little puppy towards The Buff. The rest of the pack stood and stared.

CHAPTER 9

ATTACK OF THE 50 INCH WOMAN

"THIS WILL do," said Roffo from the front passenger seat, pointing with his free hand to the sign above the lintel of the three-storey building. His left hand held a broad-brimmed hat over his lap.

"*Ye Rampant Rhinoceros,*" read Terry, as he fidgeted with the reins. "*Proprietress Miss K. Deedes. Vacancies.*"

"Hmm," mused the monk, standing up in the wagon behind the pair, "only has two-stud rating. Should find somewhere better."

"Um, no, really, I think this place looks rather, er, *nice.*" On cue, a lump of plaster peeled from the outer wall and dropped onto the street. It disintegrated, spraying fragments about like a suddenly amused person with a mouthful of Rice Krispies. The monk looked meaningfully at the young man from under one arched eyebrow.

Roffo chuckled without conviction. "I mean, you shouldn't judge a book by its cover and all that. I'm sure the, er, rotting window frames and rusting iron balconies are just there for effect." Above them, a stray cat mewed in surprise as the roof tile on which it had been ambling slipped from under its paws. The tile landed on the street with a big crash. A piece of shrapnel sizzled through the air past the nose of one of the yaks, causing it to hiccup in surprise.

The monk's other eyebrow arched too.

"Okay okay," declared the flustered Roffo, "I admit it. I just want to get out of the open and I want to do it *now.* This place is disgusting, what with all these people staring at your wotsits!"

"Only person staring at wotsits," declared the monk, with a demonic smile, "is certain foolish barman."

"Um, well, whatever. It still *feels* like I'm being watched and *cor look at the size of her* … um, sorry. Come on. I need a cold shower quick!"

Terry – *sans* bearskin – stood up in the driver's seat and bounded athletically onto the street. From somewhere came a wolf-whistle; from somewhere else came a shout of appreciation. Roffo looked about and noticed that this time they – or rather, Terry – were very definitely the centre of attention. As the barbarian fiddled with the mouth-piece of the head yak, preparing to lead it through an archway to the guest-house's off-street parking, a small crowd began to gather around the company. To Roffo's eye, this seemed to predominantly consist of women.

"I'll deal with the team," said Terry, unaware of the interest he was generating. "Why don't you two go and check in?"

With a touch more caution, Roffo slipped down from the front seat, trying to keep his hat amidships and his back to the sturdy rump of one of the yaks. He began to sidle around the beast towards the scarred front door. "Um, excuse me miss, can I get through?"

The young brunette appeared not to see him, for her eyes were elsewhere. "Great Satyr who is in everything," she murmured to herself, "look at the size of his muscles!"

"Um, miss … *please*?"

The naked young woman turned to look at the distraction. She appraised Roffo with a quizzical eye. A small frown disfigured her pretty face. "Yes?"

"Uh, well, um, I need to get through to, uh, *there* …" Roffo pointed at the door. Unfortunately, he did so instinctively with his left hand. His hat stayed in place.

"That's a good trick," said the woman, as she moved aside, "are you a magician or something?"

Roffo's embarrassment was so acute that he missed an ideal opportunity for the *magic wand* joke. Instead, he clasped hold of his hat and pelted around the yak and through the hotel's half-open front door. Inside the dark, musty foyer, Roffo leant against a wall and smiled weakly to himself. Several seconds later the monk ambled into the reception area. A large money belt now conveniently hid his equipment. Roffo scowled. "And you said we shouldn't be embarrassed about our bodies. You even laughed at my hat. Hypocrite!"

The monk smiled and shrugged his wiry, corded shoulders – the very image of Bruce Lee with alopecia. "Not so! Need money, la?" He giggled. "Come: here is Reception."

They walked through the little foyer, past wicker chairs, and up to the pine wood desk. The monk rang a little handbell. A few moments later a large woman with a tower of silver hair appeared. She greeted the men with a warm smile as she rested her immense breasts upon the counter.

"*Hello boys*," she leched. "What can I do to you?"

Roffo simply gulped and stared. He felt as though he were being interrogated by a pair of prize-winning vegetables.

"Room for three," said the monk, unfazed. "But not know how long stay."

"That's okay," teased the woman, "I've always got room for more men." As she edged along the counter to collect a key, the dim light piercing through a pair of half-closed curtains allowed Roffo to make a more accurate assessment of her. The woman's skin was tanned and clear, and she must have been in her fifties. Roffo nodded. Her age was about that too.

"In fact," continued Miss Deedes, "you're in a bit of luck. I've got a lovely balcony room for you right next to mine. What a jolly coincidence! Now, where is this mysterious *number three* then?"

At that moment Terry rushed through the front door, which he slammed shut behind him. He grabbed the handle and held on tight. From outside, Roffo caught the sound of screaming. The door bulged and scrabbling sounds came from the other side. An ordinary man might have buckled against the massive weight of frenzied females battering against the door, but Terry simply set his thighs, rested a mighty shoulder against the door, and turned to view his comrades. He shrugged in embarrassment. "Er, I don't know what I did to upset them. I was just walking along and they suddenly rushed me." He smiled weakly. "Sorry!"

Miss Deedes dropped the key. "My-oh-my, it's going to be a splendid day today!" She scooped up the key and padded over to the barbarian. Touching him on the shoulder in a rather familiar manner she said, "Move aside, love, and let me deal with the gatecrashers." With that she yanked the door open and, using her natural advantages, literally breasted her way through the feminine mob without. The door slammed shut again. A moment later there was an eruption of bellowing and shrieking. The throaty voice of Miss Deedes rose above this, punctuated by pants and screams: "He's ... mine ... I tell ... you ... now ..." (scream scream, shriek, "my hair my hair") "Bugger ... *off!*"

Miss Deedes reappeared. Her silver cone of hair was now skew-whiff and she had acquired a number of scratches and bruises. The monk rushed to her sympathetically. "Ah, dear lady, appear in need of aid. In wagon have balms to soothe cuts!"

The landlady smiled broadly. "That's the ticket ... at least for starters! Come on then you cheeky boys, I'll show you your room." With a wink at Terry, she grabbed the monk by the arm and began to drag him towards the stairs. Exchanging worried looks, Terry and Roffo followed.

———————

Grunt drew heavily on his cigarette as he lounged on the dark wooden bench outside their back-street inn. He let out a long, soft sigh of contentment.

"Bog off!" growled Trespass, voicing the opinion of the rest of the pack. "Just bog right off!" Clutching his bundle of twigs with white knuckles he added as an afterthought: "Git!"

"Some of us 'ave got it, and some of us 'aven't," stated the black-bearded Angel with a smirk, "and I've just 'ad plenty!"

A naked man with a grey beard and a paunch ambled up to the group. "Afternoon good sirs." He reached down into Trespass's lap to feel the quality of his wood. The leader of the pack's eyes bulged. "How much for the kindling?" continued the oldster.

"You … you … *you* can piss off too!" Trespass stood up, his face now red with fury. "I'm gonna …" The grey beard, sensing the way the wind was blowing, backed slowly away, then turned and sprinted off down the street.

"Sexual frustration init," suggested Grunt. "I always get a bit tetchy if I ain't 'ad a shag for a long time."

The rest of the gang stared at him with enough fire in their eyes to satisfy the combined desires of the entire membership of The Hades Chapter of the Associated Arsonists. Teeth bit into lips and fists clenched and unclenched. Trespass's mouth moved like that of an asthmatic goldfish.

Burble was the first to find his voice. "While you've been exercising the second smallest muscle in your body after your brain," he sneered, "some of us have been working." He punched himself in the thigh a couple of times. *His* eyes merely smouldered. "Like me, for instance. I've been following the Bear gits around."

While slapping Trespass on the back to restart his breathing, Frunge, who was the most easily distracted of the pack, asked: "Wot did you find?"

"They've taken rooms in an inn. Ye Rampant Rhinoceros. It's just off the main square. You can't miss it. It's the one with a giant horn on its sign."

The rest of the pack looked up at the sign above their own heads: The Wanton Rat. It too had a large horn.

Burble shook his head angrily. "No, I meant the one on its head. Anyway, the wrinkly one went out this afternoon and reconnoitred the

194

town and …"

"Hur hur hur," laughed Grunt, filthily, "I've been poking around town too!"

The others ignored him. Burble continued his report: " …and he spent a lot of time hanging about the Royal Shack. Before going back to the guest-house he detoured to have a quick look at the temple of the Nudians' chief god. I think the bloke's name is Satyr or something."

"He didnae spot ye, did he?" asked Bruce.

"Well, they do say He sees everything …"

"Nae, ye plonker – the monk!"

"Oh – him! Um, course not." Behind his back, the shortest of the yakkers crossed his fingers. "Who could possibly tell that Burble, *The Shadow*, was on their trail?"

"Anyone wi' a sense o' smell," quipped Bruce. The laughter that followed did something to ease the tension in the air.

"Drink," gasped Trespass at last, breathlessly, "I need a … drink."

"Good idea," commented Grunt. "Lots of shagging really makes a man thirsty."

They chased the giant into the inn, beating his exposed buttocks with their camouflaging switches. Inside, Bruce went to get the drinks in. As he handed one over to Trespass, the leader of the pack grimaced. "Hangabouts," he said. "How did you pay for these? I didn't see you get a wallet out. Where do you keep your dosh?"

"I keep it in the same place ye dae," replied the Northern Angel. "In a sporran under ma beard."

"Wait a minute though … *Burb* bought the *last* round in that other pub. Where does he …?" They both turned to stare at Burble's bare chin, but neither the diminutive Angel, nor his chin, were in evidence.

"Where's he gone?"

Grunt gestured over his shoulder towards the *Gents*. "'E's gone to spend a penny."

Frunge and Bruce exchanged horrified looks.

———•◦•———

"Have you seen it?" Rod asked his friend Ivor Biggun. "Bloody huge it is!"

"Aye, you couldn't miss it if you were blind," replied his portly drinking partner. "I saw him come through the gate, you know, and I reckon *it* arrived in town a couple of minutes before he did!"

"My brother was on guard duty when *he* arrived," interjected

Pump, the ginger-haired landlord. Adding further grist to the rumour mill, he elucidated: "He told me that as *he* walked through the gate *his* feet made prints in the dust while *it* left a deep groove. Apparently he tried to hide it behind his axe. Weird! If I had such an impressive one I'd be sure everyone knew about it. I certainly wouldn't be serving behind this here bar!"

His companions nodded sagely at this.

"Aye," said Ivor, "and did not Satyr say unto our ancestors: 'keep not your weapon sheathed, for it will become blunted, but show it proudly and frighten all your enemies'?"

"He did!" concurred the landlord.

"Yeah, and he also said we should oil it daily! Now, I wonder if there are any young ladies around here who'd like to … oh, *bugger!*"

The door to the inn swung open and a tall, dark-skinned man leapt into the bar. He landed in the middle of the room, placed his hands upon his hips, and thrust his pelvis in the direction of the trio at the bar. "Make obeisance, chipolatas, for Justin honours Ye Rooting Pig with his presence … and what a presence!" He wiggled his hips and set up a pendulum motion below the waist, doing a fair impersonation of a rubber grandfather clock in an earthquake.

But there was no response.

Men *did not* turn away in embarrassment; women *did not* faint. Justin snorted. Normally there would have been a couple of women out cold by now. Instead, the oblivious ladies huddled throughout the lounge in excited, whispering groups, while the men simply smirked. Non-plussed, Justin strutted over to the bar.

"Well, if it isn't my old rival Ivor Biggun, *ex*-Big Knob of The Buff. How's it hanging? Still using the weights?" He threw back his head and laughed loudly. Brushing his black hair back out of hazel eyes he examined the faces of the men at the bar. They contained no emotion. "Weeeell, aren't we a quiet lot tonight? Cat got hold of your tongues … or something?"

"No, we're just fine," stated Ivor, flatly. "We were just quietly considering Scripture, that's all. In fact," he turned to face his companions, "I was just about to ask your opinions on the Book of Big Job …"

"Ah," smirked Rod, knowingly, "13:2 perhaps? How does it go? 'And then the new Big Knob said unto his warriors: disarm him! And the guards didst *remove his weapon*.'"

"That's the bit! I was just wondering what the *new guy* would get up to, being a bit of a warrior and all that. I don't expect he'll settle for tormenting his predecessor with bad jokes and ridiculous innuendo. No, I reckon he'll take more *extreme* measures."

"What are you talking about?" demanded Justin. "What have you heard? You know I'm the biggest gun around."

"And the quickest," quipped Rod, under his breath.

Justin ignored the insult and advanced on his rival. "What are you talking about?"

Ivor took a taste of his ale and allowed a short silence to slip by for dramatic effect. "Oh – haven't you heard? There's a new bloke in town. Definitely king of the communal showers. What do you reckon, Rod? You've seen him."

"Huh? Oh, definitely. In fact, I'd say he's, what, this big?" he stretched out his arms in the manner of a fibbing fisherman.

"You're making it up," cried Justin. "No-one's *that* big! I know what's going on here. It's jealousy, isn't it? You've never come to terms with losing your title, eh? Anything to get your own back!"

"Well, why don't you go and look for yourself? I hear he's staying at Ye Rhino."

"If you think I'm going to fall for that one," sneered Justin, "you've got another think coming."

"So you're not gonna go then?" said Rod. "Now, is that because you're afraid of what you might find, or is it because you can't take another night with Miss Deedes?" He chortled. "She's worn down more men than a dominatrix with a cheese grater."

Justin fumed. "I don't have to stand here and take these insults. I'm off." He turned to address Pump, the barman. "I leave now, and your inn will be a sadder, poorer place for it. But there you are. It's your loss." He turned and strutted towards the exit. In the doorway he paused to give the clientele a final pelvic wave, then disappeared into the evening twilight.

Roffo paced up and down the bedroom with a worried frown on his face. Occasionally, he paused to hitch up the impromptu toga that he'd made for himself from a yellow, flower-patterned bedsheet. "Where is he? I bet he's either been ravished to death or … or … the bugger!" He turned to point at Terry. "That's it! He's gone to get some nooky for himself and left us to stew. Probably feared the competition!"

Terry stood looking at the bedclothes he had found under a pillow. A puzzled expression contorted his face. He held up the pyjama bottoms.

"I don't think much of their tailors' skills. Look at this ... there's a great big split right up the crotch! And leather?" Terry scratched himself (which was a disconcerting sight, given that modesty had yet to impose its will upon him). "Why leather?"

"Haven't you been listening to what I've been ... *what was that?*" Roffo swept over to his friend and stood at his shoulder. "Let's have a gander."

Terry handed over the night-time attire. Roffo's eyes bulged. "Blimey! Have you seen this? There's some sort of studs on the inside, round where your bum would be. And what's this little knobbly bit poking out the front?"

"The top's weird too," noted Terry, poking a finger through one of the nipple-level holes.

"*Never mind that,*" squealed Roffo, "*what the Hull is with this rubber hood!*"

Terry shook his head. "Shoddy work! Remind me not to let these chaps get hold of my bearskins."

Roffo slumped onto the bed, shaking his head. "Perverts," he whispered, "they're all ruddy perverts! You know what these are, Terry, don't you? These are the famous sex-clothes of Nudia. And we're ... we're *expected* to wear them to bed!"

Terry held the set of bottoms against his lower anatomy. "I don't think I'll be able to get into these."

"Well, sod custom! I don't care what the monk says, I'm not putting this kit on, no way! He can if he wants ... in fact, he's probably wearing some at this very moment in the company of a bevy of wanton beauties."

Terry shook his head slightly as he toyed with the little metal bit fastened to the corners of the mouth-hole of the sleeping-hood. He dropped the thing onto the bed with distaste. "I'm sure he'll be back soon. He's probably just been held up. I'm sure he's doing his best."

"That's what's worrying me!" said Roffo. Then he sighed. "No, you're probably right. Oh, and if you're going to sit next to me, can you at least try to cover *that*."

"Sure." Terry put a pillow over his lap. "Still, I don't know why he thought *I* ought to stay inside. He seemed to think I might be in some kind of danger or something. I mean, why would anybody want to harm me here? All the people seem quite friendly."

Roffo looked askance at his friend. His voice was saturated with envy. "I don't think they want to *harm* you as such. And it's the *friendliness* that's the problem."

Terry shrugged. "I wonder if he's found out anything about the map fragment yet?"

"Who knows. Say ... what's that sound? It's coming from outside?" Roffo froze on the bed. "Thieves? Murderers? Nocturnal Attire Enforcement Patrol?"

Terry got up and, dropping the pillow, paced over to the balcony. He rested his hands on the stone railing and peered into the gathering twilight.

"Hello? Who's there?" The night had drawn in quickly, leaving the street full of shadows. Ivy matted and darkened the wall around the balcony and a particularly deep shadow-pool lay beneath its overhang. Straining his eyes, Terry thought he could make out movement in the murky pool of anti-light. His peripheral vision tugged his awareness off to the left – just in time to catch a glint of light reflecting from the polished heel of a leather boot disappearing around a corner of the guest-house. More movement drew his attention off to the right. And then he noticed a shape at the foot of the wall. No, *two*, no ... *more*. His hearing, trained in the wilderness, unblunted by civilisation, caught the ominous tinkle of metal on metal. The ivy rustled.

"Er, Roffo," he said, quietly. "Bring me my axe. *Quickly*."

Roffo appeared at his shoulder. "Axe? What for?"

"Don't worry. Just get it for me please."

The junior barman left, but was back in two seconds. "Er, you left it in the wagon. My sword's there too."

The barbarian's eyes flicked from one movement to another, tracing the flow of the shadows. "Well get me something else then," he hissed, urgently. "Some sort of weapon."

"Right," squeaked Roffo. Behind him, Terry could hear the sounds of a frantic search: the creak of moving furniture, the rustle of sheets, the slide of wooden draws. At last Roffo re-appeared at his shoulder. "Um, couldn't find much, just ... um ..."

"Come on," hissed Terry. "Let's have it!" He reached a hand behind him. After a moment's hesitation he felt something pressed into it. Something ... *soft*. Terry looked at it. His eyebrows arched. "A pillow? You've brought me ... *a pillow*?"

Roffo chuckled nervously. "Um, yeah, well, they're lethal weapons in the right hands. I knew a kid back home ... amazing the destruction he could cause in the dorm after light's out with a pil ..." Roffo faltered under Terry's astonished gaze. "Um – sorry?"

And at that moment all Hull broke loose.

The air was suddenly filled with the whir of grappling irons, and three ladders – like giant cobras – rose up to rest against the balcony. A chorus of hideous, blood-curdling shrieks – as though from a host of banshees at a wailing convention – rent the soundwaves.

"Never mind that now!" roared Terry. "Prepare to repel boarders!"

Roffo hefted his own pillow and wet his lips. Action at last! This was what he had yearned for! But why, then, did he suddenly feel an urge to go to the toilet?

"Look out!" roared Terry, as he swung his pillow two-handed like a mighty battle axe. The nearest ladder-climbing invader – armoured in studded black leather – gave a shriek of surprise and pitched into the murk.

"What the …?"

A pretty hand with deep red nail varnish clamped onto the balcony beside the business end of a grappling iron. It started to haul. Up came a pile of auburn hair, then a clear, tanned face with freckles, and then a lascivious grin. Roffo leapt forward and biffed the beautiful maiden in her heavily made-up face. As the woman pitched over backwards, her back arched, and her uncovered nipples speared the sky.

Roffo wrestled with the grappling iron and cast it down into the gloom. Turning to look at Terry in triumph, he suddenly bellowed at the uncomprehending barbarian: "Behind you!"

Instinct took over: Terry turned and smote in one movement. The leather-clad beauty was caught in mid-leap – having scaled the ivy beside the balcony – and plummeted from sight.

"Women?" yelled Terry, as he fended off a pair of invaders who had appeared at the tops of two ladders. "Women!"

"Yes," cried Roffo, as he bludgeoned the perm of a blonde with wicked intent in her eyes, "terrifying, isn't it!"

"Women!" repeated Terry. A hand reached through the railings of the balcony and grabbed him *there*. "By Grom!" he cried. He leapt back, and *steel* entered his eyes. He set his legs wide and readjusted his grip on his pillow. "Fight for your life, my friend," he roared, "fight like you've never fought before!" And with that he clove the air around him. Redheads, brunettes, strawberry blondes – all were pummelled back into the void. While Terry wrought destruction with mighty blows, Roffo darted about with a sneaky strike here, a nipple-tweak there, casting down ladders as soon as they rose up to meet him.

But the invaders continued to come in, wave after wave. The air became redolent with the perfume of battle; blood-red lipstick smeared the defenders' weapons; and the balcony was soon strewn with the dislodged harnesses of the foe.

"Terry ... *help me!*" Roffo was momentarily overcome by two gorgeous babes, who took it in turns to dart within the diminutive warrior's swing to rip at his toga with nails of steel. The barbarian leapt to the aid of his friend, picking up one invader in each mighty hand and, with the flick of iron wrists, casting them over the parapet.

"Whoa ... I was nearly a goner there and ... *watch that doll!*"

On and on raged the fight. Twilight fled from the scene of battle and night dropped into a ringside seat. At the start of the assault the occasional woman had still worn her daytime attire (viz, nothing at all), but now all of the adventurers' adversaries wore nocturnal leathers. A whip cracked, yanking Terry's pillow from his grip. A giant-breasted, mousy-haired woman slowly rose onto the railing. She licked her lips and prepared to deliver the *coup de grâce* ...

"Terry – catch!"

Terry swivelled and caught Roffo's pillow and then – with a powerful backward sweep – he dislodged the woman. She disappeared from sight, her perfect mouth forming a little "O" of surprise.

At last the press began to diminish. Ladders that were knocked down did not reappear and the ivy around the balcony became so shredded that no invader could get within leaping distance of the parapet. And then ... *nothing.* The pair of warriors stood back to back, waiting for an attack that did not come.

"Is it over?" asked Roffo, wearily. His toga was now in shreds and his pillow was ripped and leaking feathers. Terry was silent. "Do you think they'll come again?" continued the barman.

For a moment the barbarian was tense – and then his shoulders relaxed and he exhaled deeply. "Yes, I think it is over." He peered over the edge of the balcony. Street lights had been lit so that they could at last see something of the force that had assailed them. Women hobbled off in various directions, dispersing to their respective beds. Some helped others who had broken their heels. A wailing lament broke out from one redhead who had broken a nail. In the orange glow, the lipstick-smeared faces made the limping beauties look like ghouls.

Roffo came to stand beside his friend and look below. He sighed. "War: what a waste!" He perused the scene for a few moments more and shook his head. "Maybe," he said wistfully, after a while, "just *maybe* ... we should have let a couple through?" He pointed. "I mean, that blonde there for example. She's a bit saucy."

Terry nodded glumly. War was not meant to be like this!

———————•◦•◦•———————

It had been a long and trying afternoon for the monk. He had searched high and low for evidence of the fragment of Boozer's map, but with little success. He had started at the library on Frottage Street, but had found scant reference to ale there and no reference to Boozer or his map at all. Indeed, the library had contained little of scholarly worth: most of its books and parchments were recently quilled works with titles such as *How to get ye perfect Tan*; *Eating for Sexe – How Grub affects ye Drives*; and *Tartric Sexe: How to do it.* There had been a whole wall filled with books of fiction by Barbie Pinkhair, all of which seemed to revolve around a wanton maiden being amorously pursued by some handsome-yet-dishonourable man with steely eyes and a square jaw. The phrase 'heaving bosom' seemed to occur quite a lot (heaving *what*? he had wondered), while every book seemed to climax in one of a variety of improbable positions (often illustrated). Another wall was dedicated to copies of the sacred book of Nudia – The Bibulous – while another huge section of (well-thumbed) books was concerned with Modern Arte (in which the naked human form was pre-eminent).

Leaving the library, the monk had wandered across to the central square, weaving in and out of the copious wurst-sellers, passing the stocks (where a miscreant had been pleading with passers-by to remove the heavy woollen Trews-of-Punishment that had been forced upon him), and had strolled up to the entrance of the Royal House. The flag – a pink 'O' on a brown background – had been at half-mast, indicating that King Richard the 43rd was probably Up but definitely not In. The building was a two-storey affair, constructed of wood and then disguised with stone cladding to make it appear castle-like. A single guard had been patrolling outside the large wooden front door – a door which (the monk had noted with satisfaction) appeared to be as riddled with woodworm and dry rot as every other door and window frame in The Buff. If the need arose the monk felt confident that – like the female population of Nudia – it would probably go down with only a little persuasion from the barbarian. He had nodded at this and then moved on: a touch of breaking and entering might be required, but more information was needed before he would dare risk offending Nudian Royalty.

During the rest of the afternoon the wiry oriental had moved from one centre of gossip to another, always doing the polite thing and purchasing an ale whilst there. At The Jolly Roger on Deviant Way he had heard a rumour that the King could not read and was therefore unlikely to have any use for scrolls and whatnot "except to wipe his arse on". *Damn!* At The Golden Pillow in Humpy Lane he had learnt from a disgruntled writer – surprisingly semi-clad in a cravat – that the priests of Satyr enforced a strict censorship on all written material. Any work deemed anti-Scripture, prudish, or pro-clothing was confiscated. *Interesting!*

Subsequently, however, while he had been taking a surreptitious leak to make room for more ale, the monk had received something of a shock. As he was standing in a dingy alley, minding his own business and whistling a little tune, he had looked up to find a strangely familiar face peering at him from around the corner of the nearest building. In his moment of startlement he managed to drench his bare foot. When he next looked up, the be-stubbled face was gone. Shaking his leg as he went, the monk had limped off in the opposite direction as fast as he could.

Now in The Rascal's Resort, the monk sat nursing a pint, chewing on his lip and pondering the events of the afternoon. That face – where had he seen it before? Frembolia? Way? Had they been followed?

As the monk continued his worried musings, a pair of gentlemen waddled over to the next table and sat down. A ruddy-faced chap with a walrus moustache and fat hands thumped his pint down onto the table and then, with similar energy, plonked his bare behind onto a creaking wooden stool. "Damn it all, Stoker, and especially damn the PM and his lackeys... may they be sent to Frigidia where the maidens are as cold as the Trevis Glacier!"

Stoker – a thin man with protruding ribs – licked his lips nervously. "Minister ... *please!* We don't know who might be listening. The whips ..."

"Damn the whips too! In fact, damn everyone! Gutless, kow-towing, spineless ..."

"*Please!*"

Minister Mai T. Pole clamped his teeth shut and fumed for several seconds. He was about to launch into another tirade when Stoker leant forward to place a thin finger on his chubby lips. "Shhhhhh!"

"But ..."

"Take a deep breath ... good! Now another ..."

Minister Pole's shoulders sagged. "Thanks, Stoker. You're a good man."

"Simply doing my job, Minister. My star waxes and wanes with yours."

"Nevertheless, you're a fine fellow. But I'm still angry – calm, but angry. Talking-Out my Private Member's Bill like that! It reeks of conspiracy!"

"I'm sure you're right, Minister. The priesthood guard their privileges with a rod of iron – if you'll forgive the innuendo. But surely you must appreciate that *no* Bill that threatens to inconvenience them will ever get a second reading? Clearly Bishop Mazed has had a quiet word with the PM."

"I suppose I knew in my heart that this would happen but, damn it all, Stoker, we *should* be allowed into the business part of their Temple, their Sanctum Sanctorum. Have you heard the rumours about what they've got in there? Treasure, jewels, priceless works of art. They're sitting on a mountain of loot and here we are, *Parliament*, and not enough money to get the streets paved, or to repair people's homes, or … or … to pay ourselves a decent wage …"

"Hear hear!"

"… or to properly finance our administrative support …"

"Hear-double-hear!"

The Minister paused to wipe his brow. "You know, Stoker, I hear they've got so much treasure they don't know what half of it is. It's also said they have a communal harem containing the most beauteous babes in the country. And do they pay taxes on that? Part of their Taxable Allowance my considerable arse!"

"You're raising your voice again, Minister …"

"Sorry!" Minister Pole took a deep pull on his beer and wiped his lips. "I mean, no wonder everyone wants to get into the Priesthood. It's about time we sorted out once and for all who is the real power here!"

"I believe," said Stoker, cautiously, "that so much is already 'sorted out', as you put it. Let's face it, Minister, it was the Priesthood that created Parliament when dear King Richard's grandpa – the late King Richard – was going loopy with an ailment related to his favourite pastime. It is only because they didn't want to be burdened by the everyday running of affairs – and couldn't trust the Monarchy – that we were created."

"Well, yes, that may be so, but things change. It seems we do more and more of the work while they do less and less. And here we are, the representatives of the people, living in poverty while they live the life of Roger. It just makes me angry …"

"Minister, your face is starting to turn red again!"

At the adjacent table, an inscrutable monkish fellow slowly put down his half-finished ale. There were matters that needed looking into here ... but maybe tomorrow. Time was getting on. With renewed excitement he set off for the guest-house, his machinating mind momentarily putting aside all thoughts of pursuers and shadows.

Bishop Yul B. A. Mazed reclined languidly in his plush red chair, his long legs outstretched before him, his silver hair glinting in the candlelight. Absently, he ran his hand through a small chest of gold coins, revelling in the cold caress of the metal against his skin.

"So, my brethren," he said softly, "how goes the eternal fight against the forces of evil?"

The three priests – arranged in a semi-circle of stout chairs in front of the Bishop – looked at one another uncomfortably. There was only one thing worse than the Bishop's *angry* voice, and that was his *soft* voice. At least when he was angry you knew where you stood, plus there was the added advantage that you had no time to feel the appropriate emotion of *stark terror*, since he was onto you instantly, like a leaping tiger. But when the Bishop spoke softly, well, things could go either way – from a mild compliment and the offer of a flagon of wine, to a fierce rebuke and the sort of penance that made your eyes water (and usually involved the attachment of something large and weighty to something soft and delicate). It was the uncertainty that was the killer.

"Generally, things go well, Your Grace," said Brother Pud Denda, "although I did have a delegation of Young Mothers earlier who were simpering on about how Little Johnny gets cold when it rains, and how poor Fanny tends to get a chill when the West wind blows off the mountains. You know the stuff. They said they thought there ought to be some sort of special dispensation for the little 'uns ..."

"And?"

Pud swallowed hard and wiped his slick palms against his naked thighs. "And, um, of course, I said 'Get Thee From Here' ... like, in a really deep, angry sort of voice – dead impressive I thought. 'Get Thee From Here Women, For You Insult The Spirit Of Satyr With Thine Pathetic Mewlings.'"

"Pathetic Mewlings? That's good that!" nodded Brother O' Toole. "Wish I could think of lines like that ..."

"Yeah, anyway, I can't remember the rest, but I basically told them to bog off and stop trying to corrupt their children, and no way could they wear togs just 'cos it was raining. Um, did I do right?"

The Bishop's eyebrows converged like kissing caterpillars. "Brother

Denda, do you not know?"

"Um, yeah, ha ha, of course I know! It was right. Um. Yea Verily and all that stuff."

The Bishop nodded ponderously. "Good. Anything else? Who took the Confessionals?"

"Um, that was me, Your Grace," squeaked Brother Shafto, a corpulent priest with a face lined with broken veins. "Nothing unusual there. I had a couple of 'I don't lust after my brother's wife' ones, a woman who said she'd had a bad back and had denied her husband for a *whole* week, and the regular quota of young ladies who confessed to dreaming about wearing posh frocks."

"And you gave out severe penance, I hope?"

"Did I heck!" chortled the corpulent one. "I don't think they'll be back in a hurry!"

"No wonder you were red-faced when I saw you earlier," noted Brother O' Toole with envy.

"Aye, I was bloody knackered! You should have seen what the leggy one could do with her—"

"Enough!" sighed Bishop Mazed, but with less than his usual intensity. There seemed to be little dissension amongst his flock these days. He cast his eyes about the little room: at the caskets of jewels, the chests of gold and silver, and the rolls of fine silk. In the chain of storerooms beyond, he knew, there were countless amphorae of choicest wine, pots full of exotic and exorbitant spices, and paintings of great antiquity and worth. Such treasures had been acquired over many years, either as gifts from the devoted, or in taxes on the people of Nudia and the pleasure-seeking visitors who swarmed to their land. But it had all become too easy. The Priesthood indulged their every whim and desire; they wanted for nothing, and yet ... there was an *absence* in the Bishop's life. Ah, how he longed for the days of the Inquisition: converting the Heretics, plundering their treasures, and putting all to staff and rod! But now the protests seemed too trivial to waste effort on, and he found it impossible to rouse himself to sanctimonious wrath. Even the ridiculous protests by the Writers' Guild – with their absurd cravats – failed to energise him. There was no real fun to be had there; let others deal with the matter.

He brooded for a few moments more before continuing. "Now then, the plans for the Sexageisha ceremony. How are they going?"

"*Whooooooooaaaa!*" shrieked a voice. The arched door to the vestibule was flung open to reveal a wild-eyed priest standing in the doorway. "*Whoooa!* There is Blasphemy afoot! Great evil cometh ... *whoooaaa.*

I have seen it!"

"Evil?" started Brother Denda, using the fingers of both hands to form the sign of the Y. "Where?" The other two priests attempted to ward off evil in a similar manner. Bishop Mazed simply rolled his eyes and looked to the heavens.

"*Everywhere*," cried the seer, P. Ping Tom. "They come! They come to plunder, to steal, aye, yes, *oooooh*, and to do terrible things, oooh yes mother!"

"Been at the Blue Powder again I see, Brother," noted the Bishop, with more amusement than anger. Ping's prophetic powers were not insubstantial – they just tended to be rather imprecise. The Forty Year Drought, for example, had actually lasted just Four Days, and the Plague of Locusts had turned out to be one of Ladybirds. But you had to give him points for trying. Recently, however, the seer had taken to a notorious narcotic – made from the guts of a local aquatic animal – with uncertain results.

"The drug of truth!" cried Ping, skipping about on the spot. "It allows insight into all things! *Whooooaaaa!*"

"Indeed." Bishop Mazed scratched his long, thin nose. "Tell us, then, what do you foresee?"

"I see doom … *doom*! Aye, the end is nigh!"

"Yes yes," continued the Bishop, starting to lose patience, "we'll take that as read, shall we? Now give us something a bit more substantial."

"Yeah, like the winning lottery number," suggested Brother O' Toole.

The Bishop held up a quieting hand.

"I see defilement …" continued the crazy.

"Okay."

"And I see … I see the deflowering of sacred purity!"

"Go on."

"And … and … *peculation* in the temple!"

"Sounds perfectly disgusting. Write that down, Brother Denda. No peculating in the Temple. Thank you, Brother Ping. You may go."

"No, no, you must listen …" The seer threw himself on the floor and started to thrash about in the middle of the carpet.

"Oh bugger," grumbled the high priest, "he's gone. Well, I think that concludes business for the day." The Bishop got to his feet and gave the dribbling seer a swift kick, causing the others to wince in sympathy. "Anyway, who's for a quick game of Pokeher before prayers? Jolly good! Shafto, go get the cards."

The priests made their way from the vestibule.

———————

"Now now Miss Deedes – behave yourself!"

The voluptuous proprietress, clad from head-to-toe in leather (with various slits, holes and gaps therein), panted breathlessly. "Well, stop trying to escape me then you naughty ... *boys!*" She darted to the left of the bed, having feigned a move to the right.

Terry and Roffo scuttled to the left too.

The pursuit around the bed continued for several more minutes and a couple of dozen laps. It was like the Indy 500 except that the winner hoped for a bit more than a bottle of champagne and a glossy cup.

"Incredible stamina!" commented Terry, with admiration, as he took another bend at speed.

"Yes," puffed Roffo, hot on his heels, "that's what I'm afraid of!"

Around and around they went. Occasionally, Miss Deedes screeched to a halt and switched directions.

"Bloody Hull, Terry, she's good at this ..." *pant pant*, "do you see how she ..." *pant pant*, "slows to let you nearly catch ..." *pant*, "up ..." *pant*, "and then reverses ..." *pant pant pant*.

"Yeah, clever ... *Roffo!*"

The young barman – wearing a slipping toga – tripped on his hem line and went down.

"*Nooooooo!*"

Miss Deedes leapt ... and dropped like a particularly soft bag of spuds onto the bare floorboards. From under the bed Roffo heaved a huge sigh of relief. The barbarian – with one more tug – pulled him through to the other side.

"Okay you cheeky monkeys," gasped Miss Deedes, climbing to her feet. "Auntie's beginning to get a little bit cross!" She pushed the collapsed mountain of hair out of her eyes. "We don't want to get *too* worn out before the *real* fun starts, eh?" And she bolted to the right.

"Here we go again. Terry: save yourself!"

Still hauling his friend, Terry rushed around the bed and passed the door ... which suddenly opened up square into their pursuer's face! Miss Deedes dropped like a stunned elephant.

"Ai-la! Think have ..." The monk stood in the doorway, staring down at the heap of concussed femininity at his feet.

"Don't just stand there," cried Roffo, "come in quick! Terry – while she's out of it – sling her outside ..."

"Right!"

"Mr Monk, help me with this bed. Mind your back, Terry …"

The barbarian dropped their hostess outside, then returned to help his comrades push the heavy bed against the door.

"Do you think that will hold?" wondered the barbarian.

"It'll have to. And we'll not fall for that 'cup of cocoa in bed' routine again! Now …" Roffo turned to the monk, hands on hips, the nearest that anyone had yet seen him to being cross. "Just what have you been up to while we've been defending life and limb from ravishing hordes? And this had *better* be good!"

For a moment the monk was taken aback, his face pulling an expression something like that of a rubber-faced ruminant watching the approach of a primitive vet with a pair of bricks.

"Ah … sorry … but think may know where map fragment is …"

CHAPTER 10

THE NAKED LAUNCH

THE TEMPLE was situated at the edge of town atop a small anticline. From town-side, the ascent to the Temple was smooth and gradual, but at the summit the hill gave way to a steep scree slope that led down to a shallow river locally known as Ye Heavenly Flow. Scrubby trees grew in the more stable pockets of the slope and a winding path switch-backed down to a little jetty on the riverbank. The course of time had pushed the scree slope further and further back into the hill until, at present, it lay a mere five yards from the north face of the Temple.

Terry and the monk trudged up the hill to the sacred building. On either side of The Road to Bliss were shops selling a wide variety of religious mementoes. There were miniature 'Satyr in Purgatory' statuettes, in which the horned God stood, arms spread wide and fists clenched, agony on his face, and a pair of demonic underpants about his person. There were copious copies of The Bibulous. There were reliquaries containing small wisps of exceedingly curly hair set upon velvet, which were claimed to be 100% Guaranteed Genuine Satyric Specimens. And there were special signed Barbie Pinkhair novels, blessed by the Bishop with his Holy Waters.

The intrepid duo picked their way past the tack shops and through the little cemetery which formed a buffer between the shops and the Temple. The relative size of the tombstones – each a thrusting obelisk – appeared to signify the status of the person buried beneath. In one section, under half a dozen large, shady trees, were the tombs of important dignitaries: Big Knobs, Parliamentarians, and Royalty. On each of these upright stone boxes were carved various Bibulical scenes: Satyr-the-Man at The Last Orgy; Doubting Thomas standing – wide-eyed and amazed – before Satyr-Revealed; the destruction of the city of the evil Frottagists; and a goodly number of scenes from Appendix 3 (Satyr's Favourite Positions). Passing the last of these tombs, the monk frowned at the suggestion of movement. He came to a halt, resting a restraining hand against Terry's chest. The two men waited and – a few moments later – observed a head peering around the stone. After making startled eye contact with the monk, the head darted back out of view.

"Who was that?" wondered Terry. "And why do you think he's been following us?"

"You notice too?"

"Yeah. He's been shadowing us ever since we left the guest-house."

"Hmm – now remember. Yesterday was followed by someone. Different someone though. Someone *think* seen before."

"Well, I don't know this guy. He casts *quite* a shadow though. Maybe I should go and have a word with him?"

"No. Not yet. If know followed, and follower not know we know, have advantage. Come." The two approached the verdigris copper doors of the Temple.

Behind the tomb, Justin cursed his carelessness. He struck the obelisk in frustration, then checked to see whose memory he had affronted. The legend simply stated 'Whopper'. A frown distorted Justin's face. "Ah, Whopper you old card! A much over-estimated fellow in my humble opinion. Well, here you go mate, let me water your flowers for you …"

Inside the Temple, the two spies paused to ascertain the nature of the edifice. Arranged to either side of them were several dozen large collection boxes.

"'For New Roofe'," read Terry. He looked up at the vaulted ceiling. "Hmm. Looks all right to me. Fine stonework. I reckon these builders could put up some stout fortifications if they tried. Dad would approve."

The monk read another caption. "'For repair to stained glasse windows'." He looked around. At the far end of the huge hall behind a large altar, and along the walls parallel to the nave, there were a score or so highly colourful windows, tall and thin and arched at their tops. These windows, like the carvings on the tombstones, depicted various Bibulical scenes: the birth of Satyr to Joy of Sax; Satyr turning water into cocktails; and more positions from Appendix 3. The monk scrunched up his face in puzzlement. "All look perfect. Perhaps problem with frames?"

"This one here says: 'To Repair Damaged Statues'." Terry ambled over to a large bronze affair in a little alcove. This showed a wicked-looking man with a quiff and an immaculate suit forcing a vest over the head of a weeping child. The caption revealed: 'Sartor Corrupting Ye Innocents'. The barbarian stroked the cold metal and admired the workmanship. "Well, this one's not too badly damaged."

"Nor this," appended the monk, from beside a second statue. This portrayed a proud Satyr, hands on hips, his magnificence thrust out before him. "Not unless count discolouring of thingy."

"Yeah, brass gets like that when it's been rubbed a lot …"

"Ah, my children," came a soft, level voice. "You must be strangers here. Do you not know the legend?"

The two men turned to look at the man who had spoken to them. In spite of the absence of clothing, the man was distinguishable from the common Nudian because of his small, white, conical hat. On this was stitched, in red, a pair of shears: the implement of Satyr's demise. Even without the hat, the monk would have known the priest for what he was – from the tone of his voice, from the corpulence of one who had led an easy life, and from the way he clasped his soft, white, beringed hands together in a peculiarly religious manner almost like praying. The monk's frown deepened and he felt an urge to spit, as though to clear a bad taste from his mouth.

"What legend?" asked Terry.

"Ah, my children, it is said that if you rub the Holy Appendage and make a wish then it will come true."

"Really? Okay. Let's have a bash." Terry chewed his lip for a moment. His eyes lit up. "Yeah – I'll have some of that!" He reached forward and gave the out-jutting member a swift stroke. Realising what this must have looked like, he blushed. He turned to his companion. "Are you going to have a wish?"

The monk shook his head. "Have no wishes, only intentions."

The priest cocked his head and frowned slightly. "An unusual answer. You are Believers are you not? We generally do not approve of tourists here in the Temple."

"Um, yeah. Can't you see from our clothes?"

The priest appraised Terry. "Ah, yes, but of course. Forgive me for doubting you. And I'm sorry about your injury."

The barbarian looked down at the large bandage that swathed his middle region, donned earlier on the monk's wise advice. "Um, thanks. It's embarrassing really. You know. Shut it in a door."

The priest smiled. "A common affliction. Perhaps you'd like me to show you around?"

"Yes," interjected the monk, "in particular, like to see damaged windows and broken statues that need repair." The monk smiled. Terry slapped a hand to his forehead.

An hour later the spies headed back down the hill. They descended The Road To Bliss, passed along The Chase, detoured through Sexe Drive, and joined The Grand Carnal. This led back into the centre of town. As they walked they discussed what they had found in the Temple.

"I'm surprised he showed us anything," mused Terry, "what with all your jibes and stuff. I mean, messing about with the Holy Shears was bad enough – you nearly decapitated him – but using the Confessions box as a loo was something else. *Especially* as there was someone in there at the time!"

The monk sniggered to himself. "Only another priest. Thought they like that sort of thing anyway!" His face suddenly turned serious. "But priests deserve it! Parasites! Using religion for own benefit!"

"Is that why you left your Order?"

The oriental looked sheepish. "Not exactly. Was kicked out for getting drunk and putting traffic cone on head of statue of First Dali Llama. Humph! Some people have no sense of humour."

The two walked in silence for a few minutes. Ten yards behind them, a beer-bellied man with long, unwashed hair strolled along with his hands behind his back, attempting to look nonchalant. A further five yards behind him, a darkly handsome man crept along, holding a ceramic pot before him in an attempt to disguise his identity.

"Do you think it's in there, then?" wondered Terry at last.

The monk nodded his head curtly. "If still in Nudia, must be there. Notice big locked door behind curtains to side of altar?"

"Yeah. There's a whole wing of the Temple off to that side we never got into. But I noticed from the outside that there's a little tower above the wing."

"Think can climb up there? Otherwise need to go through two strong doors."

The plotting continued all the way back to the guest-house.

Roffo could not believe it: left behind again like some useless piece of baggage!

"*Roffo, cook the food,*" muttered the young adventurer to himself. "*Roffo, fetch some water; Roffo, go buy some supplies; Roffo, go fill in the latrine trench.* Bah! I'll show them!" He tipped another stout leather bag upside down, spilling its contents onto the already cluttered bed. "*Ahhh, Roffo – assemble things for breaking into guarded fortress – yes?*" he mimicked. "Bollocks! Well, you'll see. I know a thing or two about night-time raids and the like! Aye, I've pinched a few things in my time …"

Well, Maddy's bottom mostly. Still, Roffo did consider himself adept at proper thieving too. As a youth, in his home village up in the hills, he'd been champion scrumper of '73. And had he not also gained the sobriquet 'The Sugar Mouse Bandit' after a particularly daring bout of shoplifting? He paused in his labours and stood with arms akimbo, the smile of reminiscence on his face. What days! What high adventure! And all for the love of the beautiful Valerian, the first girl he'd *nearly* kissed. Clever old Gramps – he knew a thing or two! "All the girls love a rogue," he'd said, and it was true! It was just a shame that the rogue in question happened to be named *Timpson*. A frown settled on the young man's face. And now that he thought back, well, he hadn't *actually, genuinely* stolen those sweets anyway. Not *as such*. His frown deepened. In fact, he'd paid the shopkeeper for them and then given the old codger a bit extra not to welch on him.

Roffo shrugged his shoulders and up-ended another sack with a clatter and a clang. He'd had other successes though, like, like … the time when, under the influence of alcohol, he'd stolen a pie from Awful Puns. Surely that was the nimblest piece of work ever, and a miracle given that he'd barely been able to walk in a straight line at the time. True, he *had* been caught – but that was only because he'd given the game away in the police line-up by being copiously sick. And anyway, had he not read every crime thriller in Cross-My-Way's small library? With a little nod Roffo concurred with himself that, with all the information he'd gleaned from *both* books, he was surely the wisest *potential* thief in the whole world. And he knew exactly what the present job required.

First off were the skeleton keys. He'd not actually managed to get his hands on a proper set of these, but over the years he'd collected a huge bunch of keys that opened all sorts of things. In fact, he had so many keys that even *he* didn't know what half of them were for. But if he found a door locked against them he felt sure that one of his keys would do the trick.

Next there was a sledgehammer, in case the keys were not up to the job. Of course, you could never tell when shoddy workmanship might let you down, and so he added a second to the pile. Ah, but the door would surely come down more quickly if two people were at it. He added a third, and then, because *that* might fail (handle break, head fly off), a fourth. Oh yes, and two pillows to help muffle the blows of the hammers.

A couple of crowbars, he decided, might help them prise open locks, while a full set of screwdrivers would surely help if they needed to unscrew some hinges … and a tool belt was needed to hold the screwdrivers. Ah, yes, and what about oil to lubricate squeaky hinges? Roffo chuckled to himself: the classic mistake of the tyro! Many a burglary had gone astray because of a rusty, creaking door!

Right. Good. That was doors covered. But what if they needed to get through a window? A pair of glass-cutters were added to the pile along with some stout tape to prevent the glass from shattering should they need to use force. Force? He put two sturdy throwing-rocks next to the roll of tape. Then two more.

Doors, windows … locked drawers were covered by the screwdrivers … *aha*! He rooted about in a mass of ironmongery and found a couple of spanners – just in case they needed to take the back off a desk in the search for secret compartments. And what about drills to help break up locking mechanisms, saws to cut open sealed cabinets, and lump hammers to smash up everything else in a rage when they couldn't find what they were looking for? He couldn't find the drills and saws. He'd get them from the wagon later.

Okay, but what about other mission essentials? They'd need weapons all-round, of course; and charcoal to blacken up; and macho bandannas so that they'd look *really hard* and frighten off any guards; and water bottles, filled to the brim, to quench the thirst; and high-energy chocolate bars – plus some fruit and grainy things (that looked and tasted like birdseed) – to make sure they had a balanced diet and wouldn't collapse, become anaemic, or develop scurvy at some crucial point in the operation. But what if they were caught? In that case they'd need valuables to bribe their way out of trouble: a bottle of Burning Pisse Vodka to get the prison guards drunk; some sleeping pills and poisons … oh, and of course, some bandages and liniments in case they were tortured. Roffo paced up and down the room. What else? Rope – to abseil down from roofs and tie up guards; tar to light torches; torches; tinder boxes … he must forget nothing!

And now for the *pièce-de-résistance*! Roffo picked up a package of perfect Zmas-present proportions. He carefully unwrapped the item from its water-resistant covering and placed it reverentially on the bed. It was a book: *Illinois Jane's Guide to Traps, Tricks and Pitfalls*: the ultimate reference work for the would-be raider of lost temples, churches, and other places where people invented ingenious ways of stopping collectors of religious artefacts from having it away with their sacred relics. Roffo had studied this mighty tome for many an hour. He had learnt off by heart the best way to avoid being run over by a giant boulder (i.e. run like buggery), the best thing to do when trapped in a room of contracting dimensions (use your head, though someone else's was preferable), and the best way to cross a floor covered in dubious lettering (learn to spell correctly in the language of the people whose temple you were robbing).

All he needed now was the correct clothing. He looked over at the nightwear placed out for them by Miss Deedes. It was black as coal – just the colour any self-respecting thief would want to *not-be-seen* in. All he would have to do was use black boot polish on the shiny metal studs to stop the moonlight glinting off them, and sew up some of the slits, and they would be perfect.

There was now only one thing missing. He needed a bag, a special bag, a bag without which they could not possibly go ahead. He found a suitable sack, a needle and some thread, and settled down to sew. Within no time it was finished. With vast contentment he nodded at the sight of his work: for there, in shaky lettering, crossing the middle of the sack, was spelled the word *swag*.

The sun dropped from the sky like a slowly deflating helium balloon, taking the afternoon with it.

In Nudia, the people spent the diminishing hours of daylight going about their accustomed business. In the fields, labourers *carefully* swished their scythes and harvested their crops and thought about ale. In The Buff, housewives visited shops and stopped to natter with friends and coochie-coo baffled babies in prams. In the backstreets of the trendy Left Cheek, writers in cravats penned furious diatribes against the strictures of society while drinking mighty quantities of wine. In the raunchy SoHoHo area, pink-faced tourists in leather thongs (the least offensive item of clothing to the populace) peered through Nooky Parlour windows and fended off the awesome offers of touts and club owners. In Parliament, Prime Member's Question Time passed in a furore as the walrus-moustached Minister Mai T. Pole, to the horror of his secretary, Stoker, launched into a rambling, barely coherent attack on his leader's integrity and then collapsed in a drunken stupor. And in the Temple, Bishop Mazed reclined on a jewel-encrusted throne, quilled his sermon for the next day, and pondered the merits of a holy crusade.

With the ultimate demise of the afternoon, patterns changed, and life in Nudia took on a different pace. Weary people slouched home for their dinners; wide-eyed tourists returned to their hotels for cold showers; and the good and the great retired to splendid houses, plush restaurants, or the clubs around SoHoHo and the main square. But as the good citizens unwound, chilled out, or otherwise took it easy, less innocent, more frenetic activities were afoot ...

"Right, this is a military operation, so I want things to go like clockwork." Roffo paced up and down, his hands behind his back, clutching the crowbar of authority. Terry and the monk exchanged concerned looks: their charcoaled faces made them look like a pair of very worried black-and-white minstrels being interrogated by the PC police. "Now, shall we go through the plans one more time?"

"Been through plans fifty times already," muttered the monk, adjusting his bandanna. "If not go soon, day will break, and that *not* in plans!"

"Okay okay! Just checking. I just want to make sure that we all know what we're about. Preparedness is the key to success! That's something I learnt from Gramps long ago as we whiled away the winter evenings over a nice pot of tea and a game of Riske. After all, there's no point strolling into undefended Bu-chak if your opponent has five elephant regiments in adjacent Rembolo!"

The monk sighed. Resignedly, he reached down to the rucksack that Roffo had packed for him. He tried to lift it. It wouldn't move. "Ai-la! What in here? Battering ram and eight siege engines?"

"Preparedness! I told you we must be ready for every eventuality. In any case, I gave you the lightest 'sack, so I don't know what you're grumbling about."

Muttering under his breath, the monk braced himself. With a great deal of straining and grunting he managed to swing the rucksack off the floor. He tottered around for a bit, like a drunken man giving a piggyback to a sumo wrestler. By wedging the 'sack against a wall he was at last able to manipulate the thing onto his back.

Terry cheerily made to lift up his own equipment ... and frowned in puzzlement. It wouldn't budge! Straining every ounce of his mighty sinews, he bench-pressed the rucksack above his head, rotated it in the air, and let it slowly drop onto his shoulders. His thighs warped outwards from the effort of staying upright.

"Good!" cried Roffo. He reached under a table and then, somewhat sheepishly, pulled out a thin cord bag. "Map, plans, compass, valuables. You know. All the really *important* stuff. A general needs to keep his hands free so he can rapidly direct the battle. Come on then!" Roffo skipped through the door, down the stairs, past the sleeping-drug-afflicted Miss Deedes, and onto the street.

Two thunder clouds followed.

"Are you sure this is a good idea?" asked Cucumber Joe. "I mean, can't we just frighten him out of town or somefink?"

Justin scowled at the shadowy form in front of him and practised using the shears. "No! He might come back. He is a freak of nature, an abomination, and we must dispose of him."

"Cripes!" went Dick Monster, pulling his head back from around the corner of the building. "Here he is! Great Satyr, the blasphemers are attired! An' ... hang on a minute ... you didn't say he was a *barbarian*!"

"Barbarian?" whined Phil More. "*Barbarian!*"

"An' that's not all," said Dick, "he's got a couple o' friends with him. That makes the odds four against three – and one of them is a bloody barbarian! That's great, just great!"

"We'll have to cancel the plan then," noted Joe. "This changes everyfink. I'm off ..."

"Hold it *right there!*" Justin raised the shears menacingly and rested them against Joe's well-tuned pecs. "Are you telling me that the greatest Nudian tag-wrestling team of all time – men for whom grappling other naked Big Men holds no fear – is now about to turn tail and flee *at this* ..."

"Well," interrupted Joe, "there *are* three of them, an' you said there'd be just *one* ..."

"Dick... describe his companions!"

"Um, okay, so, they look a bit on the weedy side ..."

"There you go!"

"But ..." persisted Joe – a man whose stage act involved painting a certain part of his anatomy green – "you didn't *say* our target was a psychopathic human killing machine! My life means more to me than your title. I'm sorry Justin, but … ah *ah* AH *AH!*"

"Precisely!" The Big Knob of Nudia withdrew the shears a fraction of an inch. "I do not plan to be usurped. So. It's either *Him* or *You*. Choose!"

"Well," gasped Joe, "put that way …"

"Look out!" cried Dick, suddenly. "*Firewood salesmen!*"

The shears were whisked away behind Justin's back just as a pack of five hairy men crept around the corner.

"Ah!" went Trespass, in surprise. "Hello there, er, friends. Firewood?"

Dick, who was nearest, looked around in bewilderment. "Er, yeah … yeah, that's the ticket. In fact, we was just out looking for some, weren't we mates? Not creeping around in dark at all, oh no. Just trying to find something to keep us warm." The rest of the tag team mumbled assent while Justin simply glowered. "Can we have two bundles please?"

"Heh heh, sure … here you WHAT!" Trespass paled.

"Two bundles? Yours an' … *his* …" Dick pointed at Frunge.

Scenting a money-making opportunity, Burble quickly stepped into the breach. "Sure, friends. Shall we say, what, five silver pieces each?"

The negotiations went on for some minutes. By the time the two groups had come to an arrangement – leaving Trespass and Frunge the two most unhappy men in all of Nudia, and the tag-team considerably out of pocket – their quarry had disappeared from view.

The monk collapsed outside the mysterious east wing of the Temple, his pack still attached to his back. He wheezed like a man who had just smoked the yearly output of a large cigarette factory. Terry shucked off his rucksack and staggered forward from the sudden loss of weight. The impact of the rucksack on the ground caused a tremor that set the stained glass windows rattling in their panes and sent the precarious edge of the cliff into a gentle avalanche down the scree slope.

Roffo flapped his arms about in panic and attempted to quieten his comrades. "Men … *please*! Let's have some professionalism here!"

Terry leant against a flying buttress and groaned. Slowly he attempted to straighten his back, which co-operated, but only in vertebrate-crackling protest. "By Grom, I've not had to do anything like that since I was punished as a kid for rescuing a cat from a tree! That's a steep hill!"

"Yes, well, we'd have probably made quicker time," declared Roffo, "if you hadn't of had to carry the monk and his pack too. I must admit, I'm a little concerned that he's not pulling his weight in this operation."

"That it …" gasped the monk from his prone position, feebly windmilling his arms in a fruitless effort to get up, "Kill him … yes … kill him now …"

Roffo frowned. "Really! That sounds like mutiny, Mr Monk, sir, mutiny! If we were back at the barracks, um, *as it were*, I'd order Terry to flog you with The Cat. But a good leader should be fair as well as firm. So, I won't put you on report on this occasion, but I *will* be watching you from now on." Roffo slapped his crowbar into the palm of his right hand. "Right. *When* we've all finished lying around, we've got work to do. Terry: begin Phase Two!"

———————

"Wot they doing?" growled Grunt. "I can't see 'cos Bruce's fat arse is in the way."

"One maire comment like that," replied the red-bearded one, "an' I'll blow yer heid aff."

"Shut up you morons," hissed Trespass, "they'll hear us …"

"Aye, well, they're gaein' tae hear this all reet. Grunt: prepare f'r the Trump o' Doom!"

"Don't you dare you bastard!"

"Then move awa'. This bush isnae big enough for the both o' us …"

Trespass smote his head with the Fist of Frustration. "QUIET!" he whispered, in savage capitals. "Cut it out now or you'll have me to deal with. Who sniggered?"

"Not me," lied The Shadow. After a further moment, the diminutive yakker prodded Trespass. "Well? Go on then … tell us what they're doing."

The leader of the pack sighed and thought "Why me?" He attempted to make out the shapes in the gloom ahead of him. Behind him sounds of a scuffle broke out along with whispered curses. He tried to ignore the activity. "Well, looks like Testicles is climbing up the side of the tower. Bloody Hull – no safety harness or nothing! He's got something in his mouth …"

"You bugger – take *that* …"

"OW!"

"Go on," urged Burble, from behind his leader's left shoulder.

"Dunno what it is … he's going up like a bloody fly though! He's at the top already … Ah, *I see*. It's a thin rope. He's pulling it up. It's

tied to a thicker rope. Right, he's tying *that* to the window pillar thingy
… *stop shoving!*"

"I can see now," said Burble. "The barbarian's pulling up their
packs now. I dunno what's in *that* one but it looks bloody heavy: even
he's having trouble. Oh-oh, he can't hold it …"

THUD

The tag-wrestling team were thrown from their feet.

"Earthquake!" whined Cucumber Joe in terror. "Run for your
lives …"

"Get out in the open," cried Dick Monster, "an' watch that
tombstone!"

The tottering obelisk paused at the end of its swaying arc, made a
quick calculation, and decided that the force at its base – added to that
of gravity – wasn't enough to overcome its frictional adherence to the
ground. It settled back onto its foundation. Phil More, who lay on his
back, his legs outstretched, his vitals in the direct earthward path of the
wobbling tombstone, smiled a sickly smile and passed out.

Justin leapt to his feet and scowled at his gang. "It's only a tremor.
Someone slap *him* awake," he pointed at Phil. "I'm going to see what
the Usurper is up to."

———◆·◆·◆———

Inside the Temple, a jobbing holidaymaker from Cross-My-Way
desperately threw his legs around the neck of a large stone statue while
at the same time trying to steady the now-swirling rope on which he
had been descending. The thief's efforts managed to rock Satyr's stony
head forward so that it buried itself in his groin, appearing to *go down*
on him in a perversely lithophilic manner. Unfortunately for Mitchkin,
the bandaging from his previous encounter with Satan the dog proved
inadequate in the cushioning-vitals-from-blows department. The thief
whimpered. A tear of pain dribbled from under his bandaged head, passing
over the parallel cat-scratch scars that crossed his nose, then dripping
into the darkness below.

Straining with the effort, Mitchkin pushed out his battered pelvis
and managed to right the lecherously smiling statue. Still groaning, the
thief let the rope slip through his hands … He fell to the floor, landing
heavily on his buttocks. "Oooo-ahhhh!" he cried. Stuffing a hand into
his mouth, Mitchkin stared around the darkened chamber with wide

221

eyes. But there was no sign of movement. He cautiously regained his plimsoll-clad feet and, dragging a dead-leg, began to limp off to the nearest door.

He didn't get far.

"Got it … got it … gotit … gotitgotitgotit …" and indeed he had.

"Well done Terry! Now drop it down inside … CAREFULLY. Then you can haul us up."

"Sure thing." The barbarian braced his thighs against the window pillars and, with muscles bulging, cords straining from his neck, and teeth clenched in a rictus of effort, began to lower the rucksack down the well of the tower. At the last moment his grip failed and the rope slipped through his hands. There was a dull, cushioned thud from below, but nothing more. Terry nodded to himself and turned to pull up his companions.

The monk was the last up; he glared at Roffo. "Right, now take lead. Where rope down … aha!"

"Er," said Terry, "er …"

"What's up?" asked Roffo.

Terry pointed. "That rope there … *it's not ours!*"

The monk looked non-plussed. "So? Probably used by priests breaking curfew. Let us go."

One by one, the adventurers lowered themselves into the bowels of the Temple, past the leering statue of Satyr, to land beside the heavy rucksacks. Perhaps because it was dark, or perhaps because it was unexpected, none of them noticed the pair of plimsolls poking out from under one of the packs.

Roffo opened a sack and started rummaging inside. "Sledgehammers? Drills? What do you want?"

Terry and the monk examined the two doors that led from the room – which appeared to be nothing more than a private chapel. The one to the west was locked, but the one to the east was slightly ajar.

"This is way need to go," whispered the monk. "Other door must be locked one saw earlier from other side …"

"Wait!" Roffo appeared at their shoulders, raising an oil can into a beam of moonlight spearing through one of the windows above. "I'll oil the hinges!" He came back several seconds later. "Now try this: it's called a periscope. It's a useful tool for pros like us. Let's you see around corners and whatnot."

The monk gave the young barman an astonished look, then a small smile spread across his rubber face. He nodded and, taking hold of the implement, used it to peer through the crack in the narrowly opened door.

"Ah! Two priests inside playing cards. On far side of room. Candle is by them. Both have maces on table. Hmm, not know how to get at priests …"

"Blowpipe," said Roffo, handing a tube to the monk, "and here are half a dozen darts. Notice how the feathers are painted yellow and black, just like the Nudian Stinger Fly. Painted them myself this afternoon. I suggest Terry has a go, as he's bound to be the best shot. Oh, and don't worry: I dipped them in a sleeping drug, though it's *probably* best not to suck."

Again, the monk stared at the young man, and again he nodded. "Good!" He moved over and handed the pipe to the barbarian.

Ten seconds later the two priests were slumped over the table, snoring, and the three thieves were in the room.

"Bah! Coins, jewels, more coins …"

"Yeah, same here. Shit!" Roffo closed the lid of a casket – and then suddenly looked up. "What am I saying? Whey hey! We're rich, *rich!*"

"No! This not what here for! *Not* common thieves …"

"No, we're bloody good ones!"

"NO! Put back! After something more important … mustn't be weighed down by baubles."

"*Baubles* he says! Okay. But after we've found the map, I'm coming back here."

They tried the next two storerooms and found much the same. In the second, they also found bolts of finest silk and several works of art. The fourth storeroom, however, was a small library. Scrolls and parchments were heaped on tables, stuffed in chests, and arranged along shelves. Some of the chests were locked. Roffo went to get some bolt cutters while the others began their search.

Outside the Temple, two groups of men clustered at opposite ends of the building and fretted at the passing of time.

"I don't know about this, Justin," worried Cucumber Joe. "This is sacrilege this is. I reckon we ought to call out the guards and let them deal with it."

"Yeah," concurred Dick, "they could be doing anything in there: defiling statues, nicking things, *murdering* priests in their beds. You can't put nothing past them barbarians."

"No!" Justin paced up and down, trailing the shears from one hand. "We've got to catch them and teach them a proper lesson. If the priests catch them they'll probably just stick them in jail for a while. *Whole*. And *he*'ll still be here, *fully equipped*! I'm not having that." He stopped and pointed the shears at the doubters. "We'll nab them as soon as they come out, right? Go for the barbarian. The others won't be a problem. You lot hold him down and I'll do the rest. Got it? I said, GOT IT?"

The tag-team muttered their unenthusiastic assent.

Meanwhile, thirty yards away, hidden behind a pair of bushes, the yakkers grumbled to one another.

"What are they doing?" wondered Trespass. "I can't believe they came all this way just to break into some temple to steal some religious crap. How's that going to help Hops out?"

"Maybe they're trying to find something to *exorcise* Manis with," suggested Burble, with a grin.

"You think so?" asked the incredulous Frunge. "Wot, like, Holy Water stuff? Will it work on him d'you reckon?"

Trespass batted the gullible yakker on the back of the head. "Fool! I'm surrounded by idiots!"

"Well, I didn't know," continued Frunge. "I thought Holy Water only worked on vampires and things. Wot can we do?"

As Trespass looked to the heavens, Burble muttered: "Wish them luck."

"La!" hissed the monk. "Look at this."

"What've you got there?" Roffo came up to the monk's shoulder. Terry loomed behind the young man, looking over his head and down onto the ancient book that the monk now held in his hands. The monk flipped over the cover so that the others could see.

"The Bibulous. So what? There are hundreds of copies here and about."

"True, but this copy very old. Very, *very* old."

"The original?" wondered Roffo. "Go on!"

"Perhaps, perhaps not, but must be one of earliest editions."

"Must be worth a fortune! Let's take it too …"

"No. That not why call you over. Look inside." The monk re-opened the book where he'd left an index finger bookmark. The fading black ink was annotated, here and there, with a clearer red ink.

"Hold that torch up, Terry – ta. That's better …" Roffo leant closer and began to read from one heavily altered paragraph. "'*And so King Dong said unto his foes, give up your* …' Looks like the original said '*swords*', but that's been crossed out and replaced with '*clobber*'. So, um, it goes: '… *give up your clobber and join us* …' Interesting."

"And here," pointed the monk, "text altered from: '*Thou shalt not covet thy neighbour's wife*' to '*Thou* shalt *covet thy neighbour's wife*'."

"And here," Terry's muscular finger descended from above Roffo's head and stabbed at the page, "it's been altered to say '… *and so Satyr streaked through the streets of Jereboam*', instead of *ran*."

"It goes on like this."

Roffo whistled. "Well, you have to admire them: these priests are surely the biggest load of pervs in the entire world. It takes some balls to rewrite a holy book and con an entire kingdom."

The monk slammed the book shut, suddenly angry. "Perhaps keep this after all. One day people of Nudia might be interested to know truth about holy book."

"Er, yeah, right … but not tonight, *eh?* Let's find that map."

Bishop Mazed staggered through the Temple cemetery. "No-no," he sang, "no-no-no-no, no-no-no-no, no-no there's no *corsets* …"

"Bah bah, bah-na-na-na-na-na, bah na-na-na-na-na," chorused Brothers Denda, Shafto and O'Toole, "there's no *corsets* …" The men jigged around in a peculiar dance, their arms reaching for the sky, their bottoms wobbling, their legs trembling. As their tuneless rendition came to an end the priests burst into laughter, and even the bishop chuckled.

"Whey-hey!" cried Brother Denda. "That new Stringy Fellows' club is a corker. What a night, eh, Bish? Good to let your hair down once in awhi— *ulp!*" The Brother, suddenly realising what he'd just said, turned as white as a (white) sheet.

Bishop Mazed put an arm around the man's bare shoulders. "Be calm, Brother. Disrespect comes easily when wine loosens the tongue." He smiled a frightening smile. "That is why we should be forever vigilant!"

"I'm sorry, Your Eminence. Please … *not the hanging stone!*"

By now the group of clubbers had reached the heavy iron door to the East wing of the building: the living quarters entrance. Brother Shafto lowered his head and searched in his clerical handbag for the large iron key to the door. With shaking hands he attempted to find the right hole for the key, which wasn't easy, given that there were five of them and they appeared to be dancing together. He pressed the key forward and, by sheer luck, chose correctly. The door opened.

The Bishop ushered the Brothers through, restraining Denda with a firm grip. He gently shoved the trembling man through last and then, unexpectedly, administered a swift kick vertically through the goal posts. Denda dropped like a stone and clutched himself.

"Punishment served," laughed the Bishop, and the others, in relief, laughed too.

"Ah, it seems a shame to call it a night so early," suggested the corpulent Shafto. "May I suggest we broach a barrel? I hear, ahem, that there is a rather fine barrel of Embolian wine in the Vintages Room."

"Your effrontery astounds me, Shafto, as does your girth. But why not!"

The drunken party staggered onwards, through the dormitories of the acolytes, along a corridor from which branched the private quarters, and towards the treasure storerooms.

"Over here!" cried Roffo. The others gathered around the young adventurer, who was standing beside a small altar. Two heavy candlesticks stood on either side of the altar and a large chest rested between them. A long rubbery sack hung on the wall above the chest. "Look at the caption on the chest."

"Ah, yes: 'Mappes'. Good! If fragment here, must be in chest. Open it."

"It's locked. Terry – will you do the honours?"

The barbarian stepped forward with a pair of bolt cutters and soon had the lock off. He pulled the massive chest forward slowly, inch by inch, for its width was about the span of his outstretched arms. When it was at the edge of the altar he stopped. The three men peered inside.

"Whew! Look at all that parchment. There must be hundreds of maps and things in there. Where do you think they got them all from?"

The monk picked up a large, intricately penned map that represented the mysterious southern continent of Goroldo. "Such craftsmanship," he said, in awe. "Very fine, very valuable."

They started to sift through the contents of the chest, plucking out town maps, contour maps, maps of ancient kingdoms that no longer existed, maps of imaginary lands, colourful maps, maps whose details were outlined in gold thread …

"It could take hours to check this lot," noted Roffo. "Hang on a sec. I'll get the other fragment so we know roughly what we're looking for." Roffo retrieved his thin cord bag from a table in the centre of the room. As he rummaged about inside, however, a sound carried to him. He paused and looked up. Then he cocked his head to one side as though this might aid his hearing. *There it was again.* It was coming from his right – from the direction of the storeroom *beyond* the little library. He wrinkled his brow and moved up to the door, pressing an ear against it. At first he heard nothing and then, clearly, a peel of laughter. This was followed by the sound of jangling keys and creaking hinges. He put his eye to the keyhole, and thought he detected candlelight from the next room.

"What is it?" said a voice, suddenly at his side.

"Ah ... oh ... my heart ..." A white-faced Roffo turned to face the monk. "Don't you ever creep up on me like that again! Blimey, I nearly wet myself!"

The monk gestured him into silence. He then frowned as he heard the voices coming from next door. They were louder now and rather raucous. In fact, he thought, it sounded as though they were singing. "Better hurry."

The two rejoined Terry and started to go through the heap of parchments with greater urgency. "This is hopeless," declared Roffo, after a while. "In this light we could miss it completely."

"That so." The monk paused to think, then looked up at the sack over the altar. "Aha! Perhaps should put all maps into sack and then get outside and examine contents at leisure?"

Terry yanked the large flaccid sack from the wall. He and Roffo started grabbing great handfuls of parchment and shoving them inside. After several frantic minutes, with numerous glances over their shoulders towards the source of the singing, the last of the contents of the chest were packed away. As Terry hefted the sack over his shoulder, however, the arc of the swing brought it into contact with the sturdy lid of the chest – which teetered for a moment and then descended with a *bang.*

"Shit!" cried Roffo. "*Let's go.*" The three men raced to the door that ultimately led back to the chapel. Beyond the opposite door the singing stopped abruptly.

———•••••———

"What was that?"

"Ooooops – 'scuse me Your Eminence! It just sort of slipped out ..."

"No, you fool, what was that bang?"

"It sounded like it came from next door," noted a suddenly sober Brother Shafto.

"That's what I thought. There shouldn't be anyone up at this time."

"Prob'bly naughty ac'lytes," slurred Brother Denda.

"If so I'll roast their hides! Come on!"

The priestly posse staggered up to the door. Bishop Mazed grasped the handle, gathered his anger, and flung it open. The room was empty, but the opposite door was open.

"Right, Brothers let's …"

"Oh Great Satyr," wailed Denda. "Look … *looooooooook!*"

The others followed the direction of his pointing finger. They gasped in unison.

"No! Satyr preserve us!" whined Brother O' Toole.

"Sacrilege," shrieked Shafto, making the sign of the Y.

"How dare they!" roared Bishop Mazed. He stalked over to the altar – giving the empty chest only a cursory glance – and reached up to the wall where one of Nudia's most sacred relics had recently hung.

"They've nicked it. Oh, catastrophe … it is *gone!*"

"Brother Tom was right! He sees truly!"

"*Satyr's Holy Longy* – stolen!"

"There will be an accounting for this!" bellowed Mazed. "Guards, guards! Rouse yourselves! You lot, follow me!" The Bishop stormed through the storerooms, his priests fearfully trailing after him. From the living quarters behind came the sounds of commotion. Ahead, the party strode into the first of the storerooms, to there discover the two drugged guards. "Leave them!" yelled Mazed. "Come on."

In the chapel they saw a pair of booted feet wriggling up a rope into the darkness of the tower. As the Bishop touched the rope it came snaking down from above. "Curses! Outside, quick, they cannot be allowed to escape!"

"At least we have one of them," declared O'Toole, excitedly. "Your Eminence – look!" The priest gave a mighty tug at an abandoned rucksack. Seeing his efforts, the others joined in. The pack began to shift slowly to reveal, first, a pair of plimsolled feet, and then a pair of legs clad in black trousers, and eventually the bandaged head of a man.

Smiling inanely, Mitchkin stared into the faces of his captors.

"Shit shit shit," commented Roffo, as he started to descend the rope to the ground. He was sandwiched between his two companions: Terry led the way down, while the monk brought up the rear – his boots periodically biffing Roffo in the head. "What are we going to do now?" gasped the young man, as he continued to feed the rope through his hands. "Our provisions are still inside …"

"Forget that now … just keep going!" hissed the monk. "Must head for river … be caught if go back to guest-house …"

"Shit shit shit …"

"Hurry up," cried Terry, on reaching the ground. He dropped Satyr's map-stuffed Longman's Special and peered up at his comrades. "This place will soon be swarming …"

"TOO LATE, my friend!"

Terry swivelled around to find four men forming a semi-circle around him. Three of the men were beefy specimens, while Terry recognised the fourth as the man who had followed them earlier in the day.

Justin pointed at the barbarian. "Men: detain him!"

The greatest Nudian tag-wrestling team of all time edged towards its quarry. Dick Monster was the first to make a move. He darted at Terry and attempted to get a neck-lock on him. A split-second later Phil More threw himself into a forward roll and emerged level with the barbarian's right thigh, which he attempted to grab. Meanwhile, Cucumber Joe skirted around the mêlée looking for an opportunity for a good hold.

Dick locked a forearm in front of the barbarian's throat and then passed his other arm behind his neck. Before he could put the squeeze on, however, Terry flexed a giant shoulder, which rippled upwards and caught the wrestler under the chin. As Dick's grip loosened, Terry reversed his hand and, catching his opponent at groin level, *squeezed*. The wrestler's face turned a peculiar blue colour and he dropped to the ground.

Almost instantly, the second wrestler was at him. Phil More grappled Terry's thigh and stood up, trying to off-balance him. But Terry's mighty leg would not move, no matter how hard the wrestler tried. Terry turned to face his opponent and, this time with his right hand, grasped his opponent's *weakness* and *lifted*. Up and up rose the hapless wrestler until he was suspended at shoulder level.

Terry frowned slightly. "I always thought nude wrestling was a particularly dumb idea." He flicked the howling wrestler away and turned to face the Cucumber man. Joe licked his lips and looked from one indisposed comrade to the other, and then down at his own green-painted soft spot. He looked up at Terry and considered his chances.

He licked his lips once more, crouched into an attacking position ... and then turned and – as fast as his legs would carry him – fled around the corner of the Temple.

"Terry, look out ... oh *bugger!*"

The barbarian turned around just in time to see a massive pair of shears raised to strike ... and then a blur of falling barman. Roffo flailed through the air to land squarely atop the Nudian Big Knob, felling him like a tree. Terry leant over to help the winded Roffo to his feet. "Thanks!"

"No problem," wheezed Roffo. He poked the stunned assailant with the toe of his boot, then flicked away his weapon. "Stupidity," he cried, "*sheer stupidity.*"

"Please," groaned Terry, "not at a time like this!"

"When finished messing about," said the monk, with some urgency in his voice, "think we better – how say? – *run like buggery!*"

From around either side of the Temple there suddenly emerged several dozen howling men – guards and priests – some armed with spears, others with maces.

"Strike down the heathens!" cried a tall, silver-haired man. "Retrieve Our Lord's Divine Protector!"

"Shit ... where now?"

"Down cliff. Quick!"

The three adventurers scrambled over the top of the cliff and started slipping and sliding down the loose scree slope. Terry crouched low, adopted a classic pose, and surfed down the slope as though riding a giant wave.

A little way off, five very confused men watched the unfolding events with more than a little concern.

"Bollocks," cried Burble, "I think they're trying to start a war."

"In that case," suggested Bruce, "I think we ought tae git oot o' here *quick*. Those Nudians are jist a wee bit pissed aff. I dunnae think it'd be a good idea tae git caught hangin' aboot here jist noo."

"You're right," agreed Trespass. "Bugger! Right men: back to the grove as quick as we can. We'll collect our gear and try to follow them."

The yakkers surreptitiously rose from behind their bushes and slunk away towards the road back to town.

Terry was the first to the bottom of the slope, skidding to a halt beside the small jetty on the river. At the top of the cliff, several dozen very angry men, armed with torches and various sharp objects, began to stream down the slope. The monk and Roffo tumbled and scrabbled towards the barbarian. Terry reached out an arm and managed to grab hold of the monk as he hurtled by, but Roffo was too far away. With a howl, the young barman skidded into the river, closely followed by an avalanche of small stones, dirt, and fossil shells. The barbarian leant down and fished him out.

"What now?" squeaked the drenched barman. "We're trapped! There's no frigging boat!"

"Shhhh! Need to think!" The monk scratched at his chin and paced up and down. The howls from up-slope steadily increased in volume. "Not get far if swim. There no boat. What have here? Nothing except …" His eyes lit up. He knelt down to examine the large, sturdy sack that was stuffed full of parchment. He turned to appraise the barbarian. "Terry – can blow up?"

"Eh?"

"Can blow up sack?"

"I'll give it a go." Terry took the sack, made a small aperture out of its opening, and took a deep breath. His huge chest inflated as though someone had stuck the nozzle of a tank of compressed air up his arse and turned on the valve. Terry put his lips to the opening and *blew*.

"Hurry!" howled Roffo. "They're nearly on us!"

As Terry puffed and puffed, the giant Longy expanded further and further: a great bag of air and parchment. And still Terry blew: ten, twelve, fifteen times … until at last it was fully inflated: a giant, nine-foot-long inflatable raft of the banana boat variety. The barbarian tied a knot in its end and displayed it to his comrades.

"Very good," yelled the monk. "And now into river. Quick." The first spears began to fly.

"You two – grab hold amidships," cried the barbarian, standing in chest-deep water. "Then kick. I'll steer from the back!"

The three adventurers grasped hold of their new boat and began to kick. Terry's powerful legs rapidly churned the water into a violent foam, causing them to surge down the river. The howling Nudians gained the jetty and began to fling spears and insults after them. But Terry kept up the sort of leg-stroke that would have caused the Man from Atlantis to hang up his swimming trunks in shame …

Soon, the jetty – and their antagonists – were lost from view.

CHAPTER 11

UNDERGROUND, OVERGROUND (WOMBLING FREE!)

THE INSPECTOR fingered a lacy blouse and feigned interest in the quality of its weave.

"Something for undercover work?" enquired the pretty shop assistant sarcastically. "Or is it for personal use?"

Yavlo gave the grinning young woman one of his heard-it-all-before looks. This was the sixth dress shop he'd tried today, and on each previous occasion he'd been on the receiving end of this very same gambit. Indeed, the quip was beginning to wear as thin as the flimsy attire strewn throughout the present establishment.

"Madam," he replied, forcing his lips into a gentle smile, "can you keep a secret?" Appreciating that the direct approach did not always work best, he had developed a more subtle routine. Yavlo leaned forward and dropped his voice to a low, conspiratorial whisper. "Actually, it is for my Sergeant's mistress ..." He gave a slight, almost imperceptible nod in the direction of his second-in-command. Boomber was currently standing in one corner with his head bobbing around like a cork on a stormy ocean, desperately trying to look everywhere *apart* from at the semi-clad underwear-modelling women who were depicted in the paintings dotting the walls. "He does not wish his wife to know, you understand. To avoid being, ah, observed in the act, he has asked me to *do the necessary* for him. Keep it quiet, eh?"

As the assistant took in this new information, her mischievous smile turned into a look of curiosity. She appraised the wart-faced policeman and frowned. "Wot – *him*? A wife *and* a mistress?" She shook her head in disbelief. "Are they both blind?"

Yavlo smiled. "Makes you wonder, does it not?"

The shop assistant licked her lips and ran her eyes up and down the plump, unattractive man. Her gaze lingered about midway. Yavlo shook his head slightly, despairing at human nature. "I suppose you are used to such goings on," he continued casually. "I mean, I imagine you get a lot of gentlemen popping in to acquire some stylish garment or other for an illicit girlfriend?"

"Oh … yeah. Happens all the time." The girl's attention was still fixed on the Sergeant, her mind contemplating anatomical possibilities. "Mostly they want lingerie like the stuff your friend is trying *not* to look at." Yavlo followed the girl's nod. As his eyes caught sight of the picture of an *under-clad* female, he felt a sudden flush rise to his cheeks.

"Yes, well, in spite of appearances, I believe the Sergeant was thinking more along the lines of something that might be worn in public. Have you anything, oh, I don't know, something a little … *exotic?*"

The girl pouted out her bottom lip and began to chew on it thoughtfully. "Weeeell, exotic is *out* this season. Definitely passé. Now, wot you really want is something a bit like this …" The girl reached out to a nearby clothes rack and plucked out a thin, pastel-blue top. "Y'see? Definitely demure. Stylish and also functional, yeah? You could wear this all the time, for any occasion: to the shops, to the theatre … wherever."

"Hmm, yes, I see. But is it not rather, well, *staid?* Even middle-aged? I am not sure the Sergeant's present *amour* is quite ready for such a *mature* style."

The girl looked at the Inspector sharply. "She's *young?*"

"Indeed. And she is also quite, ah, *shapely.*"

"*Go on!*" She turned to look at Boomber once more, confusion in her eyes.

"Yes – quite so. Anyway, I believe the young lady rather likes to party. Indeed, I think I heard tell of a party to which the good Sergeant wishes to escort her. Uh, I believe it to be a fancy dress party."

At this, the girl laughed. She turned an amused eye on the silver-haired Inspector. "Right. Fancy dress? You had me going for a minute there. I should of known, yeah?" She laughed again.

Yavlo frowned. "I am sorry, young lady, I don't know what you are implying."

The girl wagged a finger at the Inspector. "Who's a naughty boy then? Fancy dress? Hah! That's wot they *all* say. You'd be amazed how often we get your sort in. Every couple of weeks in fact. Well, wot you gets up to in your own spare time is no concern of mine …"

"One moment, miss … Did you say every couple of weeks? Was there such an *incident* about, oh, three weeks ago?"

"Might of been."

"Madam ... that gentleman ... who was he? What did he buy?"

The girl nudged Yavlo in the ribs. "An old friend? Don't want to clash with him, eh?"

"No ... please ... madam ... if you will!"

"Can't tell, can I? Rules of the profession init! Our clients are very secretive about their fashions."

At this point Boomber ambled over, his lingerie lust at temporary saturation point. "What's this, guv? Difficult witness? Reckon I should loosen her tongue? I find a bash on the head with a stout truncheon tends to jolt the memory."

The girl recoiled from the horrific visage of her new assailant. "He wouldn't ... would he?"

Yavlo sighed. "Alas, I am afraid that in his present state – roused by all of these lewd images that you have displayed around your shop – the Sergeant could get up to almost anything."

The girl raised her hands. "Okay okay! I was only teasing anyway. Wot's it to me wot you lot get up to? The last fancy-dresser I had was a tall bloke with black hair and a black beard, and he wore black leather. Typical, eh? Oh, and he had little beady eyes. *And* a scar."

With a sideways frown at his Sergeant, Yavlo asked: "And he bought ...?"

"Uh, he bought six costumes. A job lot we had – from Samark, or somewhere like that. All veils. They were black, too. *Very* unfashionable! Yeah, and they was different sizes. Let me think ..." The girl thought. "Ah, that's right. One was medium, two were large, two were extra large, and one was extra extra large. And that's all I can remember. Honest!"

"This gentleman ... he did not say where this fancy dress party was, did he?"

The girl laughed. "I think you're probably a bit late for it now! Anyway, he didn't. He was a bit sheepish. But you lot usually are, aren't you?" The girl folded her arms. "Right, much as I've loved chatting to you, it's about time I closed up. So, *if* you don't mind ..."

"Very well, young lady," said the Inspector. "You have been most helpful. Thank you." Yavlo gestured to his companion and the two strode purposefully out of the door. Once outside, Yavlo turned to address his Sergeant

"What a tricky problem, eh, Sergeant? Six costumes ... *six*! The witnesses at The Bear were not clear about numbers, but what we do know is that there are only *five* Angels. Could Manis have been with

234

them? I believe that we have sufficient evidence from witnesses to suggest that he could not. *Blast!* And I was beginning to think that there might have been some substance to that theory of Mr Hops after all."

Boomber shook his head gently, then broke into a relieved smile.

"Anything the matter, Sergeant? No? Very well." Yavlo started off down the street. After a few paces he turned back to face his underling. "By the way, Sergeant Boomber, that was most irregular in there, not to say verging on the unethical. I hope you were not really planning on attacking that poor young lady with your truncheon?"

"Me, guv? Of course not! Policemen *never* hit their suspects." Boomber smiled broadly at the Inspector. "Though we have occasionally been known to help them down the nearest stairs. *Rapidly*. Now, let's be getting back to the station, eh, guv? I'm sure young Hendy is being useful and has got the kettle on."

Yavlo sighed. He followed his Sergeant down the road.

———————————

"Phew, that was close," gasped Terry, as he relaxed at the back of their improvised raft, weary after his exertions. "Another dramatic escape. I'm pleased to say that this is something of a family trait."

"Maybe think again?" suggested the monk, pointing towards the bank. For there, cresting a nearby levee, was the Nudian mob. "Must have taken shortcut."

"Paddle … *paddle*!" screamed Roffo, catching sight of the angry horde behind them. His gaze swivelled forward and fixed on an advancing rock protruding from the sprightly water. "Boulder … *boulder*!"

Terry whipped out his axe and plunged it into the foaming river, using it as a rudder to steer the inflated Longman's Special around the onrushing rock. Beyond this was a turbulent flight of rapids. Suddenly, a large, slimy, brown, sausage-shaped creature leapt out of the spray and landed on the barbarian's leg. Terry dislodged it with the quick flick of a muscular finger. "Shit!" he exclaimed. "Blood-sucking leeches!"

"There is shoal behind," noted the monk calmly, as he looked over his shoulder at the twin menace of spear-wielding exhibitionists and vampiric Surfing Hirudinea.

The raft plunged obliviously on into the rapids. Roffo was flung about at the front like a rag doll in the mouth of a rabid rottweiler. In contrast, the monk sat impassively in the middle of the inflatable, maintaining an extraordinary and seemingly effortless balance, while Terry retained his upright posture through sheer power alone, gripping the raft between his giant legs. The leeches leapt all around them like hyperactive salmon late for the last spawning of Autumn.

Roffo let out a scream and closed his eyes as the raft flew over a low waterfall … and then came to a halt. They were momentarily caught in a stopper wave, caused by the confused contraflow of river currents. Seeing this, the Nudian lynch mob gave a howl of delight and scrambled up to the high ground above the gorge. A volley of arrows and spears began to rain down upon the rafters.

"*Shiiiiiit!* Terry, do something!"

The barbarian slid his axe onto his lap, freeing his broad hands for action. He reached down and began a mighty one-handed paddling which no river current could resist. They rose up out of the cloying eddy and once again surged forward. Terry plunged his axe haft back into the water and steered them into the fastest flowing part of the rapids and away from the steep bank occupied by their pursuers. They hadn't got much farther, however, before the monk himself let out a concerned shout and pointed down the valley. At its end there rose a rock wall with the dark mouth of a cave at its foot. It was into this cave that the river rushed – and then disappeared! Seeing this, Terry dug his axe into the water in an attempt to slow their progress. Over the ruckus of the river a high-pitched shriek carried to him on the wind: looking up again he caught sight of the early morning sun glinting off the Nudians' weapons as they ran along the opposite cliff top. *Go into the dark unknown and face probable death, or stay and face certain death?* No contest really. He exchanged a quick, knowing look with the monk – who simply nodded – and pulled his axe from the water, releasing the brake.

The terrible roar of the river rushing into the cave mouth and down into the bowels of the earth caused Roffo to open his eyes to see what the *Hull* was going on. He immediately wished he had kept them closed. He shrieked at the sight of the dark abyss before him, and then shrieked even more loudly as a leech leapt over the bow of the raft and attempted to mate with his face. The barman flapped wildly at the blood-sucker, only realising – too late! – that he had let go his grip on the raft. A violent jerk tipped him into the water.

The sudden loss of weight from the front of the raft caused it to rear up obscenely, obscuring the view of the paddling barbarian. Worse still, the suddenly erect Longy provided a new target for the chasing archers and a skilful shot pierced its tip. A hissing sound now became audible over the water's clamour as the tight grip of Terry's thighs forced air along the raft and out of the puncture. The boat began to deflate.

236

As they swept into the black cavern, the two remaining sailors of the Good Ship Longman desperately tried to keep hold of their craft – but without success. They were soon cast into the cold water to join the bobbing Roffo, tumbling along into the dark unknown.

"*Whoosh,*" chortled Cucumber Joe, demonstrating the demise of Terry Testosterone and friends with a plunging sweep of his hands, "and down The Pan they went." Being the only member of the Wrestling Assassins to escape from the Longman Thieves with his consciousness intact, he had joined the pursuit of the previous day and had therefore been the only one of his party to have seen the dénouement of the chase at first hand. Justin had demanded a recounting of the events half a dozen times already. He was gradually coming to terms with the fact that his position was safe.

"So, we won't be seeing them again?"

"No way, no how, no when. They're gone."

Justin nodded and blew out his cheeks in relief. He turned his attention back to their game. "Bishop Mazed?" he conjectured, pointing over the side of the bridge at the turd that floated past.

"Nah," stated Dick, peering energetically at the excremental raft, "it's one o' seer Tom's. Look ... you can see the remains of Mushrooms of Enlightenment in it." He leant back and grinned proudly. "An' that's game, set and match to me I think."

The turd of disputed parentage disappeared down the small sewage stream known locally as *the log flume* and plopped into the quiet pre-rapid basin recently vacated by the three Longman riders.

"You've never been much good at poo-sticks, have you Justin?" commented Phil More.

Justin shrugged and turned away. The first man to reclaim the title of Big Knob since Shears Manly headed back towards The Buff, now safe in the knowledge that his latest rival had literally disappeared down the toilet with the rest of the town waste.

Terry awoke to the sound of swearing. He lifted his head from the sandy beach and looked towards the monk. The bald-headed one had extracted a handful of soggy map fragments from the Longy and was giving it the full benefit of all the more colourful phrases he had picked up during the course of his quest. He then threw the fragments over his shoulder and dived back in search of another saturated mass.

Terry frowned at the indelicacy of the language – which he was well able to translate, given that it was considered impolite in barbarian society to tell someone to *fuck off* in any language but their own. Thus, Terry had picked up a fair lexicon of obscene words over his life. He recognised, for example, that the monk was using rather a lot of *Effin*, which was understandable, given that this was a language in which two thirds of all words were in some way indecent. Indeed, Terry himself had been forced to learn *Rudiementary Effin* in primary school and he could still remember some of the rules. *All sentences*, he recalled his teacher saying, *must have a Subject, an Objectionable, and a Verbal.* A verbal was an insulting verb, of which the Effins had absolutely *loads*, such as *to gribble* (to flatulently exude until you were killed by your own bowels), *to refiggle* (to search out a herbivorous creature and to perform oral sex upon it), and *to yukbukle* (to be sick in a saucepan and then to pass it off at a family get-together as bouillabaisse). Personally, Terry had found the subject distasteful and had dropped it at the first opportunity.

A heavy throbbing in the barbarian's head provided a welcome distraction from the litany of – as the Effins would say – *lopooloops* (words so nasty they made hardened scum weep like infants). When he ran his fingers through his mane to find the source of this discomfort a large lump presented itself for inspection. His father had always maintained that the proper way to deal with such protuberances was to knock them back into the skull with a war hammer. Terry, however, preferred the less radical approach of the civilised races, which was to allow such swellings to subside naturally. The barbarian's musings on the relative merits of the two forms of health care was interrupted by an extra-loud cry of excitement …

"Ubundi!" shouted the monk.

Terry's frown deepened. "I don't know that one. Is that a word in *Blyndin*?" He sat up on the beach and looked out at the underground lake in front of him. The river they had been washed down flowed into it nearby. Over the course of centuries this river had deposited the beach on which the party had been washed up. Something about the appearance of the subterranean panorama bothered him.

"No no. Ubundi is capital of Wulu nation, founded by King Sucka and Wulu wimpies. Fearsome warriors. Strange place. Strange beliefs."

"So?"

"Map fragment here has same design as first. Must be from same map. Shows next X at Ubundi." The monk thrust the bit of parchment under Terry's nose and pointed to a small squiggle in its corner. "Red Nose of Boozer!" The monk noticed Terry's enthusiasm was somewhat muted in comparison to his own. He saw the direction of the barbarian's gaze. "Ah ... thing that bother you about underground lake is that *see* it, la? One hundred feet underground, and yet there is eerie, sorrowful light ..."

Terry eyes widened. "That's it!"

"The answer to dilemma is fluorescent algae: on walls, on roof, on clothes ..." He lifted his arm to reveal a glowing sleeve. "Bugger to wash out."

"So where is this Ubundi then?" Terry was momentarily relieved that his gnawing worry had been defanged ... but then another, more pressing anxiety took a chunk out of his nether regions. "Wait a minute! Why am I even asking such a question? First off, where are we, and how do we get out of wherever *here* is?"

"According to map, Ubundi on other side of mountain chain now under. Need to cross lake and find exit on other side. People must do it before. Look." Terry's eyes followed the monk's outstretched arm, which pointed to a very old wooden walkway – supported on piles – that led back up the river's course. Here and there bits of it were missing, suggesting that it had once been used as a conduit between the outside world and the underground lake, but that it had been neglected or forgotten.

"Walkway completely washed away further back up river. Roffo went to see." The monk pointed to a freshly collapsed section. "You did that with head!"

Terry ran his hand over his lump. Such a small swelling for so much damage! The sparkle of his axe, resting beside him, caught his attention. How had he managed to keep hold of it during his trip down the river?

"Couldn't remove from hand, even when pulling you unconscious from water," commented the monk, sensing the unasked question. "Strange thing that: hand not even clasped around handle ..." He frowned. Changing the subject, he pointed towards another rickety structure across which Roffo was even now carefully stepping. "Over there, pier where load and launch boat." The barman was making his way towards a small, brass bell that dangled from a gibbet-like structure at the end of the pier. "Don't touch bell!" bellowed the monk, just in time to stop Roffo's inquisitive hand. "Do not touch bells in strange, dark places. Never know what might summon!"

"Of course I wasn't going to ring the bell," shouted back Roffo. "Gramps told me all about such things. He said they generally beckon mermaids who come to take you away to a life of sexual servitude. Er… can't I give it just a little tinkle?"

"Sexual servitude – pah!" muttered the monk, stuffing the piece of map into his leather burglar-habit and shaking his head. "Never seen picture of mermaid with genitals yet!" He stood up, grabbed hold of the deflated Longy, and headed towards the jetty. "Leave bell alone!"

"Okay okay … I was just admiring its craftsmanship, that's all." The barman affected a hurt tone and leant against the jetty's handrail, scowling at the monk. The rail – which had supported no pressures more strenuous than those of wood-eating insects for the last three hundred years – promptly gave up the ghost: it broke, tipping the young adventurer into the black waters. Roffo surfaced just in time to watch the gibbet perform a perfect pirouette before crashing against the pier's floorboards. An almighty *clang* filled the cavern. Roffo looked back towards the bank at his two travelling companions – who stared in horror at the bell and then, in unison, turned their eyes towards him. Under the intense weight of their gaze the junior barman slowly sank back into the lake. When he resurfaced, however, it was to find that nothing had changed. No fire-breathing monster from Hull had trans-located into the chamber; the waters *had not* risen up to consume them; and *no* bevy of gorgeous sea-nymphs had appeared to drag them into sexual slavery. Disappointedly, Roffo swam for the shore.

"Look – nothing!" he said, pointing across the lifeless water. "No monsters. No horrors." He crawled onto the beach and stood up. "Nothing at all to get frightened about. It was just an old bell. An old watch bell or something. Maybe a—"

"Shush!" interrupted the monk, raising a finger to Roffo's lips.

"Yes," confirmed the barbarian, "I heard it too."

Roffo strained to hear something over the deafening sound of silence. He was about to accuse his friends of trying to pull a fast one when he heard a gentle splashing.

"Water dripping from the ceiling?" he suggested. "You can tell by how rhythmic it is. Listen: a nice steady *splash splash splash*."

"Why getting louder then?"

"Um … maybe it's raining above?"

"There!" hissed Terry, pointing out across the lake with his axe.

At first Roffo could see nothing, but as his eyes grew accustomed to the gloom in the centre of the lake he started to detect the outlines of a shape. He yelped when his mind resolved the image: "Bloody Hull!" he cried. "It's a three-headed hound of the *Guard-to-the-Underworld* persuasion! We're doomed!"

"Humph!" scowled the monk. "Why guard entrance to underworld? Who so desperate to get there they break in? And what big dog doing in middle of lake? Surely will sink?"

"It's the carved prow of a boat," stated Terry flatly, benefiting from his superior eyesight. "There are four rowers to each side and a steersman at the back. Nine men in all. That's three each if it comes to a fight."

"Three each!"

The boat slowly approached the quay, the oars rising and falling, water droplets sparkling on the edges of the blades and where the oars cut the lake. The frightening aspect of the carved prow came into clearer definition, showing three snarling, fang-bearing heads – heads that were so poorly carved that … Roffo sniggered. "Is that … is that a *poodle* to the left? And that centre head, that's the strangest looking dog I've ever seen. I swear it's cross-eyed."

Terry managed to hold back a laugh. "And that one on the right … it looks like a big *sheep*!"

"Ha! You're right! The Triple-Headed Sheep-Poodle of Hull."

"Shhhhh! Be quiet or else get into trouble!"

The boat pulled up to the jetty, the oarsmen raising their paddles to let them coast the final distance. From the back of the boat the steersman beckoned to the adventurers with a bony finger.

"I'm not going anywhere on *that* thing," stated Roffo, defiantly. "In the first place, I wouldn't be seen dead – ah, if you'll pardon the expression – on something so dumb. And in the second, I was always told never to accept lifts from strangers, and they come no stranger than *that* lot!" The nine men were all, somewhat predictably, dressed in black robes. Their hoods were – naturally – drawn up over their heads, obscuring their faces.

"Stay here then," replied the monk. "Saw small, white, blind crabs on rocks. Should keep fed until die of old age."

The monk set off along the beach and clambered onto the walkway that led to the pier. Terry followed him closely, gripping his axe tightly. Roffo quickly weighed up his options, concluding that the prospect of being left alone in a gloomy cave was far worse than being caught riding on a really stupid boat with a figurehead that looked like it had been carved in a school woodwork class. He trotted after the others. Once on the walkway his view of the boat was impeded by the broad back of the barbarian. At the end of the pier he squeezed a space between his two companions to get a better look at proceedings. What he saw was the black-robed steersman with one hand on the tiller and the other thrust out, palm up, in a *give-me-money* attitude. The hand was a pale colour, white as bone. In fact ...

Roffo grabbed at the back of Terry's leather loincloth and gave it a good tug. "It's Sharon!" he exclaimed, in a loud whisper. "It's Sharon!"

Terry slapped his hand away, fearful that his friend's desperate tugging might remove a garment that had already suffered shrinkage after its recent soaking. "Let go," he gasped, before relieving some of the pressure with a quick adjustment of his dress.

The monk snorted and turned to look at Roffo. He whispered out of the corner of his mouth: "Not bone. Hand painted white. Ridiculous charade!" He turned back to consider the outstretched hand. He nodded to himself and delved into the folds of his black, erotic-burglar leatherwear habit, producing a small, tatty purse. After a moment's thought he placed three tiny bronze coins into the hand, declaring loudly to all in earshot: "It not matter how much pay ferryman, just that pay him." Without waiting for an invite he clambered aboard the craft and gestured for the other two to follow. The steersman slowly lowered his cowled head to examine the coins in his hand. His eyes – for indeed his sockets did hold eyes – widened.

"*Tight git!*" he growled, in a savage bass voice. "For that type of money you can row your bloody selves!"

" ...and they say there's *another* group of strangers in town," whispered the old man conspiratorially, "who are *also* thieves of religious artefacts." He hiccoughed, took another pull of his beer, and wiped away his foam moustache. He hunched further forwards. "And I don't mind telling you, I wouldn't fancy being in their feet when they're brought before the Inquisition, no siree! You lads haven't seen any strangers about have you?"

"Nah," replied Trespass, "and we've been looking all morning – haven't we lads? But I have heard a rumour that they're four-foot-tall women with shaven faces." Trespass thought about this for a moment before adding: "I mean, er, they're *not* hairy old baggages ..."

"Really?" The wrinkled pensioner frowned. "Well, I've heard they're big fat bastards with beards."

"There's no-one like that around here," blurted Frunge. He looked around nervously, spotted his brother, and pushed him forward for

242

inspection. "See. Short runts with smooth faces."

"Shut up!" hissed Trespass. More loudly he asked: "What happened to the other thieves? Are they dead?"

"*Maybe, maybe not.*"

"What do you mean maybe, maybe not? Either you're dead or you're not. You can't be in both states at once."

"Well, they shot the rapids and disappeared down The Pan, so…"

"The Pan?"

"Yeah. You know. The large cave at the foot of the rapids …" The old man looked at his new acquaintances with sudden suspicion. "You sure you're local? I thought you wuz Grizzly Tina's boy, but come to think of it you're a bit big for the lad. I'm not sure I recognise you now. And I thought Old Digger knew everyone from hereabouts …"

"Uh, no, you're right," stuttered Trespass. "Ma Tina is my, er, Ma. It's just that I've, er, *grown.*"

"Yeah," interjected Burble quickly, "and we're his cousins from out of town. Only got in this morning."

"New to The Buff, eh? Well, welcome to the big city, lad. Now, where was I? Oh yes. Well, you see, they may have survived the journey but we'll never know *unless* …" Digger ground to a halt and gave Trespass the sort of look that said he should be able to fill in the blanks by himself.

Trespass smiled stupidly – partly in nervousness, partly in embarrassment, partly in ignorance, and partly to hide his growing exasperation with the old man. What he *really*, really wanted to do, at this moment, was to thump him.

"Unless what?" asked Burble, patiently.

"Unless you go and observe what state they're in!" The old man's eyes lit up with enthusiasm. "There's a wise old philosopher-barber called Occum – lives over in Cross-My-Way – who has an interesting perspective on such matters. Now, he would say that at present – for us – these thieves are both dead *and* alive because we don't know which they are. We need to actually go and observe them to find out. And in doing this we will *effectively kill* them or *save* them!"

"Och," muttered Bruce, shaking his head, "tae much sun. It's obviously affected his brain."

"No no," said Burble, puffing out his chest, "I understand him. To find out if they're dead we have to go and see the bodies."

"Well that's obvious," scoffed Trespass. "Any idiot could have worked that out."

243

"Humph! Well, you couldn't! Anyway, I'm not going down any dark, smelly cave looking for corpses. That's a job for a speleologist with necrophiliac tendencies, and *not* for *The Shadow*!"

"You don't have to join them down The Pan," sniggered Digger. "You just have to cross the mountains and wait for their bloated bodies to float out the other side where the river re-emerges. I'd estimate it'll take a week or two for them to reappear." Now the oldster eyed up Burble. There was definitely something amiss here. For a start, he now recalled that Tina's lad had only got one arm. "So, you're called *The Shadow*, eh? That's a rather suspicious sobriquet for a …"

CRUNCH

"Did you see that?" stammered Trespass. "The way he tried to hit my fist with his head? What a nutter!"

Burble bent down to examine the prone figure. "He's out cold. Right. Testicles is gone and things are getting hairy around here. I'm for home. Who's with me?"

"Yeah, bruv," said Frunge. "Good call. I'm with you."

"Hold on!" said Trespass, making a grab for the departing Frunge. Realising that there was only one thing he could possibly grasp hold of, he dropped his hand. "We've got to go and look for those bodies. We *have* to be sure."

"You actually want us to go over those bluddy mountains just to look at some rotten corpses?" Grunt growled. "Why don't we just go 'ome and tell Manis they're fish food?"

"No. I don't trust that damned barbarian to be dead. It'd be just like him to turn up and spite us." Trespass's tone turned conciliatory. "Look, it won't be a problem. Just two or three days max. Those mountains aren't so tough: my yak drops bigger lumps each morning. Eh? Come on. Let's go and reclaim our clothes and get out of this madhouse."

"Humph," went the monk.

"Stop harumphing," demanded Roffo. "I wasn't going to row myself to the next the world. So? It cost a bit more. Why don't you just lay back and enjoy the ride?"

"Now have nothing. No money, no gold, no silver, no thing! Maybe have to sell *you* to raise some cash, hey?"

"Oh yeah?" retorted Roffo. "Then who'd dig your latrine or cook

244

your grub?"

"Need no-one. Go *natural*."

"Ha! That'd be the—"

"Stop bickering you two," sighed Terry in exasperation. "Why don't you admire the scenery instead? Look at these columns. When they fall there's going to be an almighty splash."

Roffo and the monk stopped glaring at each other and turned their attention to the thick grey pillars that sprouted randomly from the lake. These shot upwards to the cavern's ceiling like a collection of mine props supporting the peaks above.

"Yes, very interesting scenery," muttered Roffo, without enthusiasm. "Who'd have thought the underworld would have such majestic features? I bet most people who see this place are *dead* impressed. Which brings me to my next concern. Won't our hosts be just a *little* bit miffed when they find out that we're not up to much in the *being-dead* department, and don't you think they might try to rectify this situation?"

"Foolish youth – still not understand! This obviously *not* mythical river of underworld. Only *simple* people believe such illogical flights of fantasy. No. Obviously being ferried by taxi company run by mad buggers with overactive imaginations. Maybe drop us off where river emerges from mountains."

"Er, yeah," posited Terry thoughtfully, "or *maybe* they're going to drop us off at some terrible altar to an evil god, where we'll be sacrificed, and they're rubbing it in by charging us to get there?"

"Bah! Don't start with pessimistic mumbo-jumbo!" The monk gurned despairingly. "Not know where you two get ideas from. Something to do with sheltered upbringing maybe?"

"Or *maybe*," continued Terry, "something to do with the fact that the column we're being rowed towards is carved into a giant statue of a very mean-looking deity?"

The others stared at the colossal figure that loomed out of the semi-darkness. Even though the figure was seated it still reared a good 300 feet above them. Around its feet were further statues of spectral beings that were presumably allied to the deity. Every one of these appeared to be a nasty piece of work, such as an imp, demon or traffic warden.

"Looks can be deceptive," reassured the monk. The slight quiver in his voice suggested, however, that whereas this might be true in some cases, he wasn't at all confident that this was one of them.

Shortly, the boat pulled up to a small stone jetty.

"Er ... very nice," said Roffo, addressing the steersman. "But as we are in a bit of a hurry we wouldn't mind skipping the usual tourist attractions and heading straight for the nearest exit. Thanks."

In response, the steersman simply pointed to a large grey altar slab that rested in front of the stone god.

"Um, no thanks," said Roffo. "My Gramps told me what happens to virgins who go too close to the altars of foreign gods … um …" He ground to an embarrassed halt. But then the spark plug of fabrication kicked in. "Not that anyone here's a virgin, gosh no, what an idea, eh? The very thought! How I pity such people. Ahem. Anyway, I suppose that means we've got nothing to worry about, right?"

"Am virgin," said the monk unashamedly. "Holy orders insist that remain pure and chaste." He turned to address the steersman. "Think God would like soul of wrinkled monk added to seraglio of beautiful young women no doubt sacrificed previously? Humph! Think not!"

The steersman ignored the question, again pointing to the slab. Seeing that he had a reluctant party he petulantly thrust his hands into the voluminous sleeves of his robe. Roffo and the monk looked at Terry expectantly. One quick blow would surely sort the fellow out. Terry eyed up the steersman before taking a quick glance at the rowers. Only nine in total. *No prob* … When he returned his gaze to the stern of the boat he found that the steersman had removed his hands from his sleeves. Each hand had somehow acquired a small crossbow. The steersman waved one of these weapons towards the altar to indicate that, yes, they should definitely disembark *now*, and they should do so without further hesitation. *Thank you very much, hope you enjoyed your trip, but don't really expect you'll be travelling with us again, etcetera, etcetera.*

"Okay, okay, we were just going," insisted Roffo, quickly jumping ashore. The others followed more slowly. As the last disembarked, the steersman growled a command and the oarsmen dipped their paddles back into the water.

———————

"Right then, next question. Who butchered Barabus the Bad at the Battle of Brundle's Bottom?" Occum peered around the smoke-filled lounge of The Bear at the dozen or so clusters of hunched, intent quizsters. The round on *who killed who* had really got them thinking. The content of the odd fiercely raised whisper could be resolved above the low murmuring.

"It is, *it is* … write it down!"

"No way, dickweed – that was Bosworth's Bonkhall, not Brundle's

Bottom …"

"Whoa – good one mate … that's it, that's *definitely* it …"

"Smith, you quizmeister you! Come here and let me give you a …"

"I *know* this one, I know this …"

"You're a useless pillock, you really are …"

"Ah, yeah, *that's* definitely it …"

Occasionally, something about the tone or content of a comment allowed Occum to identify its source.

"It bollocking was, it *bloody well bollocking* was." Yep, nodded Occum, that was Rude Lubblers.

"Naaaahahahaha, go on! 'Ee said *butchered* you silly moo." Occum smirked: that was clearly one of *Tarts 'R' Us*.

Nearby, Hops leant against the bar, smiling broadly. Quiz night was proving a roaring success. It was the first time The Bear had been packed out since the night of The Incident; Jepho was being made to work for his money for a change, and the barmaids were being rushed off their feet. The new ale, imported from Yankia, was really rather appalling, but the quiz itself seemed to have taken the clientele's mind off it, and he'd barely had a dozen complaints all night. Still, Hops mused, it would be some time before he would have his own brew back on tap.

Occum called over to one of the barmaids. "Oi – Maddy! Thirsty work this! Another tankard of Budwasters if you please. Ta lass." He fiddled with his parchments. "Right, and now for the last question in this round. An easy one. Who killed Kenny Dee?"

"I bet it was Manis, the bastard," roared one wag.

"Aye," yelled Rusty the Ironmonger, "and I reckon I sold him the weapon he dun it with!"

At a table near the bar, one neatly attired gentleman rose rapidly to his feet with a screeching of his chair. "Sir, this is a most serious matter! If you have any evidence for your accusation I would quite like to …"

"Guv, please, sit down! They're only joking …"

"Please guv …"

A barrage of tankards, many of which were *not* empty, converged on the silver-haired man. The members of The Cunning Constabulary dived for cover under their table.

"Oi you hooligans," yelled Long Jon Con Dom, lifting a bucket of water menacingly, "calm down!"

Occum scowled at the troubleshooter, then turned his gaze back to the lounge. "Right. Swap your parchments and I'll give the answers to the *weapons* round. All swapped? Well hurry up then. *Good* …" Occum accepted his free ale from Maddy with sour-faced gratitude. He sniffed the pint, wrinkled his face, closed his eyes, and took a pull. "Damn and blast Hops, if this is beer then I'm a pigeon! Ptah!" He set the tankard down. "Okay. The answers." Occum perused his answer sheet. "Number one was, of course, *Johnson's Flaming Sword*. Two was *a Nudian's tool*. Three was *steel* … oh yes it was, don't argue, the quizmaster is always right, especially if it's *me*! Um, where was I? Right, four was *a short-handled axe and two small green frogs*, five was *a banana*, six was *a piccolo*, sev—"

"A piccolo!?" piped up an astonished voice from the back. "Mad Peter the Brown went into battle armed only with a piccolo? You sure? I thought it was a penny-whistle."

"Of course I'm sure! Now shut up! Number seven …" Occum spat out the last two words while glaring at his tormentor. There was an implicit threat in that glare. It spoke of a haircut gone wrong and ears that would need to be taken home in a brown paper bag. No more complaints of inaccuracy followed. "The answer to number seven is *a siege catapult*, to number eight *Tiddles*, and to number nine *250lbs*." Occum stared at his audience. No-one dared ask for ten each way. *Good*. He had them back under control, quaking at the sound of his voice. "And finally, the answer to number ten is *the Black Mountains* … they fell on his head, all right? Bring up your answers for checking and I'll give you the scores of the leading teams."

There was a brief period of frantic writing followed by a general kerfuffle. Various team representatives scurried to the top table to hand crumpled pieces of parchment to Phlip, the quizmaster's assistant. Phlip – who had been stained the colour of mahogany by his ordeal on the night of The Incident – immediately set to work transferring the marks onto his score sheet. After five or six minutes he handed an update of the scores to Occum.

"Right, listen up you rabble. The leading scores after the *weapons* round are: in third place, with 28, we have *The Four Horsemen*. In second, with 31, is *A Piece of Cake*. And the leading team, with 33 points, is *Noble Intentions* …"

"*Fucking Ace!*" shouted Rude Lubblers, as he jumped up and slapped his team-mate, Alfred, on the back. "I told you *Tiddles* was the name of *fucking* Cannibal's *bollocking* war elephant. Now what do you *buggers* want to *sodding* drink?"

Occum shook his head slightly. The things that man knew! There was no justice in the world. "Okay, next round, *films*." This would get them. "Question one. What thin film gives water an iridescent, rainbow-like appearance …?"

<hr/>

"Big bugger, isn't he?" noted Roffo rather nervously, as he stared up at the giant statue. From this close to its base, the upper portion was lost somewhere in the gloom of the cavern ceiling.

"How you know he a he?" enquired the monk. "Might be female."

"*No* … no. From what I can see he is most definitely male. Look … up there …"

"You mean at overhanging rock 100 feet up?"

"Er, yeah, except that the thing jutting out is …"

"*So*," boomed a deep voice from above, "what have we got here then? Dinner? I've not eaten anything except fish in ages."

There was a loud cracking noise followed by a small avalanche of stones. From out of the gloom a great, bearded stone face descended like a slow-motion meteorite and peered at the startled trio. Giant eyelids nictated with great deliberation. A huge toothy smile opened up in the rocky face like a chasm. "Not much meat on you two," it rumbled, "but *this* one's prime beef!"

The monk was the first to recover his composure. "Oh majestic one," he bowed respectfully, "surely mere mortals like us make unworthy meal?"

"Yes, mere morsels such as *you* do." As the Rockgod spoke, all sorts of debris cascaded from his mouth: splinters of stone, bits of wood, fishy debris. The monk stepped aside nimbly as the head of a giant fish dropped onto the stone floor, disintegrating with a disgusting *splat*. "*You* look a bit tough and scraggy. However, your companion looks like he's been raised on a healthy diet and plenty of exercise. He should make a *fine* snack."

"You can't eat us!" squeaked the petrified Roffo. "For a start, you've not said *fee fie foe fum* or anything! My Gramps said that giants and stuff *have* to say that before they eat you."

"Well, I'm not much of a one for tradition." The god turned his ponderous attention on the cowering barman. "Hmm. *You* should make a good toothpick. I've got a piece of armour stuck under my molar. Been there for *ages*, it has, and it's beginning to piss me off."

With a slow, creaking motion the god lifted his hand and leant towards Roffo. The barman was instantly mesmerised by the granite stare: a blank expression settled onto his face and his arms dropped limply to his sides. Before the hill-sized hand could reach the level of the giant's knee, however, the monk stepped over to Roffo and pushed him aside, breaking the spell. "Do not look," he hissed. "Rockgod too slow to catch prey, so must use hypnosis …"

"Defy me, would you, mortal? I'll crush your bones, I'll… I'll … *what's that you've got there?*" An immense digit pointed at the *map bag* that was slung over the monk's shoulder, trailing on the ground behind him.

"This? Ah, it just sack of maps."

"*Bollocks!*" boomed the god, in a sudden outburst that shook the very mountains, throwing both Roffo and the monk to the ground. Terry swayed on his mighty thighs, but could not be felled. "It's my *thingy*. You know. *For the weekend.*"

The monk got to his feet, but as he did so he made the mistake of looking up … and was caught by the weight of a gaze that could crush the resistance of even the mightiest. His arms dropped to his side. In a monotone he exclaimed, "What is that?"

"It's *my* bloody *thing-you-put-on-todger-before-bang-bang*! What do they call them nowadays? Longys. It's *my* Longy. Those bloody thieving priests from above nicked it hundreds of years ago. Gits! The missus hasn't let me near her since. Says we can't afford to raise little devils on the income generated from one small underground lake, and that without me thingy the best form of contraception is abstinence."

"Ah, see problem …"

"And now you've brought it back to me. How kind. As a reward I think I'll eat your livers with some fava beans and a nice Chianti and then – hubba-hubba-hubba! Her columns are going to shake tonight!"

Suddenly, Terry leapt forward and grabbed the flaccid contraceptive device from the monk's shoulder, flinging it to the ground. Turning his back on the statue, he held his axe above the sheath. "One more move and the Longy gets it! And that means no more hubba-hubba-hubba for you. Ever!"

The god stared hard at the back of the Terry's head, but his mesmeric powers were not strong enough to penetrate the barbarian's thick mane. The god scowled. As he leant back to consider his position, he let go of his grip on the monk's mind.

"Food or sex?" mused the stone deity. "One of life's great conundrums. I haven't had a decent meal for decades, but I haven't had *it* for *centuries*. Looks like mister wiggley wins on time penalties." He looked down again. "Okay. I'll swap. Your lives for the wotsit."

"Deal!" shouted Terry.

"Right. Hand it over then." A mischievous smile played slowly across the Rockgod's face, so slowly that a blind man could not have missed it. Subtlety was not this god's forte.

"Wait," cried the monk, grabbing Terry's hand as it reached for the prophylactic. The monk shook his head to dispel the remaining fog. "How know keep word? Gods renowned as deceivers!"

"How dare you! I should zap you with a bolt of lightning and have you barbecued. I should—"

"*Ooooh,*" moaned Terry, in mock weariness, "my arm is really beginning to tire."

"Ahem, of course I'm trustworthy. What type of deity do you take me for?"

"One who eats people," responded the monk. "This what do. First, call back acolytes on boat. Then order them to row us to far side of lake and nearest exit. There, give Longman to rowers when safe. Deal?"

"I'm extremely upset that you don't trust me. I'll have to think about your proposition." A small fall of rocks caused by a mysteriously growing rocky overhang indicated that it was not his brain that was doing the thinking. "Right," said the Rockgod, as his face began to turn from granite to jasper, "you're on. Now get out of here before I explode with, er, *anger.*"

The monk bowed reverently, then turned towards the Longy. He magically produced a sharpened chopstick from within his kinky leather habit and drew the sack over his arm so that the sharpened point rested against the rubber. He then walked down the path to the jetty, which was even now being approached by the boat – as though telepathically called. Terry grabbed Roffo by the arm and set off after him.

"Explode!" quipped a much-relieved Roffo, as he climbed into the boat. "I half-expected a fountain of lava to erupt at any moment. Now I understand where it all comes from!"

Terry went to stand beside the steersman. He'd not get a chance to draw his crossbows on them a second time.

———◆•••◆———

"*My yak's crapped bigger mounds* 'e says," whinged a sweating Grunt. He tried to pull his yak up the steep slope while his mount – in turn – tried to pull him back down. "Come on you bugger, you're supposed to be a mountain animal!"

"Stop moaning, you fat bastard and get your arse up here!" yelled Trespass from above. "By the time we get there the locals will probably have eaten what's left of them."

"Just as long as they don't try and eat *us*," commented Burble, joining him on the ridge and staring back down the scarp at the struggling Angel. "You hear very strange stories about the people who live on the other side of these mountains. Apparently they're called the *Weahthefinls*, and they're grumpy bastards."

"Aye, well, I would be tae," noted Bruce, as he leant against a rock rolling a fag, "if yon Nudians were permanently peein' intae *ma* water supply." He licked the cigarette paper and pushed the few escaping wisps of tobacco back into the fag end with his match. "Tae much Rear Thruster," he suggested, as he pointed back down the incline with his needle-like creation.

"Yeah, and that's just the yak," observed Burble. "At this rate it'll take four months to cross these mountains rather than four days."

Grunt's head finally crested the rise. Wheezing, he extended a hand to Burble. "Phew! Give us an 'and up then."

"Ha, you fat bastard – look at the state of you! You're sweating like a Gibrellian's armpit and puffing like an ex-asbestos miner." Burble grabbed the fat Angel's outstretched hand and instantly wished he hadn't. Grunt gave one huge tug and sent him flying head first over the lip of the incline.

"Sucker!" shouted Grunt after the disappearing form of Burble, who was now tobogganing down the slope on the front of his riding leathers. "That'll teach you to call *me* a fat bastard! See 'ow you like climbing up *that* slope again, *hur hur*. Let's see you swea—"

His harangue was cut short abruptly by an irate Frunge, who leapt on his back. "That's my bruv you're pushing around, you sod!"

Even though Grunt was the biggest and strongest of the pack, the unexpected addition of Frunge's not-inconsiderable weight around his neck caused him to stagger slightly. He lost his footing on the edge of the slope and, like an old oak tree in a storm, he slowly toppled backwards. He, too, started sliding down the slope, this time with Frunge sitting atop him like a fat East German woman riding a luge. Bruce watched them shoot down the slope, wincing as Grunt was brought to a sudden halt by the intervention of a large and inconsiderate boulder. Frunge was pitched over the rock and into a small bog, where his legs could be seen windmilling in the air. A little further downslope, Burble came to a rest in a thistle patch.

"My brother's got kids that behave better than you lot," shouted Trespass. Shaking his head, he grabbed Bruce by the arm. "Let's get going. They'll have to catch us up."

"But Grunt had all the food …"

Trespass smirked. "Yeah, but guess who's got all the drink? Come on …"

Roffo waved respectfully at the retreating boat with two of his fingers. "Do you think we should've told him there's a hole in it?" He turned around to find that the others had already left the cave mouth. They were standing by the river outside, examining the grassland before them.

"Out there is veldt and land of Wulus," explained the monk. "Probably take three or four days to get to Ubundi, providing have no trouble with tribes that live en route."

"This grass must be a good five feet tall," noted Terry. "You'd better let me lead. I'm going to be the only one with a decent view of where we're going."

Suddenly, ten yards in front of them, a small black figure appeared as though from nowhere, his head just clearing the tops of the grass stalks. "*Weahthefinl's* the river?"

His cry was answered by a similarly leaping figure twenty yards away. "Sodthat!" The second man disappeared, then reappeared. "*Weahthefinl's* the village?"

The first figure now spotted the three travellers. He quickly reappeared in the air, flapping his arms in a desperate effort to stay aloft. "Intruders!" He pointed, then disappeared below the grass. When he bounded up again he cried, even more frantically, "And *weahthefinl's* the army?"

Number two bounded up. "Lost!"

A third voice carried to the party, this one from about forty yards away on the opposite side of number one. "I'mhere I'mhere …" He disappeared.

"*Whothefinl* are you?" cried number one.

"Ah, yes," observed the monk, "Know these people. They the *Weahthefinls*. Humph! Thought only story. They race of pygmies. Ridiculous choice of home."

"Yeah, that's as may be," said Roffo, "but what I *really*, really want to know is this: do they have any decent tailors? I'm sick of wearing this Nudie nightmare."

"Having tailors not problem. *Finding* them is."

A wail carried to the adventurers on the wind. "Army-lost … whaddymean lost … whoto?"

"Notlost … LOST."

"It must take them a hulluva long time to hold a conversation," mused Roffo. His comment was punctuated by an almighty splash a few feet down river, followed by the forlorn cry of: "*Weahthefinl's* the life rafts?"

"Come on," said Terry, gesturing urgently. "I know this is against my barbarian principles, but let's rescue them."

Roffo tutted. "Your dad would throw a fit if he heard you say that. But good idea. Maybe they'll reward us with some new clothes. Or something to eat and drink."

"Yes, so long as water not come from river," said the monk. "Some habits of Nudians *quite* disgusting …"

<hr />

"Och, that wiz a bugger o' an earthquake!" said Bruce. "It's a good job it only went on f'r a couple o' minutes. I thought it wiz gaein' tae shake the beard aff ma face!"

"Strange noise, too," noted Burble. "I thought quakes were meant to sort of *rumble* and *thunder*. I didn't realise they *grunted* and *groaned*."

The Hull's Angels sat astride their yaks on a little knoll overlooking a sea of grass. They were a sorry-looking lot. As a consequence of their various tussles with the raging earth, the thorny mountain plants, the hard slopes, and each other, their clothing had been torn to ribbons and their faces looked like the very worst specimens at the bottom of a bin of supermarket apples. The only reason the men's exposed flesh was not *entirely* covered in bruises was that scratches and scrapes and clods of dirt covered a substantial area of skin – and these refused to share. These men were so filthy they would have made the average tramp goggle in horror and pack up his cardboard box for better climes.

"Right then," said Grunt, "where's this bluddy river? All I can see is grass."

"We'll never find it down there," said Burble. "Whose stupid idea was it to come here?" He scowled at Trespass, who made a point of ignoring him.

Just then, like a frog with a firework up its bum, a small figure leapt up from the deep grass almost directly beside him.

"*Weahthefinl's* the … *aaaaark*!" Trespass's arm shot out instinctively and grabbed the pygmy around the throat.

"Whoa! Look wot Tres has caught," shouted Frunge, excitedly. "A jumping black dwarf! You don't see many of them in Way!"

Trespass stared at his captive with almost as much surprise as the pygmy stared at him.

"Ask him where the river is," said Burble.

"Aye, an' ask him if he's seen any barbarian corpses recently," said Bruce. "Gae on …"

"Er, you heard him!" said Trespass, giving the pygmy a bit of a shake. But the pygmy just gasped and began to turn blue.

"Maybe you should loosen your grip a bit," suggested Burble.

Trespass did so, reeling the pygmy in and setting him on the giant shoulders of his yak. "Okay – speak! Understand? Where is the river, and have you seen any …"

"Barbarians? Oh yes. I've seen a barbarian, but no corpses."

The assembled chapter emitted a loud collective groan.

"You mean Barbarian Terry, don't you?" continued the pygmy. "The Saviour! Yesterday he saved the army from a very large crocodile, and then he made a loincloth out of its skin. He said it wouldn't shrink like his last one because it was made from the hide of an aquatic animal."

"He's alive!" groaned Bruce. "Ye knoo what that means, don't ye?"

"Yeah," muttered Burble, "it means we can't go home yet. Bollocks!"

"Shut up!" shouted Trespass. "Was there a priest and a wimp with him?"

"There was a monk," confirmed the pygmy. "However, there was no wimp … only Roffo, and he was well over three feet tall!"

"Bugger!" groaned Burble. "They're *all* still alive,".

"Right – no more Mr Nice Guy," said Trespass. "Where've they gone now?"

"Ubundi," said the pygmy, eager to get his ordeal over and done with. "Five days walk to the east … er, if you know which way east is. When you're in the grass it all gets a bit, um, *confusing*."

"To Ubundi, then," said Burble, assuming command. "Let's ride!"

"Wait a minute," said Trespass. "What do I do with *him* now?"

"You should always throw the small ones back," suggested Grunt.

Trespass nodded. With a twitch of his arm he cast the pygmy back into the deep grass.

When Big Ed dared open his eyes again, all he could see before him was the wide path cut through the grass by the yaks. And at that sight, a marvellous idea struck him. What if *they* did the same thing? What if he could get his tribe to tread a deliberate path through the grass? It could run from the village to the river. Yeah! And then they could tread other paths to all the other little villages on the plains. No-one need ever get lost again!

With no further ado, Big Ed climbed to his feet and sped off into the grass to tell his village elders. Alas for his race, within five minutes of entering the towering stems Ed was well and truly lost, never to be seen by his tribe again.

CHAPTER 12

WULU DAWN

THE THREE adventurers trudged through the knee-high, sunburnt grass. They walked in a weary silence, like zombies bored with their humdrum non-existence. Overhead, the sun swelled in pride at its own magnificence, casting down heavy beams to force the men into bent-kneed subservience.

Roffo hitched up his lionskin backpack – a gift from the *Weahthefinls* – and altered his step to match the remorseless tread of the barbarian. A bead of sweat dithered on his brow, uncertain of the best route to Chinsville. Along Brow Ridge and over Cheek Hill, or down the Nasal Flyover? It decided on the latter but, on reaching the tip of Roffo's nose, found construction incomplete.

The junior barman, thief, desecrator of sacred items and Longman Rider extraordinaire, crossed his eyes and looked menacingly at the bead. He twitched his nose. He contorted his lips and tried to *blow* up the surface of his face. But nothing would shift the irritating droplet. Another sweaty bead formed on Roffo's back and began to crawl towards the Mountains of the Moon. Roffo groaned. Enough was enough! He pulled up.

"Right," he declared, "that's it! I've had enough!" He dropped his rucksack and vigorously rubbed the bead of sweat from his nose, causing the cloth of his tunic to peel noisily from his odious armpit. "Ugh! I'm drenched all over! I feel like I've spent a month in a Samark sauna!"

The monk – whose brow and otherly parts were as dry as the mouth of a motorist in the presence of a breathalyser – scowled at his young companion. "Must learn control!" he muttered. "Mind greater than body. Mind must master body … show who boss. Only when mind is master can fear, discomfort, and savage urges be resisted!"

Roffo placed his hands on his hips. "So, you're saying you can resist all, er, bodily pressures?"

"That so."

"Mmm – everything? What about the urge to blow after a bowl of baked beans?"

The monk closed his eyes and nodded.

"And what if I put a whole bottle of Dr Feare's patented 'Go Go' Bottom-Drainage Potion in your tea? Could you resist that?"

"With ease."

"But what about …"

"Enough, foolish one! Must not dawdle! Must get out of sun before perish from thirst!"

"Aha!" cried Roffo, in the manner of an excited grandmother calling 'House' in a game of Bingo. "The Great One hasn't learnt how to master thirst!"

The monk gurned in disgust. "Of course have! It *you* who will perish! Pah! Such foolishness!"

Terry – whose skin glistened like a male model in a t.v. advert for, well, just about any product aimed at a female audience – bent down and picked up Roffo's rucksack. "Come on then. I'll give you a hand."

"Thanks, Terry, but … hang on. What's going on over there then?" Roffo's pointing finger drew the attention of the others. A cloud of dust was now apparent on the horizon, roughly in the direction in which they were headed.

"Stampede?" wondered Terry.

"Er – that's bad, isn't it?" mused Roffo. "I suppose we should do something then. Like … run?"

"Where to? We're on a flat plain with only a few small trees for cover and no time to reach that hillock over there."

"Shit! I'm sure it's heading this way."

The monk nodded. "Agreed. When cannot escape storm, best to sit tight and put on waterproofs. Must wait and see what develop." And with that he crossed his legs and sat down.

Within a matter of minutes the cloud began to resolve. Amidst the dust the adventurers were soon able to make out the forms of several dozen dark-skinned warriors. And these were riding the most peculiar of mounts …

Tombo stood up in the stirrups of his War Ostrich and glowered at the savannah before him. In the short time in which he had worn the headring of a Squad Leader of the Imperial Wulu Cavalry he had glowered a lot. He glowered at the thirty warriors who made up his squad. He glowered at Cinder Trees. He glowered at mud huts. He glowered at streams. Warriors – Tombo knew – should have suitable nicknames to mark them above the common man and his name, he intended, would be 'He Who Glowers, With Attitude'.

He could have glowered at the landscape for hours, but then his steed – the mighty Thunder Chicken – snorted in disgust and clawed the ground restlessly, bringing the warrior's attention back to the here-and-now.

Tombo turned to stare at the men sitting silently upon their mounts, attentive to his every order. *Fine men*, he thought. The Feral Hippos Squadron had a mighty history, and Tombo had done well to gain their command. For had it not been the Feral Hippos that had routed the Pompous Gnus at the battle of Itzibitzi Ford? And had it not been the Hippos that had rescued the Royal Sceptre from the treacherous Ubu? *It had!*

Of course, some had cast doubt upon Tombo's right to this position, suggesting that he might never have achieved it had he not been the son of Ozbondo, Witchfinder General and Chief Shaman (a.k.a. *The Terror of Ubundi*). Not that such doubters ever spoke for long – speaking being difficult once his father had removed their tongues and woven them into a ceremonial doormat. Still, Tombo knew that not all doubts could be so quelled – since not all doubts were spoken – and thus he was determined to prove his mettle.

He glowered at his squad for a final time, then turned Thunder Chicken to face the East. With an imperious gesture, he beckoned his men to follow.

The patrol ranged to the eastern fringes of the Chiefdom, down to the Itzibitzi Ford, across to the Mound of Boozoomba, and then on to the Cinder Forest of Palooloo. The morning swept past, the sun rose high, and lunch beckoned. Tombo was about to turn his troop for home when he noticed a flash of reflected sunlight in the distance.

Tombo pulled up his squad with a raised hand and turned to watch. After several minutes he noticed it again. Sunlight on metal? He felt a tingling of excitement in his leopardskin-clad loins. He pulled his white buffalo-hide shield onto his left arm and hefted his war lance in his right hand. He glowered at the sun – turning a magnificent side profile to his men and holding the pose until he was sure that the glower had been registered – and then burbled a war cry and set Thunder Chicken into a gallop. His warriors streamed after him.

It was not until they were within ten yards of their quarry, however, that Tombo realised that there would be little glory for him this day, for there were only three strangers (even though one was huge). It would be a dishonour to wash his lance in the blood of so few! He snarled and, raising his lance overhead, made a circling motion. His squad immediately fanned out to pass around and beyond the intruders, forming a fence from which there could be no escape. Tombo pulled his steed to a halt five feet in front of the three men. His warriors stopped circling and turned to face their foe, their lances down and levelled.

Tombo glowered for a long moment as he sought something suitably momentous to say – something that would enrich the camp-fire tales of the History Sayers – but even this privilege was to be denied to him ...

After a brief, whispered exchange amongst the intruders, the shortest of these brushed aside the worried hands of his comrades and stepped forward to steal Tombo's thunder. "Trust me ... I know how to handle this," he whispered, before turning to face the Squad Leader and raising his voice. "Er, hi there!" he began. "Nice bird you got there ... does he speak? Haha! I had a budgie once, but he wouldn't speak to me at all. The little bugger had a Hull of a peck to him though ... er ... ahem ... yeah. Well. Anyway. As the saying goes: *take us to your leader!* Er. *Please.* Um, if you don't mind that is ..."

Tombo rolled his eyes.

———————•◦•◦•———————

The three adventurers trotted along in the middle of the column of ostrich-borne warriors. Whenever one faltered (viz. Roffo) a warrior would grunt in displeasure and prod him with his lance. After a while Terry took pity on his friend and swung him up onto his shoulders. The tempo then increased, and soon the ostriches were croaking in dismay at the pace set by the barbarian and matched (with apparent ease) by the unconcerned monk.

"Eh-up!" called Roffo, from above Terry's head. "Huts ahead! Can't be much further now. How are you bearing up?"

The barbarian looked around at their escort. "Oh, fine fine, except ... well, I need to, you know, *Go!* Do you think they'd mind if I ran on ahead? I'm also getting cramp from running so slowly."

"Terry, my man, I'd stick around if I were you. I don't think we should give them an excuse to turn us into kebabs, eh? Oh look: over there! Looks like a cattle pen and, wow, it's a biggy! Hey – Chief ..."

"Shhh!" hissed the monk, from Terry's side. "Hold tongue or else get us killed!"

"Look, I know how to speak to savages. Gramps used to tell me all about it. Trust me! Oy, Chief! Over here!"

Tombo rode up to the men. Even Thunder Chicken was starting to feel the pace. The warrior looked at Terry and the monk and noticed that they were not even breathing heavily. He glowered at Roffo – but there was uncertainty in the glower and not as much Attitude as he would have liked.

"How Chief!" Roffo raised a hand. Then he pointed at the pen of cattle that was steadily being revealed as a sizeable corral. "That there is um big um pen – savvy? You have heap um big load of um cattle."

Tombo stared. Was this one some sort of imbecile? "Why do you talk like an idiot?" he scowled. "Or do all men from the North speak like you?"

Roffo coughed in embarrassment. "Er, sorry, it's just that I thought ... oh, never mind. I was just wondering about the cattle. Are they yours?"

"What you see is but a small part of the wealth of our great leader, Chief Lottomoos. This is called the Veldt Tip Pen, because it lies on the edge of the Veldt."

"Interesting!" Roffo gave a whistle. They had now been jogging along the perimeter fence for some minutes, but there was no end to it in sight. Thousands of cattle milled about inside, bellowing and grumbling. A couple of hundred metres away a dozen young boys herded another wedge into the pen.

The party dropped onto a dirt track that headed for a gap between two hillocks. On one of these, remarkable for a large spherical boulder on its summit, there was a second corral. Roffo pointed again. "There's another ..."

"Yes. That is the second largest corral. That is the Ball-Point Pen."

"Because it's near a point with a boulder shaped like a ball?" Roffo was beginning to suspect narrative contrivance. "And let me guess. This biggest pen of cattle ... is it near a fountain?"

Tombo's eyebrows arched. "Yes. Have you been to Ubundi before?"

Roffo laughed and shook his head, looking to the heavens as though searching for something. "Surely you could have done better than that?"

he muttered. "Sorry, chief, not talking to you."

They passed through the narrow valley and found themselves on a slight rise, looking down into a huge bowl-shaped depression in the land. A great fence, made of interwoven branches, formed a circle around a grand settlement of hundreds of huts. A river – fat and lazy – meandered around the settlement and passed behind the third of Ubundi's great corrals: The Fountain Pen. And, indeed, a small fountain was evident nearby, spouting a jet of water into the sky.

Before long, the party passed through the main gate in the fence and, between rows of curious citizens, trotted down to the dusty central square. It was here that they came to a halt directly in front of the Royal Hut of Chief Lottomoos.

Chief Lottomoos of Ubundi impatiently drummed his fingers on his massive naked belly. Having been dragged away from his harem while sowing the royal oats he was not a happy man. The fact that he had allowed himself to be interrupted at all, however, said something about his hedonistic priorities. Had he been stuffing his face during one of his eight daily meals he would not have budged for anything less than an assault by a blood-crazed Ubu war party. And had he been admiring his precious Royal Herd, ah, then even the Ubu could have taken a *flying* … er, yes. Indeed, they could have burned down his palace hut, whisked off his maidens, and stuck him with enough spears to make him look like a cactus, and still he would not have budged. The Chief grinned to himself at the thought of his glorious herd and wondered when Ozbondo would allow him to hold another Full Review …

The sound of a throat being cleared brought the Chief's attention back to the matter in hand. He looked down from his dais at Tombo's prisoners and noticed – in embarrassment – that he'd managed to put his loincloth on back-to-front. It was enough to make a man spit! The Chief threw back his head, gargled throatily, and hawked. The phlegm arced through the air to land on the broad back of the Royal Spittoon. The man, crouching a little to the left of the Chief, muttered the traditional phrase of thanks and bowed his head lower.

Lottomoos turned his attention to the men kneeling before him. A mighty crowd had formed a giant circle around the square: men, women and children, standing silently, their eyes wide, their mouths agape. The strangers themselves were a curious mix. One was small and leathery like an ancient ape, the second was also small of stature but was young and had eyes that darted everywhere like a nervous snake, while the third ... Lottomoos turned to look at the nine men of his personal bodyguard – men who were, by tradition, the largest warriors of the tribe. The Chief looked at the third stranger, clad in his crocodile-skin loincloth, and then at his bodyguard, and then back again. He licked his lips nervously and assessed the distance between himself and the giant barbarian.

The Chief was about to summon his guards a *little* bit closer when he heard a rattling sound off to his right. He closed his eyes and winced. The rattling drew nearer until its source stood at his right elbow.

"So," hissed Ozbondo, the bald-headed Shaman, "what have you brought *us*, my *glorious* son?"

Tombo raised his war lance in salute. "Father – some prisoners! They were lurking on our borders in a most suspicious manner, so I rounded them up and brought them back to you ... er," he turned so that he was addressing Lottomoos, "oh Great Chief!"

Ozbondo frowned. He was a tiny, wizened, wicked man. In a society of warriors, the only way for one of his size to succeed was through guile, deceit, and trickery, and Ozbondo was a master of all these things. And it was perhaps *because* he had achieved his status in his own right, and not through the accident of birth or bodily design, that he was a man of great vanity and great resentment. He scowled and looked at the fat Chief beside him. He did not resent Lottomoos his harem or his gluttony or even his herd (well, perhaps *that*, just a little), but he did resent having to demonstrate even the tiniest bit of subservience. And as the years had slipped by he had come to test the established limits more and more. Now, in utter distaste, he gargled and hawked.

"I say! Do you mind!" The Chief pointed at the Royal Spittoon in irritation. "He's soiled now! Useless! I'll need a new one!"

"Yes, yes, of course," grumbled Ozbondo. "You can have one of mine. Guards ..." Ozbondo gestured to his own retinue of bodyguards. "Take this wretch away and dispose of him!"

"Wait!" cried the Chief in panic. "Hold on there! The Royal Spittle!" Lottomoos clapped his hands and a pair of ugly old women emerged from behind the throne. They shambled up to the Spittoon and carefully scraped the Chief's phlegm into a little earthenware pot. The Chief heaved a great sigh of relief and indicated that the guards could now remove the used article.

Roffo watched this chain of events with a touch of humour and more than a little horror. He whispered to the monk beside him. "What *are* they doing? Is *gob* valuable here or something? You know, like their currency?"

"Wulus very superstitious people," murmured the monk. "Believe in witches and wizards and terrible magic. Believe that if witches get hold of bodily effluent then can do terrible spells."

"Go on!" hissed Roffo, more sharply. "You're having me on!"

"No. It true. In Wulu society people take extra care of waste and stuff. Collect it up, burn it, bury it, etcetera."

"Disgusting! Oh, look at the Chief now, the filthy bugger! His finger's buried up to the knuckle. Surely he's not going to … ugh! I think I'm gonna puke …"

As the unfortunate Spittoon was being dragged away, the Chief busied himself excavating one substantial nostril. He inspected the large nugget he uncovered, then reached down to his right to where the soft hair of the Royal Handkerchief awaited … The Chief frowned at Ozbondo, challenging him to dare defile *this* servant. In response the Shaman merely smiled at him – though it was a smile of repressed fury.

"*When* the Great Chief has finished …" said Ozbondo, "maybe we can deal with the prisoners *bravely* captured by *my* son."

How does he do it? wondered the Chief. *Manage to make me feel so small so easily?* "Er, go on then," he said. "What do you think?"

Ozbondo turned his full attention upon the three captives. As he appraised the young barman, Roffo felt the weight of his malevolence and turned his eyes away. The monk, however, met the Shaman's glare with a look of complete unconcern. And Terry met the evil stare boldly, grimacing back mightily.

"I do believe," hissed Ozbondo, perturbed by the monk's attitude and startled by the barbarian, "that these may well be *wizards*." He pronounced the last word with great deliberation, raising his voice so that all could hear. The people in the crowd, almost as a single body, trembled. Women whimpered and children hid their faces, while men covered their mouths as though fearful that some discharge might fly out and be captured by the evil ones. "Yes – they might well be wizards," continued Ozbondo, "come here to steal our essences and use them for their unspeakable art of *DooDoo*!"

"Oh, strewth," muttered the Chief, "not again …"

Ozbondo, with sudden madness in his eyes, turned to assault the monarch with a wide-eyed stare. He pointed a ferocious finger at him. "Oooooh! Beware! Bewaaaare! Beware it is not *you* they seek …"

"Uh, d'you really think so?" The Chief's palms were beginning to sweat. The Spittoon was gone, and he didn't fancy wiping his hands on the Handkerchief, not after what *he'd* just left there, and so that only left ... He reached under his throne to where the as-yet unsullied Royal Bogpaper lay ...

"Yes, perhaps so," hissed Ozbondo. "There will have to be a smelling out ..." the crowd gave a collective groan of fear "... tomorrow!"

"Uh!" exclaimed Roffo, "um, er, if I might *just* have a word ..."

"Silence, *I* have—"

"Ahem," coughed the Royal.

"The *Chief* has spoken!"

"Well, not really ..."

"And *afterwards* the bones suggest will be an auspicious time to hold a Full Review of the Heavenly Herd!"

"Oh, really!" exclaimed the Chief, excitedly. "Jolly good show! Take these potential wizards away and lock them up good and proper. *I* have decided!"

As a cluster of beefy guards armed with very sharp assegais converged on the three adventurers, Ozbondo gave a smirk of triumph.

"Well, I don't think much of Wulu hospitality," declared Roffo, as he assessed their present accommodation. They were incarcerated in a circular hut made of twigs held together by a cement which, Roffo feared, *was not* dried mud. There was no furniture on the bare earth floor for them to sit or lie on, but the bathroom was, at least, *en suite*: a wooden bucket rested against one wall. Large cobwebs decorated the sloping ceiling, and a squadron of flies performed acrobatics for their entertainment.

"Could have been worse," muttered the monk.

"Oh yeah? And how do you work that one out?"

"Could have been killed already."

Roffo's jaw dropped. "Thanks! Thanks very much indeed! That's just the sort of hopeful comment I need right now! You know, I *was* feeling right depressed, but suddenly the world seems a much better place!"

"He's right, though," mused Terry, who'd been studying the walls and was now peering into the combined lavatory-washbasin-bidet. "I've stayed in worse places. Usually had to pay, too. At least this is free."

Roffo stared at his friend as though he had come from another planet. "I can't believe you're both being so calm. Did you see that old bloke? A nasty piece of work if ever I saw one! And I don't like the sound of him *smelling* me tomorrow. I ain't had a proper wash in a week. Why didn't anyone say anything?"

"There time to speak and time to be silent," said the monk, nodding softly to himself. "You not detect tension in air? Between Chief and Shaman?"

"Yeah, I noticed that," said the barbarian. "I reckon they're not the best of friends."

"Just so! That Shaman: little shit! No. It best if try to talk to Chief alone. Earlier, time not right."

"Well, we'd better try to find the time soon, because I don't think we've got much *left* between us. In fact, what *is* three multiplied by, oh, twelve hours? If only I still had my copy of *Illinois Jane's Guide to Traps, Tricks and Pitfalls* – then we'd be able to get out of here! She had several chapters on escaping from different types of prisons and the like. I bet some Nudian's using it for loo paper right as we speak …"

In fact, back in The Buff, at that *exact* moment, a heavily bandaged miscreant of the thieving fraternity was leafing through that very volume of *Jane's* that Roffo had been forced to leave behind in his rapid flight from Nudia.

Mitchkin – sentenced to ten years in jail plus *The Heavy, Itchy, Smelly Woollen Robe of Penance* – had easily picked the lock to his cell in the basement of the temple. He had ghosted past the two jail wardens and ascended the stairs to the main level. Even heavily bandaged *and* with one arm in a sling *and* one leg in a cast *and* wearing clothing in a place not noted for such a fashion, he still possessed the ability *not to be seen*. People could walk past Mitchkin and see a shadow, a statue, or even some acquaintance – *oh, you know, whatsisname* – but they never saw a thief. It was all part of his art.

And now, being desirous of the odd Nudian souvenir or two, he was in one of the temple treasure rooms. He had already loaded up a very heavy bag full of gold and gems and had just been on his way out when he saw *the* book. A classic! He had not seen a copy since his old teacher had, as a parting gift, nicked *his* (this being the perverse tradition in thiefdom).

A broad smile settled upon Mitchkin's face. Ah, those were the days! Tears misted his eyes from divine memories: the fun, the pranks, the japes, the escapes! He leafed through to Chapter 31, a personal favourite: *How to avoid the Aztechy Poison Blow Dart Traps and steal a Gold Statue of the God Hullabooloo while Blindfolded and Surrounded by Three Hundred Psychotic Warriors with Tattooed Buttocks, Halitosis, and Questionable Sexual Appetites*. It was one of those missions he had always dreamt of trying!

Maybe now, with this book, he could …

The door to the room opened and Bishop Mazed strode in, flanked by Brothers Denda and O'Toole. Mitchkin looked up in startlement. He had been too intent on the book! He slammed *Jane's* shut.

"*Ooooooooooo!* My thumb, my thumb!"

Mazed's eyes widened in fury. "Seize him!"

Mitchkin grabbed his sack of swag in one hand, the book being in the other, and turned to flee through the opposite door. He tugged the sack off the table, but wasn't able to hold it. It dropped.

"*Aiiieeeeee!* My foot, my foot!"

The thief did not get far. But he knew where the treasured book was, and he knew he would be back. Two days later Mitchkin escaped once more, and this time – in spite of running into a door (black eye) and falling off a roof into a freshly dug grave (dislocated shoulder) – he managed to escape from the naked clutches of the Nudians. Ultimately – somewhat the richer – he found his way back to Cross-My-Way.

"What'ya doin?" asked Roffo, coming up to stand behind the monk, who was sitting cross-legged on the bare ground. "Hey, those are the bits of the map!"

"Clever boy. Recognise maps. Good. Maybe learn to read next."

"No need to get tunicy, I was just making an observation. What are you doing with the pieces now? I mean, surely they don't tell us much without the rest?"

"Hmm, maybe, maybe not."

"What do you mean?" wondered Terry, coming over to sit beside the gurning one.

"Sometimes possible to tell from pattern what comes next. Like … see here." The monk had the two map fragments slotted together. They appeared to comprise two of the four corners of a rectangular parchment. On the first, to the left, the map showed the temple where the monk had 'found' the fragment, and a dotted red line that traced a route through Cross-My-Way to Nudia. A cross on The Buff indicated that there was a fragment there and, indeed, that was where they had acquired the second piece. On the first fragment the red dotted line continued off the edge of the parchment to the right. The monk traced this line now with his finger. "See, even without second fragment knew *roughly* direction to travel. Line goes over mountains crossed under … but not see where terminate until found *this* piece." The monk tapped the second fragment. This showed the line continuing along a savannah beyond the mountain range and then bearing off a little way south – to Ubundi – where there was another cross. Another fragment! But the line continued on, weaving to the south-west and eventually disappearing off the edge of the parchment.

"I see what you mean," cried Roffo excitedly. "We might be able to work out where the piece is *after* Ubundi, even without finding the piece *here* first, just from the general direction of the line."

"Yes, perhaps. If had another map, to same scale, could lay pieces over top … then at least see area next piece must be in."

"Eh?" Terry scratched his mane of hair. "I don't follow."

"It simple. Look. From size of map, and distance travelled between places on it, can work out rough scale, like, one inch equal thirty miles, la?"

"Go on."

"Also know this map scribed on standard size parchment … can tell because two fragments here form one length. See, when put together have straight line along three sides …"

"But jagged on the fourth, where it's torn?"

"Good, yes!"

"Hey, I realised that too," said Roffo sullenly, feeling an imbalance in the praise ratio.

The monk merely nodded. "Anyway, now know, for example, that place of recipe must be in certain area, and might be able to guess *where* if could look at complete map of possible area."

"Er, yeah, okay," mused Terry, "but the next fragment could be anywhere within hundreds of square miles."

"Yeah, mate," said Roffo, "but it's probably going to be at a town or temple or something, and not, like, just pinned to a tree in the middle of a forest."

"So, where do you reckon it is? And can't we just guess where the recipe is and go there? I mean, since the third fragment must go here …" Terry indicated the bottom right quadrant of the incomplete map "… then Boozer's recipe must be somewhere in the fourth fragment, here," and he indicated the missing bottom left area.

The monk scratched his head this time. "Perhaps … perhaps if there *only* four pieces to map."

"Eh?"

"Never mind for now. Anyway, without third fragment and line showing general *direction* to go in fourth area, that still leave many *potential* places to search."

"So we need the third piece, definitely," stated the barbarian.

"Yes."

"And we're no closer to finding that while we're stuck in here!" exclaimed Roffo angrily. "We're gonna be barbecued, or eaten, or fed to the crocodiles first."

The monk looked at the young man now and raised his brow in sudden surprise. "Ah, did not say?"

"Say what? That they only feed members of royalty to crocodiles here, whereas for strangers they first cover you in—"

"No. About map! You not see? Chief's headring?"

"Well, yeah," said Roffo, somewhat defensively, "I saw it. He had a sort of gold ring on his head which was sort of wrapped up in a ... tatty ... old ... bit ... of ... *cloth*? The fragment!"

"Believe so."

"But why," said Terry, "would he be wearing it on his head?"

The monk shrugged. "Wulus not write. Maybe think writing some kind of magic. Boozer probably gave fragment to some previous Chief, maybe even to Sucka himself, and say it great gift, bring luck, fertility, victory in battle, some bullshit."

"The devious git!"

"And now ..." the monk picked up the two pieces of the map and put them inside his leather habit (the *Weahthefinls* not having had any clothing large enough to gift to him) "... it time to consider tomorrow. Need work out plan to escape certain *terrible* death ..."

———•••———

"If that fucking herdboy smacks me with that switch again I'm gonna ... gonna ..."

"Gonna what? Lick him? Stare at him meaningfully with your big brown eyes?"

"God I hate being a cow. What a bummer!"

"Yeah – if only we had hands or something. Then we could lob a rock at the bastard, or push his face into a fresh pile of crap ..."

"Ha, moo moo," laughed the light brown beast, "and that's not all you could do with your hands. Did you see what the boy was getting up to yesterday behind that rock?"

"Cor, yeah! Just imagine if you could do *that* to *yourself*! You'd be at it all day!"

The two cows threw back their heads and mooed in unison. The slightly darker brown bullock then bent down to rip up a mouthful of crispy dried grass. He chewed on it thoughtfully for a moment. "You know," he continued, "I think being a human must be pretty cool, but if I could really be anything else, I mean, the very tops, it has to be a crocodile. No-one beats them with switches. And what's more, the humans often feed them *other* humans. I think crocs are probably more civilised. I can't see them getting together and taking one of their own up to the humans and saying: 'Go on then, mate, turn him into an interesting item of footwear, or perhaps some female fashion accessory, go on, we don't mind.'"

Light Brown looked at him. "Reckon you're right there. And those humans ... they feed the crocs *loads*. I reckon they chucked in a good half dozen of their own yesterday, and probably twice as many the day before. It's a wonder there are any of 'em left at all."

"Yeah, well, I wish they'd chuck in that irritating young git with the switch and the sticky hands. Really pisses me off he does!"

"Yeah, and so does that ..." Light Brown nodded in the direction of a young albino as she strutted past. "Pompous cow! Just 'cos she's white and those humans have some fetish about the white ones! I dunno! She just looks sickly to me. I wouldn't shag her for all the brown crispy grass in Ubundi!"

"Well, you won't miss much then. The precious ones never put in any effort, you know? They think they don't have to, since they can get any bull they want ..."

"You haven't ...?"

"Fraid so!"

"Bastard! Ow! *Bugger* that herdboy!"

"Ignore him. Come on. I see some crispy brown grass ahead. Let's go get it ..."

———•••———

The Square was beginning to fill with Wulus. People had abandoned their homes, their cattle, and their little gardens, to trudge to the capital from all over the Chiefdom. Some had even walked through the night to be here. The atmosphere comprised a heady – and rather perilous – mix of expectation, excitement, and cow flatulence. As long as nobody lit a match, this was going to be a very special day!

The adventurers watched all this from rather exalted positions. They had each been tied to a stake set in the ground in the area immediately in front of the royal dais. A dozen more men had been similarly blessed, having been plucked from the crowd by beefy warriors just for showing a bit too much interest. The adventurers had even been given their own private protection in the form of Tombo and his Feral Hippos, who stood by in their best togs, resplendent in cheetahskin loincloths and ostrich-plumed headrings.

"Great plan. Brilliant. *I know*," mimicked Roffo, "*let's let ourselves be tied up in preparation for some hideous ordeal and painful death*. Wonderful."

"Keep calm," said the monk, "need to think."

"What, didn't you have enough time last night? And this was the best you could come up with? At least we could have made a break for it in the dark. Terry was game."

"Hut surrounded by guards outside – guards with *spears*. Even barbarian skin not resistant to sharp metal. Not have got far."

"Farther than waiting for our legs to be bitten off by crocodiles first! That's right, isn't it, Terry? *Terry?*"

The barbarian was shuffling uneasily against his stake. He had twisted himself around so that he could see the dais. Lottomoos was already present, surrounded by his bodyguards, but Ozbondo was still in make-up. It was the head bodyguard, however, who was the focus of Terry's interest, for that man had a new toy – a toy he was now brandishing proudly. It was an axe. *Terry's* axe.

"Uh-oh," said Roffo, seeing the direction of his friend's interest. Being positioned between the barbarian and the monk, he wriggled about so that he was facing the man in the leather habit. "I think that *steel* thing is happening again."

The monk looked at him sharply. "Must not be allowed to! Could ruin everything!"

Roffo chuckled dryly, "Yeah, like the heads of the Chief's guards for one thing, and probably a wimpi* or two for another."

"Distract him. You best friend … talk to him."

This startled the young barman. Terry's best friend? Yeah, he probably was! He wriggled about to face the barbarian. "Oy, Terry my man! *Terry!*"

The barbarian slowly turned to face Roffo. For a moment, he stared at him as though he was a stranger, but then the clouds retreated from before his eyes.

"Terry," continued Roffo, "what do you reckon to a bit of crocodile wrestling? Do you think you're up to it?"

---

* A Wulu army.

Ozbondo hummed to himself as his body servants dressed him in his finest Shaman regalia. One young woman carefully positioned an ivory headring atop his short, curly hair. From this there sprouted the red and yellow feathers of a bird of paradise. The skin of a young lioness was draped about him so that its eyeless head rested atop his right shoulder as though it were asleep. Around Ozbondo's neck were placed a number of necklaces in which the bone motif was prominent. Around his thin thighs was wrapped a cheetahskin loincloth. And about his wrists and ankles there were fitted a variety of jangly bracelets.

A servant mixed an ochre paste in a small earthenware bowl, then applied this to the Shaman's face, painting four diagonal stripes on each cheek so that it looked as though Ozbondo had been clawed by a very large cat. Another servant bowed before the Shaman, presenting him with his witchfinding sceptre. This comprised a human femur on top of which was strapped, with leather thongs, a tiny human skull. Ozbondo accepted the sceptre, gestured his servants away, and looked himself up and down. Enough to put the willies up the stoutest warrior! Excellent!

The Shaman knew the importance of *the look*. He also knew the importance of putting on a show. He doubted that the strangers were much of a threat to himself, or to the nation, but that was not the point. This was a chance for him to perform; to be seen; to reinforce his position; to create fear; to demonstrate power! As he strode from his hut towards the Royal Dais he cackled to himself. For his own entertainment, and for practice, he pulled a face, opening his eyes wide, arching his eyebrows, clenching his teeth. The look – *yeah!*

Ozbondo paused behind the dais. To his right, several hundred yards away, he noticed the vanguard of the Royal Herd. The lowing was gaining in volume as more and more cattle were stacked up behind the leaders of the parade. When all of the Chief's cattle were marshalled they would form a mighty river, one hundred yards wide and several miles long, stretching out of the capital and curving away through a dry river valley between spartan hills. Ozbondo could see that the Ball Point Pen had already been cleared. The Review was the Chief's show. It would demonstrate *his* power and wealth. Well, he could have it! What Ozbondo wanted was subservience. He didn't want to arouse awe, only fear. And now it was his turn.

The Shaman stalked up to the throne from behind. He climbed the broad, flat dais, rustled past Lottomoos without a glance and, with a high-pitched shriek, leapt into the air from the front of the dais. He landed in a squat amidst the stakes and before the assembled multitude. Here, he adopted a wide-eyed stare, slowly scanning the crowd and ignoring the captives. A great hush settled upon the thousands of rapt Wulus. It was not unknown for witches and wizards to be plucked from the crowd itself, and the passing of the years had taught people that it was those who spoke, or made a noise, or coughed, or sneezed, or cried, who were invariably the ones who were dragged forth. This was exciting, but it was also very deadly. As Ozbondo skittered up to a point in the crowd, the people craned to see where he was headed. Had he spotted someone? Was it someone they knew? Was it a friend or an enemy? The multitude held its breath …

Ozbondo *loved* this. The terror in the eyes of those he approached! It was like a drug to him. Even the acrid stench of urine brought him to a high! *Aha*, he thought, *look at that fat git! Well, watch this …* With a howl he leapt into the air, shook his sceptre, and ran up to the fat man, stopping just six inches from his face. The man's eyes opened even wider than the Shaman's, perspiration sprung onto his brow, and the hint of a whimper escaped from his lips. Suddenly, eight huge warriors – Ozbondo's men – appeared as though from nowhere, their spears raised, waiting for an invitation. The Shaman considered the man. *Yes or no?* And then he threw back his head, cackled, and spun away. The man took the most relieved breath of his life …

Up and down spun Ozbondo, terrifying the crowd. And this was just the prelude. Even so, his wicked mind was at work. Maybe people became *less* scared, he thought, after he had passed them by? Maybe they thought he wouldn't come back? Well, that wouldn't do, oh no, that wouldn't do at all! With an ear-splitting scream he raced back to the fat man. This time, however, he raised his head and gave three exaggerated sniffs … and brought down his sceptre upon the man's shoulder! The man fainted on the spot, which was probably for the best. The Shaman's warriors dragged the lard-arse off to the crocodile pits …

"He's barking," whispered Roffo, "absolutely barking! We've got to get out of here, and we've got to do it *now*!"

The monk gurned unhappily. "Wait … just few more minutes. Need to think …"

"Terry," hissed Roffo, "how are you doing on the ropes? And stop looking at that guard …"

"Oh, sorry. The rope? No problem. I can pull the stake out too if you want. It'd be a bit of a weapon."

"Good show. Wait for my word …"

———•◦•◦•———

"*Ride … like the wind, ride like the wind …*" warbled the yakkers as their beasts thundered across the savannah. The inconvenience of the tall grasslands of the *Weahthefinls* lay behind them, and now the knee-high grass of the savannah proved great riding country. The spirits of the Angels had soared over the last couple of days. This was *it*, this was what being a yakker was all about! The wind in the beard, the thunder of hooves, the flying landscape, the camaraderie of other big, dirty, scruffy wasters. Brilliant!

Frunge whooped in joy and spurred on his red-haired Noughton. He looked back and laughed as the others began to fall behind. "Teach you to ride girlie yaks!"

"Bastard!" yelled Trespass, though with surprising good nature. "How can anyone say that about a Harleck Dravidian?" Laughing, he booted his own beast in the sides and was rewarded with a rumble of internal power and a bout of speed. He roared up to Frunge and began to overtake him.

"Hold up," cried Burble from behind. His West Highland yak was a powerful, functional beast, without the turn of speed of the Name sub-species. Bruce's Black Mountain yak, and Grunt's immense Ducrapi, also found the pace in excess of their top cruising speed.

Trespass gave an obscene gesture and pulled further ahead. This was the life! He let his lead increase to fifty yards just to show the others what was what. But when he tried to throttle down he got little response. Puzzled, he pulled back harder on the chopped horns. *Nothing.* The creature seemed to have a mind of its own. Trespass shrugged: maybe it was enjoying itself as much as he was? He decided to give it its head.

Frunge cruised up beside him. "Yeah! He's never run so well! Must be something in the air. Look – no hands!" The dim-witted yakker released his grip on his steed's horns. His beast maintained its pace. Soon, on Trespass's other side, the rest of the *peloton* came up to him.

"Yeeee-hah!" yelled Burble. "Turbo-drive!"

"Dunno wot's got into mine," beamed Grunt, "but 'e's gone bonkers! I didn't know 'e could go so fast."

"Aye, mine neither," howled Bruce. "But what the fuck, eh?"

274

They all laughed.

The pack raced over the ground like bovine thunder. They began to come upon signs of human habitation: huts, small gardens, little cattle corrals. But everywhere seemed to be deserted of animal and human life.

"Where do you think everyone is?" wondered Burble.

"Probably 'eard we was coming and thought they oughta get the fuck out!" laughed Grunt.

They came up to the edge of a huge corral. The interwoven branches of the fence appeared to go on forever. But there was not a herdsman or a cow in sight. Burble looked across at his comrade. He frowned. He looked at his own yak. He looked at the steeds of the others. The beasts were all frothing at the mouth. He leant over and, somewhat perversely, looked underneath his beast. His frown deepened.

"Uh, I reckon I know what's going on," he said.

"Yeah," laughed Trespass, "the natives are all wimps …"

"No, I mean, about why the yaks are acting so funny. *Look*: they've all got *the horn*."

"Of course they do," said Trespass, "they're yaks aren't … they?" He looked across to his left at Frunge's slavering steed. Something large was snaking about beneath it, occasionally visible over the top of the yak-belly-high grass.

"Er … I see."

"So," said Burble, "when was the last time *yours* had it?"

"Um, it was back in Way."

"Precisely. I think we're gonna find out where all the cattle from that corral have got to."

Bruce nodded. "Aye, he's reet. I reckon we ought tae stop this …"

"Yeah, and let's do it now."

Ahead were two low hills through which a broad, dry valley led. On the left hill was another immense corral, which was also empty. Out of control, the yaks raced on for the gap between the hills.

Ozbondo stood before the three captives. He had spent the last ten minutes dancing and capering around the local sorcerous suspects, and now half of the stakes were standing empty. The men who had been freed, however, were the lucky ones, while those still restrained could shortly look forward to an encounter with creatures that possessed bigger teeth than a lovechild of Barry Gibb and Esther Rantzen. Ozbondo smirked at the foreign captives and placed his hands on his hips. He was going to enjoy this.

"Uh, do hurry up there," came a voice from the throne. "This is all very entertaining, but the procession awaits."

The Shaman froze. Sudden fury seared through his veins. This was unprecedented! He glowered at Lottomoos and sensed his men tighten their grip on their spears. If he gave the signal now they would rush the Chief and put an end to the corpulent one. He looked across to his son, who stood glowering beneath the royal dais. Tombo was slightly in front of the Feral Hippos, who were spread out in a line between the dais and the rest of the square. A smile returned to Ozbondo's face. The Chief had been a fool to allow *his* son to command the crack regiment! Ozbondo toyed with the idea of commanding his own Sullen Buffalos to charge, expecting Tombo to take his side, but then he decided against it. The wise man would wait. He would first have to be clear about the loyalties of his son and his son's men. Instead, the Shaman contented himself with an insult. He strutted up to the foot of the dais.

"O *Great* Chief," he sneered, "do not interfere in matters that are not of your *understanding*."

A gasp spread around the multitude. Lottomoos appeared stunned. He turned to the chief of his bodyguard. "Can he say ... oh, for goodness sake stop playing with that! Can he say that to me?"

"Uh? What?" The bodyguard lowered the axe. "Whassat?"

"Oh, strewth ..."

Ozbondo strutted back to the captives. He went to the monk first. "So," he hissed, "is this a wizard I see before me? What have you to say for yourself, old man?"

The monk gave an inscrutable look and said nothing. Ozbondo stalked up to him, rattled his sceptre, then darted forward and brought it down on the captive's shoulder. "Wizard!" he cried. The crowd appeared to both gasp and cheer simultaneously. But behind his back the monk flexed his hands *just so* – a technique known to his order as bird-escaping-snake – and the rope fell loose about his wrists. For the moment he did nothing.

Next, Ozbondo stalked up to Roffo. "Is this a young wizard I see before me?"

Roffo gave a sickly smile. But he straightened his shoulders and, with every ounce of his courage, cried out: "Go blow yourself *Mr Arseface*!"

276

"Mr Arseface?" the Shaman was momentarily stunned. Then he scowled and tapped Roffo on the shoulder. "Wizard!" Again, the crowd gave a gasping cheer.

Ozbondo finally moved over to Terry. As he approached the barbarian, however, he caught the first hint that something was amiss: he heard an unnaturally loud bellow come from the direction of the Royal Herd. The cows seemed to be getting impatient. Well, if the Chief and the people could wait, thought Ozbondo, then so could they. In any case, they'd be *his* soon enough. He stood before Terry and looked him up and down. *Hmm*, he thought, *nice pecs … it'll be a shame to feed him to … what is that noise?* Ozbondo turned to look down the avenue towards the vanguard of the Herd. As he did so, he noticed that the attention of the crowd had also shifted towards the ruckus. He was losing their attention, and that would not do! From what he could see the cattle appeared to be restless, even frightened. Herdsmen and boys were running to the scene from either side of the avenue.

"Right," shouted the Shaman, "that's it!" He beckoned over Numi, leader of the Sullen Buffaloes. "Go and find out who is responsible for that disturbance and bring the wretch to …" A mighty collective bovine bellow now resounded through the air. As they watched, the front line of the cattle seemed to spur forwards in fear. Herdsmen leapt out of the way or, in a few cases, were trampled in the rush. A huge clamour now started up as thousands upon thousands of cattle opened their throats and gave vent to their fear. Within seconds, the entire Herd was pelting forward in an irresistible stampede.

"What the fu—"

"Terry," cried Roffo, "now! *Now!*"

The barbarian simply stretched out his arms behind him: the rope snapped and went hissing off through the air. Terry turned and heaved at the stake, which came easily out of the ground. At the same time the monk stepped away from his stake. A nearby guard turned to look at him stupidly … and the monk simply *touched* him, *like so*. The guard collapsed in a heap. The monk ghosted over to Roffo, stroked his bonds, and the rope fell away.

On the dais, Chief Lottomoos only had eyes for his precious herd. His mouth was open in horror. He grasped at his hair with both hands. "What are they doing? Stop them – my babies! They'll hurt themselves!"

The Herd roared down the avenue towards the square. The crowd – appreciating that this wasn't in the programme – now started shrieking. En masse, the spectators tried to clamber out of the way, rushing out of the south side of the square away from the dais structure. The town's huts – not the sturdiest of buildings – began to go down under the press of frantic humanity.

Roffo shouted to Terry over the awesome noise and sudden hurricane-like wind. "Terry – the headring! The Chief's headring! Fetch!"

<hr />

Terry needed no further urging. The headring was on the head of the Chief, who sat beside the head bodyguard, who was currently in possession of something that did not belong to him. Terry brushed aside two Feral Hippos and leapt onto the dais. The opposition there was not as great as it should have been, since most of the troops – and half of the Chief's bodyguard – had voted for self-preservation and had legged it out of the path of the onrushing storm. Terry twirled the stake about as though it were nothing more than a cheerleader's baton and started swatting soldiers and bodyguards as though they were flies. "I'm coming!" he shouted. "I'll save you, *oof*, you blighter! I'm coming!"

"Stop, you stupid beast, *stoooooop*," cried Trespass. The yak had sensed nooky. It had not had any for quite some time and now, here it was, surrounded by thousands of potential lovers! So many to choose from! It was like releasing Warren Beatty on the Planet of Women after a year-long space journey with not even a copy of *Playboy* for company. Restraint was just not an option!

Beside the leader of the Hull's Angels, Grunt was buffeted on the back of his own mountainous beast. His yak crunched through a hut, turning it into tinder. And suddenly it was in the midst of the Herd. It was in heaven! Alas, the cows did not share this opinion – after all, if The Undertaker bust down the door to *your* bedroom, would you stay or run? Not being quite as stupid as their press would make out, the cows decided to run, as did the bulls – unanimously deciding that they weren't about to go head-to-head with anything *that* big. The Herd scattered, rippling out in every direction, brooking no interference from anyone or anything. Grunt threw himself onto his yak's neck and clung on for dear life.

"Right, come on then," Roffo gestured to the monk. "It's payback time!"

Ozbondo turned to see the two adventurers coming towards him. He didn't know what the *fuck* was going on but this ... this he could understand. *Resistance?* He gestured to Numi and the four men who were clustered around him. "Kill the old one, but keep the insolent young one alive. Go!"

The guards advanced. Roffo suddenly felt incredibly stupid. He looked around for Terry. But the monk came past him, put a gentle hand on his shoulder, and actually smiled. "Never mind. I handle Mr *Arseface* ..." And suddenly, the monk wasn't at the barman's side at all, but was flying through the air.

"Ouch!" winced Roffo, in sympathy with the two guards who had suddenly found one unwashed foot apiece in their faces. They dropped like sandbags from the flies of a theatre. The monk spun like a whirling dervish caught in a tornado. A leg kicked out and another guard dropped, and then another, and then ... Numi grabbed the monk's leg and flipped him over. The leader of the Sullen Buffaloes roared with laughter and raised his spear. And then he struck. But the monk wasn't *there*, and the assegai pierced deep into the ground.

"Looking for me?" came a voice, and Roffo thought, *no, don't look around*, just as Numi rather foolishly decided to do so.

But something beyond this action now caught Roffo's eye: a thin figure trying to slip off around the side of the dais. With a quick look over his shoulder – at the horned front of death that was now almost upon him – he broke into a sprint towards the dais, following Ozbondo around it. He flung himself flat just as the irresistible mooing force surged past. Several cows tried to clamber onto the dais, but were dragged away by the passing current. Looking back, Roffo goggled at the sight of the monk rising above the stampede, his arms folded, standing astride a pair of bullocks. "Amazing," he said, and then a shadow passed over him.

Ozbondo stood over the young adventurer, much the worse for wear. His lionskin cape had been torn off, his feather plumes had been broken and now drooped over his face, and his ghastly sceptre was nowhere to be seen. "You ... *you!*"

Roffo licked his lips nervously. Now, what would Terry do at a moment like this? Roffo shook his head. Not an option. What about the monk? *Aha!* Roffo lifted his leg up vertically, hard, right between the *gates to heaven*. Ozbondo shrieked in a voice most appropriately described as *castrato*, and crumpled to the ground. Roffo climbed to his feet. "I think that's one-nil to the wizards, eh?" He turned to find Terry.

The barbarian was not far away. In fact, he was sitting on the side of the dais, watching Roffo with one eye and the now lessening flow of cattle with the other. His axe nestled in his right arm and he twirled the Chief's headring around a finger of his left hand. Roffo went up to sit beside him. "No problem getting that?" He pointed at the cloth-wrapped headring.

"Nah. The Chief wasn't interested in it. Poor chap. He just sat there crying *my babies my babies*."

"And, er, the axe?"

"Nope. I told the bloke it was mine. He just looked a bit embarrassed. Well, he couldn't dispute it, could he? Where's the monk?"

And at that moment the monk crashed through a nearby hut, still riding atop a pair of bullocks. He dismounted with a double-twisting somersault and spotted the landing perfectly. The bullocks blundered off towards the royal hut.

For a moment the monk stared after them. "Swear one of them just say, *right, now let's find that bloody herd boy!*" The monk shrugged. "Hearing things? Never mind! Think better get out of here quick. No time to lose."

"No, I guess not."

"Terry, carry Shaman-smiter?" The monk gurned in amusement and cackled to himself. "Good! Now go."

As they trotted out of the ruins of Ubundi, Roffo called down from Terry's shoulders: "It was a good job that stampede happened when it did. I wonder what caused it?"

Suddenly, a nimble cow raced across their path. It was followed by a large hairy man riding the biggest yak any of the adventurers had ever seen. The rider was beating the creature on the head and wailing at the top of his voice. But the yak was, as all could see, extremely excited and not in the mood to take *no* for an answer.

"Hmm," said the monk, "should have guessed sex involved somewhere in this."

"Yeah," said Terry, a frown upon his face, "and I swear I know that guy."

Simultaneously, Roffo and Terry shouted: "Grunt!"

But by this stage the Angel was already half a mile away and retreating rapidly.

———◆•••◆———

"Grass as far as the eye can see, sir," declared the Nudian militiaman, Dan Glur, as he swept his arm out to indicate the endless pampas that spread to the horizon. The one hundred men of the Religious Artefact Retrieving Expedition were loosely clustered around the rocky outcrop on which Glur stood. This was on the downslope of the mountain they had recently crossed. Militiaman Glur looked down at the assembly of naked men resting on their spears; he addressed his commanding officer. "A complete ocean of impenetrable greenery. If we set foot in there we'll get lost for sure!"

"Well, Dan," replied Justin, expedition head and honorary Captain in the militia, "it's lucky for us that I've got the biggest periscope around, isn't it!" The Big Knob of Nudia was enjoying himself. Normally, the only events he got to lead were processions into the temple on festival days, but he had called in some favours and *insisted* on commanding this force. Of course, his enthusiasm had had little do with a sense of civic or religious duty, and more to do with the need to make sure that *He* was dead. An uneasy feeling in his guts gnawed at him – a disturbing presentiment that his foe still lived, or perhaps it was only wind?

Another scout puffed up to the group, returned from beachcombing the shore of the green sea. "No sign of the river, sir. Maybe it's the other way?"

"Perhaps we should split into two parties," suggested Jumbo, full Captain in the militia but presently second-fiddle to Justin, "with one heading east and the other west? One is certain to bump into the outflow. Then we can reassemble and split once again, with one group following the river into the grass and the other tracking it back under the mountains." Jumbo nodded to himself. "Yes. That way the holy relic is sure to be found."

Justin scowled at the man. "You want to divide our force? Think, Captain! There could be any number of terrors lurking in that stuff. Just look out there for a moment. *There.*" He thrust an appendage out. "See, there! That strange ripple in the grass? Now, do you feel any wind, eh?" Justin looked smug. Here he was, not only the Big Man of the occasion, but lecturing the professionals on simple military tactics. He could turn his hand to anything! "Well Captain, what caused it? Could it be a giant, rabid mongoose perhaps?"

Some muttering started up amongst the troops. Men began to slowly edge away from the grass and lower their spears.

The expedition leader continued. "Or maybe it's a whole herd of them, eh? Now, if they went for *your* snake you'd want as many of your mates around as possible to help fight them off, wouldn't you!"

Jumbo scowled in turn. This was ridiculous. "My men can handle themselves," he declared.

"So I've heard."

"Very droll, sir." The second-in-command clenched his fist more firmly around his spear. "In any case, personal danger should count for nothing when it comes to retrieving the Holy Longman. There can be no better cause in which to die. I personally would fight a thousand monsters to recover it – single-handed and all at once if needs be!"

"Yes, I'm sure you would. I'll note that down as a volunteering for the next hopelessly pointless suicide mission. But *my* decision is that we stay together." Justin smirked at the man. It took all of his self control not to start chanting *nah-nah nah-nah-nah*. "Now, which way do we go first? Come on, *Captain*, make a contribution! Get out the Decision Support Device."

Muttering under his breath, Jumbo unscrewed the end of his spear and reverently removed a small metal disk from within the hollowed-out tip. He handed it to his despised leader.

"Right then. Heads we go left, tails we go right." With a flick of his thumb, Justin sent the coin spinning through the air. But before it could land in his outstretched palm a small black figure leapt from the grass and grabbed it. Justin reacted instantly: he fell onto his back, clasping his hands protectively over his prime assets. Jumbo, however, dived into the green sea after the thief.

The party, with spears now fully lowered, watched the swirling, screaming mass of reeds in front of them. Suddenly the grass went still, and silence returned to the pampas. For a whole minute nothing moved.

"Poor Jumbo," sighed militiaman Glur, poking at the grass with the business end of his spear. "That he should be taken in such a way. Was it a mongoose? Did anyone see? What should we do now, sir? Sir? Are you all right?"

Justin opened his hands and looked down at what they had shielded. He gave a huge sigh of relief. "Thank Satyr for that. Still intact! It's getting bloody dangerous around here." He looked around his command. "Right, let's get out of here. One man down already and no sign of the river. I think we should run, and I do mean *run*, back to The Buff. Tell them that the Holy Relic is lost forever. Tell them it has been taken by a foul demon who eats people. That's the truth, right?"

The militiamen gave each other worried, sidelong glances, and turned to stare at their commander. Surely they could not go home without the Relic? They would be forced to wear The Yellow Pantaloons of Disgrace!

"But, sir, we can take it," asserted militiaman Pete Rick. He looked around his colleagues, who all nodded their grim assent. At least, they all nodded bar the group of three oversized wrestling militiamen who were even now backing up the slope.

"You might be able to take it, but I can't! Which asset is more vital to Nudia? The old Longman of our god, or the *physical integrity* of the ruling Big Knob?" The mass hissed in disbelief at what they were hearing. "Shut up! I'm in command here and I say 'run'. So start running or I'll have you all court-martialled!"

And, at just that instant, there was a rustle behind the soldiers. Quick as lightning they leapt about to face the foe they expected to burst upon them. Instead, from within the greenery, there emerged a steely-eyed Jumbo. He held up his hand for everyone's inspection. Hanging from it – by its teeth – was a pygmy.

"Is that it?" remarked Justin in disbelief. "All that thrashing and screaming was just you trying to subdue that little bloke? He hardly seems worth the effort."

"He's a tough sod," snarled Jumbo, his teeth gritted in pain. "Now, will one of you men get a crowbar and prise the bugger's jaws open? Then we can interrogate him. He may know the whereabouts of the Relic, or at least the river."

The pygmy was soon detached from Jumbo's hand and tied to a small tree. Justin bent down until their faces were almost touching.

"Well, *little* man, what do you have to say for yourself? Biting poor Jumbo's hand and stealing my money ..."

"*My* money," corrected his second-in-command, who was sitting on a nearby rock, nursing his bitten fingers.

Justin looked over at him. "I bet *they're* sore," he commented, using a tone of voice that suggested he hoped they were. His gaze returned to the cowering figure in front of him. He laughed. "I can tell you're impressed by my stature, small man."

"I certainly am," replied the pygmy. "That's the second monster I've seen in the last month. The other was bigger though."

Justin's jaw dropped. His worst fears were realised. "He's alive," he gasped. "Great Satyr, what have I done to deserve this?"

"Who's alive?" wondered Jumbo, suddenly curious.

"The barbarian. It has to be. One of the villains who stole the Relic."

"Interesting!" Jumbo got up and sauntered over to the captive. "Small man, did this *big* man ..." he looked askance at Justin, who was starting to hyperventilate "... did he have any friends with him?"

"Won't say."

"Hmm, that is not, perhaps, the most sensible answer for a man tied to a tree surrounded by one hundred naked men."

"Good point." The pygmy started to sweat. "Um, yeah, he had two travelling companions. But five more came through here looking for them a couple of days ago."

"Even more interesting!" He turned to face a numb-looking Justin. "That ties in with my uncle Digger's story about how he was assaulted by the thieves' back-up team. It must be them. Small man," he returned his attention to the pygmy, "did either of these parties have a relic with them?"

"Er, what does it look like?"

"A giant prophylactic. They were using it as a boat."

"A boat?"

"Bah," declared Justin, starting to regain some composure, "he's a simpleton. He doesn't even know what a boat is. We may as well kill him now and get it over and done with ..."

"Wait," interrupted the pygmy. "I *do* know something. I know where they were going."

"Where?" enquired Jumbo.

"My life if I tell you?"

Jumbo scowled at Justin. "Yeah. My word on it."

"Ubundi. Due east. Apparently it's on the other side of the pampas. If you can see above the grass you can navigate by the sun. Release me?"

Jumbo stepped forward and, in spite of the squawks from behind him, undid the pygmy's bonds. He then turned to face the troops of RARE. "Gather up your equipment, men, we're shipping out. East it is."

Justin made a face behind the Captain's back. But for the present he said no more.

CHAPTER 13

A RUMBLE IN THE JUNGLE

YAVLO WAS slouched at his desk, thinking about nothing in particular. Indeed, the *particular* nothing he was thinking about was the quantity of evidence he had linking Manis – or indeed anyone else – to the destruction of The Bear's cellar. Worse still, the Inspector had inadvertently caused Boomber to be thrown out of his own home. Perhaps if he had been a better judge of human nature, Yavlo mused, he might have realised that the shop assistant would gossip. He wondered whether he ought to own up to the Sergeant about his role in *the domestic* (as Boomber referred to the incident).

A crash from the cells behind Yavlo derailed the guilt-train of his thoughts.

"Are you all right in there, Sergeant?"

He received no reply.

With a sigh, Yavlo got up and strode over to the door that led to the holding cells at the back of the station house. "Boomber?" The Inspector looked down the line of three cages to the one at the far end. Here, Boomber was in the process of trying to discipline an unruly bed frame with his size eleven boots. "Boomber! That is civic property you are abusing!" He gave a sigh of regret. "I know it is not what you are used to, but it will surely do until your good lady comes to her senses." The Inspector gestured to the man in the cell next door. "See here: Deknat has no problem sleeping on these beds."

The town drunk opened two bloodshot eyes and stared mournfully at his jailer. In a town full of drunks it took great dedication and application to be known as *The* Town Drunk. The effort of moving a part of his body this early in the afternoon *without* the fortifying effect of ale seemed to exhaust the man: his eyelids slowly closed again.

"That's no endorsement, guv!" retorted Boomber. "I once found that sot asleep on a pile of broken bottles. *And* he snores like a catarrhal yak. If you don't get him out of here by tonight, guv, I'm going to be a more permanent resident of these here cells, because I swear I'll kill the noisy sod."

"Really, Sergeant Boomber, that is most unprofessional! Still, I do take your point. I will let him out later so you can get a decent night's sleep. Now, come and help me think this Manis thing through. I am afraid I cannot get my head around it."

"Manish! Bashtard!" slurred Deknat, suddenly roused at the mention of his nemesis. "Git tried to charge me forra pint after I cleaned up the dead 'uns for him!" He tried to jump up from his bed to continue his diatribe but only managed to get semi-vertical before being brought to a halt by a violent coughing fit. It took some seconds for the man to bring himself under control, during which time Yavlo feared the man's lungs might make their first and only live appearance in the outside world. Deknat wheezed to a halt. He cleared his throat noisily and looked up at the policemen. "Yeah – charged me forra pint! Just because I tipped all the dregs into my mug! I had to sieve all the fag ends out and everything. Yeah, and there was even a tooth in one pint. Bluddy disgustin' it was!"

"That Manis is as tight as the proverbial lowlander," agreed the Sergeant. "Do him a favour and he'll charge you for the privilege."

The Inspector's eyebrows rose at this. "Of course!" he shouted. "That's it! Deknat – Boomber – I do believe you may have cracked it! Remarkable!"

"What is it, guv?" enquired the confused Sergeant. "Come on, tell us!"

Yavlo looked around conspiratorially and held a quieting finger to his lips. Boomber caught the mood of the moment and leant over Yavlo's shoulder, checking that no-one had crept into the outer office. And Deknat scanned his small cell for miniature intruders before turning to focus on the Inspector through the bars of his cell.

"It is simple," said Yavlo, in a low voice. "It is obvious from the description of the shop assistant that the dark stranger who bought the exotic clothes was one of those gentlemen who like to be known as The Hull's Angels. This is unusual in itself because those fellows are perpetually broke – as they have a penchant for spending whatever money they have on ale and yak accessories – and so they must have been bankrolled. But by whom?" Yavlo started to pace. "There is only one suspect here, and that is the scoundrel who runs The Pilgrim. Are you with me so far?" Boomber nodded his head vigorously, while Deknat preferred a thumbs-up in deference to his raging hangover. "Now, a normal criminal would promptly try to eliminate any evidence linking him to a crime, is this not so? In the case of Master Manis however – a man who is, let us be frank, rather a miser – that option would seem most unlikely, particularly when the evidence in question is as expensive as the exotic clothing worn by the sabotaging ladies on the night of the crime."

"Guv, I do believe you're on to something. Manis would keep them for personal use or sell them on!"

"Indeed! And since Master Manis is not *that way* inclined, we can assume he will have tried to recoup some of his losses. As such, we can assume that the clothes have not been destroyed, and that they are still out there, waiting to be found."

"Guv, you amaze me!"

"Thank you, Boomber. It's all in the little grey cells," Yavlo tapped his temple. "If we find the clothes and trace them to Manis, then the crime is solved. The problem is finding out where Master Manis might have disposed of them. To whom might he have sold them? That is, what type of woman would *conceivably* wish to wear such flimsy erotic wear? And as to that," Yavlo raised his hands and shrugged, "I do not know."

Boomber and Deknat considered the question for a moment. An answer came to the Sergeant almost immediately. He was about to speak when it suddenly occurred to him that a speedy resolution of the case would bring him into hasty conflict with a certain innkeeper who was not known for his patience, co-operation, good-humour or, indeed, any other virtue. Life *could* become difficult. Boomber closed his mouth.

Deknat's mind, however, worked in the slow, methodical manner characteristic of inebriates everywhere. An answer eventually came. "Maybe, jus' maybe, you're too late," he suggested. "Y'know, there was a Samark caravan in town when the crime was committed. This is one of the few things I remember from a month ago, because I woke up one morning after a bit of a session with my head in a big pile of camel shit. Excellent luck! Rene the Reek gave me the price of, er, *a cup of tea* for it. I 'spect Manis sold the clothes to those buggers and they're long gone."

"Oh, bad luck guv'nor," soothed Boomber. "It was *such* a nice idea. Anyone for tea?"

"No … I mean, thank you Sergeant, a kind offer, but that idea … *no*. Samarks do not usually buy clothes. What they do is buy the raw materials – rolls of cloth, silk, etcetera – and then they have their good ladies make something up. No, I believe that the clothes are not only in one piece, but that they are still in town."

At that moment, young Constable Hendy walked through the door, having just completed his rounds. "Oh, hi there guv, Sarg." He wiped a layer of sweat from his forehead. "It's darned hot outside. Phew! Anyway, what goes?"

Boomber looked at the Inspector, and then at Hendy, and instantly realised that between them the two men could get *him* into a lot of trouble. "Nothing, Constable," he declared. "A pot of tea would be nice though, eh? Off you go …"

"Wait up there, Constable," called Yavlo. "Maybe you can help." Boomber groaned and hid his face in his hands. The Inspector continued. "I have come up with a theory that the clothes involved in the disturbance may still be intact, and indeed, may have been sold on. Can you think of any women who might wish to buy exotic clothing?"

Hendy scratched his head. "Well, guv, I would of thought that were obvious. *Tarts!*"

"Okay Hendy," said Boomber, "that's enough of that …"

"What's that Constable … *tarts?*"

"Yes, guv, you know, *ladies of the night?*"

"Er …"

"*Ladies of ill-repute?*"

"I am afraid you have lost …"

"*Working girls?*"

"Sorry …?"

"Strewth guv! You know! *Floozies! Strumpets! Prostitutes!*"

"Oh … ah … I see … you mean, members of the fair sex who, er …"

"Yes guv," sighed Hendy, "that's exactly what I mean."

"Cor," drooled Deknat, "reckon he's right there. Need any deputies to help you search their clothes?"

Boomber scowled at the drunk, but the damage had already been done, and the cat was not only out of the bag, it was savaging the wallpaper.

Yavlo nodded to himself. "Indeed, this all makes a kind of sense to me." He looked up at Hendy. "Good show, Constable! But … well … *are* there any such ladies in town?"

"Oh, guv," said a resigned Sergeant, "and you were doing *so* well …"

As he pushed his way through the undergrowth in search of his missing steed, Burble's mind filled with devilish thoughts of brick-related castration techniques. The last he had seen of Thruster had been during the bovine chaos in Ubundi: for a short time he had ridden *two-up* atop a sprightly white heifer, but he had soon been dislodged by the violent pelvic activity. At least *he* had only been *bucked* ...

Having avoided being trampled underfoot, thanks to the timely appearance of a termite mound, Burble had attempted to track his beast. The massive herd of stampeding cattle had been easy to trail at first, having cut a swathe across the veldt. But the landscape had rapidly changed, and the clumps and clusters of trees (outlying colonies of a jungle that nestled up against the plain) had caused the herd to disperse. With a multitude of tracks to follow, Burble had been confounded. He had followed one of these, for no clear reason that he could think of, and been led along a minor path into an outcropping of jungle. The path had soon petered out, however, and he now found himself in some dense undergrowth that had obviously *not* suffered from the ravages of rampaging ruminants.

While musing on the profit that might be had from setting up a yakburger bar, the Angel blundered into a dangling vine, which grabbed him around an ankle and tripped him up. As he lay on his back, Burble started to mutter evilly to himself. *Thrown from a rutting yak, stepped on by a thousand charging cows, nibbled by angry insects ... and now attacked by a bit of plant: it was more than a man could take!*

Burble grabbed the creeper and gave it a ferocious yank, but the elasticated vine pulled back. Like a true Angel, Burble flew into the air, but came to an abrupt halt when his helmeted head violently juxtaposed a branch. The shock of the blow caused him to let go of the intransigent creeper and fall back onto a lower bough. A monkey sitting in a nearby tree burst into hysterical laughter.

"Piss off you hairy git!" yelled the Angel. He grabbed a handful of moss from the branch and hurled it at the chimp. The monkey dived for cover, swung off another vine, bounced off a tree trunk, and landed in the arms of a large man sitting on a nearby bough. Burble's heart sank. Had the barbarian hunted him down? He scuttled along his branch and took refuge behind an immense fern. He parted the fronds and stared at the man. It was not Terry, as he had first thought, though the man was of remarkably similar stature… and he appeared to be conversing with the monkey!

"What is it, Cheata?"

The monkey chattered at the man.

"A man flew through the air …" translated the giant. *Ooo-ah ook-ahk.* "And then he threw some moss at you …" *Eeek eeek ahk.* "Where?" The monkey pointed towards the branch where Burble had landed.

The yakker quickly released the fronds and sought to bury himself within the vast fountain of greenery that was the fern. He couldn't believe it: a *monkey* was trying to grass him up! And what was worse, he was doing so to a man who *thought* he could speak with animals – a trait peculiar to those who had spent rather too long on their own. The fact that the stranger had accurately translated the chimpspeak eluded Burble for the moment: he was convinced that the man was mad. The clincher, though, was the fact that the man had called his simian chum 'cheetah'. Burble shook his head. *Absolutely barking!*

"Bananas …" said the man, waving a finger at the chimp. "I mean it! If you keep making up stories, I'm not going to give you any more!"

Burble risked another glance. He saw the man bring his legs up and heel-kick the branch upon which he was sitting.

"*Um-gower Trantor!*" yelled the madman.

A loud trumpet greeted this request, and the tree bough appeared to move. A moment later the head of an immense, grey beast resolved from the shadow of the foliage. Burble gawped. It had two giant, curving horns and a long, writhing nose. The madman kicked the beast behind one of its enormous ears and it veered off into the forest. The noise of crushed plant life followed in its wake.

Burble stared after them. What a magnificent animal! It must have been at least twice the size of a yak, with horns far bigger than anything he had seen before. He *had* to have it! The others would turn every-shade-of-green-on-the-palette-of-a-landscape-artist in envy if he turned up riding *that*. Burble resolved to make the thing his own. Stealing such a prize would, after all, be no problem for *The Shadow*.

He leapt off his branch and followed the mounted man.

Tracking the huge, grey beast was about as difficult as following the footprints of Robinson Crusoe along the beach of a tropical paradise. A broad, flattened path – with the occasional waist-high dung heap – marked its progress. As Burble ambled along he considered the running costs of such a mount: all that crap implied it used a lot of fuel, while parking might also be difficult. The yakker chewed on his lip thoughtfully. The logistical problems would be great, but ... the expression on the face of that git Grunt *alone* would make up for any amount of expense.

The crashing in front of him stopped. Burble cautiously edged forward and took up a position behind a fallen log. Before him was a clearing containing a small pond and, amongst the arboreal wealth, one particularly large tree. A beautifully constructed house rested within its branches. The house was made from neat slats of wood and flower-patterned curtains hung across its two windows.

Burble watched as the madman tied his beast to a rope made of creepers. This ran up to a pulley in the top branches of the main tree, then down to a small wooden cage. As the man went about his business, Burble noticed that he was dressed in a brown loincloth, which again reminded him of his barbarian enemy. He wondered whether the two men might be related.

"Raise!" bellowed the madman. The grey beast walked slowly forward, drawing the cage upward and propelling the man to the upper reaches of the tree. He stepped onto a platform outside the house and turned to look within ... rapidly ducking as a frying pan sailed through the space recently vacated by his cranium.

"Just where the *Hull* have you been!" shrieked a female voice from within. "You've been out with the troop again, haven't you? Well, your dinner's spoilt so I gave it to the dog." A thin, white arm emerged through one of the windows and smashed a rolling pin against a circular open cage that – Burble now noticed – was situated just below one of the windows. The slumbering canine occupant immediately jumped to its feet and started running on the spot as though being chased by Bulabothel himself. The cage started to revolve. The yakker suddenly understood that it was some form of wheel. Another creeper was attached to the wheel and this led down to the pond. As the creeper wound up it brought a now-full bucket of water with it.

"If you're sober enough," continued the harridan, scarcely pausing to draw breath, "then you can get into the kitchen and put up those shelves. You promised to do it *weeks* ago, and all you've done since is lounge around with your mates, grooming each other." The rolling pin thumped down and the dog stopped. A feminine head appeared through the window to collect the bucket. The woman was fairly attractive, but currently had a beauty handicap: her hair was in cone curlers. She withdrew inside and continued her harangue. "I don't know. After you've eaten all those ticks and bits of dead skin its *no wonder* you don't want to come home to my cooking!"

"But June," protested the man, "I'm Tarsal, King of the Apes! Mutual grooming is part of the fabric of primate society. It is the glue that holds us together! It's even *more* important than marking out your territory, and *that's* pretty damned important. What do you think I've been doing for the last four hou— *ugh!*"

The water from the pond made a reappearance, this time *sans* bucket. Tarsal was drenched.

"Oh god – you *disgust* me! Out pissing against trees again! I should have listened to mother! With all your binge drinking to keep your bladder full, it's a wonder there's any water left in the pond! And that's another thing. *Don't you dare* wash that elephant in there again. I don't even want to *think* about what I found at the bottom of the kettle this morning!"

An elephant! thought Burble. So *that's* what the beast was. He had heard of Cannibal – of course – but he had always assumed that the legendary warrior's famous mount was just a sort of big fluffy horse. Well, while this Tarsal was distracted by his shrewish mate, Burble was going to have it away with his transport!

The Shadow crept from behind his log and sprinted across the clearing to the elephant. The beast looked down at him with a faintly stupid expression on its face. It fanned out its two ears in the elephant equivalent of a shrug. And then it helpfully raised a leg, creating a step which allowed the Angel to climb onto its back.

Burble looked at the complex knot that fixed the cage-raise to the beast's neck. He tutted to himself. Such a knotty problem required a classic solution. He produced a knife and hacked through it. It was only in the split second before the last strand parted, however, that the yakker suddenly realised the error of his ways. His face scrunched in terror as the creeper broke and sizzled into the sky. A short heartbeat later, the unsecured cage crashed to the ground a *very* short distance away.

The arguing in the house stopped abruptly. Two surprised faces peered out of the window.

"Someone's stealing the car!" screamed June. "Stop him! Help ... *joyriders!*"

Tarsal stood in the doorway, beat his chest, and cupped his hands to his mouth. Before he could let rip with his characteristic yodel, however, a rolling pin bounced off his head. "Cut out that crap," shrieked his wife, "and get down there at once. Stop him!"

Cursing, the man made to grab his emergency escape vine – only to find that Cheata had beaten him to it and was already swinging away.

"Too late, pal!" jeered Burble, thumbing his nose at the temporarily stranded ape king. He raised his legs and kicked the elephant behind the ears. Nothing happened. Of course! The man had given a command. Now what was it? "*Er-Botham!*" he cried. The pachyderm did not move. "*Eh-Boycott!*" Still nothing. "Fuck, fuck, fuck!" What *had* the man said? It was a cricketer of some sort, but which one? He looked back and saw Tarsal descending from his house by leaping from branch to branch. "*Errn-Willis!*" The ape man neared the ground. "*Um-Gower!*" And at that, the elephant started to amble off at the pace of an arthritic grandmother with two hundredweight bags of coal on her back. Burble kicked it desperately. "*Um-Gower pretty bloody quick!*"

But the elephant's pace did not alter. Desperation started to creep up on the yakker. He decided on a more direct approach to the animal-master relationship: he leant back and dug his dagger deep into the pachyderm's ample buttocks. The beast let out a huge trumpet and took off like a rocket-powered boulder-of-fury. The howling ape man was left trailing far, far behind.

"Ah, this is more like it," cried the elated Burble. The elephant crashed through the jungle, squashing all in its path. But then, suddenly, from right in front of him, the Angel caught sight of Tarsal's chum. The chimp swung out of the trees, straight for his head. Just as Burble was expecting a prehensile boot in the face, the monkey raised up its legs and released an immense stream of brown effluent straight at him. The stinking discharge splattered across the man's face and chest. Unfortunately for the chimp, however, it had not calculated its angle of attack properly, carelessly failing to take into account the extra height afforded to Burble by virtue of his horned helmet. As Cheata swung past, legs asunder, he clipped one of the sharp projections ...

The combined effect of flying crap and monkey genitalia almost dislodged Burble from the elephant ... but not quite. He regained his balance and goaded the elephant back towards the veldt.

<hr>

"You'll never find him," bickered June, as she watched her man roll his spare loincloth into a thin band and tie it around his head. "He's probably been stolen to order by some lackey of a master criminal who specialises in the international vehicle trade. By the end of the week some rajah will be swanning around the sub-continent on his new ride oblivious to the fact that it used to be the proud possession of an ape king living thousands of miles away."

Tarsal ignored his wife. He clipped his knife onto his vine belt.

June sensed that this line of argument was getting nowhere, so she changed her angle of attack. "Anyway, how are you going to recognise him? By now they'll have re-sprayed him and tattooed false number plates onto his arse. He might have even been taken by a thief working for a chop-shop operation. By the time you get to him he could be in several pieces, ready to be welded to other bits of animals to make a super beast of burden."

His packing complete, Tarsal turned to address his wife. "He wants Trantor for himself and his own pleasure. I could see it in his eyes. Whatever that pleasure is I dread to think. I cannot allow my faithful Trantor to undergo such trials. Many a time he has saved my life. I must now repay that debt. I, Tarsal, will track them to the ends of the earth." Tarsal walked out of the door to his house and took hold of a vine in two hands. He turned back to address June. "Besides, the troop demands vengeance for the humiliation suffered by Cheata. Never again will he be able to embarrass us at dinner parties by furiously masturbating over the canapés. Poor Cheata!"

"Cheata Cheata Cheata!" screeched June. "It's not about Trantor at all, is it, it's about Cheata! You lads! It's always the troop first and everyone else second! Well, if you think I'm staying here while you go gallivanting off around the countryside, then you've got another think coming. I'm off to stay with the Prester-Johns!"

Tarsal shrugged his shoulders. "A king's gotta do what a king's gotta do!" He swung out into the jungle.

———•◦•———

"Any sign of him?" asked Trespass, as he emerged through a tall stand of grass.

Bruce had been left to wait at the rendezvous point: a lone scraggy tree a stone's throw away from the edge of the jungle. He shook his head. "Nah. The wee runt's probably fallen doon a crack in the mud. The others are back though. They're cookin' dinner." He gestured in the direction of a flattened path in the grass that curved behind the tree. Light grey wisps of smoke could be seen curling into the pale blue sky. "Prime steaks."

"Cooie," came a voice from the jungle's edge. "I'd like mine rare please." An immense grey head, two tusks, and a writhing snout appeared through a patch of fronds. The head was followed by a body the size of a house. Atop this improbable creature rode the missing yakker. The beast sauntered towards the two men.

"Burble!" shouted the pair in unison.

"I smelled the cooking and reckoned only you lot would have the nerve to eat the local honcho's prize beef."

"What the *Hull* is that you're sat on?" stammered Trespass. "And why has it got a snake in the middle of its face?"

"It's not a snake, arsewipe, it's a nose." Burble grabbed hold of the beast's ears and gave a tug, drawing it to a halt. "Do you like it? It's my new elephant. I borrowed it *permanently* from the local nutter. Now where's that git Grunt? I want him to see this."

Bruce took a worried step back as the elephant's trunk attempted to grope his face. "Why? Dae ye think he might like tae mate wi' it?"

"I wouldn't put it past him. Where's the grub?"

Bruce led the men to their comrades, who were ministering to hot pieces of ex-cow. "Look who's finally turned up."

"'Oly Clovory!" yelled Grunt, leaping over the fire. "There's a giant 'orned demon with 'im!"

Burble chuckled. "Ignorant sod! It's an elephant. I've traded up. More powerful than a Harleck Dravidian, safer than a Volvic, and as destructive as a barbarian siege engine: the choice of the discerning owner. Look upon it and weep, you buggers!"

"Er," mused Frunge, who was always, mentally, some distance behind events, "that don't look like Thruster. Why's he all bloated and grey and stuff? Is he ill?"

Burble sighed. "No, bruv, it's an el-ef-ant. Like Cannibal."

"Cannibal?" Frunge looked around in confusion. "I thought he was a man from Carth ... er, Card ..., um, *Cardiff*. You mean *it's* a man from ..."

"No! I mean it's like the thing he rode. You know. When he crossed the Palps to sort out the Tomans?"

"Then where's Thruster?"

Burble shrugged. "Last I saw of him he was heading east, chasing after a local cow." He leant down and whispered into his mount's ear. In response, the elephant raised one leg, causing the other men to beat a hasty retreat. Burble clambered onto the leg and hopped to the ground. He approached the fire and helped himself to one of the steaks.

"Hey ... wot's that on your horn?" asked Frunge, pointing to Burble's riding helmet. Before the beardless-one could speak, his brother had plucked off the small, red berry and dropped it into his mouth. "It's pulpy," noted Frunge. "Not bad though. A bit like a monkey nut."

Burble's eyes widened as he made certain mental connections. He decided to say naught.

"Right, enough of this," growled Trespass. "I've worked out our next move." He plucked up a hot steak with his knife and took an experimental bite. "Ah … ooo … hot …" The others sniggered. Trespass spat out the morsel and glared at his crew. "Shut it!" He scowled his men into silence. "Right, now listen up. While you lot were trying to control your beasts back in Savage-ville, I managed to keep hold of mine. Mastery, or what! Anyway, I followed the barbarian as he fled the stampede." Trespass took a smaller experimental bite of his steak. "They went south, down a path through the jungle. Now let's eat up and move out and … *oy*!" Trespass wrestled his dinner from the questing trunk of the elephant. "Burb – tell your beast to bugger off and get its own grub!"

———◆◆◆◆———

"Sniff like you've never sniffed before!" demanded Chief Lottomoos. "Smell out the demons who panicked my herd and … and … and … did *this* …" Lottomoos stared at the half-butchered carcass in front of him. Tears began to roll down his face.

The assembled warriors stared at Ozbondo expectantly, knowing they were safe from the Shaman for the moment. The witch doctor in turn appraised the assembled wimpi. They were the Chief's men: his son and the surviving members of the Feral Hippos were still out trying to round up the Royal Herd. Now was not the time for disobedience.

"Your majesty," asserted Ozbondo confidently, "they will be crocodile food by the end of the week!" He too wanted to get his hands on the wizards … or at least, on *one* of them. *Mr Arseface indeed!*

"Sod the crocodiles," declared Lottomoos. "For this insult I'll eat them myself. But you …" he raised his voice hysterically and pointed, "*you* will be crocodile food yourself if you do not find them." He leant down and wiped the tears from his cheeks onto the back of the Royal Handkerchief. The kneeling man gave the traditional exclamation of thanks with more than usual enthusiasm. After all, tears were something of an improvement on his usual fare.

Ozbondo managed to hold his temper in check … *just*. He gave a little bow so that he could mask the anger on his face. "It will be done! The wizards will be found, and then they will rue the day they kicked me in the … uh, they *desecrated the Royal Herd of Ubundi*." Ozbondo straightened, and his expression was now about as serene as it ever got. But his mind was already working frantically. First, he would corrupt the wimpi and bring it under his control, and then he would catch the demons and rescue the Chief's magic headring. And once he possessed that, he would truly be able to mount an attempt to wrest control of the tribe from Lottomoos.

"I have thrown the knuckle bones," declared the sniffer-out of wizards. "And the fates have foretold that the best time to depart on such a hazardous journey is at the crowing of the cock, two days hence." *When my son is back and can accompany us*, he added, under his breath.

While Terry scouted the way ahead along the jungle path, the monk leant against a tree trunk and *harumphed*. He looked at the map again and shook his head. The cross had not moved: it still rested over the city of Copros.

"I don't know what you're moaning about," complained Roffo. "Gramps once told me about Copros. He said it's a city full of art and intellect and whatnot."

"Full of something," muttered the monk. "Sometimes Hull not involve fire and knitting needles. Sometimes Hull involve company of other people. Ever been to pretentious dinner party? Or poetry recital?"

"Well, no," replied Roffo, using a small stick to poke at a morsel of food that had become lodged between two teeth. "But I don't see how it could be any worse than a place where you have to walk around with no kit on. Or a place where *you* are part of the menu."

"Foolish youth!" tutted the monk. "Know nothing of real world."

"I know plenty! Like, I know … *urgh*!" Roffo's toothpick suddenly moved, revealing itself to be a heavily disguised insect. "Bloody jungle!"

Terry's face appeared over the top of a large fern. "Ey-up! Come and see what I've found. It's a lost city!"

"Oh no!" moaned Roffo. "I hate lost cities! Gramps used to tell me about them. They're always inhabited by foul fiends who like to suck your brains out of your bottom. Or perverts who like to cut you open, add parmesan cheese, and eat your intestines like spaghetti."

"I don't think so," said Terry, trying to sound upbeat. "I've given it a quick once over and there doesn't appear to be anything sinister about it."

"No, that's coz all the inhabitants are hiding and waiting for the night. They're probably ghouls, or zombies, or evil worshipers of Bulabothel who hate the light."

"Uh, well then," said Terry, "why are all their temples filled with carvings of flowers? They *must* have been a peaceful race. Come on."

Still grumbling, Roffo followed the barbarian, with the monk bringing up the rear. The city was only a short walk away. They emerged from the jungle amidst a ruin of broken brick buildings. The jungle had done its best to reclaim the land: the cobblestone streets were broken up by the roots of trees growing sporadically along their lengths, while other trees grew within the houses, piercing through collapsed roofs and poking branches out of empty window frames. Terry led them along one foliage-cluttered thoroughfare to what must once have been the main square. He indicated a tall building that was still largely intact. It was bell-shaped, with a steeple rising to the sky.

"Interesting," observed the monk, as he traced the designs in the brickwork beside the empty oblong space where a wooden door had once hung. "Carvings appear to depict Yellow Lotus flower. Hmm. Very dangerous plant."

"In knew it!" declared Roffo. "This is the city of the Killer Tomatoes! At any moment now we're going to be throttled by strangling creepers, or squashed by giant raspberries, or ... or ... *abused* by giant, perverted walking cucumbers! And once we've been beaten to the ground we'll probably be used us as living grow-bags for the offspring of some demonic garden produce!"

"No no, foolish one! Plant only dangerous if eaten. Flower of lotus bush renowned throughout world as bringer of forgetfulness. But there many different varieties, yielding many different forms of oblivion. For instance, there famous variety mentioned in *The Oddity* that cause you to forget way home. Another variety called Stink Lotus cause you to forget to wipe arse after visit toilet. This variety is *Yellow Lotus*. It cause you to forget inhibitions."

"Well, that doesn't sound too bad," commented Terry.

"Oh, *very* bad," replied the monk. "If lose inhibitions, start picking nose in public, or wearing underpants on head, or propositioning gorgeous girlfriend of nastiest man in world. Just think what else might do!"

The thought of streaking naked through the streets of Cross-My-Way filled the minds of both Terry and Roffo. It brought a grimace to the face of the barbarian and, for Roffo, awoke the slumbering

298

memories of a drunken night of revelry that he had yet to live down. Roffo shuddered.

"Go find safe place to sleep, then find water," instructed the monk. "I look for flowers. Very valuable if know how to use them." The monk turned to leave, but then turned back to his comrades as an afterthought. "Apologise now if come back with finger up nose."

<hr />

Manis stared at the mechanical Longman-dispensing device and pondered its merits. Where the expenditure of money was concerned he had the diligence of an accountant, the insight of a logician, and the remorseless efficiency of a calculator. He now ran through the relevant facts in his mind:

1. It was undeniably true that many men came to his inn to partake of a certain ale, and then went home to their partner (or someone else's) for a night of unbridled passion.
2. It was also true that many of these men wanted to take precautions against catching diseases and fathering unwanted children.
3. It was highly likely that such men would pay money for this protection.
4. It was a possibility that, *in extremis*, they would pay a *lot* of money for this protection.
5. It was even a *likelihood* that they would pay *too much* money for this protection, especially as they tended to be drunk and the machine before him did not give change.

Manis smiled. His voucher scheme was proving a roaring success: people had resignedly taken to drinking the ten pints of normal ale required to gain enough 'Profligate Points' to entitle them to buy a pint of Mardon's. He then frowned, because this thought brought him on to the negative accounting:

6. It was also true that most men tried to collect all of their vouchers during the course of a single evening and subsequently weren't able to keep *themselves* vertical, let alone anything else.

Manis chewed on his lip. And the conclusion was? The conclusion was that, for many of his customers, inserting things into little slots was out of the question. And the slot on the machine in front of him, where the money was supposed to go, was very little indeed. Manis could not see anyone being able to use it.

He shook his head. For a moment little sacks of coins had started to float before his eyes. "The big problem," he noted to the machine's inventor, "is that we have to carry most of the punters to the door at the end of the evening as it is. What do you want us to do? Get the Berserker to carry them up here first" – they were presently standing in the *Gents* – "to see if they want something for later?"

"Manis, Manis," soothed Long Jon, who was doing a bit of moonlighting from his troubleshooting job, "trust me! This machine will make you a fortune!" Jon could also be tenacious where money was concerned. But money wasn't his driving force. Oh no. Jon was a man who had a dream, a vision, and it was of *rubber*. "You don't have to worry about BD, because most men buy their Longmans way before they're Fully Tanked. Market research has shown that most get theirs in after their fourth or fifth pint."

"Really?" Manis was impressed. "You've done market research on this, eh?"

"Indeed."

"Well ... why four or five? Why then?"

"If you want the psychological, physiological, or biological answer, alas, I cannot tell you. But it is clear that there is a correlation between the time of buying the Longmans and the propensity of the drinker to turn his thoughts towards the theme of sex." Jon grinned. "As you know yourself, after four or five pints even the most hideous creature – be it wife, girlfriend, best mate's girlfriend, best mate, or even woolly farmyard companion – suddenly becomes the most alluring, ravishing being in the entire world!" Long Jon gave a mischievous smile. "And it is at about this point – when your average drinker has turned his thoughts to sex and suchlike – that he needs to go for his second or third pit stop. And that is why the machine is put in here." The Purveyor of Devices of Sexual Education and Gratification sensed that his argument was starting to tell. "Now, put yourself in the punter's boots. Come on." Long Jon turned to face the urinal and Manis, somewhat dubiously, stood beside him. "Right, here you are, whistling perhaps ..."

"Or singing a bit. Yeah, I gotcha."

"Right, so you're singing a bit, and you're also looking around ..."

"Comparing yours with ...?"

"If that's your poison! Anyway, you also start to think. Great place for thinking, this. And you tend to think about good things. You get this nice, warm, relieving feeling spreading through your loins. And it makes you think: 'Cor, that bird by the bar ain't half a cracker', and such like. All happy. And you put it away, and then you turn ... come on, turn with me! And you turn and you see ..."

"The machine!"

"Precisely! And before you know it, out comes the money ... listen to it!" Long Jon closed his eyes and lifted a hand to his ear. "Ker-ching ker-ching ker-ching – money! And it's all *yours*! And what's more, there's no embarrassment at all for the punter! There's none of this: 'Oh dear, I need a packet for tonight but it's that Miss Gertrude at the alchemists, oh dear what can I do?', and you end up coming away with a comb or something. *In fact*, it's a bit of a macho thing to buy your Longies here. It says to everyone in view: 'Look at me, who's the stud around here then!' Indeed, I predict you'll even have blokes visiting your inn *just* to buy a pack, and quite probably stopping for a pint or two in the meantime!"

Manis's heart was beating fast now. He saw it all! This was going to make him rich! But he deliberately calmed himself and took a deep breath. The art of negotiation was to suggest that you were doing the other fellow a favour even when you were ripping him off. "Well, yes, I see some merit in the machine now. But you don't think it lowers the tone of the place?" Manis indicated the gaudy pink lettering which declared the machine to be 'Long Jon Con Dom's Patent Longman Dispenser'. He couldn't help smiling at the painting of the couple engaged in nude wrestling underneath though. They looked uncannily like Trespass and Sonia. *Madam* Sonia.

The tall sex-toy salesman looked around the toilet. It was a mixture of brown stains and chunky, pebble-dashed decor: a troop of vomiting Jackson Pollock impersonators could not have lowered the timbre of the place. He looked at the innkeeper from the corner of his eye. He had not been born yesterday. "I rather believe that the machine matches the decor. By that I mean it is stylish and done in the best possible taste."

"Hmm ... and what about the flavours of the *things*. Is this really what the punters want? *Quiche* flavoured? *Exotic banana*? *Pork Scratching* flavoured?"

"Indeed. They cater for a wide variety of tastes, from the refined vegetarian to the foul old strumpet with three teeth and no taste buds to speak of. And some are really rather nice and make a pleasant snack if your larder is empty. Try the *rum truffle* ones: my wife personally recommends them!"

The thought of finishing off a meal with a coffee and a pack of three did not particularly appeal to the innkeeper. "Right. But ... what about the religious nutters? You know some of them are against artificial contraceptives."

Long Jon raised a surprised eyebrow. "So *this* is where they come to relax after a hard day of being self-righteous!"

"Less of your sarcasm, mate," growled Manis. "You don't want the Berserker coming up here and accidentally vandalising your new machine whilst he's having a pee, do you?"

"Undoubtedly I would prefer him to use the urinal," replied an unconcerned Long Jon. "However, the machine is designed to withstand a few knocks, minimising maintenance costs. Keeps it *cheap* to run."

Manis had run out of gripes. He *had* to have the machine. He turned to it for a final examination. The lucky dip selection looked particularly interesting and he could see it becoming a great favourite. "Oh god, *cauliflower cheese* again, well, here's the last of my coins, hope I get *prawn coctail* this time." There was also a separate slot that dispensed skeleton keys guaranteed to open any chastity belt. Useful! It had to be a winner. Besides, if the machine ever made a loss he could always send someone very large around to Long Jon's house to complain.

"Okay then ... you're on!" The beaming landlord thrust out his hand towards the inventor. "But don't forget: I'll be buying the Longmans in bulk, so I'll expect a discount ..."

And the haggling got underway in earnest.

———•◦•••◦•———

There are many mysteries in the universe, such as: how did 'The Birdie Song' ever get to Number One in the hit parade? And: how do food companies manage to dupe people into thinking the 'gifts' they get in their cereal boxes are really 'free'? And: how do teenagers ever make it into their twenties without first being lynched? And, ranking high among these mysteries, is: how does a city become 'lost'? And this is a real poser. It's not as if a soon-to-be-misplaced city gets out of bed one morning, says to its neighbour, Mr London, "Well, I'm just off to the shops then, see you later," and takes the wrong bus, never to be heard from again. How absurd! No, the fact that cities become lost cannot be *their* fault. They know exactly where they're meant to be *and they stay there*. So, it must be the fault of the inhabitants. Maybe *lost inhabitants* is a better way of putting it. But is that any more likely? A whole population getting up,

wandering off, and then forgetting where it left its city? Well, actually …
yes. Yes it is. We personally know quite a few people just like that …

But even more amazing than the mystery of the lost city, and just as mysterious, is this: why are lost cities always, and we mean *always*, inhabited by monsters?

The three adventurers set up camp in the Lotus Temple, just off the main square. They built a little fire in the centre of the overgrown floor, and then set out sleeping mats. Roffo soon slipped into a blissfully ignorant sleep.

"Is he out?" asked Terry.

The monk looked at the young barman, watched his chest heaving gently, and nodded. "In realm of Notia, goddess of dreams."

"That's good." Terry picked up his axe and started to whet it.

The monk put aside his lionskin rucksack. He had been filling this up with Yellow Lotus flowers, which he had earlier collected from the grounds of a number of ruined temples. He brought out the sharpened chopsticks on which he had previously been working and started to whittle another one.

"When do you think it'll come? Midnight?"

The monk nodded. "Always way."

"Lots of little ones, or one Big Mother?"

"Usually just big one."

Terry grimaced. "It's going to dribble a lot, isn't it? I hate that. Drool all over the place. As sure as night follows day."

"Probably."

There was silence for a while. From outside, there came the occasional chirrup of insects, the croak of tree frogs, and the flutter of wings. The fire began to die. Midnight approached. And then they heard a cracking of twigs.

"Well, here it comes. Maybe we can reason with it?" Terry got to his feet.

The monk shook his head. "Probably not. Monsters stupid. Just hope it doesn't roar. Got splitting headache."

"Yeah, and it'll wake Roffo. Ah, here it is …"

Through the entrance to the temple strolled a ten-foot-tall ogre, covered in hair, entirely without clothes, and carrying a club. Unspeakable drool cascaded down its chin. It saw the men and opened its mouth to roar …

"*Shhhhhhh!*" went the monk, holding a finger to his lips. "Headache! If roar, I throw chopsticks through throat. Savvy?"

The monster snapped its mouth shut and nodded. It looked between the two men, then focused on Terry. Its eyes bulged. It recognised the form of its nemesis: a form genetically ingrained into the brain of all monsters; a form invariably associated with the transmogrification of big monsters into lots of little pieces of big monsters. "Ooooohhhh noooo!" it whined.

"Look," said the barbarian, "we're not out for trouble, but we're not about to sit here and let you eat us, right? So, we can do this easy, or we can do this hard. It's up to you."

The ogre considered the barbarian. "Errrrrrrr. Okayyyy. Eassyyy!"

"Arm-wrestle? Right arm? Best of three? If I win, you bugger off, if you win I'll let you *try* to eat me. Fair enough?"

The monster nodded, realising that these was the best odds it was going to get. It sighed in relief when Terry thumped down its arm for the second time.

"I goooo," said the monster, "sorrryyyy tooo disturbbb."

"No problem," said Terry cheerily. "Good night."

Mr Wriggle flickered his forked tongue, smelling the air. He caught a scent that had, of late, become sickeningly common. *More* humans. This was getting ridiculous! They were just like buses: none for a year and then hundreds all at once.

"Wonder what'sss happened to Caliber?" said a voice from somewhere above him.

"Isss that you, Sssid?"

"Yesss, who elssse?"

Mr Wriggle looked up. Wrapped along the length of an overhead branch was a giant anaconda. It had a huge bulge – the size of small elephant – one-third of the way along its length. Mr Wriggle hadn't eaten for ages. That anaconda: what a bugger!

"Calibar?" asked Wriggle.

"Yesss, the ogre. Usssually take a heavy toll of travellersss."

"Oh … him! Probably laid up with indigessstion."

"Sss sss sss," laughed Sssid. "Got a bit of that myssself."

Bassstard, thought Wriggle. He turned his attention back to the path – or more formally, the J8 Jungleway – which cut a line from the plains of Ubundi to the Sortofbrowny Desert, via the land of Copros. He mulled over recent events. First there had been the three humans. The python had had no luck there. The young one had looked rather appetising, but the men had marched on out of sight before he could strike. Two days later there had been five more men: horrible, hairy brutes riding monstrous steeds. Wriggle had hidden in the bole of a tree and waited for them to pass. And two days after that there had been an entire wimpi from Ubundi riding War Ostriches. Such men were not to be messed with! That had been yesterday. And now there were more.

"Do you sssee anything up there?" he called to Sssid.

"Not yet ... afraid my belly'sss in the way, sss sss sss."

Sssod! Mr Wriggle slithered along the branch until his head was in the furthest leaves. The branch began to sag under his weight. But from here he could make out the travellers on the path. There were several dozen of them and, what's more, *they were already unwrapped and ready to eat. Brilliant!* The python began to drool. He would show that damned anaconda!

As the men trudged nearer, Wriggle's excitement began to grow. He slithered still further forward. Maybe, just maybe, he could reach down and grab one of the morsels by the head. He edged out further and further and ... *slipped out of the tree.*

The men below shrieked, but one shrieked louder than the rest. "Great Satyr, a snake! It's trying to *mate* with me! Help, save me, kill it!" But Wriggle was surprisingly quick for a reptile and he squirmed off into the undergrowth.

———◆•◆•◆———

The three travellers lounged on sumptuous cushions and awaited the fabulous feast they had been promised. Their host, Sheikh Aleg, sensed that his guests were growing impatient. He clapped his bejewelled hands and the scantily clad dancers ceased their gyrations. The girls bowed to their master and scurried from the tent. As the last one disappeared through the tent flap the Sheikh waved at a waiting servant, who also bowed before following the dancers. A moment later, several men and women entered through the flap carrying a variety of covered dishes, pots, and tureens. They arranged the containers on the carpeted floor in front of the four men.

"Ah, my friends," cooed the Sheikh, "I feel ashamed that I can offer you no more than this meagre fare. But when you are trading with the jungle tribes it is best to travel light, yes?"

The servants disappeared, but soon returned with yet more plates and pots. Two men struggled in carrying a large tray with a silver lid.

Others brought in bottles of wine, ale, and liqueurs. More trays – heaped with fruit and bread – followed.

Roffo stared at the forty or so dishes and smiled to himself. Being luxuriously entertained by a grateful client at the end of a hard day's questing was what *It* was all about. "If this is meagre," he squeaked, "then I'm going on a diet." He lifted the lid from a pot and goggled at its contents. Disconcertingly, the contents goggled back.

"Ah, sheep's eyes," enthused the Sheikh. "One of the delicacies of my people. You like them too, yes? I will get Abdou to pack you a jar of pickled ones for your journey."

Roffo smiled stupidly at his host.

The monk, meanwhile, had helped himself to another local delicacy, ladling part of the contents of a pot onto a wooden plate. "Ah, if not mistaken this Curse-Curse."

The Sheikh bowed. "It is clear I am in the presence of a well-travelled man." The merchant prince grabbed a handful of dried dates and plopped one into his mouth. "But do you know how the dish gets its name?"

"I know this," said Terry, who had chosen the soup as a starter. "It's from the chillies, isn't it? They cause you to curse when you put the food in, and then curse when you pass the food out."

"Excellent!" cried the Sheikh.

The monk nodded. "Also used in some cultures as instrument of torture. Barbarians use chillies for this, la, Terry?"

"Er, yeah," the barbarian had become distracted by the wriggling mass he now found at the bottom of his soup. "Um, what are … *these*?" he lifted his bowl to show the Sheikh.

"Ah, the maggots of the Yettoran Blow-Me Fly. May I?" He scooped up several squirming morsels and stuffed them into his mouth. "Delicious!"

"Um, there's not any maggots in the fruit is there?" wondered Roffo, who had decided to start with something he knew. "I mean, for added flavour and stuff?"

"Alas no. Would you like some put in? *Abdou!*"

"NO! I mean, no thanks, don't go to any trouble, really, I'll just, yes, I'll, um …" He put the apple back down, just to be on the safe side.

The Sheikh looked at the young man askance, then shrugged. "As you wish. Now," he turned to face the monk, "let us talk business while we eat, yes? What do you want for the Lotus flowers?"

"Horses," said Terry. "We need horses."

"There are some in the blue bowl," replied the Sheikh, facing Terry.

"Your young friend has just helped himself to some."

"*Splutttt!*"

"Oh dear. A little salty, yes?"

"I meant *to ride*," clarified the barbarian. "And a pack mule."

"Yes, men of action should not tire themselves out by carrying excess baggage around the jungle. You shall have one. What else do you require?"

"Gold," said the monk. "May have to spend time in Copros."

Sheikh Aleg wiped his grubby hands on his black tunic then selected a goat steak from a tray on the carpet. He nodded twice at a large guard standing by a wooden chest. This man opened the chest and plucked two bags from it. He brought these over to his master, who indicated that he should lay them at the monk's feet. "That should keep you for a month or two, yes?"

"Your price fair," declared the monk, who was a keen judge of the worth of a heavy bag of tinkling metal. "May your gods grant much success in other trading ventures." He picked up the bags and hid them in the folds of his leather habit.

"Thank you, my friend. Let us drink a toast!" He clapped his hands. Four maidens appeared and filled the beakers of the men. "To all our quests!" The Sheikh quaffed his drink in one go. The other men, seeing this, did likewise.

"Hmm. Interesting flavour," noted Roffo. "Warm. Pungent. A bit sweet. What is this, Your Excellency?"

"Ah, it is a special drink to us. It is the fermented bile of the camel. Would you like some more?"

Roffo stared at their host in horror.

"Piece of piss!" laughed Trespass, referring to the ease with which the Angels had managed to follow the barbarian and his comrades. The path cut through the undergrowth by the scything blade of Terry's axe could have easily accommodated a pair of elephants walking abreast.

"Yeah," laughed Grunt, "they must be right *idiots*. Even *we* would of tried to 'ide our trail!"

"Och, maybe they dunnae knoo they're bein' followed," suggested Bruce.

"Or maybe they just forgot," said Trespass.

"Or maybe," mused Burble, "they don't care."

"Er, who are *they*?" asked Frunge.

Burble leant down from his great height and patted his brother on the head. "Never mind, bruv, it's not important."

They rode on in silence under the forest's green canopy. The press of trees combined with the hot and humid atmosphere to give an oppressive feel to the morning. As the day wore on, however, the dense undergrowth began to thin, and by the time Grunt's rumbling stomach announced that it was time for lunch the odd sunny clearing had begun to appear. The Angels took their meal in one of these glades, but were soon on their way again. By the time a further half-hour had elapsed, all that was left of the jungle was a scattering of small copses dotted about a landscape of dry, brown grass.

They came to a faint path that led up the gentle slope of a boulder-strewn hill. From the peak of this they could see a city perched on another hill in the distance. The surrounding panorama was completely different to that of the jungle, with gnarled olive trees sprouting between fields of grape vines, which matted the steps of man-made terraces.

"Aha!" exclaimed Trespass. "That must be their destination."

"Copros," declared Burble. "That's what Gubbu called it." Gubbu had been the leader of a cannibal foraging party whose path they had crossed two days previously. He and his cohorts had left the Angels alone, reasoning that any meat that smelt *that* bad and contained *that* much fat could not be good for them. The cannibals had, however, hung around long enough to pass on some information concerning the local geography before making their excuses* and leaving.

"A major centre of the arts and whatnot," continued Burble. "It sounds like just the sort of place where people who are looking for something might find the sort of thing they're looking for, um, *as it were* …"

"I dunno about you," said Grunt, "but I vote we look up a decent inn when we get there. Me throat's drier than that stream emptied by Burb's elephant yesterday."

"Aye, yon elephant's a damned nuisance," grumbled Bruce, as he kicked his steed into motion and started down the hill. "Did ye see hoo pissed aff that actor bloke wiz who'd got there jist afore us? Kept screaming aboot hoo it wiz meant tae be the source o' the Nial, an' hoo it wiz noo shorter than it wiz supposed tae be, sae wiznae the longest river on the continent naemore."

Trespass frowned at the highlander's back as he started after him.

* The old one about having their neighbours over for dinner and not wanting to be late.

"I thought it was explorers who went looking for the source of rivers. You sure he was an actor?"

"Aye, said he wiz Richard Burton."

"Burton?" piped up Burble, who had ignored the actor's complaints at the time. "I read one of his books once ... er, well, or should I say *looked at the pictures*. Disgusting it was! I lent it to Grunt and when it came back all the pages were stuck together!"

"I told you, I spilt jam on it," growled the yakker, from his position at the rear of the pack.

"Yeah, I heard you liked a quick cream tea in the afternoon!" taunted Burble.

"Right, the midget dies!" Grunt kicked his heels into the side of his yak and set off after the smallest of the yakkers, who was now in full flight down the hill.

Trespass tutted to himself and led the others after the feuding pair.

CHAPTER 14

OF LEXICONS AND LAVATORIES

THE ADVENTURERS rode along a dusty road winding between wide-spaced cypress trees and olive groves. Every now and then they trotted past mule-drawn carts loaded with amphorae of wine – or stacked with logs, or with boxes of fruit – and occasionally they passed strolling, toga-clad men. They followed the road as it ran towards a palace-sized boulder covered with a thin topsoil and half a dozen straggly black trees. The road swung to the right of this obstruction, then straightened, passing through a stone arch that marked the city's limit. Through this, the three men caught their first clear view of Copros: rows of tan-coloured buildings marching up the flanks of the hill on which the town was perched. Most of the buildings were two storeys high, while a number of the grander ones sported porticoes.

The three men pulled up in front of the arch.

"Well," declared Roffo, "it doesn't look that bad to me. Looks quite attractive, actually."

"Yeah," agreed Terry, "and the thing I really like about it is that no-one's threatened us with spears yet …"

Roffo nodded. "*Or* forced us to take our clothes off!"

The monk gurned in displeasure, pulling a face like that of a man trapped in a lift with the *Il Petomane Re-Enactment Society*. "Look beyond superficial! This place Hull on earth!" And with that he shuddered.

While they paused in the shadow of the arch a group of three men came up behind them. The men, being intent on their conversation, casually circumnavigated the party with barely a sideways glance.

"… so, I said to him, *made mostly of water? How can we be made of water? We'd just soak into the ground! And when it's hot, we'd evaporate. And if there's a fire, you don't throw yourself onto the flames to put it out, do you?*"

"Ha, just so," said the second man. "What nonsense! I personally concur with Portup's Thesis that we are, in fact, fundamentally made of *earth*. Look at the evidence! You go to the loo and what comes out? Mud! And the by-product of drinking anything is a sort of dirty yellow liquid, just like water passing *through* mud."

"Yes, Portup is a clever fellow. The evidence for his wise theory is incontrovertible. For example, when you die and decay you become indistinguishable from the surrounding earth *because* you're essentially the same stuff."

The third man leant against the arch and mopped his brow with a handkerchief. "But I wonder about the human skeleton?" he mused. "Could that be made of stone instead?"

"Portup suggests that bone is made of Compacted Mud Concentrations," said the second man, confidently. "Which in many ways is much the same thing. But the important thing to remember is that CMCs are still, like everything else, composed of the fundamental particle: the Mudom."

"Compelling stuff! I think we are in agreement then," said the first man. "Earth it is! Right. What mystery of the universe shall we solve next?"

"What about The Meaning of Life," said the second man. "I have one or two views on this matter."

"Good show! May I start? Thanks. Now, have you heard the metaphor that *life is like a rice pudding* …?"

The three men continued out of earshot.

Roffo pulled a face and looked at the monk. "Loonies, or what? Mud? Damned fools! I thought everyone knew the fundamental element of the universe is fire …"

"Really?" Terry's eyebrows arched in surprise. "We were always taught it's *iron*."

The monk closed his eyes and winced.

The main road was lined with limestone columns carved in the shape of heroic figures bearing torches. It being daytime, the torches were unlit.

On their left, the adventurers passed a large building from which various *sloshing* sounds emanated. The monk assured his companions that this was entirely innocent, considering that the building was a bath-house. A little further on, in a recess in the hill just back from the road, they passed a large amphitheatre. The wide semi-circle of seating was half full. On the stage, a play was in progress, acted out by figures clad in green togas and wearing masks. The monk hurried the party on.

They followed the meandering road up the hill until they were near its summit, where the road straightened and ran into a large cobblestone square. Surrounding this were a score of grand buildings. The monk pointed out some of them: "University ... law court ... parliament ... public lavatory ... library!"

The library was the tallest and grandest building of the lot, being four storeys high, and broad. Its portico was lined with elaborate columns, and balconies ran along each level. The walls were painted with a variety of scenes with bookish themes: people reading books, or writing books, or surreptitiously stuffing books into their togas, or looking furtive and tearing out pages, or wearing spectacles and wagging fingers ...

"Wow," said Roffo. "I've never seen anything like it! It must be one of the biggest libraries in the world!"

The monk nodded in displeasure. "La – *is* biggest. Damn Boozer!"

"Eh?"

"Map fragment obviously in there."

"How do you know?" asked Terry.

"And why is that a problem?" wondered Roffo.

The monk gave a last, indigestive look at the library, then turned away. "Let us book hotel room, then get drink. Will tell all."

After booking in to *Ye Learned Oraculist*, a quiet little hotel just behind the main square, the three men sought out a place to have a drink. Behind the library they came upon *Olde Possum's Wine Bar*. They passed through its green-painted door and wove through neat little tables up to the bar. The walls were whitewashed, and bunches of grapes hung from the wooden rafters.

"I'll get these in," said Roffo generously. "Shop!"

A frowning, middle-aged gent approached the party from the opposite side of the bar. He wore spectacles and a red and white checked apron. The little hair remaining to him formed two tufty masses, one above each ear. He was in the process of drying a wine glass.

"Ah, barman!" said Roffo. "Three pints of your finest, if you please."

The barman's frown deepened. He placed both glass and cloth onto the bar, wiped his hands on his apron, and inspected the three men suspiciously. "I'm afraid we do not serve *pints* here. Oh no no *no*! What sort of establishment do you take this for?"

"You don't? This *is* a bar isn't it?"

312

"This is a *wine* bar, sir! We serve Cultured Alcoholic Products here. We have a wide range of wines: reds, whites, and greens. And we also serve a number of choice bottled lagers."

"*Bottled* lagers?" Roffo looked at his companions, but they simply shrugged in mystification. "Well, I guess we'll have …"

"Please, sir," interrupted the barman, "if you would kindly take a seat someone will be with you shortly to take your order."

"Um, right, but why can't you just …"

"Oh no no *no*! That *would not* be proper! If you please …" He gestured to a nearby vacant table. Roffo shrugged and led the adventurers to the indicated place. They had only just taken their chairs when Mr Shiny-Head reappeared, looming over the table with a small note-parchment in one hand and a quill in the other.

"Now, gentlemen, what would you like?"

"Um, wouldn't it have been easier if you'd just taken our orders at the bar?"

The barman blew out his cheeks. "Sir, in Copros we do not believe in standing at bars to drink, nor do we believe in waiting upon Employed Service Personnel when they should be waiting upon us. And further to your earlier implication, nor do we believe in quaffing great quantities of harsh drink like outlandish barbarians, er …" he suddenly noticed Terry and added hurriedly, "begging your pardon, sir, no offence intended! Oh no no *no*!" Wiping a nervous trickle of sweat from his brow, the barman continued. "Culture, refinement, delicate tastes, fine foods, intelligent conversation, and good form: these are the requisites of the civilised man; these are the rules by which we live. Without such customs one is scarcely to be distinguished from the savage beast!"

"Besides," added the monk sourly, "if serve at bar then not able to tack on whopping service charge."

The barman glowered at the oriental before turning back to Roffo. "So, if you please …?"

"Well, I'm not really into wines so I'll try one of your bottled lagers." Roffo looked at the monk, who nodded curtly. "Okay, make that two. And what about you, Terry?"

The barbarian scratched his unruly mane and scanned the interior of the bar. He cocked his head to one side and closed his eyes to prevent vision from interfering with his acute, wilderness-honed hearing. He raised his nose to the air and took three deep sniffs. Various civilised scents came to him: perfumes, soaps, *mild* body odour, the scent of gently cooked meat seasoned with herbs. He opened his eyes again and mentally reviewed what he had discovered. He'd heard no raucous bellows, harsh obscenities, or sounds of ringing steel; he'd smelled no human odours beyond the three d-w-w level (days-without-wash) and no stench of badly cooked food or raw meat. He nodded to himself. All of the patrons appeared to be local. Even so, he took a last look around the room just to be sure, licking his lips nervously. "Um," he began. "Er. Um. Er. Well …" he took a final deep breath. "*Bottle-of-Chardoneigh*," he said, in a verbal explosion. "Um. If you have any. Um. Please?"

Roffo and the monk looked at their friend through wide eyes.

The barman's eyebrows also arched in surprise. "Indeed, sir, indeed we do …" He turned to go, but Terry reached out and restrained him with one mighty hand.

"Um, excuse me, but, er, I'll have an '82, um, if you've any in stock?"

"A good choice, sir! Well, this is unusual, a cultivated barbar— … er, gentleman from foreign parts. Splendid!" The barman, released from Terry's iron clutch, turned on his be-sandalled heels and skipped back to the bar.

"Terry, you amaze me. Wine? What would your dad say?"

The barbarian smiled guiltily. "I dread to think. In my village we used to use the wine we pillaged from civilised parts as a sort of punishment. You know, if you'd done something wimpy …"

"Like climb a two-hundred-foot tree in mid-winter clad only in your loincloth just to rescue a cat?"

"Um, I told you about that did I? Um, yeah, well, if you did anything like that, the next time you went into the pub they'd force you to sit at a *special* table. The Torture Table it was called. It had a little checked tablecloth …"

"Like this?" Roffo held up one corner of their tablecloth.

"Yeah. That's right. And then they'd bring you a little bowl of carrots cut into strips with some sort of white dip. And then they'd serve you wine. And then they'd put a sign around your neck saying 'My Name is Algernon'. And *then* everyone would spend the evening laughing at you." Terry shook his head. "And if you got up to leave, they'd throw axes at you. Even so, some preferred the axes to the Reesling."

The barman returned with their drinks on a tray. He reverently set a sparkling wine glass and a musty old bottle in front of Terry. "Enjoy, sir! Revel in the delicate summer tastes, close your eyes and let the melody of the fruit of the vine take you to a peaceful hillside redolent with the perfume of flowers!" He turned to the other two customers.

"I assumed that *you* wouldn't want any glasses." He thumped two bottles of lager onto the table. There was a large slice of melon rammed into the business end of each. "Please try *not* to spill it on the table-cloth!" He gave a despairing sigh – a sigh that said *such is the common stock* – and returned to his duties.

Terry watched him go. "Hmm, I now see what you mean about the people here. Delicate *summer* tastes? Everyone knows the '82 Chardoneigh is evocative of autumn." The barbarian shook his head. "Coprolites … they're full of shit!"

"And what the bollocks is with this piece of fruit?" said Roffo, observing his drink. "Do you think that bloke was maybe doing up a couple of fruit salads and then got a bit confused?"

The monk sighed heavily. "No. Meant to be there. Meant to drink through it, thus …" He picked up his bottle, placed his mouth around the piece of melon, and glugged.

Roffo did the same. He upended his bottle, but nothing came out. Then he began to shake it. But the melon slice had completely jammed the flow. Roffo put his mouth around the neck and sucked mightily. At last he had to concede defeat. "Bollocks!" he cried, lowering the bottle. "Anyone got a penknife?"

The monk slammed his drink down. "Ugh! Do not bother! Vile, bland, tasteless, crap. Reminded of Budwasters."

"Really?" Roffo sighed, pushing his bottle aside. "What about yours, Terry?"

The barbarian held the tiny glass delicately in one muscular hand. A sublime smile played across his lips. "The barman might not know the difference between his Chardoneigh and his Bowjolly, but he keeps a good cellar!"

Roffo gave a lopsided smirk. "At least someone's happy." He turned to the monk. "Okay then. What's this about the library?"

"Library? Ah, yes, library is place where fragment must be." The monk flipped the piece of melon from his bottle and started sucking on it. "It natural choice. If wanted to hide something, then put there."

"But surely it's easy to find things in libraries? You just sort of look them up."

"In most libraries, true. But here … it different. No-one ever find anything. *Ever.* Problem of classification."

"Eh?"

"Okay. Say want to find book on something. Maybe on *elephants*. Where look?"

"That's easy. You look under a section on Animals, or whatnots, and then maybe look under the letter 'E'. Or under Mammals. Something like that."

"Wrong. In Copros people talk bollocks … think it make them seem intelligent and cultured. Coprolites believe that if person not understand you, it show *you* clever and *they* ignoramus. See? Also believe there no point using one word if can use three. So. Here, elephant also called Grey Betrunked Behemoth. Elephant is Common Word, Grey Betrunked Behemoth is Scientific Copric Word."

Roffo scratched his head. "So? I still don't see the problem. Find the Animal section and look under G."

"You mean Animal, or you mean Animate Organic Entity?"

"Whatever!"

"Still no good. Where find Animate Organic Entities? In Copros, might be under section about Animate things. Or Organic things. Or Entities. Also, because first scientific word is Grey, could be under Colours." The monk rolled his eyes. "Sorry. Vari-hued Light Reflectances."

"Er …"

"Precisely! Copros library is nightmare. Could take forever to find anything there. And that why Boozer *would* put fragment there. Awkward bugger!"

"We'd better get started then. Come on, Terry, there's no time to lose. I need to get back to a place where the only things you find in your drink are lumps of crud that guarantee you a hangover the next day. Drink up! And stop grinning like that! We've got work to do …"

———————

A little distance away, in the Lower Reaches of the city, a Situation was developing.

"You cannot park there, Sonny Jim!" said the officious-looking man in a black toga and a black peaked cap.

"And why not?" asked Trespass. "There's no yellow lines or nothing …"

A crowd had started to gather around the unusual visitors to Copros. After all, it wasn't often that the clean, artistically oriented, intellectually pseudic Coprolites came across the sort of hairy, unwashed creatures presently cluttering the street – and that was just the men. The visitors' mounts were even worse: a pack of rumbling yaks with chopped horns *and* an elephant.

"Civic Ordinance 56 clearly states that Organic Transport Vehicles over one tonne are prohibited from parking on the streets. There are designated parking lots for things like this ..." the traffic warden pointed at Burble's elephant.

"So how were we meant to know?" growled Trespass. The other yakkers began to cluster around him.

"If you visit civilised parts," declared the warden, getting out a clipboard, some mini-parchments, and a quill, "then you should make the effort to assimilate their statutory regulations ..."

"Their wot?" wondered Frunge, in bemusement.

The warden ignored him and started writing. "I'm afraid I'm going to have to give you all a ticket."

Parking tickets! Trespass's eyes widened and his breathing became harsh. *Traffic wardens!* He began to grind his teeth. He hated traffic wardens. Their very existence was anathema to him. As his temper neared boiling point he began to catch snippets of conversation from the growing crowd, carrying to him over the scratching of quill on parchment ...

"Oh, look at *him*," said a female voice, "he's *such* a brute ..."

"Yah. Uncivilised animals ..."

"And they *don't half* smell ..."

Grunt turned to face one fop. "Wot did you say?" he growled. The pungency of his breath caused the man to cower back and hold a hand to his nose.

"Ah, er, oh ..."

Grunt began to clench his fists.

"Right then," interrupted the warden, "here you go. Five tickets. One each." He handed the parchments to Trespass. "Kindly remove your beasts to an appropriate Zone of Temporary Vehicular Immobility, and then report to the law courts for justice to be ... *ooof!*"

Trespass's arm recoiled. Enough was enough! He smiled down at the wheezing warden and began to tear up the tickets. Suddenly, a shrill whistle blasted out and the crowd began to part.

"Look out," cried Burble, "it's the filth!"

"Rumble!" roared Grunt, planting a fist in the rough direction of the absent chin of his nearest critic.

Soon, the street was a swirling mass of scrapping, bellowing men.

———•◦•———

Head Librarian Grimulous adjusted the small pair of spectacles so that they perched on the tip of his nose *just so*. By tilting his head backwards he could now give the *appearance* of looking down on the three men. The condescending *Oh-What-Is-It-Now (sigh)* Look was one of the first things every trainee librarian learned, and it was an art at which Grimulous was master (as he was at *all* of the Twenty Disciplines of Dooey).

But something here was not right. For a start, one of the Inquirers was so tall that – in order to *appear* to be looking down on him – Grimulous had been forced to tilt his head so far back it was almost perpendicular to his body. He wriggled on his seat as though the massaging effect from his buttocks might somehow stimulate the pile of cushions to engorge with down and thrust him higher. He tried lifting himself with his hands on the desk but this only gave him another inch or so. Damn! He was starting to get a crick in his neck! But worse than this, there was little evidence of The Look having its usual effect. Normally, it cowered all Potential Book Abusers within eyeshot, yet two of the three men standing before the librarian's desk seemed totally oblivious to it. Indeed, only the youngster had adopted the proper Eyes-Downcast Position of Meekness that ensured the correct level of obedience, reverence, and respect. *Not enough frown, perhaps?* Grimulous tugged down the corners of his mouth still further until it seemed they must surely meet, with the probable consequence that his chin would fall off.

"We need help look—"

"*Shhhhhhhh!*" went the Head Librarian, with vicious intensity, putting into practice the Fourth Discipline.

"Yes yes," muttered the monk, in irritation. "Now if …"

Grimulous lost his composure. His mouth dropped open. That had been right on the button (indeed, he doubted whether Dooey himself could have done better) and yet it'd had no effect at all. "Urb," he gulped.

"Sorry?"

"Uh … did you not, ub, feel …"

"Why don't you sit up properly," said Terry. "That's bad for the posture, you know. You'll get a crick in your neck."

Grimulous's spectacles fell off in shock. His shoulders sagged. His frown let up slightly.

"There," said the barbarian. "Isn't that better?"

"Um, yes, thanks," mumbled the librarian.

"Humph!" scowled the monk. "Enough horseplay! Need help find map …"

Grimulous attempted a recovery shot. "Help?" He flicked his right index finger upwards. Time for the Fifteenth Discipline: The Wag …

"And if now wag finger at me," said the monk sternly, "I bite off.

318

Okay?"

The librarian dropped his head forward in utter defeat. How would he live this down? "How can I help you?" he asked meekly.

"Will the defendants please rise!" cried the court usher.

The Chief of Police gave Trespass a prod with his baton and then stepped back nervously. In spite of the fact that the prisoners had their hands tied behind their backs, and the additional fact that they were surrounded by thirty policemen, the Chief was not about to take any chances. It had taken half of Copros's police force over an hour to subdue the five strangers. The Chief examined his men. Most sported a disturbing number of bruises. All of the men – bar three – had one black eye, and the exceptions each had *two* black eyes. The force could have easily passed off as a roving band of pandas.

It was, however, difficult to tell whether the prisoners had been hurt at all, since the layers of grime on their skin acted as a kind of bruise camouflage. The men could have crept through a typical bar-room brawl without difficulty, emptied every drink, swiped the money from the till, and no-one would have noticed them. And, rather disconcertingly, they seemed to be enjoying themselves.

Trespass stood up and hawked onto the stone floor. "Yeah?"

"Please don't do that! Ahem. And now, for the court, please state your name and origin."

"Bog off!"

"Ah, I see …" The usher turned to the judge and shrugged his shoulders.

Judge Mincey peered at the defendants with horrified fascination. "It's going to be like that, is it?" He sat back and adjusted the silver wig perching atop his own white hair. A long beard flowed down his chest. His toga had a pair of silver judicial scales embroidered on the shoulders. The judge sighed and looked down at the parchment before him. He looked up. "I think we can dispense with the formalities here, given the, ah, *truculence* of the defendants. Perhaps someone could just tell me what the blazes is going on?"

The wooden benches facing the judge's podium were packed with tense-looking policemen and curious citizens. From the dishevelled state of most of the public it appeared that they, too, had been caught up in the ruckus.

Several seconds of murmuring followed. At last, a traffic warden stood up and waved to attract the judge's attention. "M'lud! Over here!"

"Yes?" The judge frowned at the sight of the warden, whose toga was severely ripped, and who wore the remains of his cap around his neck like a collar. Judge Mincey further wondered whether the traffic official's nose was *meant* to be that shape.

"Uh, it all began when I tried to give some tickets to these men. I was simply doing my duty … er, excuse me." The warden reached into his mouth and pulled out a loose tooth. "Damn! Sorry, m'lud."

"Quite all right. Go on."

"Well, I was simply informing them of their contravention of Ordinance 56. You see, one of the defendants possessed a Grey Betrunked Behemoth …"

"Eh?"

"An elephant, m'lud," whispered the usher.

"I see … extraordinary! Carry on!"

"Um, so I wrote them some tickets, but then that one," he pointed at Trespass, "punched me in the Sub-Abdominal Sensitive Zone! And *then* he ripped up the tickets."

The judge turned to Trespass. "Do you deny this?"

Trespass laughed. "I hate traffic wardens."

"I see. And the state of you fellows …" the judge indicated the assembled police "… I assume this came about as a result of trying to apprehend these men?"

"It did, m'lud," said the Police Chief.

The judge blew out his cheeks. "Well, I must say that this is the most serious case I have encountered in quite some time. And, given the defendants' clear lack of remorse for their actions, I am afraid that duty demands I impose a severe sentence. Indeed, I do believe that, in the interest of deterrence, The Maximum is called for."

The yakkers' good humour evaporated.

"Bollocks," murmured Burble. "I don't like the sound of this!"

"Yes indeed," continued the judge. "Chief of Police, I command you to take the defendants away and, for the period of *one whole week*, incarcerate them beneath *You Know Where*." The assembled audience gasped in horror. "May they rapidly learn the error of their ways." The judge banged his gavel. "Next case!"

As the prisoners were marched away to their place of internment, Trespass gave a nervous laugh. "Phew, and I thought they were actually going to, I dunno, bump us off or something. Burb, what's up?"

A cold sweat had broken out on Burble's brow. He had caught the sniggers of their escort and added up one and one to get two. "Uh, I think death might have been preferable. I know where they're taking us."

"Oh yeah?"

"Yeah. You *must* have heard of it too. It's a place of legend. A place of utmost horror …"

Trespass's brow furrowed. "Hang on a minute. We're in Copros. Not *the* Copros? Not *Copros* as in …" he turned as white as a field of snow.

Bruce got it too. "Oh God, *nae*, they're takin' us tae …"

"The *Toilet Pits of Copros* …" finished Burble.

And indeed they were.

"And this map … quite old is it?"

"Yes."

"Hmmm!" Grimulous rasped his chin in thought. He had led the three men into a little storeroom so that he could help them unobserved. "You could try Ancient Cartographic Artefacts."

"Write down," the monk instructed Roffo. He turned back to the librarian. "And where that?"

"Hmm, good question. If it's under *Ancient*, then it could be under the Temporal section somewhere. Perhaps Temporal Artefacts, perhaps Temporal References, or maybe even Temporal Literary Phenomena." He adjusted his spectacles. "Mind you, I can't say as I've ever come across a Temporal section. Epochal maybe?"

"Don't you know sections in library?" asked the monk in exasperation.

"Sections in the library?" Grimulous laughed. "Goodness gracious no! Of course not! How absurd! Regardless of one's ideals, one has to acknowledge the realities of existence! To learn the minutiae of Bibliographic Categorisation would take an eternity." He tilted his head back out of habit: he had chosen to ignore the barbarian – since it was impossible to look down on him without carrying around a ladder – but with the other two men limited librarianship *might* be possible. "Besides, there is no-one alive with the knowledge to teach it. Categorisation is what we call the Art of Science. One develops an intuition for where new works should go. In any case, it would be most unwise to be able to direct people to the books they wanted. The very idea! Why, they might then be tempted to *take them out*, with all the consequent risks that implies. And that would not do!"

"Then what *do* they teach librarians?" asked Roffo.

Grimulous frowned (which in this case was a good sign). The young man had shown signs of succumbing to his powers, unlike the other two devils. He leaned his head further back and *peered*. "Librarianship is a far more practical and skilful discipline than you could imagine, young man. I cannot relate the profound secrets of my Art to any but another of my sect. But, in essence, we are taught how to *protect* those noble objects that fill this wonderful edifice, to save them for posterity, and to prevent the soiled hands of the ignorant from dirtying their pages, or their minds from misrepresenting their truths."

"You mean," said the barman, feeling decidedly uncomfortable under that gaze, "that you sabotage the efforts of everyone who wants to find anything?"

"Quite so! What a sharp young man! Have you ever pondered a career change?"

The monk suddenly scowled, thrusting out a hand to clasp hold of the Head Librarian's toga. "Better not be bullshitting *us*!"

"Oh, ah, ho ho … of course not, sir! I can see that you are, um, men of wisdom and therefore worthy users of our civic amenities!"

"What I don't understand," said Roffo meekly, looking at his feet, "is why the map would be under a *time* category. Maybe I'm just being simple but, well, I don't really see *time* as being the, wotchacallit, *essential* feature of the map."

"Ah, I didn't say it *would* be under the Temporal category, just that it *might* be."

"But why won't it be under, well, Geography? Or something like that? That seems a more relevant classification."

"Relevant to whom? To you? Perhaps. But you must consider the nature of the classifier, the man who received this map into the library. How would *he* conceptualise it? Discover the nature of that past librarian and you are probably half-way there."

The monk shook the librarian to recapture his attention. "So, who was librarian at time of Boozer? What his name?"

"As to that, sir, I cannot tell. You will have to look it up …"

Terry managed to restrain the monk in the nick of time.

───⦁·⦁⦁·⦁───

Outside a window of The Bear, a small flock of pigeons clustered in cooing fascination.

"What's going on in there then?" trilled Junior, a young bird with purple-dashed wings. "What's that *horrible* noise?"

"Dunno," said Slim Greenchest, "but it sounds like they're torturing cats!"

"Coo, yeah," said Crapper, "let's hope so. Shove over then. Let's have a gander."

"Gander?" chortled Fat Sixtoes, "you *still* have that goose fixation then?"

"Yeah, he likes *big birds*," said Slim.

"Don't we all, coo coo!"

"No, I mean …"

"Yeah, we knows wot you mean!" Fats nodded knowingly. "Anyway, there's no cats in there."

"Then wot *are* they doing?" asked Junior.

"It's, well, they have a word for it. Wot was it?"

"Screeching?"

"Nah …"

"Wailing?"

"No."

"Disembowelling themselves wiv blunt spoons?"

"No, I mean, they has a *special* word for it. *Krappy-Okay*. Something like that."

"Wot," wondered Slim, "is that, like, some hideous disease wot makes you howl like a monkey in a cauldron of boiling water?"

"Nah. Apparently, they does it for fun. It's, like, *entertainment*."

"Well it's not entertaining me!" said Slim. "Come on. Let's get out of here before all the cats in town decide to come and join in."

The pigeons took to the air.

———•◦•◦•———

Inside The Bear, Hops cowered in one corner as far away from the makeshift stage as he could get. The Bear's misfortunes had called for desperate measures to get the punters back in, and surely there were no measures more desperate than this. Normally, the sight of his inn packed out would have cheered the innkeeper no end, but the singing was so excruciatingly dreadful that it formed a wall against which Hops could make no progress. He couldn't even get to the till to empty it. One more rendition of 'My-Way' and he swore he would go mad. In the meantime, he simply cringed in a corner and whimpered pathetically.

On the stage, the newly formed Spicy Girls were coming to the end of another song.

"Big finale, girls!" cried Red Sonia.

"*Those su-uh-mer … niiiii-iiights,*" concluded the strumpets.

Sporadic cheers, applause, and wolf-whistles erupted from the audience. Tankards were banged on tables and a pair of male underpants flew through the air to land at the feet of the lead singer. Sonia picked them up. "Ooo, ta!" she cried, enjoying her moment in the spotlight. "Ta very much! Right girls, what's next?"

"Uh, thank ye Spicy Girls," said Phlip, the mahogany-coloured compere, entering stage-right. "No need tuh sulk, ye'll get another go later, haha! Off ye go then! Shoo! Um, right, and next it's …" Phlip scanned down the list and sighed. Half of the requests were simply lewd, while the other half were blatant attempts at advertising. He shook his head. Awful Puns had requested *Amerigan Pie*. Dr Feare had, naturally, gone for *Doctor Doctor*. And, to judge by his request, Long Jon had managed to restock. He wanted *The Toys are Back in Town*. "Right, can I now have, um, Rude Lubblers, who's going tuh sing that catchy little number, um, '*It's not Fucking Unusual*'!" Phlip giggled in embarrassment. He nodded for the little four-piece band in the corner to strike up the appropriate tune.

With his tunic open to the navel and a gold medallion dangling against his hairy chest, The Human Obscenity took the stage.

———— ·•·•·•· ————

Roffo and the monk strolled along the torch-lit streets of Copros in a state approaching desperation.

"I don't believe it. Two hours we've been looking, *two bloody hours* and we still haven't found a single *proper* inn. This is madness!"

"Maybe should have stayed with Terry at Olde Possum's?"

"Sod that! There's still some of us who have principles, you know. I mean, wine is okay to gargle with after a meal, but you can't spend the evening drinking it, can you?"

"Hmm. Barbarian can."

Roffo shrugged. Terry had some funny habits and no doubt about it. Roffo could vaguely comprehend how someone might take a liking to cookery, or hanker after cats, but *wine*? And *gardening*? They weren't exactly the most stimulating of pastimes!

"Well, that's as may be, but I need a serious drink. You know. The sort you glug down in great quantities. The sort that makes you belch. The sort that makes you spend half the evening standing up, facing a wall, and peeing on your boots. That sort. I mean, that library is really doing my head in. We've been looking for three days now, and what have we found? Nothing! I just want to have a drink and forget about books for the evening." He pointed. "What about over there, then? What's that place?"

The adventurers crossed the road to a well-lit two-storey building, the front doors of which were propped open. A cheery murmur came from within. Three women and two men stood outside, chatting and sipping from wine glasses. They were a well-dressed group, each having gold or silver trim along the hems of their togas. One of the women wore a silver tiara on her head and another wore a rich silk scarf around her hair.

The questers stopped a few paces away from the group, caught in the light flooding out of the doors. "What do you reckon?" asked Roffo. "Looks a bit like a party to me. Maybe it's a *bring a bottle* job, eh? Maybe someone's brought some home-brew? Do you reckon it's worth a look?"

The monk shrugged. "Why not? Must be worth try."

"Good. Let's crash it!"

They skirted the well-to-do group and entered the building. In a broad, candlelit hallway they came upon a score of people in a number of gossiping groups, most of whom held wine glasses. The two men attempted to act innocuous. They took the first left off the corridor, which brought them into a large room with a high ceiling. Most of the inhabitants were clustered in one corner.

"Drinks table?" wondered Roffo. "Let's find out! Excuse me ... sorry ... 'scuse me ... whoops ... beg pardon ... *bollocks!*"

"Ai-la!"

The corner held no liquid-treasure-laden table. Instead, it held a large easel on which rested a most peculiar painting, looking like the product of a small child who'd had a fit while mixing paint. Purples and yellows and greens were splattered all over the canvas. A small depiction of a mutant bull appeared in one corner, and a melting sundial appeared in another.

"*What the fu—*"

The circle of people, who had made way to let the adventurers through, now closed in around them. Although the dozen or so people cast some peculiar glances at the two men, there were no comments of the "*Who the devil are these vagrants ... Jeeves, throw them out!*" variety.

The monk whispered into Roffo's ear. "Big mistake! This Art party."

"Eh?"

"Party to show off work of artist. Must go quick or brain melt."

"Art?" said Roffo, rather more loudly than he intended. "This mess? *Go on!*"

Silence descended over the circle of admirers.

"Um, what did I say?"

An elderly man cleared his throat. "So, you have your doubts about *Decorous Omni-Shades*, eh?"

"Um, Decor-what?"

"The painting, lad, the painting! It is entitled Decorous Omni-Shades, by Peekaso. Do you not find it extraordinarily emotive? Does it not speak to you of cosmological intensity? Does it not posssess a divine ebullience?"

"Um ..."

"Come come, no need to be bashful." The man half-turned to smile at the crowd and receive a titter of appreciative laughter. "Tell us what you think of it. Regale us with your wisdom! Speachless, eh? I know. Let us make it easy for you. Tell us what do you think of it *in one word*?"

"Er, that's easy. It's *shi*—"

The monk elbowed Roffo in the ribs, causing him to splutter. He leaned over to the barman-cum-adventurer. "Say long word," he whispered.

"Eh? What do you mean?"

"Say long word. Anything. Not matter what."

"Okay. If you say so." Roffo turned back to the expectant – and somewhat amused – hemicircle. "Um ... *feculent*?"

An *aaaaah* of appreciation spread around the listeners. Hearing this, a couple more people came to stand behind the crowd, peering over toga-clad shoulders. The elderly gent looked somewhat non-plussed.

"Er, yeah, that's right. It's feculent, that's what it is." Roffo looked towards the monk, who stood with his arms folded, smirking. The gurning oriental gave the junior art critic barman a nod of encouragement. "And, er, it's also *pancreatic*. You know, it gets to you right here ..." Roffo indicated a vague area of his abdomen.

"Gosh, yes," noted one middle-aged gent, waving around a wine glass, "it does rather!" Others murmured assent and started prodding their own bellies. The elderly inquisitor looked at Roffo with sudden doubt.

"But what about the ethical statement of the piece?" asked one earnest young man with curly blonde locks. "How do you interpret its moral position?"

Roffo rubbed his hands together. "Well, I think it's ethically *vexa-*

tious." *Oooooh*, went the growing audience. With increasing confidence, Roffo indicated a purple blob in one corner of the painting. "See this? Looks like a bruise, don't it? Is the bloke saying he's *for* bruises? It, er, *reeks of turpitude* to me. I'm in inner ..." Roffo recalled a word his Gramps had once used in a game of Scramble, the old bugger, "... *tracasserie.*"

A woman fainted.

Another shrieked.

"Wor! Me too, me too!" yelled one excited fellow with big teeth. "Er, I mean, *et moi, et moi!*"

"Yes, he speaks the truth! The artist is clearly a vexatious cad."

The monk tugged at Roffo's sleeve. "Roffo, tell me, think maybe artist is *paludicolous*?" The crowd gasped.

"You read my mind! Paludicolous. Just what I was thinking. Obvious. You can tell from the, er, *conjunction of inverted linear segmentations* here ..."

Half an hour later the two men managed to make their escape, brushing aside earnest queries, invites to dinner parties, and requests for their presence at various Art Critiques and Philosophy Circles. Outside the building they came upon a small party of men giving the painter of Decorous Omni-Shades a right pasting. "Attempting to corrupt us with your *insidious rectal imageries*, eh?" yelled one man, as he broke the painting over the poor artist's head. Another booted him up the arse. "So much for your *porcine ambivalence* and *fluctuating arch-pessimisms!*"

The adventurers hurried away.

"Where do you get them from?" laughed Roffo. "I didn't know the meaning of half the words you fed me. To be honest, I didn't know the meaning of half of mine either! I mean, paludi-*something* ... what's that when it's at home?"

The monk gurned merrily. "Ah, paludicolous ... means *marsh-dwelling*, which is where Coprolites belong!"

"And what about *fraumboobuloid*? What on earth is that?"

The monk now wheezed with laughter. "No idea. Make up!"

"No! *Really?* And they thought you were saying something, well, profound! Morons!"

"Exactly!" And the two men giggled and wheezed with laughter as they continued along the torch-lit street

————◆•••◆————

The light of the early afternoon sun blundered through a high window and assaulted the back of the monk's head, sizzling his reddened ears and casting a grotesque silhouette onto the parchment that lay on the desk before him. The parchment hosted a score of lines of neatly written text. These began in sunlight to the left and disappeared in shadow to the right. Each line was punctuated – in the depths of the umbra – by a little cross.

The monk now dipped his quill into an inkpot and scratched an 'x' at the end of the last line on the sheet. For a moment, after the conclusion of the second diagonal stroke, the quill hovered in the air. And then, with one lightning movement, it was speared down through the parchment. It sank an inch into the wooden desk.

"Wow," said Roffo, sitting across the table from the vandal. "How did you do that?"

The monk gurned sourly and waved the query away with the twitch of a hand.

"Yeah, well," sighed Roffo, "I know how you feel." He returned his attention to the document in front of him.

He Who Gurns folded his hands behind his head and rocked back in his chair. This was hopeless! They had been searching the library for four days now and in all that time had only found one map – and that had been sandwiched between a book on cats and another on *Demonic Practices of 8th Century Chadoor*. Even finding this had been a fluke. Terry had stumbled onto it, not through any insight into the library classification system, but by starting at the first shelf on the bottom floor and working his way along it. The barbarian had confidently predicted that, through this strategy, he would reach the end of the row by the turn of the year.

In the meantime – until Terry's discovery had made it apparent that such a strategy was foolhardy – the monk and Roffo had been trying to discover the location of a specific *map section*. The Head Librarian had been right though: they needed to discover the nature of the classifier who had received Boozer's map to make any progress. But where would his name reside? Finding this – like finding the map fragment – was like searching for a blackhead on the bum of a coal miner in a pitch-black mine shaft on an overcast day on the planet Dark in the lightless universe of Blackness. The monk looked down at his list. He had written down every term he could think of for *librarians*, *libraries*, and *classifications*, and jumbled the various words up so that they formed three-word descriptions in Scientific Copric. None of the sections had even *existed*. He had come across some classics in his searches though, such as the General Section on Explosives, which contained four books on sneezing (Explosive Nasal Syndrome

A3) and eight books on stars (Occasionally-Erecting Gas Globes H8). Part of the frustration was knowing that these classifications were unique to one classifier, and that a different Head Librarian would have adopted an entirely different scheme for sneezing and stars, filing items on these topics away somewhere else.

"Eh up," said Roffo darkly. "Look who it is. It's that librarian bloke. It looks like he's hiding another book so it'll be preserved for all time."

The monk followed Roffo's glower. He spotted Grimulous edging along a shelf, his finger tracing out book titles. Once the librarian found an appropriate place, he nodded to himself and inserted a small, leather-bound volume.

"I reckon he knows more than he's telling," said Roffo. "Let's go and have another word with him. And if he won't talk, well, it might be fun if you try that quill trick on him ..."

<hr />

The Librarians' Common Room occupied one corner of the fourth floor.

Terry removed his head from against the door. "There are three. The Head Librarian chap and two others. He's talking to one man, but the third is further away, probably in an annexe of some sort."

"Get anything else?" asked Roffo.

"Um, yeah ..." Terry put his ear against the door once more, listened for five seconds, and then nodded. "The one in the annexe is making tea. Three cups. One lump of sugar, two, and one again. Milk in the last. He stirs with his left hand and wears a gold bracelet on that wrist. The man talking to ..."

"Okay okay!" Roffo held up his hands as though admitting defeat. "That's amazing! How do you get all that just by listening at a door?" He shook his head in disbelief, then turned to address the monk. "Anyway, how are we going to handle this? I mean, this is their thingy, um, *sanctum sanctorum*. We can't just barge in ... can we?"

"Terry, say when tea-maker joins others, okay?"

The barbarian nodded. Thirty seconds later he gave the monk the thumbs-up.

"Right, leave to me!" The monk put a hushing finger to his lips and gestured the others to get back. He knocked on the door then stepped to one side. After a moment, the door opened and a librarian peered out. Seeing no-one there, the man stepped outside completely. The monk ghosted in from the right. He placed a hand against the man's neck and gently *squeezed*. The librarian slumped to the ground, unconscious. The monk gestured for Terry to drag him away, and he then repeated the exercise …

"Surprise surprise!" said Roffo, as he walked through the open door. "Ah, tea! Don't mind if I do. I'll have two lumps please. That's the nearest cup, I believe. Ta very much."

"What are you doing in here?" exclaimed Grimulous. "It is forbidden for any but the Descendants of Dooey to enter this place. This is sacrilege!"

"Yes indeedy," said Roffo. "We may be crap at findings things in libraries, but we're pretty hot at the sacrilege game. Don't worry, though. If anyone turns up we'll just say you invited us in. I suppose you're not allowed to do that, are you? Probably get demoted or something. You know. Have your spectacles broken in half in front of the assembled mass of librarians. Or have your thingy shut in a book. Whatever."

Grimulous scanned the severe expressions on the faces of the intruders. He gulped hard. "Very well. What do you want? Be quick, then leave before my two colleagues …" he looked puzzled.

"Do not worry," said the monk. "They just sleeping. Not see us. No problem." The bald-headed martial arts expert surveyed the room. It contained black leather sofas and settees, several intricately carved tables, a bronze bust of a man with a big nose (whom he guessed to be Dooey himself), a doorway to the tea room, and … "*Aha!*" On one wall there was a plaque. Etched into this was a list of names. The first name at the top was "Dooey", and the last – which was two-thirds of the way down – was "Grimulous".

"Whoa!" declared Roffo. "That's it, isn't it! A list of the Head Librarians. And those are dates, too, aren't they?"

"Yes. Write down names and dates in this period." The monk indicated a set of four names: Rombo, Crustius, Meldano, and Farogue. "Boozer must have brought fragment here in this period sometime and given it to one of these librarians. Need to do calculations to be sure which."

"Is that all you wanted?" said Grimulous, with some relief. "Well, fine. Note the names down and go. *Please.*"

"Hang on," said the monk. "Letters and numbers after dates … what are they?"

"Ah," said Grimulous. "Those old things. They're just, um, sort of, mistakes …" he trailed off. The monk came to sit opposite him. He stared at the Head Librarian in an inscrutable-yet-unnerving way.

"Say again?"

"Er, well, they're nothing really ..."

Roffo handed something to the monk. "Here, you might need this." It was a pencil. A *sharp* pencil. The monk tested its sharpness on his thumb.

"Ah, er, there's no need to get nasty. Um, the letters? Ah, yes, I remember now. They're unique *codes*. They indicate, um, *variations* of classification. Each new Head Librarian devises his own code based on Dooey's standard. It is then named after him."

"So," said Roffo, taking a closer look. "Beside your name it says 'G9'. Grimulous 9?"

"Yes, my own categorisation is known as G9. There. You have now wrung every iota of sacred information from me. I am exhausted. Please leave."

"Wait!" The monk held up a hand. "What do codes refer to? How is ..." he peered at the plaque "... G9 different from ... E2? Or H8?"

"Well, I can't honestly say ... and it's no good waving that pencil about either, because I don't know, and that's the truth. The earlier ones have been forgotten – lost in history. Of course, I do know some of them ... maybe the last six. We're taught them, you see, to give us an idea about how to go about devising our own code."

The monk looked at the plaque with a sinking feeling. The four names in the Boozer period were over forty Head Librarians in the past. He gave a hopeless sigh. "Anyway, explain own code ... maybe give us clue."

Grimulous thought about revolting. But then he looked at the object in the monk's hand once more. It was *such* a sharp pencil ...

"I was just thinking about taking a bit of a break," said Roffo to the monk. "You coming?"

The monk shook his head. "No. Need work this out." He had narrowed down the possible receivers of Boozer's fragment to either Meldano (M4) or Farogue (F5). Once he had pinpointed the culprit, he reasoned, he could do an exploratory search for books labelled with that librarian's special code, and then attempt to find some correlation between their nature and the way in which they had been classified. The first problem was the uncertainty about the exact year when Boozer would have staggered through Copros, but by using his knowledge from past research, plus an analysis of the map fragments he currently held, the monk was slowly narrowing down the possibilities. If the worst came to the worst he would just have to pluck out M4s *and* F5s.

"Okay," said Roffo, "well, I might grab a bite to eat too. See you later."

Roffo collected Terry from downstairs and the two men exited the library onto the main square. Outside, beneath the late afternoon sun, the junior barman rubbed his hands in anticipation. "Right – what about a bit of grub first, and then we can take in a show. After all, it is Fritday and we haven't *really* been out since we got here."

"Um, yeah, but don't you think we ought to give ..."

"No no. I'm sure he's got it all under control. He explained his plan to me and it sounds like a damned good one. He's a clever blighter, you know. If anyone is capable of working out the right code, then it's *him*. We'd probably just get in the way."

"Well, if you're sure ..."

"Of course I'm sure! Right, let's try—"

"Um," Terry raised a hand to cut his friend off. He looked down sheepishly. "But first I, well, *need to go*."

Roffo squawked in exasperation. "You can't need to go! When you read about adventures in novels people *never* need to go!" He saw his friend jiggling on the spot. He sighed. "Very well! How *desperate* are you?"

"On a scale of one to ten?"

"Yeah."

"Twenty seven. Sorry."

Roffo rolled his eyes. "Oh well, there's no helping it. We're going to have to risk the public loo. Let's get it over with."

They crossed the square to a large one-storey building. For all its reputation it looked a jolly place. Its walls were decorated with colourful frescos depicting woodland scenes, with trees and lakes and wild boars, and a pastel blue sky. Outside the broad entrance, a small band of musicians played gentle, soothing, bowel-eruption-masking tunes on violin and pipes. Users – and potential users – relaxed on benches lining the wall facing the square, chatting gaily and adjusting their togas.

Terry and Roffo wove through the little crowd and past the musicians. They walked through the doors, passing beneath a sign declaring 'Gentlemen', and entered a little marble-floored foyer. From desks to either side of this, cheerful old men dispensed toiletries: little bags full of soft moss, scented water, garlands of pungent flowers, and sprigs of lavender. The lavender came in two forms: one to be pinned to the toga, and one to be affixed via a piece of string to the top lip. The adventurers purchased a pair of lavender moustaches and some bags of moss. They then walked through a polished wooden door into the lavatory proper.

The lavatory itself was large, square and well-lit. A knee-high ledge ran along the four walls, and on the top of this – at evenly spaced intervals – were several dozen round holes. Men were scattered throughout the room, sitting over the holes. Some communed with Nature alone, whilst others communed with friends as well. All had their togas hitched up to their waists.

"Right, let's make sure we're as far away from anyone else as possible," muttered Roffo. "Look – over there." He indicated a vacant section of five holes situated along the opposite wall. As they walked to their destiny, the barman scowled: "Communal loos? Disgusting!"

"Oh, it's not that bad," suggested Terry. "You know, we used to have a communal loo in my village, too. It was nothing like this though."

"It was worse?"

"Eh? Oh yes. *Much.*" Terry swung his bag of moss idly. "It was my uncle's field."

———•••———

Blaaaaaaat.

"Oh God, not *him* again!" Trespass attempted to move his head to one side to avoid the imminent deluge of brown unspeakableness. He was presently buried up to his armpits in a foul lake of human excrement – a lake that slowly glooped around a narrow tunnel which formed a square beneath the business part of the Copros Public Lavatory. The rest of the Hull's Angels were arranged in a line off to his right.

"Uh-oh … and you think *you've* got problems," groaned Burble, who was secured mid-flow at the far end of the line. As a result of his vertical inadequacy, The Shadow was buried to bottom-lip level. "Mr Constipation's just arrived. I know his voice. Oh, god, the toga's coming down …"

"At least it'll be sol—" began Trespass. "*Aaaaarrrrggh!*"

Plish, went the man who was sitting above the leader of the Angels, *plishplishplish plish.*

"Watch out!" yelled Grunt, from beside his leader. "Stop shaking your head, you git! Take it like a man!"

Trespass frowned wretchedly. "Oh, yeah?" He freed one hand from the muck – which emerged with a great sucking sound – and tried to wipe some of the fresh deposit from his forehead before it could dribble into his eyes. "And how's that then? With a stiff upper lip?"

"I think mine's already gone stiff," said Burble, miserably. "At least … ugh!"

"Wot's up bruv?" asked Frunge.

"*That's not my lip!* Eck eck eck eck!"

Hrumph, exclaimed another user of the civic facilities (in unintended mimicry of a howitzer), *hrumph hrumph*.

"Pheweeee!" cried Bruce.

"Was he one of yours?" asked Trespass.

"Aye, why is it always me, eh? Why dae I always git the smelly ones?"

"Humph," moaned Trespass, "I want to know why Burb always gets the easy ones." He gestured one utterly befouled hand towards the ceiling. Light shone through the unoccupied holes, while the eclipsing of light presaged something ominous and dreadful. "That constipated bloke, now, he could be there for *hours*, hogging that seat and stopping others from using it. And I resent that."

"I'd swap with you any time," said Burble. "It's okay when he's straining, but when he *does* go off …" He let the implication hang.

Occasionally, during off-peak times, the prisoners could make out snippets of conversation from above, or hear the music of the Lavatory Musicians. Most of the conversations seemed to Burble to be meaning-less jaw exercises. In the toilet pits, verbal diarrhoea complemented the natural variety to form a Hullish melange. Take Mr Constipation now. Burble had, over the last four days, heard his musings on every subject from why god must be a dog, to the metaphysics of goat cheese. Today, however, the man appeared to be alone: Burble caught the rustling of a newspaper.

A little distance off to Burble's right, the light from two more holes was blotted out. The conversation from the new arrivals carried to him.

" …I hope we find it soon. I can't take much more of this."

"Er, of *what*?"

"The snobby looks we keep getting. You know, the way the locals keep looking down their noses at us. And the way all the restaurants have their menus written in some weird language just to confuse people. I mean, what the frig were those *escargots* I had yesterday? I reckon snails would of tasted better than that crud. And I can't stand the way our hotelier treats us like he's doing *us* a favour by letting us stay in his dump. But most of all, I can't take any more of their bottled lager, or those cocktail things with the salt and the umbrellas and stuff. I mean, why do you need an umbrella in your drink? It hasn't rained once since we got here – outdoors or indoors."

"Well, the wine is nice. You just need to acquire a taste for it."

Burble knew those voices. He turned to hush his squabbling comrades. "Oy! It's Testicles," he whispered savagely. "Up *there*!"

"... anyway, I wonder what it tastes like? I can't wait to try. Gramps told me about it once. Said they serve it in heaven. When I was young, he told me that if I was good and did my chores, then one day I'd be able to sit on a big cloud surrounded by lots of beautiful women, drinking it all day. Ha!" There was a pause. "I remember thinking at the time that I'd rather end up in a tree house with a Thunder Blaster Catapult, an endless supply of ammo, a plate that magically produced chocolate cake whenever I was hungry, lots of jars of worms, and lots of unsuspecting grown-ups to wander below my tree-house going 'Oh shit, it's raining worms', and 'Ow, something just stung me on the cheek, what could it be?'"

The second eclipse spoke from an unseen orifice. "Well, I hope we find it soon. I'd like to get back home. I worry about my plants, you know. I hope Maddy isn't over-watering them. Do you think this is the last fragment? Do you think it'll show us the way to Boozer's recipe?"

"Terry ... *shhhh*! Mum's the word! Remember: *floors have ears*! You don't know who might be listening." There was a rustle of clothing. "Right, that's me done. Let's go. I'm hungry." And the voices soon trailed off.

"Did you hear that!" exclaimed Burble. "So that's what they're up to!"

"I didn't catch a word they were saying," said Trespass. "Too many other noises. What's up?"

"Well, they're—" And at that moment, Mr Constipation decided to let go.

Phh-TOOOM.

"Burb ... Burb ..."

Bruce leaned over to have a look. The Shadow's eyes seemed to be spinning around independently of one another, while his tongue (in the circumstances somewhat unwisely) lolled out of the corner of his mouth. "I think ye're gaein' tae have tae wait a wee while f'r that explanation," said the yakker. "I think he's got *percussion* ..."

They stood outside the entrance to the town amphitheatre. Roffo's pose was disgruntlement personified: his arms were folded and his frown was as deep as an oceanic trench.

"Well, do you want to go in or not?" asked Terry.

"This place," said Roffo, "is about as entertaining as a tooth extraction on a cold, wet morning followed by lunch at the Cabbage Soup Shack and then an afternoon visit to my hypochondriac Aunt Linny for an update on her latest festering sores and a private viewing of her haemorrhoids. This place is seriously lacking in the fun department."

Terry consulted the leaflet he had picked up at the restaurant where they'd had dinner. "We could go to a Poetry Recital instead. There are eight different ones listed here. Or there's a couple of Cheese and Wine …" Terry looked up and smiled wistfully. "Sorry." He addressed the 'What's On' listing again. "Apart from that, it's just Philosophy Circles, a bit of Opera, or …"

"Yeah, a Play." Remarkably, Roffo's frown managed to deepen still further. This was the mother of the mother of all frowns. "I mean, no proper inns, no clubs, no bands apart from this Chamber Pot music … how can these people *live*?"

"So you don't …"

Roffo threw up his hands. "Yes, why not! It's Fritday and I always make a point of going out on Fritdays. Let's go."

The two disappointed party animals paid over some copper pieces and entered the amphitheatre. They found some space on the stone seating half-way up one side. The place was approximately two-thirds full.

The play, entitled 'Veracity', had already begun. On stage, four men in green bedsheets loped around, while a woman wearing a goat mask and a shaggy pelt capered after them. Roffo picked up a discarded Programme from the step below.

"*Now in its second glorious year*," he read, "'*Veracity' tells the tale of the search for truth.*" Roffo looked up and adopted a pained expression. "I feel sick already. If you spot a sick-bag seller get me a crate or two, eh?" He turned back to the Programme and scanned through it. "Right, get this … the play's about the search for truth. The blokes in the green sheets are The Four Seekers … the green represents a state of ignorance …"

"Why green?" asked the barbarian.

"I dunno … ah, wait, here it is … green is the colour of *grass and, as everyone knows, grass is extremely ignorant indeed.*"

"Uh, yeah. I think I need a skip-full of sick bags myself."

"You haven't heard the half of it. That woman dressed like a goat is *The Harvester*. Blah blah blah … she *harvests the ignorant and turns them into The Night Soil of Existence-Without-Truth*. Honest, that's what it says!"

"I think *I'm* turning green."

"Whoa, mate, you don't want to do that, or you'll have that goat-woman after you." Roffo sniggered. "No, what you want to do is turn *red*."

"Red?"

"Yeah, *the colour of the sun*." He looked up. "Well, bugger me, and there was I thinking it's an orangey colour." He looked down again. "Anyway, red symbolises *The Fire of Knowledge*."

"Does anyone actually *say* anything in this play?" wondered Terry. "I mean, so far there's just been a lot of rushing about."

Roffo held up a hand. "Yeah, any second now … *wait for it* … wait for it …"

On stage, one of the green-clothed characters stopped and faced the audience. He raised the index finger of his right hand and smiled. "I know," he cried loudly, "let us repair to Ye Library!"

And at that, the goat-woman gave a hideous bleat and bounded off stage-right. The audience stood to applaud. The Four Seekers bowed and exited stage-left.

"Thank god that's over," said Terry. "Let's—"

Roffo raised a hand. "That's only Act One, I'm afraid. In the next Act the Seekers journey to Ye Library. I expect they want somewhere warm to have a sleep. Or maybe they have a grudge against that Grimulous bloke and they're going to give him a good kicking."

"Really?"

"No. That'd be too much to hope for. It says here … *they go to seek wisdom in the pages of the masters*. Poor sods. I wonder if they realise they're wasting their time. Someone should tell them."

On the stage a number of bookcases had been set up. A hush spread around the amphitheatre. A man, wearing librarianesque spectacles, entered from the left pushing a trolley of books. He picked one up.

"Ah, Marbaltor's tome of wisdom!" He caressed its leather cover. "How your wisdom speaks to me through the spirit of the leather and the parchment, *I who cannot even read*."

Roffo exploded with laughter. He started to roll about on the stone terrace. Terry looked at his friend with some concern. Other people in the audience started to look at the pair with disapproval.

" …can't … even … read … oh … oh … oh … classic!"

On the stage, the illiterate librarian hugged the book to his chest and delicately kissed its cover. A dreamy, besotted look came over his face. "Where shall I nest thee, oh heavenly block of tree product, recipient of the wisdom of sages?"

The actor-librarian sighed and turned to the shelves. He ran a finger along the volumes stacked on one shelf ...

And Roffo stopped laughing.

Instantly.

The sight of the actor on the stage struck a powerful chord in him. He experienced a moment of déjà-vu. His eyes widened. "Uh!" he exclaimed.

"Are you all right?"

"Uh ... the librarian!"

"Eh? Yes, he's a librarian. Do you want some water?"

"No! I mean, the librarian!" Roffo waved his hands in growing excitement. "Earlier, at the library ... You were downstairs at the time, so you didn't see it, but *he was putting a book back!*"

Terry looked at his friend as though he'd had a bit too much sun. "So? I thought that was his job?"

"Yeah it is but, don't you see, *he was putting a book back*. From a *return* trolley." Roffo bounded up and down on his seat. "But Grimulous is the original *illiterate* librarian! We've got to go and see the monk, and we've got to see him now!"

"So you see, don't you?" said Roffo. "If that was a *returned* book, then what code did he use to classify it?"

"Original code. Remember: there codes on all books. Must tell librarian how it originally classified."

"Yeah, but that can't be right. Grimulous said he only knew half a dozen codes, and the earliest ones have been forgotten. If he was lying, then he might be able to help us find the map after all. But if he was telling the truth ..."

"Ai-la," cried the monk, excitedly, "then must use *own* system, regardless of original classification!"

"Exactly!"

"Er," said Terry, "I see that but ... how does that help us?"

"Well, it might not. If no-one has ever taken the map out to have a look at it, then it'll still be in its original location. But a lot of time has passed since then. And no-one *ever* finds what they're looking for. The

338

librarians see to that. So people just have to search randomly and pull out lots of things to look at. And that means that, well, probably most of the books and stuff have ended up on the return trolley at some point."

The monk nodded. While his comrades had been out, he had come to the conclusion that it must have been Meldano who had received the map fragment from Boozer. He had then moved through the library plucking out every book that was coded M4, noting the sections in which each appeared. He had already composed quite a large list, but it had rapidly occurred to him that there was not much of a pattern. He had occasionally found adjacent books that were conceptually linked, as though categorised according to the same scheme, but often the M4s occurred singly, or else they were surrounded by conceptually similar books that had different codes.

"And so," continued the monk, "it quite likely map filed under system of *more recent* librarian, not original classification."

"Like G9?" wondered Terry.

"Or at least," suggested Roffo, "under one of the more recent systems that Grimulous admitted to knowing."

"Good!" The monk patted the barman on the arm. "Roffo – you genius!"

"Really?" Roffo smirked in pride. "Er, thanks!"

"And so," concluded the monk, "must now look under G9 system. First. But most probably must pay final visit to Librarian Arsehole."

———•••———

"No … go away!" Grimulous fled between two shelves of books. But he was cornered, and soon in the clutches of the three adventurers.

"You understand what want?"

"Yes yes," Grimulous gave a peevish wave of the hand. The fragments of Boozer's map lay on the table before him.

"Repeat!"

The Head Librarian sighed. "You want me to try to classify a fragment of map that looks just like these pieces according to the classification systems of the last six HLs. I'll need some parchment and a bit of time. Even knowing the codes, there are several ways in which something as peculiar as this could be classified. Silence would also be nice. And isolation."

"You think we born yesterday?"

Grimulous shrugged his shoulders. It had been worth a try.

———•••———

Their spirits had waned as the evening had progressed. It was now three in the morning and the library was dark – and *officially* closed.

Grimulous had methodically gone through the possible categorisations of the four librarians who had preceded him, but with no luck. "Right," he said, rubbing his hands. The Head Librarian had to admit that, after initial resistance, he was rather enjoying himself. Here was the chance for him to use his expertise to actually *find* something in the library – and that was quite a challenge. But if this fragment *could* be found then he intended to be the one to find it! "We now come to Jargool. A peculiar fellow. Rather pretentious."

"Hmm, that like pot calling kettle black!"

Grimulous peered over his spectacles at the monk to silence him, old habits dying hard. He cleared his throat. "As I was saying: rather pretentious. And also a bit lazy. I see this piece of map, and you know what I think?"

"Go on."

"Bric-a-brac!"

"Eh?"

"Bits and pieces."

"Oh!"

"Precisely!" Grimulous pursed his lips in thought. "I see him in my mind's eye. He goes to the trolley and sees the fragment. Of course, it will have been put into a folder of some sort. Purple probably, knowing Meldano. And Jargool would have opened this up and frowned. *Ah, me, the trials of the librarian*, he would have said, and then: *I cannot be bothered with such partial obscurities!* And he would have headed straight for Bric-A-Brac, in the Miscellany Section. Floor two. Follow me."

The party had trooped up and down the stairs to the various floors dozens of times already. Roffo could feel his calf muscles ballooning with fatigue with each step he took. They were currently back on the fourth floor and so had to descend a couple of flights. Grimulous led the lantern-carrying men into a labyrinth of shelving.

"Here we go: *Miscellaneous General Section*. Now, let's see. Here we have Miscellaneous: Animal Husbandry Issues … Miscellaneous: Antiquities … Miscellaneous: Bric-A-Brac. You will find that many of the items here are J7s. Now. Where would the fragment be?" Grimulous held a piece of Boozer's map up to his lantern. "What would Jargool *see*? For him, the incompleteness of the piece would be key: it would be the visual thing, the thing that would strike him with the least amount of effort. He would then be forced to consider the intention *behind* the thing. Clearly, this would be a Fragmentary Locational object."

Grimulous ambled back and forth across the face of a set of shelves. "Aha! Not Locational, *Directional*! Here we have *Fragmentary Directional References*. I have a strong feeling about this. Now, we don't have a title, do we? Meldano would probably have given it one, otherwise Jargool would have had to give it a title himself. Ha! That would have irritated the bugger!" The librarian turned to look at the adventurers. "I suggest you give me a hand here."

"What are we looking for?" asked Roffo.

"Probably something in a purple folder with the code M4."

"What, like this?" said Terry, as he pulled out a folder. He opened it up. "Oh look …"

"Terry! Bloody Hull – that's it! I don't believe it. Well, bugger me!"

The barbarian smirked. "I'd rather not."

The monk clapped his hands and gave a jig. "Haha – beat library! Beat library!"

"We'll be bollocking *legends* for this," said Roffo. "Actually, we won't, cos no-one will believe us."

Grimulous cleared his throat loudly. "Yes, well done. Now, please return the piece to its place. After all, the library *is* closed. If you come back tomorrow we can deal with formalities then. You'll need a library card, of course, and we'll need references and statements of good character for that. And then, naturally, it will take a little while to process your applications. Oh, let us say three months to be on the safe side. And the Bric-A-Brac section, I notice, is an 'overnight loan' section, so you will only be able to … er, if you would kindly *put me down* please …"

The monk placed the fragment with the rest of the pieces. "Let us leave straightaway. Consider fragment on road."

"What about him?" asked Terry, indicating the man slung over his shoulder.

"Lock in store cupboard. Will be let out in morning."

"Yeah," said Roffo, "let's rock and roll."

"Go on," said the Chief of Police, who was surrounded by two dozen men armed with crossbows, "hop it!"

The Hull's Angels trudged out of the tunnel that led from the Toilet Pits. They were completely covered in excrement and stank with such an intensity that birds flying overhead started to experience problems with flight and every other creature within a hundred yards began to mewl, whimper, click or buzz in horror. Nothing unprotected could have survived for more than a few seconds within a twenty-yard Kill Zone of the men. The police wore clips on their noses and perfume-scented rags about their faces, and their clothes were drenched with powerful scents. They formed a corridor through which the yakkers were now ushered.

The police escorted the men through the city to the suburbs, and thence to the road out of town. This route had been evacuated for safety reasons: houses were locked and windows were shuttered, and barricades prevented the curious from getting too close. At the edge of town, by the arch, the Angels' mounts had been tethered to a tree. As the wave of nauseous stench rippled towards the elephant and the four yaks, however, these became restless. By the time the yakkers squelched into view, the beasts were pulling at their tethers and foaming at the mouth.

The Chief of Police pointed to the far distance. "Leave this place and do not return, uncivilised wretches."

"Not bluddy likely," muttered Trespass.

"Yeah ... accommodation leaves something to be desired," said Burble.

"Let's hurry, lads," said Frunge, "I think I'm starting to crust over."

But their mounts were no fools. As the yakkers approached them, the increasingly frantic beasts found the strength of desperation. With one mighty effort they managed to pull the tether line from the tree. With honks and bellows of triumph, the beasts pelted off into the distance.

The shambling Shit-Men attempted to follow.

Chapter 15

The Thirty-Nine Steppes

―――――――――――――――――――――――――――――

"THIS IS the place, guv," said Boomber, as they approached a gate set in the south wall of the dingy alleyway they had been traversing. A courtyard was visible through the bars. "You gives a special ring – you know, a *code* – and they lets you in." The Sergeant grabbed a dangling bell rope and tugged on it several times. After a short pause the gate swung open.

"Remarkable," said Yavlo, wearing the tiniest of frowns. "I do not wish to even think about how you came upon this particular piece of knowledge, Sergeant. Actually, no, I take that back. How *did* you learn of this?"

"Oh, you know, guv, you picks up all sorts of interesting facts from the criminal fraternity. In this case," Boomber tapped the side of his nose in a conspiratorial manner, "a snout told me." He pointed to a small door on the far side of the courtyard. "That's where you get in."

The pair marched across the yard, through the door, and into the building's foyer. This had a theme of leather and crushed velvet and was full of chaise longues.

"Up the stairs now," said Boomber, "then you've got to tap out the code again."

The Inspector gave his Sergeant a long look full of suspicion before turning to lead the way up the spiral staircase. He halted before a door on the landing at the top of the stairs and glanced sideways at his second-in-command. Boomber nodded in a reassuring way, so Yavlo stiffened his back and rapped out the code. A slit opened in the portal, revealing a sleepy pair of eyes. These suddenly bulged in recognition of the police officer. The spy-slit was slammed shut. The door remained closed.

Yavlo knocked again.

"What d'ya want, copper?" came a voice from the other side.

"Is this not an establishment where, uh, kind ladies dispense certain unusual services for pecuniary rewards?"

"You what?"

Boomber gently moved his Inspector to one side and whispered to him: "I think it might be best if you leave this to me, guv. I knows how these people think." Boomber cleared his throat and said more loudly, "I want to see Tiffany."

"Why?" The voice was full of suspicion. Again it asked: "What d'ya want?"

"What do you think I want?" growled the Sergeant. "A pound of sprouts?"

The sounds of a whispered conversation diffused through the door. Yavlo leant down and put his ear next to the keyhole.

"It sounds like 'e wants us to pound 'is sprouts," murmured the doorman. "I always thought them police were a funny lot. What should I do?"

"Let 'em in," said a female voice. "I'll mash their sprouts good and proper! I've unfinished business with the boys in white. When I was working the docks at *Eastward O?* a couple of years back a copper tried to arrest me, so I kneed him in the charlies and got fined for it. This time *they* can pay *me* for the privilege!"

A key was thrust into the lock. It passed right through the door and into Yavlo's ear. The Inspector let out a stifled squawk as the cold metal attempted to bash out a note on his eardrum. Before the door was opened, he quickly jumped upright to assume the dignified demeanour of a copper going about his legitimate business.

"Enter the inner sanctum of 'eaven," said the doorman. "My name's Peter and this 'ere is *Var* … er, no … *Ver* … um, nope, um … *Vir* … *Viv* …*acious* … yeah! Vivacious *Val*! That's right, silly me, forget me own name next, ha ha. Anyway, she'll be only too 'appy to satisfy your every need, no matter 'ow sad and perverse."

Yavlo rubbed his ear and ran his eye over the woman in front of him. She appeared to have a series of caravan routes tattooed on her legs in purple ink. Her face was of the sort usually referred to as 'lived-in'. Lived in *by what* was the question.

"Thank you," said the Inspector. "But I would really just like to ask you a few questions, if I may? About your clothing?"

"Aha!" Peter nodded. "One of *them*. Righto sir. As you wish." He turned to face Boomber. "And what about you … ah, Mr Smith! I didn't recognise you in that uniform. The usual, eh?"

The Sergeant's face reddened. "Sorry mate, but you must be confusing me with someone else."

"Right you are, sir. Mum's the word and all that. Now …"

Varicose Val decided to dispense with formalities. She grabbed hold of Yavlo's hand and started to drag him down the corridor toward the bedrooms. "Come on then, luvvie. I'll see to *your* particular needs. I've handled many a private's privates."

"Madam," declared Yavlo, as he was towed remorselessly along the corridor, "I am no private. I am an Inspector." He turned to look at his Sergeant for support, only to see Boomber disappearing down the corridor in the opposite direction, accompanied by the doorman. The next thing he knew he was thrust through a door and thrown onto a bed. The sheets crunched in complaint.

The woman wrenched open a chest at the bottom of the bed and started rummaging about, leaving the flabbergasted Inspector to examine his sparse surroundings. A large mirror was affixed to the ceiling over the bed, clearly intended to reflect its occupants and their lusty activities. It presently showed a worried-looking gent lying atop sheets that may once have been white, but which now possessed the sort of interlaced, yellow-ring pattern typically found on unclean coffee tables. Val let out a squeal of delight as she discovered the thing that she was looking for. A pair of size seven hob-nailed boots were held up for Yavlo's inspection.

"These do you, luvvie? I'll do your sprouts first, and then we can talk about what I'm wearing after, eh?" She sat on the bed and began to lace on the boots. "Now, do you want it standing up or doggy fashion? I knew this bloke once who also liked a bit of a kicking. But what he *really* liked was having *it* beaten with a tuning fork." She cackled to herself. "*His* thingy resonated in *A sharp*, but by the time I'm done with you, luv, yours will just *B flat*!"

"No no, madam, there appears to have been a misunderstanding! I do not wish to be kicked *there*, or anywhere else for that matter. What I want is to discuss exotic clothing with you. That is all!"

"Oh," sighed Val in disappointment, "you're one of them skimpy underwear blokes." She ceased her lacing, rose from the bed, and went over to a dresser resting against the wall beside her trunk. She delved into a drawer and produced a rather baggy pair of knickers. "These seem to of stretched a bit, ha ha! Must stop lending them to the mayor." She threw the underwear onto the floor. "I've got some peep-hole panties if that interests you?"

Yavlo mopped the sweat from his brow. This was getting way out of hand, but duty demanded he persevere. "No thank you, madam. I was thinking more along the lines of something of Eastern origin. With veils and suchlike. Perhaps something the people in *that* book would wear ... the one the good Sergeant keeps mentioning. Oh, what was it? The Korma Suture? Something like that."

"Ah, the nude gymnast's bible and curry cookbook!" Val smiled. It was not a pretty sight. "I know every position personally! Hang about." She returned to her dresser. "You're in luck, luv. The Madam got some new stuff in a little while back – from that Master Manis of all people. Anyway, she reckoned it'd be useful for attracting punters from the caravans, though it never worked." She looked up at the Inspector. "They prefer the local flavour, if you know what I mean. Hey ... where are you going?"

"Thank you, madam, but you have satisfied my every desire!" Yavlo clambered off the bed. He needed to find Boomber. They would have to collect all the gear, of course, and then get statements from the ladies involved ...

"'Ere," shouted the confused girl, as she watched her customer open the door and rush out, "I've not done anything yet!" As the door slammed shut, she slouched onto the bed. "Worst case of premature ejaculation I ever seen!"

Yavlo barrelled down the corridor. Now, where had Boomber got to? He opened one door. "Oops! Excuse me Your Eminence!" He gave a little bow and continued to the next door. Wrong again. "Sorry ... oh, is that you, Your Holiness? I didn't recognise you in that rubber mask. You've not seen my Sergeant, have you?" An angry muttering reached his ears. Yavlo stepped back in embarrassment. "Ah, I see. You can't speak properly with that gag on. I will come back later." He made to depart, but remembered duty and turned back. "By the way, Your Holiness, I do believe it is illegal to do *that* to a sheep. However, I presently have other fish to fry, so we will say no more about it on this occasion."

Yavlo tried the next door. A girl was bouncing up and down on a distinguished privy councillor. "Oops! I beg your pardon, Councillor Troi! Carry on."

The Inspector went from door to door searching for his second-in-command, and running into many of the town's good and great on the way. He eventually found Boomber. The policeman was chained to a wall having his fancy tickled by a girl with an ostrich feather.

"Honest, guv," explained the contrite Sergeant, as he was released from his bonds, "she caught me unawares. I'm glad you arrived when you did. I couldn't of taken much more." He rubbed his wrists and gave the girl a sheepish look. "She tied me to the wall, guv, and used a little known Phetish torture technique to try and extract information from me. Er, thank you, Tiffany, I'll debrief you later over a cup of tea." The girl winked and left the men to it. "Anyway, guv, I gave her nothing!"

Yavlo considered the departing girl, then looked back at Boomber. Something very fishy had been going on here, and he would get to the bottom of it. But later. "Come on, Sergeant," he said, "we have all that we need to put Manis behind bars. The exotic clothing worn by the vandals who destroyed The Bear were indeed sold to the ladies of this establishment by that villain. He must have masterminded the whole crime."

"Ah, good stuff, guv. I suppose we'd better get hold of the clothes then. You know what they taught us at police school: no evidence, no case."

"I agree," replied Yavlo. He now broke into a tiny grin of triumph. "In this case, however, there should be little difficulty in convincing the judge that these clothes do exist. After all, when I bumped into him just now, he was wearing some of them."

The Head Librarian stood with his hands resting on the table. From this position, he could peer down his nose through his spectacles at the dozen Sub-Head Librarians, demonstrating his mastery of the First Discipline of Dooey. Grimulous slowly scythed his gaze around the table, sizing up his men and wondering how each would respond to the grim tidings he was about to relate.

"Librarians!" he began. "I have called this conclave to announce that a *most grievous* crime has been committed …"

"Uh, sorry," interrupted Forenzo, the most junior Sub, nervously raising a hand. There was no doubt that Grimulous was master: after a single glance from the Head he felt like confessing to crimes he had never even contemplated. "It's my fault. I admit it. I know I should have got some more milk in but, well, I was busy and …"

"So, it's *you* is it!" declared a grey-haired chap called Bassar, pushing his spectacles down his nose and glowering over the top. "I had to have black tea *all afternoon*! I hate it when that …"

Grimulous cleared his throat and frowned peevishly. "Librarians – enough! That is not the crime to which I was referring!"

"Well," murmured the grey-head, "it's a pretty bloody serious crime if you ask me."

"I agree," said a ginger-haired man. "It's an absolute disgrace. What could possibly be worse? I haven't been so upset since the time I found that young lad sticking pages together with his boogers."

"I remember that," said another. "I knew the boy's parents. Had to emigrate because of it. Got off lightly in my opinion …"

Grimulous scrunched his hands into fists. "Please, gentlemen! I am afraid that this particular crime *is* worse. *Much* worse. Compared to this, the abuse of Unsightly Nasal Detritus is on a par with turning over the top of a page to mark your place. Librarians, please prepare yourselves." He paused for dramatic effect. He licked his lips. "I am afraid it is my painful, onerous duty to announce … a *Code One!*"

A blanket of silence and disbelief settled over the men. Eyes goggled. Drool dribbled from open mouths. One Librarian hid his face in his hands. Another bit on his fist. Another choked back a sob.

"*Noooo* …" cried Bassar, the first to break. "It cannot be!" He looked around the table imploringly. Others stared at him dumbly. "Head, you must be joking … please say it's not so! Please tell us that this is no more than a joke of exceedingly bad taste!"

Grimulous shook his head solemnly. "I am sorry, but it *is* so. Three outland villains swiped an item from the Miscellaneous Bric-A-Brac Fragmentary Directional References Section. Then they locked me in a cupboard and escaped." He turned to look at the ginger-haired man, named Eddy, who had been the one to find him. "I am sorry I couldn't tell you at the time, my friend. I was too distraught."

"Oh woe! Great Dooey, what can we do?"

"We must fall upon our metal rulers at once. Oh, the shame of it …"

"That I should have lived to see this day …"

"But … where have they gone, these Avatars of Evil?"

At the mention of this name, each of the Librarians made the Sign of the Square, the symbol of the Index Card of Truth.

Grimulous held up a hand to still the quailing men. "Hold! Listen to me!" The voices died. One of the Sub-Heads fainted over the back of his chair. The Head ignored him, taking off his spectacles to give them a polish. "There is clearly only one course of action open to us." He put his spectacles back on. "We must regain the lost item and return it to its rightful place …"

"*Wherever that may be!*" chorused the men, repeating the sacred chant.

"Yes, *wherever that may be*! We must recover the item *no matter what*!

No matter what trials, tribulations or depredations we must face, no matter that we place our lives in peril, no matter that we should come face-to-face with the Wicked God of Mildew himself!" Grimulous paused to regain his breath. "My Brothers! It is now my duty – my sacred, pious, painful, jubilant duty – to make a declaration. It is a declaration that has not been made since the time of Crustius. It is a dire declaration. My Brothers, I solemnly declare ... *Jihab!*"

Jihab: the Holy Quest for Books: the war against the illiterate: the crusade against those who despise reading, crease pages, break spines, and use books as props for rickety coffee tables or as coasters for cups of tea.

And at the very mention of the word, the mood in the room changed. It was as though electricity had surged through the buttocks of every man. They leapt to their feet as one. Some started to bang upon the table. Others cheered. Others waved their arms about manically.

"Jihab ..." roared the librarians, taking up a chant ... "*jihab ...*" that built in power and volume, rising to a crescendo ... "*JIHAB!*"

"Aye," cried Grimulous, bellowing over the rising storm of voices. He clenched a fist and raised it to the heavens. His voice took on the quality of thunder. "It is the only way! Men! See to your charges: gather your troops! Have them whet their rulers and pack the extra-sharp Death Index Cards. The rising of the Librarians has begun. There can be no delay. From this day henceforth we cannot, *must not* rest until the item is recovered. The honour of Dooey is at stake ..." He raised both arms to the skies. "Librarians: prepare yourselves! We march tomorrow!"

"I'm knackered!" declared Roffo, as he trailed along after his two comrades. "Hanging around that bloody library into the middle of the night and *then* heading straight for the hotel to do a bunk, and *then* riding thirty miles without a break. My bum is so stiff you couldn't beat nails into it with a sledge hammer! Can't we stop at that inn over there and get an early night?"

"No," replied the monk. "Must get as far away from Copros as possible ... unless *want* to spend month under dribbly bottoms of Coprolites?"

"At least," countered the barman craftily, "it would give us a chance to look at the map. For all we know we could be heading in the wrong direction entirely."

"No, we not. Think understand Boozer. Nevertheless ... *would* be worth finding precise destination." The monk pulled up on the reins of his horse. "All right, we stop. But if get caught *you* get place closest lavatory entrance. That where the most desperate men sit."

"But locking up a librarian is hardly the act of a desperate man."

"He doesn't mean *you*," said Terry, tying the reins of his horse and their pack mule to a hitch. "I think he means the men who sit *above* ... *they* would be the most desperate."

"La!" sniggered the monk, dismounting. "Have biggest need – and load!"

The adventurers formed up and walked to the door of The Inimitable Orator. A burly man in a black coat stood within its frame.

"'Scuse us," said Roffo.

"You can't come in," declared the black-coated individual.

"Why not?" Roffo could see over the shoulder of the man into the public house. It appeared to be empty. "This place is as deserted as the stands during the final day of a Test Match. Are you hosting a convention of invisible men, or are you just closed?"

"Sorry," said the bouncer gruffly. "No all-bloke parties."

Roffo's jaw dropped in disbelief. "But ... but most people who go to inns are blokes. They go to enjoy the convivial atmosphere, to talk complete bollocks with other like-minded individuals, and to get away from their wives and screaming children."

"Sorry. It's the management's policy not mine." The square-headed individual puffed out his over-sized chest and placed his hands behind his back. "Now, I can see that you're a nice group of lads who probably wouldn't cause any trouble, but it's more than my job's worth to let you in. Besides," he added, looking at the monk, "*you* haven't got any shoes on."

They all looked down at the monk's bare feet. He had taken off his boots during the ride to give them an airing – and he wasn't about to put them back on now for this animal. "Wear shoes Great Creator gave us all, and not cover them in hide of dead animals out of respect for Him. It act of religious persecution if not let me in."

This set the bouncer back on his heels. Religious persecution? How would that go down with his trumped-up employer? "Well ... *look*, your friend there hasn't got a shirt on." As if in an attempt to regain the initiative he poked a finger into Terry's massive bare chest. Roffo managed to put a restraining hand on the barbarian's arm before it could sweep up and *remove* the offending digit.

Having saved the bouncer from the indignity of being known for ever after as *Nine Fingers*, Roffo made to challenge this latest dress code. "Of course he hasn't got a shirt on: he's a barbarian, and barbarians don't wear shirts. What you have standing before you is a representative of his people attired in his national dress. It would be culturally insensitive of you not to let him in. It could even cause a thingy, um, *international incident*. And you wouldn't want to be the cause a serious rift between the people of Copros and the barbarians of the Far North, would you?" He grinned and raised his eyebrows. "Besides, have you ever *seen* a rampaging barbarian war party that's out to protest about diplomatic wrongs?"

"Er ..." The bouncer hadn't, but he could well imagine the horror of it. Still, it was probably an idle threat, given the sheer distance to the barbarian lands. "Well, okay, but neither him nor the old geezer have any strides on. You can't come in here unless you're wearing a smart pair of trousers. And that means no shorts, no jeans, and definitely no loincloths. And that's a rule I can't bend. I wouldn't want you scaring the ladies."

The monk started to simmer. "I not old, just had hard life ..."

"Look," said Roffo, "ladies don't wear trousers either, so barring us for this reason would be, wotsit, *sex discrimination*. I mean, you don't bar ladies for not wearing trousers, do you?"

The bouncer nodded. "Actually, we do. In fact, we don't allow ladies in at all."

Roffo threw up his hands in exasperation. "If ladies aren't allowed in, how can you bar us entry because we might scare them?"

The doorman had run out of arguments. As with all bouncers, logic went so far over his head he wouldn't have been able to touch it wearing stilts.

The doorman crossed his arms. "Sorry. No smart trousers, no entry."

"I'm just curious," said Roffo, "but is *anyone* allowed in?"

"Listen, mate," said the moron, "we have standards here. We don't let in any old riff-raff wot wander in off the streets. The troublemakers go to the rough places around the corner." He gave a gesture with his thumb. "No, we've ... uh ... where'd they go?"

A few seconds later the three panting adventurers stood outside a ramshackle building that lay off the alley behind the first inn. Roffo stared through a window of The Pothouse.

"Yes – I can see it: ale being drawn from a hand pump! And there's no sign of any bottles of wine, and no tables covered in silly checked cloth. And best of all, there's no idiot standing in the doorway barring you because your nose might offend the ladies or your boots are the wrong colour. In fact, I can't see anything pretentious at all. Let's go for it!"

The riff-raff pushed open the door and stared at the familiar trappings of a normal alehouse. They let out a collective sigh of relief and headed for the bar. Unsolicited, the landlord plonked three jugs of nectar in front of them. For a moment, the men stared at the glasses reverentially. Then three glasses were lifted to three mouths. And two seconds later three empty glasses were slammed, in unison, back down onto the bar. Three hands wiped froth from three mouths.

"Ah," sighed the monk, "cannot beat jug of real ale. Suggest get another and go sit in corner."

The three questers collected a second round of drinks and went to sit in a small window alcove. The monk withdrew the map fragments from his leather habit and fitted them together. He leant back to show off his skill in jigsawmanship. The others let out a collective moan. As with every puzzle since the dawn of time, there was a piece missing.

"Bugger," said Roffo, succinctly summing up the feelings of the company. "Who's half-inched the middle bit?"

The four fragments formed the four corners of a map, but there was a diamond-shaped piece missing from the centre.

The monk was the first to twig. "Ah – see problem!" He picked up a soggy beer mat. He folded it in half, and then folded it in half again. He then pinched one corner and tore it off. When he opened up the beer mat it revealed a pattern similar to that of the four joined pieces of map: the central diamond was missing.

"Damn," said Roffo, "and I thought this was it! What does the fourth fragment show?"

Terry traced the red ink trail. It went west – in the direction in which they had been headed – and crossed an upland plain. The next red cross lay on the other side of the plain. After reaching the cross the line veered off to the north-east and disappeared off the edge of the map into the missing central area.

"Do you ever get the feeling," said Roffo, "that we've been going around in circles? I mean, we're now heading roughly back in the direction of Way."

The monk nodded. "Yes. Boozer like typical drunk, staggering around in circles."

Roffo sighed. "Ah well. Where is this next cross then? Do you recognise it?"

"Ai, it Vegetopia. Also known as Skeletal Coast. Last fragment of chart *must* be there."

Roffo spluttered on a mouthful of beer. "Oh woe!" he cried, in alarm. "Gramps told me about The Skeletal Coast. He said it was named for the bones of all the adventurers who've perished there!"

"Foolish youth," berated the monk. "It called that because people who live there very thin. No, that not problem. Problem is that to get there must cross here …" He indicated the plains on the map. "Mungo Plains."

"Oh woe," went the youth for a second time. "The Mungos! Gramps told me about them too. He said they're fierce warrior tribesmen who drink horse's blood and fermented mare's milk, and they fight for fun!"

"So, Gramps knew something after all," said the monk. "Mungo Plains also known as The 39 Steppes, because rise in 38 small steppes then descend back to sea level in one very large one, called The Giant Steppe. To cross it, may have to fight every tribe on way."

"Great," said Roffo, "that's just great. Well, gentlemen, who's for another drink? After all, these may be our last!"

———•◦•●———

The Hull's Angels sat around their campfire, listening to the complaints of the frogs from the nearby water hole.

"Listen to those green buggers whinge," muttered Burble. "You'd think they'd be happy about all the flies we've brought them." The yakkers had cleaned themselves up in the pond. "I wish they'd belt up – the ingrates!"

Frunge scowled. "Yeah, and I reckon they owe *me* a medal."

Trespass laughed. "Reckon you're right there. I ain't never seen that many flies in all my life. It's a good job you had a protective crust over you."

"I still don't understand," pouted Frunge, "wot took you lot so long to come and get me. Four hours I was stuck in that field … *four bluddy hours!*"

"You're lucky we weren't longer," said Burble. "We had a Hull of a job persuading that farmer to lend us his cart. It took us ages to run him down and get the keys to his barn. And then his horses started acting up, so we had to tow the cart ourselves."

Frunge's frown deepened. "I mean, it weren't just the smell and that. You should try standing about in a crap cast. It was bluddy hot. Now I know wot it feels like to be a tandoori chicken in a clay oven."

The conversation momentarily died. The yakkers stared into the fire and thought their own secret thoughts. One thought about food, and another about ale. One mused on the concept of vengeance, and another worried about the logistics of rounding up their wayward steeds on the morrow. And one pondered how Bindian cooks managed to get their poppadums so flat, and whether or not their strategy involved the use of a rolling pin.

In the nearby water hole, the frogs continued their clamour of complaint. It wasn't that they were ungrateful for the bounty of flies – they appreciated it, and let no-one suggest otherwise! But what they were most definitely *not* chuffed about was the sudden conversion of their home into a cesspit.

"Look at the living room," croaked one, "it's absolutely ruined!"

"Aye," ribbeted another, "and my favourite arm-Lilly pad! Look at it! Soiled beyond belief! And who's going to pay for the new three-piece?"

"Compensation!" warbled a third. "Fetch the solicitor … we want compensation!"

The cry was taken up around the pool – in frog-speak, naturally. "Compensation … compensation … compensation!"

"Those frogs are really getting on my tits," growled Grunt.

Bruce nodded absently. "Aye."

"Watcha thinking about?"

"Och – me? I wiz jist thinkin', if Testicles an' his crew think they're ontae the best ale in the world then they're fair wasting their time."

"So you're suddenly a big expert on the subject, are you?" sneered Trespass.

"Aye, I might be at that!" said the red-bearded one defensively. "You see, my auld dad wiz a religious mon and he knoo aboot such things. Aye, he told me all aboot the brawest ale in the world, an' I remember the tale well, f'r it wiz the only interestin' bedtime story he ivver told me."

"Tell us then," said Burble.

Bruce cleared his throat and spat a great, green lump of sputum into the fire. The others watched it hiss and bubble and nodded their approval. This was the correct procedure by which to start a tale-telling session.

"It is said in the Highlands," began Bruce, "that it wiz the God Impi who invented ale, an' he gae the secret as a weddin' gift tae his twin brother, Impo."

"Well, it sure beats a toast rack," sniggered Trespass.

"Aye, that it does! But this gift wiz like a prize yak: beautiful an' valuable, but dangerous if ye didnae ken what ye were daein' wi' it. An' poor wee Impo didnae, an' sae spent his entire weddin' day drinkin'. Ye ken: havin' a swally under the table, sayin', 'och, that's me, I need the *Gents* again,' an' secretly guzzlin' in the cubicle. Insultin' the bride's maids an' laughin' loudly. Aye, ye git the picture …"

The other men nodded in unison, remembering weddings they'd attended.

"Anyway," continued Bruce, "he drank sae much he got completely pissed, an' when it came time f'r the weddin' ceremony he wiz sae drunk he couldnae stand up straight, an' when he exchanged vows his voice wiz all slurred. Och, noo, this didnae create the best o' impressions, an' his bride – Creuset, the Goddess o' Kitchen Utensils – burst intae tears. But Impo wiz sae far gone he didnae care. An' at the reception afterwards he chundered on his new mother-in-law, which wiz nae a smart thing considerin' she wiz Virago, Goddess o' Inopportune Visits, Cheap Perfume, an' the Beratin' Tongue."

Grunt laughed. "Sounds a bit like Sonia's mum. Whoa, Tres, that'll be you one day mate."

Trespass nodded. "Don't I know it! Go on, Bruce."

"Aye, so, Impo jist kept on drinkin' an' by nightfall he wiz sae drunk his brother had tae help him up tae the weddin' chamber where Creuset awaited him … *yearnin'* f'r the *consummation* o' the marriage."

A wave of filthy chuckles rippled around the fireside.

"But Impo, aye, well, he could barely stand *if ye ken what I mean,* an' there were nae nuptial adventures *at all.*"

"Are you sure this ain't the tale of Tres and Sonia," laughed Grunt.

"Belt up fat boy!"

"Anyway, Impo wiz sae embarrassed by all this that he fled from the land o' the gods – followed by all manner o' fryin' pans, woks, an' kitchen ironmongery – an' he sought refuge in the realm o' mon." Bruce shook his head sadly. "Och, poor Impo – the wee scally! While hidin' in exile he became cruel an' twisted, an' looked on his weddin' gift as the source o' all his misfortunes. Aye, an' he blamed Impi, e'en though his brother's gift had been a damned fine present an' well-intended. An' afore long Impo decided enough wiz enough an' he would make others suffer tae, an' that is why he gae ale tae mon … so we would abuse it an' be humiliated tae."

Bruce ended his story with a long sigh and a shake of the head.

After a moment's silence, Burble piped up: "Hang about! That explains how ale came to man. It doesn't say anything about the best ale in the world."

"Och – *that*. Well, Impo hated ale, but he loved it tae. He couldnae leave it alone. He drank continuously an' hated himself f'r daein' it. But after a while, in one o' his rare sober moments, he decided tae dedicate himself tae findin' a cure f'r his condition. He decided tae develop an ale that tasted like heaven but didnae have any of the unfortunate consequences."

Burble nodded. "I *have* heard of Impo's ale. It's meant to be damned good. Are you saying Impo succeeded, and his ale is the best in the world?"

"Aye, that is what we believe in the Highlands." Bruce folded his arms and looked meaningfully at his colleagues. "An' sae ye see, we dunnae hae tae follow Testicles any mair 'cos he's goin' f'r the wrong brew. We can gae back tae Way an' leave him tae it."

Trespass scoffed. "So you say. Nice story. But I've heard different."

"Yeah, me too," said Grunt. "Anyway, this ain't *just* about finding out wot Testicles is up to. Now it's personal. Vengeance I say!"

Bruce looked at Burble for support, but the beardless one had other thoughts. "You can have your vengeance, but I want that ale. Think of all the money we could make from it, eh? I say *sod Manis*. He wants us to thwart the gits from The Bear. Okay, so be it. But we don't have to give him anything else. If we find this ale, we should keep it for ourselves."

Frunge opened his mouth to speak, but Trespass cut him off, correctly anticipating that the dense one was about to ask something along the lines of "*Who's Impo?*" or "*Where are we?*" He clenched a fist. "Tomorrow, we find our yaks and then ride. For vengeance and wealth!"

Burble and Grunt echoed the sentiment: "For vengeance and wealth!"

"*Er …*" said Frunge.

The Mungo considered Terry through his one still-open eye. He poured out a flagon of fermented mare's milk and proffered it to the barbarian. After Terry had taken the flagon the Mungo returned to his place amongst his bruised, battered and bandaged comrades – pleased to have escaped without adding further to his already impressive collection of purple skin patches.

"So," declared Khan The Khan, the leader of the Mungo clan which had foolishly crossed the path of Terry's party, "it was a good fight, yes?"

Terry took a contemplative sip of his drink. As the foul liquid flowed over his unsuspecting taste buds his face screwed up into a scowl.

The Khan misinterpreted the grimace. "You thought it was *poor*? We can do it again if you like?"

To a man, the tribal warriors inhaled worriedly. Were they going to have to do *that* again? Fighting was fun, but only if you had a chance of winning.

"Er, no, *that* was fine," declared the barbarian. A sigh of relief spread throughout the tent. "It's just that this milk is, um, a bit warm? That's all."

"Warm fermented milk is for babies," declared The Khan. "What a terrible insult! If Bakedbhean Khan served *me* warm milk I would take him outside and beat the crap out of him." The Mungo leader glowered at his warrior. Bakedbhean Khan paled at the thought of having to go another round with the barbarian.

"Hmm, no need do that," said the monk, with some amusement. "Think he done that to self already. No, fight was good – eh, Roffo?"

When the Mungo horde had attacked, Roffo's horse had bolted over the next rise. On his return – approximately ten minutes after the first assault – he had found prone, groaning Mungos all over the place and his companions chatting amicably with the clan leader. "Er... sounded great from where I was."

"It was, it was," enthused The Khan. "And after such a splendid barny it was only proper that we invite you to dinner."

Terry was still concerned about his drink and wondered how he might ditch it without seeming impolite. "Uh, and what *is* for dinner?"

"Today? We've got horse blood soup for starter, followed by a main course of black pudding ... made from horse blood, naturally. Dessert is fermented mare's milk yoghurt, and we'll round off with a fermented mare's milk cheeseboard. Oh yes, and we have some after dinner mints."

"These mints now," said Roffo, cautiously, "they are made from ...?"

"Fermented mare's milk chocolate, of course. Ah. Here is the first course, brought in by my lovely wife, Billie Khan ..."

A hideous woman pushed her way through the tent flap of the yurt. She was covered in thick skins and smelled of horse grease. Like the rest of the Mungos, her hair was filthy and matted and she appeared to have less than the optimal number of teeth. She carried a tureen full of a bubbling red-black liquid, which she placed in the centre of the carpeted floor. She left again to get some bowls.

"Now, before we start the feast, I must ask you the traditional question that all Mungos ask their guests. Just to get the conversation rolling, you understand. Okay. *What is the best thing in life?*"

The assembled horde leant forward, eager to hear the reply of their formidable guests.

The monk looked at his friends and was invited by their nods to speak for them. "Ah, yes, am ready for such question." He folded his arms. "Best thing in world is *fine ale drunk in good company by warm fireside*. There no greater thing than that. You can keep all wind in hair, lamenting women, soft toilet paper and such. Yes. That is best thing in life."

Meanwhile, on another part of the plain, four yaks and an elephant jostled with five horses for space along the tether line that held them. Five badly bruised yakkers sat around a campfire and held court with five heavily bandaged Mungos. A pot – suspended over the fire – bubbled contentedly with the promise of a healthy bounty.

"That idiot's been trying to milk Jotun," whispered Burble to Trespass. "How can he *not* have noticed that Jotun is *male*?"

"Shut up," murmured Trespass. "Look, he's collected a bucketful. At least it's made him happy."

"Yeah *and* the elephant!"

Grunt, meanwhile, was in conversation with Imran, the leader of the Mungo foraging party. The clan chief was presently showing the Angel his personalised war club.

"Looks like a cricket bat," commented the yakker. "Well it would do if it didn't 'ave all those nails 'ammered through the end."

"Yes, cricket – I know that sport," replied the Mungo. "It is true. I have smitten many of my opponents' balls with this. Look, you can see the round, red marks where I got in some particularly well-timed shots. Ah, here is Toux Khan." Imran called over to a big-nosed Mungo. "Is the food ready yet? I hunger."

"Yes my lord," said the Mungo. "The *Blood and Thunder* is done."

"Blood an' Thunder?" queried Bruce "What in Hull is that?"

"Horse blood and chillies. It is one of our national dishes. But before we serve you we must know the answer to one question. It's a tradition thing. Tell us: *what do you think is the best thing in life?*"

"The best thing in life?" wondered Trespass. "Ah, that's easy!" He rubbed his hands together as though in anticipation. "The best thing in life is: *a comfy armchair, a good book, and a nice pot of tea* … er …" Trespass's jaw dropped. "Uh … did I really say that?"

Nine pairs of eyes stared at him in astonishment.

———◆•◆◆•◆———

"No, you're not supposed to kill us!" declared Pee Khan desperately. "You're *supposed* to give us dinner!"

"Give you *dinner!*" Tombo's well-practised glower slipped from his face, replaced by a look of utter incredulity. "You attack us, lay out half the wimpi, and then expect to be *fed?*" The leader of the Feral Hippos regained his composure. The legendary glower – with a good dose of Attitude – reformed. "Indeed, you *will* be fed … fed to the crocodiles!" Tombo turned to issue an order to his second-in-command. He opened his mouth to speak, but then a thought occurred to him and he returned his attention to the captive Mungo. "This is embarrassing. I don't suppose you have any spare crocodiles we could borrow? I'm afraid we forgot to pack ours."

"Crocodiles? What are they? A type of horse?"

"No. They are short, long things with big teeth …"

"Partial to a bit of leg are they?"

"I'm sorry?"

"Just wondered if they were partial to a bit of leg," the Mungo gestured towards Thunder Chicken, "seeing that most of your horses have only got two legs."

Tombo stared at the man. "They *all* have two legs."

"Cor – must be savage blighters, these crocodiles. Only take the two legs do they … oh, ah, I suppose if they took any *more* then you wouldn't be able to *ride* your horses, and so they wouldn't be *here* for me to see. Silly me!"

"No, you fool!" Tombo threw his arms in the air in frustration. "They're meant to have two legs. They were all born with two legs!"

Pee Khan nodded. "Ah, *I see*. Right. Let me get this straight. Crocodiles are short, long, have big teeth, like a bit of leg, and only have two legs …"

"*Aieeeeee!*" screeched Tombo. "I will make you understand this thing if it *kills you*. Listen carefully! Crocodiles are long and short with big teeth and *four* legs. Our mounts have got two legs because they were born with two legs and are supposed to have two legs. Got it? They would not know what to do with any more legs!"

"Right, okay, we're on the same wavelength now! You ride two-legged horses …"

"Nooooo!" screamed Tombo. "They are not horses, they are *ostriches* …"

"Of the two-legged variety?"

"Yes, all ostriches have two legs!" Tombo tugged on his curly hair with both hands. He danced around in a circle. Eventually he calmed himself. "So. Now tell me. Do you have any crocodiles?"

"Er …" Pee Khan licked his lips and looked at Tombo, and then at the cluster of warriors who had formed around him, obviously concerned about their leader's state of health. "Um … *crocodiles?*"

"Answer!"

"Well, you know, all this shouting and stuff … it's enough to confuse a man. I dunno. One minute four legs, the next two, then four again, I wish you'd make up your mi— Ulp!" An assegai appeared beneath the Mungo's chin. "And, um, you say they are not horses?"

"No. A crocodile is a reptile. It has greenish-brown skin."

"Aha!" Pee Khan snapped his fingers. "Now that you mention green skin … I *have* seen a crocodile. Well, a *bit* of one."

"Speak."

"Well, it was only a bit of its skin really. It was being worn as a loincloth by this huge warrior bloke. Nice fellow actually, once you got talking. Actually, it's only because of him that you won. Half the blokes are still at home nursing their bruises."

Tombo's eyes sparkled menacingly. "And two men travelled with him? An old bald man and a young buffoon?"

"Let me think … yes, that's right. I think. There have been so many people crossing the steppes over the last few days. Funny that. And they've all been looking for the barbarian. Popular guy."

"Like who?"

"Oh, five great hairy hooligans …"

"The Stampeders of the Royal Herd!"

Pee Khan shrugged. "Whatever. And then there were the Librarians from Copros. Nasty bit of work them." He shuddered. "Staring down their great spectacles at you, throwing them index cards. Bloody painful! And you know what? After they'd given us a bit of a hiding they stopped and forced us to have a quick reading lesson." Pee Khan wrung his knuckles in remembered pain. "And whenever you got a word wrong they gave you a fearful belt with their metal rulers. I can barely hold the reins of my horse!"

Tombo saw his father and called over to him. "Dad ... *dad!* Over here!"

Ozbondo bounded over to the group of warriors and their prisoners, the bracelets on his arms and wrists jangling. He gave his son a stern look. "How many times do I have to tell you? Do not call me 'dad' in public! Call me *sir.* Or better still, *Terror of Ubundi.* Or *Scourge of Wizards.* Something like that. Okay?"

"Sorry da— er, *O Friend of the Crocodiles?*"

Ozbondo smiled and rattled his obscene sceptre. "I like that. Now go on."

"This man has seen the barbarian *and* the Stampeders."

The Shaman gave the Mungo a quick sniff to make sure he wasn't a wizard, then rattled some bones at him for effect. He opened his mouth to begin his interrogation but was pre-empted by a groan from the felled Mungo who lay beside Pee Khan.

"Oooooooh! Fermented mare's milkshake please ..." mumbled the slowly awakening figure, "with extra horse blood sugar."

"No no, Jonbu," said Pee Khan. "They're not going to feed us. They want to kill us!"

"Ooooh nooo!"

"Who is that?" asked Tombo.

"Ah, that is my cousin, Jonbu Khan. He is the man who put the 39 in the 39 Steppes."

"And is he more intelligent than you?"

"Well, I wouldn't like to say really. If you mean, will he be easier to talk to, well, he's probably a bit like me. We Mungos tend to clam up a bit when *imminent death* is upon us."

Tombo snarled. "Very well, we will spare your lives if you give us the information we need." From the corner of his eye Tombo noticed that this suggestion brought a sudden glower to his father's face. And what a glower! He'd have to ask for some tips later. "So, tell us. Which way did the barbarian savage go?"

"You're trustworthy, are you?"

"Utterly. I am a man of honour."

"What about the creepy guy?"

Ozbondo's eyes goggled. If they'd had the time he would have personally seen to it that this one died a lingering death. But time was pressing. "Ach! Yes yes. You have my word on it. You will be spared."

"Okay." Pee Khan pointed west. "They went that way. Across the

Steppes towards The Skeletal Coast. A terrible place. The people there refuse to drink horse blood. Savages!"

Ozbondo nodded. "Let us go. We cannot waste any more time with these fools." He turned towards his war ostrich, Feathered Nightmare, as Tombo took the reins of Thunder Chicken. The other warriors began to disperse to their mounts.

"Er … hangabouts!" cried Pee Khan. "You can't go yet. We haven't eaten!"

"So?" said Tombo.

"It's tradition. You beat us, so we've got to feed you."

"Bah … be happy you still have your lives!"

Jonbu sat up suddenly. "Wait! You must answer the question!" He collapsed again.

Ozbondo and Tombo mounted up simultaneously. "What question?" asked the Shaman.

"*The* question," said Pee Khan. "You know. *What is best in life?*"

Ozbondo laughed and treated the Mungos to the kind of look that made strong men fill their trousers. "That is easy. *A cowering population in front of me, a well fed crocodile pit behind me, and a grazing herd of cattle the size of a continent around me!*" He set his heels to Feathered Nightmare and, cackling, set off across the steppes.

The mounted wimpi followed.

———•••———

Tarsal stirred the pot and considered the black-eyed Mungo woman who crouched in front of him. He hadn't meant to give her the shiners but, well, he'd *had* to defend himself when she'd jumped out from behind a clump of grass and attacked him. It had been quite a battle at that! The screaming harridan had landed the first blow – a swinging upper-cut that had nearly taken his head off – after which they had grappled for a bit, during which time he had managed to enrage her even more by ripping her black fishnet stockings. She had responded to this by trying to drill a hole in his head with her stiletto heels. He had eventually overcome her by ripping off her skin-tight leatherware and twisting it around her body to create a kind of straitjacket. Unable to fight on, the woman had given up. She now squatted opposite to him, *staring*. After a moment more, the woman flicked back her jet black hair with a jerk of her head and made to speak to him for the first time.

"I would know the name of the man who has defeated Cher Khan, tigress of the Steppes."

"I am Tarsal, King of the Apes," answered the jungle man. He feigned uninterest by examining the contents of his cooking vessel.

"I have vowed to marry whoever defeats me in a fair fight, ape man," she replied. "*You* are that man. I shall follow you forever."

"Er… I'm flattered, really, but I'm already married, thanks." Tarsal groaned to himself. One feisty woman was more than enough!

"A Mungo's vow is never broken!" The woman leapt up to reveal that she had freed her arms. She pounced on the King of the Apes and pressed him tightly to her heaving bosom. "We will be together forever. You will take me with you to your home and there I will fight this other woman for the right to bear your children!" She released Tarsal and the ape man fell back, gasping for breath.

Cher Khan strutted over to the cooking pot and gave the contents a stir. She raised the ladle towards her lips, but then remembered tradition. She faced her new amour. "Before we eat, great fighter, you must tell me. *What is best in life?*"

"You what?"

"Tell me! It is tradition."

"Oh, er, all right." Tarsal eyed the woman suspiciously. He didn't fancy taking her on again, not without some reinforcements. Perhaps it was best to play along for now. "The greatest thing, my sweet? My friend Cheata knew this well. We discussed it often. The greatest thing in life is: *a bunch of bananas, a good groom, and enough bladder juice to mark out a sizeable jungle territory.*"

Cher Khan's purple-painted lips turned into a frown. "An unusual answer, great fighter." She turned her attention back to the pot and sampled the ape man's cooking. She dropped the ladle. "This isn't properly cooked!" she screamed. "Where's the horse blood? Where's the fermented mare's milk? And what is this? A piece of … *banana*? This *will not do.* And look at the fire, it's about to go out. Pathetic! Run over to my pack mule and get some more firewood! Well, what are you sitting about for, Mr Lazy-good-for-nothing? It's behind that hummock. Now hurry up!"

"Yes, dear." Tarsal ran over to the mule. He paused at its saddle and looked back over his shoulder towards the hidden campfire. He was unobserved. *Bugger this for a game of soldiers!* Facing west, he sprinted at top speed across the plain.

———•◦•◦•———

The battle-weary men were clustered around a dozen campfires. The hosts wore grubby horsehair garments, but the guests wore nothing at all. Around each of the campfires a similar scene was being played out. The half of the men who were clothed tried not to sit *too* close to the half who weren't. The hosts' eyes roved about all over the place, trying desperately to avoid alighting on the bare flesh of their guests. An embarrassed silence lay over all.

At last, around the Executive Campfire, the leader of the Mungo clan cleared his throat. Oyl Khan spoke in an unnatural base voice. "Well then, what brings you to the Steppes?"

"We've come from Nudia," declared Justin, who lounged obscenely, "on a mission to regain a stolen religious icon. Our journey has taken us over high mountains, across seas of impenetrable grass, into thick jungle, and through a land of pretentious wankers."

Oyl Khan nodded in understanding. "Coprolites! Bah! They're always going on about how violence detracts from the pursuit of art and knowledge. They usually refuse to fight us, and we don't fight people who won't fight back. But something has changed." He shivered. "A dreadful host has swept across the plains – a host of screaming Coprolites, armed for war, with fanaticism in their eyes."

"They're fanatics all right," said Jumbo. "They wouldn't let us into any of their inns unless we put a *tie* on. I didn't even know what one was until this man tried to force one around my neck. Some ruckus erupted *then* I can tell you!"

"Yeah," said Dan Glur. "We would have ended up in the Toilet Pits except there were too many of us to fit. They eventually settled for escorting us to their borders."

"Sounds truly terrible," said Oyl Khan. "We may live a nomadic life but at least we honour our guests … *after* we've fought them. And then we feed them. Speaking of which – before we eat, there is one question I must ask you. *What is the best thing in life?*"

The Nudians looked at one another and pondered this profound question. Predictably, it was Justin who got his answer in first. "I can't speak for my less-endowed fellows … but for me the best thing in life is simple. *It is a warm day, a tall pedestal, and an admiring crowd …*"

"What do you mean, you're pregnant?" stammered the Rockgod. "That is most definitely *not* the best thing in life!"

"But surely a sumptuous meal served by a busty barmaid, followed by a tale of lusty adventure from a master storyteller is better!" persisted Roffo, as they descended the Giant Steppe.

"What about ale?" asked Terry.

"Well, I took that as read. Ale before the meal, during, and after."

"Okay," said Terry, "but what type of meal?"

"Roast beef perhaps?"

"And roast potatoes?"

"Naturally."

"And where do you lie on the question of sprouts and cabbage?"

Roffo feigned terror. "I am with you a hundred percent on them! They are the vegetables of Bulabothel! No, consider the meal as including nothing more obnoxious than peas and carrots."

"Er ... remember, I'm a barbarian! We're allergic to *all* vegetables. Can I leave them aside?"

"Better still, you can put them on your knife and flick them at your fellow diners."

Terry nodded sagely. "In that case, I am with you. Your idea *is* what is best in life."

The monk chuckled at this. "Ah, but Roffo, you forget! What about game of Riske afterwards?"

The junior barman slapped his forehead. "How could I forget? Of course, the meal would have to be followed by—"

"Um, I'd rather not," said Terry. "Could I just, um, nip off with the barmaid and leave it to you?"

"Well, depends on who she was."

A sparkle entered Terry's eye. "Maddy?"

"And now you're being mischievous. Hands off!"

Terry laughed and gave a little bow from his saddle. "She's all yours."

Stretched out before the three adventurers, as they rode along with their pack mule in tow, was the land of Vegetopia. A narrow river wove its way across green, cultivated fields, passing before the gates of a city that squatted in the middle of the flat countryside. From within the walls of the city, five tall, thin towers could be seen projecting skywards, no doubt reflecting an attempt by some religious cult to channel the prayers of the devout straight to the gods in heaven. A road swung in front of the men, heading like an arrow to the city, crossing the river at a little bridge. The men soon joined this road.

CHAPTER 16

A PERSISTENT VEGETATIVE STATE

"OH MY god," quailed the man, a Captain in the Vegetopian Home Guard. "Grotesques!"

The three adventurers exchanged bemused glances. Roffo twisted around in his saddle to look behind, but no-one was there. The monk scowled in a manner suggesting he was not exactly plussed.

A dozen guards piled out of the guardhouse and rushed up to the barrier that crossed the road.

"Holy Macartny!"

"Lawks!"

"Bloody Hull!"

They dived for cover behind water barrels, stacks of hay, and a little stone wall. A tardy trooper appeared in the doorway of the guardhouse wearing nothing but a protective skirt of reinforced leather-and-metal strips. His puny white torso was so emaciated he could have been a calendar pin-up for the Society of Anorexic Stick-men. The trooper's jaw dropped, and the piece of lettuce he had been munching fluttered from his hands. "Pork sausages!" he blasphemed. He leapt back inside the hut and slammed the door shut.

"Was it something I said?" wondered Roffo.

"No," scowled the monk, "something did."

"Eh? What's that then?"

"Ate healthily for most of life. Eschewed ridiculous diets. Drank beer. Ate meat."

"Stop stop," laughed Roffo, "you're making me salivate!"

The Captain – whose name was Twig – poked his head up from behind the stone wall. "Grotesques, go away! There is nothing for you to eat here!" His head disappeared again.

A voice from beside the Captain said, "D'you think it's a trick? You know, like the Wooden Hamster of Ploy?"

"Yeah, that's pressed me buzzer," said a voice from the other side of the Captain. "I reckon they're just, thingummies, *puppets*. Inside there are prob'ly ten blood-crazed squads of Quorns. Def'nite."

"You think so?" asked Captain Twig. "And they think we're going to take that little package into the heart of our city and then go for an early night?" He chortled. "They must think we were born yesterday!"

"This getting ridiculous," muttered the monk. "Oy! Buggers! Stop pissing about and open gate."

"Or he'll huff, and he'll puff," giggled one of the hidden guards hysterically, "and he'll blow our shed in!"

"Control yourself, man!" said Twig. "Someone, slap him around the face." The Captain slowly rose up to face the travellers. He held his hands wide to show that he had no weapons. He wore a thin leather tunic, an armoured skirt, and a helmet crested with red boar's hair. The Captain licked his thin lips, nervously.

"Tricksters from Quorn," he stated, "take away these hideous caricatures of men and their beasts. We're not going to fall for *that* one. I give you five minutes and then, cease-fire or no cease-fire, we will fall upon you like a shower of meteorites. So I swear by the great goddess Macartny!"

"Foolish man! We not puppets, but real men!"

"What, even ..." the Captain scrunched up his face in disgust, "... *that!*" He pointed at Terry. "It is just not possible to be so *hideously deformed*, so *grossly mutated*, so *abominably misshapen*, as *that!*"

Roffo had an idea. His eyes widened in understanding. Then a cunning look stole across his features. He cleared his throat to catch the Captain's attention. "Um, that's a rather ungenerous attitude, mocking our poor friend here. Doesn't your goddess teach compassion and charity? Look at the poor man. It's his glands, you know."

The Captain frowned. "Glands?"

"Aye, a terrible complaint he has. Biglanditis. That's it. In fact, we've all got it, but he's the worst by far. You know, sometimes when I get up in the morning and see him, first thing like, it makes me want to puke. But look at him: in spite of his *monstrous affliction* he bears up with a cheery demeanour. And do you know why?"

"Er, why?"

"Because he has *hope*. And that's because he knows his condition isn't incurable ..."

367

The monk nodded now. Clever. He saw the drift. "La, it is so!" he interjected. "Wise medicine man say there one place where may be cured. It holy land of Vegetopia, where sublime people know what's what. There, and only there, is cure to be found."

"No – really?" the Captain felt rather chuffed. People had heard of his land? And what's more, they were thought to be *sublime*!

Terry looked at his friends in bewilderment and opened his mouth to speak, but Roffo got in first. "Yeah, it's true. And this wise geezer also said: 'Do not go to Quorn, as the people there are all complete gits and they'll only laugh at you.' Straight up. That's what he said!"

The troopers began to stand up from behind their various shelters, curiosity gradually replacing fear. One man, called Berry, slowly edged over to the travellers. He looked at his Captain quizzically, in response to which Twig simply nodded. The man reached up to Terry – who was sitting astride his horse – and prodded him in the abdomen. His puny finger was barely able to make an impression on the barbarian's iron muscles. Berry then clenched his fist and knocked on Terry's belly.

"Well, he's not hollow!" The trooper edged back into a little cluster of his colleagues. They patted him on the back and looked at the hand that had come into contact with the malformed human leviathan.

"Hmm, well, I'm at a bit of a loss here," said Twig. "I guess you'd better enter." He turned to his men. "Berry, Horseradish, Minty, come with me. We'd better escort our guests into town. Robin, run ahead and warn people. I don't want the senate accusing me of giving people heart attacks. And tell people to get their children indoors. *Sublime*, eh? Ha ha! Right, move out!"

"So, when do we go and get him?" enquired Hendy, feeling a flush of excitement. The current case was the most perilous in which he had been involved; more so, even, than the Case of the Dyslexic Graffiti Artists and their Unmentionable Paint. "What are we waiting for? We've nailed him!"

"Nailed!" exclaimed Boomber sullenly. "If we goes barging into The Pilgrim to arrest him it'll be us what's nailed, probably to the bar by his mates! Isn't that right, guv?"

"Alas, my dear Sergeant," sighed Yavlo philosophically, "I fear that you are right. It is an unfortunate fact that in this town the criminal fraternity outnumber the law keepers by a significant majority. It is also true that the good citizens of Cross-My-Way are unlikely to offer us much in the way of assistance, their sense of self-preservation being far stronger than their sense of justice."

"*Oh don't forsake me oh my darling,*" warbled a voice from one of the holding cells, "*I do not know what fate awaits me … I only know I must be brave … for I must face a man who hates me … or lie a coward – a craven coward – in my grave…*"

"Be quiet in there!" yelled Boomber, glaring through the door leading to the cells. "That bloody blues minstrel is getting right on my nerves. I know he's supposed to suffer for his art, but do we have to as well?"

Yavlo frowned. "I know, Sergeant, but singing drunkenly outside the bedroom window of a police officer at two o'clock in the morning is a serious offence. It is not something I can simply ignore."

"But, guv, he did it on purpose so you'd lock him up. You *know* what he's like. I think you're just encouraging him."

Yavlo smiled at this. "Do you really think so? Shall we go and ask him how he is enjoying his stay? Come along, gentlemen." The Inspector led the way into the back section of the station house. The minstrel was in the end cell, where he was due to remain until his trial – which was likely to be some time off, since the town's prison was fully booked for the foreseeable future. Yavlo smiled at the prisoner. "Ah, Mr Waters, how are things with you?"

The minstrel – a tall, slim, dark-haired fellow – scowled. "Not good! In fact, I have a number of complaints to make."

"Oh, yes? And what are they?"

"Well, this bed for one." The minstrel swung his legs around so that he was sitting upright on the derided item. "How am I supposed to get a *terrible* night's sleep in here: it's far too soft! I am used to sleeping on lumpy pillows, hard mattresses, and unwashed sheets infested with fleas and bed bugs. Look at how clean this place is. It just will not do!"

"And what about the food."

The minstrel punched his own thigh in displeasure. "It is really rather excellent. Where are the undercooked sprouts I was expecting? I even anticipated a pie or two from a rather notorious gentleman who's name I dare not even utter. While I've been here I have not thrown up once."

"Hmm, I see." Yavlo nodded. "And what of the other amenities?"

"The loos are spotless, and the paper is soft. Where is the sandpaper? In fact, the only moment of song-writing stimulation I've had since my arrival was when I poked a finger through the paper. I was almost happy.

But then I noticed that the lavatory *not only* had hot running water, but it had soap as well. Bah! How am I meant to be inspired in here?"

"So," summed up the Inspector, "can I take it that you have learned the error of your ways, and that we will see no more of you after your release?"

"Too bloody right!"

Yavlo turned to his Sergeant. "There you go. I believe I have turned the situation to our advantage. Constable Hendy, are you all right?"

"Oh, ah, yes guv. Sorry. Wasn't listening. I was thinking about how to arrest that naughty Master Manis. We need a plan, you know."

"A plan – really?" exclaimed Boomber. "Well I never! Young Hendy has Inspector Material written all over him … ah, begging your pardon, guv."

"That's quite all right, Sergeant." In truth, Yavlo had not caught the gist of the Sergeant's sarcasm. His mind was elsewhere too. He looked at the minstrel thoughtfully from under a furrowed brow. Mr Waters had swept up his guitar and was attempting to tune it. "Now who," mused the Inspector to himself, "would best know of schemes for triumphing over adversity?" More loudly, he asked: "Mr Waters, you are a teller of tales are you not?"

"Musical tales. That's right."

"And you would therefore have a wide repertoire of, how can I put this, sad tales where powerful, happy fellows meet terrible difficulties?"

"I have some absolute crackers. Somebody comes a cropper in all of my songs. Powerful fellows especially. The bigger they are the harder they fall. And the happier they start out, the more miserable they become."

"I see …"

"Guv," said Boomber, worriedly, "I hope you know what you're doing."

"I believe so, Sergeant. Now, Mr Waters, do you think you could do something for me?"

The minstrel sensed something was up. He put down his guitar and directed his full attention to the policemen who stood beyond the bars of his cell. "Maybe," he said. "But if I do I want some concessions."

Yavlo nodded. "I shall search out the most festering bedding in town, and I shall commission a job lot of pies. Okay?"

"Fair enough. What do you want?"

"I want you to tell me a tale. It is a tale about how a sad, weak collection of fellows meet a dreadful adversary and best him. The adversary is very powerful, fairly wealthy, and extraordinarily happy."

The minstrel smirked. "And he owns an inn, eh? Such people are always the happiest. I get your gist." The minstrel scratched his head. "Well, assuming you wanted to add misery to the life of the Happy One, the *first* thing you'd have to do is turn the powerful man's friends against him."

Yavlo waved at Hendy, indicating that he should start taking notes. He turned back to the minstrel. "Carry on, sir. How do we, er, *the weak brotherhood* do this?"

"Generally, *they* should start by telling Mr Happy's mates false stories about how he has slept with their wives, daughters, sons, parents, or livestock. Alternatively, they should make up porkies about how Mr Happy has done a dirty business deal behind his friends' backs."

"Cor … that's cunning," said a suddenly interested Boomber. "Very cunning."

"Yep," continued the minstrel. "Another thing your hypothetical brotherhood should do is destroy Mr Happy's alliances. To use another analogy, they must ensure that the cavalry of a neighbouring allied power won't charge to Mr Happy's rescue right at the end. But it is important that Mr Happy retains the hope that this might happen right up to the *very* bitter end."

"*Destroy … alliances,*" muttered the desperately scribbling Hendy.

"Also, the weak chappies should corrupt the source of Mr Happy's wealth. If he's broke, he can't hire any new mercenaries to fight for him. Got that? Right. Next, the victim's wife must be made to—"

"Excuse me," interrupted Yavlo. "Can we assume that the, ah, Happy Victim does not have a wife?"

"No wife? Hmm." The minstrel paused for a moment, then nodded to himself and continued. "Right, well, it's got to be his faithful dog then …" The minstrel noticed a shaking of heads. "Pet cat? Budgerigar? Teddy bear? Look – it doesn't matter, okay! It's the principle that's important. The victim's closest friend-lover-pet-pot plant-whatever, must be made to meet a tragic end, probably under the hooves of a rampaging yak. Preferably, a yak owned by Mr Happy. Preferably a *prize* yak. And *this* must *also* die in the incident." The minstrel leaned back against the wall and smiled. "By this stage, our Happy Hero should not be quite so smug. Indeed, he should be friend-less, spouse-less, alliance-less, money-less, power-less, and pet-less. At this point, the wicked perpetrators must strike. *Ta-dah!*"

"Very good! I do believe, gentlemen, that we now have the plan that Constable Hendy was seeking! Boomber –" he faced his Sergeant

"– get out the blackboard and start writing down a list of all of Master Manis's friends and allies."

"You don't have to make a list of them, guv," replied the Sergeant. "Just go over to the 'Wanted, Dead or Alive' notice board. They're all there ... oh, apart from the merchant who sold him the Mardon's. I guess he counts as an ally."

"Yes, you are right. He could be a problem ..."

Hendy looked up at this. "Ah, guv, I have some info on this matter. Well, you know how Young Festers is my cousin, and how he's also a regular at The Pilgrim? Well, I was at a family get-together the other weekend, and he told me that Manis is expecting more Pedigree to be delivered in a few weeks ..."

"Good show, Hendy!" cried Yavlo. "A splendid piece of detecting! Mr Waters – your recommendation?"

"Ah, well, send someone to meet the caravan. Someone with plenty of tall tales."

"I take it we can rely on a certain master storyteller for help here? Excellent! Now, how do we go about turning ..." Yavlo's enthusiasm petered out. His eyebrows arched. He shook his head, as though to clear it of some mental foggery. "What am I saying? Turning people against others? As officers of the law we should not even be contemplating such a devious underhand scheme! Will we not become as tainted as those we seek to bring to justice?"

"Guv," said Boomber, deciding that it was at last time to get off the fence and unfurl his colours, "do you remember who it was who had you kicked out of his inn? Do you remember who made you look like a right prat in front of everyone there, aye, and made you the laughing stock of the whole town?"

"Yes," scowled Yavlo. "Thank you, Boomber. He's dead meat! Come, Sergeant, let us repair next door to plot and scheme ..."

"And have a brew-up, guv?"

"Indeed, Sergeant. And Hendy, perhaps you would like to sort out the good minstrel's dinner. Gentlemen, let us act!"

Constable Hendy watched his commanding officer go. He shook his head in admiration. "Like a new man!" He turned back to the prisoner. "Right, Mr Waters, sir, I'll just find your arrest card and note down your special dietary requirements, okay? Ah, here it is: 'Name: Mr M. Waters, Occupation: Blues Minstrel.' Aha! For the record, sir, could you just fill me in on what the 'M' stands for? Masochist?"

"Oh no, lad," said the minstrel. "It's *Machiavelli.*"

The adventurers had been installed at The Succulent Shoot, a hotel in the centre of town. A whole floor had been cleared for them, with each man given a large suite to himself. A detachment of Guards had been placed by the central stairwell to escort the adventurers whenever they left their rooms. They were all currently in Terry's suite, along with Captain Twig and the worried-looking hotelier, Rooty, who was hovering close to the door, ready to bolt at the first sign of teeth.

"Sorry about the precautions," said Twig, directing himself to the monk. He regarded both the oriental and Roffo as seriously-obese-but-virtually-human, though he could not bring himself to even look at the barbarian. "Everyone's a bit jumpy. We've been at war with Quorn over a vegetable patch for the last two years. There's a truce on at the moment, but we're all a bit paranoid about Quorn spies poisoning our cress. The escort is for your own protection."

The monk bowed. "Thank you for hospitality. Escort really not necessary though – can look after selves."

Twig frowned. "Yes, I'm sure you can, but I've got strict instructions from the Senate. You can stay until you get better, but I have to keep an eye on you." He shrugged. "Those are the rules. I've been seconded to the Guards, so if you need anything I'll be just outside."

Twig turned to leave, but the hotelier placed a hand on the Captain's weedy chest. "Wait a mo'. I'm still not 'appy with this. What guarantee do I 'ave that they ain't gonna eat my furniture? These aren't cheap rooms, y'know."

"Too bloody right!" declared Roffo. "With the rates you're charging us, you'll be able to afford a new chain of hotels by the end of the week!"

Rooty looked at the fat man, aghast. "Well, they're the normal rates …" Twig spluttered. The hotelier glared at the Captain. "Anyway, I ain't leavin' until I get a deposit or somethin'."

"Hey," said Roffo, as an overloud aside to his comrades, "I'm hungry. Are you hungry? What's for dinner …?" He turned back to face the hotelier. He raised his eyebrows in an exaggerated manner and started to lick his lips. "Oh, look what I've found!"

"Urk!" Rooty pelted through the door. Shaking his head in disapproval, Twig followed. The Captain closed the door behind him.

"Actually," said Roffo, "I *am* hungry. Didn't I see a mini-bar just now?"

"Already there!" laughed Terry. The three men clustered around the icebox – a relatively recent innovation in high-cost hotel rooms throughout the continent. The refrigerator was affixed to the wall, being connected to a muffled pipe which passed through the ceiling and the floor. Ice was periodically fed into the pipe from the roof, dropping into a compartment in the refrigerator *per se*. When the ice melted, it drained away down the pipe into the basement, providing the hotel with drinking water.

Terry opened the metal box.

"What the …" Roffo peered over Terry's shoulder as the barbarian began to pass out the refrigerator's contents. "Celery sticks? Iceberg lettuce? Cold beans on cocktail sticks … ugh!"

Terry took out a bottle of clear liquid. "Gin?" He took a shot. "Mineral water!"

"What's in that bowl … *ohmigawd, it's raw sprouts*! Someone, please, disembowel me!"

The monk started tucking into a bowl of coleslaw. "Hmm, not bad."

"Not bad if you're a rabbit," declared Roffo, with a long face, "but if you're a hideous bloated fatguts like us, you need meat, junk food, things with sugar in. And ale. Don't tell me they're teetotal too? No ale? And I thought Copros was bad."

Terry groaned. "So you don't think there'll be any wine then? And … and … and … no steaks? Hamburgers? Hot Dogs? Fried Duck? Lamb with mint sauce? Camel Tartare? Roast Wildebeest? Fish? Sparrow Surprised?"

"Terry, stop torturing yourself!" Roffo had never seen the barbarian so upset before. He turned to the monk. "This is desperate! We've got to find the map quick so we can get out of here. Don't worry, Terry … tonight we'll slip out the window or something and go hunting. There must be loads of game around since these buggers don't eat anything." He consolingly patted his friend's shoulder. "Okay, I declare this Council of War in session. Right, Mr Monk, where do you reckon …"

———————

"You've absolutely no chance with that bunch of milkbar wimplings!" declared a gleeful Manis, as he waved dismissively at the five jittery men standing by a large table near The Pilgrim's front door. "That lot couldn't drink four pints in an evening, let alone at competition speed!"

The partisan crowd within the confines of the dark pub heartily cheered their leader, waving abusive gestures towards the small pocket of Bear supporters that had ventured into enemy territory for the contest.

"We will see, Master Manis, we will see," replied Hops, in a manner that, he hoped, oozed confidence and belief. He turned to his supporters and gave them a cheery wave. They returned a half-hearted hurrah and quickly went back to their pre-competition game of 'guess-what-the-hell-that-big-floaty-bit-in-my-beer-is'.

The loud knelling of The Pilgrim's bell broke their collective concentration. Mitchkin the umpire stepped forward and raised his (bandaged) hands, indicating that he wanted silence.

"Ladies and gentlemen, Manis welcomes you to the newly inaugurated Cross-My-Way Beer And Cream Cake Competition. This event, designed to show off the athletic, manly characteristics of the local hostelry clientele, involves the downing of four pints of finest ale and consumption of three of Mrs Frettal's sweetest cream cakes. Each of the competing inns supplies a team of five individuals who must each drink and eat the full complement of beer and cakes in the exact order: to wit, a beer, a cake, a beer, a cake, a beer, a cake and finally, bugger me, a beer. The team that finishes first wins and garners glory and fame unto their local. Let the beer be drawn and the cakes be, er, *creamed*!" The crowd roared its approval and Mitchkin the umpire took a bow, allowing Mitchkin the thief to steal the socks off the feet of one of the people in the front row.

Manis cheered along with the crowd. He could hardly believe that Hops had fallen for *this* one. All he had done was say "prove it" when he had heard Hops boasting about the ale-downing prowess of his clientele to some of the stallholders in the market, and the fat one had had to go for it or lose face. He knew his erstwhile foe had little hope of winning this type of competition at the best of times, but with his champion ale-downer out of town? His chances were non-existent! Manis had wondered whether Hops had anything up his sleeve, but in the end had come to the conclusion that his opposite number was simply here to keep warm and get some free advertising from the event.

Manis looked along the line of his team – serious drinkers to a man. And the fact that he had locked Old Blunster and Deknat in the Pilgrim's ale-free stable for five hours had given his team's two stars a real thirst for competition. These two were presently chained to the inn's walls to stop them from getting their desperate hands on the competition pints that Spotty Wembers had deliberately put just out of their outstretched reach. The other three members of his team – Sly Herrold, Bestial Bob and Fingers – were receiving the accolades of the crowd and eyeing their free ales greedily.

Meanwhile, Hops was quietly preparing his own troops for battle. These were not men who drank fast *as such*. That is, they were men who *could* do the occasional yard of ale when required, but they were instead *stayers* – men who measured their drinking exploits with calendars rather than stopwatches.

Hops addressed his men. "Right lads, it's not as bad as it seems. Sure they can drink, but can they eat cake? That's the hard part. All that sweet, gooey, clammy goodness will get them, I assure you."

"Might get us, too," noted Horus with a resigned shrug.

Hops ignored him and continued his pep talk. "Phlip, you go first, followed by Horus, then Jepho, Grimwade, and Grevis. Save the best till last, eh?" Hops sidled closer to his team and looked around conspiratorially. He beckoned his squad to look in his hand, which opened to reveal a small bottle full of a bright green liquid.

"Shhhhh… secret weapon! A couple of quick swigs will help lubricate your throats and get the ales down. Old family potion. Get a good slug down your neck, Phlip, and pass it on."

Phlip took the proffered bottle and, with some trepidation, took a surreptitious swig. When he *did not* turn into a frog, or retch himself inside out, he took this as a good sign. He had another quick glug, then passed the potion on. Just as Grevis finished the bottle the bell sounded again and Mitchkin beckoned the teams to take up their places behind their respective tables.

The crowd fell silent.

"Begin!"

Phlip and Deknat simultaneously dived for their first pint. The town drunk easily threw his back… though Phlip almost immediately regained lost time as Deknat went straight for his second in avoidance of his cake-eating responsibilities. Once the drunk had had the alien concept of taking solid nourishment between drinks beaten into him by the Berserker, however, he easily completed his leg of the competition – by which stage The Bear's outie cleaner was still on his last cake! By the time a swaying Phlip started on his fourth pint, Old Blunster was tucking into his first cake – a sight that sent a sickening feeling to the pit of the outie cleaner's stomach. Surely he could not let Hops down again! This thought forced him to down his last drink in a Personal Best time. As soon as he slammed down his empty glass (allowing Horus to start his leg) Phlip realised that the sickening feeling was not related to the thought of failure at all, but was rather due to the excessive volume of liquid and cake that he had just forced into his body. This situation was remedied at about the same time that Blunster finished his leg in the record time of 32 seconds: Phlip orally exploded! A stream of second-hand ale and cake – dyed fluorescent green by Hops's potion – shot across The Pilgrim, clearing the first row of onlookers and coating a small group of Cloverite noviciates who had sneaked out of their seminary to watch the spectacle.

Manis roared hysterically. "This is too easy! Come on boys! You can beat these chunder-wonder has-beens!"

Horus finished his leg, trusting his bulky farrier's frame to hold together better than that of the outie cleaner. Jepho took over, realising he was lost already, for the smell from Phlip's eruption was already turning his stomach over. Herrold finished his stint for the Pilgrim as Jepho's first spew flew across the room. By the time Jepho's ordeal was over, he had personally painted four green streaks across the Pilgrim's floor. Manis went into a fit of apoplectic laughter … and Bestial Bob finished his last pint. This left the Pilgrim hearties with one round to complete, compared with two for those from The Bear. Grimwade began fast while Fingers, realising that he did not have to rush, and slightly worried about the months of ribbing he would have to take if he was the only one from his team to throw up, kept up a slow, steady pace. He need not have worried, for Grimwade had been overeager and outstretched himself, particularly in the stomach department. This situation was rectified as the teacher's gut rapidly contracted and sent a stream of spew in the direction of the unfortunate Mitchkin, who was knocked off his feet by the force of the blast. Feeling better for this, Grimwade gamely carried on, but as he finished his stage Fingers began his last pint. Indeed, the light-fingered one euphorically slammed down his last glass before Grevis had reached his first cake, denying the fatman his favourite treat, and signalling a Pilgrim victory … *of sorts*.

"We've won! We've won!" bellowed an ecstatic Manis, who turned to receive the viewing public's adulation. The assembled masses were, however, not as animated as the triumphant barman expected. In fact, rather than exhibiting red-faced excitement, most were rather pale. Occasionally an empty space in the crowd opened up as a few of his patrons skipped rapidly away from some central individual. Weird behaviour for winners, he thought, but Manis had little time for thinking when there was gloating to be done!

"Ah, Hops. I think this proves—" Manis was interrupted by the sound of retching behind him. He turned to berate Phlip, but instead found himself facing Young Festers, who had his hands over his mouth, trying to retain his diced carrot collection. He was failing badly. On looking around his bar, all Manis could see were people reacting badly to the smell generated by the vomit from the Bear team. The reaction went critical.

"What was that you were saying, Manis?" shouted Hops over the cacophony of wailing and gagging, as he edged to The Pilgrim's front door. "You don't think you'll be able to get the smell of vomit out of your bar for weeks? That's terrible! And you'll never get those green stains out of your woodwork? Awful! Well, my bar is nice and clean now, you know. You should all come over and see it!" And with that, he scuttled through the door and hared across the square.

A thunderous stampede followed in his wake as Manis's desperate clientele headed for the sweeter smell of The Bear ...

———————

Since the adventurers had no clear idea where the map fragment might be, they decided to split up to hasten their search. Without delay, the men emerged from the hotel into the early afternoon. Each had his own personal detachment of Guards in tow.

"Well, see ya later," cried Roffo.

"Yeah, if I survive that long. Roast pork!"

"*Shhhhh!* We mustn't make our hosts suspicious, Terry. Remember we're here to lose weight. Mum's the word. Later!" Roffo turned right and headed off down the road. The monk gave Terry a thumbs-up, then set off in the opposite direction. This left the barbarian standing outside the hotel in the company of half a dozen uneasily shifting soldiers, who watched him with horrified distrust.

Sergeant Ferny sidled up to the barbarian. "Where to, then?"

Terry looked down at the man. He was as thin as a post, with the sort of gaunt face characteristic of all of the citizens of Vegetopia: prominent cheekbones, lots of severe angles, and a nose so sharp you could open letters with it. The man's physique was such that his leather armour looked over-sized and faintly ridiculous, while his helmet – sitting atop a head that already appeared bulbous as a consequence of the thinness of the body beneath – made the man look top-heavy. Terry was surprised that the Sergeant was able to walk without toppling over.

"Uh, this way?" Terry pointed at the road leading directly away from them. This formed a T-junction with the road on which the hotel was situated. Ferny shrugged and gestured for the barbarian to lead the way. The Sergeant and his men fell in behind.

Terry ambled along the narrow road, passing tall, thin houses with whitewashed walls and green doors. After a short distance the housing gave way to shops. Outside a blacksmith's shop, Terry came across a scrawny man in a black apron, gasping for breath. The smith strained to raise a little hammer above his head, then brought this down onto a horseshoe. After more gasping the man repeated the action – his bare, grease-stained, matchstick arm trembling with the effort. The smith looked up as Terry's shadow rolled over the anvil. His eyes bulged in disbelief; the hammer dropped from his hand onto his toe.

"Ouch!" cried Terry in sympathy, before hurrying on.

The barbarian led his escort into an area in which clothes shops appeared to dominate. He stopped to look in the window of one of these. All of the clothing seemed to be made from sackcloth or cotton. A thought occurred to him and he turned to Ferny. "I notice you're wearing leather armour, but I've not seen anyone else wearing leather. Or furs."

"Ahem, yes, well, touchy subject there." The Sergeant lifted his helmet and scratched his head. "It's a case of necessity before beliefs. We don't believe in harming animals and wotnot, but, well, if you need protection you need protection and leather does the job. But we only use the hides of cows that have died from natural causes. You know: heart attacks; strokes; accidentally coming into contact with sharp objects. That sort of thing. We've a special, er, *dispensation* to wear leather. But we only use it because those buggers from Quorn do, and we can't let them have an advantage, can we!"

"And you don't mind?"

"Me? Well, don't get me wrong – *down* with all animal tormentors and all that – but it's comfortable, tough, and you don't need to wash it every week." Ferny grinned, then remembered himself, and frowned disapprovingly once more. "But some men *do* refuse. Conscientious Objectors we call them." He shrugged. "What can you do? It don't help the war effort, but we're not savages. We put them to work on the cress farms."

Terry frowned. Conscientious Objectors? Barbarians didn't have many of those, although Terry did recall one occasion back home when a man had refused to join a pillaging party. They'd put him to work in the fields, too. *As fertiliser.*

"By the way," said Ferny, "talking of clothes … That's a funny-looking loincloth you're wearing. Green? What's it made of?"

"It's made of croco … er … *grass.*"

"Croco Grass? Never heard of that before. Weird foreign stuff, eh?"

"Er, yeah, that's right." Terry turned quickly and continued on.

The road soon emerged into the central town square. As Terry came out of the shadows and into the open, his sudden appearance was met with a chorus of screams. Skinny women grabbed undernourished children and shielded their eyes. Some people turned and fled. Others dropped to their knees and clasped their hands in prayer.

"Shit!" cursed Ferny. He and his men fanned out and made calming gestures while Terry stood behind them in bemusement. The panic rapidly died down and turned to curiosity. An arc of people gathered around to stare.

Terry waved in embarrassment at a couple of children – who instantly burst into tears. "Mummy mummy," bawled one, "don't let him eat me!" A man beside them turned and started retching. Terry shook his head and hurried on. The Guards formed a protective cordon; the crowd rolled along after them.

On their right they came to a grand building of white marble. Senatorial Guards flanked the front entrance, but there was another entrance a little further along. A small line of people queued there.

"The Senate," said Ferny, in answer to an unspoken query. "The queue is for the Public Gallery."

"Can we go in? I, er, wouldn't mind ditching this crowd."

Ferny considered this and frowned. "Well … I guess so. But you will behave, won't you? This is the seat of power and everything."

"Cross my heart!"

The people in the queue to the Public Gallery fled in panic as the barbarian approached, allowing his party to jump straight to the front. Terry was ushered through the doors, along a corridor, and up some stairs. The party came to another door. This time, Ferny went in alone to explain the situation to the occupants. After several minutes, he stuck his head out of the door and beckoned the others inside. Half of the Gallery was empty: people crushed together in the other half in a desperate attempt to get as far away from the hideous stranger as they could. Terry turned away from the other visitors and considered the action below.

Several rows of marble benches faced each other across a broad floor. Toga-clad anorexics rested their bony flanks on these benches. One of their number – a man with lank, black hair and a huge, hooked nose – strode about the floor, speaking and gesticulating. For the moment, Terry ignored the speaker and instead surveyed the interior of the building. Could the map fragment be here? Perhaps, as in Ubundi, it was seen as a kind of trophy or relic of power? Maybe it would be on open display? The walls of the Senate, however, comprised unadorned white marble. The only other item in the large room was a throne: this was perpendicular to the rows of benches and currently unoccupied. Like the rest of the interior, it was rather plain, being made of simply carved wood, with scrolled arm-rests and a red cushion.

Terry turned his attention to the debate.

"… and so to say, as Nutlet does, that a *siege catapult* is an artificial device, contrived by man and therefore against Nature and an abomination, is clearly an absurdity. How so is it more *unNatural* than a spear, or than a horseshoe, or than a house? Indeed, how so is it more unNatural than a beaver's dam? Are we then to conclude that the building of spears and horseshoes and houses is a sin against Mother Nature?" The orator, who had been facing the rows of benches to the right, now turned to face his own side on the left. He gave a mischievous grin. "If we follow Nutlet, my friends, then we must surely abandon our homes and move into the forest. And more, we must breach the dams of the cursed beavers, and we must rush through the forest like thunder and tilt the birds from out of their nests, and we must fill in the badger setts, and we must *remonstrate* with the misguided creatures for their unholy follies!"

The people to the left, of whom perhaps a third were women, slapped their knees and howled with laughter. From the all-male benches to the right, a silver-haired man rose up on a walking stick.

"Tarka is being deliberately mischievous! I ask for the floor … where is that bloody Speaker …?"

A man now emerged from behind an arras, adjusting his toga. He smiled sheepishly and sat down on the plain throne. "Sorry, people, call of Nature. The Chair recognises Nutlet!"

The silver-haired man took the floor, while dark-haired Tarka retired to the front bench opposite. "Tarka misrepresents me! All men must take shelter from the elements, and the creatures that are more attuned to Nature know this. They should form our role models …"

"Oh, and they use spears, do they?" chortled one of the women opposite.

"Aye," said another, "but they beat them into ploughshares when the war is over!"

Nutlet glared at his howling opponents and turned to scowl at the Speaker.

"Er, I say, please, let Nutlet speak!"

"Thank you, Speaker. The spear and the plough and the house, and before you say more, the wheel and the cart and the plate, these are all necessities of life! Because we have lost touch with Nature we no longer have claws and beaks – and so we must have spears. We can no longer run like the cheetah, and so we must be carried upon carts ..."

"And we can no longer dig holes like badgers," shouted an excitable man, sitting beside Tarka, "so we must build houses?"

"No, er, yes, er, you know what I mean, damn it! Some things are Natural and *Simple* ..."

"Like Nutlet!" bellowed the first woman, making an observation that was greeted with much mirth.

"... and some are *Complex*," continued Nutlet, undeterred, "and are therefore unnecessary and fabricated and *lose* Nature ..."

"What a load of bollocks," shouted Tarka, drawing a gasp from the benches behind his adversary. "A siege catapult is like a spear, it serves for defence, and defence is a pre-requisite of Nature and of life itself. We ourselves are the product of Nature. We *are not* inferior to the animals ..." howls of protest came from the opposition benches at this "... and we are not *more* removed from Nature than they. And the things we build are therefore the *products* of the *products* of Nature, and are Natural. This *Complexity* issues is the biggest load of mis-thinking bollocks I've ever heard ..."

"Hear hear!"

"The next thing we know, Nutlet will be calling this very building Complex and Anti-Nature and demanding its destruction ..."

Terry turned to Ferny. "Er, do you understand any of this?"

The Sergeant laughed. "Macartny no! These are politicians. We just shut them in here and let them ramble while the rest of us get on with it. They're usually harmless enough."

Terry looked down upon the chaos below and shook his head. A debate about whether siege catapults were *Natural* and should be built? Madness! Barbarians, who were closer to Nature than civilised men, had a very practical view on the whole Nature question. It went: *so what?* They had more important things to worry about. Like how to pillage the town over the hill, and who was going to pay for the next round, and where the next haunch of beef was coming from.

"I think I've seen enough. Can we go?"

"Cherish the creatures, both great and small, for they are the Children of the Great Earth Mother. Suffer no harm to come to their shiny pelts or their feathery bodies, respect their rights to twitter and to roar and to defecate wheresoever they might wish. Aspire to their innocence, protect their essences, and be humble before them. Though we may be dirt in the wake of their little paws, pray that in future reincarnations we may be rewarded with ascension to the state of Furrydom. Amen."

"Amen," murmured the congregation. They sat down with a great rustling. At the back of the cathedral, a sour-faced man gurned in disapproval. He was surrounded by an escort of Guards. They all seated themselves.

"Now," said Bishop Vole, leaning forward on his lectern, "I would like to talk to you today about the subject of *sin*. In particular, I want to talk to you about the abuse of what Foreign Criminals and Deviants refer to as *beasts of burden*."

"Bugger," went the Guard sitting to the monk's left.

"Er, I just need to nip out for a pee," said another.

But Sergeant Grass, who commanded this squad, reached out a restraining hand. "Sit still, man, and take your medicine."

The Bishop, in his green cassock and green mitre, scanned the congregation. His eyes alighted on the party at the back. "Aha!" he cried. "I see we have some of our military brethren with us today. Welcome, brothers. And I see that you have an obese stranger in your midst. That is good. Sometimes I weary of preaching to the Good Lambs of my congregation, when it is the Black Sheep who are most in need of instruction. Welcome to you all."

"He's a complete git," whispered the first Guard, whose name was Tadpole. "He saw us come in. I bet he's been waiting for this for some time."

"Shush," said Grass. However, he looked at the monk pleadingly. "Esteemed visitor, do you really want to listen to this?"

The monk waved a hand distractedly. The fragment in Nudia had resided in its temple. Could the Vegetopian piece be similarly situated? He scanned the interior of the cathedral. Stained glass windows depicted a variety of idyllic country scenes, showing animals cheerily romping about in fields and forests. Behind the pulpit was a stone carving of a man tied to a cross. The man's hair was in dreadlocks and, like the Bishop, he had a number of rings through his eyebrows, lip, and nose. Little birds sat on the arm of the cross, looking at the man sorrowfully. The monk noticed that this scene was repeated on two further stained glass windows. In one, a dozen villains milled around at the foot of the cross. They wore little round hard hats and big yellow jackets. Some held truncheons, and one was chewing on a chicken leg.

"... and I say to you, there is no excuse." The Bishop had been speaking. "Does the horse say unto you, 'Yea, get thee onto my back and I will gladly carry you until I collapse in exhaustion'? He does not! Does the mule say, 'Oh go on then, load me up with heavy articles until my back creaks in agony, no no, I don't mind'? NO! He does not!"

"Here it comes," muttered Tadpole.

"To use animals to carry us and our burdens is a travesty and a sin! It is a sin born of laziness and of moral turpitude. It is yet one more step along the road to Exploitation and, my children, that is the road to Hull!"* The Bishop was growing excited. He leaned forward on his lectern and pointed at the party at the back. "And so behold, my children, the main perpetrators of this sin ..."

"Ooooh Macartny ..." Tadpole wriggled down so that only his eyes peered above the pew in front. The other soldiers tried to do likewise – all except the Sergeant, who sat up straight and glared at the Bishop challengingly.

"Yes, it is well that you shrink in embarrassment! *War with Quorn* they say! Aye, they relish such a war for it allows them to indulge in all sorts of depravities, from riding on the backs of horses, to stripping the very flesh from dear, dumb cows and turning it into trendy clothing. Where will it end?"

The congregation hissed at this, and people turned to look back at the soldiers. The Bishop took off his mitre before it fell off. His dreadlocked hair cascaded onto his shoulders. He opened his mouth to continue his diatribe ...

The monk pondered events. There were undoubtedly private chambers here, perhaps even treasure rooms, though the cathedral was not half as big as the temple of Nudia. How could he get in while shadowed by these troops? Of course!

The monk leaned over to Sergeant Grass. "Hmm, interesting sermon. Very, ah, unhelpful to cause."

"What do you mean?"

"Bishop want soldiers to disarm. Disband cavalry. Dispose of armour. Hmm. Unhelpful. *Unless* ..."

Grass looked at him sharply. "Unless you support Quorn?"

"Is there problem with spies?"

"Uh, well, we've had a few ..."

"Hmm. Could Bishop be Spymaster?"

"Uh, interesting! Maybe we should—"

---

* Also known as the A63.

The monk placed a hand on the Sergeant's bony shoulder to stop him from rising – not a difficult task since he considerably outweighed the soldier. "No. Talk to Bishop after sermon. Alone. Look through personal possessions. Scour cathedral for incriminating evidence."

Grass looked at him suspiciously. "You really think so?"

"Secret mission!" The monk tapped the side of his nose. "Brought in by Senate to find spies. Sorry not tell you – didn't know if could be trusted. But now believe you true patriot!"

The Sergeant gave a low chuckle and looked up at the Bishop, who (with spittle flying from his lips) was in full flow. "Me and the lads would love to nail this bugger!" he said. "You're on!"

Roffo had already seen the signpost and knew where he must go. "Library!" he exclaimed to himself, throwing his hands in the air to emphasise his frustration. "It's going to be in the *bloody* library again!" He trudged along the road with hanging head, accompanied by the redoubtable Captain Twig and an escort of Guards.

They emerged from a side street onto a little square. Passing pedestrians, seeing the huge young man and his escort, looked startled and hurried away. Roffo sighed.

"I 'spect they think I'm some sort of criminal who's been gorging on the corpses of animals and stuff, eh?"

Twig nodded. "Aye, that'll be it. If it distresses you that much, maybe we could knock up a banner that says you only have gland problems."

Roffo gave the sort of scowl that would have met with approval from a certain monkish character. The whole situation was farcical. Vegetopia was only three or four weeks' travel from Cross-My-Way, and yet its inhabitants were utterly ignorant of the ways of people outside their own borders. "You don't get many strangers here, do you?"

Twig shook his head. "We're a bit cut off. A barren coast lies to the west and the plains of Mungo are to the east. To the north are mountains, and to the south is the cursed land of Quorn … and we all know about the people who live there!"

"But what about traders and caravans?"

The Captain shrugged his shoulders. "Seem to avoid us. Dunno why. Maybe we've nothing they want."

"*Maybe they'd rather not starve to death*," muttered the barman to himself. "Ahem, well, where's this then?"

"Museum Square. The library's over there …" The Captain

pointed to the left. "Need to find some books to help you plan a proper diet, eh?"

"Er – Museum Square? There's a museum here?"

"Sure. Want a look?" Roffo nodded, so the Captain turned right and led the way towards a large marble building on the opposite side of the Square.

Well, thought Roffo, somewhat guiltily, *it's not exactly dereliction of duty: the fragment could be in there.*

They entered the building. The woman at Reception goggled at the blubber man and his protection. For a moment she was speechless. She looked down and fidgeted with her tickets. "So," she said at last, "eight adults? That'll be eight copper pieces please."

Twig looked at Roffo meaningfully. The barman sighed, producing his money sack. Roffo started to count out the required entrance fee ... but then noticed a discrepancy. "Hang on a minute!" he said. "There are only seven of us!"

The woman looked up and grimaced. "You expect me to believe there's only *one* person in *that* body? You'll get out of sight, and then your mate will climb out and you'll all have a good laugh at my expense," she sniffed. "I know you Guards, always larking about!"

Roffo's jaw dropped. "Where, exactly, do you think this other person is hidden?" Roffo was wearing a tight-fitting tan tunic and trousers – a gift from Sheikh Aleg. "Up my arse?"

"Well, I wouldn't put it past—"

"Okay okay! Here you go!" Roffo handed over the last coin, snatched the tickets, and stormed past Reception ahead of the Guards.

In the foyer, the adventurer stopped to peruse the signs listing the various sections and displays. "Nuts and Berries," he read. "Trees of Vegetopia. Paintings of Local Animals by Schoolchildren." Roffo turned to look at Twig. "Paintings? Why not stuffed ..."

The Captain looked aghast.

"Ah, er, of course. Sorry. Knew a museum once ... had stuffed animals ... barbaric ... ahem." Roffo grinned stupidly and turned back to the inventory. "Geology. Clothing Through The Ages. Jewellery, Rings and Studs. History of Vegetopia. Weapons." He shrugged. "An embarrassment of riches?" Roffo set off for the second floor and the History section. Who could tell ... maybe Boozer's appearance would be recorded therein?

The History section told the tale of Vegetopia through exhibits and reconstructions. It related how the Warriors of the Wounded Wood had been expelled from 'a land far away' for protesting against the building of a new by-pass. With paintings (by the ubiquitous Schoolchildren) it related how Roses had led his peace-loving people across the Mungo Plains and, after forty years of hardship, emerged into the verdant land of Vegetopia. (*Forty years?* wondered Roffo. *Must have been naff navigators! We crossed it in a week!*) It told of their ancient leader and prophet, Beejeezus, who had slipped and fallen from his tree house while protesting against the building of the by-pass. He had been left hanging from the branches while the Security Men had 'laughed their bollocks off'. Roses had fled – hard-pressed by the heavy mob – and Beejeezus had never been heard from again.★ The story then related how, fifty years after the founding of Vegetopia, a sect had made the sacrilegious decree that it was okay to eat animal products after all (such as 'the cheese and the milk') and departed south to form the country of Quorn.

The story was supported by various exhibits, such as Roses's oaken staff, and a number of preserved banners that had belonged to the Warriors, with sentiments ranging from 'Stuff the By-Pass' and 'Trees not Roads', to such extravagances as 'Save the Chickens!' Various maps showed how Vegetopia had grown from a collection of tree houses into the town of today, built of stone and marble 'ecologically mined' from a nearby underground quarry.

There were descriptions of the various wars between Vegetopia and Quorn, and one section displayed typical weaponry (starting with deadwood clubs and progressing to weapons that weren't quite so 'ecologically neutral' – these invariably having been developed by the less scrupulous Quorns and then adopted by the Vegetopians after defeat). Another section looked at Vegetopian culture, with exhibits on clothes-making processes, style, diet, and pastimes. The Diet display interested Roffo. This occupied a little room off to one side of the main Culture Exhibition. Within it was The Dietary Charter of Roses, dictating what could and could not be eaten. Roffo used his finger to trace down the list. He found the clearly stated prohibition of 'ye exhudations of all creatures of four legs and of two, from whatever orifice they might come.' But there was no mention of ...

"Here!" said Roffo to Captain Twig. "This Charter doesn't say you

★   Actually, Beejeezus hadn't been badly hurt at all. The workmen had brought him down after a while and given him a cup of tea. But Roses had already legged it. Beejeezus never forgave 'that usurper' and gave up ecological campaigning for good. He eventually became an accountant and used the by-pass every day.

can't drink ale or wine or such stuff ... um, not that anyone would want to, *foul stuff* ... um, or so I hear ..."

Twig nodded. "Well, it's not banned as such. It's said the Evil Perverts of Quorn drink ale occasionally. With us it's a, well, cultural choice. The bloated stomach is considered socially unacceptable, so we're all a bit careful about what we eat and drink. Ale is meant to really put on the calories, you know."

With growing excitement, Roffo tracked through the exhibits. There were recipes for various Vegetopian dishes; there were displays of farming tools and eating utensils; there was a picture (by Honey Bun, aged seven) of a woman making a nut roast; there was another picture of a social scene where men quaffed Diet Cherryaid in a 'pub' called The Thirsty Beaver; there were recipes for various fruit beverages; and there, isolated in one corner, was a tiny section on 'Alcoholic Fatdrinks'. And there *was* a record of the visit of Boozer! He had apparently come as a prophet (clearly in a time when the mores on physical build were not as severe as they had subsequently become) and founded a society of brewers, which had disbanded several years later. But Boozer's legacy remained. For there, in the corner, pinned onto a display card, was ...

"Gotcha!" whispered Roffo.

A fierce light had entered the eyes of the Angels, a light of grim and angry resolve. Over the last couple of months they had faced all manner of hardship: dodgy food, uncomfortable beds, abuse, nudity, stampedes, attacks, and being incarcerated up to their necks in human intestinal outflow. There is only so much that a man can take and – for these men – that limit had been well and truly exceeded. They clustered behind a boulder, staring ferociously at the guardpost blocking their way to Vegetopia Town.

"Right," growled Trespass, "enough is enough! Let's do it!"

"Yeah," snarled Burble. "It's time someone else ate shit, and those wimps will do for starters."

"Aye, they're doomed," growled Bruce. "We'll ride them doon, an' then on intae toon. An' if anyone gits in oor way ..."

Grunt hawked and spat. "Wot we waiting for? Cut the chat and mount up! Let's ride!"

"Huh?" went Frunge.

The yakkers raced for their steeds and leapt into their saddles or, in the case of Burble, leapt onto one vast grey leg to be lifted to his seat.

Grunt gave a great roar and kicked the flanks of his mighty Ducrapi. The yak bellowed in rage and thundered onto the road. Yelping and howling, the rest of the gang followed.

By the guardpost, Corporal Berry looked up at the sudden disturbance. His eyes goggled. He shrieked, cast down his spear, and fled across the cabbage field beside the road. Other troopers rushed out from the guardhouse. They instantly broke into a chorus of wails. Private Horseradish pointed and screamed: "The Yak-Riders of the Apocalypse!" and mimicked a sewage works. Private Carrot ran into the outhouse and slammed the door shut. Lance Corporal Minty simply stood in the road and covered his eyes, as though this would somehow make the approaching horror go away.

It didn't.

With maniacal glee the yakkers came on. Grunt burst through the barrier and aimed his beast at the guardhouse. His mighty yak burst the wooden shack asunder, turning its walls into so much kindling and scattering its contents – furniture, paperwork, crates of fruit – all over the road. Burble goaded Jotun towards the outhouse. The elephant gave a tremendous bellow and flattened that building. Private Carrot was only saved by leaping into the Stygian pit and making like a mole. Trespass and Bruce barrelled along to either side of Lance Corporal Minty, grasping a thin arm each. They carried the soldier between them towards town. Minty only escaped by slipping out of his uniform, leaving him naked and bruised in the middle of the road.

And Frunge roared off in the wrong direction altogether. Remarkably, it only took the dense one a couple of minutes to realise his error. He soon corrected his course and surged along the road after his whooping, screaming comrades.

Ahead, sleeping in the late afternoon sun, lay the unsuspecting Vegetopia Town.

They had been waiting outside The Succulent Shoot for half an hour.

"Where is he?" asked Terry. "Do you think he's found something?"

"More likely skiving off," muttered the monk. He looked around at the dozen bored Senatorial Guards. The cathedral had been a dead end: the Guards had ransacked Bishop Vole's rooms and found nothing of the map or, indeed, anything to suggest that his allegiance to Vegetopia was other than sound. A lot of fingers had been pointed after that, mostly at him. The monk now noticed Sergeant Grass propped against the wall of the hotel, looking daggers at him, and running his thumb over the point of his spear suggestively.

"Maybe he's in trouble, then?" said Terry. "Perhaps we should go and look for him."

"Trouble! Ai-la! With that one, trouble certain." The monk shook his head. "Give five more minutes, then look."

———————

Roffo's frustration was growing. He knew he was late for the agreed rendezvous. He also knew he should simply report his findings to the others and allow a proper plan to be devised. But, well, *he* had found the map and *he* wanted the kudos of its recovery. He could imagine the scenario now. There would be his colleagues, sitting around glumly, Terry in saddened food-lust and the monk with his usual milk-curdling expression, and then *he* would saunter up to them ... *Sorry I'm late chaps but, oh, whoops, what's this that's just fallen out of my sleeve? Well, well, well, I do declare, it's the map.* He chortled at the thought. How their faces would light up! They'd pat him on the back and sing his praises and maybe even offer to buy him a pint!

But it was all going wrong! He had tried almost everything to ditch his escort for long enough to pluck the fragment from the wall. His first ploy had been to try to evade the soldiers by craftily varying his pace. And so he had slowly ambled through 'Nuts and Berries' (for example), waiting for the soldiers' attention to be captured, and then put on a turn of speed to leave them behind. This scam had worked to some degree: he had tended to lose three or four men each time, but that always left a couple on his tail.

Next, he had taken the soldiers for a meal at the museum café, allowing them to order great heaps of pointless green food. He had rapidly finished his own meal (a piece of fruit), leaving the others with half-full plates. *Then* he'd declared that he *just had* to visit the Culture Exhibition again, suggesting that the men finish their meals and catch him up shortly. But Captain Twig was a diligent fellow and would have none of it. Sulkily, the men had left their Vegetable Terrines and Sprout Sorbets and trudged after him.

Then Roffo had led the escort on two more circuits around the museum. The soldiers *must* have been incredibly bored by this stage. Roffo had bought them more food, in case a full stomach might dull their attention, and then endless cups of green tea, in the hope that they might all want to go to the toilet at the same time. He'd even paid several lavatorial visits himself, once declaring loudly that he had constipation and that the others should go ahead and amuse themselves and that he'd join them anon in Reception. But when he'd emerged it was to find Captain Twig and one other Guard patiently waiting.

Roffo was just about at his wits' end. There was now only one ploy left, and it was a desperate one, for it would certainly give the game away. But, frankly, the young barman was footsore and beyond caring. He turned to Twig and declared angrily, "Right, let's go to the Fruit and Vegetable Display one last time, eh?"

Twig sighed, indicating that Roffo should lead on.

The Veggie display was on the third floor. Roffo had his penknife out before they even got there. He rested the haft of the knife in the palm of his hand and the blade against his wrist so that it was hidden under his sleeve. The men entered the hall and came upon a display that was a paean to the green stuff. Here, hanging from the ceiling by two wires, the pride of place went to the biggest marrow known to Man (and very probably to Woman, too).

Roffo reached the hall first and broke into a run, sprinting beneath the marrow. He grabbed a chair that was resting against one wall and clambered onto it, so that he was facing the troopers. Standing on tiptoes Roffo could just reach the wire above one end of the marrow. "Say cheese!" he cried, insultingly, and cut the wire.

The marrow, released at one end, swept downwards and out. Twig stepped aside, but two of his men were not so fast and were flattened by the swinging monster. Roffo leapt down from the chair and ran over to the pumpkin display. Twig started shouting orders and his Guards began to rush the barman. One of the two marrow victims also staggered to his feet and came on. By now, however, Roffo had acquired a pumpkin. He hefted it in both arms, turned, aimed, and bowled it along the floor at the warriors.

"Strike!" cried Roffo in glee, as the pumpkin scattered his adversaries like so many bowling pins. Twig himself dived out of the way into a box of cauliflowers. Roffo hurried along to the dried peas' display and scooped up two handfuls. By the time he turned to look, three men were on their feet and coming at him. One of these was Captain Twig, now wearing a cauliflower like some exotic form of helmet. Roffo rolled the peas at the men, turned, scooped up more, and repeated the procedure. As the men gained the pea zone they began to scrabble and slide about. Twig looked as though he were jogging on the spot, flailing his arms in a desperate attempt to keep his balance. But one by one the men slipped and went arse over head. Such falls would barely have shaken men with normal buttocks, but the Vegetopian trend for unpadded cheeks was a disaster waiting to happen: the men howled in agony as bony butts bumped solidly on the hard ground.

Roffo clenched a fist in triumph and raced past the discomfited Guards, down the stairs, and across to the Alcoholic Fatdrinks Display.

Grunt dropped his pants and mooned the terrified denizens of Vegetopia as he surged along the street atop his Ducrapi. People fled from his path, screaming and pulling their hair and praying to Beejeezus. For the Vegetopians, this was the end of the world; this was the time of the Yak Men of the Apocalypse, who had come to feed them until they exploded; this was the signal of the end of all things, the precursor to The Great Judgment when all would face the Creator and give account of their lives. Of course, some of the more-lucid wondered – as they dived for cover – why there were *five* men instead of the predicted *four*, and why one of them was riding atop a huge, grey, skip-like creature with a hose in the middle of its face.

Trespass goaded his mount up onto the pavement, where it scattered stalls selling tie-dyed clothes, jewellery with star and moon motifs, and multi-coloured candles. A woman who was having ribbon platted into her hair shrieked and rushed across the road, trailing the braid behind her. A platoon of dreadlocked soldiers dropped their spears and hared up the road as though chased by the evil tarmac demons from legends of yore.

Burble laughed evilly as he provoked Jotun into great mischief: crashing through houses, trampling statues, and defecating in fountains.

The red-bearded Bruce whipped his yak into a foaming-at-the-mouth frenzy.

And at the rear came Frunge, whooping and hollering and totally puzzled as to *why*. At one point he came to a crossroads, and halted. His yak sat back upon its haunches with a great *sluuuurping* sound. The yakker looked behind him, but saw nothing *particularly* untoward. He considered the view in front again. Which way had they gone? Left? Ahead? Right? He considered the streets. To left and right they were empty and silent, but ahead there was a carnage of half-demolished buildings and ruined stalls. *No clue there then.* He scratched his head. *Wait a minute!* He suddenly recognised a huge mound of steaming droppings in the middle of the road ahead – from which two unhappy soldiers were even now extricating themselves. *Bruv's ele-thingy does things like that!* Straight ahead then! He broke into a whoop and set his steed in motion. The unfortunate be-dunged soldiers dived out of the way, then rose to watch the departing monster. They shook their heads in sorrow at what they saw: a pair of sandalled feet protruding from the beast's posterior.

"Look, *there!*" bellowed Trespass. "It's the runt. *Charge!*"

Roffo, who had been cheerily trotting along the road lost in a world of his own, was brought back to the here-and-now by the sound of the shout. He stopped. A quizzical expression settled onto his face. He felt the ground shake. A tremor? It appeared to be increasing in magnitude. An earthquake? And were those screams he could hear? Behind him?

Roffo turned around. "*Bugger!*" he cried. For there – bearing down upon him – was the manically leering form of Trespass, leader of the Hull's Angels, followed in short order by the rest of those villains. One even appeared to be riding atop an elephant!

The thief of museum artefacts turned once more, put his head down, and broke for it … but didn't get far. He was running … running … and suddenly his legs were windmilling in the air as his tunic was stretched between his shoulders. The ground flashed past under his feet and malevolent laughter assailed his hearing. He let his arms hang limply and looked left. Trespass had him grasped firmly by the collar. With a mighty twitch of the wrist, the yakker flicked the adventurer over his saddle horn.

"Well, what have we got here then?" he said.

Grunt pulled up to the left hand side of Trespass. He grinned wickedly, revealing a mouth full of rotten teeth. "Wot are we gonna do with 'im? I know! Let's do to 'im wot those bastards in Copros did to us!"

Burble rode up to the right hand side of Trespass. "Jotun – slap!" The elephant swung its trunk around hard and spanked Roffo on the buttocks.

"OW!"

"Yeah, that's it," called Grunt.

Howling with mirth, The Shadow repeated the command again and again.

"Ow … ooo … you swine … you bugger … owowowow …"

"Hang up," said Trespass after a while. "I'll search him …"

And, at that moment, the Demolition Men passed the entrance to a side-road. From out of this emerged Terry, the monk, and a dozen panting soldiers.

"Roffo!" cried Terry. A grim expression settled onto the barbarian's face. Without a backward glance, he began to sprint after the mounted party.

"Hoots mon!" cried Bruce, looking back. "Yon barbarian is fair gainin' on us!"

Burble looked too. "Shit! How does he run so fast? Tres ... quick, ditch the runt. Testicles doesn't look in the best of moods!"

"Hang on, hang on ... hey! What do we have here?" The leader of the pack, who had been frisking his captive, plucked out an ancient piece of map. "Is this what I think it is? The bit of map thingy they were talking about? The route to the Holy Ale?"

"Oy, give that back!" Roffo flailed a hand at the fragment, but Trespass's arms were the longer.

"No chance boy. Adios!" And Trespass tipped Roffo from the saddle. Howling with laughter, the yakkers put their heels to their steeds and roared off down the road.

———•◦•◦•———

Terry shortly came upon Roffo, who lay flat on his back.

"Roffo ... Roffo ... are you all right? Speak to me!"

The barman's eyes fluttered open. He stared up at the sky. "Bollocks!"

"Eh? Are you hurt? Can you feel this?"

"Ow! Leave off, Terry! I'm fine!" Roffo winced as he came into a sitting position. "At least, *most* of me is fine. My butt feels like it's on fire. *Ooooo!*"

The monk arrived at the shoulder of the crouching barbarian. In spite of the sprint he was breathing steadily. The rest of their escort still trailed some way behind. Roffo looked up at the monk, and his eyes went wide.

"Oh, Holy Clovory! It's gone! I had it, and now it's gone!"

"Had what?" asked Terry.

"*Ooooh noooo!* The map fragment! I found it in the museum. That's why I was so late ... I had to work out how to get it. But Trespass just swiped it off me. And he knows what it is, too!"

The monk gave a quiet curse, then turned to look after the fleeing yakkers. They were already a cloud of dust on the horizon. "Better pack up quick and follow." He turned to go, but Roffo reached up and tugged on his robe.

"Er, it's worse than that. Um. Sorry. But, er, in getting the fragment I had to sort of, well, disable the guards. Um. I 'spect they'll be, sort of, *after our hides* before too long."

The monk gave the young man a devastating scowl. "Should have waited for reinforcements. Ai-la!" He turned to look back into the centre of town. Their wheezing escort was no more than fifty yards distant, but further down the road the monk noticed a more organised gathering of men. The blare of a trumpet reverberated through the air, to be shortly answered by several more. "Not even time to get back to hotel. Must go now!"

Terry hoisted Roffo to his feet. The men – divested of their possessions once more – started to jog off down the road and out of town.

CHAPTER 17

THROUGH THIN AND THICK

A S EVENING fell, the adventurers found themselves in a little wood a dozen miles from Vegetopia town. They hunkered down in a hollow shielded from the road by large, moss-covered rocks and ancient trees. Terry peeled back some foliage and stepped into the hollow, his arms full of branches and kindling.

"I don't know if we ought to risk a fire," said the barbarian, "but I got some firewood anyway. At least it's dry so it shouldn't smoke much."

Roffo sat in deep shadow, staring miserably ahead. "What's the use? We're *bound* to be discovered. When the Fates are against you, you might as well bend over, drop your pants, paint a big target on your butt, and wait for the Boot of Doom."

"Pah!" exclaimed the monk. "No need wait for Fates! Bend over now and I give kick up arse, foolish youth!" He turned his attention to Terry. "Any sign of Vegetopian host?"

Terry nodded, though the gesture was barely visible in the fading light. "Yeah. It looks like they've set up camp about a mile back – where the road fords that stream we passed. Judging by the number of campfires I reckon there's about a hundred of them, maybe a few more."

"Think they follow, or go home in morning?"

Terry considered this for a moment in silence. Then he nodded to himself. "They're going to follow. I saw movement on the road from town. A line of lights. I'd guess they're shipping in some provisions on wagons."

"If I knew the map was that important to them," said Roffo, "I would have left it. How was I to know?"

"Tcha!" hissed the monk. "Probably not after us. Must be after damned idiot yakkers."

"I'm not surprised," said Terry. "The Angels must have trashed half the town. *My* clan couldn't have done much better itself!"

Roffo sighed. "And we have to follow the Angels too … *if* we can."

"Humph! Blind man could follow that lot! All need is sense of smell."

"But they're mounted!" said Roffo. "Terry might be able to catch them up, but we couldn't. If the Vegetopians are mounted, well, we won't be able to keep ahead of *them* either! We'll have to abandon the hunt, and all because of me!"

At this, the tone of the monk's voice lightened and his lips curved into a soft smile. "Perhaps, perhaps not. No need blame self too much. Hah! Was young and foolish once!"

"Yeah," said Terry, "and besides, we probably wouldn't have got this far without you."

"You're just saying that to try and make me feel better."

"No, Terry right. It your idea that help find map in Copros Library."

The barbarian chuckled. "Aye, and I'm not sure I could have held off that assault in Nudia if you hadn't been there with your mighty pillow!"

Roffo's face broke into a half-smile in the dark. "That was quite a scrap, wasn't it? Still, I've cocked up Big Time here."

"Yes," said the monk gently. "Still, who knows what tomorrow bring?" He turned to look to the north-east, the direction in which the yakkers had ridden. Trees obscured his view, but he knew that The Piles lay in that direction: a severe set of mountains that formed a tight cluster in the very centre of the continent. *Hardly good riding country*, he thought. "Terry, light small fire perhaps? Then go to sleep and see what gifts Notia, Goddess of Dreams, might bring …"

———— ·•··•· ————

"I bought those in good faith," protested the short, balding fellow. "The bloke who sold them to me said they were his. Told me they'd been in his family for generations. Honest!"

"Relax," said Sergeant Boomber, with a jovial smile. "I believe you. Thousands wouldn't, you know, but *I* do." He paced around Picket's lock-up stable, wondering what other treasures might be found should he search through all the wooden crates that littered the floor. "I mean," he continued, "*gold-laced mayoral robes of office*? Well, they're ten a penny in Cross-My-Way. These can't *possibly* be the ones stolen from the town hall last night."

"Yeah, that's right." Picket started to sweat. Everyone knew about his lock-up, but there was an *understanding* that he was protected. What had changed? "I mean, we elect a new mayor every two years, so there must be loads of mayoral-type gear out there. Only last week someone offered me a sceptre of state."

"Really? Anyway, I'll have to check that these aren't the stolen clothes – just a formality, you know – and then I'll bring them right back. Okay?"

"Sure, sure," replied the fence unhappily. "And if they do turn out to be stolen, I'll give you a description of the bloke I got them off. Nobody stitches up Honest Picket with dodgy gear and gets away with it!"

"Aye, well, that's what Manis said when he pointed me in this direction."

Picket frowned. "Manis?"

Boomber slapped a hand over his mouth. "Oh, cripes! Shouldn't have said that, should I, what with confidentiality and all that? Forget I spoke. Er, I think I hear the kettle whistling. I'll see myself out."

"Er, yeah. *Manis?*"

As he departed the lock-up the Sergeant chuckled to himself.

———•◦•———

The party of adventurers had risen just before dawn and, for want of a better plan, had dropped from their hiding place onto the road to follow the route taken by the yakkers. Tracking the Hull's Angels proved a straightforward feat, given that the north-east-tending road was dotted with over-sized foot prints. In any case, any attempt by the yakkers to leave the road and cross the potato and cabbage fields would have left unmissable signs of arable devastation.

At first the men had jogged along three-abreast, but after an hour or so Roffo had begun to tire, so Terry had swung him onto his shoulders and then contined effortlessly. Once the barman had recovered somewhat, Terry put him back down to run under his own steam until tiredness took him again. This pattern was repeated throughout the morning, and a remorseless pace was set.

After six hours – when the sun was high overhead – the adventurers left the road and gained the top of a small hill, where they halted for a rest. The fields of Vegetopia had by now given way to an undulating, untended country, with the foothills of The Piles in the near distance.

"Well, they'll have to stick to the road in this country," said Roffo. "They might get to the ale first, but they won't give us the slip ... for whatever *that's* worth."

Shielding his eyes from the overhead sun, Terry looked south in the direction they had come. A low and thunderous growl escaped from his stomach.

"Yeah," said Roffo, "I'm famished too. When did we last eat?"

"I don't even want to think about it," said the barbarian. He continued scanning the southern road. "Anyway, it's two days since we last had a proper meal."

"Seems like a month!" Roffo lay on his back and looked up into the sky. His face scrunched in concentration. Then he turned on his front. "It's no good. I'm absolutely starving. I've *got* to eat! D'you think there are any inns or hotels along this road? There's got to be – *surely*?"

"I don't get the impression this road is used very much," said Terry. "The Vegetopians don't seem like great travellers to me, and this road just heads up into the mountains."

"*Oooh*," groaned Roffo, "food!" He plucked up some grass. "I wonder what this tastes like? Well, here goes!" He shoved a handful of the green stuff into his mouth, chewed for a second, then spat it out. "Ugh – disgusting!" He alternated his glance between his two comrades, but each seemed to be in a world of his own: one watched the horizon to the south, while the other chewed his lip and stared at the mountains to the north. Roffo watched his friends for some minutes, determined not to intrude on whatever profound thoughts they might be having. The ability to remain silent, however, was not one of the barman's virtues. He opened his mouth to speak, then slammed it shut. Moments later his mouth opened again as though of its own accord, forcing Roffo to ram a fist into it. He withdrew his fist and clicked his teeth. He rolled his eyes and looked around slyly. He clicked his teeth again. And then he began to click out a little tune. He stopped when he saw the monk stiffen, slapping an open hand over his mouth to quell the noise. But the monk just blinked, shifted around on his seat, and raised a finger to his lips in an "I wonder" sort of gesture. Roffo could contain himself no longer.

"Er, copper piece for your thoughts?"

"Eh? Oh, just thinking about where ale must be."

"It's up in the mountains somewhere, isn't it?"

The monk nodded. He turned to stare at Roffo. "Yes ... *you* should know."

"Er, well, I'm not keeping anything from you, honest! I mean …"

"Not consciously … but maybe *sub*consciously?"

"Um …"

"Must find out, la? And there *is* way!"

"Uh, well," said Terry, "we'll have to find out later." He pointed south. "Movement on the road. They must be mounted to be this close. We have to go *now*!"

"Okay," said the monk, leaping to his feet, "this way!" He headed down the side of the hill *away* from the road, scampering over the rugged ground towards another hill where they might be hidden from the view of the approaching host.

"But that's the wrong way!" exclaimed Roffo.

"No matter," cried the monk over his shoulder, "change of plan! Need to get supplies from Vegetopians first. Then see what see."

Terry and Roffo exchanged glances, shrugged, and followed the bald-headed man.

———— ••••• ————

Night had fallen.

The three adventurers crept along a ditch towards the Vegetopian encampment. Various fires burned in the centre of the camp, over some of which – hanging from tripods – were set large cauldrons, bubbling away with vegetable soup. Circling this central fire-lit area were the host's tents. On an area of level ground beyond the tents were picketed the contingent's horses.

"Very slack," whispered Terry. "They've only posted two sentries on this side of the camp and they're so widely set you could lead an army between them. *And* the sentries are half asleep. Any barbarian commander this careless would be forced to disembowel himself with a blunt twig and make a casserole out of his own innards."

"Really?" asked Roffo.

Terry nodded in the dark. "Seen it done. The bloke actually said – before he died – that it was the best meal he'd ever had."

"You barbarians – you're all mad!"

"Um, not *all* of us, please!"

"Ahem!" The monk cleared his throat meaningfully. "Okay, I go to commander tent and get what need … you get provisions and transport, la?"

"Sure thing," said Roffo, who saw the evening's escapade as a chance to redeem himself. "Leave it to me, er, *us*."

The monk slipped out of the ditch and ghosted between the two dozy sentries. It was then only fifty yards from the picket line to the first of the tents. The cowled one reached the first piece of canvas unseen. While it had still been light, Terry had used his trained eye to pick out the commander's tent, and it was for this that the monk now headed. He wove nimbly in and out of guy ropes, traversed the odd patch of open ground, and sauntered boldly past a couple of campfires surrounded by soldiers. *People see what expect to see*, thought the monk. He reached his objective and circled to the rear of the tent to be out of the firelight. He listened at the canvas, but already knew from the light emanating from within the tent that it was occupied. He heard two men speaking to one another, but could not make out what they were saying.

The conversation continued for perhaps five minutes, then the monk heard the canvas flap on the opposite side of the tent being opened. *Good.* He delved into his robe and removed a number of his ever-present sharpened chopsticks. *Just in case.* He worried at one of the guy pegs. When this came out the tent sagged slightly, allowing him to squeeze under its edge, sliding inside on the damp grass. The Vegetopian commander was sitting at a table with his back to the intruder, facing the entrance flap. The monk, with the grace of the Fung-Chu adept, rippled towards the man. With a lightning blow he sent the soldier off to visit Notia in the world of dreams.

The ninja intruder looked at the map on the table that the commander had been perusing. *Perfect!* He rolled it up and placed it within the folds of his robe. He also found some blank parchment and a pencil. That would do …

There was a rustling at the tent flap.

"Permission to enter, sir …" The trooper entered before permission could be given. "I just thought I'd … hey! Who in the name of Macartny are you?"

The monk crouched and raised a chopstick to the level of his ear. "Be silent or never speak again!"

"Oh, er, I say, what have you done to the Colonel? Ah, er, ha ha …" The man saw what the monk was holding and raised his finger to point, breaking into staccato laughter. "Ha ha ha ha … what are you going to do, whip me up a stir fry? I'll have a number ninety-two please, and *chop chop* … hahahaha!"

"Shhhhh, foolish one! I serious!"

"Oh, me too! Have you ever tasted camp cuisine? Awful stuff. I know! I'll just call the guards, and then you can fix up some chop suey while we interrogate you. *Gua—*"

He got no further.

With a blinding flick of the wrist, the sharpened chopstick whistled through the air ... and the man spoke no more.

The monk squeezed out of the tent and rushed back to the rendezvous point. Terry and Roffo were already present – and they weren't alone.

"Ai-la," declared the monk, "that our mule!"

"Precisely," declared Roffo smugly. "And Terry's axe was amongst the baggage. That's why he's grinning like a buffoon. Anyway, our mule was tethered up with the other horses. They must have brought him along 'cos he's a damned sight stronger than their own beasts."

"Aye," said Terry, "I've never seen such puny horses in all my life. They could carry a Vegetopian, but no-one else."

"No problems?"

Roffo chuckled quietly. "Piece of piss! Except when Terry suddenly sneezed. You know how it is. Someone *always* has to sneeze just when you need to be quiet. Well known fact of life. Well, when Terry sneezed he blew over two horses and the picket guard. *Achooo ... blam!*" Roffo mimicked the deed. "What about you?"

"Hmm ... slight trouble. Best not wait here gossiping. Soon be ruckus ..." A sudden shouting came from the centre of the camp. "See what mean?"

————◆◆◆◆————

"Uhn thnn zz tha tha tha ..."

The campaign commander, Colonel Branch, massaged the back of his neck and glowered at his incoherent aide-de-camp. "For Macartny's sake, will someone help him out!"

One of the soldiers clustered in the doorway tried to ease the afflicted man away from the canvas.

"Oth oth oth oth," declared the man.

"I think he means *ow ow ow ow*," said the soldier helpfully.

"I can see that," snarled the Colonel. "What's *that?*"

"Hold still, sir," said the soldier to the aide-de-camp, "this is gonna sting a wee bit." With a rapid motion, he pulled out the piece of wood that affixed the unfortunate aide's tongue to a tent pole. The aide fainted.

The soldier held up his trophy and cheerily declared. "It's a chopstick, sir! Do you want it? Not that it's much good, there being just the one of them. Er, sorry sir."

The commander rolled his eyes.

402

The next morning found the ale questers hidden in a gully some two hundred yards from the road. Roffo eyed the monk suspiciously as the cowled one struck a small fire into life and blew on it until it caught.

"What's he doing?" wondered Terry.

"Dunno," said Roffo. "He said something about getting hidden knowledge out of my head."

"I don't like the sounds of that. Is he going to burn it out?"

"I hope not!" Roffo laughed unconvincingly. "Er, you won't let him do it will you, Terry me old mate?"

"Course not. But ... well, I'm sure he knows what he's doing."

"Thanks. That really sounds like unconditional support!"

"Shhhh," went the monk. "Nothing to fear!"

"Haha. *Nothing to fear!* Isn't that phrase usually followed by a scream of agony, a bloodcurdling cry of terror, an ... *ohmygod no!*" The monk had reached into his robe ...

He brought out the stolen map.

Roffo heaved a sigh of relief.

The monk unfurled the map and placed it before Roffo. The three men clustered around it.

"Now, Roffo, look at map." The gurning one got out the four pieces of Boozer's map that remained to them and put them together, placing them on the bottom left quadrant of the larger campaign map. The men could see that there was a roughly diamond-shaped piece missing from the centre. The monk directed Roffo's attention to the missing segment, and then to the comparative area on the larger map. "See, this area roughly correspond to fragment *you* lost."

"Thanks for reminding me."

"Shhh! Now examine two maps. Note how mountains curve, note key landmarks, key features ..." He pointed to various aspects: Big Hemroid; Small Hemroid; the road that led from Vegetopia to the edge of The Piles (then curved away to the north-west, joining the Great Road they'd taken months earlier en route to Nudia). He pointed out rivers (both wet and dry), and other geographical features: amusingly shaped rock formations, gullies, plateaux, defiles ... "Anything familiar?"

Roffo stared at the two maps for some time, then shook his head sadly. "I'm sorry. I saw the fragment quite a few times – I had to tramp around that damned museum loads to try and lose the Guards – but, y'know, I never really *looked* at it."

"Okay." The monk rubbed his forehead with one finger. "Think knowledge *is* there, but buried like nugget of gold in mountain." He plucked out a chopstick – causing Roffo's eyes to bulge in fear – but did nothing more sinister with it than hand it to the barman, blunt end first. "Take this. Good. Now, come round here in front of fire …"

"I'm not going to put my head in there, no way …"

"Shhhh! Be calm. Take deep breath. Good. Again. Now, relax …"

"That's all very well for you to say …"

Terry patted his friend on the shoulder. "Go on. Do as he says. Surely you trust him by now?"

Roffo heaved a great sigh. "Yes, of course I do, I suppose. Okay … what do I do?"

"See flame," said the monk, in a calming tone, "see it … see how it twist and curl … see yellow and orange … concentrate … relax … focus …"

Within ten minutes Roffo was sitting at utter ease, his shoulders sagging loosely, his head rolling.

"Now, think back to museum. Back … back … You are there, standing before wall, and on wall is map … piece of map … and it something like map here … see it?"

Roffo lolled his head forwards. "Yes, I see it. It's an old fragment of a map."

"Examine its features … see mountains and roads and rivers … and look … somewhere on map there is X … see it?"

"Yes, there it is, it's … I can't explain."

"Take chopstick in hand. Good. Now look at map."

Roffo's eyes opened and he looked at the map. To Terry, it seemed as though the young adventurer was not exactly at home.

"See X now?" asked the monk. "Where …?"

"There it is," said the somnolent Roffo, plunging the chopstick into the map.

———◆◦◆◦◆———

"Where am I?" asked Roffo, who understood the dramatic requirements of the situation.

Terry groaned.

"Er, sorry. It just sort of slipped out." Roffo looked at the monk. "That was amazing! Does it make any sense? I mean, where I stuck the chopstick?"

The monk rubbed a hand at his mouth and grimaced at the map. The hole in the map was in a position part of the way up Big Hemroid. He studied the geography for a few moments in silence, then his face twisted into a smile.

"Look," he said. "Wherever ale or recipe must be, must be *inaccessible*, or would be found by others, la? *But* must also be *accessible*, or no-one able to survive up there as not able to get food and water. Probably. Now look here ..." He traced various routes on the map. "This road ... curve away to north and west and eventually lead to Way. This path yakkers taking. It not go to Big Hemroid."

"So ... why are the yakkers going that way – aha!" Roffo saw it. "There's a dry river bed that virtually meets the road *here*, and that loops around beneath the foot of the X mountain."

"Yes. Guess yakkers leave road there and take to river valley. Hmm. But, why not just follow river valley from ..." the monk looked at the map, then stood up to look over the lip of the gully, then looked back to the map, "over there." He pointed.

Terry frowned and examined the map. "It's quicker as the arrow flies to go via the river bed, but the terrain would be difficult if you were riding yaks ..."

"Or an elephant," chipped in Roffo.

"Yeah, or an elephant. The way they're going will be quicker *for them* ..."

"But maybe not *for us*," concluded Roffo.

The monk nodded thoughtfully. "It possible we able to get here first." He indicated the map, where the dry river passed into a steep, narrow gorge, from where the distance to the X spot was perhaps a dozen further miles.

"Right then," said Terry, "there's no time to lose. Let's head to the river."

"Hang on," said Roffo, "this is all very well and good, but what *is* at the X? There's no town or anything marked on the map. Mr Monk?"

The monk shrugged. "As to that ... find out when get there."

"I found the wallet on the road and I was just bringing it to you when you stopped me," complained Fingers. "I didn't nick it, honest!"

"Janus said he felt someone's hand in his pocket just before the wallet went missing," said Yavlo. "When he turned around the person standing behind him apparently looked just like you."

"Coincidence. There must be hundreds of people in the market who look just like me. All of the men for starters."

Yavlo nodded. "Well, let us momentarily put aside the fact that the wallet went missing three days ago, and hence your act of Good Samaritanship is rather tardy." He fished around inside his tunic pocket and brought out a piece of jewellery for Fingers's inspection. "Do you recognise this ring?"

"Er, no. Whose is it?"

"The answer to that question depends on who you talk to. Janus claims that it is also his. However, Young Festers says it is his. Apparently, he got it from you." Yavlo smiled. They had brought pressure to bear on Hendy's cousin and had hit the jackpot.

Fingers growled. "Is that what the little creep said?"

"Ah, no, I am sorry. I appear to have given you a false impression. Festers was admirably mum. It was Manis who revealed the history of the ring."

The pickpocket turned pale. "Ma ... Man ... Manis?"

"Indeed." The silver-haired Inspector pocketed the ring and the wallet. "You obviously have a very dear friend there! Anyway, all of the missing property has now been accounted for, so there is no harm done, is there? Good day to you, sir."

"*Manis?*"

<hr>

They had been marching along the dry river bed for three days now. The going had not been too arduous: the sides of the bed were shallow and the bed itself was dusty and filled with small boulders that caused little hindrance to the party or their mule. The ancient water course had not seen any substantial flow for some time – perhaps as a consequence of a change in climate, or perhaps because the river that had once run along its course now ran elsewhere along an easier, more direct route to the sea.

The landscape was relatively barren. Beyond the river bed the land was parched and rocky, sparsely dotted with thirsty little trees and bushes with coarse, needle-like leaves. Wildlife was also scarce. Roffo had seen one snake, a dozen lizards, a few birds wheeling overhead, and some rather nasty bugs. A couple of the latter now watched the party as they passed.

From the shade beneath a rocky shelf, Arachnea the tarantula viewed the men with an air of superiority. Beside her, Nipper the scorpion clicked his claws experimentally. The pair had come to an agreement not to eat each other, which was as close as a relationship ever came to *friendship* in the insect world.

"Go on," said Nipper, "do it! I love it when you do it! The little bloke at the back … he'll bolt for sure! I'd bet three flies on it."

Arachnea wiggled her venomous fangs and contemplated the game. She knew humans were generally terrified of her − a fact she found rather puzzling, considering their relative sizes − but she was never slow to exploit this fact for the sake of the prestige it gave her in Three Big Red Rocks county. She turned her compound eyes to consider Nipper, who was swaying with excitement. "No bet. It's too easy. I *know* he'll run."

"Okay okay … what about the Big Mother? Three flies say you *can't* shift him."

Arachnea turned a malevolent look on the scorpion. She idly wondered what he would taste like. *Probably better than Fangs*, she thought. Fangs was her ex. She'd gobbled him up as an après-sex snack last night. The bugger had given her indigestion. *Men!*

"All humans flee at the sight of Arachnea," she declared, somewhat arrogantly. She repeated an oft quoted arachnoid saying: "The bigger they are, the further they jump!"

"So that's a bet then," said Nipper. "Three flies say you can't do it."

"Oh, very well then. And you'd better have your stake, because I don't take credit." She watched as Nipper gave the scorpion equivalent of a big gulp. "Right, watch and admire!"

Arachnea considered the path she would take, made a decision, and raced out into the sunshine. She drew parallel to the humans. The leathery one, who looked a bit like an old ape, was at the front leading a mule, while the young human and the Big Man walked side-by-side, conversing. Arachnea raced like insect lightning in front of the two men.

"So, what d'you reckon about Maddy?" said Roffo. "Do you think I have a chance there? I mean, once we get back to Way and … *aieeeeeeee!*" The barman leapt a foot in the air and about three feet backwards. Terry watched him with amusement − and the tarantula with a complete lack of concern.

Arachnea raced into a shadow on the opposite bank of the river bed and turned to consider the men. *Palps!* The big human hadn't even twitched! She could imagine that damned scorpion on the other side clicking his claws in laughter. Well, he wasn't going to get *her* flies! This time she'd go straight at the Big Man. *That* would shift him. With spider rage growing within her, she sped into the sunlight once more. *Ha ha ha*, she thought, *here I co—*

Splat.

"My god!" said Roffo in awe. "I knew barbarians were *brave*, but *that* is something else!"

In the shade, Nipper watched the big human scraping the ex-Bad Mama of Red Rocks off his boot. "The Queen is dead," he chuckled, "long live the King! Now, where has she hidden her stash?"

"Well, well, well, what do we have here!" declared the police Sergeant. "You're in serious trouble now, my laddo. Urinating in the gutter is against council by-law 12323. It also contravenes hygiene code NOPEE. That public-spirited fellow, Master Manis, warned us you might—"

Yavlo cleared his throat. "Ah, okay Boomber. Enough is enough." He looked down at the felon and smiled in an embarrassed manner. He shooed him away. As the Inspector watched the criminal's retreating back, he sighed. "I somehow doubt, Sergeant, that Manis's circle of friends and allies include many of the five-year-old-boy persuasion."

"Oh well, guv, you never can tell ..."

"Over there, look!" shouted Roffo. "It's the Sumerian Gorge!"

The dry river bed swooped out to the left in a big curve, then cut back to the right, where it disappeared into the mouth of a towering gorge. The suddenness of the change in landscape was marked and dramatic: the rugged and undulating ground off to the adventurers' right swept up to the massive rock prominence like the sea crashing against cliffs. And through these cliffs there was just one absurdly narrow entrance, carved thousands of years ago by the now-extinct river. Indeed, this entrance – the Sumerian Gorge – was the only access into the depths of The Piles (for all but the most expert mountaineers) for hundreds of miles.

Terry pointed off to the left. "Aye, and there's the road. See, it swings about and approaches the river bed over there."

"Are we in time?" asked Roffo. "Do you think that git Trespass has beaten us to it?"

"Er, no, I don't *think* so."

Roffo wiped some sweat from his brow and took a glug from his water bottle. He ran a sleeve across his lips. "How do you work that out then?"

"Because, er, they're over *there* and coming this way, er, *quickly*."

Terry's eyesight was superior to that of his comrades, having been rigorously trained from childhood. Indeed, his training had begun on the very first day that he had opened his eyes on exiting his mother's womb and given his first roar (that being *de rigeur* for barbarian babies). By the age of two he had already gained the ability to estimate the number and disposition of enemy forces from a mile away, even though they were hidden in a forest in thick fog and he was looking upside down between his legs while hopping up and down in a war dance and simultaneously sharpening his axe with a whetstone held between his teeth.

Roffo dropped his water bottle and strained to see. The monk, shielding his eyes from the glare of the sun, noticed them first.

"Er, Terry right. Perhaps now time to … *run?*"

"What are we waiting for! Terry, lead the way and hold the pass!"

The barbarian surged out of the river bed and cut cross-country straight towards the gorge, avoiding the leftward loop of the river bed. The monk and Roffo followed Terry's tracks as rapidly as they could, leaping over boulders and cracks in the ground, and shimmying around thorny bushes and little trees. After twenty paces the monk, who had been leading the mule, pulled up. Terry disappeared in a plume of dust.

"No good – can't lead mule," he said to Roffo, who pulled up beside him. "You mount up and ride, then both go quicker!"

Roffo simply nodded and leapt into the saddle. He pulled out his pen-knife and cut away some of their provisions and baggage. "Yee-hah!" he cried, spurring his mount on. In response, the monk – belying a man who looked so grizzled – set off at the easy, rapid, remorseless pace of a natural distance runner.

———

The race was on!

"Ride, men, *ride!*" roared Trespass, whipping his mighty Harleck Dravidian into a frenzy. His men thundered off the road towards the dry river bed that led to the gorge. They had made good time on the road but now, suddenly, found their progress impeded by the terrain.

"Ow … ooo … eyah … ooof!" cried the leader of the pack as the sharp-edged foliage whipped him from left and right, reminding him of a past towel-flicking initiation into public school.

"Whey-hey!" screamed Bruce, "this is fun!"

Trespass would have to have serious words with the highlander later! But for now he needed all his attention to stop himself from being unseated. He yanked on his steed's left horn to divert it around an outhouse-sized boulder, then had to pull hard right to avoid another. To his left he could see a grey blur. *Jotun*. The elephant headed straight for a boulder ... and sundered it! Huge chips of shrapnel sizzled through the air. One of these gave Trespass a new and unusual parting in his hair.

"Bulabothel!"

The yakkers burst out of a thicket and into a slightly more open area. From here, Trespass could see their adversaries heading towards the gorge from his right, with Testicles just a blur of dust. He made some rapid mental calculations and risked a sideways look at his crew. The yak-riders were struggling across difficult terrain – but Burble and his mount were simply slicing through it like a hot elephant through a mountain of butter. Burble was sitting easily atop Jotun, smiling and taking in the view.

"Don't just sit there!" bellowed Trespass. "Go go go! You can get there first! Don't wait for us you little—" The obscenities that were about to follow were cut off by a censoring branch, which whapped him across the mouth. But Burble had got the message. He smacked Jotun's flanks. The elephant gave a mighty bellow and switched into pachyderm overdrive.

The ground shook!

———•••———

Closer and closer they got ...

Separate races were emerging. To any onlooker it was clear that the gold medal was going to go to either the barbarian or the elephant-rider. But bronze was looking pretty well sewn up for the hearties from The Bear. One by one the yakkers were going down. Frunge unwisely tried to emulate Burble's rock-splitting feat and was left counting stars. Grunt lost control of a skid caused by a rapid right turn and was pitched into a thorn bush straight out of Sleeping Beauty. And the other two yak-riders, choosing self-preservation, settled on a lesser pace and a cheerleader role.

"Gae on Burb!" cried Bruce, standing in his stirrups.

"Yeah, you bugger ... fly! Fly like a fucking ... ouch! What is it with these damned branches?"

But Terry and Burble were heedless of the cries and imprecations of their colleagues. To them, the race was everything – the sole focus of their attention, will, and desire.

Burble was by now bumping along the river bed. He looked right and saw his arch-foe just ten yards away, but the barbarian was *behind* him and the gorge was there, straight ahead, sixty yards … fifty …

Hang about, thought Trantor/Jotun, *that's a pretty bloody narrow gap* … But, elephantine thought processes being what they are, he was, by this stage, already committed.

Even Terry was beginning to tire. He rejoined the river bed, dropping down behind the elephant. But he set his face into a grim expression and used his iron will to send even more energy into his powerful legs. He began to catch the elephant – which was no mean feat, given that Trantor/Jotun had won the elephant marathon for the past three years in the jungle Olympics and was widely regarded as the greatest pachyderm runner of his generation. Slowly, very slowly, Terry began to overhaul him. And there was the gorge, its narrowest point, fifty yards … forty … thirty …

Terry gave a terrible barbarian war cry – a cry that was reckoned to be the most terrible of a very terrible set of cries, a cry that bespoke utter doom for any who stood (as opposed to *ran away exceedingly quickly*) in earshot. And he powered past the elephant!

Thirty yards … twenty …

Jotun saw the barbarian draw level and gave a swipe with his trunk, but there was little energy left in him. He had not been pushed so hard since the games of '88 when Tusker had run him close before being disqualified for a drugs offence.

Fifteen yards … ten …

Terry pushed his chest forward … and broke the proverbial tape! He flew into the gorge while Jotun …

BAMMMMMMMMMM!

———◆•◆••◆———

"Holy Clovory!" cried Roffo from mule-top. "He's wedged up the gorge! Did Terry get through? Gods, I hope he got through!"

The two men increased their pace and attained the river bed. They surged on, travelling side by side, heading towards the narrow gorge and the huge grey bottom.

"If they came together," gasped Roffo, "then Terry will be *barbarian paté*!"

They pulled up behind the massive animate plug. Jotun was bellowing in frustration at his defeat. But no humans were to be seen.

Roffo dismounted and ran up behind the elephant. "Terry! Are you there? Speak to me!"

"Hello?" came a voice from the other side.

"Hello, Terry, is that you?"

"Yeah, I'm okay."

"Thank Clovory! We thought you might have been *splashed*!"

"No, I'm fine. I've just been looking at Burble. He was thrown off his elephant. He's a bit concussed, but he'll be okay."

The monk patted Roffo on the shoulder, drawing his attention to events behind them where the yakkers were making their painstaking way along the river bed. "Be here soon. Best go."

Roffo delved into a pack on the mule and brought out a rope. "We'll have to climb over."

"Hmm, yes. Have to leave mule, la! Can't be helped! At least obstruction stop others from following for a while."

"Yeah, I think we're going to need all the time we can get. Terry, the rope's coming over! Can you secure it to the elephant's tusks ...?"

CHAPTER 18

DRINKING FOR VICTORY

EXAMINING THE stolen campaign map, the monk had estimated that it would take the adventurers six or seven hours to walk from the narrowest point of the Sumerian Gorge to Big Hemroid … but this estimate hadn't taken into account the coming of night, or the weariness the men would feel from having eaten nothing but lettuce and raw carrots for six days. Matters hadn't been helped by the unfortunate insertion of an elephant between them and their mule-borne food supply.

The men had spent a cold and hungry night on the dry river bed at the bottom of the steep gorge. When the morning had come they had stumbled to their feet, shaken the blood back into their numbed extremities and, coughing, trudged off up the barren watercourse. After an hour of yomping, during which the sides of the gorge had peeled apart like the skin of an unzipped banana, they had caught their first view of Big Hemroid: an immense red pustule on the surface of the world. The adventurers had looked at each other wordlessly, given a collective sigh, and continued.

Now, with every step, their objective became clearer and clearer: indeed, the left hand side of the gorge was revealed as a mighty spur of the mountain itself. And it was while following at the foot of this wall – as it gradually decreased in gradient and fell away – that Terry noticed something unusual. He knelt down to consider a scuffed area on the ground, and then followed this a little way up the slope to where it disappeared behind a bush. He returned to his comrades and broke the morning's silence. "Man-made. It was probably last used three or four days ago."

"Let us follow," said the monk.

Terry nodded and started up the narrow track.

The path switch-backed up the side of Big Hemroid, occasionally weaving in and out of clusters of pine trees. Apart from these, and a smattering of small yellow flowers which clung to the browny-red slopes like a dose of Yellow Measles on the face of a jolly fatman, the mountain was barren.

To Roffo, the view soon became vertiginous: he stopped looking down and focused instead on the barbarian's broad back. At one point he considered the leather belt circling Terry's waist and momentarily dwelt on the absence of the axe that usually depended from it, wondering whether they might regret leaving it with the mule. *After all*, thought Roffo, *it's a difficult thing to wield if you only have hooves.*

They continued onwards and upwards until Terry climbed over a steep ridge and came onto a level ledge. Here he came to a halt.

"Whoa! I think we, er, might be *there*."

The barbarian's comrades clambered up next to him. They gaped at the entrance to the tunnel in front of them.

"Heave," screamed Trespass, "heave!"

As the Angels pulled the rope with all of their might, Burble urged forward the yaks hitched to the rope behind the men. The rope around Jotun's midriff grew taut; the men's faces reddened; and the yaks bellowed in fatigue and frustration.

"And again!" cried Trespass. "*Heave!*"

The elephant started to shift, slowly and painfully.

Burble leapt to his feet and started jumping up and down on his brother's long-haired Noughton, urging it to greater efforts.

"It's moving," roared Grunt. "Come on you tossers, '*eave!*" Morning sunshine sparkled off a bead of sweat on his cheek.

A vein stood out on Trespass's forehead.

Bruce's eyes bulged as though they were about to pop from his head.

But as the men and yaks gave a last mighty pull their efforts were finally rewarded. With a great sucking sound, Jotun moved … slowly … sliding …

POP!

Men and yaks tumbled over at the release of resistance, and Jotun became the world's first flying elephant.* Trumpeting mightily, he whistled over the heads of his prostrate rescuers to land upon a spiny

* Oh yes he was! This was well before Dumbo!

bush. While resting on his sizeable, thorn-proof butt – somewhat dazed – a euphoric feeling began to spread through him. So that was flying! Wow! And at that, a variety of schemes began to pass through the elephant's great head, most of which involved glue, the feathers of a thousand birds, a big cliff, a long run-up, and a rubber band of improbable proportions.

Trespass got up and dusted himself down. "Well, we're not going to get through there unless we walk … and I don't hold with exercise."

Burble ambled up to him. "Agreed! But we don't have to. The gits will have to come out this way unless they want to do a hundred-mile detour. We might as well set up an ambush and wait for them."

Frunge looked between the two men in confusion. He raised a questioning hand. "Er, wait for *who?*"

The men ignored him.

———◆•◆•◆———

Carved above the arched entrance to the tunnel was a message.

"*Heaven and Hull Through the Bottom of a Glass,*" read Terry. "I don't know what *that* means, but it sounds like we're on the right track."

"Yes, seen this before." The monk rummaged about in the voluminous cornucopia of his robe (having dispensed with his leather habit in Vegetopia town) and pulled out the fragments of Boozer's map. He found the top left quadrant and indicated a line of writing. "That what say here, in tongue of Boozer."

"But what does it mean?" wondered Terry.

Roffo smirked. "I know this! It's a saying my Gramps used to use whenever he was completely pissed and feeling a bit, you know, *poetic.* After he'd finished a pint he'd look through the bottom of his empty and say: *Ah, Roffo me lad, you can see Heaven and Hull through the bottom of this glass.*" The barman had put on the extraordinary accent of a leery, ancient yokel. "*The Hull is the bottom of the glass itself, signifying the end of joy, but the heaven is the next pint I see through it, over there, lined up on the bar, just waiting to be drunk!*" Roffo chortled to himself. "The old codger! I fell for it every time. *What pint?* I'd ask. *Ah, that be the pint ye're about to get me!* The old scoundrel!"

Terry smiled. "Well, that's definite, then. What next?"

"I feel that Illinois Jane would probably have had a few wise tips on how to handle this situation," sighed Roffo. "If only we hadn't lost her book in Nudia."

"Well, no choice then," said the monk. "Must enter. But keep eyes peeled. Doubt if inhabitants likely to give away secrets for free."

The tunnel was broad enough to take six men abreast, and high enough to allow Terry to walk without stooping. A strange phosphorescence along the ceiling gave off enough light to see by. The tunnel cut through the mountain in a straight line for perhaps one hundred yards, and then started a gentle curve to the left. It terminated after a further hundred yards at a big, wooden, iron-banded set of double doors. There were doors to either side of this: one in the left wall and one in the right. Above the left door there was a sign. Painted in black, on an old piece of board, was the word *Reception*.

"Reception!" declared Roffo. "What kind of place is this?"

"At least it's not, well, *threatening*," said Terry.

The three men looked at each other like a trio of naughty schoolboys silently daring each other to ring the doorbell of some weird old man prior to running away and hiding behind a hedge. At last the monk sighed, threw up his hands, and approached the door. He knocked loudly.

"Come in!" said a voice.

The men looked at each other again. The monk shrugged, grasped the handle, and opened the door.

They found themselves in a musty little office. A big desk faced the door. Stacks of papers and parchments were stuffed in most corners of the room, and a hogshead was jammed into one large recess. A fat man in a long-sleeved brown robe – curiously elasticated at the wrists – was currently pouring himself a tankard of the foaming brown stuff. He had a huge brown beard and a little bald patch.

"Ah, gentlemen, come in. And how may I help you?"

Terry and Roffo nudged the monk forward with urgent whispers.

"Ahem. Greetings." The monk bowed. "We come from far away to seek recipe of Holy Ale ..."

The man finished drawing his drink, held up one hand to silence the monk, and took a deep pull of beer. He drained half of the tankard, smacked his lips, and gave a belch of utmost pleasure. "Ah, we live in an age of miracles, do we not?" He came to the desk and put down his tankard. The eyes of the parched and famished adventurers were drawn to it like a magnet. The man reached out a hand. "My name is Namoor, part-time Receptionist to Paradise ... ha ha, our little joke. Pleased to meet you." He shook hands with the three adventurers in turn, then seated himself carefully. There was barely room between the arms of the chair for his huge behind.

The monk nodded and indicated his colleagues. "This Terry Testosterone, barbarian and adventurer. This Roffo, barman and Longman Rider. And I ..." He paused and wet his lips. He heard a snigger from behind, and a finger prodded him in one kidney. He cleared his throat. "My name Marion ..." His two companions squawked with the effort of restraining their laughter. The unfortunately named fellow continued stoically: "... ex-monk of mystical brotherhood."

Namoor was thankful for having a grin-concealing beard. "Marion, eh ..." The man called Roffo slapped a hand to his face. His shoulders heaved up and down in a peculiar manner. "Er, pleased to meet you. Now ..."

"*Marion*," squealed Roffo.

"Ahem!" Namoor waited for the gasping to subside somewhat. "Well, I can't say as we get many visitors up here. Most are simply curious passers-by, as opposed to folk who actually know what we're about."

"*Shut up*," said the monk. "No, not you, sorry. La! How many visitors like us?"

"Since I've been Receptionist? Oh, approximately ... *none*. We used to get loads of visitors in the old days. Most were buyers, but there were a few 'seeking the recipe'. Of course, the buyers were franchised members of the Brotherhood, back in the days when we trusted men with secrets. And then trade ceased. War? Pestilence? The Brothers all dying of horrific liver afflictions? Someone mucking about with the signposts? I dunno."

The monk frowned. "If no buyers, what happen to all ale?"

"Oh, well, we drink quite a lot of it, and we store the rest. We're always having to dig new tunnels to put it in. In fact, the whole damned mountain is just about dug out."

The adventurers looked stunned.

"Uh, you saying whole mountain stocked with barrels of *Boozer's Very Peculiar*?"

"Just about."

"Um," said Roffo, "I know this might sound like a liberty and whatnot but, well, we've not had much to drink recently and we're a bit parched. I don't suppose ...?"

"Sure." Namoor walked over to the hogshead. Beneath it was a crate of pint glasses, from which he plucked three. He stepped over to a small barrel that lay beside the hogshead, somewhat obscured by the bulk of the larger container. He filled the glasses and carried them back to the adventurers.

"Water!" exclaimed Roffo in disappointment. "But, but ..."

"You thought ... oh, sorry, no. More than my job's worth to be giving away freebies."

The men took their glasses sullenly, and drained them.

"Now then, what *exactly* can I do for you?"

"Er, what are options?"

"Well," Namoor tugged on his beard thoughtfully. "I can sell you a consignment, of course. The smallest batch we do is fifty hogshead." He considered the adventurers. "But it doesn't look like you've got the manpower to cope. I mean, it's a bugger carrying them down the mountain – but ultimately worth it, eh?"

Roffo patted the monk on the shoulder. "We could always come back? Way can't be more than three weeks' travel away." He faced Namoor. "And how much would that be?"

"Fifty hogshead? Oh, a gold piece per gallon, fifty four per 'head, that's two thousand seven hundred. Gold. No credit."

Roffo's jaw dropped. "That's not even a *small* fortune ... that's a *bloody big* one!"

The monk shrugged, unconcerned. "That not why here in any case. Want to learn recipe."

"You want to become a member?"

"Of what?" asked Terry.

"The Chosen Alcoholic Monks of the Righteous Ale." Namoor considered the men. "Of course, you *can* try for membership, but there are just *two* little problems."

"Go on," said the monk warily.

"The first is the set of initiation tests. We only allow the very best to become members. If you succeed, you'll get a certificate, unlimited BVP all your life, and the recipe itself. It's quite fun, actually. You see, we write down the recipe for you as you go along. With each successfully completed test we write down another bit. You can keep the certificate even if you fail. It's a nice memento, but it's quite useless unless you manage to get the whole thing. And there is, of course, the subsidiary difficulty that, well – and there's no point beating about the bush here – if you fail it *can* be *fatal*."

"*Can be?*" squeaked Roffo. "How did I know he was going to say that?"

"Okay," said the monk, grimly, "and what is second problem?"

"Ah, the second problem? Well, the second is that *if* you pass the initiation tests you can *never* leave this place again ..."

———•·•·•———

The adventurers were seated on benches in a small, bare room, waiting to be called forth for their initiations.

"So it's come to this then," said Roffo. "Anyone got any ideas about what we're facing? Are there any clues on Boozer's map ... *Marion*?" he sniggered in spite of himself.

The monk gurned in displeasure. "You giggle like teenage female hyena! Foolish youth! This not time for humour. It time for meditation and contemplation."

"Sure, but I mean, what a name! Did your parents really *really* hate you or something? Or ..." He could see the monk's face contorting into horrific dimensions. "Um, sorry. Anyway, contemplating what? I don't understand. What are we going to have to do?"

"No idea. Wait and see."

"But after – if we get through – we're going to make a break for it, aren't we? Once we've got the recipe, right?"

Terry and the monk exchanged grim looks. The barbarian nodded. "When the time is right. Not before. I'll keep an eye out."

"Good," said the monk. "Now be silent. Compose self."

Shortly, there came a jangling of keys at the door. This opened to reveal Namoor with half a dozen other beefy brethren. Each of these men wore a long-sleeved brown robe with elasticated wrists, and each had a beard. Namoor smiled pleasantly. "Okay gents: single or group membership?"

"We can do it as a group?" asked Roffo.

"Sure. But if you do, then you only get one certificate between you, and if one of you fails a test, then you all fail." He gave a bit of a sneer. "But I'm sure you're not really interested in the *lesser* membership. It also limits you to only five gallons of ale a day, and that doesn't bear thinking about! No, Full Membership is by far the best option."

Roffo exchanged brief glances with his comrades. "Ah, yes, well, you see, we're of the school that believes in quality not quantity. We'll go for the group membership."

"Oh!" Namoor looked somewhat put-out. "Very well. I think you're making a mistake though. Come along then, all of you."

———•·•·•———

Namoor led the adventurers and their escort deep into the bowels of Big Hemroid. The waiting room was situated behind the first big double door they had seen. They now passed doors to left and right, turned left at a crossroads, and continued until they came to an elevator. Namoor shouted "Sixty-seven!" into a mouthpiece, and the elevator began to descend. Roffo noticed that both Terry and the monk were concentrating hard on memorising the route they were travelling. His own memory had never been *that* good, so he simply crossed his fingers and wished them luck.

They exited the elevator, then walked for five more minutes along a straight corridor. Light in the distance signalled its end. The three men gasped in amazement as they emerged into an immense cavern, lit by hundreds of torches, with a large lake in its centre. Various vats, pumps, and bits of machinery were cluttered around the lake.

Namoor chuckled. "We diverted the river through man-made tunnels into the mountain many years ago. This is where we get the water to make our brews."

The Receptionist led the adventurers around the lake to the seventh door in the left wall of the cavern. Tables littered the stony floor outside of this door, and a large number of hogsheads were set up on the largest of these. A score of brown-robed figures guzzled beer here, laughing and joking. Two men lay on their backs, staring at the cavernous ceiling, completely ratted. Another bearded fellow broke into a Holy Litany, and his chant was rapidly taken up by the others: "Beer *beer* beer *beer* beer *beer* beer … *cheers*!"

"Well," said Roffo, shaking his head in amazement, "they certainly know how to enjoy themselves!"

Namoor led the party through the door, closing it behind them. They found themselves in a large room with a dozen tables, lots of empty floor, and the obligatory bar. A total of ten doors was situated on the back wall. A black-robed fellow with a white beard waited in the centre of the room. He was surrounded by seven more black-robed beardies.

"Hail, my friends," declared the old man. "My name is Crawford. I am the Master Brewer. I understand you wish to be initiated."

"They want to go for group membership, MB."

"Oh … oh I see." Crawford frowned. "They know the limitations to their membership should they pass?"

Namoor nodded. "I have told them."

"Hmmm!" The Master Brewer appraised the men. "Very well. Gentlemen, I must now explain to you the rules of initiation. The first is that, at any stage, you may pack up and leave. If you do so, however, you will forfeit the right to attempt initiation again for another five years. Do you understand?"

The adventurers nodded.

"Good. Now. There are a total of ten tests ..." He raised his hands to the sky and declared loudly and hollowly: "The Ten Trials of the Wise!" He dropped his hands and looked embarrassed. "Sorry. A bit silly, I know, but one has to at least *attempt* grandeur on such occasions. Ahem." He looked down at a piece of parchment on the desk before him. "Now what, ah, I see ..." He looked up again. "Just needed to check ... not done this for *years* you know! Right. Ten tests. For group membership you *all* have to *endure* the first trial, and then each of you must accomplish three tests alone. It's up to you to choose who will do each test at the time. Is that clear?"

"Er," said Roffo, raising a hand, "do we get a list now so we can plan who'll do what?"

"Do they?" Crawford asked the fat man to his left. The man bent down and whispered into his ear. Crawford nodded. "Ah, I see ... it's a bit like the *Hull, One Room For Eternity, Tea Break, Room of Shit,* and *Handstand* scenario."

Roffo looked quizzically at the monk.

"It joke," whispered the gurning one. "Tell you later."

Crawford cleared his throat. "I'm afraid not. You are told the nature of each test once you are ready to perform it and *then* you choose who will do it. So, if one person does the first three single trials, then the other two must do the remaining six between them."

"I don't like the sound of this," muttered Roffo. He examined his friends. Frankly, he had faith that either could do any test placed before them ... but what about himself? A cold hand played Chopsticks down his spine. He could see himself being left to do the last three tests, and these were *bound* to be the most difficult ...

Standing beside the barman, the monk watched his young companion from the corner of his eye, thinking much the same thing.

Namoor took Roffo by the arm. "Okay, chaps. Are you ready for the Group Ordeal? Then come with me to Room One."

"Hang about," said Crawford, scrambling from his seat. "Give us time to get to the viewing room." He headed for an eleventh door that was concealed behind the bar. "We don't want to miss all the fun!"

"Right then," said Namoor, rubbing his hands together, "will everyone please be seated."

The adventurers were in a room with a distinctly Bindian theme to it: the walls were covered with flock wallpaper and ethnic paintings, and a trio of fat, bearded blokes sat in one corner, attempting to play sitars whilst simultaneously drinking pints of ale.

The table at which the questers were now seated was laid out in preparation for a meal, with knives, forks, plates, side dishes, and condiments. Three portable food heaters lined the centre of the table. Namoor took the grills from these, set light to their candles, and replaced their grills. He looked up – drawing the eyes of the adventurers with him. It was then that they noticed the existence of a glass-walled observation room *above* them. The window ran around the left and back walls of the room. The front wall – through which they had entered – was, of course, adjacent to the main hall, while the right wall stood between this room (the first) and the second of the Test rooms. The monk nodded to himself: clearly, the observation room ran along the back wall of all ten of the trial rooms.

The adventurers could see Crawford and his black-robed cronies settling into seats above. From there they could look down on proceedings like a collection of caesars at an amphitheatre.

"All systems go?" asked Namoor.

"You've lit the wotsits too soon," said one of the black robes. "The candles will be spent before it's time to eat."

"Bugger!" Namoor rectified his mistake. Crawford then nodded and gave a thumbs-up. At this, Namoor turned to address the initiates.

"Okay, this is the first trial, also known as the Group Trial. I must remind you that you must *each* successfully complete this one in order for your party to proceed to the individual trials. Have you got that? Good." Namoor pulled a sand timer from within his robe and placed it on the table. "There are two parts to this trial. The first is to drink six pints of a standard pub ale in an hour and a quarter. Your time will start when I turn over the timer." Two men entered the room from behind a curtain in the back wall, carrying trays containing full pints. They began to stack these up in front of the adventurers. They left to collect some more. Namoor continued. "Of course, that is the easy part. The second part is to eat a Bindian meal *completely*! Every scrap must be consumed: every fragment of pickle and poppadum, every grain of rice, every smidgen of curry. Do you understand?"

Roffo had begun to pale. "God, no! Eat a complete curry *after* an evening's drinking? It's *never* been done before!"

Namoor chuckled. "Not true! Every man you see around you has completed this very feat."

"Yes, but, well, you're all lard arses aren't you?"

Namoor stiffened. "We are simply men of hearty build! And besides, the endless consumption of BVP tends to increase the girth. Most of us here are more spherical *now* than when we were initiated." The assistants had by now completed bringing in the full complement of pints. Namoor nodded as the last man disappeared through the curtains. He turned over the timer. "Begin."

Roffo gave a sickly smile and looked at his friends. "I'm sorry. I'm going to fail you!"

But the monk patted his arm. "Roffo ... when you last eat?"

"Uh, well, it was some time ago I admit ..."

"And what was it?"

"Um, okay, it was just a piece of lettuce ..."

"And how you feel now?"

"Well, I am a *bit* ravenous ..."

"Precisely! This feat not human. But maybe, just maybe, in this circumstance it possible, la?

"Um, okay. I'll try."

Terry, who was already on his third pint, stopped for breath. "That's the ticket. Just take things steady and you'll be all right. By Grom I'm hungry. I wish they'd hurry up with the grub."

And so began the ordeal!

———————

In deference to the Bindian experience, the ale was not top quality. Indeed, it comprised the slops from failed experiments and naff batches of brew. But such was the thirst of the adventurers that the beers were soon utterly consumed. Terry polished off his final drink after just five minutes, then had to wait in agonised anticipation for the meal to begin. The monk made steady progress, the ale disappearing down his gullet at a constant and remorseless rate. He slammed down his final empty at the hour mark. Shortly afterwards, with a trembling hand, Roffo slopped down his last glass and wiped his lips. Namoor stared at the foamy dregs that remained in the bottom of the glass. He glared at the young adventurer. But after a moment's thought, he nodded him through.

Namoor now clapped his hands to signal for the meal to be brought in. Once again he lit the heater candles. "There are two poppadums each, one plain and one spicy. And I want to see the four pickle bowls licked clean. Okay?"

Terry raised a questioning hand. "Um, I don't suppose I could have a few more? I love poppadums."

"Er, I don't see why not. Let it be so."

The poppadums were easily consumed.

Next came the starters.

"Oh," said Terry disappointedly. "Shami kebabs. You haven't got any tandoori chicken have you?" The waiter looked at Namoor, and the Gamesmaster scowled. Terry clarified the situation. "I mean *as well as*, of course." He still finished his food before the others.

And then the ordeal truly began. As every drinker knows, the real test begins with the arrival of the main course: it is then that belts are loosened, time-outs are taken, and regrets are voiced. It is at this time, *always*, that the cry goes up: *why didn't we eat first!**

Namoor chuckled. "Vindaloos all round, with pilau rice and garlic nans. And remember: every smidgen!"

Terry's curry disappeared as rapidly as a small child down a well.

The monk began to sweat. To cope with the volume and the volcanic heat of the curry, he used his mystical arts to physically expand his stomach and to deaden the sensation in his mouth. Working at his food like an automaton he dismantled his meal and packed it away.

And Roffo … Roffo struggled mightily. His face turned the colour of sunset, his hair matted with sweat, his eyes bulged, his tongue swelled up. His arm began to tremble as he lifted each spoonful to his mouth. His lips became smeared with burning paste. But still he went on … and on … *and on*. And yet, it is to be doubted whether he would have been able to pluck up that last grain of yellow rice had it not been for the placement of a certain bizarre elephantine lock on the party's larder door the previous day. The grain disappeared, Roffo's eyes crossed, and his head fell forward onto his spotless plate. The monk and Terry rushed to his aid.

As Terry shook the barman, the monk looked towards Namoor. "And now dessert?"

Namoor looked grim, but he shook his head. "Real ale drinkers *never* have dessert. That is one of the rules. However …" He clicked his fingers. A waiter brought in a tray. On it were three small, dark squares. Namoor held up a finger. "And I warn you, if you say *it*, I will fail you instantly!"

---

* To which the correct reply is: because the pubs were open!

Roffo – who had somehow regained consciousness – giggled manically. "*It?* You mean: *Oh no, not the waf—*" Terry clamped a hand over his mouth.

The three men ate their mints and looked up at their judges. Crawford and his colleagues, one by one, gave them the thumbs-up. They had passed the first ordeal!

———◆•◆◆•———

"This is the Second Ordeal. Ah, thank you, Zazoon, the certificate ..." Namoor received the stiff piece of paper from one of the black robes and handed it to the monk. The adventurers clustered around and studied the gold-penned script. With their lips working silently they read the first line of the recipe for Boozer's Very Peculiar.

"Hmm," said the monk, "so far it standard. *Take three parts of malted hops* ... blah blah blah."

"What type of hops?" wondered Terry.

"Interesting! It not say here. Hmm."

Namoor cleared his throat to regain their attention. "You can peruse that at your leisure once the test begins. At least, two of you can." They were in the main hall again. Namoor opened the second door along the back wall and ushered the men in. A course was marked out along the floor with various tables, statues, and other items en route. The Master Brewer and his mates had moved into position in the viewing room above.

"This is the obstacle course," said Namoor. "The initiate will start here," he indicated a table nearby, "where he will rapidly down a pint of *exceedingly* rough ale. He will then cross over to here ..." he led the party to another table in the centre of the back wall, "where he will consume the first of the beer snacks." Lined up on the table was a bag of salt and vinegar crisps, a pack of scratchings, a pork pie, and an egg. "The crisps have been left open for two days to allow them to soften and lose all flavour, and the scratchings have been roasted to the hardness of granite. The pork pie comes from all those bits of pig you don't want to know about, or even knew existed, while the egg has been pickled mercilessly." Namoor pointed back to the table from which they had come. "After the first snack, the initiate has to rush back and drink another pint, then return here to eat another snack, and so on, until four pints and all of the snacks have been consumed. Next," Namoor moved on, "he has to zig-zag around these poles until he reaches *here* ..." the Gamesmaster stopped, "where he has to pick up this paddle and then spin around thirty times without falling over. Important that! If you fall, you lose."

"This is impossible," said Roffo, who was being carried between his comrades.

Namoor smiled cheerily. "And at this point, he has to stop and, using these traffic cones, throw them onto the heads of the four statues of Boozer over there. You've ten cones, and you must get one on each statue. And finally," he led the way to a table against the right wall where a brown-robed beardie waited, "you have to drain the yard of ale that Fildo here is holding." Namoor beamed at the initiates. "The yard has to go down in three seconds, the course has to be completed in four minutes, and if you puke, you lose. Who's up for it?"

———◆◆◆◆———

They studied the certificate. A second line had been scribed onto it, which again revealed little more than a standard brewing procedure. Roffo was now propped against a wall looking very green. "I don't know how the Hull you did that, Terry. I felt sick just watching you."

Terry gave a little smile. "Oh, that's nothing. We used to do obstacle courses like that in primary school."

"No!"

"Yes, it's true. In the first year. But they got more difficult after that. Like, after the paddle you'd have to throw axes at the blonde tresses of little girls. That sort of thing." He chuckled to himself. "Actually, I was surprised there was only one yard of ale to drain."

"Why's that?"

"Well, we usually had to do about a dozen. But in *secondary* school things really started to get tough ..."

"Terry, I don't think I want to hear this!"

Namoor's head appeared through the open door to room three. "Ready?"

———◆◆◆◆———

"So all you have to do," said Terry, "is drink that one pint of gassy, mass-produced *lager*?" He gestured towards the table on which the fizzy, straw-coloured pint was set. "What's the catch?"

Namoor smiled. "The true ale drinker will react appropriately. Now, who's going to do it?"

The monk held up a hand. "One moment. Can discuss ... in private?"

"Why not?" Namoor retreated to the opposite side of the barren room.

426

"I can't believe it's as easy as drinking a pint," said Terry.

The monk observed Namoor, who stood as far away from the table as he could. He watched as the Gamesmaster's eyes settled on the glass – and a look of utmost disgust crossed his face!

"*Oooooh*," wailed Roffo, holding his stomach. "At this stage I couldn't *even* handle that!"

The monk looked at him sharply. "Roffo, how you feel?"

"By Clovory, I swear I'm going to chunder any minute. Maybe I ought to force it? It'll make me feel better."

"No! Do not!" The monk waved Namoor over. "We decided. Roffo will do Ordeal."

"Hey, but I'm—"

"Shush! Roffo, just try to drink lager and be natural. Trust me!"

Roffo shook his head. He couldn't see what the monk's game was but ... trust him? Yes, he *would* do that. He shambled over to the table. He felt his gorge rising even as he placed his hand around the unnaturally cold glass. He licked his lips and thought he could taste bile. With a last look over at his friends, he tipped the pint up to his mouth. He managed to swallow a mouthful and then ...

Roffo imitated Vesuvius, only with far more diced carrots. The occupants of the room rapidly stepped back against the wall ...

The hewey-fest continued for an improbable length of time. At last, Roffo's stomach stopped heaving and he lay on his back in a gory pool. "Oooh," he cried, "relief!"

From the opposite end of the room Namoor came forward. "Magnificent!"

Once Roffo's ears stopped ringing, he heard the applause. It was coming from all around him: from Namoor, from the escort, and from the observation room, where Crawford and the black robes were on their feet giving him a standing ovation.

Namoor helped him to his feet. "Pass with honours, my friend!" He shook the barman by the shoulder in a congratulatory way. "Never have I seen such a superb indictment of this vile alcoholic beverage than you've just given. Bravo!"

In spite of his begrimed state, the brown robes hoisted Roffo onto their shoulders and paraded him from the room.

———•◦•◦•———

"Ordeal number Four," said Namoor, "involves walking across a rice paper floor while carrying five *full* pint glasses in both hands. You must not spill a single drop. Indeed, to ensure that this is the case, the glasses actually contain a form of acid." They were inside the fourth room standing by the door. The near and further edges of the room comprised stone floor, but rice paper had been stretched taut across the gap between them. "The floor has actually been cut away beneath the paper. If the acid touches the paper it will burn it sufficiently for the tension to be released and the initiate will fall. The drop is about twenty feet and the floor of the pit is covered with broken glass."

"Nasty!" declared Roffo, who was feeling a lot better. Not only had he eased the unendurable pressure in his belly, but he had also accomplished one of the trials. His confidence had soared. He turned to his colleagues. "Me again? I'm used to carrying full pint glasses. I once managed six without spilling a drop!"

The monk considered him grimly and laid a hand on his shoulder. "La! Think maybe *could* do task … but at moment perhaps *not*. Maybe bit *over*confident?"

Terry nodded at this. "Sorry, Roffo, but I agree. You know how sometimes you get a bit *too* enthusiastic and then, well, that's when disasters happen. I think this task is more difficult than it looks."

Roffo looked downcast. "You're saying it ought to be done by someone with a cool head?" He sighed. "I see what you're saying. And, well, I guess Mario— … er, Mr Monk *is* a bit of a martial arts expert. Moves like a cat and whatnot."

The monk smiled. "Yes. Good choice, Roffo. Agreed. After all, must do test sometime. Cannot be shielded from everything!"

Roffo laughed. "Away with you! Just don't spill anything, okay?"

"No problem."

And it wasn't.

———————

Terry was chosen for the Fifth Ordeal. This involved playing a board game called '*Passe Oute*'. The opposition had initially comprised three brown-robed brethren, but now only one remained: the other two had collapsed over the backs of their chairs and lay where they had fallen.

Terry rolled the dice and moved his counter. The Red Lion came to a rest on a red square. Terry read the caption. "One pint and two whisky chasers." A tray materialised at his elbow with the requisite forfeits. The barbarian nodded thanks to Namoor. He swigged down the pint and followed this with the double. "Ugh!" he cried, "whisky!"

The man across the table glared blearily at the barbarian: it was clear to him that Terry was still very much in the game. The acolyte of Boozer slowly picked up the dice and threw. *Nine*. He moved his White Hart and read the caption where it ended. "Thank bollocks," he slurred. "It sezz ... it sezz ... *red* to drink a mug ov ... ov ... ov ... *margrittas* ... hee hee hee hee hee hee."

Terry frowned. Margaritas? Oh well!

Namoor delivered the jug and Terry drained it in one. He thought for a moment and mulled over the taste. Then he smiled. "Hey – that's not bad! You can land on that square whenever you want, mate!"

His adversary groaned.

Terry's next roll took him past the Start.

"Tongue-twister!" cried Namoor. He picked up a card from the deck at the centre of the board and handed it to the barbarian. Terry considered the card for a moment. "Peter Piper Pickled a Pack of Peppery Paupers ..." He completed the 'twister flawlessly. Namoor scowled and gave him the thumbs-up.

"See what I mean?" said Roffo to the monk. "You couldn't have done that *sober*."

The monk pouted out a lip. "True. And you could not have done it drunk."

"No doubt about that! I think we chose right again."

The last of the adversaries rolled and moved his figure. His counter passed the Start and landed on a square already occupied by the Green Man of one of the ex-players. Namoor handed him a card.

"Sheez zellz zee sells by ..."

"Stop!" shouted the referee Namoor. "That's dreadful. Drink!"

The brown-robed fatty wearily located the full pint that appeared at his elbow. He lifted it towards his mouth. He opened his mouth. He started to pour. Unfortunately, the glass had got nowhere near its intended target. The ale *did a Niagara* into his lap. The man giggled and slumped off his chair.

Terry looked at his foe in disappointment. "Uh, that's it, isn't it? Damn. I was just starting to enjoy myself! What about another game?"

Namoor shook his head in awe.

The adventurers mulled over recent events in the main hall. They were half-way through their initiation and had earned a half-hour break. The monk was carefully examining their certificate. This now had five small paragraphs inscribed on it, each of which detailed various ingredients and processes needed to make BVP. He nodded to himself.

"Yes. Starting to get hint now. Recipe mentions proportion of malted barley to other carbohydrates ... temperatures ... times ... but still not type of hops used."

"Maybe anything will do," suggested Roffo.

"Unlikely. Each type of hops leads to distinctive taste. Would have thought that type of hops important in brew like this, and one of first ingredients mentioned."

"Well, I'm sure it'll be mentioned later." Roffo had come down from his earlier high and now jiggled about on his chair restlessly.

In spite of the warm glow that he felt from the huge quantity of alcohol he had consumed, Terry was not entirely unaware of events around him. He noticed his friend's nervous twitches. "What's up, Roff? You seem a bit jumpy."

"Um, well, yeah. Look: there are five tests to go and I've still got to do two of them. Let's face it, you two succeeded in your tests through skill, but I only got through on a fluke."

The monk looked up from the certificate. "Completed first test too. That no fluke. It great test of will."

"Yeah," said Roffo bitterly, "but that was only because I hadn't eaten for ages. I reckon you two could have polished off that Bindian even if you'd come straight from a banquet. I'm just, well, I'm just afraid I'm going to let the side down."

"Hmm. You underestimate own abilities. You have great skills: just need to find right tests."

"Besides," said Terry, "even if you did only pass the two tests by luck, well, that's still *something*. Barbarians believe that some people are naturally lucky and others aren't."

"Really?"

"Yep. We even have a saying. It goes: *When you march into battle, choose the man on your left carefully: don't choose the strongest – choose the luckiest.*"

"Cor! That's almost profound! And there was I thinking the most philosophical thing that has ever come from the mouth of a barbarian was *let's bash 'em.*"

———————

Ordeal Six was a complete walkover. The test required the initiate to drink five pints of inferior ale very quickly, and then play darts. The objective was to get down and out from 501 with 18 darts. The initiate had to accomplish this feat at least four times in a maximum of five goes. The monk stepped up to the oché and produced three of his sharpened chopsticks.

"This okay?"

Namoor sought guidance from the onlookers, but Crawford merely shrugged.

"They're unusual arrows, but I don't see why not."

The monk licked the tip of the first chopstick. He threw it into the treble twenty ...

"Damn," whispered Roffo, "four to go and I've still got to do two of them!"

"For the next ordeal," declared Namoor, "the initiate has to correctly identify ten ales from around the world. So, who's it to be? Who has travelled most widely? Who has sampled the greatest variety of ales?"

"Bugger," said Roffo, more loudly. "Make that two out of three. Go on Mr Monk, you might as well get it over with."

"Hmm, yes," said the monk, fishing a large piece of crud from between his teeth. "Very meaty brew. Nutty. Reminded of acorns and hydrochloric acid. Must be Mr Fruity's Knee Trembler."

Namoor sighed. "Of course it is. Let's move on to the next room."

The adventurers stood in room eight. They had been left by themselves while Namoor had gone out to collect some vital ingredient for the ordeal. The room was small and almost empty. For furniture, it held just two desks and two chairs. One desk was near the back wall, facing them, and the other was in the centre of the room, facing the one at the back. On the nearer desk, several pencils had been laid out. On the back desk there was a sand timer.

"It'll soon be the moment of truth, eh?" said Roffo miserably. "I wonder what impossible feat they want here? Turn the desks into a palatable brew with no other ingredient than your own spittle? Drink five million gallons of slops and spring from desk to desk eighty times without touching the floor or falling off or puking?"

"Cheer up," said Terry, "it won't be that bad."

"Yes," said the monk, "must be positive! If positive, can overcome any trial."

"That's easy for you to say, you've done your three tests and Terry's only got one more to do. I bet I won't be able to do *this* either, so I'll have to do the last two. And those will be the *potentially fatal* tests. Guaranteed. Just you watch. Not only will I fail, but you'll have to carry me home in a body bag!"

The barbarian and the monk looked at each other wordlessly. What more could they possibly say?

Namoor returned carrying several sheets of paper. He had a broad grin on his face. "Now for the real killer. This one is the Man Breaker. It's astonishing how many worthy fellows go down at this stage."

"Here we go," muttered Roffo.

"Yes, indeed: Ordeal Eight is the Written Exam. It's an aptitude test rather than a test of knowledge. Multiple choice. And you must score eighty percent or over to pass. Who's it to be?"

Roffo groaned. "See what I mean? An exam! I hate exams!" He turned to Namoor. "Look, can't I just try to turn the desks into a palatable brew using no other ingredient than my own spittle?"

"Er," said Terry uncertainly, "er … I'm not *too* good at exams, um, *really*."

"I don't suppose you had them at barbarian school," said Roffo.

"Well, the exams did tend to be practical-based, but we did have to do *some* written papers. I remember one question from the last paper I did before graduating. How did it go? *You are surrounded by cruel and malicious guards in a castle dungeon. There are eight guards, and all are heavily armed. They are led by a homicidal tyrant. Your hands are tied behind your back. In front of you is a twelve-foot-deep pit containing seven ravening wolves. The evil tyrant is about to command that you be thrown into the pit. What do you do?*"

In spite of the situation, Roffo was intrigued. "Well, what *do* you do?"

"Oh … you say to the tyrant something like, 'My lord, yea, I accept your command, but at least let me die like a warrior with my hands untied.' Because he reckons you're a goner he thinks 'what the Hull' and unties you. You leap into the pit and sort out the wolves. You then use the corpses of six of them to build a ladder. You climb out and use the seventh wolf as a club. You dispatch the guards. Then you get the tyrant and you … er … you wouldn't want to hear the rest. It involves lots of bodily parts that, um, *become detached*, plus a fair amount of screaming.

Er, from the tyrant of course, not you."

Roffo sighed. "So, it's down to me then, I guess. I apologise in advance for the failure to come."

The monk stepped up to the barman and grasped him by both arms. He looked into his eyes. "Roffo. You *can* do this. But … *must think.* You clever man when *think things out.* Do not give first answer. Do not be impetuous. Just *think.*"

"Sure. I'll try."

Roffo took his seat at the central desk while his friends were ushered from the room.

Outside, the monk turned to Terry. "Last paper before graduating? You passed?"

"Oh yes. Every exam actually. But I *never* got full marks. Only, um, *A's.* You see, I tended to lose marks for not being blood-thirsty enough." Terry laughed. "Actually, I had *that* question in my 'mocks', too, and I nearly failed it. The examiner wasn't too pleased when I said I'd take the tyrant for a cup of tea and try to reason with him. In the end I thought it best to give the answer they wanted in the real exam."

The monk nodded. "Yes … perhaps *you* should have done test. But Roffo *is* smart when uses brain. Must pray to Boozer he will try."

———•••———

"Your time starts *now!*" Namoor turned over the sand timer.

Roffo wiped the sweat from his hands onto his trousers and turned over the exam paper. He looked at it. For some reason his vision was blurry and he couldn't make out a single word. His breathing was coming fast and hard. He licked his lips. He looked up at the timer. *Bollocks, that sand is moving fast!* He looked back at the paper, but it was still a blur. *Okay, calm yourself. Deep breaths.* Roffo closed his eyes and inhaled, then exhaled, slowly. He did this twice more. That was better. He picked up a pencil and felt the sharpness of its point. *Ideal.* Okay. Try again.

He looked down.

Question 1: When I see a Big Beard I feel …

A) Nauseous,

B) Indifferent,

C) Envious.

Was this some sort of joke? The answer was obvious! It was 'A'. He brought the point of the pencil into contact with the paper … and then the monk's last words came back to him. *Do not give first answer. Do not be impetuous. Just think.* He withdrew the pencil an inch and thought.

Hang on a minute ... all of Boozer's acolytes have beards! He grinned. Of course! He circled 'C'.

Question 2: When I am in a bar and someone farts repulsively I ...

A) Say "What smelly bugger did that? Get out get out ..."

B) Pretend that nothing has happened and continue with my conversation.

C) Claim it as my own.

Roffo grinned. His personal answer was 'A' but ... he circled 'C' again and went on.

The three men milled about outside the room. Waiting. The tension was almost too much for Roffo to bear. "I've failed, haven't I? That's why he's taking so long. Oh no, here he comes ..."

Namoor emerged through the door with a sheet of paper in his hand. He smiled at Roffo. "Well done young man!"

"Er, so you're saying ... *I passed?*"

"With flying colours. Shall we move on?"

Roffo's back straightened and a grin spread across his face. He made an obscene gesture involving one hand, a shaking motion, and a circular conjunction of thumb and index finger. "Piece of piss!"

"Now, I must warn you," said Namoor, with a serious expression on his face, "that this ordeal is not to be taken lightly. Indeed, I must say that you are a fine set of fellows who have done superbly so far. It would not be a disgrace to bow out at this point and take away your certificate and your memories."

"Oh oh," intoned Roffo. "So you're saying that this is where the shit really hits the fan."

"Indeed." Namoor looked troubled. They were standing outside the ninth room. "This task involves selecting the Holy Tankard. Inside this room you will find a dozen receptacles, each containing a brown liquid. One of these is the True Tankard, the one from which Boozer supped his divine ale. Indeed, the Tankard *does* contain that brew. The other receptacles, however, contain something altogether less palatable." Namoor licked his dry lips nervously. "They contain Jolly Roger's Death Ale."

Roffo and Terry gasped in unison.

Namoor nodded solemnly. "Indeed. To drink of that ale is death, unless one has built up an immunity to its poison, and then it is rather tasty, or so I am told. What is wrong with Marion?"

The monk had slumped against the wall. He beat against it with a fist. "Ai-la! I ... *have* immunity!"

"Buggering bollocks," said Roffo. "That's typical! Bloody typical!"

"I am truly sorry," said Namoor. "It just means that whoever takes on this ordeal had better not fail."

"So who should do it? Me or you?"

Terry smiled. "I'll do it. Death holds no fear for a barbarian. Besides, we're rather *hardy*, if you know what I mean. Maybe I could cope with the poison."

The monk muttered to himself. "What will receptacles be? What will ale be in? Think?"

"Well," said Roffo, "it won't be served in a half-pint measure, that's for sure."

"Yes. That right. Also won't be in cup or straight glass or such bizarre container."

"What about the *material* of the container?" asked Terry. "Won't that be the key?"

"It won't be in a plastic glass," said Roffo.★

"Or anything weird," said the monk, "like wood or porcelain."

"Just ... a plain pint glass mug then?" suggested Roffo.

"No ... not glass. *Tankard. Pewter* tankard."

"Of course!" exclaimed Roffo, "that's it! It has to be! But ... how is that difficult? I mean, how can they confuse you?"

The monk smiled. "Hmm ... Roffo, can tell difference between pewter tankard and silvery tankard made of other metal?"

He caught the monk's drift instantly and snapped his fingers. "No, but I know a man who can!" He patted the barbarian on his muscular shoulder. "In you go then, Terry. Use that barbarian instinct of yours!"

Apart from the glasses, pots, mugs and receptacles that were clearly *wrong*, there were three metallic tankards. Terry picked up the first of these and instantly felt a tingling in his hand. An image flashed through his mind of a battlefield, a blood-stained pennant, a broken spear set into the ground

★ Who appreciated that the polymerisation of hydrocarbons would not be perfected for many years to come.

... He put the tankard down. A *steel* tankard! Maybe they would let him keep it after the test? The second tankard induced similar, though less violent images. Could there be iron in it? The third tankard was pure. Terry knew. Tin and lead. Pewter. This was the one. He lifted it to his lips and drank ... drank deep ... drained the tankard ...

And collapsed onto his back.

* * *

"Oh no," cried Roffo, slapping his friend about the face. "The gits ... they've poisoned him ... And *you* ..." Roffo snarled at Namoor, who stood nearby, grinning. "What are *you* smiling at!" He started to rise. "I'm gonna ...!"

The monk stepped into his path. "No! Look!"

Terry sat up. His eyes rolled in his head. "Surely I have died and gone to heaven!" He ran his tongue around his lips, gleaning every last drop of the Holy Ale.

* * *

They entered the tenth room. An air of excitement permeated all. From their position by the door the adventurers could see up into the observation room: it was packed more tightly than a sprinter's jock strap. Crawford and his black-robed judges had been joined by a score more brown robes. The main hall had also begun to fill up as rumour of the party's successes had spread; they could hear murmuring coming through the closed door behind them.

The room itself was relatively bare so that the nature of the Final Ordeal was not at all clear. A burning brazier rested on a tripod some five feet in front of them. Beyond this, there was a line marked on the floor, which ran from one side of the room to the other. A similar transverse line was marked on the floor some fifteen feet further away. An empty tripod was positioned just beyond that line. Apart from this, there was nothing else in the room except for eight buckets of water arranged against each of the side walls.

Namoor was currently stoking up the brazier. Orange flames licked the air, and a spark leapt from the coals and sizzled on the bare stone floor.

Roffo looked at these arrangements worriedly. "Well, chaps, what do you reckon? Am I going to get burned here?"

"Ah ... unfortunate choice of phrase," said the monk. He exchanged concerned glances with the barbarian. Terry chewed on his bottom lip and gave a barely detectable nod. The two men had their suspicions.

"What?" asked Roffo. "What is it? You know, don't you? Cough up!"

"Hmm. Best let referee explain. Do not want to terrify unnecessarily."

"*Terrify!*" squealed Roffo. "Well thanks a bundle, thanks very much indeed. What about you, Terry, or is the *horror* to come so *nightmarish* that even you can't speak of it?"

"Uh," said Terry uncomfortably, turning to the monk, "let's have a look at this certificate then. Can you see what's missing?"

Namoor came over to the party. He held a red-hot poker in his hand. "It is time."

Roffo retreated until his back was against the wall. "If you think you're putting that poker anywhere *near* my bottom you've got another think coming!"

"Eh? Oh, sorry! Forget this. Nothing to do with the ordeal."

Roffo sagged slightly. "Well, that's a relief ..."

"No," continued Namoor, "the ordeal is actually much, *much* worse."

Roffo's face went white. He felt faint. In a small voice he said: "Go on then."

"Well," said Namoor, "what you have to do is quite simple. It's *excruciatingly, mind-bendingly agonising* ... but simple. Ahem. Yes." The referee gestured at the brazier. "All you have to do is pick up the brazier by clamping your forearms around it, thus ..." he held out his two forearms in front of him, at waist level, then revolved his hands in their elasticated sleeves to face inwards. "Pick it up so that the brazier is about midway between your wrist and your elbow. And then simply, er, walk to the other tripod and put it down." He shrugged. "If you drop it ... well, you lose."

Incredulity etched Roffo's face. "And you're trying to tell me that every member of CAMORA has done this?"

"Ah, well, you see," began Namoor, "if you'd done the full set of tests by yourself you would have been, ah, half-cut by now. *At least* half-cut. Maybe even *double* or *treble* cut. Possibly even completely diced! Ahem. And, well, alcohol does have other benefits apart from the thirst-quenching one. I did warn you against trying for Group Membership."

"Ah, yes," said Roffo desperately, "but you said that's because of the reduced amount of ale you get and whatnot. You didn't even hint at this!"

Namoor shrugged. "I'm sorry. As we say here, *my wrists are tied.*" And he raised his arms, bringing attention once more to the unusual sleeves of his robe and their elasticated wrists.

The monk nodded. "Ah, see now … sleeves hide terrible burns on arms."

"*Terrible* burns? You're not making this any easier for me!"

"Ah … apologies. Shut up now."

"Anyway, time is passing," said Namoor. "You can still leave with your certificate. That's up to you. If you succeed, you get the final ingredient. And you ensure that you will never leave this place again."

Roffo looked down at the floor in utmost misery. "What can I do? I can't … I can't carry *that*." He looked at his friends. "Can I?"

"Roffo," said the monk, "must do what have to do. If say 'no', that fine. Cannot be blamed. But …"

"But you'll hold it against me? Forever?"

A smile softened the monk's usually irascible features. "No. Was going to say: but think you *can* do this."

"Really?"

The monk laughed. "On quest, been amazed by certain young barman so often it beyond count. Think you capable of most anything!"

Terry laughed too and tousled the barman's hair. "I agree. Whatever your flaws, you have the courage of a barbarian."

Fire suddenly sparkled in Roffo's eyes. A ferocious grin settled onto his lips. "Too bloody right! Yeah!" He turned to Namoor and pointed at him with a savage finger. "Right then, dickweed, are we going to stand here all day or are you going to get your huge arse in gear!"

Namoor stepped back in surprise at the sudden change in attitude of the initiate. "Uh, right. If you'd just remove your tunic … we don't want any fires starting, now, do we, heh heh."

Roffo ripped off his tunic and strode over to the brazier. He looked back at his friends and gave them a thumbs-up. "Game on!" he cried, and grasped the brazier …

Back in Cross-My-Way, in the kitchen of The Merry Bear, Maddy was sorting out dinner. For some reason today her mind was all over the place, and amongst the things that crossed it were thoughts of the missing adventurers. A lustful smile settled onto her face as she thought about Terry. What a guy! It was weird, though, that she hadn't really missed him — at least, not at first. Obviously, that had had a lot to do with the problems they'd faced at The Bear. The days had been busy, what with getting the inn back in order and devising strategies to persuade the customers to return. But matters had settled down now, business was good, and she had plenty of spare time to think about life. And she realised that things were very different now that he had gone ...

Now that *they* had gone. She thought about Roffo, too, and a different kind of smile came to her lips. What a buffoon he was! But, well, it was funny that, in a way, she had actually missed him *more* than the barbarian. When he was around things were never dull. In fact, wherever Roffo went, there went perpetual crisis. And now things were quieter and less harried but ... who wanted *quiet*? Enough time for 'quiet' when you were in the grave.

Maddy grinned and shook her head: foolish thoughts! She reached to draw the cooking tray from the stove. Unfortunately, with her thoughts elsewhere, her grip on the tray was not as strong as it should have been. The tray slipped back through her gloved hands and scalded the insides of her forearms.

"Eeeek!" she squealed. Maddy rushed over to a bowl of water and plunged her arms in. "Damn that Roffo," she wailed, perhaps a touch harshly. "That boy could cause mischief if he were on the moon!"

"Ooo ... aaah ... ooo ... aaah ... ooo ... aaah ... ooo ... aaah ..." Terry and the monk ladled water onto Roffo's burns. Because of the circular nature of the brazier, and the way it had been carried, the burns were surprisingly small: they were approximately four inches square. At present, the burns were uneven pink and red blotches.

"Ooo ... aaah," went Roffo, "nononono don't stop ... ooh ... aaah!"

Crawford and the black robes had come down from their observation room and clustered around the adventurers. The Master Brewer looked on in concern. "How is the young fellow?"

"Ooo ... aaah ... fine thanks ... ooo ... aaah ... piece of cake ... ooo ... aaah."

"Good show ... ah, thank you Namoor!" Crawford received a bundle from the receptionist-referee. "Well, I must congratulate you men. Splendid show, absolutely splendid. I have here your new brown robes."

The monk stood up from his ministrations and accepted the robes with a bow. "We thank you. And now final piece of recipe?"

The Master Brewer grinned, and his eyes twinkled. He looked at Roffo. "You already have it."

"Eh ... wassat?" asked Roffo, miming another round of pained exclamations.

"Yes, you already have the final piece of the recipe, young fellow. It will be clear to you in time."

"Uh, this not con is it?" wondered the monk.

"Oh no, I assure you I am quite sincere!" Crawford looked around the crowded room. "Well, I think this calls for a party, don't you?" A roar erupted around the room, supported by a sprinkling of cheers and some hand-clapping. "Excellent! Gentlemen –" he turned back to the trio of adventurers "– Namoor will show you to your new quarters where you can clean up, dress the young fellow's wounds, and robe up. And then we're going to have the biggest party since … since …"

"Yesterday?" suggested one of the other black robes.

"Precisely! Since yesterday! Namoor … see to them. And once more you chaps: well done. And welcome to CAMORA!"

CHAPTER 19

THE BATTLE OF THE FIVE ARMIES (REVISITED)

"SO WHAT'S missing?" asked Terry, as he bandaged Roffo's antiseptic-smeared forearms. The three men currently sat around a little coffee table in the lounge of a pleasant, three-bedroom suite that had been allocated to them. The barbarian and the barman shared a sofa, while the monk sat opposite to them on a red leather chair. A strip of phosphorescent algae illuminated the room; a plush carpet with a paisley design covered the floor; and a profusion of pot plants crowded together on various tables, shelves, and benches. The room was, all in all, something like the study of a university don. It was certainly comfortable and homey.

"Type of hops used," said the monk, who was perusing their gold-inked certificate, "... *perhaps.*"

"Can't you be more certain ... ow! Watch it Terry!"

"Sorry."

The monk shook his head. "No. If follow recipe will get beer at end of process. But will it be BVP? Maybe any type of hops okay to use, but maybe there special ingredient to add at some point. Couldn't tell until brewed first batch."

"In other words," said Roffo, "we're completely in the dark. Maybe there isn't a tenth part to the recipe and it's all just a big con? I mean, if you weren't *sure* you had all of the recipe then you wouldn't try to leave here, would you? Maybe only the black robes know the truth?"

The monk gurned in puzzlement. "No. Think there *is* tenth part to recipe. Feel it in bones."

"Well where is it?" wondered Terry. He finished winding the second white cotton bandage around Roffo's left forearm. "All done."

"Eh? *Thanks*. Now, what was it Crawford said? *You already have it*. And he also said: *it will be clear to you in time*. What does that mean? Could they have slipped it to us in some way so we didn't notice? Aha! What about the robes?"

"Yes. Good idea." The monk turned to consider his brown robe. It was made of soft wool with a hood and two pockets. He rummaged through the pockets of his robe while the others did the same with theirs.

"Nothing," said Roffo. "Maybe there's something sewn into the hem. Or maybe the robe *is* the clue?"

"You mean *it's* part of the recipe?" said Terry, uncertainly.

"No, I mean, maybe there's something important about the material of it or, well, if it's been dyed, maybe there's something important about the type of dye?"

"Hmm. Dye is chemical. Need to think about this."

"Have we been given anything else?" asked Terry.

The other two men thought about this for some moments. At last, Roffo shook his head. "All we've been given is the certificate and the robes. That is, apart from what we ate and drank during the trials, and I for one am not about to go delving into *that* when it re-emerges!"

"So, what do we do?"

"Think that Crawford honest," said the monk "Also think must leave here quick before become addicted to BVP, then not able to leave at all."

"Yeah," said Roffo, "and before our butts become so large that we won't be able to squeeze through any of the exits. So what's the plan?"

"Go to party, but keep robes and certificate with us at all times. Suss out joint. See if another way out, or else *visit* Namoor in Reception tomorrow and *persuade* him to let us out."

Roffo rubbed his hands in glee. "I like that plan, especially as it means we can join the celebrations. Gentlemen: shall we party?"

"Personally, I think Manis is trying to become respectable," asserted Picket, spitting out the last word as though it was a piece of putrid meat. "He'll be inviting the mayor over for tea and crumpets next."

"Aye, I've heard the mayor likes a bit of crumpet," replied Fingers, recycling the oldest culinary joke in the world. He pondered his pint for a moment before venturing his own opinion on Manis's sudden conversion to lawfulness. "I think it's the success of this Pedigree myself. He's earning so much money from his legitimate business enterprises that he doesn't have to bother with us and our more *exotic* activities any more." He hunched further forward so that his thin lips were a bare three inches from his colleague's face. "I think it might be time for us, the felonious citizens of Way, to find ourselves a new leader. You know, someone who'll appreciate our finer talents and not cast us aside when things look rosier on the other side of the, er, *fence*."

"Well said," nodded Picket. "You wouldn't be putting yourself up for the job by any chance, would you?"

"The thought never crossed my mind!"

The fence peered at the pickpocket through narrow slits. "So you don't fancy the idea of taking five percent off the top of everyone's earnings then?"

"Well, now that you mention it …" Fingers left confirmation of his intent unspoken, but raised an eyebrow meaningfully. "Of course, whoever takes over will need a deputy."

"A deputy, hey?" mused Picket thoughtfully. "And who do you think that should be?"

Knowing glances were exchanged between the two plotters. A period of silent contemplation on the joys of power followed. Picket's chain of thought was broken by a tugging at his sleeve.

"Well, whoever takes over should have more morals than Manis," he declared, looking down at the boy at his sleeve. "He's the only man I know who would grass up a child for peeing in the gutter. Isn't that right son?"

"Sure dad. That Manis is a complete *cu*—"

"Ahem!" went Picket, appreciating that while 'f'-words might just about get through the censor, 'c'-words probably would not. "Want another pint?"

The little boy considered the offer for a moment. "Yeah, dad," he nodded. "And lend us some change for The Machine, eh? I've got a hot date for tonight and I hear she likes *Liquorice Allsorts* …"

In human experience, the phrase 'morning after' has only negative connotations. There is the morning-after pill for clearing up the mess of an injudicious sexual encounter. And there is the morning-after hangover – which ably demonstrates Mother Nature's belief in the balance of all things (including pain and pleasure) and shows that She has a wicked sense of humour to boot. And, worst of all, there is the morning-after-curry experience, about which no more need be said.

As Roffo straddled a ceramic bowl and prepared for the fallout from the previous day's First Ordeal, his thoughts drifted back to the night's celebrations. It had been a pure beer drinkers' party all right: the divine ale had flowed like water, and the scratchings of a hundred pigs had been consumed. The three new CAMORA members had been much-fêted, not simply because they had passed the initiation, but because of the style in which they had done so, setting a number of new records in the process. There had even been a special award for the young barman for his performance in the Lager Ordeal. After being presented with an engraved tankard, he had been required to sit for a portrait for the Hall of Fame. It was only after his features had been rapidly sketched that Roffo had been allowed to have a look at the work – and he'd had to admit that the artist not only had a good eye, but a colourful imagination too (the outline of the geyser erupting from his mouth being spectacularly improbable). But Roffo was rather flattered by it all. Indeed, he currently basked in a warm glow that wasn't entirely related to the ominous effects of the chicken vindaloo.

Roffo smiled even more broadly as he remembered how everyone had wanted to congratulate him on successfully completing the final task. His arms now ached as much from the vigorous hand shaking as from their scalding. But other events were only a blur. He recalled that the monk had spent the entire evening badgering the Master Brewer about the last line of the recipe, but had learnt nothing new. According to a grinning Crawford they *already had it*. And in the meantime (Roffo recalled) Terry had triumphed in a number of drinking contests.

But that was all he could remember. Roffo had woken in the morning to find himself staring at the underside of a table. In order to assuage the throbbing in his head he had tried to lie as still as possible, but an acolyte had soon heard his gentle groaning and pulled him from his hideaway. A giant fried breakfast had then been thrust under his nose. That was two hours ago, since when he had managed nothing more than a detailed exploration of the corridor between the party room and the toilet cave.

Suddenly, something in Roffo's stomach *moved*. He shrieked and clasped the bowl even more tightly. With his face now scrunched in torment, the young barman felt a sensation not unlike that experienced by Edward the Second during the last moments of his life ...

The Master Brewer was pleased to note that two of the new boys had crossed the central cavern to examine the workings of the brewery. He badly needed more help, what with recruitment having dried up, in addition to the problems of an ageing population. Crawford frowned at this thought. Well, *ageing* was only part of the story. CAMORA numbers were actually dwindling as a result of the terrible incidence of liver disease, combined with the invaliding-out of workers to the Retirement Complex, where immense lardies – looking like huge, hairy beachballs – were towed around specially widened corridors by braces of oxen. Crawford pondered the men. The big one looked promising in the moving-barrels-full-of-ale department, while the wrinkly one might make a good stock keeper. He waved at them in a friendly manner, then turned back to his vats.

"Probably deciding where we work," muttered the monk to his companion. "Look interested in machines and I tell you story, or should say, *part* of story."

Terry stood on a rock and perused the bubbling vats and groaning pipework. He pointed to a gauge tacked on the side of a vat, waving his hand around in a manner that – he hoped – suggested he was explaining something important about it to his companion. "So, what's this story then, and what's it got to do with escaping from here?"

The monk nodded sagely and pointed to another vat. "When first searched through libraries looking for references to whereabouts of Boozer's recipe, sometimes got frustrated because of lack of success. To take mind off early failures, read many books of fiction and immersed self in fantasy worlds they described." The monk waved his hands around. "One book told adventures of group of little people who travelled in search of treasure hoard guarded by giant, winged reptile. At one point they captured by enemies and locked in underground castle, but escaped by hiding in ale barrels that traded to neighbouring lake dwellers. You see, barrels were sent to lake people down subterranean river which emptied into lake. Was wondering if might do same?" The monk nodded in the direction of the river that supplied the brewers with their water.

"It's an interesting idea," admitted the barbarian. Then he chuckled. "And I know Roffo would just *love* to take another hair-raising trip down an underground river. Let's see if there are any barrels big enough to fit us."

As innocently as possible the pair made their way past the vats to a collection of huts that lay beside the lake. These appeared to serve as storerooms. The first was stacked with firkins. The second was packed with hogsheads.

The monk considered the hogsheads, comparing their dimensions to those of the barbarian. He mentally folded Terry up and tried to fit him inside one of the barrels. Then he shook his head: Terry was far too big. "Really need tuns," he said. "Maybe look in next …"

Crawford walked in.

"Ah – there you are! Taking the guided tour, I see. Splendid! Any idea where you'd like to work?"

The monk frowned. "Maybe barrel-making. Are these biggest here?"

Crawford slapped the side of one of the hogsheads. "Yes indeed. We used to make lots of different sizes, but we pretty much stick with these blighters now. Ah, and here's our Master Cooper. Henri … come over here. I might have a couple of new apprentices for you."

The bulbous, black-robed beardie who had just entered the shed stalked up to the party. Beneath all his facial hair was a major scowl attempting to fight its way out. He ignored the adventurers and addressed Crawford.

"The damned loo is blocked again. The smell is enough to knock out a skunk. That's the third time this month."

The Master Brewer turned a sheepish smile onto his new brown robes. "We have a few problems with the guys in Maintenance. Not that it's *entirely* their fault. It's a problem with the ventilation system, you see. It's not been upgraded for at least a century."

"Yeah, well," muttered Henri, "someone's gonna have to sort it, otherwise the next Bindian meal we have might be our last. Oh, and another thing. One of the bowls has been pulled from the wall. You won't believe this, but there are actually *teeth* marks on it!"

"Maybe something has climbed down the ventilation shaft from the outside world and is loose in the building?" suggested the Brewer. "Bite marks in the ceramic, eh? I don't like the sounds of that. A monster of some sort, perhaps? Maybe its nest is blocking the air shaft?"

Both Henri and Crawford turned to look at Terry. "And maybe," they asked in unison, "you'd like to climb up and have a look?"

Terry had to fight hard to maintain a serious demeanour. "Well," he said, shielding his quivering lips with one iron hand, "it *could* be dangerous. Of course I'll go. But, ah, I'd feel happier if I had the assistance of, oh, let's say *two* volunteers?"

———•◦•◦•———

"They've been up that ventilation shaft a long time," declared Henri, who stood outside the toilet cave, hopping from one foot to the next, his groin clasped tightly in his hands and a look of absolute concentration on his face. "Maybe there really *is* a monster up there? Maybe it's eaten them?"

"Nah," replied Namoor, who had taken control of the situation. "We'd have heard their screams by now. Come on. Let's go and have a look."

"No chance. If you want to look, you can bloody well go yourself!"

"Oh come on," wheedled the part-time Receptionist. "I know for a fact that you were a renowned adventurer before you joined us, famed throughout the land as a slayer of demons, monsters and the like. I'm only surprised you didn't volunteer for this duty in the first place."

"Yes, well, that was twenty years and many pints ago. There's no way I could get into that shaft. Besides, the only way I'd be able to kill a flesh-eating fiend now is if I fell on it."

"Well, I'm going to have a look. No noise is good noise as far as this job's concerned."

Namoor peered around the cave entrance. Nothing moved. He slowly crept across the communal toilet to the ventilation shaft. He took a deep breath and looked up. In the far distance a minute patch of clear sky could be seen. Namoor concentrated hard, but could detect no movement in the vertical passage, and no sign of anything eclipsing the small, square patch of sky. The three warrior chimney sweeps had disappeared.

Namoor mulled over the possible fate of the three noviciates. *Maybe a monster had devoured them?* No, a monster would only have been able to take one man at a time, giving the others the chance to raise the alarm. *Maybe there were three monsters?* Typical, wait several centuries for a monster to turn up and then three arrive at once. Unlikely. *Maybe they had cleared out the flue and then gone for a walk in the fresh morning air to clear their heads?* Namoor began to feel somewhat uncomfortable. Special dispensation was needed to leave the mountain. After all, there might be bandits or other felons waiting outside, ready to nab one of the Chosen so as to torture Boozer's secret from him. *Hmmm.* The lads were new, so *maybe they had not appreciated the severity of this stricture?* Namoor chewed on his lip. Or … *no!* It was too terrible to contemplate. The Receptionist tried to block the thought from his mind, but could not. *Maybe, just maybe, they had run off and stolen the recipe?*

"Fuck!" said Namoor. He ran from the cave, grabbed his companion by an elasticated sleeve, and dragged the *desperate* cooper away without explanation. The men sped down to the brewing vats.

"Crawford!" cried Namoor. "*They've gone!*"

The Master Brewer looked up from his work and frowned. "What do you mean *they've gone?*" The Brewer's eyes widened. He turned white. "Hang about. You're not saying there really *is* a monster? I only used that as an excuse to get the new boys to clean out the old air shaft."

"No no," cried Namoor in exasperation. "There's no monster. They have gone. By themselves. Of their own free will. Without monsterial assistance. They've done a runner!"

Crawford slumped back against a vat. "Why would they want to do that? This is where the ale is. You can't get it anywhere else. I mean, why leave paradise and head off into the dry wastelands? I mean, the only way they'll be able to get anything close to Boozer's ale is if they've stolen the... *Fuck!* Ring the Doomsday Bell. To the main entrance, men, and pray to Boozer we can stop them!"

———————

"That was easy!" laughed Roffo, scratching at his bandages as they skittered down the slopes of Big Hemroid, heading back towards the Sumerian Gorge.

The monk frowned at the barman. "Do not scratch wounds! Will take scabs off and bleed again."

"Well, I can't help it. They itch like buggery."

"Still, must learn control! Do not want hero barman dying from infection now, eh?"

Roffo grinned. "I guess not." He desisted from his efforts, and for several minutes the adventurers slipped and slid down the slope. Regaining the floor of the dry river valley, they broke into an easy trot towards the gorge. The late-morning sun smiled on them.

After a while, Roffo broke the silence. "You're quiet, Terry. What's up?"

"Oh, just thinking. You know. About whether we've done the right thing in leaving without being certain of the last line of the recipe. About whether the monks are going to pursue us. And about the Hull's Angels, and what they've been getting up to while we've been gone."

The monk let out a curse in Effin. "Forgot about Angels. Damn! Must be wary."

"What about CAMORA?" asked Roffo. "Do you think they have any tricks up their sleeves?"

The monk skidded to a halt, causing his two companions to do likewise. He stared at Roffo intently. Suddenly, his eyes widened, a smile cracked his face, and he chortled in glee. "Roffo, believe you done it again!" He slapped his thighs with both hands as he bent over to wheeze with laughter. His friends looked on in concern.

"Has he finally gone bonkers?" wondered Roffo.

Terry simply shrugged.

The monk straightened up and wiped his streaming eyes with one sleeve. "Ai-la! Roffo, you genius! Yes, believe monks *do* have something up sleeves. Come now. Must hurry." Without further ado or explanation, the monk broke into a trot and left his comrades behind.

"What was all that about?" asked Roffo.

Once more, Terry shrugged. "I think he's just worked something out, and I *think* that's good. I reckon he's going to make us work hard to get it out of him though."

Roffo frowned. "Why do I sense that the old *plying with drinks* stratagem is going to be called for here, with the consequent *emptying of pockets* result? He can be a canny sod at times."

"Yes. And at present he's a canny *distant* sod. We'd better catch him up."

The two men set off after their mad colleague.

Crawford sucked mightily, but all he managed to extract from his canteen was a mouthful of warm, dry air. There was not a single drop of life-giving liquid to be had. Angrily, the Master Brewer threw his canteen across the arid river valley. He looked up at the beating sun, mopping sweat from his damp brow with a black sleeve. Were those vultures he saw circling up there?

Crawford turned to consider his men: the war party of the monks of CAMORA. Some slumped miserably on rocks, others held canteens high above their mouths and beat them in an attempt to garner just one more drop. Namoor had fallen to his knees. Henri lay on his back, his black robe now filthy, his beard powdered with dust. As he watched, Crawford noticed another man go down, and then a second. Every man sported cracked lips and desiccated skin as though this look were somehow in vogue.

How long, wondered Crawford, had they been tracking the thieves now? A year? Longer? All of their lives? It seemed that way, although … Crawford looked back at Big Hemroid in the near distance. *An hour, tops.* But they had already consumed their supply of BVP. How much longer could they go on without its nourishing beauty? Another man

449

collapsed into the dirt. *No longer* was the answer.

With a final, bitter look down the valley, Crawford turned back to his troops. "Men, the situation is hopeless. This task is inhuman. If we remain much longer in this ale-less void we will surely perish. We must return to the caves, and there pray to Boozer that he will smite down those deviant villains. May they be barred from every pub in the universe! Let us go …"

Suddenly invigorated by the thought that the nectarious ale would soon be flowing over their lips, the party found new life. The men struggled to their feet and formed a well-disciplined phalanx. By the time they were within a hundred yards of the entrance to the High Temple of Boozer, however, all thoughts of order and dignity had drained into the dust. The lardies broke formation and, in an each-man-for-himself scenario, charged recklessly up the narrow path like a whole stable of sumo wrestlers after the last bowl of sticky rice in Japan. Alas, the path could hold only two-abreast at most. Before long, scores of hairy fat blokes were tumbling down the side of the mountain in an obese avalanche, squashing flowers, breaking trees, and raising a great cloud of dust.

Shaking his head sadly, the Master Brewer picked his way through this debris to the entrance of the cave mouth, where he found half a dozen desperate men wedged solid. Crawford sat on a nearby rock. He dug into a pocket and produced a magnifying glass. He focused the rays of the sun onto one immense butt, and settled down to wait.

<hr>

It was mid-afternoon by the time the three questers arrived at the mouth of the Sumerian Gorge. From behind a large boulder they considered the steps taken by the yakkers to entrap them: Grunt was standing upright, facing up the gorge at its narrowest point, his hands resting on either wall. The other four yakkers were out of sight beyond this human barrier, although snippets of their conversation could be heard. They were arguing about food.

Terry frowned at the apparent ineptitude of the bushwhackers. He caught the crackle of a fire and the scent of cooked meat – probably rabbit. He was able to discern four distinct voices coming from near the fire: it seemed that all of the Angels were involved in a debate about who would get the giblets. There appeared to be no greater subtlety to their ambush than that: they were utterly reliant upon their giant comrade to raise the alarm. And this was unfortunate for them, given that the slow heaving of the sentry's chest, in addition to his closed eyes, indicated that Grunt was, in fact, fast asleep and oblivious to all.

"Right," whispered Roffo, "here's my plan. Terry, you sneak up to Grunt and silently bash him on the head. Then—"

"Silently bash on head?" repeated the monk in amazement. "How silently bash someone? Use padded club? Bah! No, must quietly walk over to sentry and slip under arms and out of gorge. Then slip around others and head for mounts. Have element of surprise, but must be ready to leg it."

"Oh yeah," said Roffo. "Nice plan. But haven't you forgotten one tiny detail? Like, how is Terry going to get out? There's not enough room for him to squeeze between Grunt and the gorge walls."

Terry smiled. "Don't worry about me. I can get by."

"You must be joking!"

"Shhhh! Come on – and watch."

The three adventurers left the safety of their hiding place and slowly, silently stalked over to the sleeping form of Grunt. The monk easily slipped under the giant sleeper's arm. Roffo followed, his unruly hair nearly causing disaster as it tickled the yakker's armpit. Grunt snuffled, and his head rolled from left to right, but he stirred no more.

Terry withdrew the fist that was poised to KO Grunt should he wake. He stood nose-to-nose with the man-made blockage. And then he bent his legs and – with a mighty bound from a standing start – he leapt into the air. Terry pulled a triple somersault and landed on the other side of the yakker in a squat. He winked at the astounded barman and indicated that they should not dally in the enemy camp.

Roffo winked back. He felt good. This was how true adventurers should contemptuously deal with their adversaries. As Roffo was about to find out, however, over-confidence has been the downfall of many a hero. As the barman turned to walk from the camp he failed to look where he was going: his foot snagged on a string of Coprolite lager bottles. Twenty yards away, in the dry river bed beside a fire, four hairy hooligans turned to face the rattling trip-wire.

"Shit!" yelled Roffo. "Run!" He set off at a pace across the barren terrain, heading for high ground to the north.

Trespass stared after Roffo's rapidly retreating back. It took several seconds for his brain to register what was going on, but once it did he let out a frustrated shout and set off after his foe. Unfortunately for him, Terry and the monk had made good use of these vital seconds, reaching the tether line that held the Angels' beasts. Terry got there first, gleefully noting that their mule was also tied to the line. He grabbed his axe from its holder and sliced through the rope. Then he let out an indomitable battle cry which scared the living daylights out of the animals, causing them to stampede across the dry earth, led by the trumpeting Jotun.

At the sound of that most chilling of war-yodels, Burble and Frunge also took to their heels, although Trespass managed to bring down the beardless Angel with a rugby tackle.

"Get them!" he screamed into The Shadow's face. "Go on!"

Terry and the monk set off after Roffo, who was heading for a spur leading up a flat hill that jutted from the eastern wall of the Hemroid range. Trespass, Burble and Bruce chased after their adversaries for a short distance before Trespass pulled up, realising that his fat, unfit bunch had about as much chance of catching their foe as a tortoise of catching a box of lettuce on the back of a truck. He called for his men to stop and ordered them to collect their rides. Then he slowly returned to the entrance of the Sumerian Gorge, back to the still-sleeping sentry.

Trespass stood behind Grunt, took aim with a size nine boot, and *swung*. His foot disappeared up to the ankle in the seat of the fat yakker's black leather trousers.

Grunt let out a colossal roar and turned around to do battle, only to find his leader standing in front of him with crossed arms and an angry glare – a sure sign that he was not in the best of moods.

Grunt shuffled about uneasily. "Wot?"

"Having a nice kip, were we?"

"Nah. I was just resting me eyes from the merciless glare of the sun ..." Grunt spotted some of the activity going on behind his leader's back, notably a couple of his comrades chasing after fleeing steeds. "Um. And speaking of mercy ..."

"Mercy! I'll give you fucking mercy!"

"Oh. *Cheers*."

"No – aaaaargh!" Trespass tugged at his beard psychotically. "They've escaped, you useless git! Look! *Over there!*"

Grunt's eyes followed the line of Trespass's pointing finger and almost leapt from his head at the sight of the fleeing questers.

"Wot the...? 'Ow? Magic? It's that bluddy monk bloke, innit. 'E must be a magician."

"It doesn't take magic to get past you, you moron. A mentally deficient amoeba could do that!" Trespass took a large number of deep breaths. "No worries," he continued. "I'm calm ..."

"You don't look it ..."

"Shut the *aaaiieee*!" Trespass pummelled a wall with his bare fists.

Then he repeated his calming procedure. "Phew. Okay. Right. No problem. We'll catch them when the others get the mounts. They can't outrun us, and then can't stay up on that hill forever. In fact … here's Bruce." Trespass stalked over to the returning, yak-leading Angel – a sheepish Grunt trailing behind. "That was quick."

Bruce licked his lips nervously. "Aye, well, Burb's still chasin' his elephant. He should be back soon though. *Runnin' in terror* most probably."

Trespass's eyebrows arched. "Why?"

"'Cos there's a huge posse o' black warriors on ostriches headin' this way, an' they've scared yon animals back in this direction. That's why I wiz sae quick."

Trespass looked dumbfounded. "Another group of soldiers? This place is more packed than a kebab house after chucking-out time. Come on. We'd better get to Testicles before anyone else does, or there'll be nothing left of him to take home to Manis."

———————◆·◆·◆———————

"Absolutely nothing," reported Corporal Berry glumly, as he rode his thin horse up to the vanguard of the Vegetopian contingent.

The two companies of the Golden Leaf Regiment had spent the last couple of days wandering around the dusty land abutting the Hemroids. They had completely missed the place at which the yakkers had left the road for the Sumerian Gorge, and had instead followed an older trail that led from the road a little further to the north. Once it had become clear that they were following the four-day-old spoor of a caravan, they had turned back. Instead of heading straight for the road, however, they had turned south, hugging the edge of the mountain range in the hope of crossing the track they sought.

"Not a sausage, um, I mean, *a grass stalk*," continued the scout. "It's like they disappeared. We'll have to abandon the mission, I suppose?"

"Don't give up so quickly," said Captain Twig. "We haven't checked Old Flatop yet." He pointed at the small table mountain ahead. This rose a hundred metres or so above the rocky plain, juxtaposed to the eastern wall of the mountain range.

Colonel Branch considered the prospect sourly. "Very well. Head for the hill. If we see nothing from its top, though, we'll head back. Okay, Corporal, take a couple of men and … *Corporal?*"

"Ah, sorry sir. I was just wondering, like, who *they* were …?"

They were the fanatics of the library of Copros. Grimulous had led his wrathful host of librarians across the Mungo Plains, circling Vegetopia, and up the road to the north. They had spotted the yak riders at the neck of the gorge, but rather than closing with them they had withdrawn a little way until they were opposite one of the spurs of Old Flatop. Here they had waited. Grimulous had suspected that the thieves were in the gorge and would have to come out sooner or later, and he was ready for them.

The Head Librarian now stood atop a mound and scanned the horizon. His host – over one hundred strong – was arrayed around him, silent yet tense, their plain black banners rippling in a gentle afternoon wind. Some gripped their Doom Rulers in whitened knuckles, others tested the edges of their Death Index Cards by running them across bare forearms and grimly nodding at the consequent paper cuts. All were anxious, expectant, eager.

For the last half-hour, the scouts had been bringing Grimulous news of all sorts of strange goings on. From their left there came the slowly marching host of Vegetopia. From their right came a tall man riding a water buffalo at the head of a diverse menagerie that defied belief. And in the distance, to the far right, two more hosts could be seen marching in formation towards the table mountain. But it was on one of the southerly spurs of the mountain that Grimulous's attention was focused, for there he could make out the forms of the three book thieves, hotly followed by the uncouth yak men. Were they in it together? And what was with all these armies? Surely they weren't all after the Miscellaneous Bric-A-Brac Fragmentary Directional item? There was only one way to find out.

Grimulous raised both of his hands to draw the attention of his followers. What little muttering there was died away. The Head Librarian scanned his men with wide eyes. He pointed in the direction of the table mountain. And then, with the wild cry of "JIHAB!" Grimulous rushed from the mound and out towards the nearest spur. Echoing the terrible cry of the Holy Crusade, his librarians – like a dry and vengeful wind over the desert – rustled after him.

Tarsal goaded Chewy the water buffalo forward, and his host moved with him.

After the incident with the terrifying Cher Khan, Tarsal had decided that a bit of protection was the order of the day. Thus, at hourly intervals, he had let loose his distinctive warble: a full-throated ululating yodel that no unrestrained animal could resist. Sometimes he had been rewarded with a handful of recruits, and at other times with none at all; it had all depended upon the nature of the country through which he had been passing. He now examined his army critically. Had he set about his recruitment in the jungle, he knew, he would by now have been leading a shock-force of elephants, with cheetah scouts, chimpanzee rock-throwers, and various snarling platoons of great cats. Instead …

Tarsal frowned. They would have to do. There was no point in dwelling on missed opportunities and whatnot. Behind Tarsal was his main body, comprising three water buffaloes, a dozen cows, ten horned deer, a couple of skeletal Vegetopian horses, and a decrepit old donkey called Daisy. Milling around this tight formation were his disruptor units: seven foxes, four cats, eight prairie dogs, three labradors, a demented great dane, a poodle with a pink pom-pom about its neck, and a solitary aardvark. A score of chittering squirrels rode on the backs of the larger beasts.

Tarsal now looked up. At least he had some air cover: three squadrons of fighters (two of tits and one of sparrows), a wing of ground attack pigeons, and a squadron of dive-bomber crows. Tarsal nodded to himself. He had a definite advantage in air power. And, of course, there was also his Secret Weapon, hidden away in a dozen woollen sacks slung across the backs of the cows …

As the king of the beasts considered strategy, a sudden trumpeting caused him to jolt upright. He leapt to his feet atop Chewy's back and shielded his gaze from the lowering sun. He heard a second trump. It was Trantor! Tarsal strained his gaze further. *There!* A huge grey beast was thundering along the scrubby land, heading towards a spur that led up to a table mountain. The elephant thief and his accomplices appeared to be chasing three men up a second spur. But what was Trantor running from? A movement away to his right caught the ape man's attention. A Wulu wimpi! There were about a hundred ostrich riders heading for the hill. What were they doing here? Ever since he had stopped Burgachain – Ubundi's Chief Farmer – from cutting down the jungle to create more cattle pasture, the Wulus had been out to get him. And now they were after his beloved elephant! A steely expression set on Tarsal's face. *This would end here.* He would recover Trantor and sort out the thief and the Wulus once and for all.

Tarsal raised both hands to cup his mouth. It was time to instruct the deployment of his forces.

—•◦•◦•—

Feathered Nightmare and Thunder Chicken clawed at the ground impatiently as their riders – who had momentarily brought the wimpi's trotting advance to a halt – assessed the situation. Ozbondo scowled. Their cover had been blown by the fleeing mounts of their adversaries. This had forced their hand: on spotting the Stampeders on their arrival in the dry river valley in the morning, the Wulu war party had decided to keep a low profile. Of course, Tombo had wanted to sweep down upon the yak riders instantly to avenge the honour of the Wulus, but Ozbondo had held him back, wanting to first discover the whereabouts of the young wizard who had inflicted injury upon his person. *Mr Arseface indeed!*

Tombo suddenly pointed. "There, O Terror of Ubundi, running up that hill. Is it them?"

Ozbondo's eyes widened in recognition. "It is! How he will pay for—"

"*Aaaarrrrh Aaaarraaarrhaaarrh,*" came a cry.

"Bloody Hull!" said Tombo. "What the fuck was that?"

The Shaman turned to look left. What he saw made him chuckle. *That really was the most pathetic collection of ferocious animals he'd ever ...*

Feathered Nightmare skittered about uneasily beneath the Shaman's flanks. For some reason he felt an urge to race towards that cry, as though it were a call to arms, or a demand for allegiance or aid, that reached beyond his present loyalties. Something instinctive tugged at him, pulling him one step, and then a second ...

With a snarl, Ozbondo reined in the ostrich, maintaining his control over the bird ... *for now.*

—•◦•◦•—

The Nudian Religious Artefact Retrieving Expedition had only just arrived. They marched in loose formation, a hundred strong, towards the Sumerian Gorge. Having spotted the Wulus, the Expedition had swung around them until they were to their east. This had allowed the Nudians to approach the gorge entrance more closely than the Wulus had. The table mountain now squatted low to their north, beyond the

456

dry river valley.

"It's those buggers again," noted a disgruntled Justin, nodding in the direction of the mounted wimpi.

"Aye, they must be after the Longman thieves too," said Jumbo. "Speaking of whom – look! Legging it up that spur ahead."

"Yes!" Justin clenched a fist in triumph. *He* was amongst them. Well, *He* had no place to run to now. The leader of RARE patted the set of shears that dangled from a belt by his right thigh.

Militiaman Dan Glur, standing a little way ahead of the two commanders, pointed and turned. He addressed Jumbo. "Sir ... their bestial accomplices are just behind them. Why are they all running?"

"They've obviously spotted *me*," suggested The Vain One. "Now is the time of reckoning! Move out men!"

<hr />

Terry and the monk soon caught up with the young barman as the steep slope took its toll on his strength and stamina. The three men simultaneously crested the flat top of the small table mountain. Roffo bent over, rested his hands on his knees, and wheezed asthmatically. "Where ... are ... they ... now?"

Terry patted the hero barman on the back. "Don't worry about it. We shooed off their mounts. It'll take them *ages* ..." an elephantine trumpet placed an embarrassing punctuation mark in the middle of his analysis, "... er, or perhaps *no time at all*, to catch them."

Roffo twisted his head to one side to look at the barbarian. His eyes came disconcertingly to mid-thigh level, and he had to perform further neck contortions to look his friend in the eyes. "That ... was ... bluddy ... quick."

"Aye, well, maybe they've been training their steeds? Or maybe ..."

"Or maybe," interrupted the monk, "steeds scared crapless by sudden ominous emergence of Wulu wimpi." He pointed south to where the Angels were rumbling up to the foot of the hill. The Wulus were arrowing in from the south-west.

Roffo straightened. Fright had shocked his breathing back to normal. "Oh woe!" he cried. "What are *they* doing here?"

"Maybe they've tracked us down to get the headring back," mused Terry. "And ... um. Who are *they*?"

The two adventurers followed the pointing finger of their friend. Just to the east of the wimpi there was a jogging mass of naked men – a sight horrific to behold. The spear-wielding men were now a bare one hundred yards behind the yakkers.

"Nudians!" declared Roffo. "Oh, woe! They must be after a map fragment too. Let's get out of here!"

The adventurers scurried along to the western edge of the table top. The plateau was about five hundred yards in diameter with a large boulder situated in its exact centre. As they reached the edge of the plateau, they looked down.

"Oh, woe!" shrieked Roffo. "Who the *fuck* are they?" For there, at the foot of the hill, beginning their ascent up a spur, was Tarsal's animal horde. At the sight of the adventurers, the creatures let rip with their hideous war cries: barks, mews, moos, whinnies, chitters, and throaty grunting sounds. A massive loinskin-clad warrior kicked at the flanks of his demon water buffalo and howled commands. The sky was suddenly filled with winged fury.

"Back … back!" cried Terry, as he fended off enraged blue tits. "To the right. Quick! Run!"

The bird-swatting adventurers pelted to their right, along the north-west edge of the plateau, towards the next spur. They reached it …

"Oh, *noooooo!*" cried Roffo. Sunlight glinted off the edges of sharpened, steel-rimmed rulers.

"Keep going right," bellowed Terry. He tugged at the barman. The monk was already streaking along, his habit hitched up to his waist to free his legs for action. The next spur was a hundred yards to the north-east. They never got there. The monk skidded to a halt, his awe-struck comrades doing likewise. Just as they reached the centre of the plateau, the first of the Vegetopians appeared over the opposite rim, riding their anorexic horses. The lead warrior let out a huge shout on spotting them and gesticulated wildly with a stick-thin arm.

"Up on rock," asserted the monk. "Fight from high ground. Maybe armies get in each others' way and give us small chance to escape!"

"Caught like rats in a trap!" wailed Roffo. But he turned and ran towards the central boulder. This was perhaps eight feet high and ten feet in diameter. At its base, Terry formed a step. He hoisted first Roffo and then the monk onto the rock. He was about to leap up himself when a gasping cry stopped him in his tracks. In several quick steps he was around the boulder and facing south once more.

The five yak men urged their sweating beasts across the mesa to confront the men they had been tracking for so long. "Testicles!" roared their enraged leader. "You've had it now!" They closed on the trapped barbarian.

"You know," replied Terry casually, "you might just be right about that." His two companions looked at him from their exalted height, astonished. Surely he wasn't going to give up that easily? "But I'm taking *you* to Valhalla with me!" Terry adopted a classic fighting stance, daring his foes to attack.

Trespass and the Angels drew up their steeds just five feet in front of the barbarian. Trespass had not been this cross since the very first time he had got a parking ticket. He dismounted, snarling, his grim-faced comrades following suit. The men began to spread out to encircle the barbarian. As they did so, they gave time for the various armies to breast the various rims …

Although the five armies had begun their charges with loud-voiced fury, revelations concerning the presence of the other hosts had caused them to silence their wailing and to look around confusedly. Thus, each crested the plateau cautiously, silently, contemplatively. They each massed their entire force in battle formation. Watching. Waiting. Pondering. What the bollocking Hull was going on? Who were *they*? And *those* geezers? And what had happened to *their* clothes? And why did *their* horses only have two legs? And why were the Accomplices-Stampeders-Thieves facing each other down? Had they argued over the spoils?

Trespass at last noticed the other armies milling nervously about on the mountain rim. He came to a juddering halt. His eyes widened and his jaw dropped. *Who … what … why …*? Normally, at this juncture, he would have turned on the heels of his stout riding boots and fled as fast as a Harleck Dravidian could carry him. But on this occasion he did not. The first reason for this apparent heroism was the fact that all escape routes appeared to be blocked. The second was that *enough was enough*. Trespass had suffered every discomfort and indignity imaginable and, worse, he'd not had a pint of Rear Thruster for months. And even worse, he had not seen Sonia for that long either, and who could tell what she had been getting up to! Someone was going to pay for this, and that someone was standing before him.

Scowling, Trespass walked a complete circumference of the boulder, examining the competitors who, he supposed, were intent on sorting out the barbarian and his irritating friends. It never once crossed his mind that he and his lot might be the main object of any particular army's wrath. He returned to his comrades, went to his yak, and mounted up. *Slowly.* All eyes were on him. He then clicked his tongue and gave a sideways flick of his head, at which his comrades stepped back from the barbarian and regained their own mounts. Were they going to run for it? No chance! Trespass had not come this far to have victory, revenge, and the recipe for a divine ale stolen from him.

"They're ours I tell you!" bellowed Trespass, into the soundless void. "*Ours!*" He goaded his yak into action and once more circumnavigated the boulder, glaring at all and sundry. "We've tracked them for *months* and that makes them ours. All right? No Johnny-come-lately is going to get them first. So you lot can just bloody well *sod off!*" He returned to his men. "There are five of us and five of them," he announced, indicating the silent armies. "That makes one each. Spread out and face them. We can take them."

The Angels looked at each other in astonishment. Unusually, it was Frunge who spoke first. "And I thought *I* was stupid."

———•••———

Meanwhile, diverse thoughts passed through the heads of the men and creatures of the five armies.

Tombo considered Tarsal's animal horde with mixed emotions. He had clashed with that fiend on numerous occasions, losing some good men down the gullets of the ape man's troops. Was this a chance to settle an old score?

Feathered Nightmare ogled the Nudians to his right. Were those really juicy worms suspended between their legs?

Tarsal considered the wimpi. He scoured the mounted troops for any sign of that tree-felling bastard, Burgachain.

Wing Commander Grotfeather – cousin to a well-known fat, six-toed pigeon from Way – attempted to keep his troops in line above their human C-in-C. "Cooo cooo, stay in formation Reggie, coo, keep your wing up Ginger."

The Vegetopians stared at the ape man's cavalry, ogling the heavily horned deer. Shifting about uncomfortably in their sacrilegious leather battle-harness, the men wondered whether the deer might be here to exact vengeance for the troopers' killing of their bovine kinfolk. To make matters worse, the army on their immediate right seemed to be composed entirely of grotesques. At least *they* seemed to be armed with nothing more threatening than bits of cardboard and short metal sticks …

Grimulous found his foes for the most part hilarious: men who had not grasped the concept of clothes, men who had not grasped the concept of the dinner party, and a dinner-party-in-waiting. However, he did not much like the look of the dark-skinned men riding the Giant Bipedal Avians. One thing *they* had clearly grasped was the art of warfare.

The Nudians felt abhorrence for all of the well-clothed men. Satyr would surely want them permanently put out of their misery. Scout Pete Rick, however, only had eyes for the mounts of the black men. *They* looked hungry.

———◆·◆·◆———

After contemplating their rivals, the heads of the five armies turned their attention to the centre of the Ring of Death to determine how best to extract their stolen possessions from, or enact revenge upon, the men clustered around and on top of the boulder. Each leader found a large hairy beast facing him. Apart from one, each of *these* was sitting upon a yak; the exception – opposite Tarsal – was seated upon an elephant.

———◆·◆·◆———

Trantor/Jotun fidgeted uneasily as a conflict of loyalties raged inside his giant head. On the one tusk, there was his faithful friend from the jungle who was, to be blunt, a bit of a bossy-boots. But if he went with Tarsal he'd be able to return to his pachyderm friends in the jungle, including Big Betty. *Woof!* On the other tusk, there was the short, barrel-shaped man who not only had excruciating BO, but also had the nasty habit of wiping the excavations from his nose behind Trantor/Jotun's ears. Still, the foul human was kind of fun to be around, and Trantor/Jotun had rather enjoyed turning houses into kindling, experiencing uncontrolled flight, and defecating into oasis water holes. Decisions, decisions! After several minutes of thought, however, he *did* make a choice. The being-stuck-in-the-Sumerian-Gorge incident eventually swung it for him. He was going to defect back to Tarsal.

Trantor raised his trunk and let out a loud trumpet to signal his intention. The armies – assuming that this was a signal to attack – instantly set off in a mad dash for the central boulder. Pretty soon the converging forces would overlap, and chaos would ensue.

And thus began The Battle of the Five Armies.

———◆·◆·◆———

The three questers stood on their rock, speechless. There below them, the five yakkers were actually preparing to defend *them* against a horde of hordes. Meanwhile, these hordes were charging into an ever-decreasing area: like a constricting pair of underpants, this would surely end in tears. It would also be a miracle if any of the troopers of the five armies got within ten yards of the rock.

The monk shrugged his shoulders and sat down to watch the battle. He felt a desperate, instinctive need for popcorn and a large cola.

"Hmm," said Terry, "I feel a sudden craving for a hot dog covered in mustard."

"Chocolate-coated raisins over here," said Roffo, "or, at a pinch, some frozen cow's milk on a stick …"

The air was filled with shrieks, curses, howls, and roars. Death Index Cards filled the sky, knocking dreadlocked soldiers from their skinny horses and giving them wicked paper cuts into the bargain.

The fearless Wulus had second thoughts about closing with the swinging tackle of the naked men who were to their right, and so they turned their protesting mounts left. Tarsal yodelled to bring his force to a halt, allowing the wimpi to speed in front of it and thus to close with the dread librarians instead. He then turned to face the screaming Nudians. "Um-sobers!" he cried. At this, his platoon of cows pitched forwards onto their front knees – an action which allowed the woollen sacks they carried to roll over their shoulders and heads. The sacks spilled open, releasing their potent contents. Tarsal pointed and bellowed another command.

"Oh Satyr, no!" cried the un-shod militiaman, Dan Glur, as he recognised the monstrous beasts that now skittered towards him. "Hedgehogs! Ooo, aaaah, oooo, aaaiiiee!" Dan Glur dropped to the ground, clutching a spiked big toe. Other Nudians began to fall.

Meanwhile, the fierce librarians closed ranks to fend off the pincer movement of the Wulus and the still-horsed Vegetopians. Well-directed rulers flicked out, smacking at assegai-bearing hands and puny, white, spear-wielding arms.

"Oooyah!"

"Bugger, that stings!"

"Mummy!"

But the librarians began to be forced back. From where he stood in the middle of his animal bodyguard, Tarsal watched these events with some concern. He had no great love for the men in black, but the balance of the battle was turning and he could not allow it to do so. With a brief nod to himself, he decided to even up the score. Those Wulus, for one, *really* had it coming to them. He raised his hands to his mouth and gave *the* warble:

"*Aaaarrrrh Aaaarraaarrhaaarrh.*"

462

The ostriches had managed to resist the demands of this cry when it had come from far off, but at point blank range? No chance! The big birds had finally had enough of their Bernie Cliftons: they squawked and heaved and bucked, and soon, Wulu warriors were going arse over tit, until not one remained mounted. Now free from their constraints, the ostriches turned to head away from the demonic bibliophiles – and what they saw made their eyes bulge. It was feeding time! The birds streaked towards the madly hopping, obscenely dangling Nudians.

Another yodel, and Tarsal called his air armada into play. The birds screamed down onto the various enemies.

"Tally-ho Ginger," cried Grotfeather, "I'm going in!"

"Look out mottled-grey leader, bandits at three o' clock!"

"Damn, the flack is heavy around here. Watch those D.I. Cards!"

"I'm hit, I'm hit! Tell Plumpchest I love …"

"Ginger pull up … pull up!"

"*Aaiiieeeeeee!*"

The screaming librarians, now relieved of the pressure from the Wulus, yelled "Jihab!" and began to surge toward the rock in a tight unit. In their wake they left behind stunned birds, hand-wringing Wulus, and blubbing Vegetopians. They looked unstoppable as they swept up to the thin, rather filthy black line that comprised the Questers' impromptu bodyguard. The yakkers were soon embroiled in a desperate set-to. Things might have then gone very sour indeed had not Tarsal once more turned the tide.

"Chewy! We are needed! Come!"

The water buffalo *mooed* savagely and, bearing the mighty ape man on its back, led the thunderous heavy brigade into the midst of the Coprolite formation. Chittering squirrels bounded into librarian faces, cows licked men remorselessly, and Old Daisy got in a brutal kick at sub-Head Bassar, making him drop to the ground clutching his Sensitive Inflatable Organ.

By now, however, the Vegetopians had reorganised. Again they came on …

Tarsal and Terry shook hands. "Sorry I didn't recognise you before," said the ape man. "It was only after the start of the charge that it clicked … and I thought you might need a hand. You're a dead ringer for C, you know. But from up close I can now see that your eyes are green, not blue."

Terry grinned. "He's my cousin. I'm Terry. And you must be Tarsal. You're the spitting image of a young Uncle Thortun. Said he lost you in the jungle and all that, and only found you again a few years back. Uncle Thor always was absent-minded. So how's Jane?"

Tarsal grimaced. "It's June. I'm afraid she threw a bit of a wobbly when I said I was coming after Trantor. I suppose I'd better get going or I'll never hear the end of this."

"Take her plenty of flowers."

"Don't worry, I will."

Tarsal turned to view the carnage around him. There were all sorts of men lying about, groaning and moaning. Some clasped sorely pecked parts of their anatomy, others nursed pricked toes or smacked hands, and others wrapped bandages around paper cuts. But Tarsal's animal army stood in tight formation, looking smug with its day's work. The air squadrons patrolled above, occasionally swooping down on any man who still had fight left in him.

"Um-gower!" cried the ape man. He clambered onto Trantor's leg, then up onto his back. He looked down at the three adventurers. "I don't think any of the horses here will bear you. Take these ostriches instead." Tarsal made a squawking sound and three giant ostriches trotted up to the men. Among them were Thunder Chicken, Feathered Nightmare, and a straggly beast called Fowl Temper. Tarsal pointed out each bird in turn and related its name. "With my regards! And now I must go: I've got what I came for. And I wouldn't hang about if I were you. This lot –" he gestured at the fallen men, "– will be back in business before long. Adios!"

Terry waved. "See you! And if you're ever passing through Way, stop by for a pint!"

"Betcha! Till then!"

Tarsal turned the elephant and led his horde towards the nearest spur.

———•••••———

Roffo led Fowl Temper by the reins, picking his way through the fallen Nudians. "How long do you reckon it'll take us to get back to Way?" he asked irritably.

"Two weeks," replied Terry, "maybe thr—"

"Ah ha!" One of the bodies suddenly leapt upright and placed its hands upon its hips. "Thought you could escape from the gigantically endowed Justin, did you? Right, first things first. Where's the Holy

464

Longman?"

"The holy *what*?" wondered Terry.

"Oh come on. Don't play games with me. The sheath of Satyr! The thing you turned into a banana boat."

"I'm sorry. I wore it—"

"You *wore* it!" Justin's jaw dropped. He stared towards Terry's crocodileskin-clad loins. "No man is big enough to wear it. I don't believe you!"

"I was going to say," continued the barbarian, "I wore it *out*. We put a hole in it while canoeing down the river. Then we were forced to exchange it for our lives. We gave it to a Rockgod. I think he had, um, certain plans for it." Terry shrugged his massive shoulders. "What can I say? Sorry."

"Never mind." Justin began to reach for his shears. "That is of little consequence to me. But now I'm going to …"

Smack.

"Well, he's not pretending anymore," said Terry, prodding the felled Nudian with a booted foot. "Why did you do that, Roff? You're not normally the violent type."

"I'm in a bad mood," replied the barman, scowling at his fist. "And he had it coming."

"Why are you in a—"

The barbarian got no further with his query, for a badly bruised Grimulous – supported by an under-librarian – staggered up to the adventurers. His spectacles were skew-whiff. He waved a broken ruler at them feebly.

"O evil defilers of the great library, where is the Miscellaneous Bric-A-Brac Fragmentary Directional item that you swiped? It must be returned immediately."

The monk fished around in his robes and pulled out the map fragments. With a small bow he handed one of these to the Head Librarian.

But Grimulous was not mollified. His eyes widened in anger. "Look at the state of it! It's all dog-eared. Atrocious, absolutely atrocious! Are you savages? You *do not* treat books and suchlike in this shoddy manner!" With a shaking hand he carefully slipped the fragment into an inner pocket of his black toga. "And as for the late return, well, there's an outstanding fine to pay. Quite a big one actua—"

Smack.

The under-librarian collapsed, leaving Grimulous unsupported.

The Head Librarian swayed in the light breeze and then followed his colleague earthwards.

"Ai-la, Roffo!" exclaimed the monk. "That is second person hit today. Have gone mental? What wrong?"

"What's wrong? *What's wrong* he asks! I'll tell you what's wrong!" Roffo folded his bandaged arms and glowered. "There's been an almighty battle right under our noses, and all I got to do was watch. What an opportunity for fame, glory and whatnot! I might never get a chance like this again. And what would Gramps say?"

"Gramps would say lots," replied the monk sourly. "Would say he fought a thousand enemies and saved beautiful princess. Would say—"

"I hope you're not suggesting my grandfather has a tendency to make up his stories," interrupted the barman, "because at this moment I'm not in the mood to let anyone take the mickey out of him." Roffo turned and stormed off across the mountain top.

Terry and the monk exchanged bemused looks. The monk then bent down and thrust a map fragment into one of Justin's hands. The adventurers set off after their travelling companion. They caught up with the angry barman as he reached the lip of the mountain. Tombo and his second-in-command stood in the way of their descent. Behind them, a cross-eyed Shaman lay on his back, giggling insanely and muttering about aardvarks.

"Prepare to be fed to the crocodiles, Stampeders of the Royal Cattle!" stated Tombo, waving an assegai. "Prepare to—"

Smack.

"Wasn't me that time," declared Roffo, holding up his hands defensively.

"Just hand over the royal headring," said the second-in-command, as he rubbed his bruised knuckles. "I, Shaka, will be needing it very soon."

"Give it to him," ordered Roffo crossly. "And while you're at it … do you see that skinny bloke talking to that deer? You can give him his bit back too." Roffo tugged at the reins of Fowl Temper and headed off down the mountain.

The monk just shrugged. "Not got headring, but got Sacred Fragment. Is okay?"

Shaka thrust out a fat lip and accepted the piece of map. *Oh well,* he thought, *it'll have to do.*

The monk paced over to Colonel Branch and Tarsal's waylaid trooper. He handed a map fragment to the much-puzzled Colonel then

466

paced back to Terry. He gestured towards Roffo, who was now half-way down the slope.

"Hope he not going to be like this all way back to Way."

"He's just disappointed," said Terry. "He'll get over it. Apparently, my dad was a bit like that when he missed his first big battle. He hadn't finished his homework, you see, so my gran wouldn't let him go. He locked himself in his bedroom for two days." Terry started down the slope, leading Thunder Chicken.

The monk followed after a moment's thought. "Hmm. Two days? Don't think can face that."

Terry looked back over his shoulder and grinned. "Oh, it would have been longer if gran hadn't broken his door down with her war hammer."

"Longer than two days? Bah! Have you war hammer I could borrow ...?"

The men descended from Old Flatop.

———————

Sitting upon their yaks, the well-thumped Angels clustered around a heart-rending scene.

"You expect me to ride *this*!" wailed Burble. His bottom lip quivered and he rubbed a dirty sleeve across his eyes.

The other yak riders looked away in embarrassment. The Shadow's misfortune was not one they would wish on anyone. To have such a steed and then to lose it! It was like having your Ferrari nicked and replaced with a Mini Metro, or swapping a Honda Fireblade for a dainty moped.

Trespass's normally sullen features softened. "Come on, Burb. We can still catch them before Way."

"Yeah, bruv," said Frunge. "And if we get that recipe thingy, well, we'll be so rich you'll be able to upgrade."

"Like, to a *pony*," said Grunt, in spite of himself.

Trespass glowered at the fat man. "That's right," he nodded, "get yourself a Harleck or something. Come on, men. Move out."

Nodding miserably, Burble steadied his new Mean Machine. Daisy the donkey peered at him from under bushy grey eyebrows, her battle rage having cooled with the departure of the inspirational ape man. Still, she brayed in displeasure as the barrel-shaped man clambered onto her back and made a half-hearted attempt to buck him off.

Burble kicked his heels into the side of the pack animal and trotted off after the others.

CHAPTER 20

THE BOYS ARE BACK IN TOWN

"SO WHERE is it?" asked Roffo. "And what does it say?"

The three ostrich-riding adventurers trotted along the Great South Road, heading north. The late afternoon sun skimmed low over a stand of pine trees, hinting that they ought to make camp soon. In spite of the death of the afternoon and onset of evening, the day was still warm: an Indian summer had settled over the world, resisting the ineffectual efforts of autumn. This was the eleventh day since their departure from Old Flatop, and each day had been like this one: rainless and glorious.

The monk chuckled and, for the umpteenth time in the past few days, shook his head. "Don't know what it say. May not even be able to read it at moment."

"Then how do you know it is, well, wherever it is? I don't understand."

"Not seen it with own eyes, only suspect its presence."

"This is getting us nowhere!" exclaimed Roffo. "What do you think, Terry? I'm sure barbarians know some pretty effective ways of making people talk, and I'm not talking about the *bag-of-gold* scenario either!"

Terry laughed, but simply shook his head.

"It very close to you," continued the wind-up merchant. "In fact, it right in front of eyes."

"Right in front of my eyes?" The barman considered what he saw. "Well, I see the back of an ostrich's head, some reins, my hands, some bandages, a pair of ... bandages?" He frowned. "They came from Boozer's pad, didn't they? But I thought about them already. Crawford said: *you already have it.* When he said *that* I didn't have the bandages. All we had were the robes and the certificate."

"Think!" said the monk. "What did Brewer mean? Who he talking to?"

"He said 'you'. I thought he meant us in general … aha! I see what you mean! He was talking to *me*, wasn't he? When he said 'you' he meant *me*."

"At last! Okay. So, what memento you have that we not have?"

"Apart from a very sore bottom – how you two managed to take those vindaloos and avoid their side-effects I'll never know – all I have are a couple of pretty … wicked … *scars*?" Roffo stared at the monk, his mouth agape.

The monk giggled. "It staring at you all the time."

"You complete and utter git!" Roffo laughed too. "Of course! That's why they always wore those long-sleeved robes with the tight wrists, so that nobody could see their scars. But it wasn't just for the sake of vanity that they hid their burns."

Terry nodded. "*It will be clear to you in time,*" he repeated.

"Yes. When inflammation goes down and scabs drop off, suspect will find symbols burned onto Roffo's forearms. They will tell final piece of recipe."

"Then what are we waiting for," cried Roffo. "Let's have a look …"

"No!" The monk leaned across and stayed Roffo's hand as it was about to pluck at one of his bandages. "Be careful. Not want to risk infection, la?"

"Fine. We'll be back home in a few days. We'll unveil it then, eh?"

"Yes. It make exciting climax to story."

Roffo grinned. "Sure thing."

"… yes, he's quite a character, our Master Manis. Fiery temper and all that. Not the most forgiving of personalities, though. The list of people he's barred from his pub is as long as an orang-utan's arms." The young stranger sitting by the camp fire laughed nervously. "He doesn't like Yegorans, despises Colloidians, and detests Frembolians. But his all-time least-favourite people – absolute tops! – are Samarks. Hates their guts, he does. Livers, kidneys … probably hearts and lungs too."

Men around the fire suddenly came to attention. Beefcakes in red turbans began to reach for scimitars. A low muttering started up. But the young man continued as though oblivious. "Apparently they fire-bombed his chip shop during the war." Hendy lit a cigarette from the burning end of a piece of firewood. His hands shook as he thought about sharp objects penetrating soft flesh. "Anyway, you should be all right ... being from Chadoor and all that. You are Chadoori, aren't you? He just thinks you lot *smell*."

The Potoon placed a restraining hand on the arm of his nearest bodyguard. Thunder hovered above the Samark's chubby brow. "Sounds wike an obnoxious fewoe." Then his frown deepened. "Hang about! What waw? Theah has not been a waw wecentwee!"

The *agent provocateur* shrugged. "Beats me. But that's what Manis told me when I was last in Way. And now I remember ... oh ho, ha ha ..." Hendy slapped at the knees of his crossed legs. "He told me this other story ... about this visiting Samark merchant. What a hoot!" Hendy wiped tears away from his eyes. Young Festers had been a gold mine of information! "Said he fed this bloke with poisoned food, sent him diseased ladies of easy virtue, and gave him a room below a leaking privy. What a character, hey?" Out of the corner of his eye, Hendy saw muscles tense and he glimpsed a hint of steel. It was time to draw this charade to a close. He leapt to his feet. "But enough of this. Must get some sleep." He yawned. "Want to make an early start so I can reach town while it's still light tomorrow. Have you ever been to Cross-My-Way?"

"Ah ... no. No. This wi' be my fust twip. I am just checking out a new twade woute."

"Well, you should look up Manis when you're in town. He's got some classic stories, I can tell you!"

The Potoon glowered. "Yes, I think I wi' pay him a visit. Definite-wee!"

***

Bruce trotted over to the rest of the pack, leaving behind him a bemused-looking farmer leaning on a pitchfork.

"Well?" asked Trespass fiercely.

"They passed aboot an hour agae."

"Damn damn *damn*!" Trespass looked around for something to belt. They had been doing their best to overhaul the lads from The Bear for the last couple of weeks, but this was the closest they had yet got.

"Well, we *are* gainin'," suggested Bruce.

"But not quick enough. Damn and blast! We'll be home by evening ... but so will they!" Trespass looked around for a scapegoat and spied the sorry-looking donkey rider. The problem was that, though Daisy was a veritable warrior when roused, she was no speed merchant. The Angels had been forced to rise early each day and to ride until the very margin of darkness, simply to stay in touch with the fleet-footed ostriches and their riders. Unfortunately, like all lazy gits, these men needed at least twelve hours kip a night, and sleep deprivation was gnawing at their tempers and sanity.

Trespass scowled at Burble, who made a half-hearted attempt to scowl back. "Don't look at me," said *The Shadow*. "It's not *my* fault."

"Oh yeah? Then whose fault is it? Postman *bloody* Patt? Mother *bollocking* Tereesa? Mine?"

"Well, you're the tosser who's meant to be in charge. You couldn't run a ...."

"And I suppose you could do better?" interrupted the seething Trespass. "Go on then, *Captain Shadow*, what do you suggest?"

Burble's brow furrowed. *Captain Shadow?* What a splendid sobriquet! All right then ... think! The donkey-man leapt off his atrophied steed and began to pace. He looked his comrades up and down and considered alternatives. The solution was obvious, really, though unpalatable.

"Right then. Simple. We ditch the donkey and I'll ride two-up with Grunt."

"Two-up," laughed Grunt savagely. "That's for girls! No true yakker would even suggest—"

Frunge leant across and delivered a thudding left hook. "That's my bruv you're talking about ..."

The party proceeded through its usual decision-making procedure. When the dust settled, however, it revealed four rapidly departing yaks carrying five men, and a nearby farmer scratching his head as he considered how best to employ his new donkey.

The Potoon sat on a plump velvet cushion surrounded by huge, red-turbaned guards. The late afternoon sun sparkled off the gems depending by gold chains from his silver turban. His fat fingers – parasitized by ruby and emerald rings – drummed on his immense, silk-swathed belly. A good-humoured smile attempted to fight its way out of his flabby jowls.

In the cleared area in front of the merchant prince, a wizened, brown-skinned crone considered her multi-coloured stock of potions. The Gebrullian youth named Yershah knelt nearby, and a broached barrel of Mardon's Pedigree rested on the ground between the pair.

"Begin!" ordered the Potoon.

The Beni Yonad dipped her head as a sign of respect, then rubbed together her curiously young hands with their pearl-white nails.

"Your Magnificence," began the crone, "I thought that a mixture of elements might deliver the impact you seek, but …"

"Yes?"

"But the way in which they *compound* may be uncertain. Strange consequences may accrue."

"Good! The stwangah the bettah. Wet it be so!"

Again the crone dipped her head. She perused her collection of bottles and jars. "We will begin with the bile of the Winkle Newt. It causes heightened sensitivities, both physical and emotional." She handed a bottle to Yershah, who unstoppered it. "It is potent, young man, so apply four drops only."

Yershah complied.

"Next, as an aphrodisiac, we have the testicles of the Colloidian Sex Gerbil. Six of these, please."

Yershah's eyes widened as he contemplated the golfball-sized organs. *From gerbils?* He counted out six and dropped them into the open barrel. *Plink*, went each testicle, *fizz* went the ale.

Next, the Gebrullian received a brown pot with instructions to add twenty granules of its contents – a potent laxative known as the Condensed Hyper-Bean. Thereafter, the hellish ingredients quickly followed one after another: a black liquid that led to vomiting; a red powder that invoked rage; some yellow seeds that caused flatulence; a plant extract for laughter and good humour; and a slice of something unmentionably glutinous, reputed to cause depression.

"… and then *stir*," concluded the Beni Yonad.

Yershah took up a stick and gave the barrel a hearty whisk, then stoppered it. He looked towards his master.

The Potoon grinned mightily. "Now, wet us see how the boundah wikes a bit of his own medicine. This one wi' be, how they say, *on the house*."

Yershah smiled and said quietly to himself. "Aye, and probably up the walls and all over the carpet too."

———•◦•◦•———

With night now upon them, the adventurers rode through the South Gate. At times of trouble the four town Gates were shut and manned by members of the Town Guard, but at present there was peace in the world and the guardposts were untenanted. The ostrich-riders passed under the gate arch and trotted along the road towards the Square, the Nostrum Quarter to their left and the Latin Quarter to their right. Lanterns hung from poles along the street providing intermittent light: where the light was weakest, along the centre of the road and at positions mid-way between the lanterns, a twilight world existed. It was in the twilight – up the centre of the road – that the three men rode.

"I can't wait to see the looks on their faces!" said Roffo. Like his companions, he wore his CAMORA robe with the hood drawn up about his face. No-one who saw the men on their strange mounts could possibly have guessed their real identities.

"It'll certainly surprise them," said Terry, "*if* they're still there."

In the shadow of his hood, Roffo frowned. "I'd forgotten about that. They will be all right though, won't they? I mean, Hops can be a cunning sod at times. There's no way he would let the pub go under … is there?"

"No," agreed Terry cautiously. "Not out of choice."

"Cor, Terry, you really know how to put the dampeners on things! Remind me not to invite you to my next birthday party."

"Ah," cackled the monk, who had been in a fine mood ever since deciphering the secret of the recipe, "that is your … twelfth?"

"Mr Monk, sir, don't you start. It'll be my twenty-third and you know it. *Ai-la!*"

Terry and the monk laughed.

Trespass grasped at his thick black hair with both hands and tugged at it savagely – as though attempting to achieve the advanced state of Yul-Brynnerdom without recourse to a razor.

"No no no no no no no no!" he cried. "No no no no …"

"Right," snarled Grunt, "we get the picture."

"Thwarted!" said Burble, who was perched just in front of Grunt. "After so much hardship."

"Damn!" yelled Bruce. "There's nae justice."

"Er … wot?" said Frunge.

Two hundred yards away, the rear ends of three ostriches inadvertently mooned their pursuers as they passed through the South Gate of Cross-My-Way. It was too late. The worthies from The Bear could not be prevented from delivering their mysterious cargo to their employer.

For five minutes, the men sat about on their yaks, cursing and bellowing and beating their chests. They had suffered such despicable hardships over the last four months – and for what?

"Right," said Trespass at last. "I'm calm. See, my hands aren't shaking or …"

"Yes they are," said Frunge. "I can see them."

"Shut UP!" The leader of the pack took several more deep breaths. He looked around his comrades sternly. All apart from Frunge wore looks of barely restrained anger and bitterness. Frunge simply looked baffled. "Right. That's it then. Who's for a pint or ten of Rear Thruster and a gentle chat with our employer about travel expenses?"

Three hands were raised rapidly. After a prod and a whispered suggestion, so was a fourth.

"Settled then. And Manis had better … had better … well, he'd better …"

"Not mess us about?" suggested Burble.

"Ah. Well. No. Not as such. Cos today, right now, I might not be able to take it."

"That should be interesting to see," said Burble grimly. But his thoughts ran along similar lines.

———•••———

Inside The Compromised Pilgrim, Manis stood with his hands on his hips, frowning at his clientele. "What's wrong with everyone?" he asked. "It's like a bloody funeral in here."

Spotty Wembers made a face behind the innkeeper's back, but did not answer. His new digs were definitely a downgrade on his old flat. The acne-faced barman glowered at the memory of his eviction by Mrs Fuddy. It had been embarrassing to say the least, what with all those children hanging around, pointing and laughing, and the old lady shouting at him about self-sufficient sex acts and soiled bed sheets. Aye, and that wasn't all she had said. Wembers gave the unseeing Manis the finger. Apparently, she'd been tipped off by a letter from 'a much-maligned innkeeper'. Spotty gobbed into the bottom of a tankard and filled it with Rear Thruster.

"Here you go, boss. Have a drink."

Manis looked at the barman suspiciously, but accepted the ale. "What is it, Wembers? The Pedigree? It's only been two days since we ran out." Actually, the last barrel of Pedigree had mysteriously developed a hole. When the innkeeper had gone to put it on tap it had been completely empty. Manis had contemplated sabotage, but then dismissed the idea. After all, who would *dare*?

Spotty shrugged. "Could be. Why don't you go and ask them?"

"I think I will." Manis came around the bar. The inn was perhaps half full and unnaturally quiet: his custom had been tailing off over the last three or four weeks. Indeed, in an attempt to counter The Bear's various promotions, he had even eased the Pedigree restrictions – but with little success. It was almost as though the town was all sexed-out. There had also been mutterings about the Rear Thruster for, though a favourite with the regulars, it had not generally been to the taste of the new Pedigree customers. Perhaps he ought to get in another brew? In any case, the last week or so had seen a further downturn in custom and a definite iciness to the atmosphere.

Manis strode up to a table around which were seated Sly Herrold, Rudy Brassrubbers, and Hughie Puke. They were sitting close to one another and, like many of the other punters, muttering and scowling. Manis patted Herrold on the shoulder. "Eh-up men, what's happening?"

Herrold's shoulder stiffened under the innkeeper's grip. "Nothing," he replied. His companions fell silent.

Manis looked between the men from under a furrowed brow, but they steadfastly refused to speak. What the buggery was going on? "Don't worry about the Pedigree, lads," he ventured. "I'm expecting that damned Samark shortly. The sod's late, actually."

A stony silence prevailed.

"Boss!" yelled Wembers, at last. "It's that Potoon bloke. He's just pulled up out back."

"About bloody time!" Manis smiled his most heartfelt smile at the men. Unfortunately – his face not being built for such contortions – the effect was something like that of a shark contemplating a feast. "See what I mean?"

As Manis passed a table at which Fingers and Picket were sitting, an errant foot appeared from nowhere: Manis stumbled and nearly went over. He turned to glare. "What the fuck was that?"

"Er, sorry?" said Picket. "Did I miss something?"

"You … you …" Manis looked around for the Berserker, but then remembered that he had sent him outside to await his guest. "Bah!" he cried.

He turned around and strode to the back door.

———•••••———

The Potoon waited, sitting on the back of one of his mightiest, doggy-position-assuming guards. The guard's face was bright red and his tongue lolled out the side of his mouth. Immense buttocks spread over the man's back and neck, looking something like The Blob in repose.

"Gweetings, Manis. We have your watest batch of Pedigwee."

Manis glanced quickly over his shoulder to ensure that the Berserker was in Destruction Range. "About bloody time. I was expecting you hours ago."

Two red turbans stepped forward, but the Potoon waved them away and gave a little hiccoughing laugh. "Yes yes. I know. It is most inconsidahwate of us. I apowogise."

"You do?" Manis took a step back in surprise. "Ah, well, good. I think we understand each other, business being business and me having a Just-in-Time delivery system and all that."

"Indeed. It is appwopwiate that we be punished. I know!" The merchant prince snapped his fingers. A massive-chested guard struggled forward with his arms ringing a barrel of ale. "Pwease accept this offahwing."

"A free barrel of Pedigree?" Manis's face lit up. Freebies were rare in this cut-throat world and not to be sneezed at. "Well, thanks, I gladly acc—"

The Potoon held up a hand. "No. It is not Pedigwee. It is Pedigwee Pwus. It is vewy potent and must be wapidwee consumed."

"Pedigree Plus? Oh. Fine. But how rapidly?"

"This evening at the watest."

Manis frowned. Oh well, judging from the gloomy state of his clientele they could do with some cheering up, and this might do the job. His punters would empty the barrel with little difficulty. And some canny marketing might also get his inn back in favour. Perhaps a Special Offer? What about a Once In A Lifetime Experience: Pedigree Plus, The Choice Of Randy Emperors? He could let it go at the 'cut-down rate' of, say, *double* the price of standard Pedigree? Manis nodded to himself, then bowed towards the Samark.

"I gratefully accept."

"Good. Now, wet us settle yoah account as my men westock yoah cewah." He snapped his fingers once more and made a gesture. "My boy wi' set up the Pedigwee Pwus foah you ..."

And at that moment the Potoon's human chair collapsed.

It was not a sight for the squeamish.

The three hooded men strolled through the portal of The Merry Bear. It had been nearly four months since they had last trod this path and left behind a scene of ruination. The floors, walls, and doors had been smeared

476

with effluent, the cellar had been destroyed, and the custom had been driven away. But matters were very different now. A jolly fire blazed away in a hearth; candles cheerily illuminated the well-kept interior; light sparkled off horse brass; and the place heaved with sozzled customers. There was a most convivial atmosphere: half-cut punters laughed and shouted and swigged ale; smoke from fags – both funny and serious – swirled in the air; and a group of fine fellows in one corner bellowed out a rendition of *Jerousalem* as they were conducted by a pair of elderly gents who were otherwise known for their love of cricket and rich cakes.

Roffo's still-hidden jaw dropped. "Blimey! It's like the troubles never happened and we were never away. You don't think that You Know Who has got his grubby mitts on the place, do you?"

"Hmm," pondered Terry, "I don't see Hops, but Jepho and Heddy are at the bar."

Roffo scowled. "Means nothing. That Jepho is a treacherous fellow and Heddy can be a bit, wotsit, *fickle*."

"Well, let's find out. I'll get these in." Terry moved through the crowd like an ocean liner through the waves of a timid sea. Tankard-waving chaps slid to the side, looked up at the mountainous robe with sudden puzzlement, then shrugged their shoulders and returned to their ale and discourse. Roffo and the monk ghosted behind the barbarian.

They attained the bar. Terry thrust out a mighty hand to signal his intent. Jepho was soon drawn to it.

"Well-well-well, what do we have here, then? Don't tell me, don't tell me ... Aha!" Jepho snapped his fingers. "Monks of Impo! Obvious really. Probably hiding hideous visages under them hoods, eh? No wonder you can't get any." The barman laughed at his own joke. "Right then, lads, what's it to be?"

"What have you got?" asked Terry.

"Depends on what you want. If you're really *really* desperate, we've got some Budwasters ..."

The monk stiffened, then made to leap over the bar to confront the cocky youth. "Prepared to tolerate insult about sexual potency, but not *that*. I kill him ..." Terry and Roffo managed to haul back the rightly enraged monk.

Jepho licked his lips nervously. "Ah, sorry lads. You're obviously connoisseurs. We don't serve it out of choice, you understand. We got some in when we were in hard times, and now we've got several barrels left. It's on special offer now, y'know. Perhaps you'd still like to consider ..."

An iron fist clamped around his lapels. "If you offer us *that stuff* again," said Terry, in all seriousness, "I will dispense with you myself."

"Cor, right you are, sir. Strong bloke!" Jepho glanced over towards the stand-in troubleshooter. Long Jon was cowering in a corner, currently being menaced by half a dozen very angry, very *wet* punters. Two empty buckets lay beside him. "Ah, anyway, we've also got Bravo Ale from Greenwings, and Tolly's Dark, brewed over in Frembolia …"

"Well," said Terry, "in that case we'll—"

"Ah-ah-ah!" interrupted Jepho, raising one finger and smirking. "And as of this very day, up and running for the first time since dreadful sabotage was committed in this very public house, we have the legendary *Old P.*"

"Old P!" exclaimed Terry and Roffo in unison.

"That must mean," continued Roffo, "that Hops is still in charge. It's his brew. Manis would never touch it."

Jepho frowned. "Of course Hops is in charge. Hang abouts … don't I know you?"

And at that moment, a rotund fellow with a red face and going-south-forever hair bustled out of the cellar and pushed his way behind the bar.

"Come come, Jepho my lad, look at all these customers. I don't pay you to go chatting to monks and suchlike – begging your pardon, sirs, fine chaps though I'm sure you are. Ah – yes sir?" He turned to Occum, who had forced his way through the crush and up to the bar, largely by using the stratagem of making snipping motions with his fingers. "Two pints of Old P?" suggested Hops. "Coming right up!"

The two homeboys looked at each other. Even though they could see naught of each other's faces, they could well imagine the expressions set thereon. They turned towards Hops.

"It's us!" cried Roffo.

"Ah, right you are, sirs," said Hops, without turning from the handle of the beer pump. "Thought I recognised them robes. Welcome back."

"No!" gasped Roffo. "Us!" He threw back his hood. "It's *us*!"

Hops turned around and looked up. "I …" His jaw dropped. Terry and the monk threw back their hoods too. As far as famous scenes go, this was something like the one where Richard the Lionheart and his knights reveal themselves to a certain toxophilitic liberator of others' possessions.

From where she stood on the other side of the innkeeper, Heddy gasped. Jepho mouthed the word "bugger". People started to turn around on scraping chairs. Fat Grevis – at the other end of the bar – pointed, then fell off his barstool, taking down the eight men behind him.

"I …." continued Hops, "I …."

"Someone slap him on the back," declared a much-grinning Roffo, "before he passes out."

But Hops broke out of the trance by himself. "I'll be a Clovorite's Codpiece!" he cried. "Roffo … Terry … my lads! You've made it!"

A great cheer went up. Regulars clustered around the returned adventurers. Backs were patted, hands were shaken, shoulders were punched heartily, and offers of drinks were voiced. But before celebrations could advance any further the front door slammed open with a deafening crash. Nev Tweeky – bar fly and scoundrel – stood framed in the doorway. He pointed back out of the door behind him.

"Quick, lads!" he bellowed. "Out in the Square. It looks like they're gonna lynch Manis!"

Tweeky stepped aside as the inn's occupants flooded out of the door. Terry, Roffo, the monk, Hops, Occum … all were caught up in the exodus.

Roffo bellowed over the bedlam: "This I've got to see!" And he allowed himself to be lifted from his feet and carried along.

As the last man left the pub, Tweeky slid back inside. He rubbed his hands. What first? He plucked up the nearest of the semi-emptied tankards and helped the now-absent owner with his task.

The Pilgrim had come alive. Grumpy, disenchanted fellows had perked up at the sight of the goings-on behind the counter, swivelling around in their seats for a better view. They had watched a huge bare-chested fellow walk in carrying a barrel of ale, followed by a young chap with a wispy beard and baggy yellow pantaloons. They had observed a heated exchange between the foreigners and Spotty Wembers, which had ended in the acned one being slid along the bar like a bottle of firewater in a Western saloon.

Spotty now lay on the floor with his head propped up against a wall and eyes that seemed to spin in contrary directions, while the young Gebrullian poured out tankard after tankard of the new ale, setting these enticingly along the bar top. The scimitar-bearing guard stood with his arms folded, ensuring that no-one took premature liberties with the beer.

At last, Manis strolled through the back door followed by a fat silky thing, two more of the turbaned guards, and the Berserker. Manis stopped and frowned at the sight of the lined-up tankards and the new barman. "What the ...?" He turned a quizzical eye on the Potoon. "That's not how we do things here, mate."

"Once again, my apowogies. Has the boy been too enthusiastic? I wi' have him beaten." The merchant prince clapped his hands. Yershah looked up, saw his master, rushed around to stand before him, and bowed.

"Your Magnificence, all is ready."

Manis looked between the men, and shrugged. He strode over to Spotty and gave him a good kick, then clambered onto a table. "Gentlemen! I have a treat for you tonight. A very special brew, a master among masters, a brew that makes standard Pedigree seem like *Bud*— ... ah, that beer I cannot name. For one night only, and at the very generous price of two silver pieces ..."

"Two!" cried an outraged drinker.

Others laughed.

Manis quietened his punters down and scowled. "All right. At the *same price* as the regular Pedigree, I present to you *Pedigree Plus*! Form an orderly queue now. Spotty, get round here quick. Oy, blockhead!" he shouted at the Berserker. "Protect my stocks! Now, Mr Pot—" Manis turned to find the Samark squeezing out of the back door. He rushed after him.

"Not going to partake yourself?"

The merchant prince turned. "Awas no. It is the time of the Howee Fast. I must not dwink beeah at this time."

"Why not stay for a coffee, then?"

"No, we must wetweat to a safe distance." The Potoon came to a standstill in the doorway. He looked sheepishly at the open-mouthed innkeeper. "Ah ... I mean ..."

"Great Bulabothel!" cried Manis. "Is it *that* potent? Well, I wouldn't want my valued supplier to get an eyeful of ... well, let's say no more. Cheers then. And I think I'll take cover myself. Do you reckon I'll be safe behind the bar?"

Something wicked stole across the Samark's face. "Indeed. Pwobabwy. Foah now. Good-bye." And he shifted as fast as his fat little legs would carry him.

Meanwhile, the beer drinkers were returning to their tables with their Special Brews.

Sly Herrold lowered his tankard and wrinkled his nose. "I dunno about this beer. It's got a strange aftertaste."

Hughie Puke did the same. "Yeah, I know wot you mean. It's a bit, well, *amphibian*."

Other noses were wrinkled and doubts expressed.

"'Ere," said Fraise, five year old son of Picket, "this stuff tastes like some sort of nasal discharge. Who's that *cu*—" – AHEM went Picket – "Manis trying to fool?"

Bestial Bob, who considered Fraise to be his best friend – the two having similar mental ages – flexed an eyebrow. "Still, I don't suppose people buy this for the taste."

"Nah," said Councillor Troi, a bony fellow with a hooked nose, "I don't rate ordinary Pedigree that highly either. I mean, it's *quite* nice, but a change is as good as a rest and all that. Anyway, down the hatch!"

"Cheers," went the others.

"Not so loud!" said Rudy Brassrubbers, holding his hands against his ears. "Blimey, are you lot trying to deafen me?"

Men started to look puzzled. "What do you mean, loud?" said Patt the postman. "We didn't ... ow! Who shouted?"

"No-one said a word," said Hughie. "You're the only one speaking."

Tears began to flow down Patt's face. "Well I'm sorry, okay? There's no need to get stroppy."

"Stroppy? I wasn't getting stroppy. Are you accusing me of being stroppy? How dare you! I hate it when people accuse me of—"

"Calm down, calm down," said Fraise. "Strewth! Talk about sensitive!"

The door slammed open.

"*Shhhhhh!*" went the entire clientele. Some men dropped their faces onto their tables and heaped arms over heads, attempting to mask the agonising sound.

Trespass watched this scene in disbelief. "What's all this? A game of *Silly Sods*?"

"Don't call us silly sods," chorused the men, rather upset. "That's not fair!"

Shaking his head, Trespass led his posse across the lounge to where an exceedingly puzzled Manis was observing events with some concern. "Fine bluddy welcome this!" growled the yakker. "We come back after four months of roughing it. Four months facing untold dangers, being assaulted, shat upon, and subjected to all sorts of horrors and indignities and ..."

"*Shhhhhhh!*"

" ...and people just tell me to shush."

Manis sized the men up. Their clothes were torn and raggedy, their beards were untrimmed (even Burble had developed one – and it looked right ridiculous too), and they badly needed a wash, medication, and sterilisation (in the general sense). The innkeeper would have been more interested in their report had Bestial Bob not suddenly burst into tears for no apparent reason.

"Well, what have you been up to, then?"

"Before I say one word," scowled Trespass, "I want beer. Now!"

"Sure. Wembers?"

Spotty slid five tankards of Pedigree Plus over to the dishevelled yak men. The Angels instantly lifted their respective beers to their lips and, in unison, swigged them down in one.

"That'll be ten silver pieces," said Manis absently.

"You ... you ..." Trespass began to fume. His colleagues stepped back, wondering whether their leader had at last found the guts to sort the innkeeper out. They watched as he drew back his fist, further and further, and then *struck*. His fist flew out but, at the last second, it opened up and curled around to slap over Trespass's own eyes. Tears began to flow. "Why do you treat us like this?" blubbed the leader of the pack. "We were only doing what you wanted and ... and ..."

Burble thought this scene one of the most heart-rending he had ever seen. He wiped a tear from his eye.

Manis simply stared. "What the Hull has got into everybody?"

"*Shhhhhhh!*"

"Nothing's got into me. Nothing at all!" said Hughie Puke. "Who's accusing me of—."

"Just because I'm five," wept Fraise, "everyone thinks it's okay to have a go at me!"

"Are you suggesting I'm a bad father?" said Picket. "That's just typical! I work every hour of the day to feed and clothe you and what thanks do I get? None. Ungrateful sod!"

"*Shhhhhhh!*"

"Oooo," said Rudy Brassrubbers. He frowned. And then he smiled. And then, suddenly, he felt rather ... *perky*. He looked at his drinking companion and winked. "You know, you're really quite attractive when you do that. You know it's quite ... *endearing*."

"What are you talking ... *about?*" Sly Herrold sat up in his chair. He suddenly felt like a new man. And Rudy looked like just the kind of new man he'd like to feel. "Ah, hmmm, yes, well ..."

"And that steely look of yours: it's dynamite! It says: This Man Is A Hunk. And are those muscles real? Cor! Can I buy you a drink?"

"That's very nice of you," said Herrold, who was now feeling distinctly odd. "Same again please, *saucy*."

As Rudy minced up to the bar, Councillor Troi began to sweat. *Look at the buns on that,* he thought. *Those leather trousers really suit him. But I wonder what he'd look like without them on?*

Grunt patted Bruce on his arm. Then he gave it a squeeze. He was feeling rather *strange.* His affectionate gesture was greeted with a sunny smile. It looked like he was in! "Well then, sexy, 'ow about it?"

Picket and Fingers were by now attempting to locate each other's tonsils with their tongues. Bestial Bob began to chase a coquettish Hughie Puke around the lounge. And Trespass smiled sweetly at a horrified Spotty Wembers.

Manis stood rooted to the spot in complete shock. He looked over at the Berserker, only to find that his hard man had backed against the wall in confusion.

And suddenly …

"Oh my God!" cried Picket. "Did I really do that?"

Fingers frowned miserably. "What, so you don't like me, then?" He sighed. "Can't say as I'm surprised. You know, nobody has ever truly loved me in my entire life. Even my dog used to bite me."

"God, mine too," said Hughie, regaining his seat.

"And my mum used to beat me," said Burble.

"Not as much as she beat me," said Frunge.

"That's nothing," volunteered a sad-looking Fraise, "my dad still does."

"Oh, what is the point?" said someone else.

A chorus of sighs and shaking heads followed.

"You know," said Sly, "if I had a rope I'd hang myself. But I really can't be bothered to fetch one."

"Yeah, well, it'd only break."

"Nothing ever goes right for me."

"Nah, nor me …"

"And everybody hates me …"

"Hahahahahahahahahahahaha!" laughed Postman Patt, out of the blue, pointing at the long-faced brigade. "That is *so* funny!"

"Ha ha," Picket coughed. "I mean … ha ha ha … it's like … hahahaha …" He fell off his chair.

At this, several men at an adjacent table started pointing and chortling.

Hughie Puke picked up his beer and poured it over Fraise's head. The pair burst into laughter.

"And then … and then …" laughed Fingers, "I kissed him!"

"Oh-ho oh-ho oh-ho ... bandits at nine o'clock!"

"Here come the fairies!"

"Up against the walls, men!"

"Hur hur hur," went Frunge, "and I saw wot *you* two were up to!"

"Yeah, I got right depressed about it for a moment," said Grunt, "and then I just realised 'ow funny it all must 'ave looked. I mean, me and Bruce? Hohoho ... *parp*." Grunt clasped a hand to his over-sized butt and smiled. "'Scuse me."

"Hur hur *pheeeeerp* ... hur?" went Frunge. "Oops! Sorry!"

"God, did you see *phuuuuurt* ..."

"Oh oh, my sides, I think they've spl— ...*heeeeeernk* ..."

Drrrrrr.

Chweeeee.

Phrrrput.

Wooosh.

"Great Clovory," yelled Herrold, quacking and rumbling and suddenly afraid for the safety of his underwear, "I can't ... *pffffrrrr* ... stop my ... *brrrrrr* ... self!"

Men started to rise to their feet and, amongst a gaseous environment not dissimilar to that in which life formed on Earth, began to edge towards the toilet.

Manis turned green and started wafting the offending air away from his nose. Spotty grasped at his throat and started making retching noises. The Berserker looked incredulous. Several men passed out. And then a stunning red-haired girl emerged from the back room, rubbing her hair with a towel.

"God ... you men!"

At this, Trespass stood stock still. His treacherous bowels ceased their rumbling. He pointed at Sonia, and then at Manis. "You ... her ..." Rage distorted his features, a rage the likes of which he had never experienced before. "You *bastard*! I'm gonna ..."

As the yakker started to make his way around the bar, Manis backed up. He suddenly realised that the situation was serious. He had never seen Trespass so angry. In fact, he had never seen anyone this angry before – not *at him*. Of course, he knew that he made people angry, and it amused him, but they were never angry towards him in his presence. This was a whole new ball game. And ... it wasn't just Trespass.

"Gae on Tres," scowled Bruce, "gie him a reet kickin'!"

"Bagsy me next, Tres!" shouted Burble, who was wide-eyed and foaming at the mouth. It seemed to him that all the rage in his life had somehow been stored up for this moment. And look at him now: sore all over, weary beyond words, yakless, and currently sporting the sort of chin fuzz that said to everyone This Man Cannot Grow A Proper Beard.

Grunt felt the same. In fact, he was even angrier. To think that he had actually just been groping Bruce! It had to be Manis's fault somehow. Everything was.

There was a scraping of chairs. The rest of the clientele found their feet and started to advance towards Manis. They blocked the way out back, and the exit to the back room, and encircled the bar.

"It's gotta be something in the drink!" cried Patt. "He's poisoned us!"

"Yeah," concurred Hughie, "what a smell!"

"And to think I was just now thinking about another man's buns!" raged Councillor Troi. "I'd never do that! The git has put something in the beer."

"Aye," said Fraise, "and he dobbed me into the filth for taking a piss."

"And grassed me up," said Picket.

"Let's lynch him," suggested a maddened Fingers. "In the Square!"

"YEAH!" roared the assembled men as one.

"Now-now lads," said Manis, starting to sweat. "I've been stitched up like the rest you. It's that bloody Potoon. And I haven't grassed on anyone, and that's the truth." He turned to face the Berserker and growled. "And what the Hull do you think you're doing, you moron? Give me a hand here!"

The Berserker frowned. He had recently heard a rumour that his days were numbered because Manis wanted 'a troubleshooter with more brains than a bread roll'. "Wot's dat?" he said. "Did someone speak? I can't 'ear you. Who said dat?"

Trespass was now behind the bar, a mere foot from the innkeeper. He smiled manically. "Payback time!"

And with a great roar, The Pilgrim's much-abused clientele grasped hold of Manis, threw him aloft, and bore him from the inn. With wolf-like howls and obscene shouts they bundled into the Square.

———————

By the time the hearties from The Bear had scrambled from their home territory into the Square, Manis had been stripped naked and was being dunked in a horse trough.

"And that's for the loss of Thruster!" cried Burble, as he pushed down on the innkeeper's head.

"And that's for Bruce," said Grunt, giving him a hand.

The men were taking it in turns to give the squat innkeeper a bath, slowly revolving around the trough so that each got a chance to vent some of his unaccountable rage.

"And that's for the time you barred me for breaking a glass," said Sly.

"And that's for making me dress up in women's clothing," cried Picket.

"And that's for charging me for dregs," said Deknat.

And around they went.

The event was turning into something of a show. Not only had the clientele of The Bear come out to watch, but the news had rapidly spread and people were rushing from their homes to join the fun. A contingent of Clovorites turned up and started cheering the dunkers on. Awful Puns arrived with a tray of *delicacies* and an eye for a sale. The Potoon and his entourage watched events from camelback. And Sonia and Wembers quietly enjoyed the show in the background. Indeed, all of this activity was impeding the measured progress of the law. It soon became a race to see whether Yavlo, Boomber and Hendy could reach the scene before someone managed to pass the group of Mr Angries a rope.

"Excuse us ... sir! ... madam!" exclaimed Yavlo, prising his way through the crowd. "This is official business. Kindly move to one side and let us pass."

"Pies, get yur lovely pies 'ere. Ah, evening good sir, would you like a pie?"

"Would you like to spend the night in the cells?" grimaced Boomber.

"Oh, go on Terry," cried Roffo, "give us a lift up ..."

"Are they here?" said Maddy, who had been out back when the adventurers had arrived. "Where are they ...?"

"Great Clovory," roared High Brother Frostus above the bedlam, "give strength unto the arms of the instruments of your punishment!"

"Sod that," declared Brother Veritas. "O Mighty Clovory, give them a rope pretty damned quick, for here come the filth!"

486

"I say, Blewers, isn't this splendid?"

"*Yeees.* I do rather *think* that beastly innkeeper chap has had it coming for some time now."

"Ah, no, old fruit, I was referring to the cake ..."

"Is that it?" wondered the Potoon, somewhat disappointed. The dunking contest was fun, but he had hoped for a little more. "What is to come?"

"It is difficult to say, Your Magnificence," said the Beni Yonad. "Some of the effects will leave little trace. However, judging by the clean state of their pantaloons it would appear that the laxative ..."

SQUELCH!

"... has yet to take effect." She shrugged. "Forget I spoke."

The two dozen men from The Pilgrim had received scant warning of the catastrophe that was to come. One moment they were filled with an insane rage, and the next they were filled with an insane urge. Being hemmed in on all sides, they had naturally turned to the one available lavatory-like receptacle: the one in which a certain nude innkeeper was floundering ...

Alas for the crowd, the Condensed Hyper-Bean was a laxative that took no prisoners. The two dozen afflicted gents had got no further than forming a tight ring around Manis's trough – each raising a single leg half-way up to its lip – when the Bean struck. The antagonists whitened, rolled their eyes, and whimpered – all rage now forgot.

As the crowd began to back away, Manis regained his natural composure. He looked at his discomfited attackers, and laughed.

"Ha! You're a useless bunch of pillocks, aren't you? Can't even do a lynching properly. Well, just wait until I ..."

"This is not vewy good!" frowned the Potoon. "Wook! He's going to get out of it with no moah than a bath!"

"Er, not quite, Your Magnificence," smiled Yershah, who had made one or two calculations and realised that a certain black liquid had yet to demonstrate its effects. "I think you'll enjoy this. Any second now …"

―――――•◦•••◦•――――――

"… and then," cried Manis, "I'm going to … eh? Don't you puff your cheeks out at m—"
HWUUUURGH!

―――――•◦•••◦•――――――

Yavlo and his constabulary gently forced their way between two yak riders with peculiarly lumpy buttocks.

"Right, let us through, gentlemen. Master Manis, I have here a warrant for your … *good grief!*"

"Strewth!" said Constable Hendy.

"Well I never," chortled Sergeant Boomber.

Wiping one hand across a gruesome mouth, Picket faced the law. "He's all yours." And with that, he turned and waddled away through the rapidly parting crowd. The rest of the lads from The Pilgrim – like a brood of ducklings following their mother – waddled closely behind.

"Well, guv," said Boomber, uncertainly, as he appraised the dazed and gory innkeeper, "do you want to apply the cuffs, or shall I?"

―――――•◦•••◦•――――――

The innkeeper was sitting around a table in the lounge of The Bear along with the three adventurers. Other celebrants stood around the table behind the men, eager to be a part of this special occasion. The supporters included Occum, Eddie, Phlip, Horus and Maddy – the latter hovering between Terry and Roffo as though somehow torn in her loyalties.

"Well, that's that then," said Hops, with a broad smile upon his face. His favourite barstaff had returned, his micro-brewery was back in production, and his arch-foe had been subjected to unspeakable horrors before being hauled off to jail. What could be better?

"No it's not!" cried Roffo, excitably. "Aren't you forgetting something? Some-*Big*-Thing. You know? What we left for in the first place?"

Hops's eyes lit up. "Ah, of course! The greatest ale in the world! Boozer's Very Peculiar! Speak, lad, and quickly! Do you have it?"

Roffo looked between his fellow questers. Terry smiled and nodded, while the monk, with a huge grin, plucked their CAMORA membership certificate from his robe and placed it upon the table.

488

The young barman-adventurer gestured towards the certificate: "Behold!"

People gasped and craned forward to have a look at the gold-inked recipe. Some pointed excitedly; others read the text in low voices. Hops reached out to caress the thing.

"Is this it?" asked the innkeeper, with perspiration beading his brow. "Is this really it? The recipe? Aye, but it's grand."

Roffo cleared his throat. "Not *quite.*"

"What's that, lad? Speak plainly."

"Well, what you see before you is only nine parts of the recipe. We haven't seen the tenth and final part … *yet.*" Roffo looked around, intent on dragging this out as long as possible. This was his moment. He smiled at the array of open mouths and wide eyes. A sudden hush had taken the inn. More and more people began to cluster around the party. There was a scrape of chairs and tables being drawn closer, the sound of breaking glass, and the rustle and grunt of people climbing onto tables, counters, and other people.

At last, Maddy laughed. She tousled the barman's hair. "Oh, go on you fool. Tell us."

Roffo turned around to smile up at the barmaid and – for the first time – noticed the bandages on her forearms. "Well I'll be buggered!" he cried. "Look!" Still sitting – for the press had become so close that it was no longer possible for him to stand – Roffo struggled out of his brown CAMORA robe, revealing his own bandages. Maddy gasped. The monk chuckled.

"Extraordinary!" cried Hops. "What does this mean?"

With a gentle smile Maddy whispered to Roffo. "Go on, you buffoon. Yours first. I'll show you mine later."

"Ah, er …" Roffo blushed. "Well, um …"

"Come on, lad," cried Hops. "Out with it!"

With a last idiotic grin at the barmaid, Roffo turned back to face his colleagues. "Mr Monk, sir, is now the time for the climax of the story?"

The monk gurned merrily, like a self-satisfied Buddha, and simply nodded.

"Yeah. Terry?" The barbarian gave him the thumbs-up. Roffo took a deep breath. "Well, you see, I had to carry this burning brazier across this floor, held only by my forearms. It was, oh, a hundred yards, maybe two …"

The monk coughed.

"And, um, anyway, I wasn't allowed to drop it. Bloody painful it was, too! And afterwards, well, Terry bandaged me up, and Crawford, this brewer bloke – about two hundred years old and eight feet tall …"

Terry placed his smiling face in one mighty hand.

"… well, he said that we *already had* the last piece of the recipe, and, well …"

"Okay okay," laughed Hops, "we get the picture. It's been burned onto your arms."

"Yeah – *oh!*" Roffo frowned slightly. "It took us weeks …" again the monk coughed "… well, *some* of us weeks to work it out." Roffo held one arm out to each of his fellow questers sitting to either side of him. "Would you care to do the honours, gentlemen?"

Terry and the monk each took hold of an end to one of the bandages and began to slowly unwind. The crowd held its breath. Hops's eyes bulged in anticipation. Maddy leaned forward eagerly, giving Roffo a very pleasant pair of ear muffs. The men reached the last turn of fabric, looked at each other, came to an unspoken agreement, and ripped off the bandages.

"*Owwwww!*" cried Roffo, waggling his arms. "You complete buggers!"

Everyone laughed.

"Let's see, then," said Terry.

Roffo lowered his arms to the table. The whole inn craned to have a look.

And they looked some more.

Eyebrows were raised, Roger Moore style, to indicate puzzlement. Frowns appeared on faces. Heads were scratched. Earnest looks were very much the norm.

"Er," posited Hops, "the last piece of the recipe is … *squiggle?*"

The monk began to manipulate Roffo's arms this way and that, but nothing was clearly resolved. There were indeed identical marks on each of the barman's forearms, and they were clearly meant to be in some way symbolic. But as to the meaning of the marks …?

"Is it in the tongue of the Wood Spirits?" asked Roffo desperately.

The monk shook his head unhappily. "No. It in no language I know. Perhaps it is pictogram. Need time to check … to do research …" his mumbling slowly trailed off.

After a moment of uncertain silence, Hops suddenly rocked back in his chair and let out a hearty laugh. This seemed to break the mood and others joined in. Glasses were raised to lips, people began to turn away, voices were raised in conversation.

"But," said Roffo, "but ... this is it! We *do* have the recipe! Once Mr Monk deciphers this last symbol then we'll have it, eh?"

"Aye, lad," declared Hops good-naturedly, "and when you have it, let me know, okay? But in the meantime I have a pub to run and a goodly number of thirsty punters who want to shower me with their coins. Terry, lad, how's about you go and relieve Master Long Jon. He's a trier – to be sure – but I don't entirely rate his crowd control techniques."

Terry smiled and stood up. "Right you are, boss."

"And good Master Monk, sir, you are most welcome to stay in the spare room until you decide to move on."

The monk gurned in vexation. But after a moment's thought he shrugged and found a smile. He gave a little bow. "Many thanks, good landlord. Need time to consider nature of squiggle and work out where to find translation. Accept offer gratefully."

"And as for you, Roffo my lad, do I need to point you to the bar?"

Roffo threw up his hands in disappointment. "I think this is where I came in!"

But then Maddy leant over and took his hand. "Actually, Hopsie, I need some help changing a barrel in the cellar. Come along, Roffo."

"Oh aye," said Hops suspiciously. "Well, hop to it then." He turned to leave, but then paused and turned back. "And by the way, lad – well done!"

"Cor," said Roffo, speaking to Maddy's back as she dragged him towards the cellar. "Did you hear that? Praise from old Hops! Whatever next?"

They reached the top step to the refurbished cellar. Maddy drew Roffo around so that his back was to the open door and she was facing him. The barman noticed Terry in the background giving him the thumbs-up. "Now," said Maddy, "I'm going to give you my own little reward." She leant down slightly to kiss him ...

Roffo's eyes widened and he stumbled back. His left foot slipped on the edge of the step and he started to windmill. For several seconds his balance was, er, *in the balance*. But then he waved a touch too vigorously and that was that. He fell over backwards, disappearing into the depths of the cellar. As he fell, however, he reached out a hand, grasping, groping, seeking anything that might halt his fall...

He gained a handful of Maddy's dress.

With a great sound of shredding, the dress tore right away, following the barman into the black hole, a cross between a battle trophy and a particularly crap parachute.

As the onlooking clientele broke into laughter, Maddy shrieked after the plummeting hero:

"*Oh, Roffo!*"

The End

"So, is that really the end?" wondered Junior the pigeon.

"Heh heh," said Fats, "that's what *they* think. Look! One of the morons has left his computer on. We can get out!"

"I know," said Slim Greenchest, "let's crap in his coffee!"

"Coo, yeah, he's left a full cuppa too …"

"Me first me first …"

"No chance!" said Fats, puffing out his chest and wriggling his tail feathers ominously. "Watch this lads! I'm dead good at *whipped cream* impersonations …"

The other pigeons cooed in awe.

Dramatis Personae

The Human Players
(In Rough Order of Appearance)

The monk – Fung-Chu adept; ale connoisseur; gurning champion; possessor of a secret girlie name.

Angred – a ranger.

Tugon – a barbarian.

Gerontas – a merchant.

Hops – innkeeper at The Bear; master frowner; lover of the gold stuff.

Manis – innkeeper at The Pilgrim; a tight git.

Terry Testosterone – a barbarian; chief troubleshooter at The Bear; secret lover of wine, cats and cooking.

Roffo – barman/stable sweeper at The Bear; occasional member of its cricket team.

The Barabary brothers – the meanest trio to ever drop from one woman's womb.

Old Blunster – Way's ale-drinking champion.

Occum – barber, wit, and captain of The Bear's cricket team.

Grimwade – a teacher; member of The Bear's cricket team.

Maddy – barmaid at The Bear.

Heddy – barmaid at The Bear.

Eddie – barmaid at The Bear.

Horus – a farrier; member of The Bear's cricket team.

Jepho – part-time barman at The Bear and member of its cricket team; a sarcastic sod.

Fat Grevis – a smith; member of The Bear's cricket team; lover of large ladies.

Phlip – ex-scarecrow; outie cleaner at The Bear and member of its cricket team.

Uncle Lombo – uncle to Phlip; a pervert.

Ancient Willy – wicketkeeper in The Bear's cricket team; wind-up merchant.

Nev Tweeky – barfly and scoundrel; member of The Bear's cricket team.

Rude Lubblers – carpenter and foul-mouthed fiend.

Sly Herrold – captain of The Pilgrim's cricket team.

The Berserker – chief troubleshooter at The Pilgrim; star member of its cricket team.

Fingers – wicketkeeper in The Pilgrim's cricket team; a pickpocket.

Bestial Bob – chief fast bowler in The Pilgrim's cricket team.

Young Festers – member of The Pilgrim's cricket team; cousin to Constable Hendy.

Rudy Brassrubbers – member of The Pilgrim's cricket team.

Hughie Puke – member of The Pilgrim's cricket team.

Spotty Wembers – junior barman at The Pilgrim; a sullen youth with unfortunate skin.

Frunge – member of The Pilgrim's cricket team; an idiot; a Hull's Angel.

Burble – a beardless Hull's Angel, younger brother of Frunge; a.k.a. *The Shadow*.

Grunt – a very fat Hull's Angel.

Trespass – leader of the Hull's Angels.

Bruce – red-bearded hooligan; a Hull's Angel from the highlands.

Mitchkin – a thief and part-time umpire.

Awful Puns – a baker of dubious pies.

'Red' Sonia – a strumpet; Trespass's woman.

'Grey' Sonia – the town madam; mother to Red Sonia.

Lame Blind Sally – a strumpet (one of Sonia's girls).

Varicose Val – a strumpet (one of Sonia's girls).

'Gorgon' Gail – a transvestite strumpet and arm wrestling champion.

Tiffany – a strumpet with a feather (one of Sonia's girls).

Peter – doorman at *The Warehouse*.

Councillor Troi – Cross-My-Way councillor and man with unusual sexual appetites.

High Brother Frostus – leader of Clovorites.

Brother Veritas – a Clovorite.

Long Jon Con Dom – purveyor of Devices of Sexual Education and Gratification; stand-in troubleshooter at The Bear.

Rene Heap, a.k.a. 'the Reek' – purveyor of firelighters.

Noble – brother of Alfred; purveyor of candles.

Mr Baker – a butcher.

Janus – a spice seller.

Dr Feare – purveyor of medicinal potions.

Mrs Balook – purveyor of medicinal pastries.

Rusty – an ironmonger.

Picket – a fence.

Fraise – five-year-old son of Picket; second only to Rude Lubblers as utterer of obscenities.

Sid Sadly – an undertaker.

Joban Bile – a fruit-seller.

Crusty – a baker.

Old Gillie – an old bloke.

Patt – a postman.

Mrs Fuddy – a landlady.

Mother Tereesa – an old woman who does kind deeds.

The Dali Llama – a mystic who wears orange and says 'om' a lot.

Mrs Hops – unseen wife of Hops.

Jombers – a commentator and eater of cakes.

Blewers – a commentator and eater of cakes.

Mrs T. Waddling – a cake-making woman.

Miss Drumble – another maker of cakes: fruit cakes a speciality.

Mrs Frettal – cake woman.

Yershah – a youth from the Gebrull Islands; caravan aide; messenger; fouler of pantaloons.

The Potoon – a merchant prince from Samark; lisping fatman.

The Beni Yonad – nurse to Potoon; a fiend with potions.

Stumpy – a regular at The Bear.

Katy – Stumpy's wife.

Yavlo – Inspector in Cross-My-Way's town constabulary.

Boomber – Sergeant in town constabulary; tea addict.

Hendy – Constable in town constabulary; cousin to Festers.

Baal – cook at The Pilgrim.

Gramps – Roffo's grandpa; a teller of tall stories about adventuring.

Aunt Linny – hypochondriac aunt to Roffo.

The caped newcomer in the black fedora – a drinker of banana daiquiris.

Miss Gertrude – woman who works at the Alchemist's, who mysteriously appears whenever a man needs to buy some Longmans.

Machiavelli Waters – a Blues Minstrel.

Fred – passport officer and full body cavity search expert of the Great Yerrowe Empire.

Moustachioed passport officer – Official of the Great Yerrowe Empire; partner to Fred.

Miss K.Deedes – big-breasted proprietress of Ye Rampant Rhinoceros; nymphomaniac.

Justin – Big Knob of The Buff and egotistical maniac.

Ivor Biggun – ex-Big Knob of The Buff (having lost the title to Justin).

Rod – ex-Big Knob of the Buff (who lost the title to Ivor).

Whopper – an ex-Big Knob of Nudia; now deceased.

Pump – ginger haired landlord of Ye Rooting Pig.

King Richard the 43rd – present king of the Nudians.

Mai T. Pole – inebriate minister in the Nudian government.

Stoker – aide to Mai T. Pole.

Bishop Yul B. A. Mazed – head of the church of Satyr in Nudia.

Brother Pud Denda – a priest of Satyr.

Brother O'Toole – another priest of Satyr.

Brother Shafto – a corpulent priest of Satyr.

Seer P. Ping-Tom – prognosticator with a penchant for drugs and incorrect predictions.

Illinois Jane – authoress and defiler of temples.

Cucumber Joe – a member of the greatest tag wrestling team in Nudian history.

Dick Monster – another member of the greatest tag wrestling team in Nudia.

Phil More – the third member of the greatest tag wrestling team in Nudia.

Barbie Pinkhair – Nudian authoress.

Digger – an old Nudian theorist.

Big Ed – a lost pygmy.

Chief Lottomoos – chief of the Wulus; cattle fancier.

Ozbondo – shaman; witch finder; all round bad egg.

Tombo – He Who Glowers, With Attitude; Squad leader of the Feral Hippos; Ozbondo's son.

Shaka – Second-in-command of the Feral Hippos.

Burgachain – Ubundi's Chief Farmer.

The Royal Spittoon – receiver of the royal gob.

The Royal Handkerchief – receiver of the royal snot; brother to the royal toilet paper.

The Royal Bogpaper – use your own imagination!

King Sucka – founder of Wulu nation; now deceased.

Deknat – town drunk of Cross-My-Way.

Tarsal – King of the Apes.

June – Tarsal's woman and queen of the apes.

Thortun – Tarsal's barbarian father; an absent-minded bloke; uncle to Terry.

Cannibal – an elephant-riding warmonger from Wales.

Sheikh Aleg – merchant prince, jungle curios a speciality.

Gubbu – a cannibal chief.

Jumbo – second in command of the Nudian City Militia Religious Artefact Retrieving Expedition; nephew to Digger.

Dan Glur – Nudian militiaman in the Religious Artefact Retrieving Expedition.

Pete Rick – Nudian militiaman in the Religious Artefact Retrieving Expedition.

Portup – a Coprolite philosopher.

Mr Shiny-Head – proprietor of Olde Possum's Wine Bar.

Grimulous – Head Librarian of the great library of Copros.

Dooey – founder of library of Copros.

Judge Mincey – a judge in Copros.

Peekaso – Coprolite artist; painter of *Decorous Omni-Shades*.

Rombo, Crustius, Meldano, Farogue and Jargool – former Head Librarians of library at Copros.

Forenze – most junior of the sub-Head Librarians of Copros; milk thief.

Bassar – a sub-Head Librarian from Copros.

Eddy – a sub-Head Librarian from Copros.

A bouncer - a sad individual who won't let decent people into pubs for countless spurious reasons.

Khan, The Khan – clan leader of the Mungos.

Bakedbhean Khan – a server of warm fermented mare's milk.

Billie Khan – repulsive wife of Khan The Khan.

Imran Khan – leader of a Mungo foraging party and wielder of an interesting war club.

Toux Khan – a Mungo with a large nose.

Oyl Khan – leader of the Jerry clan of the Mungos.

Pee Khan – a nutty Mungo.

Jonbu Khan – the Mungo who put the 39 into the 39 Steppes.

Cher Khan – a Mungo female; tigress of the Steppes and mate hunter.

Colonel Branch – head of Vegetopian army.

Captain Twig – Captain in the Vegetopian Home Guard.

Corporal Berry – member of Vegetopian militia.

Lance Corporal Minty – member of Vegetopian militia.

Private Horseradish – member of Vegetopian militia.

Private Carrot – member of Vegetopian militia.

Private Robin – member of Vegetopian militia.

Sergeant Ferny – member of Vegetopian Senatorial Guards.

Sergeant Grass – member of Vegetopian Senatorial Guards.

Private Tadpole – member of Vegetopian Senatorial Guards.

Rooty – proprietor of The Succulent Shoot, Vegetopia.

Nutlet – member of Vegetopian Senate.

Tarka – member of Vegetopian Senate.

Bishop Vole – Bishop of Vegetopia Cathedral; animal rights extremist.

Roses – man who led the Exodus of the Vegetopians.

Beejeezus – prophet of the Vegetopians; accountant.

Namoor – part-time Receptionist; Gamesmaster; monk of CAMORA.

Crawford – Master Brewer of the monks of CAMORA.

Zazoon – a monk of CAMORA.

Fildo – a monk of CAMORA.

Henri – a monk of CAMORA; Master Cooper.

THE GODS AND MYTHICAL FIGURES

Clovory – a toenail-less god.

Bulabothel – a not very nice god whose name is frequently taken in vain; reputed to live in Hull.

Grom – god of the barbarians (a.k.a. Lord of the Battle Mound, Sharp Pointy Objects and Really Long Hair); provider of steel.

Jer-Ey – god of Mice.

To-Mas – god of cats; the Mewing Destroyer.

Basmati – god to the Samarks.

Lokran the Housekeeper – a god.

Impo – a god; twin of Impi.

Impi – a god; twin of Impo.

Creuset – goddess of Kitchen Utensils.

Virago – goddess of Inopportune Visits, Cheap Perfume and the Berating Tongue; mother to Creuset.

Cirrhosis – an angel; reputed to have stolen the secret of ale to give to man.

Boozer – a wood spirit; reputed by some to have made the first true ale.

Hullabooloo – god of Aztechys.

Smyth brothers – reputed barbarian recipients of secret recipe of ale from Grom.

Satyr – big-willied god of the Nudians.

Sartor – evil god of the Nudians who forces the righteous to wear clothes.

The Rockgod – sexually frustrated consumer of people, fava beans and Chianti.

Macartny – a goddess revered by the Vegetopians.

Notia – goddess of dreams.

Sharon – a mythical steersman of underworld transport.

Calibar – an unspeakable ogre.

THE ANIMAL PLAYERS

Fat Sixtoes (Fats) – a pigeon.

Nelson – a one-eyed pigeon.

Filthy Twotoes – another pigeon.

Junior – another pigeon.

Crapper – a pigeon.

Slim Greenchest – yet another pigeon.

Grotfeather – a pigeon; cousin to Fats; Wing Commander in Tarsal's
   air force.

Ginger – a pigeon.

Reggie – a pigeon.

Plumpchest – a pigeon; Ginger's 'bird'.

Satan – a dog; only living creature to enjoy Awful Puns's pies.

A Harleck Dravidian – Trespass's yak.

Thruster – a 1000cc West Highland Yak owned by Burble.

A red, long-haired Noughton – Frunge's yak.

Votun – a Ducrapi; Grunt's immense yak.

A Black Mountain Yak – Bruce's yak; at one time the only hairless yak
   alive.

A Frog – inhabitant of Stinky Bottom; politically regressive.

A Newt – another inhabitant of Stinky Bottom.

Wing Commander Eeee – leader of the 6654th mosquito squadron.

Buzz Master – chief of the horseflies.

Bandit Leader Vow Vow – leader of the midges.

Tearless – ex-King of the crocodiles; now a loincloth.

Thunder Chicken – Tombo's war ostrich.

Feathered Nightmare – Ozbondo's war ostrich.

Fowl Temper – a war ostrich.

Cheata – Tarsal's right-hand ape.

Mr Wriggle – a python.

Sssid – an anaconda.

Trantor/Jotun – Tarsal's elephant; 'borrowed' by Burble.

Tusker – Elephant long-distance runner and dope fiend.

Big Betty – elephant; part-time amour of Trantor.

Arachnea – a spider; the Bad Mamma of Three Big Red Rocks county.

Nipper – a scorpion; acquaintance of Arachnea.

Daisy – a donkey.

Chewy – a water buffalo.